MORE SEAMUS McCREE

U.P. NORTH

A Compendium of Tales set in Michigan's Upper Peninsula

James M. Jackson

Introduction

This volume contains reprints of two Seamus McCree novels, *Granite Oath* and *Hijacked Legacy* set in Michigan's Upper Peninsula. The earlier compendium, Seamus McCree U.P. North included previous Seamus McCree novels and stories set in same locale.

ISBN-13 Trade Paperback: 978-1-943166-42-8

Granite Oath Fever (2022) and *Hijacked Legacy* (2024) are the seventh and eighth novels of the Seamus McCree series. Those who prefer to read a series in order should put this book down and start with the first novel in the series, *Ant Farm.* If you'd like to read just the U.P. novels in order, then you'll want to first read *Cabin Fever* and *Empty Promises* (or Seamus McCree U.P. North, which includes both novels plus two short stories).

James M. Jackson
Amasa, Michigan

Printed in the United States of America
10987654321

GRANITE OATH

A Seamus McCree Novel

James M. Jackson

First Edition
Trade Paperback Edition: August 2022

Wolf's Echo Press
PO Box 54
Amasa, MI 49903
www.WolfsEchoPress.com

This is a work of fiction. Any references to real places, real people, real organizations, or historical events are used fictitiously. Other names, characters, organizations, places, or events are the product of the author's imagination.

GRANITE OATH

A Seamus McCree Novel (#7)

DEDICATION

For Jack Olson and his tractor.

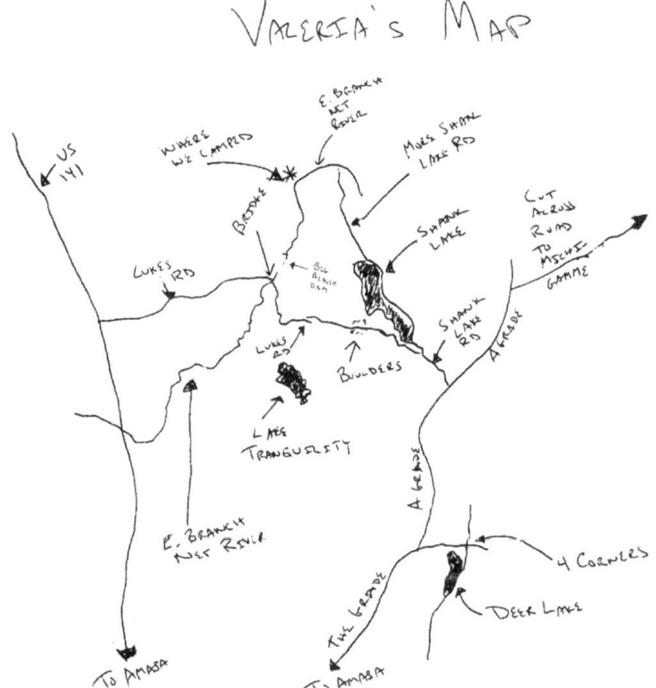

ONE

MY WORDS FROM THE MORNING shamed me. "Megan," I'd said when my granddaughter was dragging her feet. "People are late for two reasons. Either they think their time is more valuable than the other person's, or they don't care about breaking their promise." She looked at me like I was speaking Urdu. "Which one are you going to tell Mrs. Belanger when you're late?"

That got her moving. Now, I was late to pick her up at the Amasa Summer Creative Arts Academy. I boiled up the long gravel driveway and skidded to a stop in a parking area next to Kim Belanger's backyard, where she held the Academy. Megan and another girl sat at a picnic table in the shadow of an ancient yellow birch, their backs to me.

Kim was perched on the other side. At my approach, she folded a page corner of the book she was reading and shaded her eyes from the sun. "Seamus McCree." She drew my name out: Shay-mus Muh-kree. "You're the last person I *ever* expected to be late."

"I'm so sorry. I got stuck behind logging trucks coming down The Grade. That's no excuse. I should have left earlier. And I couldn't call because the card with your phone number is sitting on my refrigerator, and I never entered it into my contacts. Can I pay you for your extra time? Come on, Pumpkin. Put away your coloring book and pencils. We need to get out of Mrs. Belanger's hair."

Megan looked up, surprise painting her face. "Grampa Seamus, look at my unicorn."

She had finished the horn and was working on the mane, each lock of hair a different color. "Beautiful," I said. "How did you become such an expert?"

Megan laughed at our joke. She adopted a solemn face, wove her torso back and forth, and deepened her voice. "Practice. Practice. Practice." Then she giggled. "Can we wait with Valeria until her mommy comes?"

Kim said, "You know I was just busting your chops. You don't owe me anything. But you could do me a big favor and take Valeria home. Her mother works in Iron Mountain and sometimes can't get here until five. Problem is, I can't wait that late today because I have to cart my own kids to the library. The Friends of the Crystal Falls Library is sponsoring a YA author they want to see."

"I'm a little uncomfortable driving someone's kid without her parent's permission."

Kim waved away my worries. "I've taken her before. I'd do it again, except the road's tough on my Prius. If we could take your Subaru, I'll go with you." She asked if that was okay with Valeria, whose answer was a squeal of delight that she and Megan could play longer. We sent the kids in to use the bathroom before we left.

Kim handed me the coloring materials and Megan's backpack. "I'll be sorry when your granddaughter's visit is up. Before Megan arrived, Valeria was pretty much the outsider. You know, everyone else grew up together. Megan bullied her way past the cliques and brought Valeria with her. Those two are besties."

My face broke out with grandfatherly pride. "Megan is a force of nature. I was worried how to keep her entertained for an entire month while her parents are rafting down the Colorado. Your summer academy is perfect for giving her time with kids her own age. Before I forget, let me get your number into my contacts."

Kim dialed me, allowing me to capture her information, and then she called Valeria's mother. Her brow furrowed, and she left a message to say she was bringing Valeria to the trailer.

"Problem?" I asked.

"It's probably nothing, but Kat—that's what Valeria's mother wants me to call her—usually lets me know if she'll be late, which she hasn't this time. And she *always* picks up my calls."

Two

THE KIDS HAD A WHEE of a time bumping and thumping down two miles of a long-abandoned logging road to get to Valeria's trailer. Frost-heaved rocks threatened to dent a rocker panel or remove a muffler. How Kim brought a Prius in was beyond my comprehension. We drove through parklike areas of mixed mature hardwoods. As the road worsened, I slowed further and marveled at a stand of majestic hemlocks so large that, even with joined hands, the four of us couldn't have circled their trunks.

A mile in, we crawled through a section of road gullied by past spring flows from the surrounding tamarack swamp from which the dry spell had sucked any sign of standing water. Another mile of dodging rocks the size of Gibraltar and potholes deep enough to swallow a VW Bug brought us to a spot used as a turnaround.

Valeria called, "Mister, Mama stops here."

I pointed to the rutted tracks straight up a hill. "I can drive that. How much farther?"

Kim said, "She's right. It's maybe four hundred yards, but there's no place to turn around at the trailer."

Valeria unlocked her door. "I can get out here."

Not on my watch. Plus, we had the minor matter of the four gallons of water Kim had brought with her. I released everyone to bathe in mosquito dope and parked the car with one side scraping encroaching tag alders to allow Valeria's mother room if she returned while we were here. A horde of mosquitoes attracted by the car's exhaust buzz-bombed me before I could spray. I hate bug spray smell, and if I had known I'd be tromping through the woods, I wouldn't have worn shorts and sandals. Megan and Valeria skipped up the road. Kim and I split the water jugs and trudged after them.

The road curved past a vernal pond, then bent around a knob covered with mature popple. I smelled the woodsmoke before I saw the camp. Hidden in a dense thicket of white birch was a rusted travel trailer with an extended awning roped to the trees. A curl of blue smoke rose from a firepit with a saucepan on a grill perched on four legs. Sitting on rocks were a cast iron frying pan, a coffee pot, and a ten-quart kettle. Nearby was a stump with a hatchet embedded in it and a stack of branches lying beside it. A smaller pile of chopped wood waited, ready to burn.

The trailer looked level and had a couple of hundred-pound propane tanks covered with spider webs attached at the rear. Two card tables and four camp chairs had pride of place under the awning. Three settings of glasses with water, empty bowls, and spoons occupied one table. The other there, ending their segment with "and then." Megan delights in twisting stories beyond all recognition, such as her contribution, "and then a dragon with flames shooting from its mouth flew down to the fairy village, and then."

I responded, "and then the fairy fire department extinguished the flames and brought the dragon to the fairy doctor who diagnosed the dragon with *flamous erruptus*, a hereditary disease passed on only to females who eat blue moon ice cream before dinner, and then . . ."

The fifteen minutes flew by in dragons and fairies and giggles and groans until the next camper arrived. Megan extracted a promise from me to wait and talk with Valeria's mother. Mission accomplished, she grabbed her day pack and lunch bag, and she and her friend sprinted to the massive tent Kim had set up in the yard for rainy days and to act as a midday sunscreen. I read the latest William Kent Krueger on my Kindle, losing my place each time a vehicle pulled up to discharge a child. Ten minutes after the camp's official start, I hopped from my car and dashed to the tent.

The kids sat in a circle and shared their morning check-in, their voices raised to hear above the rain pounding the canvas. Kim motioned me to the edge, where we had some privacy. "I called Kat Serrano," she said. "Still no answer. I'm getting really concerned something happened to her. I don't want to worry all weekend. Will you drive up and make sure everything is all right? I have two water jugs for them."

SIX

THE STEADY RAIN BECAME A downpour, obliterating previous vehicle tracks and transforming parts of the two-track to the Serrano trailer into a stream. The Subaru's all-wheel drive worked like a charm, but I hit several rocks hidden by pooling water. My hope of seeing Kat's truck at the turnaround bore no fruit. I parked my Subaru pointed toward civilization, then zipped my raincoat, pulled up its hood, and pressed into the rainstorm. When I bent into the car to retrieve the two gallons of water, my slicker hitched up and drained cold water down the seat of my pants. *Dumb move, Seamus.*

Footing was slick going up the hill, but despite more than an inch of rain, the vernal pond remained dry. At least this precipitation would lessen the fire hazard, and there were no mosquitoes. At the trailer clearing, I called to announce my presence. The saucepan remained on the grill above the drowned fire. They'd have no fire until the rain stopped, and even then, it would take work to start one with soaked wood. I found no evidence of breakfast dishes.

The awning sagged with collected rainfall, straining the trees holding it up. Water poured through a slit in the awning over the trailer's steps. The force of the water running off had knocked over three empty gallon containers.

I called again. Valeria stepped out wearing a faded yellow raincoat with too-short sleeves and a broken zipper. She held the raincoat together, exposing the black bear attached to her wrist to the water dripping through the awning. Over the drumbeat on the trailer's metal roof, she said, "Grampa Seamus, you can't come in."

Her use of Grampa Seamus sent a shiver down my spine. I suspected she didn't know my last name—kids rarely knew surnames unless adults used them and they picked them up. "I'll stay here. Did your mother get home last night?"

She swiveled her head, as though she was listening to something from inside the trailer, then spoke rapid-fire Spanish. I wished Megan were here to translate. Valeria closed the door behind her. "Nana says we have everything we need. Can you please leave?"

Her quivering bottom lip gave the lie to her brave front. I was unwilling to depart until I knew whether Kat had returned. I framed the question in a way I hoped she'd answer. "Megan's worried about your mom and asked me to find out if she got home okay yesterday."

Valeria heeled water off her cheeks. She looked at her feet and shook her head.

Now what? I didn't know if Kat's no show was unusual or a common occurrence. Despite her grandmother not wanting me here, my Good Samaritan genes kicked in. "Okay if I take your water containers and fill them for you?"

"Yes, please." Valeria picked up the three jugs at her feet and traded them for my two filled ones. She scampered back to the relative shelter of the stoop.

Fine, smart guy, you gave yourself an excuse to come back. What do you do if Kat still hasn't returned?

SEVEN

SHERIFF LON BARTELLE GREETED ME in the tiny reception area secured from the main facility and led me down a hall smelling of disinfectant. At his office, he said, "I'm fully vaccinated, so you can remove your mask. Long time no see. What's up?"

I ignored his offer to remove my mask since I didn't know who else had been in his office. I passed him a memory card. "This came from my trail camera on Shank Lake Road. I heard of the break-ins on Cable Lake and thought you should see these."

"Hey Tex," Bartelle shouted into the hallway. "McCree's here. Bring a card reader."

I had met Tex, then a deputy, now a sergeant, eleven years ago. Because of a hitch in his step, I had bestowed him with the Tex nickname. Others had picked it up. He entered and plugged a card reader into the computer. "What's up? Love the bird motif on your mask."

Bartelle installed the memory card and a new window opened, displaying a long list of files. "Point me in the right direction?"

"The six pictures from Tuesday."

Bartelle brought one up and whistled. "First time we've seen them on the east side of the highway." He tapped on a picture showing a blurry license plate. "Bet they're using an opaque cover to obscure the registration. Seamus, you mind accompanying Tex to check your neighbors' places, see if anyone was broke in? Knowing which trails to take or ignore will save him a bunch of time."

I bristled at the suggestion I required Tex's help. "Once the rain stops, I was planning to use my daily run to loop around the lake and do exactly that."

Bartelle crooked his arm over his head, which I knew meant he was thinking. "Normally, I'd say fine, but I want Tex to join you this time. When are you free?"

I wondered why, but figured he had reasons. "Anytime until three-fifteen when I leave to pick up my granddaughter in Amasa. Bring a four-wheeler if rules don't allow you to borrow one of mine. Got a plat book handy? I can show you which neighbor properties I know have cameras up. Maybe you can sweet-talk them into letting you download their memory cards."

Bartelle liked that idea and deputized me for this work. "So I don't lose a case on chain-of-custody or some such."

At his mention of handling things, I pumped his sanitizer dispenser and rubbed the cool gel over my hands. He was not telling me everything that was happening. Why?

Eight

MY MAPLE TREES PITTER-PATTERED THE last drops from the rainstorm while Tex and I unloaded the Sheriff department's ATV in my driveway. The sun already warmed my neck, and I enjoyed catching the earthy scent of moist woods in the shaded areas while driving the ATVs to the first trail camera. The fun stopped the moment we discovered a camera that covered a neighbor's gate was missing. It had been there for years, and I offered to call the owners to confirm it should still be there.

"Let's walk and see what we see. I sure wish it hadn't rained last night. Washed away any tracks."

Doors and windows locked. Nothing seemed to be missing from their boathouse, but I admitted I might not know everything that was supposed to be there.

Tex pointed to the grass at one corner of the boathouse. "The overhang protects that area and someone's recently trampled the grass. Yeah, call them."

The husband didn't answer his cell, but I connected with the wife. She was pretty sure the camera had been up, but she'd have her husband call me. They had another camera attached to the pole with the solar panels, and yes, we had permission to look at the memory cards.

We spotted the camera high on the pole. Tex and I dragged over a picnic table and a dented fifty-five-gallon barrel that we set on the table's top. I was taller and climbed onto the wobbly barrel and retrieved the memory card. Even though Tex steadied the barrel, I didn't think OSHA would approve our technique.

Tex inserted the card into his reader and skipped past deer and some of the fattest raccoons I had ever seen chowing down on corn dispensed from a timed feeder. On the night in question, a false trigger at 11:37 p.m. provided three pictures of nothing. At 11:41, the camera caught two people, one big, one small, wearing night goggles.

I said, "Those goggles use infrared, right? They'd see the infrared flash of the cameras?"

Tex chewed his top lip. "If they were looking at it, maybe." He checked the next picture. "They've moved to the window."

Several false triggers followed, which we speculated meant they were walking at the periphery of the camera's sensors. The final shots caught one of them striding away at 12:52.

I did the math. "What took them more than an hour?"

"Let me copy this card. We'll put it back and take another look around."

This time, Tex checked locks for evidence of tampering. He found scratches on the generator shed door lock. "What kind of generator do they have?"

"A portable they use for projects and a big one for charging the batteries that are part of their solar system."

"Call your neighbor again. Most people keep a spare key around. I want to know if anything's missing."

The wife told Tex where they hid the cabin key, and that the genny shed key was hanging on a hook inside the back door. The cabin looked fine, but the entire battery bank and the smaller generator were missing from the generator shed.

I left Tex at the crime scene talking on the phone to the distraught wife and walked up the driveway to open the gate for the crime scene guys. The driveway had to be 300 yards long. No way I would want to hand-carry those batteries that distance. How did they do it?

On my way back, I found where the crooks had cut through the woods on a four-wheeler to circumvent the gate. I back-tracked the path of broken branches to the road, where tire tracks suggested they had parked a truck. They had hauled the batteries out on the ATV. I showed Tex the damage. He agreed with my analysis. He wanted to secure the crime scene and sent me with his card reader to check the other camps around the lake.

They'd stolen one more trail camera, but others had caught their activities at three camps. At the nearest neighbor's, the truck and trailer had turned around in the yard. A camera at the second captured a blurred picture of two people walking through the woods at the road's edge. Sneaky. At the third, the truck and trailer were parked in front of a cabin for three minutes—long enough to check the windows and doors.

I returned with the news to find Tex with another Iron County deputy taking pictures of the generator shed and surrounding area. Using the plat book, I showed Tex what I had found.

"Thanks," Tex said. "I know you caught shots of these guys driving by your place. If they had scouted your buildings, would you have known?"

Goosebumps rose on my skin. "Not the cabin, but there's nothing there to steal. I'm guessing they skipped me because I had a night light on in the upstairs bathroom for Megan."

"Yeah," Tex said, "and maybe not. Make sure nothing's missing from your garage and generator shed. Let me know."

"My batteries weigh two hundred pounds each. It took two muscular guys to lift them off a truck and set them in place. No one would lug those suckers through the woods up to the road."

Tex blessed me with his you're-a-fool-Seamus stare. "Guys motivated by drugs do stuff no rational person would consider. Besides, don't you have an inverter, and controllers, and copper wire?"

NINE

TEX'S WORDS WORRIED ME ALL the way home. He'd mentioned drugs. Did they know, or at least suspect, who these guys were? Like every rural county, we have our share of drug issues between the opioid epidemic now featuring fentanyl-laced products, meth, and heroin. Just what I wanted were strung-out addicts needing money for their next fix.

My check of the garage and genny shed proved everything was copacetic. Walking past the Subaru, I noticed the empty water jugs on the passenger seat. I scrounged two five-gallon containers from my basement and filled them too.

I left early to make sure I wasn't late to pick up Megan again. Seamus's Corollary to Murphy's Law was in full force. My corollary states that if you have planned for every contingency, none of them will happen. I arrived with a half-hour to spare and opened all the car windows to catch the breeze. A distant fire brought a sniff of woodsmoke. I listened to a singing cardinal until it became background noise, then lost myself in the Krueger novel.

Megan opening the passenger door returned me to the real world. I asked if Valeria had ever gotten to camp. As I suspected, she had not. "Then let's take the water to them."

"And invite her for an overnight."

"You can ask if her mom's there, but I wouldn't get your hopes up, Pumpkin."

TEN

THE TRAILER'S TURNAROUND WAS DEVOID of vehicles. I handed Megan a one-gallon jug of water and grabbed two five-gallon containers. Megan's burden slowed her footsteps, but not her mouth. She was full of plans for what she and Valeria could do over the weekend. Schlepping forty pounds of water in each hand, I kept up with Megan, but my arms protested by the time we reached the clearing.

Since I had been there, someone had added freshly split wood to the pile near the firepit. But there was no fire nor any signs of food preparation. Megan called and Valeria appeared from the trailer. She squealed and ran to give Megan a big hug. I set the containers down and shook out my arms. "I brought some extra water."

It occurred to me that the kid couldn't lift the forty pounds, and I didn't know her grandmother's capabilities. "Let's find a place strong enough to support them off the ground." I looked for anything suitable other than taking up the limited table space. "I'll gather rocks to put under them. Where's a good spot?"

Valeria pointed to a level area near a rope swing similar to the one I had hanging from a white pine. I gathered rocks. The kids added handfuls of pebbles to my pile—too small to help. "How about you two go get the other two water jugs from the car?"

Valeria removed the stuffed bear from her wrist and wrapped its arms around the trunk of a sapling. Magnets clicked together to hold it in place. What will they think of next? The girls sprinted down the trail. My lack of Spanish forced me to dismiss my desire to find out how the grandmother was doing. I built the two rock piles high enough to work and placed the heavy containers on them. Rickety. I used the Swiss Army knife I carried in my front pocket to carve several stakes that I pounded into the ground with the hatchet. When I tried again, the containers were level and stable. Hooray.

From behind me, I heard Valeria say, "You ask him."

Megan responded, "No, you ask him."

The kids appeared, supporting the gallon jugs against their stomachs.

I stayed squatted next to my completed project. "Ask me what?"

Valeria put down her water. "Is it true you're a detective?"

"*Private* detective," Megan said. "That's what Seamus means. Momma says it's Yiddish for a private detective."

Valeria tilted her head. "What's Yiddish?"

Megan placed her jug next to Valeria's and put on the face of a college professor. "Momma says it combines German and Hebrew spoken by Jewish people. But Grampa Seamus isn't Jewish. He's Irish, which is close to the same thing, 'cause they sound alike, and he has a Jewish name."

I covered my smile, then controlled my expression. "Well, not exactly. They're spelled differently even though they sound the same. I spell my name S-e-a-m-u-s and the Yiddish word for private detective is s-h-a-m-u-s."

Megan shrugged. "Momma says it's because you solve mysteries for people. Valeria and I want to hire you to find her mother. I'll use my allowance." She misunderstood my frown. "If that's not enough, we can both pull dandy-lions."

Valeria nodded vigorously.

"Dandelions. Valeria, what does your nana say about your mother?"

Valeria's mouth formed words, but none emerged. Megan rattled off some Spanish; Valeria replied, looked at me and said, "Megan says if we hire you, you can't tell anyone things we tell you. Is that true?"

I caught myself rubbing my eyes until they hurt. I'm not a doctor or a lawyer or a priest. "Well, I don't gossip, and I won't repeat anything you tell me unless I must. Like if I had to tell someone something so they could find your mother."

That triggered another Spanish conversation between the kids. Megan said, "Valeria's worried you might talk to the police, and then ICE will deport her nana and put Valeria in prison because Texas wouldn't give her mother a birth certificate for her. You can't let that happen, Grampa Seamus. I promised you wouldn't."

My memory spit out a factoid that Texas had lost a suit about not providing birth certificates for children born of illegal immigrants. Valeria was three or four when the suit concluded, but Texas didn't track you down and say they were sorry for your trouble and here's your paperwork. Guardians had to apply for the documentation, and how many knew they could or how to do it? I could not imagine at their age knowing what deportation meant. What must it be like to live in fear of the government? When I was eight, my father was a sergeant in the Boston Police Department, and jail was a place I visited on take-your-child-to work day. Even as a teenager, after he died on duty, and I joined a gang and didn't want them to catch me, I never feared the police.

"Valeria," I looked her square in the eye. "I promise I will not talk with the police unless your nana gives me permission. Your mother has left you with your nana before?"

Valeria hoisted herself onto the swing and set it to a comforting rock. Three, maybe four, times since they had moved to this trailer, her mother had been gone for a weekend. Those times, Kat had picked up Valeria from the camp Friday afternoon and brought groceries and ice for the weekend. Without a refrigerator, they couldn't keep food long because the ice melted. Kat had always hugged Valeria goodbye and returned before Valeria went to bed on Sunday night.

"Valeria, I know your nana is in the trailer. Will you ask her if she wants anything from the store? I have to shop anyway. If there's something I can pick up?"

"We don't need anything. Just Mama." Tears streaked down her cheeks.

Megan tugged my arm. "Grampa Seamus, do we sign a contract?"

The kid knew about contracts? "Pumpkin, the laws say you have to be an adult."

"I knew that," she said. "We can pinkie swear."

Eleven

I WAS THINKING AND NOT paying attention to the rocks in the road on the way out. My right front tire caught the edge of one and nearly jerked the steering wheel from my hand. The seatbelt snapped tight, and I instinctively threw out my arm to prevent Megan from getting hurt. She squealed from some combination of delight and fear. I was going slow enough that I didn't lose control, but I recognized it as a precaution that I should not think and drive.

A minute later, Megan pointed to a jutting rock. "Grampa Seamus, don't hit that."

"I already hit my quota of rocks for the day, Pumpkin. We're good."

We weren't good. The low tire pressure light glowed soon after we reached paved road. I found a level spot and pulled onto the shoulder. Megan offered me the tire gauge from the glove box. We agreed I had no use for it. The front right was fast becoming a pancake. "Ever change a tire, Pumpkin?"

We made it a team project. I showed her where to position the jack, and she ratcheted it up until it met the frame. At that point, the car's weight was more than her muscles could handle. She stomped on the tire iron to loosen the nuts, but was too light. I loosened the nuts and jacked the car high enough for the task.

Megan untwisted the nuts and kept them in her pocket, waiting for me to remove the flat and install the donut. She threaded and tightened the nuts. We took turns lowering the car, and once it was down, I cranked the nuts tight. We stored the tools and tossed the tire into the hatch. Job completed. Now she knew how to change a tire and had the dirty clothes to prove it.

It was after five o'clock and past normal closing time for the repair place in Amasa. On my arrival, the owner and four dogs the size of buses boiled from the house. He found a slit in the sidewall and declared it dead. He could order one, but it would take at least a week. With the price of gas, I preferred the Subaru over my F-150, and had another idea to get the car roadworthy again.

TWELVE

I HAD PRAYED MY WAY home on the donut and wouldn't risk driving the Subaru until it had new treads. The next morning, I secured the dead tire in my F-150's bed, boosted Megan into the cab, and, with promises of a restaurant meal, pulled out before seven-thirty.

The store in Iron Mountain tried to sell me four tires because "with all-wheel drive vehicles, they should have the same wear." I insisted I would buy one and keep it slightly under-inflated to match the other three. Suddenly, my tire was out of stock. I'd have to order it. You bet I would—from my guy in Amasa.

Megan and I chose a local restaurant for breakfast. While she scarfed down French toast loaded with a "mixed berry" syrup that was thick, sweet, and sticky, I ordered my replacement tire. It would arrive in seven to ten business days. The Iron Mountain tire dealer might be quicker, but they had lost my business forever. I next tried Kim Belanger. "Which motel did Kat work for and what did she drive? I'm going there to see what I can learn."

Kim gave me the place's name and told me Kat drove, "a rusted Ford Ranger, originally red, but now it has black fenders and a blue door."

The motel belonged to a national chain. We surveyed its lot, saw nothing resembling the multicolored Ranger, and parked. We entered the lobby and detoured to the hand sanitizer stand inside the door. Megan bathed her hands in the stuff. I used one squirt to minimize the rotten garbage stench from its denatured ethanol. Didn't help.

Megan delighted in tapping the bell—only a fairy could hear her first try. She nailed it the second time. Its ding brought a harried woman running from the office, tucking a loose hair behind her ear, and arranging her face into a smile. "Do you have a reservation?" Her hand hovered above a slotted rack with pages poking out like porcupine quills.

"Looking for information on one of your employees. Kat Serrano? I understand she works in housekeeping."

She froze like she was playing the game "Mother May I" and did not have permission to move. "I'm sorry, sir, we can't provide information about our employees."

I gave her my friendliest smile. "My granddaughter, Megan, is best friends with Kat's daughter. She and Kat's mother begged us to ask you if Kat left here on time on Thursday, because she never made it home." That wasn't accurate on several accounts, but the clerk didn't need to know we already knew Kat had arrived home early, left, and *then* disappeared.

Management had schooled her well. "I'm sorry, sir, but I'm not allowed—"

"Actually, although we're friends, I am asking as a deputy of the Iron County Sheriff's department." I pulled my shield from my pocket and allowed her a good look. "I'm trying to do this with minimal fuss. You know, no one wants an *embarrassing explanation* written up in official records."

Her flush suggested she could imagine several embarrassing explanations. "If you'll leave your name and number, maybe the bosses will call you back?"

Leaving my information did not strike me as my finest plan. "I can make it easy on you and call them." What a kind person I am to offer.

"Oh, I don't think the Crenshaws would want me to give out their numbers."

"Understood." I memorized the name Crenshaw and squatted to Megan's level. "Shake the lady's hand and thank her for her time."

"Momma says we're not supposed to shake hands because it spreads germs."

"She's right. Mind if we use the restrooms before we leave?" I tilted my head to show I was asking for my ever-so-smart granddaughter.

"No problem. Turn right at the elevators."

I snagged Megan's hand and led her past the elevators, peeked back at the receptionist, and saw she had returned to the office. "Come on, Pumpkin," I whispered. "Let's hurry upstairs."

She slammed on her brakes. "The bathrooms are here." She pointed to the marked restrooms.

I put my finger to my lips and whispered, "We're being detectives and need to be quiet and fast." That did not seem to register. I added, "It's what you hired me to do."

Magic words. In a silent flash, we were down the hall and into the stairwell with the door closed behind us. The motel had three floors. I figured we'd start at the top.

Thirteen

A HOUSEKEEPING TROLLEY STOOD OUTSIDE an open door four rooms from the stairwell. The whoosh of a vacuum suggested the housekeeper might be close to finishing that room. She—I had met only a few male housekeepers and those only in the fanciest hotels—probably had a certain number of rooms to finish in a fixed time. If we waited by her cart, we could talk and minimize interrupting her work.

I told Megan we would ask about Valeria's mom and hope we found someone who worked with her Thursday to learn what happened that day. The vacuum cleaner silenced after a death rattle. The housekeeper, a thirtyish Hispanic, wheeled the beast into the hallway.

"Excuse me. We're trying to find Kat Serrano. Her daughter is—"

"No English." She said and turned away from us.

Megan ran in front of her, blocking her way into the room. "*Por favor, señora,*" which I understood, followed by a bubbling stream of words. The woman smiled at my granddaughter and replied in a flood of Spanish. They conversed for a minute, ending with Megan saying, "*Muchas gracias, señora,*" and giving the woman a little curtsy.

Megan clued me in. "She knows Mrs. Serrano, but she wasn't working on Thursday, but Gretchen was." She pointed toward the trolley at the other end of the floor.

We found a ropey white woman dumping bedsheets onto the carpet outside a room. From down the hall I called, "Excuse me, are you Gretchen? Can we talk a minute about Kat Serrano?"

She kicked the sheets to the wall, crossed her arms over her chest. The sleeves of her uniform top rose, exposing blue butterfly tats. "Who wants to know?"

"I'm Seamus McCree and—"

"My best friend is Valeria, who is Mrs. Serrano's daughter. She left after coming home early on Thursday, and she's missing, and everyone's worried sick for her, and Valeria and I hired my Grampa Seamus to help us find her, and he drove us here to talk to people who worked with Mrs. Serrano, but he doesn't speak Spanish, but I do, and I talked to Juanita and she said you were working here with her on Thursday."

Megan ran out of breath. Gretchen's wide smile showed gaps from missing teeth. "Girl, you talk faster than a used car salesman. I gotta keep working, but you can come in. Your Grampa Seamus needs to stay where he's at." She looked me up and down. "Safety. Door will be open. I'll mute the TV. He can listen. You help me dust. Deal?" She held out a duster.

Megan scrunched her face. "Is this a trick to get me to do your work?"

Gretchen's laugh was deep and changed into a coughing fit. Her face grew red, and I worried she would hack up a lung. Eventually, she regained control. "No trick. They pay me to work, and you're slowing me down." She shook the duster at Megan. "I heard a lot of names, but not yours."

"Megan Nelson McCree." She accepted the duster and followed Gretchen into the room.

I leaned against the door frame and listened to the two-way interrogation as Megan and Gretchen traded questions. Gretchen knew of Valeria because Kat often showed pictures of her daughter. Thursday, Gretchen and Kat had started at opposite ends of the floor. Some time before lunch break, the boss lady came and taped shut one room in Kat's half. Kat seemed upset at lunch, but wouldn't talk. Then mid-afternoon, Kat apologized to Gretchen for sticking her with extra work, but she had to leave early. They hadn't been full, and Kat was such a nice lady, Gretchen didn't mind cleaning a few extra rooms. That was the last Gretchen saw her.

Gretchen's questions of Megan elicited information I didn't know: my granddaughter wanted to become an astrophysicist and discover where black matter went. How she learned of black matter was a mystery I'd explore on our ride home.

The two of them returned and stored their dusters in the trolley. Gretchen unwound the cord for the vacuum. I hurried my questions before she turned the beast on. "Did Kat have any close friends? Boyfriend?"

"Not that I saw. What with working three jobs, that girl didn't even have time to join me and Juanita and the others for any fun. But she dances at the Silver Fox. You know the place?"

"I've driven by it. Never been in."

"You don't want to go in by yourself? You could buy me a drink after my shift. But not with your little chaperone. They got a pole and nude lap dances. I hear there's private rooms, but I don't know how private."

"And you think Kat?"

"All she said was she hated working there. I got to get at it, honey." She plugged the vacuum cord into the wall socket.

"Thanks, Gretchen. Do you know what her third job was?"

"Kat joked once that she got to dress up instead of down. Kinda like it was super hush-hush?" She bent down to Megan. "I hope you find your friend's momma, sweetie." The vacuum's whoosh meant I'd have to find my own answers to my remaining questions about Kat's third gig.

FOURTEEN

THE FORECASTERS CALLED FOR GREAT overnight weather. Clear skies, low of fifty—perfect for sleeping in a tent. We set up one in a grove of cedar trees a few feet from the lakeshore. I lugged down sleeping pads and bags. Megan carried a book to read with her flashlight. A fresh breeze brought water lapping against the shore, and the kid was soon fast asleep, giving me time to research the motel's owners.

The official owner was a limited liability company controlled by Randolph Michael Crenshaw, who went by "Mike." He was a former board member of the Dickinson County Chamber of Commerce and through his LLC also owned a grocery store, bait shop, the Menominee Rapids Resort, the Silver Fox, and a gazillion acres of land in Dickinson, Iron, and Baraga counties. I'd often wondered who was behind the R M Crenshaw Family Trust I saw while flipping through the plat books looking at land to buy for a trust I had created for Megan.

His local home was an eighty-acre property outside Randville. The satellite view showed two big blobs on either side of the driveway where it met the road. Google's walking man hadn't made it down his country road, meaning I couldn't get a ground-level view of what I guessed were stone pillars. His drive ran through well-tended fields and led to a house, garage, and barn. His official residence was in the Moorings area of Naples, Florida, with easy access to the Gulf through Doctor's Pass. The satellite picture showed a private dock and a boat large enough to swallow my house. I exaggerate, but the dude had money.

He had married Anita Palumbo two summers ago, wedding and reception at his resort. My first thought seeing her picture was "trophy wife." Calling her that does not reflect well on me. It's caused by my deep skepticism about reasons a woman with a Barbie-doll figure would marry a rich guy forty years her senior. She might be a wonderful person and the couple deeply in love. Really.

She had no children, but he had four kids split between two former wives. Three daughters, all married, lived in expensive houses in Naples. One son, Randy, owned a modest mid-century ranch in Iron River. There had to be a story about the disparity.

Questions buzzed in my brain. Why was a room on Kat's half of the floor taped off? We knew she left early on Thursday, but why? She had not returned to work. Where had she gone?

Something upsetting had happened at the motel. I tried out the idea that the reason Kat had not said goodbye to Valeria before a long weekend away was because she had to leave earlier than usual and Valeria was at camp. Possible, but she would have told Nana. Nana appeared upset. Was that because Kat was missing or because she knew why Kat wasn't at home? How could I know if she was lying when I couldn't speak her language?

With luck, Kat would show up tomorrow with an explanation. In my gut, I didn't feel that was a winning bet.

* * *

I WOKE TO A FAMILY of otters breakfasting on the lake. They were a chatty bunch. I peeked out of the tent and spotted one flipped on his back, chomping on a fish like it was a corncob. My stirring woke Megan, whose first words were, "Grampa Seamus, will you call Valeria's mom? I want her to come home."

Five-thirty was way too early to call anyone. We had time to enjoy the otters. Then I'd cook pancakes and bathe them in the maple syrup I had created this spring from my sugar maples. Given most kids wake by seven, that was the earliest we would try her mother.

At 6:59 Megan handed me my phone. My call to Kat Serrano dropped into a filled voicemail box. Who else had been calling her? Megan wanted to drive immediately to Valeria's trailer. To prevent us arriving before eight o'clock, I prolonged breakfast cleanup. Sunday was Megan's day to wash the dishes and mine to dry. A good drier can make up for spotty washing, but that morning I insisted Megan rewash until I couldn't find anything to complain about.

They say, "timing is everything." I do not know what would have happened had we left earlier, but I'm thankful we didn't.

FIFTEEN

WE MET A BLUE SILVERADO with super-sized tires and a jacked-up frame on the two-track leading to Valeria's trailer. I pulled my F-150 far to the right and retracted the side mirrors. I risked mosquitoes and stuck my arm out the window and offered a friendly "after you" wave. The truck squeezed by us. Sun reflected off its windshield, and I couldn't get any sense of the driver. I hoped this meant our timing was perfect, and Kat had returned.

I drove to the turnaround. No sign of Kat's Ranger—not surprising, assuming the Silverado brought her home. My hopeful feelings tanked seeing new tracks continuing up the rough grade to Valeria's trailer. If Kat were with them, she wouldn't have directed a truck that big to drive up there because it was too large to maneuver easily. Either she wasn't with them or something, like an injury, necessitated driving to the trailer. I didn't care for either option.

I kept my fears to myself and had Megan lug a one-gallon jug while I carried two more. Our approach hadn't been silent, but the woods we were walking through were. No fire smoke, no chopping wood, no kid playing. My feet dragged to a halt and Megan rammed into my legs. The clearing containing the trailer was a war zone with smashed-in windows, deflated tires, shredded tarp, overturned outside table, and plates, glasses, and mugs shattered against a boulder. Someone had smashed the antlers from the bull moose carving. Valeria's swing hung in two pieces, chopped in half by the hatchet.

Deep ruts gouged the earth where the Silverado turned around.

"Valeria." Megan's wail expressed her angst.

The wind shifted and the smell of propane gas reached me. "Megan," I employed my rarely used do-not-mess-with-me-right-now voice. "Go back to the truck. Now!"

She dropped the gallon jug and flew down the path to my F-150. I ran toward the trailer, making a megaphone of my hands and yelling, "Valeria. Valeria's nana. It's Seamus McCree and Megan. We're here to help."

Propane hissed from the severed line between the propane tanks and the trailer. I shut down the gas at the tanks. It hit me: propane in the tanks meant the attack had to have been by the occupants of that blue Silverado.

I pulled open the trailer door. More destruction: mattresses slit; dishes broken; orange tree paint sprayed on everything. I came back out and again called for Valeria and her grandmother. "It's Grampa Seamus. Megan and I are here to help."

Not even a curious chickadee responded to my calls. With a chest tight with fear, I rushed around looking for bodies—nothing. Had the Silverado taken them? I leaned against a tree to calm my racing pulse and consider what to do. Make sure neither Valeria nor Nana were around and needed help.

My next call for Valeria brought a scuffling of leaves in the distance. Too steady for a squirrel or deer. I cupped my hands behind my ears and swiveled my head as owls do to determine the sound's direction. I soon spotted Valeria leading her nana through the trees. As they came closer, I kneaded my hands to burn off the worry of seeing the child dressed in a thin nightgown. Her grandmother wore a shapeless dress. Neither wore shoes.

I waited until they were in conversation range and tamped down my urge to ask what had happened. "Are you hurt?"

They were not, but they shivered in the morning's cool air. With Valeria giving me her grandmother's permission, I entered the trailer and found their coats—slit by knives. I recovered shoes and socks for both, a sweater for Nana, and jeans, tee shirt, and sweatshirt for Valeria. "Megan is in my truck. I'll get her while you change, and we can decide what to do."

Valeria translated, and her nana gave me a curt nod.

Megan waited for me inside the truck with the doors locked. I told her how proud I was of her mature actions. "If this happened to us, we'd call the police. These folks won't want to have cops look into this because Valeria's nana isn't supposed to be in the country. They'll worry the police will arrest her or at least report her to the immigration service."

"That's not fair." Her face flushed in anger. "If they arrest Nana, what happens to Valeria?"

She gets swallowed by the bureaucracy of child care services, which, despite their best efforts, couldn't help but add to the child's trauma. And I would not add to Megan's by telling her that, at least not now. "The first thing is to get them to safety. Whoever did this might return and trap all of us. I need your help to convince them. Can you do that?"

We climbed the hill, Megan silent, me strategizing. I could check them into a motel. Across the border into Wisconsin might be better. But if we couldn't find Valeria's mother, how long would that work? And then what?

At the sight of Valeria, Megan raced ahead of me, and the two girls met in a long hug. Nana was sorting through the broken dishes as if they were a jigsaw puzzle she could make right. "Valeria, is there any place you can go for several days?" At my question, Nana stopped sorting through the pottery and asked a question in Spanish to which Valeria and Megan both responded. The three engaged in a rapid-fire discussion that involved handholding between the girls. Nana crossed her arms, shook her head. When she hid her face—I suspected to hide her emotions—Valeria ran and threw her arms around the woman's legs.

"Megan, what's everyone saying?"

"There is no safe place they can go, and Nana refuses to leave with Valeria's mother still missing."

I understood the sentiment, but they couldn't stay in this wreckage. The three resumed talking. I zoned out until I realized they were staring at me. I felt guilty, of what I didn't know. "What happened, Megan?"

Valeria answered, "Nana says to tell you thank you."

I asked Megan for an explanation.

"They'll stay in our guest cabin if we promise not to tell the police anything, and I can stay with them while you find Valeria's mom, and tomorrow you can take Valeria and me to the arts academy."

I should have seen that coming. Megan had made logic leaps I couldn't fault since I hadn't mentioned my plan to find a distant motel to keep them safe. If the shoes were on other feet, I would want someone to make sure Megan stayed safe. Ah crap, Sheriff Bartelle still had me deputized. Michigan has no law against not reporting a crime, only for actively concealing one. Was that true for deputies? I could claim I didn't know *for a fact* that Nana was an illegal alien. Anyone could see this was a crime.

A cynic's line goes "No good deed goes unpunished." I would pay for whatever decision I made. I chose people over the law. It was only temporary, I told myself. I'd find a better solution once I got them away from the present danger by their trailer.

Sixteen

It was afternoon by the time we settled Valeria, Nana, and their belongings in our cabin. Everyone was hungry, but Nana refused my suggestion for all of us to walk to the house where I could make something. The kids explained Nana had only agreed to come here because we had the guest cabin. She would not consider entering my home. She had a line that she wouldn't cross—and that I didn't understand.

Nana used a camp stove to heat cans of soup we had rescued from the trailer. While we ate, I created a shopping list for two days' supplies. Nana shooed me out of the cabin proper and onto the screened porch to get out of her way while she washed dishes. Megan went to collect coloring books and pencils from the house for the girls to use while I traveled into town.

Valeria followed me and tugged my elbow, motioning for me to duck my head. She whispered, "Grampa Seamus, is my mother dead?"

The possibility was real, but we had no evidence of what had happened to her. I matched her tone. "What makes you ask that, Valeria?"

"Mama's never been gone this long before. What are wetback horses?"

"Wetback horses? Where did you hear that?"

"The woman was yelling before they. . ." Her lip trembled and a single tear curled down her cheek. "Before they wrecked everything. She kept yelling for the—she used the f-word, Grampa Seamus. For the f-word wetback horses."

F-ing wetback whores. "Were they all women? Did you hear men's voices?"

"No. Just her."

The destruction had all the rage of male testosterone. I hadn't considered that women had done it, but I knew better than to think rage was the sole province of men. What had Valeria's mother done? They were looking for something. How did they know where Kat lived? She might have told them, willingly or under duress. Or was this housing some kind of *quid pro quo*? I told Valeria I had heard the word before. "Telling me what they said is okay. Can you remember their exact words?"

Tears streamed down her face. "Why were they so angry? What does it mean?"

"Can I give you a hug? I know it won't make it better, but it might help a little." She gave a nod, and I wrapped her against my chest. I would not tell her what they were saying, but I owed her some kind of answer. "Some ignorant people call people who come to the US from Mexico wetbacks. Did you see any of them?"

Her head shook a no against me. "We were hiding. Grampa Seamus, please find my mama."

"I will do my best, sugar." I wanted to take her mind off her mother. She had been wearing the stuffed bear around her left wrist. I pointed to it. "You haven't introduced me to your friend."

"Mama gave him to me. He doesn't have a name."

"Oh, we need to change that," I said. "Everyone should have a name."

SEVENTEEN

I STOPPED AT THE END of the cabin's driveway to install the chain to prevent the off-chance of someone pulling in and spotting Nana. I unwrapped the chain from around the quaking aspen where I stored it and stretched it across the driveway, looped it around a second mature aspen. Instead of locking it, I hooked a link on a nail to keep it tight. The point was to make it uninviting for any looky-loos without being a pain in the butt for me when I returned.

I used the half-hour drive into Amasa and its reliable cellphone coverage to plan how to ask my ex-wife for help. I didn't know for sure that helping Valeria's family was dangerous, but given Kat's disappearance and the trailer trashing, the potential was obvious. My first responsibility had to be Megan's safety. Her parents wouldn't reemerge from rafting the Colorado River for another two weeks. A drunk with six previous DUIs who was driving without a license had killed Megan's maternal grandparents. That left my ex, Elisabeth Lane, as my best shot. After years of a broken relationship, we were friends again. Plus, Lizzie loved spending time with Megan.

Her first words were, "Is Megan okay? What trouble have you gotten yourself into this time, Seamus?"

Busted. "Good afternoon to you, too, Lizzie. She's fine, and I'm trying to avoid trouble." I related recent events regarding Valeria and her family. "I don't understand what's going on, but I'm concerned I've created an unsafe environment for our granddaughter. She'll hate me for it, but can you take her? Could be just for a few days, but it might have to be until Paddy and Cindy return from their vacation."

A long sigh came down the line. "One of the most lovable and most frustrating parts of you is your willingness to take on other people's battles. Megan has you wrapped around her little pinkie-swear finger. I don't want to be the one to point out the obvious, especially since I want to congratulate you for thinking of our granddaughter's safety, but Valeria's nana may not be comfortable staying with you if Megan isn't around. I agree, you can't go to the police."

So far, so good.

"You should contact organizations that provide sanctuary to illegal immigrants under threat. Your silence right now means you won't do that because you've promised not to tell anyone."

My silence was simply me waiting to find out if her self-talk would lead her to accept my suggestion.

"You damn McCrees turn a pinkie swear into a granite oath that nothing less than a glacier can crush. Given all that, have you considered that instead of shipping Megan out, bring someone to your camp to look after and protect the kids until you spirit them away?"

"You're willing to come here?"

"A chance to visit the Holy of Holies? I'd love to, except I'm traveling all around the state organizing voter registration drives. I can't come there, and I can't have Megan here on such short notice."

A twitch of disappointment surprised me. "I understand."

"Ask Colleen Carpetti. She's dying to spend more time with you since you guys discovered you are half-siblings—or whatever you're called when you have the same mother and different fathers. Thanks to you, she's got a job she can do from anywhere. She speaks Spanish. Megan thinks Colleen is cool. Coming from a law enforcement family, she knows how to use guns a lot better than I do. Not that I hope it comes to that, but with you, it often seems to. A woman might convince the grandmother to seek help in a way you can't."

Everything Lizzie said made sense, and I kicked myself for not trying to put myself in Nana's shoes and look at this from her perspective. Her daughter was missing—although I still kept a smidgen of hope that Kat could return this evening, ready for work on Monday. People had destroyed most of their possessions. Nana was under threat of separation from her granddaughter and deportation. I'd fear making waves, too.

"Look, Seamus. I'm training trainers in all-day meetings next week. If there is absolutely no other way, of course, I'll take Megan and deal with the consequences. But you have alternatives."

"Thank you, Lizzie. I'm sure it won't come to that. And thanks for your suggestion to try Colleen. If you don't hear from me, assume I have it under control. Good luck with your voter registration training."

"Wrong, Seamus. You created my worries. Now you owe me the courtesy of telling me your solution. Unless I hear from you otherwise, I will assume you *don't* have it under control."

Ex-wives know too much.

I liked Lizzie's suggestion of bringing Colleen Carpetti here. I'd enjoy spending time with her, but I knew someone with more skills and experience dealing with the shit I routinely found myself in. Ashley Prescott, whom I thought of as Niki, was a former FBI undercover Special Agent who now worked secret assignments for the government. To my knowledge, she was between missions.

EIGHTEEN

NIKI ANSWERED MY PHONE CALL with, "If this is a booty call, I'm in St. Paul, not D.C."

I took her booty call mention to mean she was not in a relationship, but her reference to D.C. didn't compute and I said so.

"My cellphone says you're calling from D.C. Where are you?"

"At camp. I just figured it out. When the cell signal is bad, I use the internet to make calls, and I set my VPN for Washington. I'm glad you're in St. Paul. It means you're closer and I have a favor to ask."

I gave her the lowdown on the situation, mentioned Lizzie's suggestion for my sister to help, but if Niki were available, I'd prefer her assistance.

Niki cleared her throat. "You and your ex still trying to work things out again?"

"Like I told you before, that experiment failed. The entire clan is just glad we're friends after decades of being estranged. So what do you think?"

"That you should have left a note for the mother to tell her you have her family and they're safe. When you correct that, why don't you set up a trail camera on the road in to the trailer so we can monitor visitors."

I cringed at the thought of being Kat and returning to find my home destroyed and my child and mother missing. I had been too worried about getting Valeria and her grandmother out of there before the Silverado returned to think through the ramifications. "I'll take care of both things. Does that mean you'll come?"

"I am *bored out of my skull*. And will be until I get my next assignment. Next thing on my calendar is dinner a week from Tuesday with three Pendergast Holdings board members. The meeting's the next day. I can do the prep work from your place."

I considered it prudent to keep quiet. It sounded like she was thinking out loud, not that she had committed to coming. At least she wasn't yelling at me for pushing her to join the corporate board. I waited for her to continue.

"Yep. That'll work. Need to rent an SUV for your roads and pack a bunch of stuff, 'cause I never know what will prove useful. I should get there before nightfall—by midnight, anyway. Regardless, you'd better be up for me. Double entendre intended."

Message received.

Megan acted happy to hear Niki was coming and translated to Nana my intention to correct my blunder of not leaving a note for Valeria's mother. Nana agreed to my plan for her to watch Megan and Valeria while I was gone.

I stopped first at the Iron County Sheriff's office to return the deputy badge. Given it was a Sunday afternoon, neither Sheriff Bartelle nor Tex were in. No one knew how to do the paperwork, so they didn't let me leave the badge. Wasted effort.

I found a perfect spot on the two-track to the Serrano trailer for the trail camera. It had cell coverage, provided a clear view of the road, and was not obvious to someone driving past it. I triggered the setup. Moments later, a notification whooshed on my phone. I opened the app to see a triptych of myself. Perfect.

To avoid getting trapped if the Silverado showed up, I parked on a skidder trail a mile before the trailer and hiked through the woods. The stench of propane had dissipated. Otherwise, everything looked the same. I reread the note to make sure it would reassure Kat, but not point other people to my place.

Your family is safe. They're staying with your daughter's best friend from the summer creative arts academy. I'll bring the girls there tomorrow morning.

I used a broken plate to force the door to stay shut and tucked the note under the plate. She couldn't miss it—if she returned.

NINETEEN

NIKI ARRIVED AFTER EVERYONE ELSE was asleep. We unloaded the bare minimum from her rental SUV and fell exhausted into bed. I awoke twice to the buzz of my phone announcing pictures from the trail cam I left monitoring the route to Valeria's trailer. The first time a doe and fawn sauntered up the road. The second captured a barred owl in flight, carrying a rodent in its outstretched talons. No trucks or cars or people meant Valeria's mother had not returned.

With breakfast dishes washed and put away, Megan and I took Niki to the cabin to introduce her to Valeria and Nana. The four chatted in Spanish, making me a fifth wheel. Nana's shoulders relaxed. Good, Niki was having a positive impact. Then they all shifted their gazes to me and laughed.

A secure person wouldn't care what had caused that laughter. I plotted how to get Megan to let me in on the joke.

"Okay, you two Munchkins, meet me at the road in ten minutes to leave for the Arts Academy. It's looking like rain. I'll tuck your raincoat into your backpack, Megan. Anything else you need?" She didn't.

On the drive to town, the kids stuck with Spanish. Since I couldn't eavesdrop and the day was warm, I lowered the window and bird-watched. Chickadees called their names, nuthatches ank-anked, an undulating flight of a dozen goldfinches twittered past. I startled a broad-winged hawk into the air and flushed a covey of ruffed grouse. I encountered no delays and had time to pick up mail at the Amasa post office—all junk.

At the intersection to Kim Belanger's, a kerfuffle of turkey vultures worked on the remains of something medium-sized—raccoon? If I hadn't looked in that direction, I wouldn't have noticed a blue truck semi-obscured behind a patch of red pines a hundred yards from the road. And a guy watching us through a spotting scope.

Maybe the turkey vultures interested him, and maybe it was not the blue Silverado responsible for trashing Valeria's home. Or it could be as bad as my imagination made it.

I accelerated and ignored Megan's shout that I had missed the turn.

TWENTY

NOT REMEMBERING WHERE THE MICROPHONE was in my F-150 to pick up my voice for the Bluetooth connection to my phone, I pointed my words to Niki toward the screen display. "It may be nothing, but I'm not taking any chances. We're headed back. I don't think they're following me. But if they know where I live, they might beat me there because I'm returning the long way."

Niki made humming noises like she often does to show she's thinking and doesn't want you to interrupt. "You're saying Nana may not be safe here. Where do you suggest I take her?"

"Remember the Deer Lake Campground? Let's meet there. I know a spot to hide our guests until we come up with something more permanent."

"Got it. On my way in last night, I spotted a perfect surveillance spot on The Grade. Nana and I will watch from there to see if instead of following you, they're headed to your place using the normal way. If we pass them before we get to our spot, we'll head directly to the campground. Call me when you get there. And Seamus, make sure they aren't following you."

We signed off. Thank goodness I had called Niki for backup. How could I make sure no one was following me other than stopping and waiting for them to catch up? Even with the rain we had three days ago, dust boiled up behind us. Someone could follow my dust cloud, and I'd never spot them. I couldn't make a quick turn off the roadway and watch to see who passed because the dust would give me away.

Got it. I'd wait to encounter a vehicle going the other way. It would create its own dust cloud and provide cover for me to find a place to turn off and park out of sight. I could run back to the road and watch for followers.

Brilliant plan, except I reached the campground without encountering any traffic. The idea to meet there had been lousy. It had only one entrance, which doubled as an exit, making it a potential trap. I drove past, continuing to the Four Corners intersection, where I had multiple routes I could take to escape if the Silverado showed. I pulled to the road's edge and called Niki. We kept the connection open while I waited for the dust to settle and learn if I had escaped their surveillance.

In a minute's time, the dust cloud had thinned sufficiently to see nearby shapes. The kids were deathly quiet. "It's okay to talk, you guys. No one can hear us." Sixty seconds later, I flicked on my turn signal and reported to Niki. "Looks like I overreacted. I hope I didn't scare you—"

Niki's voice boomed in the truck. "Hold on, Seamus. Something's coming."

The kids hugged each other, fear painting their faces. If Niki didn't say something soon, I might have a stroke.

"False alarm," Niki said. "This one's dirt-covered silver with a GMC logo on the front. Pulling a trailer with a side-by-side. You're good—hang on."

The tick, tick, tick of the turn signal measured the time. Thirty seconds. A minute. The connection remained open, but I heard nothing from Niki. I reached behind me and patted the kids on their knees. Ninety seconds.

Niki's laughter burst from the truck's speakers. "Well, isn't that special? I thought I had a situation. That GMC stopped, blocking the little trail I used to get to my observation post. Two guys got out. One's a hirsute bear eight feet tall and the other one is your size. They started up the two-track I'm parked on, each taking a side. I had my gun drawn when they unzipped and took a whiz. Let me tell you, neither of those guys has a prostate problem. Sorry for the delay. I couldn't say anything until they left."

"You damn near gave me a heart attack. I'll head home with the girls and start packing. How long will you hang to watch our back?"

"Half-hour should do it. If they were coming, they should already be here by now." She cleared her throat. "Unless they're waiting for reinforcements."

TWENTY-ONE

HALF-WAY TO THE INTERSECTION FOR Shank Lake Road, we caught up to the truck towing a long trailer carrying the side-by-side. I dropped back as an extra precaution to prevent anyone from seeing the two girls. The kids were oblivious, making plans for constructing a schoolhouse in the "fairy village" Megan had built near the white pine by the lakeshore where her swing hung. Good, that would give them something to do while I packed supplies to go along with Valeria's and Nana's scant belongings.

Intruding on my creating a mental list came Niki's words describing the truck as a silver GMC. I peered ahead but did not see a trailer plate. I dialed Niki's cell and asked, "Did you catch a plate number on that silver GMC?"

"Nope. Why, they look suspicious?"

I slowed to put more distance between us and filled Niki in on the break-ins and the trail cameras showing a light-colored GMC towing a trailer with a side-by-side UTV.

"And you think it might be them? Pretty bold being out mid-morning."

"Not if we have nothing to ID them with. If they drive down Shank Lake Road, then I'll keep going north. I realize it sounds paranoid, but I'm getting that way."

"Makes sense. Let me know."

The trail cam images of the thieves had captured a big guy and a little guy. Those were relative descriptions. If the big guy was huge, then the little guy could be my size. Did Bartelle already know that?

When I reached the Y for Shank Lake Road, the dust assured me the truck and trailer had continued up the A Grade. I drove to my house and told the girls to have fun at the fairy village. "Take turns on the swing and no going out on the dock without an adult. I'm sorry this is scary for you guys. We still have to be careful. If you hear my horn honk—" I gave it a blast to demonstrate, "—there's trouble." Their eyes widened in fear.

I hated to make them fearful, but it was better than being complacent. "You hear the horn, Megan, I want you to take Valeria by the Lake Path to the log bench we sometimes sit on to watch the trumpeter swans. Go slow and be quiet. You *do not* want anyone to see or hear you. Got it? And stay there until Niki or I come and get you. Or I send someone who knows your secret word. Do not come if I call or Nana calls or Niki calls. Repeat it to me so I know you heard me correctly."

Megan's eyes were owl big, but she had paid attention. I sent them on their way with, "And take your raincoats."

I loaded the bed of my truck with the portable generator I use to run a window air conditioner when it gets too hot, three full five-gallon gas containers, sleeping tents, a twelve-by-twelve screened tent with rain screens, all my sleeping bags and air mattresses, a camp stove and two 20-pound propane tanks, two long folding tables, a bevy of camp chairs, water purifier, a picnic basket with dishes, and silverware for six.

What important things had I forgotten? I toured my garage, spotted water pails, and packed two, along with a portable potty, a skein of rope, and a couple of tarps. I dumped the ice I had in the freezer into a cooler and added food until it was full. Not perfect, but it would suffice for several days, after which we'd need more supplies.

I drove the loaded truck to the cabin. Niki's call caught me packing Valeria's and Nana's stuff. I asked if she was ready to head in.

"Negative. I'm following a gray Tundra and big blue truck with huge tires that make it look like it should be in some kind of mud race. Each vehicle carries two white suspects. Going slow. Michigan plates, and I've recorded their numbers."

"Their ETA, assuming they're coming here?"

"Six miles away, traveling twenty to thirty miles per hour. So—"

"Twelve minutes. I can block the road with my Bobcat and get the kids to a safe spot. Tell me your plan while I'm moving." I ran to my garage, where I stored the skid-steer.

"Park it where the road narrows at the top of your highest hill. They can see it from the earlier hill and turn around okay. If they keep coming, I'll have them covered from a distance."

"Roger. What do you want me to do?"

"Get the kids the hell out. I don't want any collateral damage."

"And Nana?" I engaged the Bobcat's ignition key. The machine generated a piercing warning pitch, telling me to wait nine seconds for the glow plug to warm the engine. I should have donned ear protectors. Deafness arrives on a series of such mistakes.

"I've got a rifle for her. Make sure you block that road."

The nine-second countdown finished, and I fired up the Bobcat. Without letting it warm up, I pushed the throttle from turtle to rabbit and roared up the driveway at its maximum speed of seven miles an hour.

Five minutes later, I parked the skid-steer perpendicular in a narrow spot between two banks that wouldn't allow any cars or trucks to pass. I stuck the key in my pocket. Niki had chosen the placement well. The surrounding trees were sufficiently open that she could see from the other hill. Given her expert marksmanship, she outmatched the guys, provided Nana could provide covering fire.

I ran to the cabin, hopped into my truck, and drove it to the house. I left the motor running and raced down the path to the fairy village.

The girls weren't there. They had constructed a new building in the fairy village, walls, a door, not yet a roof. The susurration of rope on wood drew my attention to the swing, still rocking slightly from earlier use. I peered past the swing to the single dock section poking into the lake. Empty.

I cupped my hands to my mouth and bellowed Megan's name.

Twenty-Two

I'D TOLD THE GIRLS NOT to answer, and they didn't. Had they gone into the house to use the bathroom? I flew up the trail, ignoring the sting of branches slapping my face. The basement door remained locked, and those lights weren't on. I sped up the hill to the kitchen door, stuck my head in, and yelled for the girls. Not there.

Where the hell were they? Megan knew the property well and could have taken Valeria to see the hollow tree, or the blue-headed warbler nest we'd found with the mother still on the nest, or the bald-faced hornets nest attached to branches of a sugar maple, or—too many choices, too little time. I ran to the pickup and honked two long blasts, grabbed the fob and sprinted toward the agreed meeting place.

My phone rang, and I slowed to answer it. Niki said, "Unless they take Ned Lake Road, they'll be to you in four minutes."

"Kids are missing. Try to stall them if you can."

"Roger that. Niki out."

I paused at the main dock. The girls weren't there, and I didn't hear them moving in either direction along the path. The corner of my eye caught sight of the boathouse, a roofed structure with open walls. I changed plans and dragged the canoe to the lake, dumped in two kid's life vests, three seat cushions, and two paddles.

I shoved off and paddled toward the meeting spot. Assuming the girls were waiting for me—I sent a prayer heaven-bound—I'd take them across the lake to a neighbor's camp, which was safe behind a locked gate.

The girls were not at the meeting spot. I tied the bow rope to a yellow birch and clambered onto land. The shoulder of the hill blocked anyone on the road from seeing the shore, making this spot excellent for hiding from the guys in the trucks.

Where the hell were the kids? They should have gotten here.

A horn honked a friendly toot-toot—what I would do if someone blocked my way and I figured they hadn't seen me. I scrambled up the hill, keeping low to the ground, and found a spot in a group of cedars where I could observe both the Bobcat and the meeting site. I crawled under the lower branches, browsed bare from the deer, and crab-walked sideways until I nestled against an uprooted tree and peered around the root ball.

The top of my Bobcat and most of the jacked-up blue truck were visible. The same horn sounded a five-second blast, then multiple vehicle doors slammed. I could only see the gray truck's roofline, but I thought its doors were open. I scanned for Niki at the top of the other hill. No furtive movements. No flash of light catching a scope. If she and Nana were there, they were ghosts.

The click of the Bobcat's door latch returned my attention to it. Someone was climbing in. "No keys," a guy yelled.

"Anyone got a screwdriver?" another asked.

To jimmy the lock. Why not? What's felony vehicle theft if you had come all the way out here to—do what? Why were they here?

A third person tossed something to the guy in the Bobcat. Moments later, the high-pitched beep announced the glow plug's nine-second countdown. I'd focused on what was at my front and had ignored what was behind me. I spun around, expecting to see the girls. No kids. What had gone wrong?

The skid-steer turned on with a throaty roar. I texted Niki, "Game plan?" The phone claimed it had sent the message, but I wouldn't know if Niki got it unless she responded.

Where the hell are those girls? We should be safely across the lake. Now, my only choices were to wait for Niki to engage the four guys or play dumb and apologize for leaving the skid-steer on the road. I could say I had a case of the shits. Sorry for the delay.

No text from Niki.

No idea where the girls were.

The Bobcat lurched like a drunken stock market as the operator struggled to point it forward. Whether by random luck or learning, he succeeded. In thirty or forty feet, he could leave it in a wide spot and allow the trucks to pass. Time for me to intercept them and pretend to make nice.

I used the fallen cedar for support and hauled myself to standing, then proceeded up the hill. No sense calling. They couldn't hear me over the Bobcat's diesel. I was halfway to the road when the Bobcat shut down.

A whistle, like a football coach trying to get his team's attention, cut through the quiet. I couldn't tell where it came from. Two guys got into the blue truck. The gray truck's driver ran and closed its passenger door and circled around to the driver's side.

A rifle shot cracked the air, causing me to flinch and duck. A maple tree branch dropped onto the road in front of the lead truck. "Yo, dudes," Niki called, "Next time won't be a warning. Turn those trucks around and leave. Now!"

I dropped to the ground and hoped no one saw me.

"What the hell, lady? We're just trying to get to our fishing spot." The gray truck crept forward.

"Tell that to the Sheriff's deputies when they get here. Last warning." Another crack of her rifle brought a second branch down, this time on the gray truck's hood. "Back out now. I'll forget the felony you boys committed taking that Bobcat. I'll flatten your tires if you move another inch forward." Seconds later, Niki yelled, "You realize this is a dead end, right? And don't even *think* about trying to flank me if you want to see tomorrow."

That must have convinced them this was a fight they did not want to have. The guy who had moved the Bobcat walked up the road holding his empty hands above his head. Got into the gray truck. The rear lights of both trucks engaged, and they reversed in a hurry.

With rear cameras, it was easy for them to stay on the road and reverse at speed. Were they trying to catch Niki in the open?

Nothing I could do to help. I shifted my thoughts to my other concern: what had happened with the girls?

Twenty-Three

I TRIED THE MEETING PLACE again—no kids. Returned on the lake trail to the fairy enclave. The swing had stopped moving, and the area was deadly quiet. I retreated to my house—no kids. My phone dinged. Niki's message reported the trucks had retreated. She planned to wait and watch, and Nana was walking down the road to the cabin.

I texted: *The girls are missing.*

Niki responded: *Didn't interact with the dudes in the trucks.*

I opened the house door and called, "Megan? Valeria? You guys in here?" Only the ticking clock answered.

I ran down to the tree house. No kids. Nana would get to the cabin soon. I didn't know how to communicate to her that I had lost the kids. Google Translate wouldn't cut it. I could get Niki on the phone, have her translate—I should have learned Spanish.

I met Nana coming down the cabin driveway. She carried the rifle comfortably, and a brief vision of her shooting me for letting our grand-daughters out of sight flashed through my brain. I asked, "*¿Cómo estás?*"

"*Bien. ¿Dónde están las niñas?*"

I figured she was okay, remembered *dónde* meant "where" and guessed she was asking where the kids were and responded with "*No sé.*"

Her eyes widened. She nearly dropped the rifle. "You not know, señor?" She tilted her head and called in a powerful voice. "Valeria, *¿dónde estás?*"

"*Aquí,*" came a tearful voice from the direction of the cabin.

I ran ahead of Nana, yanked open the screen door. They weren't on the porch or in the cabin itself. I called their names. From underneath me came Megan's strong, "Grampa Seamus, Valeria's stuck in the basement."

Only then did I notice they had moved the picnic table on the screened porch, and the trapdoor to the half-basement under the cabin was open. I reached the opening in two steps and squatted. Below me, Valeria lay on the cement floor gripping her ankle. A plastic step stool lay shattered next to her.

Nana stood over my shoulder and flung spitfire Spanish at the girls. Ignoring Nana, I dropped into the hole and asked Valeria what hurt.

"I jumped wrong and broke the stool and my ankle hurts and the back of my head where I hit the floor but mostly my ankle and I can't stand on it and then—"

"And then," Megan said, "I couldn't get her out. We heard the horn, but I couldn't leave her here. Are we in trouble, Grampa Seamus? It's all my fault. Please don't send Valeria away."

"I'm not mad at either of you. I need to look at Valeria's leg before I move her. Pumpkin, once I boost you up, get me a flashlight. And tell Valeria's nana what's going on." I gave her a hug. She refused my offer to help, jumped, caught the opening edge and hauled herself out, all the while jabbering Spanish to Valeria and Nana.

I performed the how many fingers routine with Valeria. She was seeing fine, tracked my finger right, left, up and down. I tapped the minor bump on her head to judge her pain. She sucked in a little breath. I asked her how badly she hurt—from a little scrape to the worst pain she could imagine. Her head felt like she'd run into a door, but her ankle hurt like the time last year she broke her arm falling off her bicycle.

Megan handed down a flashlight. I had Valeria lie on her back and stretch her legs. I gingerly pushed up her pant leg. No protruding bones. Her ankle was twice its normal size, but she reported more pain from the fleshy parts of her leg than the bone. I'd experienced sprained ankles as a kid and broken ankles as an adult. This seemed to me to be a sprain.

An x-ray could tell for sure, but it would raise all kinds of issues if we went to the local emergency room. I had nothing to show I had permission from her mother. Nana probably couldn't prove she was Valeria's grandmother and even if she could, she probably couldn't prove guardianship. Plus, they had no insurance—I could pay the costs, but anything that exposed Nana to scrutiny was a problem.

"You have a sprained ankle, Valeria. You're a big brave girl. I'm going to lift you up. It might hurt a little because we're putting some pressure on your ankle. Tell me if it hurts too much, okay?"

She nodded.

"I'll place one arm under your legs and the other behind your back. We can't both fit through the hole. I'll lift you straight up and set your bottom on the edge. Then hold your hurt foot up and scoot away from the edge. I'll hop out and carry you inside the cabin."

The picnic table covering the hole complicated the process. Valeria gave one little yelp when I bumped her ankle on the trap door frame. "Sorry, sorry," I said. "Almost there."

Megan continued talking with Nana. Whatever she said worked. I hauled myself up and found Nana sitting on the floor supporting Valeria, and Megan shoving a pillow under the knee of Valeria's injured leg.

I scooped Valeria up and laid her on the futon, arranging pillows to support and stabilize her leg. Megan followed my instructions to wrap a hand towel around ice from the cooler I had in the truck's bed.

Nana gently poked and prodded Valeria's ankle, causing the girl to suck in air. The kid was tough. Nana reached for a shoelace. I stopped her hand and shook my head. We needed to control the swelling with ice before we removed the shoe or she wouldn't get it on for a week.

Time was ticking away. Kat had done something that had caused people to go ballistic at her trailer and to bring two trucks and four guys out to my property. Did they think Kat was here? If so, that meant maybe she was hiding somewhere. Or had Kat stolen something they wanted back? Under that scenario, she could be hiding, or they could have her, or she could be dead.

I didn't know what the guys in the trucks planned to do, but we needed to assume they'd return with reinforcements and act accordingly. The number one priority had to be to get Nana and the kids somewhere safe.

Nana kept the ice firmly on Valeria's leg while Megan and I packed the truck with their belongings. I kept a line open with Niki to give me as much lead time as possible if the bad guys returned. She again encouraged me to contact Iron County's Sheriff Bartelle. "We're outnumbered and probably outgunned. If they show up again, I can delay them. But if they have enough guys and are willing to leave bodies, I can't stop them."

"I've been trying to guess what could make them that desperate."

"I'm not saying this is anything close to the actual scenario," Niki said, "but imagine Kat disappeared with a shit-ton of drugs she stole from locals who are tail end of a long cartel supply chain. The cartel wants its money or its drugs, and they don't accept excuses. Saving your life is a big motivator. You see?"

"Too well. I want to move them to Lake Tranquility. Between here and there, a timber company's placed boulders on Lukes Road to block vehicle access. My Bobcat can move them, but it means I have to shuttle back and forth to move rocks, transport people in the truck, then replace the rocks with the Bobcat." I paused to give her a chance to offer to help. When she didn't, I said, "I had counted on you as the second driver."

Niki couldn't find Lake Tranquility on her GPS. I explained it isn't the name on any official maps. I had taken Megan on a tour of the 4,000 acres I purchased for the trust I created for her. She had fallen in love with a private lake. Displaying a vocabulary ten years ahead of her age—or so her proud Grampa thought—she exclaimed she loved it because it was tranquil, with no motors within earshot. She proved she knew what tranquil meant, and I agreed she could name it Lake Tranquility.

"Sounds good," Niki said. "Does Nana drive?"

Embarrassment burned my face at my implicit prejudice. Nana not knowing much English and being here illegally didn't mean she couldn't drive.

TWENTY-FOUR

THE FIRST HITCH IN OUR operation was that the Bobcat's key would not start the skid-steer because of the damage they had done to the ignition slot. I knew the screwdriver blade on my Swiss Army knife solved that problem when the high-pitched glow-plug warning hurt my ears. I swapped the Bobcat's bucket for pallet forks to move the rocks. With Nana and the kids following in my F-150, I jounced at maximum speed down Shank Lake Road and hung a right on Lukes Road.

The Bobcat moved the rocks and replaced them to re-block the road once the F-150 was past. No longer needing the skid-steer until I brought it home, I hid it and drove the truck to the nearest of the three gates guarding entrances to the property. Megan unlocked the gate and closed it behind the truck. We soon arrived at a quarter-acre clearing I'd constructed on a rise overlooking Lake Tranquility, only a stone's throw away from a pier and boat house built to shelter a rowboat. I figured we'd set up the kitchen tarp near the firepit that I had surrounded with several stump stools.

I wasn't worried about Nana and her granddaughter camping. They had used the trailer only as a place to sleep, get out of the weather, and store their few possessions. With the tents and stuff I'd brought, they'd have more room, and the generator and propane would provide a few comforts they didn't have in the trailer.

I placed a camp chair and footstool next to the firepit for Valeria to rest her leg, although it was too warm for a fire. While Nana set up the serving tables, I re-iced Valeria's ankle. She'd kept it elevated during the ride. It had stopped swelling, and she flexed it a little for me. Both good signs, and I felt more secure with my diagnosis and decision that she did not require medical attention.

"Okay, Queen Valeria, where would your majesty like her tent set up? Megan loves it under those evergreens close to the lake. That means hopping. I don't want you putting weight on your ankle for at least a day. I can put it closer if you think that's too far."

She giggled at my silliness, and after conferring with Megan, agreed it was a fine spot. Nana chose my usual place: near her granddaughter's tent, but with enough separation to allow her granddaughter a little independence.

An hour's work had me sweating, but happy that I had thought of everything they required for at least one night. I left Megan to help Nana bring her clothes into her tent, and I walked to the bench bolted onto the end platform of the thirty-foot pier jutting into the lake where I had privacy and good cell service. I closed my eyes and let the sound of waves slapping against the shore relax me. When I almost dropped my phone, I jerked awake.

Niki answered my call. "I have to return my truck and Bobcat to camp, and you and I want to talk where little pitchers and their big ears can't hear us. Do you figure it's wise for you to leave your position and help me transport vehicles?"

Niki asked how safe I thought Lake Tranquility was.

"Nothing is as safe as Nana leaving the area. Lukes Road is the only road that provides access. The boulders I moved block the road coming from the east. You either have to move them or use four-wheelers. Lukes Road from the west has two sketchy areas that stop most people. Even if someone braved the obstructions, all three entrances into the property have locked gates.”

“You’re not convincing me, Seamus. A bolt cutter can take care of those locks in a flash. And all someone has to do is follow tracks from your house. Your Bobcat doesn’t exactly hide where it’s been.”

I agreed. “Once I get the truck and skid-steer back home, we’ll use ATVs to transport us. A couple of trips will help obscure the Bobcat tracks. To prevent wearing a trail they can follow from my place to the lake, we’ll vary our routes using logging trails I know.”

Niki said that was not good enough. “We’ll pray for rain. I think I should remain on guard here, at least until dark.”

In case they come back. “Understood. I’ll take care of moving the truck and Bobcat.”

“Excellent.” She sounded chipper. “Leave Megan with Valeria for the night. You can join me here, and we can strategize. We need a plan.”

“I have some ideas, but I didn’t pack Megan’s stuff.”

“She’s a kid. She’ll be happy to share a sleeping bag with Valeria, sleep in her clothes, and pretend to brush her teeth with her finger. Ask Nana to cook dinner for the three of them. Given all you told me, I’ll feel better if you and I overnight at Lake Tranquility.”

An involuntary shiver tightened my back. “You’re that worried?”

“I’m that careful.”

I was just thinking that sounded reassuring when she added, “And that worried. Get your vehicles back home and then bring food so we can talk and eat. And keep your damn eyes open.”

That was not reassuring.

Twenty-Five

It took damn near forever to tow the F-150 home with the skid-steer, but that was still faster than if I had shuttled them back.

I was hungry, and tired, and discouraged that the day had been a net negative. I filled all the ice cube trays with water to make more ice for Valeria's ankle, then packed the two-up with the supplies Niki and I needed. Besides an extra layer of clothes and a change of underwear, I included our toothbrushes, toothpaste, and her birth control pills. I reconsidered letting Megan wear the same clothes a second day and brought a change for her. I didn't bother with her toothbrush; she'd be asleep before we got there.

For dinner, I chose blocks of three different cheeses, a box of Triscuits, a bowl of mixed fruit, and two apples. Alcohol was a lousy choice given the circumstances. I packed two water bottles and a six-pack of Megan's apple juice boxes.

I grabbed my headlamp from its place on the hallway pegs and spotted a charger plugged into the wall. A sweep of the house netted various chargers, my laptop, and the burner phone that related to Niki's undercover work. I tossed them all into the computer backpack. What else would I need if I couldn't return here for a couple/three days? I packed Megan's and my passports, a guarantee we'd be back in the morning.

Niki's spot on a logging road used a curve to allow her to see vehicles driving toward my place, but hid her SUV from them unless they looked over their shoulder as they passed her. To prevent anyone noticing the four-wheeler, I pulled it deeper into the woods.

Niki delighted in the pop that came by stabbing the apple juice boxes with the miniature straw. Simple pleasures to reduce stress. Between bites, I poured out my concerns that my plan to locate Valeria's mother was like trying to follow cloud wisps. We had no clue who or what we were up against. My instincts told me Kat had not gone missing of her own volition, which meant every second we didn't find her was a second they could kill her.

I had tried to convince myself Kat might have left to protect her mother and daughter. Problem was, the more I learned of the Serrano family dynamics, the more certain I became that Kat would have warned them of the danger.

I rambled on. "Assuming those two trucks have something to do with Kat's disappearance, what do you think about us reporting the damage to the Bobcat? We could mention seeing the two trucks. Problem is, we probably don't want to mention you shooting at them, and officially, I'm still deputized, which means I should have called all this in hours ago."

She reached around and retrieved a camera with a telephoto lens. "That house of cards won't stand in a summer's breeze. I got pictures of three guys and their plates."

"I didn't realize you were a Nikon person, too."

"The difference is you buy yours, and I get mine from Uncle Sam. I prefer Canon, but I can't argue that black lenses make more sense than those white barrels of Canon. Back to business, check the pictures. Recognize any of them?"

I did not.

"Then answer me this: how did they know to wait for you in Amasa at that arts academy camp?"

Good question. "I didn't tell anyone I was bringing Valeria to the camp. Someone must have read my note outside the trailer and knew enough about Valeria to piece it together."

"Or," Niki said, "they saw the note, didn't know who it was, lay in wait, spotted her in your truck, and followed."

"Not directly, though. They waited for help and drove straight to my place."

"Which means they figured out who you are. I could ID you from your plate. How did they?"

"Maybe they asked Kim Belanger, the Amasa Summer Arts Academy owner? She's pretty protective of information, though. But the other kids all know who Valeria's best friend is."

Niki chewed on her bottom lip. "Meaning one of the guys has a kid at the camp? That's a stretch."

"Agreed. I'll call Kim and apologize for not telling her the girls weren't coming today and inform her they'll also be absent tomorrow. I'll slip the question into the conversation."

Niki rubbed her buzz cut. "You really should consider getting all the civilians the hell out of here and report the mother missing. Since the Iron County Sheriff's department is small and Kat worked across lines, they'd most likely call in the Bureau. They're good at missing persons."

"I gave my word I wouldn't."

"So we convince Nana."

"Feel free. Problem is, if we hide Valeria and Nana somewhere and report Kat missing, the first question is why are you reporting this and where's the family. I can't imagine your former associates at the FBI would take it well if

I told them, 'Don't worry, I have the daughter and grandmother in a safe place, but you can't talk to them.' No—"

Her deep chuckle silenced me. "Got it. But I'm telling you, Seamus, if we don't figure this out PDQ, Nana will face two ugly alternatives. She sticks to her guns, stays until she learns what happened to Kat, and risks being exposed and deported as an illegal alien. She loses Valeria to the system. Two, she tries to find somewhere to raise Valeria when she doesn't even have a green card."

I agreed Nana was between the proverbial rock and a hard place. "Then we'd better discover what happened."

TWENTY-SIX

KIM PICKED UP MY PHONE call on the second ring and turned the table on me. "Any news on Kat?" I said I was not aware of any change and asked whether anyone had asked about Kat or Valeria.

"No one's asked about Kat. Some kids wondered where Megan and Valeria were."

"But no adults asked about Valeria?"

"Why would they? What's going on?"

Kat had trusted Kim enough to share that Kat was a Dreamer. I took a chance and told her someone had threatened the Serrano family.

"That's terrible. Are Valeria and her grandmother okay?"

"For now, but the kids won't be returning to the academy. Let's leave it at that." I hung up.

Niki patted my arm. "Good try, Seamus. I will ask you a question that you will answer yes. Got it?"

"Yes."

She swatted me. "Not that question, you jerk. This one: did the assholes in the trucks act like they might be part of a local militia?" She waved her hand to indicate I was to respond.

I squinched my face to let her appreciate I didn't understand what she was up to and dutifully answered, "Yes."

She pulled up a secure encrypted browser on her phone and entered a website I recognized as the one only five of us had access to: Niki, me, an FBI agent nicknamed Rick the Prick, FBI Deputy Director Ambrose, and Averell Harrington Park, the Assistant Director of National Intelligence. She typed a message for Park's eyes only but showed it to me before she hit send.

CI identified three suspects in a new domestic terrorist cell. Permission to use Rembrandt to identify.

"Rembrandt?" I asked.

"A super secret database and facial recognition software system. Not only can it identify most of the people in the US, it maps eighteen months of the target's whereabouts."

"Meaning what?"

"Any interactions with law enforcement reported to the federal government. License renewal, court cases. Social Media posts or tags with time or location stamps. I don't know what all else they access."

"Ignoring whether your *confidential informant* had his head up his ass when he said yes, isn't spying on Americans illegal?"

"National Director of Intelligence has authority to approve. If he wants to add information to the database from credit card purchases, bank account records, *et cetera*, he must get a special court order. I'm not asking for that."

"You know I contribute to the Southern Poverty Law Center, Amnesty International, ADL, and a bunch of other groups like that, right?"

"Yep. And I also know you are harboring an illegal immigrant and you've lied to local, state, and federal law enforcement. You and Rick the Prick are my cutouts to give Deputy Director Ambrose and ADNI Park deniability for my undercover operations. It's not like you're a virgin here."

I held up my hands in surrender. "I trust you, Niki. How long 'til we get answers?"

"Tomorrow, if they're in there. Hello, what do we have here?" She pulled binocs to her eyes and scanned the road. "Is this the GMC? It's pulling a trailer. Grab the camera and go take pictures. Don't let them see you."

I waited until they had passed before racing to the road. Using a tree as a blind, I took a series of shots as the truck and empty trailer pulled away. The brake lights flashed. I froze. Had they spotted me? The brakes released. Must have been slowing for a pothole.

Niki and I reviewed my images. Niki spotted red tape covering a hole in the trailer's right rear brake light. I didn't recall that detail from the trail camera pictures, but felt pressure to act. "I should alert Bartelle. If he has someone close to Amasa, maybe the officer can pull them over for a safety check."

"You do that," Niki said, "and you definitely can't *ever* tell him about the two trucks and what they did to your Bobcat."

It hit me. "Because even if I could come up with an excuse for delaying until now, I would certainly mention it when I reported this. I gotta call this in. Bartelle deputized me on this. I can't let—"

"So call."

I chose Sheriff Bartelle's personal cellphone number rather than going through the hassle of calling the office and having to bring someone up to speed.

"Lon," I said, "this might be nothing, but earlier today Niki—" *Oh crap, I hadn't meant to say her name.* "You remember the undercover FBI agent from years ago?"

"Of course, I do. Who could forget? Niki was like her childhood dog, right? What was her real name?"

Not my place to tell him. "She saw a silver GMC pulling a trailer with a big side-by-side UTV going north on the A Grade past Shank Lake Road earlier today. Just now, we spotted the truck returning toward Amasa with an empty trailer. Someone used red tape to repair the trailer's right taillight. Did any of the trail cam pictures of those guys stealing generators and propane tanks show anything similar?"

"Give me a sec." He put me on hold for two minutes. "Dispatch says we don't have anyone who can get to Amasa before that trailer reaches the highway. But yes, that was a detail we did not release to the public. Thanks for the heads-up, Seamus. What's Special Agent . . ." He continued after I didn't supply her name. "What's she doing up there?"

"A brief vacation to clear her head."

"Tell her that if it's a working vacation, I'd appreciate a heads-up."

"Nothing like that."

"Good. Why don't you make another circuit of the trail cams in your area and check for overnight activity?"

I should have ignored the receptionist and left the damn deputy badge on his desk. I agreed—how could I not without raising questions?—and ended the call.

Niki had a shit-eating grin on her face. "Oh yeah, just a brief head-clearing vacation. Score another one for white lies in the cause of justice."

TWENTY-SEVEN

TUESDAY ARRIVED WITH MEGAN CALLING outside our tent, "Grampa Seamus, Niki. Time for breakfast."

"Be there in a minute," I said. I eased Niki's leg off mine. "We overslept," I whispered and kissed her neck.

"Amazing how well I sleep after a fine roll in the hay. So much for seconds." She whipped the sleeping bag off us. "Oh good, not broken. We can do this again." She rolled away, and we donned clothes and exited the tent to discover the sun scraping the tops of the trees. The air was moist with fog, no fire. Five-thirty, for Pete's sake.

"Grampa Seamus, are you going to find Valeria's mother today?"

Nothing like the focus of a kid.

"She had nightmares and was crying for her Mama during the night. I didn't know what to do and pretended like I didn't hear."

I squeezed Megan's shoulders and realized she was a coiled spring. "It's hard to know the right thing. Sometimes the best we can do is listen. It's not like you can understand exactly what she's going through, but you could imagine how bad you'd feel if your mother disappeared."

She could.

"Tell her that and give her a hug. I don't know if we'll find her mom, but we'll try. Won't we, Niki."

Niki knelt and looked Megan in the eye. "I heard your grandfather pinkie swore with you."

Megan grinned.

"Then that's your answer, isn't it? You two hired him, and I have every confidence he will do everything in his power to find Valeria's mother. I have something for Valeria to keep." She pulled a nickel-sized stone from her pocket. "Know what this is?"

Megan did not.

"It's pink granite. Your Grandmother Elisabeth told your Grampa Seamus that his pinkie swear was as solid as granite. It's not indestructible, but it withstands a lot of pressure. Give that to her to keep as a reminder. I see Nana is about to start the fire. Maybe you and Valeria can help gather wood?"

Megan held the rock like a talisman and ran to Valeria.

I offered Niki a hand to stand. "You remembered me telling you that, and you thought to find a piece of granite? You'd make some child a wonderful mother."

"Oh, hell no. Nieces and nephews are more family than I desire."

"No ticking clock?"

She looked at me speculatively. "What, you want another kid?"

I tripped on a rock. That was the farthest thing from my mind.

"I see the answer is no. Then let's agree we never have to have this conversation again." She called to Nana in Spanish, and the buzz saw I had fired up marched away.

I'd bet good money Niki had been asking herself the exact question I had posed.

BREAKFAST CLEANUP COMPLETE, NANA REFUSED help washing the dishes. I sent the kids to catch dinner from the pier. Megan loved fishing and was a pro at baiting hooks and dehooking ones she caught. Megan raced toward the lake, raising the dead for a square mile with her whoops and hollers. Halfway there, she stopped and galloped back to take Valeria's arm and help her to the dock.

Niki declined to join me in fulfilling my promise to Bartelle to check the trail cameras around the lake. She wanted to run the portable generator, set up a satellite internet link, and download material Rembrandt developed based on her photographs.

"I'll kick on the generator for you. When I get back, we'll take the offensive and shake things up. Let's meet Mike Crenshaw and take his measure. He could prove helpful—or a danger. I assume you brought your supply of undercover disguises."

TWENTY-EIGHT

NIKI AND I CHOSE ONE of the obscure tracks to drive the ATV from Lake Tranquility to my house. While Niki pulled together the supplies she wanted for this trip, I watched the road from the upstairs bathroom window to make sure no company surprised us.

"Ready?" she called up the stairs. For her outfit she chose short shorts, open-toed sandals, and a flowered bikini, covered by a sheer top that displayed her six-pack. A shoulder-length brown wig with purple highlights hid her clippered hair. She'd made up her eyes to look big and startled. She flashed her hand to show off an engagement ring with a rock the size of a softball.

"That's what you're wearing?" I shook my head at my inept way of phrasing my question. "The mosquitoes will love you."

"You said you planned to approach Crenshaw as fellow land barons. He has a trophy wife. You, my dear Seamus—" She batted her mascaraed eyelashes "—have a trophy fiancée. Don't you agree?"

Choose your words carefully, Seamus. "How much did that engagement ring set me back?"

"A quarter million at a Sotheby's auction."

"I went to an auction?"

A grin crept onto her face. "Well, a minion bought it for you."

"I sure can't tell the difference between diamonds and zircon or whatever those fake diamonds are."

She reached past me and scraped the ring down the edge of the bathroom window, leaving a scratch. "No, you can't. It's undercover bling I wear at high-end parties where I act as the dumb escort on the arm of some rich guy. Surveillance subjects talk freely in Mandarin because escorts are eye candy, not smart enough to understand their language. Try this on."

She handed me a shorter-haired blond wig. "It's just to get us out of the woods. You want to surprise Crenshaw, right? That means if those guys are working for him, we need to slip past, so they can't warn him. And if they don't work for him, we don't want to bring a tail to his house. We'll take my rental, but that won't do any good if someone recognizes you. Find an old pair of glasses with a different look. And put on a hat. You can return to your normal charming self before we meet Crenshaw."

"A quarter million? Really? They let you just keep it?"

"The diamond used to belong to a Mexican cartel until the DEA seized it. Sotheby's is a cover story. One more thing. You need to wear my ankle holster." She shimmied her hands down her bare legs. "I obviously can't, but I do not want to be far from a weapon."

"I don't have a concealed carry permit."

"So don't get caught. Let's go, Mr. Sugar Daddy. Time's a-wasting."

WE DID NOT SEE ANY suspicious vehicles during our drive to Valeria's trailer. Someone made finding my trail camera easy. They had tied orange logging tape to nearby branches to mark it. Huh. At least they didn't steal it. Maybe they thought it would transmit their location if they did?

I discovered another trail camera strapped low on a black cherry tree. Niki gave me a pair of evidence gloves, and I swapped its memory card with one of mine, slipping theirs into an evidence envelope. With the disguises, makeup kit, weapons arsenal, and evidence kits, it was little wonder she used an SUV to travel. There may have been more trail cams, but we agreed the risk of having our pictures taken outweighed whatever we might discover from their memory cards.

I left Niki in her SUV for my stop at the Iron County Sheriff's office. Bartelle was out, but Tex was there. I reported my morning survey of the Shank Lake area trail cameras and returned the deputy badge. He tried to get me to keep it, but I held firm and escaped before he pressed for my reasons.

While driving to Mike Crenshaw's place, Niki asked what it was I hoped to accomplish with this visit.

"He owns the two places we know where Kat worked, and maybe had something to do with the third. What better way to find out if he's feeling guilty than to observe his reaction when we show up at his door? If he knows me, don't you think he'll show surprise, give himself away?"

She tapped her lips like she was considering the idea. "And if he's not home?"

"He will be." At her skeptical head tilt, I added, "Irish intuition."

TWENTY-NINE

THE GATE TO HIS ESTATE stood open. A good start. His half-mile driveway wound past fields planted in corn on one side and canola on the other. I caught myself licking my lips. Nerves. Niki patted my leg. "Just be your charming self."

The garage doors were closed, an older John Deere tractor, bucket resting on the ground, stood in front of the barn. The windows on the house were open to the gentle breeze and mid-seventies temperatures.

I helped Niki from the passenger seat. Like besotted love birds, we linked fingers and swung our arms on our walk to the house. Mrs. Crenshaw met us with a smile and a "Help ya?"

She wore a crop top a size too small. Her bleached hair was strategically messy, designed to make you think she'd just come from bed or wanted to take you there. Her stretch pants hugged stick legs, a wide belt drew attention to her pelvis. Unlike Niki, who was solid muscle, this woman bordered on anorexic. Whether she kept her weight low by starving or drugs, I wouldn't bet. I widened my eyes with feigned interest because she would expect that reaction. While I was sizing her up, she gave Niki the once-over.

"We were driving in the area, and I hoped to catch Mr. Crenshaw."

"Does he know you, Mister . . . ?"

Good. He was home. I dropped Niki's hand like a dead fish and offered mine to Mrs. Crenshaw, along with a big smile. "McCree, Seamus McCree. I'm interested in talking to him about some land. Won't take but a couple of minutes."

She didn't shake my hand so much as allow a touch. From inside the house came the rumble of a voice scratched by years of tobacco smoke. "Who is it, Bunny?"

I called past her, "Seamus McCree, Mr. Crenshaw. I hoped to steal a minute of your time to talk about our mutual interest in land. If my proposition intrigues you, we can discuss details later at your convenience."

He appeared behind her shoulder, a suntanned face carved by fault lines. His smile, a knife slash over his square chin. His gravestone eyes performed a CAT scan of my upper half. A big man, maybe an inch taller than my six-two, he had a broad chest and massive arms furred with gray hair. He offered a hand with the distinctive tanning of a lefty who plays a lot of golf. "It's Mike. Heard you're buying up land in Iron and Baraga."

His handshake was solid, with no extra pressure to show me he was the stronger of us. My immediate reaction was relief that I was meeting him as myself. He'd lay bare any act I tried to put on. I hoped he couldn't see through Niki's.

He released my hand. "Still have big northern in Shank Lake?"

So he knew where I lived. I assured him my fishing neighbors said the pike were plentiful. "Not a good year for perch, though."

"I got some time now. Bunny, why don't you give the little lady a cocktail on the veranda while Seamus and I talk business in my study? I was about to get something to wet my whistle. What's your poison?"

Not a time to ask for a glass of wine. "Beer would be great."

"Follow me."

Bunny stepped aside. He led me into a country kitchen, opened the refrigerator, and pointed to a shelf of beer. Miller Lite outnumbered the other choices two to one. Not my favorite, but likely his, so I chose a Lite and twisted off the top. He pointed under the sink for the trash can. I'd guessed right. He grabbed a Lite and drank from the bottle.

He led me through a living room dominated by dead animal heads, down a hallway into a dark-paneled office that featured a burl-wood desk, which I admired. "Had that made from a sugar maple I found on my land." He pointed to a pair of two-seater couches framing a coffee table. "Grab a seat. Did you have a particular property in mind?"

No idle chit chat with this guy. "I've been acquiring land to leave something for my granddaughter. The U.P. forest tracts are being chopped up, and I wish to keep the open space that brought me here. I donate the development rights to assure it stays the way we love it—and I get the tax deduction."

He chuckled at that. Good start, one businessman talking to another.

"My long-term plan is to improve the woods to combine sustainable timber harvests while increasing plant diversity. Probably too much information. I wanted you to know that if you ever considered selling, I'm interested in buying. For now, I'm adding land only in northern Iron, southern Baraga, and the southwest sections of Marquette County."

He took a long pull of the Lite, and those captivating eyes held mine like a tractor beam until I blinked and looked away. He set the bottle down. "That's interesting. I couldn't tempt you to buy a motel in Iron Mountain, could I? Good cash flow, recently updated. Wants a better manager than my son."

I used drinking beer to cover my surprise at the non sequitur. "Not his thing?"

"I'm a nuts and bolts kind of guy. He's developed all kinds of package deals for the resort, but the motel is too mundane for him. I'd be willing to price it based on current cash flow and share what we were doing before I put him in charge. Maybe add that to a few sections in Iron and Baraga?"

I matched his earlier pull on the bottle. "Only way I could do that is if I had a buyer for the motel lined up. I have zero interest in learning that business. Especially now. Getting workers must be tough."

His wave dismissed my concern. "Not if you know where to look, but I hear you." He drained his beer and set it down on the coffee table. "Well, keep your eyes open for someone interested in a motel, and I know we can make a deal."

I finished my beer and placed the dead soldier next to his, making sure not to let his eyes capture mine. "I appreciate your time, Mr. Crenshaw."

"It's Mike. If I'm willing to tell you that my son sucks at managing the motel, you can call me Mike, don't you think? Let's rescue the girls from each other before they tear themselves apart with their kindness."

THIRTY

KNOWING CRENSHAW WAS WATCHING US walk to the SUV, I maintained my possessive fiancé role and tucked my hand in Niki's rear pocket.

She wiggled her butt, leaned in, and nibbled my ear. "Having fun, are we?"

I kept my voice quiet. "All for show."

"Yeah. A bulge in your jeans says otherwise." She laughed and twisted away from me, slapping my hand. "I'll give you a show." She ducked herself under my arm.

Ruh-roh. Niki had an exhibitionist streak and a devil-may-care attitude. "Remember, we might have to deal with him again."

"Seamus, would you put the sunroof down? I think I'll work on my tan."

I assisted her into the passenger seat. By the time I got in on the driver's side, she had removed the sheer top and was arching her back in a stretch, fingers locked behind her head. I turned on the engine and opened the sunroof. Niki unfastened her bikini and tossed it and the top behind the seat, giving Crenshaw a fine view of her firm breasts. She lowered the seatback and stretched out with the sun caressing her.

"Drive, Seamus. And lick the drool off your chin."

I STOPPED BEFORE CRENSHAW'S DRIVEWAY reached the street. "Better get decent."

"I must be losing it if you're not planning to jump my bones."

"Such a sick attempt to solicit compliments. Learn anything from Bunny?"

Niki retrieved her clothes from the rear and dressed. "Close the damn sunroof. I don't want to lose my wig in the wind. Bunny's Bloody Mary was high on vodka, low on tomato juice. She either has the metabolism of a shrew or she's doing drugs."

"Her eyes looked fine to me. She could be anorexic or bulimic."

"Could be. She'd be disappointed that you were looking at her eyes and not her rack. She's originally from Illinois. Hates winter. Is not fond of the U.P. Loves the yacht crowd in Naples and can't wait for their return at the end of August. Her mouth smiled a lot. Never made it to her eyes. I would not turn my back on that woman. On a brighter note, she wanted to know if we were 'friendly' with other couples. You into wife-swapping?"

She cut her eyes toward me and laughed at my raised eyebrows. "Not leaping at that opportunity? I told her you were a prude and left her the impression I was up for other possibilities."

I related my discussion. "You don't trust Bunny, and the hair on my neck tingled every time I caught Mike's eyes. That's a scary combination. You up for a visit to his resort on the Menominee river?"

She browsed their website on her phone. "Strikes me more like a party than a family place. I'm dressed fine. What's your cover story?"

"Party place? Somewhere Kat might dress up for fancy entertaining? Cover story—how about we're shopping for a place to hold my bachelor party?"

"Oh, you handsome devil you, and you plan to talk to the manager while the little lady is not in earshot. Well, that might get you thrown out on your ear."

"Bet?"

"Sure. You win, I'm on top."

"So now who's the horny one? And if you win?"

"I'm still on top. Twice."

THIRTY-ONE

THE MENOMINEE RAPIDS RESORT INCORPORATED a main building, a maintenance area, and twelve "rustic" cabins.

An overly endowed barmaid gave us a tour. I wondered if Mike Crenshaw had hired her. The main building housed reception in the middle, the public dining area on the left, a taproom on the right and through it, a separate private room that could accommodate a couple dozen folks. Tour complete, she led us to the office.

Randy, as he introduced himself, was not impressive. He was golfer tan, several inches shorter than his father with none of his old man's solidity. At thirty, he had gone to flab.

Rather than walking to the cabins set a quarter mile from the main building, Randy insisted we use a golf cart. The cabins fit the definition of rustic only in their exterior rough-cut half logs. The inside had hardwood floors with underfloor heating, wide-board pine walls and ceilings, and a cedar-lined sauna. In the one we toured (the guest was rafting today, a friend of Randy's who wouldn't mind if we took a quick peek), a real bearskin rug had pride of place before a crackling wood fireplace that provided a whiff of woods smoke. A stocked bar featured premium beers and liquors. A massive flat-screened TV with satellite hookup covered most of a wall, with a love seat and two recliners providing the viewing spots and access to an entertainment center. "Just got Starlink," Randy bragged. "Faster internet than in town."

The single bedroom had enough room to walk around a king-sized bed. Mirrors covered one wall. A skylight above the bed allowed for star gazing or, as I discovered when I twisted a knob, converted into ceiling mirrors for viewing other delights. Randy gave me a wink. *Really?*

The bathroom was the same size as the bedroom and provided a two-person jacuzzi that looked onto the river if you raised the blinds, and a shower with two showerheads and grab bars strategically placed for non-cleansing activities.

Niki oohed and aahed her way from room to room, squeezing my arm at each new discovery, shooting me lustful looks. Given our earlier conversation, I wasn't sure how much was acting. Since Randy had to show us an occupied room, I assumed there were no vacancies and risked asking if they had a room available for tonight. Alas, they were booked until after Labor Day.

"Hey honey," I said, "want to check their fire ring and barbecue pit?" Niki wiggled her ass out the door. "So," I tried to sound conspiratorial, "do you ever book the entire resort, like for a bachelor party?"

His wide smile grew wider. "When were you looking at?"

"Next year. Sometime around bird season. Ten, twelve of us."

His smile faded. "Well, we haven't started taking reservations, so it's wide open. We'd have to insist on a minimum three-day stay, and at that time of year, our residents typically book guide services, that sort of thing."

"We were thinking four or five days. Time to do some hunting, some fishing, run the river." I thought he would pee his pants. Time to jiggle the line and hope he grabbed the bait. "Do you supply entertainment or is that something we'll have to arrange ourselves? Hunting and fishing are better without female company, but you know, a little dance-band combo to go with a little dancing." No bites yet. I dropped more chum into the water. "And no one wants to waste water showering by themselves." I gave a shrug. Like what could you say?

He could respond that they did nothing of the kind. Instead, he rubbed his hands like he was already feeling the money. "We'd reserve the private dining room for your group. The band is no problem. We have an arrangement with an escort service to supply dinner companions. The main area is family friendly, but what happens in the cabins is between consenting adults. Once we determine what add-ons you want, we'll require a fifty-percent deposit. The rest paid a month before the event. That does *not* include tips." He flashed a shit-eating grin. "Our escorts prefer their tips to reflect the services they provide."

I knew his kind from Wall Street. Hookers were not a problem, and for the right fee, I suspected nothing else was either for this guy. Making money was all that counted. I would not want to stand between him and a dime lying in the gutter. Niki burst in, glowing with excitement. "I'm so pissed you guys found this first. Randy," she drew out his name. "Do you have any sister facilities I could use for a girls' weekend?"

The minuet played out with our good buddy Randy buying us a beer at the bar, ogling Niki whenever he thought I wasn't looking. I apologized that I couldn't commit today. We had one place to visit in North Dakota, where we could combine elk hunting with other activities. I promised to talk with him before I decided. And Niki hinted she'd be the one talking to Randy if I chose North Dakota. He gave us both brochures and his business card. Written on the back of mine was his private phone number to "continue our discussions to make sure we fully satisfy your guests."

On our exit, Niki surreptitiously used her phone to photograph all the visible vehicles and their license plates. No gray Tundras or silver GMCs, jacked-up Silverados or rusted Ford Rangers with different colored doors. I asked which car she figured was Randy's.

"The blaze orange Caddy Blackwing. Not prime for U.P. winters, but it's the only vehicle registered to him."

I did not ask how she had learned that. "He strikes me as sleazy. I wanted to wipe my hand on my pants after we shook. He bears investigation."

Niki drove away from the resort. "Have you asked yourself why he works in Iron Mountain but lives in Iron River? While we know he's here, let's pay his house a visit."

"You think we're going to find Kat's truck parked in his garage?"

"Doubt it, but who knows what we'll learn until we get there?"

THIRTY-TWO

RANDY CRENSHAW'S HOME WAS AT the edge of what locals still called Stambaugh two decades after it and Mineral Hills had both merged with the city of Iron River, making it the most populous city in the county. During the last decade, Iron River's population had shrunk six percent to 2,800, leaving a lot of scars.

A screen of planted evergreens shielded his vinyl-sided split level from its neighbors. One story in the front, its rear showed two stories overlooking a patch of woods. No vehicles in the driveway. A two-car garage featured a solid garage door and a pedestrian door with a clear window at the top. Not what I'd want if I were hiding something in my garage. Occupying the half-acre yard were a few mature trees and a metal swing-set with twin worn tracks under the swings. At the edge of the yard stood a solitary outbuilding, large enough to store a ride-on mower and a few tools—or act as a crude prison.

My quick online search had found no marriages, but that didn't mean he didn't have a girlfriend or children to explain the kids' equipment.

We pulled into the driveway. Niki ambled up the concrete walk to the front door and rang the bell, prepared to ask about children in the neighborhood and the house for sale down the block. I sidled to the garage and peeked in the window. Crammed to the gills, leaving barely enough room to fit his car.

We saw nothing unusual through the house windows and called into the storage shed. A scared robin flew off her nest under the roof, squawking in protest. A bust. Nothing suggested Kat had ever been here.

On the way home, we picked up crutches to replace the heavy branch Nana had crafted for Valeria, a block of ice to use on Valeria's ankle, fresh veggies and salad makings, and worms at Luckey's Sports Shop for the kids to drown or catch fish as luck determined. On the first straight section of Shank Lake Road, we set up the trail camera I had retrieved from the road to Valeria's trailer. Creeks and marshes created a pinch point, assuring that if someone planned to get to my camp or Lake Tranquility using Shank Lake Road, they had to pass that spot.

I asked Niki, on a scale of one to ten, how productive she thought the day was.

"A solid three. Could have been a four of five if I'd gotten laid this morning."

"Still time." I waggled my eyebrows.

"Not if you want ice, not water, to put on Valeria's ankle."

Thirty-Three

WE CHECKED TRAIL CAMS NEAR my house on the way in. Nothing had passed while we were gone. Niki again stored her rental SUV behind the garage. We took separate ATVs to Lake Tranquility to provide more flexibility. Besides the supplies we brought from town, I grabbed two decks of cards and a cribbage board.

"Let's strategize about tomorrow," I said. "I plan to take the kids on an ATV ride and in the process create tracks all up and down Lukes Road to obscure the ones into Lake Tranquility."

"Smart, but every time we go to town is one more chance for them to spot us and follow us to Lake Tranquility."

I granted that. "But Nana won't leave until she knows what happened to her daughter. On a scale of one to ten, with ten being severe danger and one being minimal, what do you think our current risk is?"

"What's this with the number quizzes?" She squinted one eye and tilted her head. "Another three. But it could go up in a hurry. After we get back, I'll check to see if Rembrandt made any matches. That may inform our plans. After dinner you entertain the kids—you're better at that than I am—and I'll have a woman-to-woman conversation with Nana. Even though she's a grandmother, I'll bet she's only a few years older than me."

I gave Niki a look of confusion. "She looks older even than me."

"She's had a much harder life. Regardless, you represent authority to her. I bet I can do better."

"Plus, you speak fluent Spanish, and I need a translator." And not to mention this eliminates you discovering that the kids love doing stuff with you.

I led the ATVs to the third, most western, approach to Lake Tranquility from Lukes Road. To get there required crossing corporate forest properties before looping south and east to enter Megan's land through another locked gate—the only green one I owned.

We found everything fine at the camp. Nana had skinned and filleted the perch. She sat on a stump, carving a stick of wood. Megan was reading her Kindle to Valeria, who was icing her ankle.

Niki handed Nana the groceries and slipped away to learn what Rembrandt had found.

"Look what I got you, Valeria." I held up the crutches. "How's your ankle? May I look?"

She unwrapped the dishtowel, spilling a few remaining chips of ice onto the ground. Her face contorted into worry lines.

"We're fine, Valeria. I brought a block of ice. You tell me if it hurts." I poked the purplish swelling and triggered only one "Ooh." Terrific progress. I had forgotten how quickly kids heal. "Have you put any weight on it?"

"Nana said I shouldn't."

I offered a white lie. "That was good advice, but now you have crutches. Make sure you take it easy with them and put only a little weight on that foot. It shouldn't hurt. And when you're not active, still keep your foot raised. Megan may have told you I've had ankle injuries before."

Her eyes grew curious. "Do you really have metal holding your ankle together?"

"You want to feel it?" I removed my boot and sock and twisted my foot to expose an edge of the plate where only a little muscle covered it. "Go ahead. It doesn't hurt."

She was reluctant, but Megan poked it, then lapsed into giggling. Emboldened, Valeria prodded and asked me to rotate my ankle to see how it worked. Both girls' curiosity satisfied, I put one of my clean socks on Valeria's foot and set her up on a blanket near where Nana was starting the evening fire. I should have grabbed more pillows from the house, but I hadn't thought of that. I collapsed two of the camp chairs and used them to support her legs.

"Whatcha reading, Pumpkin?"

"Momma gave me the first Harry Potter. I'm re-reading the beginning for Valeria because she hasn't read it."

I'm no dummy, but I am amazed at how Megan speaks and what she knows compared to me at her age. Some is because of the times. What was X-rated in my day is practically PG these days. But it's more than that, and joy fills me watching her engage with the world. Glass ceilings are higher and more fragile now. Good thing, because I suspect that girl carries a sledgehammer with her. I do not envy anyone who tries to stand in her way.

I heeled away drips at the corners of my eyes. Sentimental Grampa Seamus. Concentrating on something other than Valeria's missing mother gave my subconscious time to work on a plan to determine if the Crenshaws, Randy in particular, were involved in Kat's disappearance.

I had the gray edges of an idea and knew just the person to call to bring it into focus.

THIRTY-FOUR

COLLEEN CARPETTI GREETED MY CALL with, "Elisabeth told me to expect your call. Before I forget, Robert Rand offered me a fifty-thousand-dollar bonus to convince you to come back to Criminal Investigations Group."

Never happen. "His hope springs eternal. You're still enjoying your work?"

"Oh God, yes. I can't believe how fast the time flies. Do you realize it's been nearly five years since we met and discovered I'm your half-sister? I am forever grateful you introduced me to forensic accounting and CIG. I am many, many times happier than if I had stayed with the accounting firm and become a partner."

"That's why—"

"Elisabeth tells me you have Starlink. I can work while my grandniece is at day camp. Grandniece makes me feel so old. Elisabeth said you were worried Megan might need protection. She says you don't have guns. I'm sure I could borrow one from my dad. When—"

I wanted to get in front of this conversation. "Hold on, Colleen. Everything has become much more complicated in the last two days. Let me tell you the story. After, you can decide whether to risk your ass in another of my convoluted messes."

"You can tell me why I should say no, but the answer will still be yes."

Colleen, who had been adopted through private channels, had been delighted to discover she had blood relatives. We have the same mother. Last I knew, Mom had not told Colleen who her father was. I was curious as all get out but had kept my nose out of that. If either wanted to tell me, she would. An only child, Colleen's enthusiasm for her newfound relatives meant she had a tendency to discount the danger. I emphasized that facet of visiting me. The only thing I left out was what went on in my tent with Niki. I ended with, "Questions?"

"Okay, I'm booked on a flight. Leaves Logan tomorrow morning at five twenty-nine and gets into Iron Mountain at nine twenty after a stop in Detroit."

"Wait. Wait. Wait. I need to contact the guy who owns the motel and see if he'll agree to let me have someone review his books. I'll look anxious if I do that tonight. Even tomorrow morning is pushing it."

"Hey, old man. Cool your jets. The first aspect of any forensic audit, as someone I admire once told me, is to understand the business and how one might manipulate it. I'm online now, booking a room. By the time you receive permission for me to talk to them, I'll have done the legwork. Am I correct you think the Silver Fox might be the source of the party girls?"

Using my own words against me wasn't playing fair—but it was playing like a McCree. I needed to keep that in mind. "I have nothing to indicate that. But the Silver Fox is the only business of its kind for many miles around. It wouldn't surprise me if they and the resort share employees or clientele."

"Excellent. I'll introduce myself there as a down-on-her-luck girl who is living off credit cards."

"Colleen, *that* was not what I had in mind."

"Are you implying I'm not attractive enough?"

"I'm saying my mother and my son and my ex-wife, not to mention your adoptive parents, would string me up if I let you take that kind of risk. May I remind you, the reason we're looking into this is because a woman is missing?"

"Hold on. Let me check something. Look at that, would you? My driver's license says I'm thirty-seven. Which means you don't get to tell me what risks I will and will not take. I'm single. No partner. No kids or grandkids. Tell me the truth: don't you want to know if there is a link?"

Of course I did. Talk about the law of unintended consequences. "How about Niki goes with you? It gives you someone to go to the ladies' room with, since women always travel there in pairs."

"Deal. Once I'm settled, I'll call you, and we can agree on a safe place to meet. See you soon, Boomer."

I clasped my hand to my chest. Not that she could see my dramatics. "That hurts. Flap your wings hard to keep the plane up."

I told Niki what I had done.

Niki loved the idea of Colleen reviewing the motel's financials and didn't think Colleen ran any danger by checking out the Silver Fox. "It's not like she's pretending to have experience as an exotic dancer or anything. There's nothing that ties her to you. I'll wear a different disguise from the one I used for the Crenshaws and Bunny. We'll make sure Colleen doesn't ask questions about Kat. Maybe we learn something. Maybe it's a waste of time. But we need leads if we're going to find Kat."

I had no winning arguments and pointed to her computer. "Rembrandt?"

"Two out of three ain't bad. We have a local boy, no arrests, no warrants." She tapped her screen and pulled up a social media picture of Glenn Korpi. I remembered his name from his high school days. He'd been a big-time athlete at West Iron High. Drove logging trucks for a local outfit. Married, no kids. Owned a two-year-old blue Silverado registered to him and his wife. Had she been part of the group who trashed the trailer and called the residents wetback whores?

At my nod, Niki pulled up the second individual's mug shot. "Different kettle of fish with this one. Name is Aaron Rogers. Alias Aaron Robinson. Alias Aaron Riddle. Busted as a teenager for drinking and driving, and dealing dope. He earned several domestic abuse arrests in his early twenties. Last one sent him to prison where during a huge brawl, he stomped a guy to death. Clean since his release eighteen months back."

A shiver hit me when I looked at his mug shot. Hard flat eyes. I could see him as a killer. "Just means no one has caught him."

"Most likely. Last known address was Chicago. No known vehicles registered in his name. Makes me wonder what he's doing up here."

I tapped his mug shot. "How did he link up with Korpi? The third guy's a mystery?"

"I took that photo through a windshield at an oblique angle. Too much distortion for Rembrandt to make a match. Rogers/Robinson/Riddle isn't big enough to hit the FBI's database of known associates. And we have the fourth guy, who we never got a look at, let alone a picture."

"Okay, we got an asshole from Chicago working with a local boy. I assume Korpi is still local?"

Niki referred to her computer. "Dude is an Instagram nut. I've got him renting a house in Iron River in Randy Crenshaw's neighborhood. Korpi loves hunting, fishing, trapping. One interesting change. Several months ago, his social media feeds stopped showing other people. Now he's all scenery and fish."

"You think that's when he hooked up with Rogers and/or the Mystery Man? Assume it is. How do you think we should proceed?"

"While you do your grandfather thing with the girls, I'll help Nana clean up from dinner and try to convince her the best way to learn what happened to her daughter is to let us contact the police. It's been what?— five days since Kat and her truck disappeared. That trail is getting cold."

"Good. If you understand the root of Nana's worries, we can figure out how to address it. I sense a big part of her thinks Kat is dead and fears the government will deport her and take Valeria away."

"You're a good man, Seamus McCree, but in this fight, even that may not be enough."

Thirty-Five

The night was clear and cool enough that I wore another layer to prevent goosebumps. Megan begged me to take her and Valeria onto Lake Tranquility to see the Milky Way, spot satellites, and maybe catch a shooting star.

Sometimes Megan's requests to stargaze were an excuse to delay her bedtime. Her father had used the same pretext as a kid. I aided and abetted, eager to let them view night skies with so little light pollution you could believe that, if you were only a foot taller, your fingers would touch the necklace of the Milky Way. If it distracted Valeria from missing her mother, they could stay awake until dawn.

The girls lay in the cocoon of sleeping bags and blankets I made at the bottom of the skiff. I sat in the stern and rowed into the lake.

Megan pointed Valeria to the W of Cassiopeia. They worked together to locate the Big and Little Dippers. Cepheus was the only other constellation I could find. I couldn't remember the Greek mythology surrounding it. Besides, it's not all that impressive. I gave the girls a break from Grampa Seamus education and let them ooh and aah at the satellites that streamed overhead.

I zoned out from their chatter and considered Niki's report of her conversation with Nana. In the week before she had disappeared, Kat had grown more worried and remote. Nana thought Kat's distress was caused by something more serious than the everyday worries all Dreamers had, despised by one political party, ignored by the other, and used by both to score points. Nana believed Kat was dead. If her daughter were alive, she would have contacted her family. She was certain that if the police knew Kat was missing, they would rip Valeria from her arms and put Nana on a plane to the drug-torn countryside of Nicaragua, from which they had fled many years ago.

Niki had nailed Nana's age. She was sixteen when Kat was born. Married at eighteen, the family slipped across the border into the US. A roundup at a meat-processing plant ensnared Nana's husband, resulting in his deportation. An uncle later reported the drug cartel had killed him because he refused to be their mule.

Nana had remained under the radar, using a fake Social Security card and a legal individual taxpayer identification number to pay federal taxes. Kat graduated from high school, attended college, fell in love with another Dreamer, and got pregnant. Catholics, they would not consider an abortion and were married in a simple church wedding. Kat quit college to earn money to take care of Valeria, named for her husband's mother who'd drowned crossing the Rio Grande.

Kat's husband had a good job lined up as an engineer for an automaker but made the mistake of celebrating with friends and getting nailed for OWI. ICE was on a mission to deport everyone they could and kicked him into Mexico within a week. Kat sent him money to hire a coyote to sneak him back into the US. The coyote left him to die in an Arizona desert. A rancher found him. ICE deported him again. Kat heard once from him in Mexico. Silence for the last year.

Their close relatives were dead or missing. Valeria probably had cousins still in Nicaragua, but Nana didn't know for sure. Nana knew families where Immigration had deported the mother for a minor crime and deported the grandmother when she tried to gain custody of the child. She believed that if the police searched for Kat and found she had done *anything* illegal, no matter how small, they would deport her.

How could Niki or I argue against Nana's justified fears? I might make a different decision, but that was not the point. Nothing we could say could give her peace of mind. We had no sanctuary to offer.

All those galaxies and stars and orbiting planets, and yet on this blue orb we call home, Nana had no safe place. I had to ditch that train of thought, or I would slip down depression's siliconed slope.

I focused on bright Venus, which stared back, unblinking. My watch said we'd been on the lake for three-quarters of an hour. The kids would sleep in the boat if I let them. I'd give them another fifteen minutes before I brought them in and sent them to their tent.

A minute later, Niki's shrill whistle sounded over the water. "Seamus," she yelled, "your trail camera just sent a photo of a side-by-side towing a big trailer running down Shank Lake Road."

THIRTY-SIX

NIKI MET US AT THE dock and lit our way in with a headlamp. I lifted Valeria to Niki, steadied the boat for Megan and asked her to help carry bedding. The girls did not utter a sound. The intruders had spoiled the tranquility of the lake's sky viewing, and I wanted to wring their necks.

We tucked the kids in and planted kisses on their foreheads. Niki handed Nana a rifle and provided rapid-fire instructions that had her looking determined.

I threw on a vest to counteract a chill caused by anger and nerves. As Niki strapped two rifles across her chest, I prodded her for a plan.

"Depends on what they do. If we see them on Lukes Road, I want you to lead them on a merry chase away from here and somewhere we can ambush them."

My face must have projected my alarm at the thought of her shooting guys because they were chasing us. She flicked my scalp with her fingers. "To make them stop and identify themselves, you dumbass, not to kill them."

Why had that not been my initial assumption? "I have a couple of spots in mind."

"If we don't see them or their tracks on Lukes, we'll assume they're going to your place and follow them on Shank Lake Road. Whatever happens, follow my lead."

The trails from Lake Tranquility looked different at night. Twice at intersections, I had to slow to get my bearings. We lost more time unlocking and locking the gate behind us. Niki ground her teeth so hard when I fumbled the gate lock, I could hear them. Tough, I thought. I will not permit anyone easy access to Megan, Valeria, and Nana.

We blasted down Lukes Road, past the rock barrier, and all the way to Shank Lake Road, where two sets of fresh tracks ran toward my place.

Niki doused her ATV's headlights and shouted for me to do the same. "We'll see theirs before they see ours."

"Maybe," I said. "No way they won't hear us."

"I'm counting on that."

Say what?

She putt-putted a quarter of a mile to a straight section of road and pulled her ATV into the woods on the right. She pointed me to the left. I followed her example of leaving the engine running and ran across the road to her in a crouch.

"Plan?"

She released the safety on her rifle. "Forty-five minutes until we have decent night vision. We wait. If they are anywhere on the lake, they'll hear our ATVs."

Ah-ha. She wanted the psychological pressure on them of knowing someone was around. "You giving me the other gun?"

"Have you stopped shaking yet?"

I held out my hand. Almost steady.

She checked the load on the second gun. "You willing to shoot it?"

"If they fire first."

She handed me the rifle, reminded me how to disengage the safety. "Keep in mind, I have the easy part. I get to kill them after they perforate you when you tell them to stop."

THIRTY-SEVEN

AN HOUR LATER, WE MOUNTED our ATVs and crawled forward, following their tracks. As we approached Ned Lake Road, I crossed my fingers that they had gone that way. They had not. Nor were they stopped at the next two camps before mine. I motioned for Niki to stop. "Isn't it safer for us to park and walk in to check on my camp?"

She agreed, and we tucked the ATVs down one of the many trails crisscrossing my property and walked in using what I called the ridge trail—my son and I had constructed it years ago running along a ridge that paralleled the lake and was never more than five hundred feet from the road.

We kept low to avoid presenting a target above the horizon and jogged the trail. My heart raced much faster than the exercise justified, and I cautioned myself to remain calm and not react if I found people taking or destroying my property. I did not like even the *idea* of carrying the rifle because in the heat of the moment, it was too easy to use it and become prosecution, jury, judge, and executioner.

And yet, my parents had taught me to stand up against the bullies of the world. These days, adult bullies relied on semiautomatic weapons. All my life, I had refused to own a gun. Despite that, I had used one to defend myself or others more than once. I mentally slapped my head. *Pay attention to where you're running and leave the angels-on-pinhead discussions to the theologians.*

The trail ended at the guest cabin driveway. We reached the cabin, having heard and seen nothing. As it became more likely my place was not under attack, my anxiety dropped several notches. I motioned for Niki to follow me to the hill overlooking my house.

Everything quiet. While Niki remained on top of the hill, I clambered down and checked the doors. Buttoned up tight.

That left the camps at the foot of the lake. One part of my brain argued that since my neighbors weren't around, any crimes being committed were only property crimes. Bartelle would tell me to stay away and check the camps in the morning and call in anything I found.

Years before, I had suffered the mental anguish of having my Cincinnati property destroyed. If we proceeded, we might prevent my neighbors' experiencing that sense of psychological loss of no longer feeling safe that comes with a break-in. My parents had instilled in me before I could walk the philosophy that "If not me, who? If not now, when?"

Niki would support whatever decision I made, but her training made her prefer stopping the crooks—if that's what they were—I didn't know for sure.

Our eyes had adjusted to the dark, and we had no difficulty following their tracks down and around the foot of the lake. Before we reached the outlet, I led us off-road, and we parked the ATVs behind a short rise screened by a growth of balsam fir.

I quietly let her know the layout of the camp and that the road would reach a pinch point where a bridge spanned the outlet creek. We could follow the road, which kept to high ground, or cut into the woods beyond the bridge and work through an area that, although dry this time of year, flooded in the spring, leaving holes and root tangles to navigate.

A barred owl hooted from a nearby tree. Its mate responded, and soon a pair farther down the lake joined the chorus. We used their caterwauling to cover our footsteps and followed the road across the bridge. Niki stopped and crouched without warning. I nearly plowed into her.

Silent as a stalking cat, she flowed from her crouch to lying flat on the ground. I did the same and saw the reason for her actions: a headlamp shone from the far side of a pole barn building. Its glare exposed a massive guy—Niki's hirsute bear—holding what looked like an automatic rifle. He paced near the camp's 500-gallon propane tank.

He had to be close to seven feet tall, had a barrel chest, and weighed 350 pounds. My mouth went dry. Any physical tussle with these guys would not go well for us. If he even got a paw on me, I was in trouble. I checked Niki's reaction. If she was feeling the same fear as me, it didn't show.

Nature's conductor signaled the cut-off, and the two pairs of barred owls silenced their verbal duel. The headlight moved toward the giant, the crunch of gravel marking his progress. Part way there, he said, "Nothing at that other camp. You finish filling the tanks?" The baritone voice had a local accent, but not someone I recognized.

"One twenty-pounder left, but there's not enough pressure. You hear those engines? Sounded like two four-wheelers. Stopped not far away."

"Huh. I thought it was you turning the trailer around. Well, whatever. Let's load these suckers and get the hell outta here."

The four-wheeler's headlight flicked on, displaying a dozen 20-pound propane tanks and four 100-pounders. That's how they transported so much stuff: they piled their stolen goods on the same trailer as the four-wheeler. My recollection was this camp kept one or two twenty-pounders for their grill. They never had a hundred-pounder and ran their generator using propane from a 500-gallon tank. The thieves were stealing propane from that tank to fill the portables.

Given current propane prices and the cost of the portable tanks, the total theft had to exceed $1,000—the minimum loss in Michigan to justify a citizen's arrest. Walking up and politely asking them to submit to arrest was not an option. The more armed people they thought we had, the less likely they'd choose to fight. And we had to catch them with their hands full of something other than automatic weapons.

Thirty-Eight

As though acting on my mental suggestion, the big guy set his gun down, picked up a hundred-pounder like it was a cigar, and carried it to the front of the trailer. The second guy used both hands to tip another tank and spin its bottom on the ground. It would never get better than this. I let the smaller one get halfway up the ramp and yelled, "Stay where you are. Let us see your hands."

The smaller guy fumbled the cylinder but held on. The giant put both hands on the trailer rail as though he planned to jump off. Niki fired a round over their heads. "Next one goes into those tanks, and you can roast in hell. Get on the ground. Now!"

I pointed my rifle in their direction. My rapid breathing and the adrenaline coursing through my body made it hard to keep the gun steady. The whole fire-a-bullet-into-a-propane-tank-and-make-it-explode was overhyped. I knew it, did they? What am I to do if they made a break for it? We should have agreed on a plan.

I sucked in a lungful of air and held it.

Niki barked out, "Now, assholes."

Whether these two were less sanguine about their chances of burning to death than I, or Niki's command voice and shot over their heads scared them, they lay face down on the ground and on Niki's order, spread their arms and legs.

"I have them covered," Niki said in a quiet voice that wouldn't carry to the men. "Move far enough away so these assholes can't hear you and call Iron County dispatch. Don't mention me. Okay?"

It wasn't a question. I ducked behind the pole barn building to shield my voice and report I had under control two suspects caught stealing propane. I guessed the dispatcher knew my name and thought I was acting as a deputy. She recorded my detailed directions to get to the scene and kept me on the line as she contacted the available cars. A state trooper was closest. He would arrive in forty minutes. Iron County deputies were at a two-car accident with injuries. She was alerting an on-call deputy. Be an hour-plus for him.

Figuring Niki would prefer to tie the guys up—at least their legs—I found an old piece of rope hanging on a game hoist and another piece underneath the cabin's deck.

Niki laughed at my offered rope and directed me to retrieve four zip-ties from her backpack. "Do the beanpole first. I don't want him to escape if the bear tries something. Make them tight, but not too tight."

I knew what too tight felt like on me, but what did that mean when I was the one putting them on someone else?

The bear turned his head to look at me. "If you know what's good for you, you'll keep the propane and let us go free."

"Shut up, douchebag," the beanpole yelled.

Beanpole gave me a wicked grin. He may have been thin, but his arms were corded with muscles. I secured his wrists first, fearing his arms more than his legs, and made sure the ties were plenty tight. Then I zip-tied his ankles. As I approached the bear, Niki moved closer to us and changed her angle. She laid down her rifle and pointed her pistol at his head.

"You're right," she said. "You think when my partner gets close enough you can grab him or knock him down with a leg kick and use him as a hostage. And you can."

What the hell? I stopped five feet away on wobbly legs.

"Thing is. It's the last thing you'll do." Her voice had the edge of sharpened steel. "Tasers are for pussies. You so much as twitch, and I will put a slug in your skull. Your buddy won't testify because I'll gun him down and claim he was trying to escape. No jury will convict me." She let loose a maniacal laugh that put a shiver down my back. She nodded me over to him. "Truss him up like a pig. Wish I had an apple to shove into his mouth."

Niki sounded so feral, so wicked, if I had been the bear, I would have pissed myself. I formed the zip-tie into a loop and approached from his side, eliminating the possibility of him butting me with the back of his head or whip-kicking me. His hands were the size of catcher's mitts and pressed hard into his back. Menace flowed off him like steam from boiling maple sap. I loosened the zip-tie loop, leaving only enough tail to pull it tight. Even with that adjustment, I had to get him to lift his hands to lasso them.

"Keep your hands together and lift them off your back."

The bear snorted and grabbed his shirt, making it hopeless for me to secure him without wrestling his hands. Trained police might know how to overcome his tactics. I could try to pry his arms up, but unless I could keep them up, how could I tie him? An idea popped into my brain. Make him think I was crazy, too.

"Listen asshole, raise your damn hands or I'll kick you in the head and do what I want. Your thick head won't stand up to my steel-toed boots and a soccer kick that made me a pro." I walked around to where he could see me and practiced taking corner kicks. "Make your choice."

Beanpole yelled. "You can't do that."

I backed up a dozen paces and began my sprint.

THIRTY-NINE

I'D TAKEN THREE STEPS WHEN the bear raised his arms over his back. The extra distance I'd given myself was for show and to give him time to stop me, so I kept coming until he screamed his submission. I broke off my attack and secured his hands, which were shaking. He offered no resistance when I tied his feet. A guy that big had maybe never been in a position where he was helpless.

"Okay guys," Niki said. "Let me read you your rights." Niki recited the version of the Miranda statement I assumed she learned in FBI training. "You have enough stolen stuff to warrant a felony charge. For you, I have a limited time offer. Tell us who you work with and where you're cooking the meth, and we'll recommend the prosecutor knocks it down to a misdemeanor. With your cooperation, you'll get a suspended sentence. Worst, a little community service."

"Don't say anything," the beanpole said. "We'll bail out before breakfast."

Niki continued like she hadn't heard him. "Don't talk, and once we take down the operation, we'll consider you full partners. Fifteen to twenty years for manufacture and distribution. Probably get out in ten if you behave yourselves and don't leave feet first with a shiv in your neck. The State guys won't agree to this. That means you need to deal with us before they get here and take charge of the scene."

She waited. I don't know whether she wanted to discover if they would start talking or arguing between themselves or if she wanted pressure to build. I kept switching my headlamp from one of them to the other. Partly, I wanted to gauge their reactions. I also wanted to make it difficult for them to learn what Niki looked like. I guessed them for early twenties. The big guy looked like he would crap his pants. The beanpole looked at ease. They didn't bother to deny they were cooking meth.

Niki broke the silence. "It could be worse, I suppose. You don't tell us anything and after we nail the leaders, they decide you ratted them out. No reason for us to protect you then. Probably end up in the same prison.

Normally, we'd separate you two. I'd talk to one. My partner would talk to the other. We'd compare stories. We might lie and tell you the other one was spilling their guts even if they weren't. But I can tell you guys are too sophisticated for that kind of bullshit."

She clucked her tongue. "If you talk to each other, we'll separate you. Once you're separate, only the first one who talks gets my deal. Half an hour until the state trooper gets here. That's your window. My friend is going to document your crime with his cellphone, but I'll be right here if you decide to save your asses."

To my surprise, they remained quiet. I shot photos of each propane tank, the tubing and gauges they used to siphon the fuel from the 500-gallon tank, the side-by-side, and close-ups of their faces.

With time available until the police came, I figured I'd collect my ATVs. I sidled to Niki and explained my plan quietly to prevent the culprits from overhearing.

"Here's the thing," she said. "I do not want any personal publicity. Before the state trooper gets here, I'll fade into the woods. I'll leave you a rifle to make it look good. Since I don't want the trooper to hear me leave, I'll walk to your house and take the spare ATV to Lake Tranquility. That means you need to bring your ride here. While you're at it, hide the ATV I used somewhere they won't find it. You and I can pick it up tomorrow."

"And what am I supposed to say if the guys mention a woman reading them their rights?"

"I doubt they'll say anything. Someone has scared the bejesus out of them, and it's not either of us. If they do, suggest they get tested for psychedelics. You've got a fast mouth, you'll come up with something. I'll talk to Bartelle tomorrow—well, later today. You'd better get going."

I stored the ATV Niki had used at the next camp, which was less than a quarter mile away. On the way to ditching that four-wheeler, I thought better of collecting my ATV. If I was supposed to be alone, how could I have collected it and kept the crooks under guard?

Lying is such hard work. All I wanted was to hand the miscreants to the pros and curl up and sleep. Never having performed a citizen's arrest, I didn't know how much paperwork was involved. A lot, I'd bet, and I had to make the details hang together. Oh joy.

We heard the faint sounds of an engine a mile or more away. Niki pecked my cheek. "That's my cue. Do not provide any personal information if those guys can hear. Their lawyers, who they will talk to, might work for whoever runs the operation. The bosses might decide to take revenge."

I hadn't considered that minor detail.

FORTY

LATER THAT NIGHT, TWO CARS from Iron County—guys I recognized but had never worked closely with—joined the state trooper's car, flooding the crime scene with their headlights. I kept out of the professionals' way while they verified the thieves had not broken into any camp buildings. I answered questions and avoided using the word "we."

Because I could not say for sure which propane tanks belonged to this camp, they would need to contact the owner to go over everything with Tex, who would perform the official crime scene investigation the next morning. One sheriff's deputy stayed behind to secure the scene.

After four hours, they told me I could go home. "Tex will pick you up and bring you here. Be ready by seven."

The fresh air smacking my face on the ATV ride home woke me up. I unlocked the chain to my driveway and realized I might want a handy reason to explain my locked driveway if any of the police officers had noticed—more lies to anticipate and remember.

The eastern sky was lightening, and the first robins were already cheerily singing. I wasn't sure whether I'd be more alert if I grabbed a cat nap or toughed it out until Tex showed up. I chugged a pint of water to stave off a dehydration headache. Then I had to pee and decided I was up for the duration.

Tex found me sawing wood, slumped in a rocking chair on my screened porch. "I gotta say, McCree, I am impressed you nabbed these guys. When did you start toting a gun?"

Tex knew I had not owned guns in the past. This conversation was a slippery slope I did not wish to take. "Have the guys talked? They didn't say boo to me."

"Lawyers don't get up this early. Hop in. You can catch me up on the way down to the crime scene."

"I need caffeine. Let me grab a soda, and I'll catch up on my ATV. That way, once we finish talking, I can come home and grab some proper sleep. You know your way?"

He had directions, and I avoided the first bullet. Temporarily.

Diet Dr Pepper in hand, I caught up to Tex and followed him to the crime scene. The deputy guarding the scene got out of his car and started swatting mosquitoes. He informed Tex he'd had no visitors and left. Tex had me walk the perimeter of the crime scene with him. "Did you see them siphoning the propane?"

"Nope. Heard them saying there wasn't enough pressure in the big tank to fill the last twenty-pounder." I pointed to the empty small tank.

"Guess I should check the other camps around here, too," Tex said in a weary voice.

My stomach clenched. He'd find the ATV Niki had used the previous night. "Can I do it for you while you process the scene?"

He pointed to the tubing and tools the guys had used to create the siphon. "Thought I'd dust those for prints. If these two aren't the only ones stealing propane, we might get lucky. Yeah, you could save me time and check those camps. Don't touch anything, okay? Leave anything that looks suspicious for me."

I felt like I had won the lottery. Not only did it get me away from Tex's questions, I had a police-sanctioned reason to run over the ATV tracks I had left last night while hiding the other four-wheeler.

I confirmed no break-ins had occurred at those camps. My cellphone rang while I was returning to report to Tex. Colleen Carpetti on the display. I checked my watch. She wasn't supposed to get into Iron Mountain for another hour-plus. I answered with, "Something happen?"

"We're in Detroit, ready to board our flight. Someone wants to talk to you. Just a sec."

I was too tired for games. She must have run into someone who knew us both. A voice I'd known all my life said, "Surprise."

FORTY-ONE

"CAT GOT YOUR TONGUE?" MY mother asked at my lack of response.

Then, I figured it out. At 83, my mother no longer took part in darts tournaments, but she was still a star at charity events, entertaining folks with the story of her life and taking on all comers at darts. She often traveled and must have run into Colleen in Detroit. "What charity are you helping this time? And are you coming or going?"

She released a hurricane of air. "I'm coming to see you, Seamus. How many times have you wanted me to see this place? Colleen told me she was helping you with an audit, and I figured it was the perfect opportunity."

And Colleen didn't talk you out of it? "What did Colleen tell you?"

"Nothing. She's as surprised as you are. I was talking with Elisabeth—you know, your ex-wife—and she was saying you were looking for help caring for my one and only great grandchild, and that Colleen had mentioned she was taking the first flight in the morning. I booked myself on the same one. When you picked up Colleen, *ta-da*, I'd be a surprise bonus. Colleen got on the plane later than me and was closer to the front. She didn't even know until she saw me at the gate here in Detroit. She insisted I call you. Apparently I didn't bring you up right, and you weren't planning on meeting her."

I did a quick count to ten, not that I couldn't have used more time to get control of myself, but if I didn't say something, she'd fill the silence—and to my detriment. Sometimes I wished my mother would return to her self-imposed muteness that had kept her institutionalized for decades. Not really. I loved this feisty mom, but sometimes I could throttle her.

"Here's the thing, Mom. We're not at home and Colleen wasn't coming to the lake. It's complicated." I waited out a boarding announcement before continuing. "Book a room for tonight in the same motel Colleen is staying at. You'll have to pretend you just met her. Colleen will fill you in."

"I see." Her disappointment dripped down the line. "I have an open ticket. I can go back today if it's too much of a bother."

My Jewish friends have claimed that no one can lay on guilt better than a Jewish mother. I'd be willing to enter Mom into that competition. "Mom, get a room. We'll make it work. And even though it doesn't sound like it, I'm pleased that you wanted to surprise me." A thought tried to surface, but I couldn't grasp it. "Could you give me back to Colleen, please?"

I expected some sort of acknowledgment from my mother, but the next I heard was Colleen chuckling into the phone. "It was on speaker. I got to see a side of our mother I had not experienced. I'll make it look like she was expecting someone to meet her at the airport—no acting necessary there—and offer to give her a lift in my rental. Maybe you and I should get together sooner rather than later. I leave that up to you. I'll call once we're in the motel. I got to say, being part of the McCree clan ain't dull."

McCree—that's what had been bothering me. "Mom needs to pay cash and not use her real name. We don't want anyone named McCree appearing on their guest register."

"Good you thought of that. I'll hit an ATM in town."

I verbally gave Colleen my thanks and silently extended her my prayers.

FORTY-TWO

WITH MOM'S SHENANIGANS, I ABANDONED any thoughts I'd had of catching a few Zs. After reporting to Tex that all was well at the neighboring camps, he gave me permission to leave. They'd write up their notes and ask me to sign them or make corrections in the next couple of days. I drove the ATV to Lake Tranquility. Breakfast dishes were drying on damp dishtowels.

Megan heard me arrive and came squealing up from the lake. "Grampa Seamus. We're training an eagle."

I must not have heard that right. I killed the engine and asked her to slow down and enunciate her words. Wrong again, I had heard it correctly. She grabbed my hand and leaned her entire weight, pulling me toward the pier. Megan had devoured the *How to Train Your Dragon* boxed set I had given her. I figured she and Valeria had combined their imaginations.

I should have known better.

As we approached, I heard the high chirping calls from a pair of eagles who had a nest across the lake. They had fledged a single bird but were still at the stage where they were its primary providers. We often saw one, two, or all three fishing the nearby lakes.

"I got one," Valeria called from the lake.

Megan ran ahead of me, helped Valeria unhook the fish. Megan grabbed the perch by the tail, gave her hand a quick flip, and whapped its head against the cedar planking of the pier. Okay, that wasn't how I stunned them, but it worked. Megan helped Valeria stand and settle on her crutches. Megan laid the fish near the end of the pier, grabbed the fishing pole, and followed Valeria onto land.

"We hide there," Megan pointed to a massive hemlock that had blown down decades earlier and was well on its way to becoming a nurse tree. Hiding was not accurate. They used the downed log to lean against. "Watch."

I asked what I was watching for.

Her shush would wake the dead. "It doesn't work if you aren't quiet."

I sat down and jerked awake from falling asleep. I forced my eyes wide and, to stay awake, kept track of all the animals I could hear or see. Megan's bald eagles, chickadees, a nuthatch—not sure if red-breasted or white-breasted—robins, a least chipmunk exploring my boot, purple finch, goldfinch, two chattering red squirrels in a chase, the plink of a downy woodpecker, a white-throated sparrow scratching in last year's moldering leaves.

Valeria tensed. I followed her gaze and watched an adult eagle at least five years old, its head and tail pure white, glide on bomber wings from across the lake toward us. It banked, wings and tail feathers flaring to brake its flight, and dropped onto the edge of the pier. It hopped like a crow, grabbed the fish with its talons, and jumped into the air. Its wings pressed against the air in audible whooshes, wingtips touched the water once, leaving expanding circles in its wake. Two more struggling beats, and it was up and cruising away from us.

I did not move a millimeter, not wanting to spoil whatever was keeping the kids statue still. They waited to clap and cheer until the eagle landed in a massive white pine. Megan stuck two fingers in her mouth and produced a major league whistle.

I hugged the girls, making sure I didn't bump Valeria's ankle. "How did you guys figure that out?"

"Yesterday," Megan said, "Nana called for us to come eat. We accidentally left a fish on the dock and saw the eagle grab it." She slid me a look. "Pier. You told me. Piers stay in the water, docks come out for winter. We did a science experiment and left one on purpose. The fish have to be keepers. They won't come for the little ones."

The eagle is training the kids. "Now *that's* a science experiment. How many fish has it taken?"

They traded looks. Valeria answered. "That was five. It was the fastest ever. Let's do it again."

"That is extra special." I ruffled their heads. They spun away from my hug, and I steadied Valeria. "I'd love to get a video of that. Right now, I want to peek at Valeria's ankle. How's it feeling, hon?"

I boosted her onto the hemlock log, rolled her pant leg up past her knee, and removed her sock. The purple was fading to putrid yellow-green. The swelling was lower, and when I squeezed her ankle, she said it hurt only a little.

While putting her sock on, I noticed a red rash on her calf. It was warm to the touch, and on closer inspection, she had the classic bullseye suggesting Lyme's disease caused by a deer-tick bite. I asked her if she had recently pulled off a tick.

"Momma found a baby one before she—" Valeria stifled a sob.

"Can you describe its back or the color of its legs?"

She shook her head. No reason to question her further. Given the bullseye and that it was a "baby" tick—meaning smaller than a typical wood tick—I figured it was a good bet she did have Lyme's.

If so, Valeria needed to undertake a multiple-week course of antibiotics to prevent the disease from getting into her joints, heart muscle, and nervous system where, like chicken pox, it could hide for decades and return with debilitating effects. I helped her put her sock on. "We need to show this to Nana." The kids objected—they had to catch another fish for the eagle before it flew away.

"Tell you what, how about Megan catches fish while Valeria and I talk with Nana? It won't take long. She can join you for the next eagle flight.

You'll record it, right?" I handed Megan my cellphone. "Be careful with that."

I suspected the compromise worked only because it was Megan's turn to catch the fish. Valeria didn't want me to carry her even if it meant she could play with eagles sooner and insisted on crutching to the fire ring area. My kind of kid. I called for Niki and Nana.

Niki saw us and hopped off the swing she'd been pushing back and forth with her feet. "Neat trick the girls have, isn't it? You look like something the cat barfed up. Did you get any sleep?"

I hooked her arm, and we walked a few paces away from Valeria. "Did Nana agree we could report Kat missing?"

"Kat hasn't ever been away this long. Nana's heart tells her she has lost her daughter. Even though she might be right, I told her someone could be holding Kat, and if Kat had any chance, we had to find her soon. I know she understood me, but her fear of losing Valeria is too great. I pressed her just a little to ask what she would do if Kat were dead. She thinks she'll have to take Valeria to a place she knows where the meat-packing plants help people get fake documents. But she's not there yet. Maybe we should talk to the people at the motel again."

"There are two complications. My mother surprised me with a spur-of-the-moment visit." I related what had happened.

Niki snickered. "Yep, that's a complication. What else?"

I informed her of Valeria's bullseye tick bite. "I can't let that go. There must be somewhere that will treat her without reporting Nana, right?"

Confusion painted Niki's face. "Why would they even care?"

"Because she's a minor and they have forms, and they need payment. The issue isn't the money, it's the paper trail. In a tight community, the wrong people could hear." I pointed to Nana's approach. "Wish me luck that Valeria's tick bite is enough to change Nana's mind."

Forty-Three

I USED VALERIA'S LEG FOR show and tell, then sent her to play with Megan.

I explained, cajoled, pleaded. Niki translated and added her own pleas. Nana would not budge.

Despite my frustration and lack of sleep, a little voice of reason told me I had no right to judge or feel put upon or anything else. I had not walked a single step in Nana's shoes. Being a white male citizen with money gave me privileges that made it impossible for me to appreciate her position.

I was out of my element and overwhelmed with uncertainty. Nana's fearful expressions and handwringing showed the situation also stressed her. If they had been Christian Scientists who rely on prayer for healing, what right would I have to impose my beliefs on them? Unlike smallpox or polio, where vaccinations are required for the wider community to be safe, no one would catch Lyme's disease from Valeria. She alone would suffer the consequences of Nana's decision to avoid the medical community.

Yet the consequences of doing nothing for the kid could be severe and long-lasting. I would not impose my values, but the only way I could live with myself was if I removed every obstacle I could to Nana changing her mind.

"Niki, don't over-promise, but tell Nana that I will do everything in my power to make sure Valeria stays with her. I'll hire the country's best immigration lawyers. Faith communities exist that provide sanctuary for illegal immigrants. If that's what she wants, I will find her sanctuary. Valeria's rights as a US citizen will help with this."

I released a long breath before verbalizing my thoughts. "I know Nana believes she can not have any dealings with the police or with health officials. I will take that on for her. Whenever Megan stays with me, her parents give me a signed document giving me parental rights in their absence. I'll create one for Valeria that models Megan's. I can say the mother left her with me while she was gone."

Niki shook her head, but I bulled over her potential objections. "I know it's totally illegal. I can not live with myself if I don't do everything I can, legal or not, to get Valeria the medical attention she needs."

Niki scowled. "We're not talking a little misdemeanor, Seamus. These are felonies that could put you in prison for years, decades."

"Tell her what I said." My voice came out rock hard. I softened it. "Please."

In the end, whatever Niki told Nana partially won the day. Nana would not leave, but I could take Valeria to a clinic. A mixture of elation and dread filled me. I had won, but at what cost?

FORTY-FOUR

THE EARLIEST APPOINTMENT I COULD get at the urgent care clinic in Crystal Falls was 1:30 that afternoon. I left everyone else at Lake Tranquility and used back ways to return to my house, where I constructed a document to give me temporary parental rights. Not knowing Kat's signature, I scrawled Katrina Serrano and an illegible date at the bottom.

I enjoyed a quick shower, put on town clothes, and patted my pack to confirm I had my phone. I couldn't feel it. I dumped the pack's contents onto the table, confirmed the phone wasn't there. Then shit-for-brains remembered he had given it to Megan to record her eagle training.

I threw everything in the pack, raced the ATV to Lake Tranquility, retrieved my phone from Megan—first she had to show me her eagle-fish-snatching video. Niki and I transported the kids to the house. I piled them into the F-150 and prayed I didn't get stuck behind a logging truck on the way in because if I did, I'd be late.

"Okay girls. It is really, really, really important we have our story straight. Valeria, why are you staying with Megan and me?"

"My Nana broke her hip, and my Mama had to take care of her."

"And . . ."

"Mama asked you to keep me because I was already spending the weekend with Megan."

"Have you talked with her since she left?"

She shook her head.

"Because . . ."

"I don't know her telephone number."

"Right, and I didn't think to trade numbers with her." Or ask Kim for it, or take the girls to the Amasa Summer Arts Academy where they'd met, or done a thousand other things a reasonable person would do in a similar situation. Fingers crossed, no one would think to ask those questions.

FORTY-FIVE

AT THE CLINIC, THE RECEPTIONIST gave us surgical masks to replace our cloth ones and handed me several forms to complete before we could see the nurse practitioner. Valeria wasn't a lot of help. She didn't know what allergies she had—I scrawled none known. I used my address, put down my name as the responsible party, considered adding something about Valeria's mom coming in next week with insurance information, and caught myself. This family had no insurance other than whatever Medicaid provided—and maybe not even that.

I turned in the clipboard and played paper, scissors, rock with the girls while we waited. The longer we waited, the more nervous I became about what would happen next. I'd had to leave so many lines on the form incomplete. Would they even see her? The kids had a blast beating the stuffing out of me because I couldn't concentrate.

"Valery Sea-ran-io?"

The receptionist mangled the name, and I didn't realize she had called Valeria until my charge snagged my hand and pulled me out of the chair. Rules being rules, Megan had to stay in the waiting room with a wailing baby while I accompanied Valeria as she crutched into the examination room. The nurse practitioner knocked on the door and entered. "Didn't they tell you the X-ray tech isn't in on Wednesday afternoons?"

"That's not what we're here for. Valeria has a tick-bite bullseye on her left calf. She has no other symptoms of Lyme's disease." I boosted Valeria onto the examining table and pulled off her sock.

The nurse unwrapped the ace bandage. "How did this happen Valeria?"

"I was running away and fell."

"What were you running away from?"

Ice froze my heart. We had not discussed the ankle because I had been thinking only of the Lyme's disease, not the whole of Valeria as a medical professional would do.

Tears filled her eyes. No doubt she was reliving the attack at her trailer, her missing mother, our escape. I had better come up with something fast.

"No one's mad at you for jumping with Megan when you weren't supposed to. I'm not, and your mom won't be either."

Valeria nodded and blessedly said nothing.

The nurse gave me a side glance I couldn't interpret. "The ankle looks okay, although I can't be sure without an x-ray. You wrapped it?"

"I had experience from playing soccer years ago." That sounded lame to my ear. "I was a professional until an ankle injury ended my career."

"Huh." She turned her attention to Valeria's calf. "Yep, classic bullseye. You're the third one this week. Did you pull off a little tick?"

"Mama did." A sheen filled her eyes. She snuggled her nose into the bear attached to her wrist. The dread of impending disaster filled my core.

The nurse rewrapped the ace bandage. "When was this, Valeria?"

I cleared my throat to invent something plausible. The nurse ignored me and handed Valeria a tissue. "What's wrong, sweetie?"

"I miss my mama."

The nurse pulled a cellphone from her pocket. "Let's call her and see if she remembers exactly when the tick bit you."

Valeria stared at her feet. "I can't," she blubbered.

I wanted to feed her our practiced line and hoped against hope she would think of it on her own.

"Why not?" The nurse's voice sounded sharper.

She looked up at me, her mouth a grim line. "Because she's missing. Grampa Seamus says—"

Her cutoff left the nurse giving me the stink eye. "You're her grandfather? What is this girl's mother's name and number?" Her cellphone came alive with the press of her finger.

"Grampa Seamus isn't my grampa."

I talked over Valeria. "I'm the grandfather of Valeria's friend, who is sitting outside. Valeria's grandmother fell and broke her hip. We'd planned for Valeria to spend the weekend with my granddaughter, Megan. Kat asked if I could take care of Valeria until she returned. I said sure."

I rushed on, keeping the nurse's attention on me, not Valeria, who was shaking her head. "My own kids give me *in loco parentis* for Megan. I made up one for Kat to sign. But in the rush, I neglected to get her telephone number and Valeria doesn't remember it."

The nurse positioned herself between Valeria and me. "Do you feel safe?"

In a cracked voice, Valeria said, "No."

The nurse dialed 9-1-1 and asked for an officer to investigate a "situation with a man and a young unrelated girl that does not sit right."

For Valeria's sake, defuse the situation. I settled on the chair farthest from Valeria and crossed my legs. "Can I ask my granddaughter to join us? This is taking longer than expected, and I suspect the girls will both feel better if they're together."

While that was true, I also hoped the kids' demonstrating their friendship would de-escalate the situation.

The nurse jumped at the chance to separate me from Valeria. "I'll put the girls in another room while we wait."

"Great." I pulled a coloring book from my backpack. "Valeria, do you want to color? I have books and pencils, or would you rather Megan read more of the Harry Potter?"

She preferred to color, and I watched the nurse lead her into the room across the hall and wait until Megan joined her. The nurse propped the door open and positioned herself to watch both the kids and me.

Keep acting like nothing is a problem. "Could you call in the script to the local pharmacy? I appreciate your caution, but given the delay, I'd prefer not to have the kids wait a long time for us to collect the prescription." Mr. Cool Calm Collected on the outside presenting the air of imperturbability had acid burning a hole in his stomach.

To have any chance of keeping Valeria with us and away from Child Services, or whatever they called it here, I had to stick to my story and hope Megan's presence would buck up Valeria so she could get her part straight. With any luck, the deputy who answered the call would know me, which would give me a leg up in escaping this mess.

FORTY-SIX

A CRYSTAL FALLS CITY POLICE officer who didn't know me from Adam arrived with a professionally dressed woman—late twenties, early thirties. They talked in hushed tones with the nurse before the three split up. The nurse bustled into another patient room. The woman entered the room with the kids, gave me a hard stare, and shut the door with an ominous click. The officer adjusted his service belt—another inauspicious sign—and joined me.

I handed the guy my ID and the forged document that "gave" me permission to handle Valeria's medical issues. He asked if I had the same for Megan, and I provided it to him. He weaved between three questions: how Valeria came to stay with me, why I had no way to contact her mother, and whether anyone could verify my story.

Then he posed a question I had not anticipated. "Would it be okay if I called one of Megan's parents and verified that they gave you permission to have her with you?"

"I'm fine with that, but they're rafting down the Colorado River, and I believe incommunicado. I can give you the name of the outfitters. Maybe they have a way to reach their guide. If nothing else, they should be able to confirm my son and daughter-in-law are on the trip."

I pulled up the outfitter's website on my phone. The officer copied their main number and made the call without bothering to step outside. From his side of the conversation, it was clear he had no luck contacting Megan's parents. The officer said, "And I am to understand that you require a court order to verify Patrick McCree and Cynthia Nelson are on one of your rafting tours?"

"I know I'm their emergency contact," I said. "Tell them it's an emergency and you need to get in touch with that contact."

The officer gave me a thumbs up, repeated the request, and wrote the information in his pocket notebook. He disconnected, dialed a number, and the phone in my hand rang. "That, at least, checks out. Please wait here. I'll be back, Mr. McCree."

Those words did not reassure me. Twenty minutes that felt like twenty hours passed before the officer returned. "I have a few additional questions. Where did the girls meet?"

"The Amasa Summer Creative Arts Academy. I signed Megan up to let her spend time with kids her age and not be stuck with her grandpa twenty-four/seven." Please, please, don't ask for Kim Belanger's name and call her because she'll tell you Valeria's mother is missing.

"Where have you been staying with the kids?"

Given he asked that question, I assumed the kids had mentioned they were camping. "Most recently, we've been camping on land I own. The kids have enjoyed sleeping in a tent and fishing." An idea struck me. I opened the video storage on my phone. "And they're training an eagle to retrieve fish they leave for it. Have you ever heard of such a thing?"

He watched the video and watched it again. The great distraction would work for only so long. "I know you must be vigilant about kids. I've worked with the Iron County Sheriff's department several times. Talk with Lon, Sheriff Bartelle. He's met my son and can vouch for me."

He stepped from the room. On his return, he seemed more relaxed. "Sorry to take up your time, Mr. McCree. Have a good day."

I got up.

"Oh, and Sheriff Bartelle asked you to please stop by his office. I don't think it's a request you want to ignore."

Forty-Seven

PRESCRIPTION FILLED AND STARTED, ICE cream bribe delivered and consumed, I took the kids into the library. The head librarian knew both girls and assured me it was fine to leave them. She didn't care if they browsed the books and borrowed an armful or Megan read the Harry Potter to Valeria. The first unmitigated good news all day.

I left my truck in the rear courthouse parking area and walked to the sheriff's complex. I secured my mask and entered the outer lobby. The door buzzed open, and the receptionist motioned toward Bartelle's office. "You know the way."

I gave his door a polite double tap, walked in, and plunked down on the chair.

"Shut the door, why don't you?"

I closed the door, took two pumps of his antibacterial gel, and rubbed my hands. The office filled with the biting scent of ethanol. "You wanted to see me?"

"Had a pleasant chat about you with my city colleagues. They were afraid you were molesting young children. Where are they? The children, not my colleagues."

"Library, which won't hold them forever. You have my statement ready to review?"

He leaned back, laced his hands behind his head, and stared down his nose. "Only you could construct a statement that's totally true and a crock of shit. How do I know this?"

My gut spasmed like he'd punched me in the solar plexus. *Here it comes.*

He leaned forward, placing both hands on the desk. "You hate guns. Someone who didn't know that would read your statement and think you single-handedly took down those two boys. A careful reading never says you were by yourself. I need the truth, the whole truth, and nothing but the truth before I get the prosecutor to sign off on charges."

He paused. Most people would start talking, but I can do silence like a Trappist monk when I choose.

Lon knew that and gave up that tactic. "Not only would you not use a gun, you wouldn't even *think* to pick up a gun—of which, last I knew, you had none. Plus," he held up a finger, "it is extremely uncharacteristic of you to leave two eight-year-old girls alone at your house or camping, if that's what you were really doing. Which means, not only was someone else at the crime scene, another someone else was watching the kids."

His face wrinkled into a frown. "This smells like skunk fart. It has all the makings of something your undercover agent, Niki—I looked in the files and couldn't turn up her name—would do. Why are you covering for her? So help me God, Seamus, you don't come clean, I'll tell that wet-behind-the-ears City officer I didn't believe your story, and you'll be in a world of hurt."

Busted. "You're right that I didn't lie. And you're also correct that Niki and her guns were there." I leaned toward him and lowered my voice. "I'm sorry I wasn't entirely forthcoming about her. Whatever undercover assignment she's on means her name cannot appear in any paperwork. I could either let those guys get away or live with her conditions. She hopes to catch you later this afternoon to explain. I don't know the whole story, but my guess is someone she's looking at is a law enforcement officer. Rather than speculate, I'll leave it to her to fill you in."

He stiffened at my mention of law enforcement officers. "That's your story? If both of you were there, it still doesn't explain who was taking care of the kids. And you didn't give me her name."

And that investigative expertise, combined with caring about the men and women working for him, is why Bartelle is one of the better cops I know. "Above my pay grade, Lon. Those two talking yet?"

"Nope, and not likely to. They're bailed out. One's mother paid for both."

"You didn't tell me?"

"How's it feel to be kept in the dark?"

A cheap shot, but I was in no position to call him on it. "The side-by-side and trailer?"

"The skinny one paid cash for them a couple of months ago. We have them dead to rights on possession of stolen property, and that's all we have since no one saw them filling the tanks. Prosecutor dangled a plea bargain for information and got nothing."

"Who are they? Any known associates?"

Bartelle rose, telling me the interview was finished. "I look forward to seeing Niki and learning her name. If she can't get here before six, have her call." He handed me a card.

I had bought a little time. Given this conversation with the sheriff, I knew how I was spending the next few hours.

FORTY-EIGHT

MY PLANS DID NOT LAST the drive to camp. The girls were using the bathroom at Tall Pines while I pumped gas. My phone dinged a notification that the Shank Lake Road trail camera had downloaded pictures.

The first two shots of the triptych captured the front and rear end of a jacked-up blue Silverado. The third caught the tailgate of a gray Tundra. Mud obscured the license plates on both trucks.

I texted Niki a warning that the two vehicles were in the area and requested she call me once she had a good signal. My phone buzzed seconds later.

"Well, isn't that special?" Niki said.

"To avoid running into them, I'll use Lukes Road coming in west from the highway to get to Lake Tranquility. Remember the sketchy area where that timber bridge rotted out?" She knew the place. "If I get stuck there, I'll text you and you can come on the two-up and transport us in. They can't get their trucks through those rocks. No four-wheeler in the Tundra, but with the Silverado jacked up, my camera didn't see into its bed. They might have one there."

"Then keep the kids out until they leave. I'll make sure Nana's safe."

Well, that was the obvious answer, and the fact I had not come up with it proved how diminished my brain functions were. "You're right. We'll go meet Mom and Colleen somewhere near Iron Mountain. If it weren't for Nana, I could keep the kids in Iron Mountain at another motel. Better yet, go to Marquette, where no one is looking for them. Ah shit, I'm babbling."

"I'll let you know if they come this way, and your camera will alert you when they leave. Give your mom a hug for me."

Colleen answered my call with, "What's the scoop?"

"The scoop is I have two eight-year-olds bored out of their tree, and the guys we think are searching for Valeria and Nana are sniffing around my woods. Niki is staying to protect Nana. We can't come to your motel because Megan and I have been there—in fact, we shouldn't be together anywhere around Iron Mountain. Let's meet at a walking trail that runs along the river on the Wisconsin side. We can talk while the kids burn off some energy. Let me look it up on my map app."

I found the parking lot for the Menominee River Walking/Cross-Country Skiing trails and gave her directions. "We're an hour away. Your bodies are on Eastern time. Why don't I stop and get food for an early picnic? If we don't find a place to eat there, I know a rest area south of town."

The kids helped me buy supplies for a cold-food picnic and snacks to maintain them until then. I considered buying energy drinks to help me stay awake, decided that was asking for trouble. A six-pack of diet Dr Pepper would keep me sufficiently buzzed to stay on the road.

The map app offered multiple driving routes. I chose one that used county roads and avoided Iron Mountain all together.

Mom and Colleen pulled in three minutes after our arrival. Megan swarmed them and waved Valeria over to make introductions to her Geema, as she had called her great-grandmother since she was two. Valeria turned shy until Mom asked her about her crutches and sprained ankle. Then, in no time, Valeria was showing off her rash and asking my mother if she knew I had a metal plate in my ankle.

While the youngest and oldest were making nice, I edged Colleen aside. "Everything go okay?"

"Not bad, considering our mother does not like anyone to tell her what to do. I'm thinking I may have gotten the best of this whole adoption deal."

I had no clue what that meant and said so.

"Well, my adoptive parents raised me, and they were great. Trudy was in no position to look after me."

True. Back then, Mom couldn't even care for herself.

"But I get her genes. I want to be that active at her age. Look at her. Eighty-three and walks two and a half, three miles a day, lifts weights, does an exercise routine. Sharp mind. Hands steady enough to do darts exhibitions. And feisty enough to tell the world to go—" she glanced at the kids "—tell the world to pound sand if it thinks it can stop her."

"Remember, she had a heart attack five years ago."

"Yep, a wake-up call. Did you remember to contact the seller?"

I tapped the sides of my head with the heels of my hands. "Never crossed my mind. That's how crazy things have been. Let me do that right now."

I used my contacts list to dial Mike Crenshaw's number and put it on speaker. A woman's voice answered. I introduced myself and asked if Mike was around.

"Nope. This is Bunny. He said you were interested in buying some land."

I had not recognized Bunny's voice. "Mrs. Crenshaw? Yes, I am, but I hoped to talk to him about the motel. In Iron Mountain?" I let my voice rise in question. Had he talked with his wife about that, too?

"He'll be pleased to hear that. He's always back from golf in time for his five o'clock cocktail. Let me jot down your number."

I disconnected and said to Colleen, "Let's pry Mom away from the kids, and I'll give you both the scoop on the deep hole I've dug."

Colleen bribed the kids with a movie she streamed on her phone. It had them in stitches, laughing so loud we couldn't talk until we walked further away. I told Mom and Colleen everything: the propane thieves who were out on bail and knew I had instigated their capture, the little we knew of Kat's disappearance and the Crenshaw business practices, Nana's illegal status and her fears for herself and Valeria, along with her unwillingness to engage the police, and her intransigence about remaining until she knew Kat's fate. I closed with the threat by the guys in the Tundra and jacked-up blue Silverado.

The more I talked, the more still my mother became. Her response surprised me. "No one knows how far a mother will go to protect her children."

Did she mean Kat or herself?

"I have to take your word for it," Colleen said. "I assume you have a plan, Seamus. How can we help?"

"The more we flail around, the more dangerous it seems to get. The guys in those two trucks will figure out we haven't left the area. They're hunters. Given time, they'll track us to Lake Tranquility. I feel obligated to keep my charges safe, even if I can't convince them to leave for a sanctuary situation. That means I'm stuck guarding Nana. But I can't do that with Megan around. Mom, will you take Megan with you to Boston? Lizzie can help once you're there."

Mom gave me a skeptical look. "While you do what?"

"Move Valeria and Nana to a safer property I own until I understand Kat's disappearance. While I do that, Colleen and Niki can work the Crenshaw angle. I'll take Megan away if I have to, but—"

"But," Mom said. "You think the new place is safe?"

"If no one sees us going there. That buys time until I have to resupply them. Each trip to the site increases the risk."

A smile lit Mom's face. "That settles it. Move them with enough supplies to last several days. Megan and I will stay with them. You know I can use a gun. That way, you can concentrate on solving the Kat mystery. Maybe as a grandmother and great-grandmother myself, I'll have more luck convincing Nana to listen to your concerns.

Shit, I stepped into that cow pie. "It's rough camping, Mom. Have you ever been camping?"

"Are you suggesting I can't do it?"

I threw up my hands. "Far be it from me to suggest—"

"Then that settles it."

From behind Mom, Colleen rolled her eyes and mouthed, "You are so screwed."

FORTY-NINE

WE WERE FINISHING OUR PICNIC dinner when Niki's text arrived: *Trucks found the rocks. Rogers and Korpi looked around and left.*

Ten minutes later, the trail camera sent pictures of both trucks heading out Shank Lake Road. I conferred with Niki by phone. She chortled when I told her how my mother outfoxed me. We agreed Lake Tranquility was safe for one more night, provided I avoided any risk of running into the guys in the trucks. I'd drive north through Republic to M-28, take that to Covington, and drive south on US 141 to catch the western end of Lukes Road.

Colleen took Mom back to the motel to grab her clothes and check out. The trip to Lake Tranquility was uneventful, although I required four-wheel traction to drive across the area on Lukes Road where the wood bridge lay rotting in a stream bed.

The kids were asleep when we arrived. Niki and I carried them to their tent and made sure Valeria took her next dose of antibiotics. We left them to pretend to brush their teeth before crawling into their sleeping bags and letting the frogs lull them to sleep.

We returned to the fire ring to find Nana stoking the fire. Mom rubbed her hands over it while they chatted. Niki joined in their conversation. How much in life had I missed because I'd learned French, not Spanish, in school? Well, Seamus, it's not like you couldn't have fixed that over the last forty years.

The heat relaxed me, and I startled myself awake. "I hate to interrupt," I recognized the irony of my statement. "I am falling asleep on my feet. We need to make plans. Mom, I'll give you my sleeping bag. It's warm enough I can sleep without it. We don't have an extra tent. You can sleep with the kids—they won't mind that you snore like a chainsaw. Or you can inflict your sonorous torture on me, and Niki will share Megan's and Valeria's tent."

Niki was translating for Nana, who interrupted her. "No." She pointed to Mom and herself and rattled off something in Spanish. Niki said, "You're safe. Nana insists the grandmothers will sleep together."

Thank you, Nana. "Now for tomorrow. We have several problems to solve. The rocks stopped Rogers, Korpi, and friends today, but they'll be back tomorrow with a way to move the rocks or drive something around them. Plus, I'll bet Sheriff Bartelle is steamed that Niki didn't show at his office today. He's sure I haven't told him everything, but he knows we're camping on my land. I wouldn't put it past him to systematically check our properties. We need to relocate."

Niki's translation elicited questions from Nana. Her face grew worried at Niki's answers. I waited for a pause and added, "Borders are magic because people don't look across them. The Iron County Sheriff's department's jurisdiction ends at the county line. I have several hundred acres in Baraga that I only recently purchased. Even if Bartelle thought to consult the Baraga County plat book, he'd find the prior owner, not me. He'd have to go to the Baraga County records to find the sale, and he won't do that. A river runs through that property. No bridge. The only way to get to the land on the other side of the river is by boat or wading."

To Mom, I said, "Not too late to make me happy and take Megan to Boston." I could hear porcupine bristles rising. "This is luxury compared to where we're going. You're eighty-three years—"

"Seamus Anslem McCree. I'm well aware of how old I am. I know I'm a city mouse, not a country mouse. But something told me it was time to visit you, and now we know why. I have my medicine and my rosary. If I become a burden, I will take Megan and leave. Until then, you're stuck with me."

Exactly so.

FIFTY

IN MY DREAM, IT WAS the last day of college. One course had a term paper I had forgotten about, and I had to turn it in before midnight or I wouldn't graduate. I struggled to wake from the semiconscious state of knowing I was experiencing a stress dream. Couldn't do it, and now I sweltered in a prison cell with loud noises piped in to torture me.

I blinked my eyes open to light baking the tent and the sounds of kids squealing. My phone claimed it was past ten. With a gazillion things to do today, why had Niki let me waste five hours of daylight sleeping? I pulled on clothes and stumbled out of the tent to discover the camp was packed in the truck or stacked next to it.

Niki stepped from behind my truck. "Rip Van Winkle has arisen from his twenty-year nap. I was considering requesting the coroner."

"Comedy Central is not calling. Where are the others?"

"The kids are playing with their pet eagles. I told them it was their last chance for now because we'll soon have a new adventure. Nana and Trudy are watching them while I finish striking camp."

The two of us confirmed our plan for the day and made quick work of cramming the remaining stuff into the truck. While I drove everyone else to the new spot, Niki would cut through the rocks on the ATV and stop at the house to launder the dirty clothes we had strapped to the four-wheeler. We'd meet back up at my house for the last part of the trip.

Plans in place, truck packed, we allowed the girls to catch a final fish. Megan held the perch up for the eagles to see. The immature eagle launched from its perch, no longer waiting for the kids to hide. The kids had to hustle away before the bird swooped in for its meal.

Niki and I herded the kids toward the truck with the women following behind.

Megan tugged my arm. "Grampa Seamus, I'm going to miss George and Martha."

"And Gonzo," Valeria added.

At my obvious confusion, Megan explained. "George and Martha are the parent eagles, like George and Martha Washington, see? And Gonzo is like the Muppet, trying to get attention but not doing things right. We don't know if Gonzo is a boy or girl, so we can't give it a real name."

"And you can tell the adults apart?"

"Don't you remember? The girl eagles are bigger than the boy eagles."

I remembered and should have realized my granddaughter, the knowledge sponge, would not forget. "You guys are too smart for me. It's forty miles by truck to our new spot because I don't have the Bobcat to move those boulders. It's only four miles as the eagles fly. Maybe we'll see them there. Valeria, how's the ankle feel?"

She handed Megan the crutches and walked with shuffling steps.

"Super," I said. "Don't overdo it." I waited for the kids to go ahead and my mother to catch up. "You sleep okay?"

"Like a newborn baby."

"Meaning you woke up several times during the night and cried for someone to feed you and change your diaper?"

Mom looked up at the cloudless sky and released a dramatic sigh. "I thought I raised you better. Speaking of, what were you thinking, giving Valeria that rock and telling her you'd find her mother?"

Pointing out that Niki had given Valeria the rock, not me, avoided the main issue, which I needed to address. "I promised *to try*, Mom. A big difference from promising *to find*. I remembered how badly I wanted answers after Dad died. I simply knew I had to help Valeria learn what happened to her mother. At first, I hoped it was an accident or something."

Mom squeezed my hand. "It's been nearly fifty years and I still miss him."

FIFTY-ONE

MOM RODE SHOTGUN WITH NANA, Valeria, and Megan in the back seat. With supplies crammed everywhere, everyone had their knees tucked to their chins. The truck bed contained the generator, propane tanks, and everything else that didn't fit inside the cab. We weren't as overloaded as the Dust Bowl refugees arriving in California from their parched, foreclosed farms, but I took care to avoid bumps and make gentle turns.

My phone dinged while I was praying us past a muddy section of Lukes Road. Four-wheel drive pulled us through. I stopped and checked the notification. The trail camera had new pictures of the gray Tundra with a driver, a passenger, and an ATV in the cargo bed. I called Niki.

"That puts a crimp in my plans," she said. "I can't exactly pass them unnoticed with a rifle strapped to the ATV on top of a pile of dirty clothes."

We agreed she would wait to see if they arrived at the rocks. If they offloaded their ATV, she'd retreat and take a twenty-five-mile detour to get behind them. Then she could provide a rear guard for us. I would risk driving part way, stopping where I had multiple ways to avoid them.

It didn't take long before Niki reported Rogers and Korpi were at the rocks and unloading the ATV. "No sign of the blue monster. You should hang loose."

"If we don't do this now, we'll have to set up in the dark. Instead of you taking the long way around, I vote you hide and allow them to drive past. Then drive through the rocks and deflate a tire to slow them down."

"Pro tip, Seamus. Vehicles have spare tires. If you choose to declare war, let the air out of at least two. I'll see what happens. From now on, only text. I'm silencing my ringer."

Mom waited until I had disconnected. "Where did you pack the other guns?"

"No way. We're not bringing loaded weapons into the cab where we have no room to use them."

"They don't do any good if we don't have them."

"Then we'd better not need them, right?"

FIFTY-TWO

NIKI'S TEXTS KEPT ME INFORMED of what the Tundra guys were doing.

ATV unloaded

Testing drone

Loading drone on ATV

One staying with truck - I gotta go around

Wait until I catch up to you

I responded with check emojis. No reason to tell Mom and Nana I was ignoring Niki's advice—well, she probably considered them orders—to wait for her. The two guys and the Tundra were looking in the wrong area. Nothing suggested the Blue Monster or the other two people were around. I couldn't do anything to figure out where Kat was until I got people set up at the new site. And the window for Niki to help before she had to return to Minnesota was closing fast. Now was the time for a quick dash.

If I ran into the jacked-up Silverado, I'd have to rely on my knowledge of the local roads, two-tracks, and connected skidder trails to lose it. My aching hands alerted me to my death grip on the steering wheel. I shook out my fingers and told myself to relax. Who the hell was I kidding?

More than an hour later, I triggered the camera on Shank Lake Road driving by, saw no one on the road to my house. The chain was still up at the driveway, garage doors closed, meaning Niki wasn't yet there. No way I was putting off setting up the new camp until we had clean clothes. Niki would have to do the laundry on her own and bring it later.

At the turn toward the river, I stopped at a gate. Megan did the honors of unlocking and relocking it once I had driven through. A quarter mile farther on, we did the same thing with the gate that marked the boundary of my Baraga property. With the two gates locked behind us, tension melted off my neck and shoulders. When we reached the river, I adopted a jovial voice. "Oh oh. The bridge is missing. I guess we'll have to swim across."

"Grampa Seamus, Valeria can't swim with her ankle."

Mom looked back at the kids. "Megan, he's pulling your leg. I'll bet there's one right around the bend."

"I told you, Mom, no bridge. That's the whole reason we're crossing. I have a canoe and the river is shallow enough I can wade it. A quarter mile from here is a rise with a lovely growth of hardwoods where we'll set up camp. It's surrounded by swamps with no back roads in. You'll have excellent cellphone coverage up on the hill. For extra safety, I'll move the trail camera between those two gates to alert us if anyone is snooping."

"I see," Mom said. "And if we had to, we could defend it against someone trying to cross the river. Can you transport everything across? The generator? Propane tanks?"

"I'll leave them in the truck until Niki can help. We can handle the rest. Let's go see the spot I have in mind."

With two canoe crossings, I transported the girls, Nana, my mother, and sufficient supplies for everyone, other than Valeria with her crutches, to carry. I expected more pushback, but the kids were up for finding a perfect tent site, and Nana proved to be a packhorse. I kept forgetting that although she looked like she was in her sixties, she was only in her mid-forties with arms made of ironwood. Valeria and Mom set our pace, and we arrived in half an hour.

"Seamus," my mother said, "this is lovely. It's so open. I thought we were going to have to—I don't know—pull brush or something to make a spot for the tents."

The grove included twenty acres of mature sugar maple, cherry, a few white and yellow birch, and a smattering of evergreens. "I suggest y'all choose tent sites on the old logging road. Fewer stones sticking in your back. Find a flat spot or a gentle slope and point your feet down. Mom, why don't you and Valeria collect loose rocks for a firepit while Nana, Megan, and I bring the remaining gear?"

In three trips we humped everything up. While Nana set up her "kitchen" supplies and inventoried the food, I helped the kids pitch their tent and move their stuff.

Valeria rooted through her bag. "Grampa Seamus, have you seen my bear? I can't find it." She tapped her wrist where she wore her stuffed animal.

We double checked the tent. "Maybe it's still in the truck? I'll check later." Valeria's lip quivered. "Let me set up the tent for Nana and my mother, then I'll cross back over the river and check." Valeria agreed that was fair.

With Mom's help, we erected that tent. I motioned Mom inside. "Lie down and check for poke-y things. Maybe take a rest."

Her face became stone. "We still have lots to do."

"And if you get overtired and trip and break your hip, where are we? You have nothing to prove. You're already doing better than ninety-nine point nine percent of your peers."

Her tongue worked her way around her mouth like she was checking for missing teeth. "Well, I should make sure it's comfortable." She lay down on the bedroll, rocked back and forth. "You did a good job, Seamus. No rocks or sticks. Do I have to worry about snakes?"

"No poisonous snakes in the U.P. and the others will stay away. The breeze is keeping the bugs down now, but if you let them into your tent, they'll keep you up all night. The kids will collect you for dinner. Anything you're missing?"

"You have a dartboard and darts in the guest cabin, right? Can you bring them? We could hang the board on a tree?"

Funny what each of us needs to make a place a home. Darts had been the one constant for Mom wherever she had lived. It had facilitated her return from mental illness. Only in the last two years had she stopped treating as a permanent accessory a fanny pack that contained a set of darts my father had given her shortly before his death. Setting up a dartboard and measuring the distance to draw an oche on the forest floor was the least I could do. "Next trip," I said. "And thanks, Mom. You're a trooper."

I created a list on my phone of things to collect from home: clean clothes, food, a splitting maul, chainsaw with gas and bar oil to construct seats and work up some of the larger limbs into firewood, the first-aid kit from my truck. The list grew with dartboard, darts, sharpener—sure as rain, Mom would get the kids playing and that meant darts missing the board and hitting a tree or the ground or a rock. I'd need a hammer, nails, tape measure to place the board at the exact height—Mom would know if I was a quarter inch off—and to draw the oche the correct distance from the board.

I set the kids to gather kindling and downed branches for Nana to burn while I looked for Valeria's bear in my truck. No luck. I texted Niki to ask her status and if, by any chance, she had the bear. Her reply was immediate.

Folding laundry

No bear

Waiting for gray Tundra to leave area

Come here

Which meant we did not know where they were. With an involuntary shudder, my body reacted to the thought of meeting them. I asked if she thought I should wait until we were sure they were gone.

Nope.

If they kill you, I'll get them on 1st deg murder.

She followed with a laughing emoji.

FIFTY-THREE

NIKI MET ME ON THE screened porch with a glass of wine in one hand and a semiautomatic rifle in the other. Alcohol and guns did not make me happy. I shook my head.

"This is for you, asshole. I'm not drinking." She thrust the wineglass at me, slopping a little over the edge. "You're tense and you're not gonna like what I have to say. Drink some wine, grab a shower, get into clean clothes. No arguments, or I won't tell you what I learned."

That tone brooked no discussion. I enjoyed a refreshing shower and found Niki rocking on the porch. She pointed me toward a chair. "The Tundra just passed your camera."

"Excellent. Now I can move that trail camera."

She waved off my enthusiasm with a whatever hand flip. "They used their drone to survey a lot of ground. I'll bet they would have found you at Lake Tranquility. Your binocs are nice. I used them to watch the drone fly over the lake and past your house several times. It's a fancy model that allows the operator to swivel the cameras and zoom in."

I'd already figured out that using a drone extended their reach and allowed them to check out my house. I would if I were them. "Did they spot you? Is that what I won't like?"

"How long can your mother pretend she's not eighty?"

I chose not to call Niki on sidestepping my question. "Mom's like a child, except in reverse. Tell a kid they're too young to do something, and they'll kill themselves to prove you're wrong. Mom will never admit that coming here was a lousy idea. Her body won't hold up long, and I can force the issue. If you keep delaying telling me the bad news, you'll lose any positive effect of the shower and the wine."

She pointed to my F-150 in the driveway. "I can't help you get the generator and propane tanks across the river this evening. Colleen and I agreed to a girls' night out. We're having drinks and dinner before we wander into the Silver Fox. After a few more drinks, we'll see if we can audition for a pole position, maybe even an impromptu lap dance or two."

I pushed down my anger that they would subject themselves to hands pawing their bodies and perverted hard-ons poking them, even if they stayed in the guys' pants. In a voice that sounded hard to me, I asked, "What do you hope to accomplish?"

"You thought there might be a connection between the Silver Fox and Kat's disappearance, right? As Megan knows, you don't catch fish without bait. And you—" She punched my chest with a strong finger. "—aren't the right lure."

She rose, ran her hands down her sides, and shimmied. "Whereas I surely am. And dressed right, Colleen looks even hotter than me. We'll meet for dinner in Norway, make our plans, and visit the Silver Fox together. The place doesn't close until two, two-thirty. Rather than drive back here, I'll stay the night with Colleen in Iron Mountain."

During my work on Wall Street, I found excuses to miss the strip-club outings where the bigwigs entertained clients and hauled some of us analysts along to justify deducting the expense. My feelings became well enough known that the bosses had stopped inviting me years before I quit the business in disgust.

I would make an exception to keep Niki and Colleen away from that place, especially since they were attractive bait.

"This is such a bad idea. Colleen doesn't know what she's getting herself into. She doesn't even like guys. What if someone recognizes you? That could screw up the whole deal with Crenshaw. I'll go."

"And do what? Ask the girls while they're doing a lap dance if they know what happened to Kat? You couldn't hide your feelings. Just because Colleen is gay doesn't mean she can't be looking for a side gig. Who said all dancers were straight?"

She nudged the wine glass toward me. "Relax. Nothing will happen while I'm there. And no one will recognize me in my disguise. I'll make sure Colleen's safe. To make you feel better, I'll text you when we're done for the night. Let's talk about tomorrow. You still jog?" I did. "Let's meet in Iron River. There's a high school with a track, right?"

"West Iron," I said. "I'd rather run in the woods."

She released a dramatic sigh. "For a really smart guy, sometimes you are dumber than a musk ox. If we kick something up at the Silver Fox, we'll change plans. Otherwise, we should check out Randy Crenshaw's and Glenn Korpi's places. If they drive away, we might discover they forgot to lock their doors. You have a better idea?"

"Maybe try talking to the motel maids again?"

"And if Crenshaw hears of that, where are you?"

I finished the wine. "You win. I don't want to drive into town with the generator in the bed. Can you help me store it and the propane in the cab? I'll put up the back seat. What time do you want to meet?"

"Ten, unless you hear from me otherwise. I'll stop on the way for my long overdue personal chat with Sheriff Bartelle. Having a time to meet you gives me an excuse to escape his third degree." She checked her phone.

"I have to leave soon. While you were showering, I took the liberty of folding down the bedspread to save time for more interesting things. Let's get that generator moved, so I have your *full* attention."

FIFTY-FOUR

MY PHONE'S WHOOSH ANNOUNCED PICTURES from the trail camera now set up between the two gates guarding our new hiding place. I fumbled on my glasses. The phone said 1:07 a.m. and new images continued to arrive. A light breeze had stirred a thin weed that triggered the camera's sensor. I checked if I had missed any messages from Niki or Colleen—I hadn't— and put the phone in airplane mode to kill the notifications. I was awake and needed to pee. A squadron of blood-thirsty mosquitoes accompanied me. I killed most of those that followed me into the tent. The survivors tortured me with their hypodermic proboscises and incessant buzzing throughout the night. The first pink etched the eastern sky and further sleep was hopeless.

I chased down the living remnants from the night's aerial battle and completed my pyrrhic victory. Red splotches and squished carcasses marked the nooks and crannies where they had hidden until I dispatched them. At least these gals wouldn't lay a gazillion eggs to populate the next generation.

I released the phone from airplane mode and notification whooshes ran for a full five minutes. I ignored the obnoxious sound and opened my messenger app to learn if Niki and I were still on for ten o'clock. No new messages. Her last message, sent at 10:30 p.m., had shown Niki outfitted in a Dolly Parton blond wig and a sheer blouse—more unbuttoned than not—revealing a lacy black bra. Colleen leaned in, her patterned blouse opened to show lots of cleavage. Niki had captioned the selfie "two hot girls on a hot summer night."

Where the hell was the message telling me they had returned safely? Was the trail camera hogging the phone's capabilities and not letting Niki's messages through? Or had she not sent a text after they returned to the motel? Assuming they had returned. I'd drive myself nuts worrying about everything that could have gone wrong. I silenced the phone.

Nothing to do but pluck the weed triggering the trail camera.

FIFTY-FIVE

THE LONGEST PART OF ELIMINATING the offending weed was getting there and back. I zipped through the trail camera's pictures. At 3:47 a.m., the camera captured a handsome male wolf in mid lope. Wait until Megan saw that. On the return walk to the camp, I kept my eyes on the ground, finding several wolf tracks. It had crossed the river the same place we had.

With the brighter light, and knowing what I was looking for, I followed the wolf tracks on the far side of the river to within fifty yards of where we had camped. Curious, but not bold—a good way to know what was going on and not get in trouble. I entered our compound quietly, not wanting to wake up the sleepers.

Last night's dishes left to air dry glistened with a light morning dew. Once people woke up, I'd use the chainsaw I brought to make portable seats for around the firepit, freeing up the camp chairs to be used elsewhere. And I wanted to create drying racks for the dishes. I added twine to my list of stuff to buy.

Nana's and my mother's tent was nearest the firepit, its lines taut, rain tarp in place. An occasional snort told me Mom was still alive. The kids' tent was forty yards away from the snoring. Their tarp was also taut, but in front of it lay soggy coloring books. Nature had provided a better lesson than I could about what happens to stuff you leave out when the air temperature drops below the dew point.

From inside I heard Megan whisper, "You awake? Something's out there." In a louder voice, she said, "You awake?"

I shook a guy line and snorted through my nose, sounding like a wild boar—not that I had ever seen evidence of feral pigs in the U.P., although I had read there were some in a neighboring county. Both girls screamed.

I wanted to kick myself and said in a stage whisper, "And I'll huff, and

I'll puff, and I'll blow your tent down." I gave the dripping guy line another shake.

"Grampa Seamus," Megan said, "you didn't fool me."

You betcha, Pumpkin. "Never know," I said. "Trail cam has a wolf, and I found lots of tracks." That got her attention. "Since you're awake, you want to come with me while I get a couple of pails of water from the river? I can show you a spot where I've seen fish."

"Can Valeria come, too?"

"Good by me, if she can manage her crutches."

Valeria used only one crutch. Although she could put most of her weight on her ankle, she'd have to guard against twisting it again before it healed.

The spot I showed them was downriver from the campsite and not visible from where the road met the river. "Bring down camp chairs and mosquito repellent and you can fish all day."

Megan peered into the clear water. "Perch? Bass?"

"Suckers, for sure. I'm told the river has brook trout. I haven't seen them here, though."

Valeria, who had been quiet, piped up, "Nana will want to know if she can cook them."

"Suckers? For sure. Filet and fry them like perch. And if you catch a trout—yum!"

By the time we returned, me carrying the water, Valeria carrying her crutch, and Megan carrying a renewed enthusiasm for outdoor life, Nana had breakfast cooking. I closed my eyes and inhaled the combined smells of woodsmoke, boiling coffee, and frying bacon.

Perfect, if only it weren't closing in on seven-thirty and still no message from Niki. I had to steady my hand to type. *You okay?* I hesitated before hitting send. The question presupposed she was not, and that was not what I wanted to suggest. I erased it and tried, " *We still meeting at 10?* "

Not wanting the kids to pick up on my nerves, I told them to replace the firewood Nana had used. I wandered to my tent, which I had erected under several towering hemlocks. *Come on, Niki. Don't do this to me.*

I planned to count three hundred seconds before switching to Plan B. As the moments ticked by, my stomach knotted tighter and tighter until it felt like a hockey puck.

At three hundred, I texted Colleen. *Niki with you?*

No response.

Now I wished I hadn't texted them. During the walk back to the fire, I extinguished the molten lava burning in my stomach to project a positive posture and voice. Megan was scrambling eggs with a fork while Nana looked on. "I'll be gone for a while. You do what Geema says, Pumpkin, and help her and Nana and Valeria, okay?"

Her mouth formed a pout. "Why do *you* have to leave?"

The lava in my stomach threatened to erupt. "You hired me to do a job. I couldn't get back to it until I made sure Valeria and her nana are safe. Do you agree it's safe to hide here?" She thought so. "Good, that means I can work real hard to find Valeria's mom and not worry about you." *But first, I need to learn what happened to Niki and Colleen.*

Fifty-Six

AFTER CROSSING THE RIVER, I hauled the canoe into the woods several hundred yards distant from the river, the road, and any of the paths I maintained. It would take a miracle for someone to find it. Even if they did, nothing would suggest that I was using it to supply people hidden across the way.

I cursed everything that slowed me down, starting with the seventy-two-point turn to do a 180 with the truck on the narrow trail. At each gate guarding the property, I had to stop, get out, fumble open the locks, prop the gate open, get back into the truck and drive through the gate, hop out to close the gate, and return to the truck. With the engine running, the mosquitoes had their way with me. Slapping at the buzzing bastards who had joined me in the truck, I cursed the rational speed dictated by dodging protruding rocks and sprawling holes on Shank Lake Road.

I released my frustration and hit the accelerator when I got to my smooth driveway. And slammed on the brakes to avoid hitting a deer. With wide eyes and fearful snorts, it bounded away, its white tail flashing a danger signal. I closed my eyes, let my heart settle. Thank goodness the deer had been alert. It was a timely reminder that whatever had happened to Colleen and Niki, I couldn't help them if I didn't make it to them.

Inside the house, I changed into running clothes, grabbed breakfast to go and a couple of bottles of diet Dr Pepper from the refrigerator. Couldn't think of anything else I needed and locked the door behind me.

I used my phone to get directions to the track and saw the icon showing I had a text message. I fumbled through the phone's security to open the message app and read from Colleen:

sleeping

do I need to wake her

???

Bam—instant headache. I pulled my head down until my chin pressed into my chest and counseled myself to be happy they were okay, not angry because they couldn't find thirty seconds to let me know they were fine. Telling myself what to feel and feeling it are two different things. Keeping my chin pinned, I pulled my elbows behind my back. The iron bonds of tension gradually released.

I texted, *Don't wake Niki. I'll see her at 10:00 unless I hear otherwise.*

Colleen replied with a thumbs-up emoji. As if that made everything okay.

FIFTY-SEVEN

I PARKED CLOSE TO THE West Iron County High School football stadium and used its oval to warm up. From there, I followed a route I'd plotted on my phone that brought me past the house Glenn Korpi rented, on to Randy Crenshaw's home, which was less than a half mile away, and looped back to the track.

Korpi's driveway held no vehicles, nor were any parked nearby on the street. My disappointment vanished when I spotted the blue jacked-up Silverado parked on the grass next to a sad one-car garage several doors down. It faced out, preventing me from capturing a plate number without being obvious. The likelihood of there being two such trucks in town seemed minuscule. Had Korpi moved and the records Niki tapped were old? Or was Korpi so lazy he'd driven his truck to visit someone that close?

I noted the address. With a reverse white pages search, I could learn who lived there.

On the half-mile to Crenshaw's house, I rolled the possibilities around in my mind and came up with more questions than answers. How could a working guy like Korpi spend so many daylight hours wandering the woods? Where did Aaron Rogers stay, and was the gray Tundra his?

No sooner had I thought of the gray Tundra than it steamed out of Randy Crenshaw's driveway with tires squealing and headed toward me. I wanted to know who was in that truck, but I did not want them to get a good look at me. I moved to the side of the street and kept running, hiding my face by using both hands to swipe away streaming sweat.

At Crenshaw's driveway, I faked checking my shoelaces. No vehicles or people around. What an enormous piece of luck. It's not like Earth only contained one gray Tundra, but odds were I had linked Rogers with Crenshaw. Crenshaw was not the blurry picture guy Niki's camera had caught, but he might be the fourth person.

I continued my planned route, which in eight minutes brought me back to Korpi's street in time to see the Tundra driving away with the jacked blue Silverado following. Each had a passenger. The gang of four were together and moving fast, and I was on foot.

I returned to my truck at a brisk clip. To get my phone to recognize my fingers, I had to towel-dry the sweat. I wrapped the towel around my head to keep my eyes clear and texted Niki to the effect that when she finished her beauty sleep, I had info, and we needed to talk. Call.

The phone buzzed. Niki's caller ID. "I am so sorry, Seamus. I was so exhausted last night, I didn't hit send for the message I typed after we returned to the motel. I hope you weren't worried. We've got news. What's yours?"

Rather than admit her mistake had caused me massive angst, I suppressed my feelings and detailed what I had witnessed and asked what she had learned.

"As luck has it, Aaron Rogers picked us up. He admitted he spelled his name differently than *the* Aaron Rodgers of Packers fame. His pal, the fuzzy picture guy, was with him. Went by the name of Bobby last night. I pickpocketed his wallet and took it to the ladies for a little look-see. The Indiana driver's license had him as Drew Dombey, address in Gary, age thirty-one, brown and brown, six even, one sixty, wears contacts, not an organ donor. Sources tell me that Mr. Dombey has led a charmed life for someone who has been pimping since he was a teenager. Also has several battery charges. Zero convictions. I'll bet there are a lot of frustrated prosecutors because his girls recanted or disappeared."

"Disappeared?" A realization struck me like a gut punch. "As in he killed them?" *As in he killed Kat?*

"Or sold them. Or they ran away to another city, changed their name, and found a new pimp to supply them with drugs. More likely, he scared them so thoroughly they wouldn't testify. His knuckles had the scars you get from hitting teeth. Last night, he got the manager—woman named Felicity St. Agnes—to agree to interview Colleen this afternoon. Felicity is a Florence, Wisconsin local with one DWI, one leaving the scene of an accident, both a decade in her rearview mirror."

My gut tightened to a walnut at the thought of Colleen interviewing at a place like that. I could fight that battle with more information. "Given Dombey, do you think the place is legit or a front for prostitution?"

"Parts are legit. It's a nude bar, but they still have to keep their liquor license. The girls work the pole, encourage patrons to buy them drinks. I'm sure the bartender has a special watered-down bottle for them. Nothing illegal with that, provided they don't sell it to customers. Some, not all, girls went into rooms screened by heavy curtains. Colleen will learn tomorrow what goes on there. I did not see any drug deals, but we did nothing to suggest we were interested. The parking lot smelled like a herd of skunks had passed by."

"Why smoke weed there if it's legal across the border in Michigan?"

"Seamus, in Michigan you can buy and carry a certain amount for personal consumption, but you can't smoke it in public places or in the great outdoors. For a Thursday night, the place was hopping. I assume it'll be packed tonight."

"You know I think this whole thing with Colleen is a terrible idea, even worse now that we know this guy Dombey's involved. I understand that the interview might give us insight about the operation." It was all I could do to not say something stupid like, "But I forbid it." That line rarely worked on my granddaughter. It didn't stand a chance with my thirty-seven-year-old sister. "I can't stomach the thought of her going through with it. You'll be there?"

"I'm on my way to talk with Sheriff Bartelle. I thought you and I should pay another visit to The Menominee Rapids Resort. Try a couple of different meals for lunch, maybe take a peek into the private area."

"You can't do that and go to the Silver Fox afterward. That begs people to ask questions."

"Yep, it does, which is one reason Colleen should go alone. It's been more than a week since anyone has heard from Kat. We have to shake things up, which is why you and I are going to the resort, and she's interviewing at the Silver Fox."

"I suppose nothing much can happen at an interview. But to visit the resort, I need to shower and change clothes."

"For Pete's sakes, Seamus, shower in Colleen's room. She can sneak you in so no one sees you. Buy new clothes in Iron Mountain. You can afford it."

Such a thought would never have occurred to me.

"Donate them to St. Vincent de Paul," she said, "and get a tax deduction. Do I have to teach you everything?"

FIFTY-EIGHT

I FINISHED CLOTHES SHOPPING AND texted Colleen. She met me at the motel's back door. We trooped up the stairway to the fire door on the third floor. While I remained hidden, she made sure the cleaning ladies were not around to see me enter her room and held her door open. I executed a mad dash down the hallway, my backpack slapping against my shoulders.

The shower's steaming water massaged away the tension in my neck. I dressed in the bathroom and emerged, looking like someone ready to go to the resort.

"Don't you clean up nice," Colleen said. "Have you scheduled an appointment for me to examine the motel's books yet?"

"I'll call right now."

Mike Crenshaw picked up on the first ring. The holdup was because he had been waiting for his son to arrange a time for our accountants to get together to look at the financials. Since it was already midday on Friday, I asked if Monday morning, say, eight o'clock might work.

"I'm tired of waiting on that little pissant. I'll call our accountant and make sure it happens. Do you have children, Seamus? I wanted the twerp to take responsibility for this."

"One son. He's doing okay on his own, and we don't share any business responsibilities." I remembered his daughters had children. "The best part is I get to spoil my granddaughter. You have grandkids?"

We shared pleasant recollections of our next generational progeny. He was looking forward to seeing his in Florida. I thought it was a good idea to mention that I planned to have lunch with my fiancée at his resort. He sounded glad to hear the news and wondered if my investor might want to buy the resort, too. Regardless, he'd meet us there and treat us to a meal. His offer provided Niki and me excellent cover and might yield information regarding how hands-on daddy still was and the extent of his son's involvement with the resort.

I claimed I didn't know when we'd get there. My betrothed was shopping for something—I wasn't sure what, but it would cost me a pretty penny. His brayed laugh hurt my ears.

"Bunny's shopping, too," he said. "Maybe the two of them are plotting behind our backs."

Oh yeah. For sure. "That's a scary thought. Shall I call you before we head over?"

"No reason to. I'll putter around, stick my nose into everyone's business until you get there." His laugh made it seem like he was joking, which I doubted. We disconnected.

Despite the fact that the guy might be involved in multiple illegal activities, I kind of liked him—until I remembered the look in his eyes. I sat at the desk while Colleen reclined on a bed. I asked her to tell me about her appointment with Felicity what's her name.

"St. Agnes. She gets in at four o'clock. I know you're not happy, but I won't do anything stupid. Trust me on this, Seamus."

I said all the right things about trust and that she was a big girl and that I appreciated everything she was doing to help. To avoid allowing my true feelings to surface, I shifted the conversation to how our mother, who Colleen called Trudy, was doing as a new camper.

"So what you're saying," Colleen said, "is that you may have to carry

Trudy out on a backboard because she'll never admit she was wrong not to take Megan to Boston?"

"Oh, she'll admit it was a mistake, but only after I summon the medivac. You don't have to tell me, but did you ever ask who your biological father was?"

She cocked her head. "Is there someone you're rooting for?"

"The two people I thought were potential candidates are both dead now. I can't see any resemblance between you and either of them. Rooting? No. Curious? Yes. I'm not like my sister—my older sister—who thinks Mom betrayed dad. He'd been dead for years. Mom didn't owe him anything other than raising the two of us well. I have no complaints. I take it she's said nothing to you."

"Haven't asked. The Carpettis will always be my parents—I've told you that. Fingers crossed, the guy had good genes. I want to live a long, healthy life. I'm happy Trudy's still going strong. If she wants to tell me, I'll listen. If she doesn't, that's okay, too."

"That's a fine attitude."

A key tapped on the door. "Housekeeping."

It sounded like Juanita. I considered using Colleen to translate and ask if Juanita had any news of Kat. The risk of my presence here getting back to someone was too high. I ducked into the bathroom and waved for Colleen to send her away, which she did.

We listened to the key tap on the next door and the squeak as that door opened. Colleen played lookout, and I escaped without being seen. I texted Niki and asked if I should wait for her in Iron Mountain or we should meet somewhere along the way. She responded that her meeting with Sheriff Bartelle had gone splendidly—whatever that meant—and she'd meet me at the first gas station on the Wisconsin side of the border.

I arrived and found her parked at a far corner of the parking lot. She hopped into my truck, blessed me with a million-watt smile. "Things are going to get very interesting. Soon."

FIFTY-NINE

I WAITED TO SPEAK UNTIL I had the truck cruising along the highway. "Explain interesting."

"Bartelle was pissed because I hadn't given him a heads-up I was working in the area. So I built on your suggestion that it related to militia and police officers were involved and served up a whopper. I said my investigation focused on how the militia was getting its funding. They had tasked me to look into certain relationships to determine if those individuals and their illegal activities were the militia's money source."

I asked how he had taken that.

"He was all kinds of bothered until I assured him I was unaware of any officers in his department being under investigation. To make him feel better, I gave him a few names I was checking out."

I risked a glance to gauge her expression. She looked like a little kid who had just entered a candy shop with a five-dollar bill in her hand. "Whose names did you give him?"

"Aaron Rogers or Aaron Robinson or Aaron Riddle, Glenn Korpi, and that new guy we just kicked up, Drew Dombey. He had never heard of Rogers or Dombey. He had run across Glenn Korpi at a minor altercation at the logging outfit he used to work at. By the time officers got there, they had settled the dispute. Other than that, Bartelle was of little help. But now those guys are on his radar."

"Meaning what?"

"I gave him the recognizance photographs, but I did *not* tell him where I took them. I also provided him with Rogers' and Dombey's records. He saw the geographical connection—Rogers from Chicago and Dombey from Gary. He had heard rumors of an out-of-state criminal element moving into the county, but these were the first names attached to that intelligence. Let's say I wouldn't want to be speeding, or have a taillight out, if I were driving the Tundra or that jacked Silverado."

Now I understood why she reminded me of the lucky kid in the candy store. "Did you happen to mention that these guys might be funding the militia?"

"Bartelle made that connection all on his own and concluded it was likely drugs. He asked to share this information with UPSET, the joint drug task force that covers the entire Upper Peninsula. I said it was too early, but if we came up with evidence of drug-related offenses, we'd turn that intel over to him and UPSET. I enquired about prostitution or sex-trade rings in Iron County."

She paused, rubbing her eyes with both of her fists. I asked her what was the matter.

"He was adamant that he would have heard of any prostitution rings operating in his county, and he had not. Hell, it's here. It's everywhere. He's overwhelmed with drug crimes and people ODing. Anyway, it means he's unlikely to hear about us looking into the Silver Fox."

"Speaking of, let's drive by it and check if we spot any known cars there."

"You think Randy Crenshaw is the fourth guy?" she asked.

"If we see that orange Caddy Blackwing and it's not with either truck, then no. Otherwise?" I shrugged. "How do you see our meeting at the resort playing out?"

She patted my arm and laughed. "Hey, this is your play. I'm just the hot-babe fiancée, remember?" She hooted at the concept. "You two business tycoons should talk about how the resort works and what kinds of changes Randy has instituted. Find out if Mike thinks they're good ideas. I can disappear to the ladies' if you want to ask more man-to-man questions regarding what goes on in that private room."

SIXTY

THE SILVER FOX PARKING LOT had a smattering of vehicles, but none owned by my targets. The resort's parking lot was half full and didn't include any of the target vehicles either.

Mike Crenshaw must have seen us drive into the parking lot, because he was waiting at the reception desk. "Seamus, and Niki was it? Your timing's perfect. My stomach was just grumbling." He led us into the dining room and the server ushered us to the table farthest from the kitchen doors.

"Good afternoon, Mindy," Mike said to the waitress. "Please put this on my account. And add a twenty-five percent tip for yourself."

"Thank you, Mr. Crenshaw. Can I get you folks something to drink while you look at the menus?" She handed them around and took our beverage orders. Mike had his favorite beer. Niki went for a glass of Chardonnay. I stuck with water and asked whether he had reached his son.

Crenshaw shook his head. "Someone from the accountant's office will meet your accountant at the motel Monday morning at eight. Our guy will have access to the electronic accounting records. Plus, your guy can look at our reservation book for two fiscal years, and anything else he'd like to see on site."

I effused about how much I appreciated his making it happen. "My accountant is a she, by the way. Name's Colleen Carpetti. She's been staying at your motel for the last couple of days to get a feel for the place. I hope you don't mind."

He looked amazed. "It makes it seem like your buyer is anxious."

"It's me that's anxious. The opportunity to purchase some or all of your landholdings has me excited. The guy I know who might be interested in the motel and resort is a savvy investor. You two will either agree on a price or you won't. That has nothing to do with me. Although I'd like to think my enthusiasm for your property could influence him, I know it won't."

Mindy brought the drinks, took our orders, and the conversation shifted to his landholdings. I asked if there were any particular pieces of property he was unwilling to sell. His belly laugh caused the other diners to stare at us. "Everything is for sale for the right price." He was reluctant to lose a favorite forty acres nestled within thousands of acres of state land. He had bought it decades ago and built a small camp, off grid, where he and a few of his friends could get away and leave civilization behind. The hunting was terrific because no one else had access to that land except by walking in. "Hunters these days," he said, "are too damn lazy to walk a couple miles. They want to drive up to their deer stand, park, and shoot the deer. Not my kind of hunting."

He gave me the coordinates for those forty acres to eliminate them from my places to visit. He had no issue with my checking any of the other land he owned. We could come to his house, and he'd lend us a set of keys to the gates that block several of his holdings. I claimed we had another appointment that afternoon. I'd have to take a rain check on his most generous offer. If nothing else, this gave me an opportunity to follow up with him if I wanted to see him.

Over an excellent lunch, I steered the conversation to resort operations, and even recorded notes on my phone to demonstrate my interest. He was circumspect about changes his son had made, but I got the notion he did not approve them all but was giving his son rein to make the business work. Mindy cleared away the dishes, and Niki excused herself to "powder her nose," leaving me alone with Mike.

I waited until Niki was out of hearing range before mentioning that Randy had said they often used the private room for bachelor parties. I pointed across the dining area to the room. "He gave me the impression that he could bring in women to entertain my friends. I forgot to ask how those services would appear on my credit card. I don't want the little lady to see any—let's say extraordinary entertainment charges—if she looked at my statement."

His eyes glinted, and his mouth pinched before broadening into a smile. "Well," he said. "I don't know how Randy does it, but in my day, we had some outlandishly expensive bottles of champagne that we sold at a considerable markup. No one ever drank them, you understand."

Sixty-One

I ARRIVED HOME WITH FRESH produce for the campers and an uneasy feeling I was running on borrowed time. My trail cameras had shown no traffic past my house since I'd left that morning, but for all I knew Aaron Rogers and friends had drones surveilling it.

Given that uncertainty, I should minimize the number of trips we took to the Baraga camping spot, which meant I'd wait until Niki and I could go together. I stored the groceries in my refrigerator and the ice in its freezer.

The forbidden fruit is always the most interesting one, and the forty acres Crenshaw wouldn't sell roused my curiosity. With Google Earth software, I zoomed in and explored the image. He had downplayed the size of the compound. It included a two-story house that had to run at least 3,000 square feet, a pole barn building spacious enough for three or four vehicles, and a smaller building that I guessed was a sauna. He'd cleared an acre around the buildings.

Crenshaw had to be spending a lot of money to maintain a place he claimed to use only a couple times a year with friends. It shouldn't have surprised me. The rich are different from the rest of us. Now that I saw its size, I was more eager than ever to explore the one area he didn't want me to see. Round trip from my place was three hours. Too far for today, and I had no reason to think it related to Kat's disappearance.

Better I should find out who owned the property and trailer that the Serrano family stayed in and ask them questions. Iron County records showed a limited liability company owned the land. I tracked its registration to Delaware. My heart sunk. Delaware does not require the true owner's name to show on the filing documents. The Registered Agent was a lawyer whose entire practice was setting up LLCs. Another dead end.

With time before Niki's arrival, I called Lizzie to provide her an overdue update.

"Colleen's been filling me in," she said. "With your mother surprising you, I figured you'd be too busy to call. You caught me heading out the door for a registration drive. Gotta go. Stay safe."

Niki showed up at 5:30, bursting with news. While we packed my truck with the groceries, she filled me in: Colleen had gotten the job. Besides Felicity St. Agnes, she saw Randy Crenshaw, but not Rogers or Dombey. Colleen would start Saturday night.

"You can't keep going with her," I said. "She—"

"I didn't this time, remember? The only way Colleen can learn what's going on is if they accept her as what she presented herself to be: a woman scratching for a few extra bucks. She won't ask questions about Kat—because *that* could be dangerous. It's only two nights. She'll blow her cover on Monday if Randy Crenshaw shows up with the motel's accountant."

She was missing my concern. "Maybe earlier if his daddy tells him her name. We can't send her in there with no backup."

"Let's go, Seamus. We can discuss this later."

Good, I thought, I'll enlist Mom's help. In some ways, my mother was a feminist before the term became popular; in other ways, she was more conservative than the Pope. I figured she would not be in favor of her daughter working in a strip joint.

SIXTY-TWO

NIKI AND I MOVED THE generator, propane tanks, and all the other stuff to the other bank of the river. Schlepping them the quarter mile to the campsite was another issue. It took us several trips to cart everything up the hill. Task completed, we moved camp chairs out of the fire's smoke and relaxed onto them. A rich smelling stew bubbled on the stove. Nana and Mom were working together in the "kitchen," chopping veggies for a garden salad to go with the dozen suckers the kids had caught.

Niki closed her eyes and dropped her chin to her chest. If I followed suit, I'd be asleep in a second. I asked where the kids were.

"Resting before dinner," Mom said and called their names. The kids boiled out of their tent. Megan in a mad, squealing dash, followed by Valeria, who was walking without crutches.

"Grandpa Seamus! Niki! You'll never guess what!"

Megan was right. I would never guess what, but that is not how we play the game. "You caught twelve suckers," I said.

"Geema told you that. That's not what I want you to guess. Niki, you guess."

Niki opened her eyes and rubbed her chin like she was thinking hard on the subject. "You found a secret fairy village."

Valeria caught up with us. "The eagles found us. We left them a fish, and they came and took it. How did they know we were here?"

I said I didn't know for sure. "They have excellent eyesight, you know." The eagles were just the thing to help lessen the kids' trauma of having to move from Lake Tranquility. I sent the birds a silent thanks. If only I could enlist them to find Kat.

Dinner was uneventful. Rather than go back home, we stayed the night to allow time to talk to Mom after the kids and Nana went to bed. Mom reported that Nana remained firm about not contacting the police. Mom thought if Nana believed she had a safe place to take Valeria, they might persuade her to do it.

Given the fantastic progress I had made on determining Kat's whereabouts, maybe I should concentrate on finding that safe place so we could get the police involved. Who was I kidding? If someone had taken Kat, the chances of her still being alive were minuscule. The only reasonable chance she had of remaining safe was if she had left of her own accord. Being resigned to bad news did not mean I could stop searching for the truth. Which brought me to Colleen and the Silver Fox.

I was correct that Mom would blow her stack about Colleen wanting to work at the Silver Fox. I was wrong about who she targeted with her anger. "First, Seamus, it's your own damn fault she's doing this. Second, she's a big girl. It's not like the first time she's ever been to a bar with strange men around. Third, what makes you think she wants you, or anyone she knows, to watch her dance?"

Just because the women were all against me didn't mean my concerns weren't legit. "Niki, you told Bartelle you were looking into possible prostitution. Maybe you could talk him into having a deputy at the Silver Fox while Colleen's there? I know it's not his jurisdiction, but that might make it more effective."

"No way," Niki said. "Jurisdiction is everything. And don't try the drug angle with UPSET. Wrong state."

So Colleen was on her own. Crap. I hated that. Maybe I could sit in the parking lot. I asked Niki if we had a game plan for tomorrow.

"We do, but it involves breaking a few laws."

Mom let out an exasperated sigh. "I do not need to hear this. I'm heading to bed."

We said our goodnights. Once Mom couldn't hear us, Niki told me her plan. "First thing, we go to your house and pack a full day's worth of supplies. Your job is to follow Randy Crenshaw wherever he goes. Fingers crossed he sleeps in his own bed tonight."

"How can I do that without him seeing me? It's not like we're in Boston, and I can hide in traffic."

"I don't care if he sees the car, Seamus. But I don't want him to see you driving the car. I'll give you a wig and you'll take my SUV. Bring your Kindle. You're gonna have lots of waiting. Bring snacks and water and something to pee in."

"And while I am having a blast, what are you doing?"

"Knocking on doors to learn who lives where and with whom."

"And they'll tell you because you're such a pretty face?"

"No, they'll tell me because I am a US Marshal looking for information on a dangerous fugitive."

I had forgotten that as part of her undercover work, they had made her a US Marshal with an official badge and everything. "And that's the illegal part of our day?"

"The first part."

SIXTY-THREE

I PARKED DOWN THE STREET from Randy Crenshaw's house, where I had a good view of his porch and driveway. After finishing the William Kent Krueger, I started a new-to-me Michael Connelly thriller featuring Renée Ballard. What would happen if Renée and Niki met? They'd be best friends or two cats in a burlap sack. That visual put a smile on my face.

Crenshaw's appearance interrupted my reading. He walked from his front door to the garage. His engine roared to life, and a puff of white exhaust wafted past the opened door. I followed Crenshaw's orange Caddy Blackwing to a local restaurant. I had no sooner found my place in the thriller, when he exited carrying a brown paper cup. His next stop was gas in Crystal Falls. From there, he drove to the Menominee Rapids Resort.

Although Niki didn't care if Crenshaw saw her SUV, I couldn't remain hidden if I followed him into the resort parking lot. Unless I put down a huge deposit on a bachelor's weekend, I had run out of excuses to visit the resort. I performed a U-turn and pulled under the shade of a massive pine. After losing my place several times while reading, I decided to explore on foot.

I found a spot screened by thick bushes that afforded a view of the parking lot. Crenshaw was loading supplies into an eight-person passenger van. Five guys, all white, all in their mid-30s or early 40s, stood around chatting in a way that suggested they knew each other. This outing wasn't to hunt, nothing interesting was in season. No fishing poles or tackle in sight. They weren't birdwatchers. I knew those folks. They'd be peering into the treetops and underneath bushes to see what birds were around. Whitewater rafting?

I didn't want to lose them, which was likely if they left while I was just standing there. I gave up spying and returned to the SUV. Several minutes later, the van passed. I gave them a thirty-second head start and followed.

My whitewater-rafting theory unraveled after we crossed into Wisconsin and left the river behind. We passed the Silver Fox, reentered Michigan, and I ran through the various events happening in Iron County this weekend but couldn't come up with anything to justify this trip. Earlier in the month we'd had Bass Fest—I'd run in the "Run Your Bass Off" race. Next month was the Humongous Fungus Festival celebrating the largest plant by size, not weight, in the US—a thirty-eight-acre fungus. My next idea was they were traveling to Alpha, Michigan, known as the smallest village in America with a brewery.

They passed the cutoff to Alpha and drove through Crystal Falls. On our way toward Iron River, I let two trucks get between me and the van and immediately the pinch in my shoulders disappeared. If I had Niki's job, I think I would die from stress within six months. I texted her to ask if she was still in Iron River, got an affirmative, and asked her to call if she could. Seconds later, my phone rang.

I explained the situation. Did she want to join me in a tag-team to decrease the possibility of being spotted?

"I'm not done here. Use common sense, like you did at the resort. We want to know where they're going, but not let on that you're following. Got it?"

You betcha boss. Easy peasy. The pain between my shoulders returned at double strength.

They left US 2 to take a narrow road that soon became what I realized was the forest road leading to Mike Crenshaw's remote forty acres. I'd wanted to learn more about this place and Crenshaw was providing me that opportunity. With only one way in, I chose a good hiding spot to determine what other vehicles traveled to the compound or left. Bonus—I could pee in the woods, not in a bottle, and I could stretch away the stress.

SIXTY-FOUR

I SPENT THE AFTERNOON IN the car, alternately sweating and freezing. I didn't dare open the windows to catch what little breeze there was because when I had stopped, the car's exhaust had attracted a horde of mosquitoes. Each time it got so hot my head ached, I turned the car on and left it on until I shivered. Each boil-freeze cycle lasted about forty minutes.

At 1:30, a delivery van drove past, going too fast for me to capture its registration or the lettering on its side. It returned two hours later with Crenshaw, driving the passenger van, following on its heels. No sign of the five guys.

Niki finished sleuthing and joined me at 4:00. To give ourselves more flexibility to have one person drive while the other took pictures or whatever, we decided it made sense to ride together. That required a strategic retreat to park the F-150 on the paved road. We returned with Niki's SUV. She used her phone's map to direct us to a closer observation point, where we waited, and waited, and waited. I asked how she had gotten people to talk to her.

"Told them the US Marshals service had gotten a tip about a man wanted for jumping bail while appealing his conviction on breaking and entering and aggravated assault. We believed he was hiding with an unknown associate someplace in the Upper Peninsula, and sources had him in town. I showed them a picture of a guy who's deceased and described him as medium height and weight. He might have grown a beard and dyed his hair brown and might disguise himself with glasses. Basically, he could look like almost anyone. We didn't know whether the person he was staying with was also new to the area or had been a longtime resident.

"I had to calm down some folks who worried they weren't safe. I told them that his crimes had all been out-of-state."

"And people opened up to you? I've found most people are fairly reserved with folks they don't know."

"I had some of that, but most people talk to badges. Aaron Rogers has been in town for only three months. He and Glenn Korpi seem to be best buds, although no one could say how they'd gotten together. The big scuttlebutt was that Korpi's wife caught him screwing around and threw him out last week. He's staying a few doors down with a friend. Seems the wife found a map to the other woman's trailer in the woods. Made me wonder if Mrs. Korpi drove the blue Silverado up to Kat's trailer and went apeshit not finding anyone there."

"Which would explain the screaming woman," I said. "But was Korpi having an affair with Kat, or was he putting the screws on her because of her immigration status?"

Niki sighed. "Or both. Until we find Kat or can question these guys, I don't think we'll know the answer. Seems another guy sometimes lives with Aaron Rogers. No name. Descriptions varied, but it could be Drew Dombey. Or maybe the fourth guy? More work to do there. I saved Mrs. Korpi for last and asked the same questions. She was not in a sharing mood. She became flustered when I asked if her husband was home. Told me the asshole didn't live there anymore and slammed the door in my face. Interesting, right?"

It struck me as odd and unenlightening. Niki figured the wife had to know something about her husband's illegal activities. No one mentioned anything suspicious concerning Randy Crenshaw. Most thought he was a nice guy because he let neighborhood kids use the swing-set. Disappointing. I wondered out loud what we would do with that information.

"It's all part of the stew, Seamus. All part of the stew."

My stomach growled and I laughed. "Can't eat that stew. How long do we hang here? They could stay for the entire weekend."

Niki handed me an apple. "It's not like you have anything better to do. Besides, what are they doing there? No place to fish. No nearby ATV trails. This looks to me like a place you come to screw your brains out where no one can see you. If the women aren't already there, my guess is they won't arrive until evening. If someone shows up after dark, I have night goggles." Niki waggled her eyebrows at me.

"What the hell don't you have in this car?"

"Answers."

SIXTY-FIVE

DUSK ARRIVED WITH NO ADDITIONAL traffic. Time to reconnoiter. It took us the better part of an hour to find a safe spot to observe the compound. Long before we got there, we saw light shining above the trees.

A generator ran at full tilt, providing an underlying burr to the thumping bass from a sound system that pounded the air. At least we didn't need to worry about being quiet.

We stationed ourselves in the woods several feet from the mown area. The house was lit like a torch, and several exterior lights attached to the buildings illuminated the front of the house and the surrounding grounds. Light bounced off windshields of two vehicles in the driveway. The garage doors were down, and that building blocked our view of the sauna. A faint hint of woodsmoke perfumed the air.

From our distance, my binocs picked up only glare from the house windows. We watched for outside movement. A half hour showed no exterior guards or roaming dogs.

"Looks like party time to me," Niki said. "Guess I'd better see what I'm missing. You stay here. I don't want you to have to make a fast retreat through an open field with your ankle."

She couldn't see me shaking my head. "My ankle's fine. It's been fine. The plate they put in makes the odds of me re-injuring it way less than of you breaking your skull. Let's consider what happens if I go. You can observe with your night goggles, and you can cover me with your rifle. If you see anything, you have that incredible whistle to alert me of the danger."

She grabbed my shoulder. I kept making my case. "Whereas, if you go, we both know I'm more likely to shoot you than someone else. And I can't whistle for shit. Well, I have a pleasant whistle, but it carries only about three feet. So, it's my job to sneak."

I shook off her hand and trotted down the tree line until I could use the garage to shield my approach from the house. Closer in, the country-western music blaring from external speakers was so loud I couldn't hear anything else. The only reason to have outdoor speakers is if people were outside. Just because we hadn't seen them didn't mean they weren't there, and it was unlikely I could hear a warning whistle from Niki should she try to alert me of danger. I was on my own.

The wolf had been curious enough to scout out our camping spot and smart enough to keep his distance. I was not as smart and sprinted from the woods to the corner of the garage without incident. I knelt, my heart a thumping tympani in my chest. I brought the binocs to my eyes, used my elbows to steady myself, and scanned the area.

The two vehicles were between me and the house. One was a passenger van larger than the one Randy Crenshaw had used to transport the five guys. That fit with Niki's guess that women were already here. The other was a well-used Dodge Ram.

A paver walk led from the driveway to a centered front entrance two steps above ground level. Light poured from the first story's floor to ceiling windows. When I focused on the windows, all I saw were shadows of movement behind some kind of material that reflected the outside lights. The same floodlights that didn't allow me to see in made it easy for someone inside to spot me if I got careless.

I pushed away that negative thought. The only way I could see inside was to be close enough to shield a bit of window from the glare, which meant being right next to the window. With no ability to know if someone was looking out, I could not approach the house from the front. Before I tried a different side, I used the vehicles as cover and crawled across the gravel and copied the license plate numbers. I retreated, circled around the garage, discovering it had no windows, and explored the sauna. Its external firebox was warm, not hot, and the inside was dark and quiet. They had used it earlier in the day. Parked behind the sauna was a five-by-eight trailer stacked with split maple. A fenced area occupied 10,000 square feet between the sauna and the woods. Rows of vegetables filled the garden except for a recently tilled rectangular plot in the far corner.

I used an oblique angle to reach the back corner of the house with little chance of anyone inside spotting me. From there I eased to a position that allowed me to peer into the nearest rear window, which, I was pleased to discover, did not have the reflective film. A middle-aged couple worked in a massive kitchen. The woman was up to her elbows in a soapy sink. The man dried dishes, storing them into open cupboards well supplied with dinnerware, glasses of all sorts, and paper products. This was not a facility used by Mike Crenshaw to entertain a few friends only a few days each year. No wonder he wanted me to stay away. Fine, Seamus. So what are you going to do about it?

SIXTY-SIX

AFTER CONFIRMING MY CELLPHONE'S CAMERA was in no-flash mode, I positioned its lens just above the windowsill and snapped their pictures. Between the truck tag and Rembrandt, Niki had a good chance to ID them. Maybe I should leave while my luck held. But if Kat was in the house and I chickened out, I'd feel like I had let everyone down.

I crawled along the foundation to the next window, which was dark. When I poked my head up at the remaining two, I was disappointed to see they had the frosted panes people use for bathrooms.

I reached the corner and scanned the open area on that side of the house. With the corner of my eye, I caught movement inside the tree line but beyond the reach of the house lights. My heart seized, then kicked into a high gear as I willed my eyes to find whatever it was. I dared not move and staring didn't help. I very slowly turned my head and my peripheral vision again caught movement. Was he/she/it trying the same thing with me? Neither of us could hear over the music. I sipped in air and eased it out, hoping my chest didn't move.

A white flag rose and the ghost of a deer trotted away, it's tail waving a warning to any who would pay attention. I remained frozen, concerned a guard had frightened the deer. The deer soon reappeared, closer in and chowing down on the grass.

I told myself to trust the deer's instincts and moved around the corner to the first window, which looked into an L-shaped dining room that ran the entire width of the house. A wooden table polished a warm gold remained piled with the detritus of a feast. Saliva flooded my mouth as I surveyed the remains of a carved roast, tossed salad, fresh vegetables, and what I'd bet was cherry pie. I counted fourteen place settings, complete with linen napkins.

Given the five guys I had seen get into the van at the Menominee Rapids Resort, even if the help ate with the guests—unlikely—that left seven people I hadn't identified. With no lights on upstairs, everyone needed to be in the room off the front of the dining room. Unless the door was closed, I should be able to see in from the last window on this side.

After elbow-crawling to stay below the windows, I reached the final window and slowly raised my head enough to see in. Separated by open pocket doors, the dining room flowed into a parlor. Light from a wood-burning fireplace danced on the ceiling. A setting of two stuffed love seats at right angles blocked my view farther into the house. The tops of two heads close together rose above one sofa. One had long blonde hair. Not Kat.

Movement from the other love seat drew my attention. A tiger-striped six-inch stiletto heel bounced at the end of a long, bare leg. The foot stopped tapping, and a head, covered by Irish red tresses, rose. Green eyes stared into mine.

She winked.

I sprinted toward Niki and the safety of the woods. Arms pumping, thighs burning, I didn't stop until I was five yards into the foliage. I squatted next to a downed tree to catch my breath. A dozen or more people poured from the house, wandering around, lights from their flashlights looking like spotlights at a fairground.

Niki stepped next to me. "What the hell happened?"

I waved a finger to signal I needed a minute. Once I could speak, I explained.

"How much is truth and how much is fantasy? No way you could see that lady's eyes were green."

Well, yeah. "Educated guess. Anyone with that hair either has green eyes or wears green contacts. How do Peeping Toms do it? I'd die of a heart attack worrying about getting busted. What if they had shot through the windows at me?"

Niki gave me her what-the-hell-am-I-going-to-do-with-you look. "Well, they didn't. And since Rembrandt requires sharp pictures, not educated guesses, we'll wait and try to get them. And we need your good cameras."

SIXTY-SEVEN

I OFFERED TO LET NIKI call the coin toss to determine who had to drive to my place and retrieve my camera gear to get the sharp pictures for Rembrandt. With the quarter doing lazy loops, she said, "Not edge."

I snagged the coin midair. "You're supposed to choose heads or tails."

"You're sore because I found the winning call. Off you go."

Someday I'll learn. When I returned, the outside lights and most of the inside lights were dark. Niki had scouted a better spot for our surveillance, this one providing an unobstructed view of the front door from an angle that avoided having the morning sun reflect off my telephoto lens. I set two cameras on tripods, one fitted with infrared equipment, the other with a standard lens.

As consolation to my "losing" the coin flip, Niki took the first watch. She woke me at 4:30 and reported nothing had happened. Two hours later, the kitchen crew dumped a dozen garbage bags into the bed of the Dodge Ram. I captured sharp pictures of both of them.

My next picture opportunity came after another three hours. The five guys Randy had brought from the Resort and nine women, all wearing flip-flops and bathrobes or dressing gowns, paraded to the sauna. I zoomed in on individual faces and kept my finger on the camera trigger. The rapid-fire shutter woke Niki.

Photo opportunity complete, I said, "I wonder what happened to the other woman."

Niki's look told me I needed to explain. "You know: two girls for every boy. Golden oldie. Jan and Dean. Surf City." I sang the refrain and got the don't-be-an-ass look. She was right. She hadn't yet been born, and the only reason I knew the song was because, as a kid, I had found it in my mother's collection of 45 rpm records.

"Ignoring your prehistoric references, you have a valid point. I wonder if Kat was supposed to be the other woman. If that's the case, it puts another nail in her coffin. It's been—"

The synth-pop beat from the Wonder Woman 1984 trailer stopped her dead. She answered her phone, listened, then said, "Yeah. Here he is, Sheriff Bartelle."

I had been finishing Niki's sentence with "nine days since Kat disappeared" and accepted the phone like it was a rattlesnake. "Hey Lon, this is Seamus. What's up?"

"You avoiding me? Why didn't you answer your phone?"

"It's turned off. You got me now."

"Where are you?"

I didn't lie, but I didn't choose to tell the truth, either. "A ways outside Iron River. Your tone of voice is getting me worried. What happened?"

"Is your granddaughter with you?"

My heart clogged my throat. Something had happened to Megan. "No. I sent her away with my mother. You're scaring the shit out of me. What the hell happened?"

"Better see for yourself. Make sure Niki is with you. I expect answers from both of you."

Sixty-Eight

As Niki packed the gear in our vehicles, I found several messages from Bartelle on my phone, each more curt than the previous one. None from Colleen. I dialed Mom, got no answer, and left a message. Unlike me, she didn't forget to charge her phone. One more worry burning an acid hole in my gut.

Niki led, and I followed in my truck. She carved the ninety-minute trip down to an hour. That probably saved me going even faster and winding up in a ditch. A county patrol car blocked the road at my property line. The deputy contacted Bartelle, who said we should walk down to my guest cabin.

I ran with Niki in my wake.

We found Bartelle and Tex pacing the cabin's screened porch. Bartelle asked if I would give them permission to search my property, vehicles, and look at my trail camera pictures. I tossed Tex the keys to the house. "Garage is unlocked. You need a card reader?"

Tex caught the keys with a "Thanks, we're good."

Bartelle ordered Tex to take Niki to the scene; he'd talk with me here. Tex and Niki left at a jog.

I sounded calm, although I had to choke down the spew burning my throat. "Now that you've separated us, will you stop dicking around and tell me what the hell happened?"

"In time. Your granddaughter and mother aren't here?"

Sure hope not. I walked around the picnic table to put Bartelle between me and the porch door in part to see if anyone was coming, but equally to assure Bartelle I wasn't a threat. It took both my hands to support me as I sat down, making it shortly before my shaking legs collapsed. I crossed my arms. "Why don't you believe my mother took Megan?"

"Tell me where you and Niki have been since I saw Niki yesterday morning."

"Niki speaks for herself. I've been following a lead on the prostitution that doesn't happen in Iron County. I refuse to answer another question until you tell me what's going on."

"When and where did you last see the two guys you made that citizen's arrest on?"

My conscience was clear about them. My stomach unwound a quarter turn. I gave him a little head shake. "Not since then. Why?" He leaned over me. I countered his power move by folding my arms, putting a blank look on my face, and staring past his shoulder.

His eyes became resigned. "You can be such an asshole sometimes. Fine. Follow me." He spun on his heel and marched out the door, not looking to see if I was coming.

I scrambled past the picnic table, caught the screen door before it slammed, and followed him on the path from the guest cabin to my house. He would have delivered any bad news concerning Megan or my mother while I was alone and sitting down. Right? My stomach flipped, then settled. This was something else.

The hill between the guest cabin and my house provided my first opportunity to see vehicles filled my driveway. My lungs stopped working while I scanned the collection for Colleen's rental. Two state vehicles, the state's portable evidence trailer, another Iron County cruiser, and one unknown truck. I couldn't see the area blocked by the garage. The last time I saw this many police resources, dead bodies were involved.

Sixty-Nine

I ASKED BARTELLE'S BACK, "WHO called this in?" Whether he didn't hear or pretended not to, it had the same effect of adding to my angst. He led me past my 1,000-gallon propane tank, which had the same siphoning equipment attached as the bear and the beanpole thieves we caught had used. Stolen propane did not explain this many cops. He strode around the garage corner and pointed to tarps covering two bodies sprawled next to my Subaru Outback, still up on its jack, waiting for its replacement tire.

My feet forgot how to move. "The same two? Who killed them?"

"I was hoping you would tell me. I'll ask again, when and where did you last see them?"

"When your officers drove them away in separate patrol cars. How did they get here? Who called it in?"

"Text message supposedly from your neighbors across the lake."

"They're not around."

"Yep, plus it was a spoofed number. Someone wanted to stick this on you—unless it's you trying to make it look like someone wanted to frame you."

The smell of excrement, and piss, and blood reached me. I sucked on my cheeks to generate enough saliva to swallow and tamp down my desire to puke. "I assume they didn't walk."

"Truck with a bunch of propane tanks and a wheelbarrow is parked at the end of your driveway. We removed the lock on your chain. Sorry about that."

I positioned myself to see the rest of my driveway. Colleen's rental was not there. "It happened after 11:30 last night. I might not have seen the bodies because my car is blocking them from the house, but I couldn't have missed the truck."

He stepped into my space. "I thought you said you were gone since yesterday morning?"

I retreated a step and waved away the implication I was lying. "I returned briefly to pick up camera equipment for our stakeout." Past Bartelle's shoulder, I saw Tex and Niki walking down the driveway, their heads together in conversation. What had Niki said we were doing?

Bartelle motioned toward the tarps. "Want to see them?"

My stomach flipped. "Hell would I want to do that?"

"You're right. Gunshot victims are never pretty." He raised his voice to address Tex. "Anything from the trail cams?"

"All missing," came the reply.

"Well," Bartelle dragged out the word. "Isn't that convenient, Seamus?"

SEVENTY

NIKI WANTED TO VIEW THE bodies. Now that I was over the shock of knowing two people had been killed on my property, I wanted everyone to finish up so I could find out what was going on with my mother not answering the phone. I swallowed the acid of my saliva and held my counsel.

Bartelle performed the unveiling while Tex checked with the officers searching my house. Both bodies lay face down. The big guy had a shotgun blast in his back. The shorter fellow had taken one in the shoulder. Someone had dispatched them with small-caliber shots to the head. The muzzle held close enough to burn the skin.

Niki pointed to a pellet under my car next to an evidence flag. "Looks like zero-zero buckshot, but it's a bogus clue. The blast caught the bear from behind—best way to deal with someone that size. The beanpole was probably second and was running, which is why the blast caught his shoulder. Didn't happen here. Someone moved the bodies."

With Niki's words I looked more closely and couldn't find the bits of skin and blood I should have seen if the murders had occurred there.

Bartelle said it didn't prove anything. "Seamus here is smart enough to frame himself to throw off the scent. Any idea how much propane you should have in your tank?"

"Around six-fifty."

Tex rejoined us, holding something behind his back. "House is clear. You're still at six-fifty, so no theft. Tell us about that package you left under your passenger seat?" Seeing my confused expression, he added, "Your Subaru?"

I couldn't imagine what Megan had left under the seat and said so. Tex displayed an evidence bag holding another clear bag filled with a white substance with a yellow tinge. "Never seen it. My Subaru's been sitting like that for days waiting for a new tire. Doors are unlocked. I assume whoever did this," I waved at the murdered men, "planted it."

Bartelle jabbed his crooked finger at me. "Because murder isn't enough?"

Niki stepped between us. "Give it a rest, Bartelle. We all know Seamus didn't do this, and he's not running around with drugs under his car seat. His granddaughter's only eight. She didn't accidentally leave her stash of meth or whatever lying around. I gave you some names. You do anything with them? I'm pretty sure one of them flew a drone over Seamus's property two days ago."

My phone rang and displayed Colleen's name. I pressed the do not answer button and muttered, "Possible Spam."

"That's news you should have told me," Bartelle said. "They are on my list for a little chat, but we've been busy."

"I won't tell you how to do your business," Niki said, "but the State's got the crime scene. You and Tex should talk with those guys, and I wouldn't mind tagging along." She flashed him a flirty smile. "I'll drive myself, if that's okay?"

Bartelle squinted at her. "Is this the Feds way of sticking their nose into our tent? You plan on commandeering this investigation?"

"Absolutely not. Three heads are better than two."

Tex gave Bartelle a slight head bob. Bartelle crooked his arm around his head, massaged his neck with his hand. "Okay, but while we're together, you will tell me everything about this alleged prostitution ring and what you and Seamus were doing. Deal?"

"Deal" Given the way Niki faced, only I could see her give me a wink.

Whatever the hell that meant. I had bigger worries: learning why Colleen had called and running to the river to find out why my mother hadn't returned my phone call. "How much longer before I can use my house?" By which I meant, how long until everyone finishes, and what can I accomplish before they leave?

Bartelle addressed the larger question. "We'll check with the State boys, but I'm guessing your house is fine. The outside may take a while yet. Stay available. We may have more questions."

I gave him my most sincere smile. "Of course."

SEVENTY-ONE

MY FIRST QUESTION TO COLLEEN was whether she was okay.

"Bored. I have the day to myself until I dance tonight. I thought maybe I could visit your camp. Love to see it. I learned a couple of things. Nothing major. Did I mention I'm bored?"

For a woman who enjoyed living in Boston, I could see how Iron Mountain might get a little confining. Especially with no one to do stuff with. I tried to scare her away by telling her what had happened here. She reminded me she was a cop's daughter and did she tell me she's bored? "Problem is," I said, "I need to check on the campers. Mom's not answering her phone. I don't even know if I'll be here."

"No problem. At least I'll enjoy a pleasant drive in the country. Hopefully, I'll see you soon."

I gave her directions from the motel and explained where I hid a key if she found the house locked.

The State police confirmed they didn't need me around. I installed a spare trail camera on the road near my home, then armed with a pair of old binoculars to back up my story about going birdwatching, I hiked through the woods and rejoined Shank Lake Road a half mile north. From there, I ran to the river, crossed, and arrived at the camp to find Mom and Nana throwing darts at the board I had set up.

"Mom," I called once I was in hailing range, "is everything okay? You never called me back."

Mom's wave acknowledged she had heard me. She waited until I was closer to tell me her electronics had died, and none of them had figured out how to start the generator. She handed Nana the darts and fisted her hands. "The line for the oche isn't square to the board, and you set the board three-eights of an inch too high."

"I triple measured it, Mom. It is exactly five feet eight inches to the bullseye. I drew the line in the dirt with a stick. Give me a break."

She shook her head at me like I was ten-years-old. "Not possible. It looks too high and my darts are landing low. Maybe your measuring tape is wrong."

Mom had thrown a bazillion darts over the years. If she said the board was too high, it was too high. But not because the measuring tape was wrong. This wasn't my first rodeo. I had picked that tree because the ground surrounding it was level. I stood next to the tree and compared the bullseye to the height of my eye. It was not too high.

I turned to look at Mom and laughed when I realized the problem. "I hung it the right height, Mom. The ground slopes down from the tree to the oche. My fault. I should have thought of that. When I get a moment, I'll drop it for you."

"Soon as you fix the generator. You should get one of those laser-level thingies and do it right the first time."

You betcha, Mom. A lot of call to install dartboards to tournament specifications outside in the woods. I checked the generator set up and found they had somehow flicked the switch that changed the fuel source from propane to gasoline. I showed them the solution, and the generator roared to life. Megan came running from her tent, electronics and charging cables in hand. Valeria, crutchless, walked at a slower pace.

Once we plugged everything in, a snake's nest of cables running everywhere, the kids wanted to drag me down to show me how well they had trained their eagles. I sent them to catch fish and promised to join them in a few minutes.

With the kids gone, I asked my mother how things were going.

"You saw how well Valeria's ankle is doing. She puts on a good face, but she cries a lot in her tent. No news on her mother?"

I figured that meant Nana had not yet agreed to leave. Now was the wrong time to spring my newest idea to get Megan and Mom onto a plane to Boston. I'd have two McCree females, three generations apart, digging in their heels. I chose not to mention the murders at my house. Not knowing how much English Nana understood made me reluctant to go into any detail in her presence about the Crenshaw compound. That left subterfuge as my weapon of choice.

I told Mom that Colleen was coming to visit me and wondered if she'd like to take Megan to my house. They could get a decent shower—or run a bath if she wanted—and spend time with Colleen. It would also give Valeria and Nana space from McCrees.

"Might not be a bad idea, but you'd better go check on the kids. I was with them yesterday, and we got an eagle to catch a fish in the air. The girls don't have strong enough arms to throw the fish high enough. I barely could. You could do a good job. I'll make sure Nana is okay with us leaving."

SEVENTY-TWO

WITH THE POLICE AT MY house, I was not in a hurry to depart. And I feared Megan's reaction to leaving Valeria. I figured to let them have a long final play time. "And ask Nana what she wants for extra supplies. While I'm here, do we need more drinking water?"

"There's plenty. The kids take turns running water through the filter. Nana is a real workhorse. Have you seen her woodcarvings? They are *gorgeous*. She could sell them for good money."

The girls had beaten a trail to the river. I arrived to find they had caught two suckers. The eagles called from downriver.

Valeria hauled in another fish. Megan removed the hook and stunned it on a rock. "Grandpa Seamus, watch. The eagles come when I call."

This I had to see. Megan grabbed a fish and walked to a hummock of grass that stuck into the river. She waved the fish above her head and yelled, drawing out each word, "George. Martha. Gonzo. I've got fish." To my amazement, two of the birds called back. Seconds later, Megan identified the one that landed in a nearby dead tree as George. Martha, who I agreed was the larger of the two adults, did lazy loops overhead.

"Grandpa Seamus, can you toss the fish?"

"Geema told me about your new trick." I accepted the fish from Megan. "Anything special before I toss it?"

She instructed me to hold the fish high above my head to let the eagle see it. When it flew near, I was to throw it as high as I could over the water to allow the eagle to retrieve it if it didn't catch it on the fly. I channeled throwing-in a soccer ball and used both hands whipping past my head to chuck it. Martha swooped down but missed; the fish plopped into the river and started flowing downstream. Martha circled, swooped down, and grabbed the sucker from the surface without missing a wingbeat, carrying its meal to a high exposed limb of the tree in which George perched.

Gonzo flew in and tried to swipe the fish. The adults' rebukes were loud and shrill. Eagles aren't like herons that swallow fish whole. They use their hooked beaks to tear the fish apart. It did not take it long to consume the offering.

Megan brought me another fish and told me to wait to throw it until an eagle was closer. I waved the fish by the tail. Nothing happened. "Not working, Pumpkin."

Megan let loose with her George and Gonzo calls, and George launched from the tree heading toward us. The thought of a bird with a five-foot wingspan and talons that could rip me apart flying toward me had my heart thumping against my ribcage. I bent down and flung the fish high into the air. Whether it was the higher throw, or George had better talon-eye coordination, I don't know, but this time the eagle snatched the fish from the air. It gave a kri-kri-kri call and, instead of returning to the tree with the other eagles, flew upriver. Gonzo saw a potential meal flying away and pursued. Martha stayed on her perch, her piercing stare directed at us. Did she hope for another fish?

I asked Megan if she thought she could video the action. She wanted to be in the video with me and suggested Valeria do it. Sounded like a great idea. I let Valeria take a couple of selfies with Megan to get the feel for using my phone before showing her how to record a video.

At Valeria's okay, Megan called in Martha. I reared back and launched the fish into the air. In my enthusiasm, I released the sucker early and lofted it overhead. I watched Martha swoop toward the fish, the fish drop, and realized the trajectory of the two met at my head. I took Megan with me to the ground. We slid across the grass hummock and into the cool embrace of the river. Megan was on top of me and only got a little wet. I came up sputtering and laughing. Neither Megan nor I had seen what happened with Martha and the fish. Valeria laughed so hard she dropped my phone into the water. She retrieved it, and I yelled at her to dry it on her shirt.

Megan grabbed my arm with both hands and told me not to be mad at Valeria for dropping my phone. I assured her all was good. It was my fault we fell into the river. I was glad I hadn't hurt her and that the eagle had avoided both of us. The phone was okay, and we played the video. Martha caught the fish right where I had been standing. It was a terrific video, even if I did look the fool.

A motor's high whine interrupted our second viewing of the video. Megan agreed it was coming from downstream. Valeria spotted a drone flying above the distant tree line, working its way up the river toward us. Aaron Rogers had to be close enough to control the drone.

Crap on a stick. I hustled the kids into the woods.

Seventy-Three

MY INITIAL REACTION WAS TO call Sheriff Bartelle, but I had promised Nana I wouldn't contact the police. I stomped on that temptation and did the next best thing, texting Niki that Rogers' drone was getting close to the hidden camp. She replied with a check mark and "working on it."

I sent the kids to the campsite and stayed hidden behind a screen of cedars, watching the drone scan both banks of the river. I could hide, which meant the first thing Rogers would find interesting would be the road we followed to the river. After that, it would soon discover the canoe on this side of the river—evidence someone was over here. I'd have to risk drawing Rogers' attention to my movement to haul the canoe into the woods. If his lens wasn't too wide . . .

Damn. The kids' fishing poles and bait box remained at the river's edge—a dead giveaway that we were here. I parted the cedar's branches and spotted the drone 100 yards downriver. *Screwed.* I had no safe way to grab them. When Rogers saw them, he would broaden the drone's search area and find the tent compound.

My phone buzzed with a text. I looked down, expecting to see something from Niki. Instead, Colleen informed me she had reached my house. *Police say they're nearly done.* I sent a thumbs up.

Across the river, Martha ruffled her wings and called, her head focused on the drone. Had it ever seen one? The eagle launched into the air, flapped several wing beats headed upriver, did a lazy U-turn and spiraled up, gathering height. Soon it was high above me, circling and calling. The drone continued its search pattern. Martha circled several hundred feet behind the drone and glided down on flat wings to match the drone's elevation over the water. With powerful wingbeats, Martha caught up to the drone and rose above the spinning blades.

The eagle hovered above the machine and slammed its talons into the metal contraption. My stomach flipped at the loud crack. I feared what the drone's blades had done to the eagle's feet. The two split apart. The drone's bent blades dead, the contraption plummeted to the ground on the far side of the river. Martha circled the wreckage twice before flying upriver. Man, I wished I had videotaped that.

Okay, now what? Niki had mentioned Rogers could watch the drone's live video stream. He'd know it was down, but since Martha nailed it from behind, Rogers wouldn't know what happened. Rules state you're supposed to have your drone in sight. I doubted he felt constrained by rules. Regardless, he couldn't be far away.

A new text hit my phone from Niki. *Sorry ur on your own.* I had guessed that, but confirmation was still a letdown.

The mix of tag alders and wet marshes covering much of the river's edge would make it hard for Rogers to follow the riverbank to his downed drone. He might waste more time looking for nonexistent roads or trails leading to the river near where the drone crashed.

Okay, Seamus, you have time before he gets here. Use it wisely.

I collected the poles and bait bucket and ran them up the hill to the camp, where I gathered everyone together. "Nana and Valeria have proved they can hide well in the woods. Mom, that's not your superpower. I need to move you and Megan to the house. Get your walking shoes on. It's our only way to get there."

Mom looked like she was going to argue, but after a moment's hesitation, she gave me a nod.

I continued with instructions. "Valeria, you and Nana must be quiet.

No noise. No fire. Very, very quiet. If you hear anyone coming toward the camp, hide in the woods like you did at the trailer. Mom, make sure Nana understands that."

While my mother translated, I told Megan to grab her and her grandmother's electronic stuff. Nana and Mom engaged in some back-and-forth discussion. Mom asked me if I planned to leave the rifle with Nana. "No. It will only slow her down. The only thing that will keep her and Valeria safe is not being found."

Nana nodded agreement with Mom's translation.

"Tell her I will return once it's safe. I will not leave them here by themselves."

The look in Valeria's eyes was enough to make me cry. No child should be that scared. Yet it was their prior experience that gave me confidence they would be okay. "Remember to take your medicine, Valeria. Promise me you won't forget."

She pulled the piece of granite from her pocket and held it up to me. "I promise, Grampa Seamus. Hurry back."

That tore my heart.

SEVENTY-FOUR

ONCE WE WERE ACROSS THE river, I gave Mom the rifle and told her to walk far enough up the road to ensure no one could see them from the water and wait for me. To hide the canoe to prevent it from giving Rogers ideas that Nana and Valeria were on the other side, I paddled several bends upstream and hauled it into the woods.

I found Mom and Megan fretting under a hemlock. I texted Colleen to learn whether the police had left and she could drive down and pick us up. Not yet. We'd start walking, and she would meet us on the way. Mom made me lug the gun. Wandering around with a loaded rifle when the police were in the area didn't strike me as my best plan. But if we ran into Rogers, maybe I did want it. I relented and brought it along.

We soon lost cellphone coverage. I wouldn't know if Colleen was coming until she arrived, but as Mom said, it was only two and a half miles and the day was mild, with enough breeze to keep away the biting bugs. The longer we walked, the more I wondered what was preventing Colleen from picking us up.

A couple hundred yards before my driveway, phone coverage returned and brought several messages from Colleen.

They towed the truck and trailer. I parked your F-150 down by the house.

Cops pulling out now.

I'll give it five minutes and leave.

Nope. Company.

I propped the rifle against the shady side of a broad maple and told Mom I didn't know what to expect. I'd never spoken truer words. From the head of the driveway, I saw the jacked-up blue Silverado by my house, facing out, blocking in my vehicles and Colleen's rental. Leaning against the hood were Glenn Korpi and a guy I had never seen. The fourth guy?

"Okay, Megan. Take Geema to the dock, and not a peep from either of you. They can't see you on the road. You'll be safe if you stay quiet. Mom, wait until you get there and call 9-1-1. Leave a message for Sheriff Bartelle. Tell him Glenn Korpi—two Ns in the first name. Last is spelled K-O-R-P-I—is at my house. You got that?"

She repeated it. I told Megan that she was to lead Geema to our safe spot from before. I waited until they were a ways down the road, then strode down the driveway like I owned the place, which I did. "Hey guys," I said in a friendly voice. "What's up?" I was relieved Colleen was not with them.

I took the measure of the guy who was not Korpi. We looked to be the same weight, but he carried his weight on a squattier frame. At my approach, he flipped out a badge holder and flashed a shield. "Agent Carpenter with ICE." He tucked his badge holder into his pocket. "We're responding to information regarding an illegal immigrant. Young girl named Valeria, and the illegal is her grandmother. Family goes by the name of Serrano. Might have adopted false names. They often do."

These two were no more ICE agents than I was the man in the moon. Interesting that they didn't mention Valeria's mother. I saw no reason to let them know I didn't believe them and said, "My granddaughter went to a day camp in Amasa with a girl named Valeria. Good friends, but my granddaughter hasn't been there for more than a week."

"You know where they live?"

"I can give you directions. One time Valeria's mother was late picking her up from camp, and Kim—Kim Belanger, the proprietor of the day camp? Anyway, she and I took Valeria to a trailer far back in the woods. To get there, you—"

"Abandoned," Agent Carpenter said. "Our sources think you are hiding the girl."

Time to fake aggravation. "You need more reliable sources. Why someone fed you that bullshit is beyond me. Was it somebody I fired because they came to work drunk? I hire lots of people to help manage my forest land, but every single one is a US citizen or has a legitimate green card. You want to check my records? My accountant will be delighted to show you proof. I don't have to hire illegal immigrants because I pay higher wages than almost everyone around here." Academy award time for the heat I added to my voice.

They shared a look. I spotted Colleen watching us from an upstairs window. Good, she was safe.

Agent Carpenter broke the silence. "You mind if we have a little look around? Talk with your granddaughter. Maybe she heard something from her friend about their plans?"

"Yes I mind. You come waltzing in, accusing me of I don't know what. This is private property. You want to search it, show me a warrant. You've wasted enough of my time. Please leave my property now and don't come back until you have that search warrant."

Korpi stiffened and reached behind his back. Going for a gun? "Sounds like you got something to hide."

I stepped toward him, forcing him backwards. "Maybe you need a refresher on the Constitution. Specifically, the fourth amendment prohibiting illegal search and seizure." I held out my hand to Agent Carpenter. "Got a card? I hear anything about this Valeria or her grandmother, I'll be sure to call."

To my absolute shock, Agent Carpenter pulled a card from his badge holder. "I appreciate that. Let's go," he said to Korpi. "We're done here."

Korpi gave me a long stare. "You sure you shouldn't bring him in for questioning?"

Agent Carpenter said, "Not yet. We know where he lives, though."

SEVENTY-FIVE

I RACED INTO THE HOUSE, past Colleen, who asked what was happening, and to the upstairs bathroom window to confirm Agent Carpenter and Korpi had indeed driven up the road. "Tell you as soon as I retrieve Megan and Mom."

I found them on the log bench watching a pair of trumpeter swans feeding in the waters off the grass island. I accompanied them to the house and told Mom to pack all Megan's things. They were leaving today.

"Grandpa Seamus," Megan whined, "I don't want to leave Valeria. You—"

"Megan Nelson McCree, this is not a negotiation. You will help Geema pack your stuff. If you don't, I will tie you to a chair, and Geema will do it for you. Mom, everything is in the upstairs bedroom."

Mom bent down and took Megan's hand. "There is no reasoning with him when he's like this. If I could, I'd put him across my knee and spank him. I'd let you help. But he's bigger than us both, so let's do what he says."

Megan tried to stifle a giggle and let Geema lead her upstairs. I asked Colleen if she had her computer. She did, and I gave her the password to my Wi-Fi. "Go online and find the earliest flight to Boston. Check Marquette, Iron Mountain, Green Bay, even Milwaukee. It's an hour and a half to Marquette and Iron Mountain, three hours to Green Bay, five to Milwaukee."

I wanted to determine if Carpenter was an ICE agent. Calling the phone number on his card was like clicking on a link in an email. You never knew what was real or fake. My online search for ICE offices in the Upper Peninsula came up blank. Homeland Security Investigations had an office at Sault Ste. Marie, but no information on employees. I texted Niki and asked how to verify someone worked for ICE. Her return text said, *Contact ADNI Park. Tell him I told you to get the information.*

Brilliant. Averell Harrington Park, an assistant director of national intelligence, was one of her two bosses, and I served as a cutout to shield their relationship from prying eyes. I thundered upstairs two at a time and retrieved the secure cellphone from a desk drawer. I logged into the messaging app and requested him to confirm whether ICE employed an agent named Carpenter who met the description I provided.

Nothing more I could do with that. I called downstairs, "How we doing on those flights?"

"Found a United flight leaving Green Bay at five-thirty this evening. One stop in Chicago, but doesn't arrive in Boston until almost one a.m."

"Perfect." I pulled up the United site and booked tickets for my mother and Megan and asked Colleen for her information to get her a ticket too.

"No, Seamus. Don't you remember? I have an appointment to review the motel's books tomorrow."

"This has become way too dangerous. I'm not risking any family with whatever's going on."

Her hoot echoed off the cathedral ceiling. "Don't waste your money. Even if you buy a ticket, you can't force me on the plane. I'll accompany you to Green Bay. Gives us time to strategize. Come with me to look at the motel's books if it makes you feel better. But I'm not backing down, Seamus. Give it up."

I shouted into the bedroom, "How's it going in there?"

Mom responded they were almost ready. "Megan and I both have clothes at the campsite."

Megan stormed over to me and stamped her foot. "If you're deporting me, I want Atalanta and Cheech and Chong with me."

I had almost laughed at her stamped foot. Her words sobered me. She and Valeria must have been talking about deportation, even if Megan didn't use the word precisely. "Pumpkin, you know I don't want to do this, but I have to. Your hound and your cats are at their own sleep-away camps. Besides, they hate to fly, and Geema has no room for them. Do a last check to make sure you found everything." She stomped back to the bedroom.

Mom came out and motioned me to follow her downstairs. In a low voice, she said, "You know I can't keep Megan at my place. A day or two, I could do, but her parents don't return for another week, right?"

"Lizzie has plenty of room and even if she's not around, I'm sure she'd be happy to let you both stay there. I'll express mail your stuff that's at the campsite. This will work."

The app on my secure phone notified me I had a message. I entered my password to the messaging system. ADNI Park had responded much faster than I expected. A Matthew Carpenter, who fit my description, was employed as an ICE agent assigned to the Chicago area. Another Chicago connection.

Whatever his game, I didn't wish to meet him until I had moved Mom and Megan to safety. Instead of driving the normal way into town, I followed an obscure track through the neighbor's property and onto the A Grade. From there, I used the Cut Across Road and continued up to Michigamme. It added an extra forty-five minutes to the trip but avoided any possibility Carpenter would spot us.

Seventy-Six

MOM AND MEGAN MADE IT through Homeland security's screening around 4:30 p.m. My ex-wife, Lizzie, agreed to meet them at Logan Airport. Mom thought it was unnecessary. She knew how to take a taxi; she'd been doing it since before I was born. I ignored her. Mom might be capable, but I was uncomfortable with an eighty-three-year-old woman and an eight-year-old child unaccompanied at Logan at one o'clock in the morning.

On the way back north, I asked Colleen to take the wheel to allow me to have my hands and mind free to work. I had deferred talking to Niki to avoid further worrying Megan. I waited until Colleen made it to the highway and put Niki on speaker. Niki, being Niki, interrogated me about what had happened at my house and gave me an attaboy for shipping Mom and Megan to Boston.

I steered the conversation to learn about her excursion to Iron River with Bartelle and Tex.

"Total bust. First problem, I couldn't tell Sheriff Bartelle about Aaron Rogers and the drone without giving away your location. Then dispatch called with your message that Glenn Korpi was at your house. Bartelle and I did a one-eighty and drove all the way to your place. Never saw hide nor hair of the blue Silverado nor the gray Tundra—not that Bartelle knew we were looking for it. You were gone—I let Bartelle in to do a wellness check. Meantime, Tex struck out finding anyone in Iron River. They'll turn up. You've had time to concoct a plan. What are you thinking?"

Colleen snorted. "You're giving him too much credit."

"Thank you, sis. Colleen still thinks she should dance tonight at the Silver Fox." My voice carried all the enthusiasm of opening my mouth to accept a tablespoon of castor oil.

"Wait, you guys," Colleen said. "I haven't told you what happened last night at the club."

She described the atmosphere among the girls as friendly. She had worried about catty women, claws extended, competing for tips or special services. They split general tips among the dancers. The house took fifty percent of whatever a dancer earned behind the curtains. They allowed zero hanky-panky in the pole-dance room. Catcall requests for provocative behavior were fine, but no touching. A guy touches a girl in that room, he's escorted out the door.

I wasn't sure I wanted to know the answer, but I asked anyway. "What goes on in the curtained rooms?"

"Can't tell you from experience. It's optional, although only one other girl opted out. I felt zero pressure from management or the other women. Maybe that comes later. One thing that surprised me was they'd fire me on the spot if they caught me buying, selling, or using drugs on the premises."

I asked Niki if that was unusual from what she understood. "What? You think I have a vast knowledge of pole dancing and nude bars and private curtained rooms?"

Her phrasing it that way told me I was in danger of digging my grave. "I thought maybe you covered stuff like this in your FBI training."

Niki chortled. "Good try. Maybe they had past problems?"

Colleen said, "It's not like the place is totally clean. One girl told me she could get me anything I wanted. I got the feeling something hinky was going on. Is it possible they don't want drugs there because they're using the place for something worse?"

I asked if there was any place they wouldn't let her see.

Colleen read my mind. "You mean where they could keep Kat prisoner? The place is built on a slab, so no basement. I've been in the office area, and they showed me around the detached storage area because it also has a small space where the girls can lock their purses. Sorry, no. Anyway, I see no reason I shouldn't dance tonight, and I might learn some more from the girls."

Niki asked, "Did you see Aaron Rogers or any of the other people we've been targeting?"

"No, but I forgot to mention that the manager who hired me wasn't there last night. Another woman—Bonnie, maybe?—was in charge. Not tall, well put together, thin as a pipe cleaner."

Niki and I said together, "Bunny?"

"Possible. It was noisy. Yeah, could be Bunny."

Colleen gave us a detailed description. Yep, Bunny Crenshaw. Wasn't that interesting?

Niki volunteered to do a background check on her, which reminded me that she had intended to run my photographs from the Crenshaw compound through Rembrandt. I asked if she had.

"The five guys are from the Chicago area. One's getting married in two weeks. The other four are his groomsmen. The women are an interesting group. One is a Yooper. The rest are also from the greater Chicago area."

"Chicago," I said, "seems to come up a lot. Rogers is from there, and Dombey comes from Gary, which isn't all that far away. But we have nothing to link the Crenshaws to the Windy City. We're missing the bigger picture."

Niki agreed and mentioned the Chicago women had various arrest records, drugs and soliciting, but none of them had ever done time. Some traffic violation stuff on the guys, and one had a sealed juvie record. The married couple in the kitchen were born and raised in the Iron River area, had four kids in school, and the woman's mother lived at the same address. He had a couple of old DWIs; she'd been arrested a decade earlier for shoplifting, but the charges were dismissed.

Niki would forward the pictures to Colleen's phone to look at before her shift started in case any were dancing tonight. I used that opening to argue Colleen should skip the Silver Fox. Niki pooh-poohed my fears. Colleen dances, keeps her eyes open and her mouth shut, and we learn if any of the guys or gals showed up.

Was I the only one who saw danger? "If she's going, I'm going. I had planned to take supplies to Valeria and Nana. Make sure they're doing okay and try once more to convince them to let me take them away from the area. That will have to wait."

Niki said, "Already did that, Seamus. They're fine and have everything they need for now. Valeria is taking her medicine and has no symptoms other than the rash. And Nana has not changed her mind. Seamus, you or me showing up at the Silver Fox will endanger Colleen more than her going alone."

I pointed Colleen toward the left fork in the highway.

"People are looking for you. That's why you took that circuitous route down to Green Bay. Nothing links Colleen to you until she shows up tomorrow morning to review the motel's accounting records. It was fine for me to accompany her to support her when she was there to ask about a job, but it would draw unwanted attention for me to show up by myself while she dances."

Niki's logic had no holes, and I had no argument to keep Colleen from her appointed pole at the Silver Fox. "Fine. Then we should research the hell out of everybody we've come in contact with and find the damn linkages. We use those to drive some sense into Nana so we can get her the hell out and give the information to Sheriff Bartelle."

Colleen gave me a thumbs up. Niki told me she'd have more info when I got home. I dropped Colleen at her motel and, again to minimize the chances of running into anyone who was looking for me, took the long way back to my place. That gave me time to reconsider every piece of evidence we had uncovered.

The more I thought, the glummer I became. I put the odds at twenty to one that Kat was dead, and we were no closer to knowing what happened than we were a week ago.

SEVENTY-SEVEN

NIKI AND I WORKED LATE into the night. She tapped into various databases to pull up prior addresses, social media posts, arrest details, etc. Every quarter hour, she'd dump her most recent findings onto my desk. I took the data and looked for connections.

The U.P. woman lived in Norway, grew up in Bark River, had been a cheerleader, and did not have an arrest record. She danced at the Silver Fox.

The Chicago folks helped paint the picture. The groom-to-be was a heavy hitter on Chicago's commodity exchange, worth a billion dollars. His groomsmen were guys I'd expect in a wedding party: the groom's brother, two high school best buds, and the guy's college roommate. Nothing more than speeding tickets on any of them. I guessed they had their bachelor party so far away from home because they knew the area from fishing or hunting and had learned of the Menominee Rapids Resort.

The first thing I found that linked any of the eight Chicago women was three of them, and—surprise, Drew Dombey—were witnesses at a stabbing in a northern suburb of Chicago. Two drunks at a party in Lake Forest had gotten into a fight. One stabbed the other with a cocktail fork.

I brought that intel to Niki. "Lake Forest is a pretty ritzy neighborhood, and the cocktail fork is telling. With the groom's money and this tidbit, I bet these women are high-class hookers, and Dombey is their pimp or manager or whatever."

"Bingo." Niki pointed to her computer screen. "They're high-end escorts. This website quotes their weekend services as ranging between twenty-five and forty thousand. Each."

I whistled at the rates. "I guess if you're a billionaire, spending that much on a bachelor weekend is chump change. Do they work for an agency, or what?"

Niki backed her browser to show one woman's website. "That's my assumption. Their websites are similar. If your son were here, he could apply his computer expertise to determine where the links go. All I can tell is that they're dummy addresses and forwarded to an offshore server. These girls are not just pretty faces either. One is a PhD candidate at the University of Chicago. Two are minor actresses. One was Miss Nebraska, another an Olympic downhill skier hopeful who blew out her knee at the most recent trials."

She clicked on the contact form and used her finger to highlight her points. "This takes you to a secure server—at least that's what they claim—on the dark web. You select your level of service, check their calendar for availability, and upload a copy of your driver's license. And look at this: you have to tell them who referred you to the client."

I did some quick arithmetic. If the average weekend cost thirty grand

and each girl worked once a month, that grossed $360,000 a year. Split 50-50, each girl grossed $180,000. The nine women working one weekend a month grossed management $1.6 million a year.

Niki rubbed her eyes. "They don't have this set up for just these nine women. This is a multi-million-dollar operation."

I blurted out the thought before I considered it. "Kat sure didn't have that kind of money. I guess that could have been the motivation, huh?"

"Or," Niki said, "they were forcing her into it if she was indeed the missing tenth woman. My badge and I could pay a visit to the one who lives in Norway."

We concentrated on trying to connect either Mike or Randy Crenshaw to Chicago. Not a whiff. Anita "Bunny" Crenshaw, nee Palumbo, was born in Rockford and had grown up in Libertyville, a Lake County village north of Chicago. No arrest record on her.

I gathered the notes into a pile and squared them. "We've got bupkes. It's Mike's property, Randy brought out the guys, and Bunny has a hand in at the Silver Fox. We know they're involved, and now we know they're talented at hiding their tracks. The local woman is the one outsider who could tie it all together for us. She might even know Kat. Let's double-team her tomorrow before she leaves to dance at the Silver Fox."

"Remember, after tomorrow, I have to go back to St. Paul. Is that the best use of my time?"

I pulled my elbows back to stretch. Everything was taking longer than we wanted, and no lead had produced enough data to give us direction. Without Niki, Colleen and I were left with trying to find something actionable with Crenshaw's businesses.

"I'm all ears if you have a better idea."

Niki shook her head. "I don't even have enough energy to drag you to bed. But I have a feeling things are going to break tomorrow."

SEVENTY-EIGHT

"COMPANY'S COMING," I YELLED UPSTAIRS to Niki. "I don't recognize the

Jeep. I'll meet them outside. Why don't you keep watch from the window up there?"

With our late night working on the case, we'd slept in and woken up a half-hour ago with plans to visit the local dancer early afternoon. Nine in the morning was a weird time for an unknown visitor. I threw on a wool shirt and walked into the cool of the morning of what should be a spectacular day with enough wind to keep the bugs down and temps hitting the mid-70s. The air smelled clear and dry, although wispy clouds in the west suggested rain might arrive within forty-eight hours.

The dark green Jeep pulled into my turnaround and backed down the driveway, giving me a view of the driver.

I greeted Agent Carpenter after he got out of the car. "What brings you here early on a Monday morning?"

He stretched his hands high above his head, then reached into the car and pulled out a sheet of paper.

"Mr. McCree." He handed me the document. "A judge agrees with us that you have been less than forthcoming. Here's the search warrant you wanted."

That he hadn't believed me wasn't a surprise—I had not been entirely forthcoming. His convincing a judge to issue a search warrant was a shock. That required probable cause, and I didn't think he had that. I bought time to think by telling him I wanted to see what it said.

The search warrant allowed ICE agents to seize all electronic equipment, including cellphones, laptops, desktop computers, and any audio recordings. I asked what audio recordings meant.

"Answering machines, dictation devices, cassette players, that sort of stuff. A judge signed this. It's legal."

While scanning the warrant, I replayed my last conversation with Carpenter. I didn't think I had lied, even if I hadn't told the entire truth. The document allowed them to search my house, garage, generator building, unattached cabin, woodshed, and personal vehicles. I had three woodsheds and wondered whether he had to choose one—not that I had anything other than wood and tools in any of them.

They could seize *any* property belonging to Katrina Serrano—so this time, they mentioned the mother—her minor child, Valeria Serrano, and any family members. They didn't know Nana's name? I was confident neither Valeria nor Nana had left anything in my house. However, he couldn't help but notice the neat pile of last night's research notes on my desk. Those were off limits to him, but he'd find plenty on my computer and know what to look for.

Oh boy, explaining that would be—my stomach did a back flip—*nothing compared to what was on my phone.* Its location history would show everywhere I had been. Sure, they could eventually get that information from the carrier, but the selfies Valeria took were damning.

A judge's scrawled signature on the bottom made it seem legit. "I always comply with legal requests, but I don't know jack about search warrants. I need to call my lawyer."

"You can call your lawyer. But this search warrant is legal. If you obstruct me, I will arrest you. You'll stay handcuffed in my vehicle while I proceed with the search. Let's start with the house. Things will go faster if you show me where everything is."

I pointed the papers at the house. "That's my house. And there," I waved the papers toward the pole barn building, "is my garage. The generator shed is behind it. Feel free." I headed toward the screen porch.

"Not so fast," he said. "You got your cellphone or any electronics on you?"

"Nope. You gonna strip search me?"

He scowled. "If you won't cooperate, you stay outside."

To prevent me from destroying evidence. "It's a beautiful day for it. May I sit on the screened porch?"

He followed me onto the porch and checked behind the wood rack, underneath the chairs and tables, peered at the ceiling. He pursed his lips and shook his head. "Two entrances into the house. You'll have to wait outside. When did you say you last saw Valeria?"

"You can lock the doors to keep me on the porch."

"You last saw Valeria when?"

"I insist that my lawyer be present before you question me."

He invaded my space, standing inches from me. "I've never heard an innocent person say that. Never."

I wanted to avoid a conversation in which he could later use my words against me. "May I get something to read?"

He tilted his head, squinted an eye, straightened. "Sure," he said with a chipper note, "we can do that."

He followed me inside. *Where's Niki?* Nothing stirred upstairs or in the kitchen. I retrieved my Kindle from the drum table, and he said, "Electronic device. I'll take that."

Well, you fell into that, dummy. All he'd find was my eclectic bookshelf. I never use it to browse the internet. "Whoops, my bad. I have some books down in the basement. Shall we?"

He followed me down and looked around while I chose an essay collection from Outdoor magazine. I had enjoyed reading them several years earlier. "This will do." I marched upstairs with him scurrying behind me. Didn't want me alone upstairs. Still no evidence of Niki. Interesting.

"You got your book, now get." He pointed to the door as though I didn't know the way. "And if you want to use the facilities, find a spot in the woods."

I gave the asshole a jaunty salute that may have included an extended middle finger. I walked to the Wildlife Viewing Platform at the lakeshore, plopped onto one of the swivel chairs, and checked the water for ducks. None in view. I opened the book to the first essay.

And couldn't concentrate on a single word. Where the hell was Niki?

Seventy-Nine

Fifteen minutes later, Agent Carpenter came grumbling down the path, holding the secure cellphone I used for Niki's undercover work. "Unlock this for me."

I considered saying something snarky to the effect that his mother hadn't taught him to use the magic words: please and thank you. No reason to antagonize him any more than I already had; I didn't want him trashing my house. "Before that happens, my lawyer will have to agree."

He thrust the phone at me. "So, call him."

I waved it away. "Nice try. You finished?"

He stomped off, and it was all I could do not to laugh.

Niki appeared soon after Carpenter left and copped the other chair. I asked where she'd been.

"Let me read the search warrant first."

I waited in silence for her to finish, wondering what she thought humorous. She returned it to me. "When I saw him hand this to you, I guessed what it was. While you kept him occupied outside, I put your laptop, your cellphone, and our work from last night in a large garbage bag and hid everything in the outhouse."

I leaned over and bussed her cheek.

She waited until I had settled in my chair before continuing. "I hoped he wouldn't think to look down into the shitter. Turned out even better because his search warrant doesn't include the outhouse. Once he realizes his mistake, he'll correct it. The thing is, he can't do that over the phone."

"Which means," I said, "if he's working by himself, he'll have to leave. That's great for last night's workpapers, but my computer and phone records automatically back up in the cloud. All he has to do is subpoena them. Is your stuff with mine?"

"Nope. In the rental's backseat. You're right about your cloud backup. To gain access, he has to figure out who your cell provider is and where you back up your computer. Then dealing with Microsoft or Amazon or Verizon or any of those guys means jumping through more hoops."

"Which means we have a little time before he can use my cellphone to learn where we've hidden Nana and Valeria. My truck can rat me out, though."

She ducked her head in agreement. "Again, it takes time. After Carpenter leaves, we need to check the vehicles for trackers—legal or otherwise. If I were crawling up your ass, I'd stick one on anything that moves."

The net enclosing Nana and Valeria was closing fast. "He can't legally tag your rental, right?"

Her smile flattened. "Not legally. Yet. Look, Seamus, if they're doing the full Monty on you, they'll be monitoring your credit cards, your bank records, when you change your underwear."

Meaning they'd know everything I did as soon as I did it. I'd have to find another way. "And they'll soon know who you are. Colleen is our only source of a clean vehicle."

Niki nodded. "Unless you borrow or steal wheels. Speaking of Colleen, I called her after I hid the stuff. She said the only people of interest to us at the Silver Fox last night were Bunny and Randy Crenshaw. Those two got into a heated discussion, and Colleen chatted with some of the other girls about it. They said that happened often, but either didn't know or wouldn't say what the disagreements were about. I wonder what Colleen's finding in the motel's records."

"Time will tell. Besides fretting about where you were, I've been down here wondering what makes the Serrano family so important to justify this level of attention. First from Rogers, Korpi, Dombey, and friends. Now from ICE Agent Carpenter? Nana's illegal immigrant status nominally justifies Carpenter, but don't you agree Kat triggered this? Did she steal something? I don't mean their drugs, incriminating evidence. And the reason they want Valeria and Nana is they think one of them has it?"

"Another fine theory," Niki said, "with nothing to back it up."

Eighty

AGENT CARPENTER'S NEXT APPEARANCE CAME with him holding a power adapter for my laptop. He saw Niki and asked, "Who the hell are you? I didn't hear anybody drive up."

"That's because I walked."

"Let me see some identification." He held out his hand.

"No." She waved the search warrant at him. "I'm not entering your search zone, and therefore you do not need to know who I am. You're a little understaffed, aren't you? I've never seen a search conducted by only one person. At the Bureau, we'd assign a ton of people to swarm a place like this."

The flash of his eyes widening before drawing into slits told me Niki had surprised him. He recovered and arranged his mouth into a gash. "I will not have you interfere with this legal search."

Niki offered him a contrite smile. "Never crossed my mind. Make sure you leave a detailed inventory of anything you take. Seamus may not know a search warrant from a hole in the ground, but I do."

Carpenter stabbed his finger at me. "I'll find your laptop even if I have to bring a backhoe and dig up your eighty acres or drain the whole damn lake."

I sent him back to the house with a comment that before he could disturb the soil, he needed a soil erosion permit, and draining the lake would require a DNR permit. He did not appear to appreciate my sense of humor.

As noon became one o'clock, my stomach started grumbling. Niki and I returned to the house. I stuck my head inside and called to Agent Carpenter. "Can you take a break long enough to watch us grab lunch from the fridge? I'll be happy to get you a yogurt or something."

He clumped down from the upstairs bedroom. "Make it quick."

I opened the refrigerator, gulped when I spotted Megan's juice boxes on the top shelf, and grabbed four Greek yogurts.

Carpenter threw out a hand to prevent me from closing the door. "How long were the kids here?"

I gave him my best puzzled look. "Huh?"

Carpenter pointed. "The juice boxes are for the kids, right?"

"Granddaughter loves them, but they're perfect for a quick pick me up while hiking. Lots of sucrose and they wet your whistle."

He shook his head in disgust. "You're only digging your grave deeper."

"Nope," I said. "No soil conservation permit."

An hour later, Agent Carpenter left the house, told us we could go inside. He entered the garage. If Korpi had related the Bobcat incident, he'd now know for sure that it belonged to me. I counted the days since that confrontation. A week. Carpenter spent a brief time in the garage, then visited the generator shed and trooped up to the cabin. After a half hour, he joined us on the house's screened porch.

"I've compiled a list of items on my phone. Give me your number and I'll text them to you."

Hoping I'd cough up the number? "Email me, but I want to see the list before you leave."

"Sorry, doesn't work that way."

I gave Niki a side glance. She nodded an affirmative. I guess I didn't have the right to an immediate list. In which case, who was to say he had listed everything he confiscated? Not a perfect system, for sure. I provided him the email address I used for junk mail. He could troll through that to his heart's desire.

Carpenter left with a sealed box containing my things. I'd seen him take my Kindle, desktop computer, the secure phone—good luck with that—

and a digital recorder I hadn't used in a decade. I wouldn't know what else he had taken until I received the complete list or realized something was missing.

Niki and I watched him roll up the driveway and down Shank Lake Road. "So what—"

"Don't say a thing, Seamus, until I check this whole place for bugs."

EIGHTY-ONE

THE HOUSE CONTAINED NO AUDIO bugs, but Niki found trackers on my truck, Subaru, and the ATVs. She saw the gears clicking in my head. "With one, you could leave it lying on a rough stretch of road and argue that it must've fallen off. They could still arrest you and make you go through the hassle of getting bail. If they all disappeared, they would charge and convict you with obstructing an investigation."

I held my hands in surrender position. "They provide us an opportunity to leave false trails. You're sure your vehicle is clean?"

"I think so, and it convinces me that he had a legal warrant for those trackers. No judge would allow him to stick a tracker on any old vehicle that he found parked at a particular address."

"We need to gather as much intel as we can and decide how to play this. Before we can get to the local call girl's place in Norway, she'll probably be at the Silver Fox, and we couldn't talk to her there. I'll call Colleen and find out what she learned from her review of the motel's books. Why don't you squeeze Bartelle and Tex for an update on Aaron Rogers and Glenn Korpi?"

Niki reminded me I should retrieve my phone, computer, and papers from the outhouse. I used a rake to snag the garbage bag and haul it into the light. No one had used the outhouse in years, so the bag was almost clean.

I washed my hands in the lake and called Colleen from the dock. She'd found shortages in the motel's reported revenue. For example, the records did not reflect the cash my mother paid for her one-night stay. Colleen couldn't know if the cash had vanished at the time Mom checked in or whether the night clerk was blameless and the money evaporated later.

I asked if she had any idea how much was involved.

She cleared her throat. "Normally, cash payments are rare, and you wouldn't expect it to amount to squat. Running a prostitution ring that uses the motel could create some serious bucks. Unless we get our hands on a second set of true financials, we won't discover the answer from the accounting. Not much gets by the motel's housekeepers, though. Maybe that's what precipitated Kat's disappearance?"

Given what was going on at the Crenshaw compound, a prostitution ring could work several ways. The girls could pay off someone with cash to allow them to use rooms. Or if management ran the hookers, they could provide the rooms for free. With enough time, the accounting records should show discrepancies. They'd use more cleaning supplies than justified by the bookings. Same for the quantity of breakfast-buffet food. An analysis to uncover those inconsistencies would take more resources and time than we had.

While I had gone into my silent considerations, Colleen had continued talking. I asked her to repeat what she'd said.

"Crenshaw's accountant also brought information for the Menominee Rapids Resort. I guess he hopes your buyer might be interested in that, too. The hotel part of the resort breaks even, maybe makes a few bucks. The restaurant does much better than I thought most restaurants did. Referral fees for arranging outings are their big money-makers. River rafting, fishing, hunting, even birdwatching. Who knew birdwatching was lucrative?"

I mentioned my suspicions that some of the "entertainment" was being run through the restaurant's books. "Was Randy Crenshaw there?"

"Just me and Mike Crenshaw's 180-year-old accountant who asked me to dine with him. What's our next step?"

I explained our recent situation with Agent Carpenter, his search warrant, and the bugs on the car and truck. She offered to drive to camp and swap her rental for my truck. "I like your thinking. We might be able to fool them once. Let's reserve that trick until we need it."

"I have nothing on my dance card, so to speak, until the Silver Fox tomorrow night. Since Randy wasn't at the meeting, I guess I can still do that. Maybe I can strike up a conversation with that woman from Norway."

Not the time to refight that battle. "I have something more important than that and it requires a phone ICE could not have tapped." I told her what I wanted.

She said she was on it. "One question, Seamus. What if they've already tapped your phone?"

"Then you'd better buy a burner."

Eighty-Two

NIKI HAD LEARNED VERY LITTLE. Iron County deputies had not set eyes on Aaron Rogers or Glenn Korpi. Sheriff Bartelle was unaware of any ICE activity in the area. I mused whether it was time to approach Mike Crenshaw and see his reaction to Colleen's suspicions about the motel's books and my belief his son was involved in a high-end prostitution operation using his compound.

Niki chewed on her upper lip. "It's hard to fathom he would agree for you to look at the books if he knew they had issues. And what do we have on the prostitution ring other than that his son drove the five guys to the compound? The rich husband-to-be could have arranged bringing the girls up from Chicago on his own. And even if Randy Crenshaw is involved— well, he probably is, given the one local woman was there—what do you accomplish if you convince the old man?"

"Whacking hornet nests? Okay, Kat worked at the motel, danced at the Silver Fox, maybe worked parties at the Resort, and maybe hooked at the compound—explaining the occasional weekends she was gone. We could try talking to the motel housekeepers again, but if something *is* going on and they think Kat got in trouble, they aren't likely to talk, are they?"

"Nope."

"And Colleen has seen nothing in the Silver Fox that would justify making Kat disappear. Not that Kat couldn't have stumbled over something."

Niki filled in my thoughts. "Given the time, we—meaning you—can't talk to the woman until tomorrow at the earliest. And we've poked around at the resort as much as we can."

I blew out a long sigh. "Which leaves Crenshaw's compound for tonight."

Niki slapped me on the leg. "I wondered how long it would take a bright boy like you to figure out our next step. Then, like it or not, I have to take off tomorrow for my St. Paul commitments."

I hadn't forgotten, but a piece of me had hoped Niki would blow them off and see this through. "Understood. Right now, I'm going bear hunting and take Carpenter on a wild goose chase."

She shook her head. "You are nothing if not a mixed metaphor."

I LEFT NIKI AT HOME to pack and then follow more leads from Rembrandt and took the two-up ATV on a meandering route starting in the opposite direction from where Valeria and Nana camped. After a couple of hours of leading Agent Carpenter's tracker hither and yon, I reached Lake Tranquility where I searched the tent area for Valeria's missing bear. No luck.

The flat calm lake attracted me, and I kicked off my shoes and dangled my feet off the end of the pier in the cool water. The eagles called from across the lake, and soon one adult was flapping hard toward me. As it came near, I yelled, "No fish. Sorry. Next time I'll catch some before I visit. By the way, thanks for downing that drone. If it wasn't you, thank your partner. I hope you didn't get hurt."

It was like the eagle understood. It circled once above my head, wings audibly compressing the air, then flew to the far shoreline. While staring into the lake, my subconscious brought up a memory of Valeria. To gather rocks at her trailer, she had wrapped her bear around a slender tree. Had she done something similar while fishing? I laced my shoes, walked to the spot I'd last seen the girls fishing and found it strapped to a sapling looking as though it was shimming up the tree.

The bear's weight surprised me. The magnets that held its paws weren't that heavy. I poked the critter and found a small rectangular solid inside it. A capital U of tiny stitches marred its stomach. To focus on the threads, I pushed my glasses on top of my head and brought the bear to my nose. The thread's color didn't match the bear's fur.

I snipped the stitches using the Swiss army knife scissors, dug my finger into the stuffing, and found a USB flash drive.

EIGHTY-THREE

NOT WANTING TO LEAVE ANY trace on my computer of whatever was on the thumb drive, we plugged it into Niki's laptop. Pictures. We scrolled through selfies of Kat in a party dress taken on the Saturday before she vanished. She was an attractive young woman with a quizzical smile. Next came a loaded buffet table and one of a tuxedoed waiter handing a drink to another woman attired in a dress identical to Kat's.

I tapped the screen. "That's the private room at the Menominee Rapids Resort, right?"

Niki moved my finger. "That's the painting above the door." She quickly scrolled through many pictures of people enjoying themselves at the party.

"Wait," I shouted. "Go back. I think I recognize that guy."

Niki scrolled back two pictures, and Vincent Otto stared at me. "You remember my daughter-in-law, Cindy Nelson, is an investigative reporter in Chicago?" She did. "A year, maybe two years ago, she did an exposé on this guy's law firm. Not only are they the go-to defense counselors for the mob, Cindy found proof they were a major conduit for bribing Chicago and Illinois politicians. Several of the junior partners pleaded out or were convicted. Otto ended up with a hung jury. Everyone believed he'd paid off somebody. What the hell is a Chicago mover and shaker doing at a private party in Iron Mountain, Michigan?"

We scrolled through Kat's party photos. The only other people we recognized were Randy Crenshaw and Mindy, the waitress who had served Niki and me during our lunch with Mike Crenshaw.

The next picture had me dry-swallowing to keep from throwing up. Lying face up in a motel room bed was a young woman. Nude, her eyes stared at nothing. Tongue protruded through foam leaking from her mouth. Ligature marks around her neck. Kat had a picture of a murder victim.

Niki scrolled to an earlier picture at the party. "It's the woman who was dressed like Kat."

She was right, and a scenario formed in my mind. Somebody at that party had taken this young woman and strangled her in one of the motel rooms that Kat cleaned. It could have been a sex act gone wrong or something else. This photograph could explain why people wanted to find Valeria and Nana. What had Kat done after she found the dead woman? I urged Niki to let me see the remaining pictures.

The next one showed a room number. The last was a blurry shot of the printed bill for that room, naming Vincent Otto as the responsible party.

A heavy weight settled on my shoulders. "Kat, what did you do after you took those pictures? The date stamps say these were Sunday morning. As far as we know, nothing changed in her routine until Thursday. Someone calls her into the motel's office. Then, she comes home early, leaves again, and vanishes. Sometime between Sunday and Thursday before she left home, she downloaded photos from her phone onto this thumb drive and hid it in Valeria's bear."

"Wait," Niki said, "did she have a computer?"

"Nope, which means someone did it for her. Friend? Office supply place? One of her workplaces?"

"Good questions." Niki brought up a browser, made several searches, and announced, "No stories featuring a dead woman found in the motel. Kat didn't report this to the police. Neither did whoever Kat told. Or if Kat didn't tell anyone, whoever later found the body didn't report it either."

"Look at the time stamps. She snaps the body at 10:06 a.m. Was she cleaning rooms or was she checking in on one of her party friends? She doesn't take the picture of the room number until 11:25 a.m. The printed bill picture occurred fifteen minutes later. Something happened that made her take those last two pictures. Do an internet search for 'missing woman from the Upper Peninsula.' And if you don't come up with anything, try Northern Wisconsin."

Northern Wisconsin hit pay dirt. A two-inch article said Peggy Dowson's sister reported the Pembine, Wisconsin woman missing. Police discovered Peggy's car in a nearby park-and-ride and were looking for any information, blah, blah, blah. It was dated the day after Kat disappeared.

This changed everything. I said, "We have to take this to the police. Which means we inform them Kat's gone missing. And that requires moving Valeria and Nana to a safe place unknown to me. I have Colleen working on a plan, but we must convince Nana to leave now. I assume Carpenter could have received a judge's approval to tap into your rental's GPS?"

"Unlikely, but not impossible."

I pointed out the windows to gathering thunderheads. "Storm's coming. We'll get wet walking, but I don't think we should wait."

Eighty-Four

THE HEAVENS OPENED WITH A blowing rain that soaked us even with rain gear. I was a little nervous in a metal canoe on water with thunder and lightning in the distance, but no harm came to us.

We found Nana and Valeria hunkered down under a tarp, eating a cold dinner. I placed myself between them to distract Valeria while Niki worked to convince Nana to leave. "I found your bear down by where you were fishing at Lake Tranquility."

Valeria sprang to her feet, knocking over her cup of water.

I handed her the soggy bear. "I'll bet you didn't realize your critter is a fantastically special animal. He's a panserbjørn, an armored bear whose hands can clasp, who keeps great secrets, and who never lies. His name is Iorek Byrnison. When you're a little older, you and Megan can read all about him."

I hugged Valeria. "I'm sorry I hurt its tummy. Your mother hid something super important inside. We have to give it to the police and tell them she's missing."

Valeria examined the bear and my sloppy stitching. "Thank you, Grandpa Seamus. Iorek is a funny name, but I like it." She slapped it around her wrist. "You're not gonna find my mama, are you?"

"I haven't given up, honey. I promised to try, and I promise I will keep trying. Once we tell the police, they'll start looking, too."

She pulled the granite stone from her pocket and rubbed it between her hands. Tears leaked from her eyes. I felt awful that this little girl would probably never see her mother again. The uninterrupted sound of rain on the tarp made me realize Niki and Nana had stopped talking. I switched my focus to them.

Niki said, "I told Nana about the murder, that we had to tell the police, and that I have to leave tomorrow. She's petrified she'll lose Valeria, but she agreed to let us send them away."

I half rose.

Niki stilled me with a finger. "First thing tomorrow morning. That's the best I could do."

That changed the order of things. I thanked Nana for trusting us and told her that since we were not leaving immediately, my plans required Niki and me to return to my house. Our walk home was miserable. Even though temperatures were in the high sixties, Niki and I were bone-chilled on arrival.

I waited until I'd warmed up with a hot shower and a change of clothes to call Sheriff Bartelle's cellphone. I informed him I had information concerning a probable murder and a missing woman. The woman lived in Iron County; the crimes had likely occurred in Dickinson County. Could he please contact the Michigan State Police and have them send a detective to talk to me at Bartelle's office? I'd be there in forty-five minutes.

He cleared his throat. "You won't tell me what this is about, will you? Why am I your intermediary?"

"Because if I'm thrown in jail, I want it to be yours."

"Won't that be special?"

Niki arrived from her shower in time to hear the last bit of my conversation with Bartelle. She blocked my way to the door. "I understand you wanted to get them away before you told Bartelle about the murder. And given it is murder, I agree with your decision to tell them tonight. But since you might not make it home, you'd better tell me your plan for Valeria and Nana."

"I already set Colleen looking for a UU congregation that belongs to the sanctuary movement and will take them in. Can you work with her and lock that down tonight?"

"That I can do, but I need to know how you're intending to get them past ICE and Rogers."

"Whatever time I get back tonight, I'll walk to the river, cross over, and sleep there. In the morning, we'll paddle downriver. At eight o'clock you'll drive my truck to the river and lead ICE to them, except, by that time, we'll be long gone. I'll give you keys to open and lock the gates behind you—we don't want to make this look easy. Wait an hour and return. If Agent Carpenter shows earlier, no problem. Either way, your part is done, and you can bring my truck back here and drive your rental to St. Paul."

"Fine, and while I act as decoy, what are you doing?"

"Two or three miles downriver, the river flows under Lukes Road. No one is tracking Colleen's car, so she can meet us there and take Nana and Valeria to whatever sanctuary you find. Make sure that on her way out, she drives north to Covington to avoid all but two miles of Iron County. I'll walk home—it's only six miles—and deal with the fallout."

"And if they throw you in jail?"

"You and Colleen will have to create a new plan."

She smacked me on the arm and wished me success.

EIGHTY-FIVE

I MADE IT THROUGH THE Michigan state police interview following the advice a lawyer had given me about testifying at a deposition. If I did not absolutely, positively know something, I should say so. No guesses. No suppositions. Do not respond to speculative questions. If I once knew an answer but no longer did, I must say, "I do not recall." Great advice. That was the same lawyer who had told me under no circumstances should I speak to the police without having a criminal defense lawyer present—a luxury I had no time for.

The central fact I could attest to was how I had discovered the thumb drive. I gave them precise details covering who, what, where, when, and how. To that, I added hearsay evidence that Valeria said her mother gave her the bear, and that Nana claimed she had last seen Kat leaving the trailer that Thursday afternoon.

I maintained I had not reported Kat's disappearance or the trashing of the trailer because Nana did not want me to. No, I did not know why (who knows why anyone else does something?) and refused to speculate about her reasons.

I was on safe ground until they asked where Valeria and Nana were. I admitted they had stayed with me. My statements that they had stayed in my guest cabin and camped with me at Lake Tranquility might not sway a judge of my veracity. I stated truthfully that I did not know where Valeria and Nana *currently* were. I'm sure I was supposed to tell them they had also camped on my Baraga County property, and I had last seen them there a few hours earlier.

The state trooper went into bluster mode at that point. I let his threats wash over me. Sheriff Bartelle interrupted the trooper's tirade. "Seamus McCree can do silence like Charlie Chaplin. He won't tell you, even if you jail him as a material witness. If the grandmother or the kid was involved with the mother's disappearance, you can arrest him later for impeding the investigation. Seems to me, you have a missing woman to find and a murder to investigate, and they both revolve around the motel in Iron Mountain." Turning to me, he said, "Anything else you can tell us that will help find the murderer or Katrina Serrano, assuming they're not the same person?"

That thought had never occurred to me. I told them Mike Crenshaw owned the motel and provided them the name of his accountant. "They have a records management system that should verify who booked that room where the woman was killed." That led to more questions about why I knew that. I related my interest in buying Crenshaw's forest property and that my sister, Colleen Carpetti, had reviewed the motel's books on Monday.

The state trooper gave me the bullshit line, "Don't leave the area without telling us." I said I understood what he was saying without agreeing to anything.

The last thunderstorm had long passed by us, leaving a smear of wispy clouds turning pink in the east during my drive home. Niki met me at the door with a hug and a kiss. "Couldn't sleep, not knowing if you were coming back or not." She had been working with Colleen for much of the night and reported success at finding Valeria and Nana sanctuary.

I wanted no details. "Talking with the police took longer than I hoped. Nana must wonder what happened to me."

"Take your old red ATV," she said. "Pull off the tracker that's stuck to your hitch and leave it on the floor of your garage, as though it fell off. Unlike your car and truck, there's no way ICE can follow it using its embedded GPS, because it doesn't have any."

That would save time and energy compared to walking. While we reviewed the plan, I changed into a quick-dry shirt and shorts, Keen water sandals, and found my Tilley hat. I brought up a satellite photograph to show Niki the exact spot I wanted Colleen to wait for us. She enlarged the map and pointed to a white area of the river near where it crossed under the bridge at Lukes Road. "What's this?"

"Rapids, which reminds me, I need to bring them life jackets. It's the only one, but we'll have two or three beaver dams to navigate. Have Colleen park in that cleared area west of the bridge where you see that truck." I tapped the truck visible on the satellite photo. "I don't know how long it'll take us. It's only a couple of miles, but the beaver dams will slow us down. We'll pull out before those rapids and walk to the meeting spot. It doesn't matter who gets there first. If we do, we'll wait in the woods for Colleen. She knows how to get to the sanctuary?"

"Our end is under control, Seamus."

I detached the tracker from the ATV, strapped lifejackets for Valeria and Nana onto its rack, filled three water bottles, and kissed Niki goodbye. "Drive safe. With luck, I'll be home before noon and will call you."

"Forget something?" Niki shoved my cellphone into my rear pocket. "Frankly, I'd prefer we didn't require luck."

EIGHTY-SIX

I LEFT THE CANOE PULLED up on the shore where Megan and Valeria had fished and played catch with the eagles. Nana was cooking on the propane camp stove. She spoke Spanish slowly in a raised voice, like for someone you thought was not very bright. Her accompanying gestures showed she wanted me to join them for breakfast. She woke Valeria, who had slept in her clothes. Nana divided the omelet and home fries into three portions. I inhaled the food, which was delicious. Nana ate with more restraint. Valeria pushed hers around her plate.

I told her she should eat. "You'll feel better with a full stomach." I pointed to the bear attached to her wrist. "Iorek wouldn't want your tummy growling later on."

My phone dinged with a text message.

Green Jeep blazed down the road in your direction. Get out NOW!!!

Crap, Agent Carpenter was coming. "Valeria, please let your grandmother know we have to leave right this minute. No time to clean up."

Fear blossomed in Nana's eyes. Fortunately, she had everything packed. I grabbed much of their gear and ushered them before me. Nana shook her head and motioned for me to take Valeria. She ignored my objections and ran back to her tent. I hustled Valeria to the canoe and loaded it with the stuff at hand. I tossed Valeria a life jacket. "Put this on, hon, and snug it tight."

On my return to the campsite, I met Nana hauling a pillowcase stuffed with clothes in one hand and the rifle in the other. I collected the last of their things and ran after her.

The growl of a heavy engine let me know Carpenter was getting close. Valeria had not figured out her life jacket, and I helped her step into its leg straps. I clicked her buckles closed, tightened her belt, and gave Nana's belt an extra tug. As I handed them into the canoe, the truck engine quieted— at the first gate? Given its shoddy construction, it would take him little time to lift the gate off its hooks and drive through.

I settled into the stern and pushed away from shore. The relative quiet ended with the truck engine cranking up—it was heading toward the second gate, which was much more substantial. I sent a "thank you" to the heavens for my foresight in deploying the gates. Their presence had delayed Carpenter and provided us with extra time to escape.

Paddling with the current was easy. Nana picked up the paddle I had left in the bow. With beaver dams in our future, I wanted to be in total control of the canoe. I had Valeria tell Nana to save her strength for later. She tucked the paddle behind her and picked up the rifle. Maybe I should have let her paddle.

Behind us, the engine roared, followed by a sickening crunch of metal on metal. The truck had attempted—succeeded?—to bust through the second gate. The engine was still running. Even if the lock held, he could run to the river in three or four minutes.

We entered a long S-curve that provided cover from anyone upriver. I released my breath, only then realizing I had been holding it, and rolled my shoulders to work out the tension. How had they known? Unless Niki had missed a second tracker on the red ATV, I must have triggered a trail cam similar to mine that forwarded images to my phone. Given how quickly Agent Carpenter got here, he couldn't have been any farther away than Amasa.

Carpenter was waiting for me to make a move, and I had let him play me. I resisted the urge to smack the paddle on the water.

Soon Carpenter would find the red ATV where I left it at the river crossing. How he reacted was key. Once he guessed my plan, it became a race. We had to meet Colleen and for her to escape before any of the bad guys reached Lukes Road. If he wasted time and crossed the river to look for us, he'd find proof Nana and Valeria had been there, but it would add at least twenty minutes to our head start. I could hope.

We would pass several camps before the Lukes Road bridge, and instead of stopping, we could continue through to US 141. They'd have to guess where we planned to leave the river and get there before us. Niki might slow them down. Even if they got past her, they had fifteen miles to Amasa before they could drive the highway north to Lukes Road.

Unless they had people waiting in Amasa.

Or launched long-range drones to follow us.

Or something happened to Colleen.

Eighty-Seven

THE CURRENT PICKED UP AS we approached a narrowing, and the murmur of water trickling through a beaver dam grew louder. I slowed us going around a bend. Good thing. The dam was right there. I reverse-paddled to break our forward progress and steered the craft to shore.

"Valeria, tell Nana you two have to walk around the beaver dam. I'll haul the canoe over it and we'll get back in."

Nana grabbed the tag alders while I scrambled out and secured the canoe. I helped Nana and Valeria onto the shore. The footing was terrible.

"Remember, your ankle is still weak, so be real careful where you walk." I carried Nana's rifle, allowing her to use both hands to maneuver, and led them to a place where we could get back into the canoe. This damn dam was costing us more time than I had expected.

A new text dinged on my phone. Once I had them on stable ground, I checked it.

Colleen on her way

She was ninety minutes away. In returning to the canoe, I missed a step and soaked my left leg to my thigh. Slow down, you jerk—getting wet is fine, but breaking a leg won't help anyone. I tucked my cellphone into my shirt pocket before wading into stomach-high water below the dam and pulling the canoe over. The water was still cool. The sun wouldn't crest the tree line for at least an hour. We should be off the water by then.

Once we passed the confluence of the East Branch of the Net River with Shank Lake Creek, the journey was new water to me. We worked around two more beaver dams. After progressing through a section of the river that on the satellite map looked like a snake, my arms threatened mutiny. I went on full alert as we passed the first camp and underneath a bridge that provided access to it. No ambush.

Soon, my ears pricked at the distant whoosh of another beaver dam. I slowed in preparation, but with each bend, the dam didn't appear and the sound grew louder. And louder. And louder. The first three beaver dams had drops of between six and eighteen inches. This one was *much* larger.

The river widened, counterintuitive since we were approaching an area in which the beavers had constructed their dam. We floated around a curve into a broad valley that the beavers had flooded with a dam at least three feet high. Beyond, great swaths of Canadian shield burst through the soil on a hill that rose seventy-five feet. A log cabin perched on the top of the hill. I remembered this place, having dropped in on the residents years ago on an ATV expedition with my son, Paddy. It was the perfect spot for an ambush. A decent marksman could rock on the porch, spy us coming into the open water, and easily nail us.

Previous canoeists had created a 250-yard-long path to portage around the obstruction. It required three trips to transport the canoe and their gear, but that effort allowed us to stretch our legs. We loaded the canoe, Nana, and Valeria settled onto their seats. I pushed the canoe into the water, keeping only the tip of the stern still on land, and stepped in.

Valeria flung her hand out and shouted, "Look. The eagles!"

The next seconds happened in slow motion. Iorek, the stuffed bear, launched from Valeria's wrist. She grabbed for it, throwing her weight against the canoe's right side. Nana shifted the same way to look for the eagles. The grounded stern acted as an anchor point around which the canoe rotated, shifting my weight to the right. The physics said we would flip if I tried to stay in.

I followed my center of gravity into the water. Soccer players learn how to roll as they tumble to the ground. I tucked my chin into my chest and levered my feet over my head, landing on the water flat on my back. The judges scored my roll as a two on a ten-point scale. My feet settled on the graveled creek bed, and I stood in water up to my waist.

The world was a fuzzy blur. Without my glasses, I can see okay up close, but the big E on an eye chart is only a smudge. I'd saved the canoe from capsizing and kept all their gear from drowning, but at the cost of my vision. Nana jabbered away in Spanish. Valeria cried. I needed to find my glasses. Before my back flop with one-half twist, the river was clear to the bottom. Now, the surrounding water was opaque, filled with swirling bits of forest sediment.

I told Valeria in a no nonsense tone I really wanted her help. "Can you stop crying and translate for Nana?"

To my surprise, she quickly controlled her tears and wiped her nose with her sleeve.

"I've lost my glasses. You've lost your bear. We all need to stay still to let the water clear. When it does, we'll try to spot your bear and my glasses. Can you do that for me?"

Her choked words broke my heart. "It's the only thing I have left from my mama, and Nana put your special stone inside."

Eighty-Eight

While I stood still, waiting for the water to clear, the sun peeked over the hill to the east. I appreciated its warmth, but it made it more difficult to see anything underwater. The bottom became visible in fifteen minutes. I stuck my face into the river to eliminate the glare and searched for any blurred hint of gold frames. Nothing.

At my failure, Valeria offered to swim and search.

With the life jacket, she'd be fine. "Here's how to get out of the canoe without dunking your grandmother. Think of yourself as a snake with four legs. Keep low and your hands and feet wide. Good girl. Now one limb at a time move towards the back of the canoe, like you're slithering across the bottom, except only your four limbs touch. You're doing great, nice and slow. Perfect."

"Let's look for my glasses first. If we find them, we can both look for your bear."

Good in theory, and the kid was willing, but she also struck out. Time was ticking by, and Colleen should reach the meeting place soon. Valeria spotted her bear ten feet from me. "Keep your eye on it, and I'll get it for you." I wanted to avoid stirring up the sediment and set my right foot down next to my left—and felt it crunch something.

I stepped sideways, lowered my face into the water, and saw shimmering gold. Crap. They had been underneath me all along. I squatted, submerged my head, and grabbed them. I lowered the glasses with their cracked frame and broken ear piece onto my nose. The world returned to focus—more or less. I held the glasses in place with a finger and walked to Valeria. I handed her my glasses and retrieved her bear. "Trade you," I said. She hugged the bear to her chest.

Valeria swam to shore, and I waded behind her. She used her new four-legged-snake technique to position herself in the middle of the canoe, and I got in without incident. I couldn't paddle and hold my glasses flush to my face at the same time. I had to paddle, I could fake seeing. I tucked my glasses into my shirt pocket.

The pocket that was supposed to hold my phone. Unlike the glasses and the bear, we could not find the phone anywhere. Now we had no way to communicate with the outside world.

EIGHTY-NINE

WITHOUT GLASSES, THE WORLD LOOKED like a Monet painting. I kept the canoe in the main channel of the river. The distant burbling of the rapids became too loud to ignore, and I edged the canoe near the left bank and asked Valeria and Nana to look for a path to the camp that overlooked the rapids. I followed Nana's pointed finger to shore. We landed, and I put on my mangled glasses, bringing some clarity to the world.

"We'll need two trips to bring all your things to the cabin. I see Valeria is limping a little. I'll go ahead. You two take your time." The trail climbed the hill, and my spirits rose with each step. The cabin was only a few minutes' walk away from our meeting spot. Without my phone, I didn't know the time, but I thought Colleen should be waiting. A sixth sense told me to check a side trail that ended at an overlook commanding the rapids and the bridge beyond. I peeked through foliage and my optimism evaporated.

The jacked-up blue Silverado sat on the bridge. Aaron Rogers stood on the road near the cab and Glenn Korpi in the bed, both looking upstream. I tamped down the panic whirling in my stomach. Where was Colleen? Had they discovered her or had she arrived after them?

Even if she were waiting for us, we were on the wrong side of the river. Worse, their allies might be at the cabin we were walking to. I ran and caught up to my fellow travelers, telling them to wait until I returned. A few more steps brought me to the edge of the woods, where I could scan the area around the cabin.

No vehicles. No people. No sound. I placed their things on a wooden deck that faced the river, hustled back to Valeria and Nana, and told them to continue to the cabin. I retrieved the rest of their belongings from the canoe and raced up the hill, praying no one had shown up while I was gone.

Prayer answered. I described our situation and gave them a contingency plan: If I did not return before suppertime, they were to break the glass window in the door, let themselves in, and stay the night. Eat whatever food they found inside. I would not abandon them. Valeria was crying, and

I got down on my knees. "Do you remember this place? You and Megan and I visited here on our ATV ride."

She sniffled but stuttered a yes.

"I want to tell you and Iorek something, a secret just for the three of us. Can we do that? Share a secret?" She nodded. "Iorek has special powers. Whoever holds your bear can never become lost. That's a special skill! But Iorek needs help. So here's what you can do if I can't get back by tomorrow morning. You can lead Nana back to Lake Tranquility. Iorek will help you remember how to do that."

I pointed down the driveway toward Lukes Road and gave her detailed directions to a reference point I hoped she would recall. "Do you remember what comes after that long stretch of standing water?"

She screwed her eyes shut. "The green gate?"

"Smart girl. And you remember where that takes you?"

Her eyes shown with confidence. "To Lake Tranquility."

To reinforce it, I made her tell it all to Iorek. "And now tell Nana about your magic bear and how to get the Lake Tranquility."

I don't know if it was belief in a special bear or feeling responsible or something else, but I knew Valeria would face up to whatever came next. Nana hugged Valeria and shoved the rifle at me.

My mouth went desert dry as I faced the opposing elements within myself. I did not want to be part of a culture that solved problems with guns. And yet, I had used them in the past. I'd bet the people on that bridge were armed. A gun might be the only way for me to rescue Colleen, to keep Valeria and Nana safe. I shredded another piece of my soul and accepted the weapon.

NINETY

I PADDLED UPSTREAM, CROSSED THE river, and beached the canoe. I cut through thick woods and found the driveway to the camp we had passed. It would bring me to Lukes Road at the spot I had suggested Colleen park. Along the way, a red squirrel chattered at my presence—a good sign that no one else was around. Walking down the road whistling Disney tunes was not prudent. Instead, I paralleled the gravel until I spotted Colleen's vehicle backed into the parking area I had recommended.

She would not have parked if she had seen the truck, so what did she do when the Silverado arrived, and where was she now?

I waited for the dub-dub of my heart to quit pulsing in my ears before silently toe-heeling through the woods to get close enough to see into Colleen's car. Empty—unless she was lying on the backseat or hiding in a foot well. I had to check without being seen.

I used her car as a screen from the road and duck-walked to her vehicle. My knees and thighs burned with the effort. Stomach in my throat, afraid I would see a body, I rose and looked inside. The car was empty with no bloodstains and no signs of a struggle. She'd left the doors unlocked with the fob sitting in a cup holder next to a cellphone.

Colleen either planned to return or had left unwillingly. She would have made her presence known if she had been watching her car. My throat constricted, making it hard to swallow.

I inched forward held my glasses to my nose with a finger while I bent down and read the faint vehicle tracks on the ground. She had pulled past the parking area and backed in. A set of wider tire prints had looped in front of her car—the Silverado? Ground too hard to show footprints.

My body was telling me they had her. I released the rifle's safety and returned to the woods. Halfway to the truck, I picked up mumbled conversation, not heated enough for an argument. I inched forward to see the open front doors of the Silverado. The mumbled conversation resolved into WIKB's Telephone Time on the Silverado's radio.

Open doors meant they weren't worried about Colleen escaping. Dark thoughts gnawed at my intestines. They had killed her.

Aaron Rogers came into view walking toward the truck. Over his shoulder, he said, "You want more too?" Korpi replied, "No, it'll only make me pee. Which makes me ask, do we have to walk her—you know, like a dog?"

Rogers leaned into the truck, displaying a pistol strapped to his hip. "Not my problem. She's fine." He exited with a cardboard cup of coffee.

At least Colleen was alive. If Korpi also had only a pistol, the rifle might give me the fire-power advantage. But how to use it to—

Metal jabbed the base of my skull. "If you move, I'll put a bullet in your head."

NINETY-ONE

"OVER HERE, YOU GUYS," BUNNY Crenshaw said. "I've got McCree. No sign of the fucking wetbacks. Drop your rifle, McCree, and lie face down."

Bunny was the woman who had trashed Serrano's trailer. And probably was the fourth person.

Rough hands patted me down. "Clean," Aaron Rogers said. He jerked my wrists together behind me and zip-tied them. The plastic cut into my skin.

Bunny nudged the sole of my left boot. "Roll over. I want to see your face. Where are they?"

I obeyed, and my glasses settled slightly skewed on my face. I noted the Sig Sauer P226 semiautomatic in Bunny's hand—Niki's favorite model. She had another pistol in a shoulder rig. Aaron Rogers also held a pistol. Glenn Korpi stood a few paces away, holding an AR-15-style rifle. They had me outgunned, outmanned, and outsmarted. Bunny repeated her demand to know where they were.

"I lost it all," I said. "I flipped the canoe at the beaver dam and lost it all."

Bunny kicked the bottom of my foot with the steel tip of her boot, jarring bones up to my knee. "What the hell are you talking about? I want to know where the kid and her grandmother are."

I put on my puzzled face. "What the hell are *you* talking about?" I looked at Rogers. "I saw your drone searching for my grow operation. Doesn't matter now. The whole damn harvest is at the bottom of the river."

My lies led to a confused two minutes of them talking over each other while I tried desperately to think of some way to talk myself out of this situation. The discussion ended with Bunny shouting, "enough," and slicing the air with the knife's edge of her hand. She kicked my foot once more. "Last chance before I drill you. What have you done with the girl and her grandmother? I know you had them." She widened her stance and took a two-handed aim at my head. Korpi retreated several feet. Rogers gave me a wicked grin.

I opened my eyes wide, mimicking that I had experienced a revelation. "You mean Valeria? Valeria and her grandmother. Them? What do you want with them? The kid was friends with my granddaughter. I have no idea where they are. Are you telling me you weren't trying to steal my plants? Did I lose forty thousand dollars of quality product for no damn reason?"

"When did they leave? Where did you take them?"

"Late afternoon Sunday. I dropped them at Tall Pines—in Amasa, you know? Forty thousand." I smacked my forehead on my knee. "For nothing? Ah, man."

Korpi continued retreating, as if to disassociate himself from the current scene. I had to find a way to exploit his weak link. "I can't believe I pissed away all that work and money and you two didn't find it with your drone?"

Bunny gave my foot another love tap. "Shut up about the weed. Where's your canoe?

"I saw the truck parked on the bridge. How'd you know I was coming down the river? Wait a minute. I get it. You sicced ICE on me. Like I told that agent, I haven't seen them since I dropped them off."

"You two check his canoe," Bunny said. "Tell them where you left it, McCree."

I described the place and suggested they follow the shore to make sure they didn't miss it. That would take them longer than walking up the cabin's driveway and cutting in to the river—time when Bunny wouldn't have their guns supporting her.

Bunny shooed them off with instructions to "use your phone and bring me pictures and be on the lookout for the wetbacks." All they'd find in the canoe were two paddles and river water. I needed to disarm Bunny before the guys and their long guns returned.

She took two steps back and ordered me to stand with my back to her. Too far away for me to charge her. She might have read my mind. "I can give a squirrel a new asshole with this baby from thirty feet, so don't try anything stupid. How does your accountant, Colleen Carpetti, fit into all this? Her car's here. Where is she?"

My question, too. If Colleen was nearby and if Niki had given her a gun, the odds might even be in my favor. Big ifs. I kept my movements easy and wracked my brain to sort through the implications of Bunny knowing that was Colleen's car. She had either spotted Colleen, who escaped, and put two and two together or she already knew it was Colleen's car. How could she? I had to keep playing nice and spinning my story out, pretending I was playing "And Then" with Megan, except fending off Bunny's curveballs.

"She was here to collect me and the weed. I assume your guys with the guns scared her off."

Bunny marched me up the road toward the Silverado and said, "Get in the rear."

I waggled my zip-tied hands at her. "Can you open the door?"

"Do it your own damn self."

I backed up to the truck, found the latch, and struggled the door open. I turned around and my legs buckled. Colleen lay hogtied on the backseat with a bandanna stuffed in her mouth.

"Silly me," Bunny said. "I guess I knew where your accountant was all along."

Ninety-Two

Unless Colleen and I could escape, we were dead. I crawled into the rear seat. Bunny slammed the door, leaving us alone with WIKB playing on the radio. Colleen's eyes were open. "You hurt? Shake your head yes or no."

She signaled no.

That was a relief. "Duck into my hands, and I'll remove your gag."

Easier said than done, but I did it. She coughed and cleared her throat. "Well, here's another nice mess you got me into."

That she could toss out a Laurel and Hardy line was a good sign she had not succumbed to fear. I said, "Not to put too fine a point on it, the guys are temporarily gone. To escape, we need to remove the zip-ties. Can you reach the pocketknife in my right front pocket?"

We aligned our backs, and her fingers slid into my pocket. Pressing into my thigh, she inch-wormed her way down.

"Too tight, but if you remove my tennies, I can slide my hands underneath my feet and see what I'm doing.

With my imperfect vision, it took me multiple tries to remove her double-knotted sneakers. Once I did, she slipped her hands around to the front but still couldn't reach the knife.

I told her to undo my belt.

She barked a tight laugh. "I'm not into kinky sex, or did you want it for self-flagellation?"

Now I got it. Colleen's coping mechanism was to use humor. "To loosen the pants. And pull down the zipper too."

She unfastened the belt, undid the snap, and worried the zipper down. I lay down on the seat and raised my legs over my head, concerned Bunny would see the movement. Still no go.

I dropped my legs on top of her. "Grab my waist and we'll pull the damn pants down to my ankles.

That allowed her to grab the knife. She used her teeth to open it and sawed the plastic zip holding my wrists, apologizing each time she nicked me. My blood-slicked hands separated with a pop covered up by the radio's chatter. I severed her wrist-ties without bloodshed and hauled my pants back up.

I couldn't see Bunny from my position. Colleen leaned forward to look out the front. "She's at the railing looking up the river."

"Get down," I hissed. "If she sees you, she'll realize your gag is gone."

I checked underneath the seats for useful weapons and came up with a tire iron and two Snickers wrappers.

Collen asked if we should rush her.

"Too risky. Keep low and crawl into the driver's seat. When she turns her back, slip out the door and run like hell. If she reacts, I'll draw her attention away from you. Drive like your life depends on it. Soon as you're safe, call 9-1-1, and get the Sheriff's deputies here."

"She'll kill you."

"Not when I tell her I have the thumb drive and haven't given it to the police because I wanted to clear out my marijuana plants first." Seeing confusion on her face, I said, "I'll explain later. It'll buy me time. Maybe I can get lucky with the tire iron. We don't have much for alternatives."

Colleen slithered over the center console and tucked herself low behind the steering wheel. Bunny cocked her head like something on Telephone Time had caught her attention. She took a hesitant step toward the truck. And a second. One more and I'd have to open my door and distract her.

The announcer concluded Telephone Time and cued the minute-long jingle, which they played with extra volume. Bunny gave a little shrug and returned to the center of the bridge and looked at the water.

"Now."

Ninety-Three

COLLEEN WAS OUT AND RUNNING low, the radio commercial providing auditory cover. Next would come the noon news and the daily funeral report. I did not like the implications of that timing on my current situation. Bunny's head swiveled. I yanked down on the handle and flung the door open. I hid the tire iron behind my back.

She held her Sig Sauer in a two-handed grip and hurried toward me. "What the hell do you think you're doing? Get back in there or I'll shoot you."

"I know where the thumb drive is," I shouted.

She slowed but kept the P226 leveled at me. To keep her focused on me, I scooted toward the door, pretending my arms were still tied behind me.

She wagged the gun. "Stay there. What did you say?"

"That I found the pictures of the dead girl." I inched forward, stopped, and added, "I couldn't give the drive to the cops until I took care of my grow operation, so I hid it, but if I go missing or show up dead, people will find it."

She came closer. One or two more steps and she'd discover Colleen was gone. I jerked forward and placed both feet on the running board.

"So where is it?"

"This is where we negotiate, right? We figure out how to guarantee our mutual destruction if either of us talks. Colleen and I keep on living, and you never have to worry about the pictures. Everyone lives happily ever after." I scooched my butt closer to the edge, preparing to jump down. Gears clicked behind her eyes. "This should be easy," I continued. "You know where I live and your associates can kill me if I break my part of the deal. I retain a copy to make sure you keep your side."

With her next step, her eyes opened wide in shock.

Crap. I leaped past the door, losing my balance and my glasses. She fired wide, and I whipped the tire iron at her. She had quick reflexes and ducked under the spinning bar. Before she could bring the gun to bear on me, I employed a move from my soccer days and unleashed a scissor kick at her hands.

She sensed my movement, but her response was wrong. Instead of leaning away from my kick, she ducked again. My toe nailed her neck.

A well-executed scissor kick has a lot of power behind it and leaves the kicker lying on the ground, which is where I found myself. I scrambled to Bunny, prepared to slug her before she could shoot me. That was unnecessary.

She was rigid with pain, grabbing her throat, the gun beside her. I kicked the weapon aside, and my relief changed to horror as she turned blue. I had crushed her windpipe.

Colleen materialized next to me, scaring the bejesus out of me.

"I heard shots." She held out my glasses. "Here."

I shoved my glasses in my shirt pocket and pushed her. "Go get help while I try to save Bunny's life. "

Colleen took root. I punched a hole in Bunny's throat with my penknife. But when I extracted the blade, the hole pinched closed. I tried different attachments and positions. Nothing kept the incision open.

Bunny died a death I wouldn't wish on anyone.

Ninety-Four

I cursed Bunny for dying on me. And I cursed Colleen for standing around when she should have been calling the police. *Snap out of it!* Rogers and Korpi might be back at any moment, and we can't let them catch us mooning over a dead body. I removed the P226 from Bunny's shoulder rig and handed it to Colleen. I grabbed from the ground the one she had fired at me. "Let's take cover and consider our options."

"No." She expertly checked the pistol. "We're in this mess because you promised to get Valeria and Nana to safety. If we don't do that now, they'll never get out. The police will tie us up for a month of Sundays. There's no place you can keep them. Niki didn't answer when I called her while you were trying to save Bunny's life. It's now, Seamus, or you have to hope the police choose to let Nana go. Which way?"

"But if Rogers and Korpi return—"

"We deal with them if they don't drive off and leave Bunny lying in the dirt. Tick-tock."

We ran to her car, drove it to the chain across the road to the camp where I had stashed Valeria and Nana, and parked it facing out. The faint strains from the Silverado's radio accompanied us as we trotted down the driveway and into the cabin clearing. Valeria's and Nana's stuff was on the covered deck where they had left it, but they were gone. I bellowed their names.

The front door opened several inches. "McCree," Aaron Rogers called out, "what took you so long?"

He couldn't see me because of the door. Where was Korpi? I motioned Colleen into the woods and backed away. "You were expecting me?"

"When Bunny didn't call me after the gunfire, I figured she was a goner. Now you're here, so I was right. She said you're smart. I have two somethings of yours to trade. If it comes to a shootout, I'll kill them and take suicide by cop over life behind bars. Got any brilliant ideas?"

I backed into the woods, looked for Colleen and couldn't see her. Good. I dropped to the ground to minimize my chances of being hit if he sprayed his automatic rifle in my direction. "I need to know they're okay."

"They're alive, bound and gagged. You call the cops, or is it just us?"

Could I make him believe we had a common cause? "You know, I don't give two shits about you. All I want is for the girl and her grandmother to be safe."

"Where are the cops in this, McCree?"

"Cops would just get in the way. My goal is to take the two of them out of state. Bunny and Colleen are both dead. What about your partner?"

"I tied the chicken shit to a tree down by the river. Here's what we do. The four of us walk together to Korpi's truck. I take it and the girl. If no one stops me or follows me, I'll drop the kid someplace safe."

"I can't say I much like that idea. I have Colleen's rental parked at the road. Keys are in it. Take the car and grab the keys to Korpi's truck as you go past. Leave us here."

"And run into a roadblock? No way I'm leaving without bringing a hostage." He offered to take Nana too if I was worried about the girl being by herself.

Nice guy. No doubt, he'd kill any hostages as soon as he didn't need them. Had Colleen finally called the police? And was Korpi really tied up to a tree, or was he circling around to get behind me? The whole situation could blow apart if some innocent drove down Lukes Road and discovered Bunny's body. I had to separate him from Valeria and Nana and time was not my ally.

"You want a hostage? Fine. I'll go with you, except it's mutual destruction if something goes wrong. We take Colleen's car. If I lied about the cops, you shoot me and they shoot you. You drop me off at the highway, and I'll come back and free your prisoners."

I expected an immediate response but heard only my heart pounding. How could the two of us in a car work? Whoever was driving was at a disadvantage because they couldn't watch the road and the passenger. Even though I have quick reflexes, I couldn't respond fast enough if he tried to shoot me while I drove. That means no guns in the car—at least not loaded.

"You think I don't know rentals have tracking devices?"

A little, I admitted to myself. "Fine. Take Korpi's truck. Of course, it's easy to describe. Fact is, any way out of here requires you to get new wheels or arrange for someone to pick you up. Right?"

Behind me, something shuffled through leaves. I pressed a finger to my glasses, flipped from stomach to back, and sat up, pointing my pistol at the intruder. A red squirrel chattered at my sudden movement. I resumed my prone position. The door had not moved. "We've got the canoe. We could paddle out to somewhere you could steal a car."

"That's crazy."

His quick response dismissing the canoeing idea when he hadn't reacted the same way to my suggestion to take a car or truck meant he considered escaping in one of the vehicles at least somewhat plausible. It was the only chance to break Valeria and Nana free of him. "Aaron, you gotta shit or get off the pot. Somebody will discover Bunny, and they *will* call the cops who *will* find us here. If you plan on dying today, just do it already. Otherwise, tell me you have a better plan."

"You sold me, McCree. Come here and we'll walk together to Korpi's truck."

Like I'd get halfway there. "Now you're the crazy one. We need a way to make sure we both behave. Take the grandmother with you to kill if I try something."

"Good idea, McCree. Except I'm taking the girl."

Ninety-Five

ROGERS CLOSED THE DOOR BEHIND him. How would Colleen react to this plan? If she had Niki's skills, I'd want her to take out Rogers before we got to Korpi's truck. But instead, all I could hope was that Colleen made sure Korpi didn't get the jump on me.

The cabin door reopened two minutes later with Valeria visible. Rogers, protected by the door, gripped her arm with one hand, and held a pistol to her head with the other. "Tell him your grandmother is fine."

In a shaky voice, Valeria told me the man had gagged them and tied them to a bed. I asked if anyone else was in the cabin. With no hesitancy, she answered no. Meaning Korpi wasn't there.

Rogers pushed Valeria onto the stoop and pulled the door shut behind him. "Time to get this show on the road."

No long guns. If Korpi got me in his sights with either rifle before I got close enough for mutual destruction with Rogers, I was a goner. I hurried through the woods and met Rogers where the driveway entered the woods. Because I was on his right, it forced Rogers to pull Valeria tight to him with his right arm to keep her between us. His left held the pistol at her head, his finger inside the trigger guard. He was right-handed, but with the gun inches from her, it didn't matter. He couldn't miss killing her if he decided I had betrayed him.

Rogers shuffled down the road using baby steps to control Valeria, who had shut her eyes tight. I faced them, holding the Sig in a two-handed grip and matched his pace to keep my gun aimed at him. I kept far enough away to assure him I didn't plan to make a grab for him or Valeria. To maintain that distance, we steered wide of Colleen's rental.

I could not read Rogers. He seemed patient, methodical, and in control. Unlike me. My heart was clawing its way out of my chest, my teeth ached from clenching my jaw, and a wall of fire rose from my shoulders to the top of my head because I could not envision the next step.

He stopped at Bunny's sprawled body, using quick glances away from me to read the scene. I kept my attention on him, although flies buzzing loud enough to be heard over the truck's radio let me know they had found her. Thank goodness Valeria still had her eyes closed. She did not need to add Bunny's corpse to her nightmares.

"Where's your accountant?"

"Fell off the bridge." I nodded to my side of the road, hoping he would not want to cross in front of me to look. He didn't, but the moment for which I had not yet conjured a solution was upon us: how could we assure his escape while keeping everyone alive?

NINETY-SIX

ROGERS HAD APPARENTLY COME TO the same conclusion. "I don't see it working, McCree. You've made it clear you won't let me leave with the girl, and unless I have her as a safeguard, there's no reason you can't shoot me when I let her go. And as you say, if someone drives down the road . . ."

His silence fed my despair. "There's only one way. We have to trust each other, or you're right, this will never work. Truthfully, my only goal is to see no harm comes to the child and her grandmother. Take the truck and leave. I'll go back and release the grandmother, then we'll drive out of here."

Our eyes locked, and I realized he planned to take Valeria with him in the Silverado. His arm tightened around her at the same time I shifted my weight so I could block his path to the truck.

Valeria let loose an ear-piercing scream, and she stomped her heel on Rogers' toes. His grip loosened, and she elbowed him in the nuts, using her momentum to twist out of his grasp. His pistol fired with a single crack— a reflex contraction of his finger. He grabbed for her, giving me a window to shoot him without endangering Valeria. But if I didn't kill him with the first shot, all three of us might end up dead.

I stepped toward him and yelled, "You're dead if you pull the trigger again. Don't do it."

He swiveled his pistol toward me and steadied it with both hands. We stood eight feet apart, death a finger twitch away. He was bent over slightly from pain, and his face expressed confusion.

I pressed for my words to reach him. "Get in the damn truck and go. I told you all I want is for Valeria and her grandmother to be safe. I could have killed you if that's what I wanted. Just go."

"Listen to the man," Colleen said from somewhere behind me and to the left. "You pull that trigger and I'll empty a full clip in you."

Rogers didn't look at Colleen either. "So you lied about the accountant. I can't trust you."

Valeria was safe for now, but there were so many ways this could still go wrong. I took a deliberate step away from the truck. "You're alive, aren't you? I'm moving back." I took another step. "Get in and go. I don't want your death on my hands. Please." I continued backing away, each step making it less likely he could hit me. I hoped Colleen was doing the same, but I dared not take my eyes off him.

Ninety-Seven

VALERIA, COLLEEN, AND I STOOD in a group hug, watching the jacked-up Silverado disappear around a bend. "You're a hero, Valeria. How's your ankle?"

"I'm sorry, Grampa Seamus, I can't walk too good."

I mussed her hair. "You'll heal again. Where did you learn that move?"

"My mother took me with her to a place where they teach women to protect themselves. I got to practice too."

"Right now you get to horseback ride, except I'm your horse. We'll go collect your Nana, and then Colleen will take you to a safe place."

Colleen said, "You two stay here. I can get Nana by myself."

I was glad I had my thinking cap back on. "When Rogers and Korpi left to find the canoe, they had both the AR-15 and Niki's rifle that they took from you. Rogers left the AR-15 at the cabin, but Korpi might wait with Niki's rifle to ambush whoever comes for Nana."

"No, Grampa Seamus." She pointed in the direction Rogers had driven. "That man left two rifles in the cabin with Nana. He and the other man had a big argument after they tied us to the bed. He hit the other man in the head with a frying pan and dragged him out of the house. I never saw him again."

Had Rogers killed Korpi? Tied him to a tree, as he claimed? Something else? "Until the three of you are on the highway, we're sticking together."

I hoisted Valeria onto my back. In short order, we released Nana from the duct tape holding her to the bed. I used some of it—handy—to repair my glasses. Colleen found Niki's rifle leaning against the wall next to the AR-15, both loaded. Neither smelled like anyone had fired it. The frying pan lay on the dining room table. I didn't pick it up, but I couldn't see any signs of blood or hair on it. I hoped Korpi was alive, but worrying about him needed to wait until Colleen was safely off with her precious cargo.

We stored Niki's rifle in the trunk, and, on the off-chance Rogers was lying in ambush, I carried the AR-15 on my lap as we drove down Lukes Road to the highway. He wasn't. I gave Valeria and Iorek smooches on the tops of their heads, shook hands with Nana, and gave Colleen a big hug. "Good luck. Two miles north and you're out of Iron County."

I stood there, the AR-15 strapped over my shoulder, an unfamiliar emptiness in my heart, and watched their car disappear over the distant hill.

Ninety-Eight

I HAD BEEN SO FOCUSED on getting Colleen on her way with no interference from Rogers that I had not thought to use Colleen's cellphone to call Niki—or the police. I considered walking to the nearest house and asking to borrow a phone. But I didn't know where anyone lived, and they might not be home, and I convinced myself the best course was to walk back and use Bunny's phone to call the cops.

It wasn't until I reached the bridge and Bunny's body that I remembered I had tossed her phone into the Silverado Rogers had escaped in. My stomach threatened revolt at the buzz and constant motion of insects around the body. The gravity effects of livor mortis had drawn her blood away from her front, leaving her face and neck preternaturally pale under the dried blood remaining from my attempt to keep her breathing. That sight would fertilize a million bad dreams.

What now, Seamus?

Find Korpi. If he was injured, I could give him aid. If he was dead, at least I could lead the police to him.

I followed drag marks from the cabin and found Korpi prone, secured to a tree behind the outhouse. Rogers had looped Korpi's belt around his neck and buckled him to a tree. He had stuffed part of Korpi's torn shirt into the guy's mouth and used the rest to tie his hands behind his back.

Korpi had heard me and was kicking the ground to gain my attention. I pulled the shirt from his mouth but left him tied to the tree in what had to be an uncomfortable position. "I'm glad to see you're alive, Glenn. Let's have a little chat." I sat with my back against another tree and rested the AR-15 across my legs.

Fear bloomed in his eyes. "Where's Aaron?"

"Bunny's dead. Aaron took your truck. That leaves you holding the bag." To pry open the guy I considered the weak link, I told him I knew he was a minor player who'd gotten involved in something bigger than he'd expected. The real culprits were everyone else. I aligned myself to him by sharing some truth. "That whole story I told about the marijuana patch and trying to leave with my product? Total bullshit. I was protecting the little girl and her grandmother from Bunny. Did Bunny tell you what she was looking for?"

"Nuh-uh," he stammered. "I just did errands. Drove for them."

"Exactly. You're not one of them. But let me tell you how deep the shit is that you're in. Bunny wanted a thumb drive that contained pictures of a murdered woman. The person who took those pictures disappeared. Her name is Katrina Serrano. Friends call her Kat. The little girl is her daughter. Now, Bunny didn't know this, but the police have that thumb drive. Anyone they link to the murder is going down hard. That's you, my friend, unless you can help me."

His unfocused eyes shown white with fear. I pressed on. "You help me, and I'll convince the police you did not know squat. That Rogers kidnapped the girl and her grandmother. He knocked you out and tied you up because you wouldn't go along. But," I made an exaggerated shrug, "you don't help me, I won't help you. Simple, right? You understand what I'm saying?"

"But I wasn't any part of that."

I brought up my hands to suggest surrender and enunciated my words. "Glenn, I totally understand, but the cops . . . I'm trying to help you, but I need information." I tilted my head and scratched it, like I had come up with a new idea. "Well, never mind. I guess you don't know anything after all. Problem is, I need time to take care of some things. My only choice is to leave you here. Scream loud enough and long enough, maybe someone will hear you."

"You can't," he whimpered.

He was right. I couldn't, but I needed him to believe I could. "Let me ask something you do know. How did you learn I was canoeing down this river? Did that ICE guy tell you?"

"Bunny figured it out. She was sure you were hiding them. She had me and Aaron use a drone to scout the properties you own. We found that spot on the small lake you camped at, but you were gone. Then she got that ICE agent involved. I don't know what she has on him, but it must be good. She snaps her fingers, he jumps. He put trackers on your stuff and called her this morning to tell her you went to your river property. I was following your accountant, and she—"

"Wait, why were you following my accountant?"

"Bunny told me to. 'Glenn,' she said, 'you get to the motel early—before dawn—and tail the broad wherever she goes.' She and her husband were comparing notes, and she figured out the accountant was the same person the Silver Fox hired as a dancer. So, I'm doing what she told me when Aaron and Bunny catch up to me and signal for me to pull over. They join me in my truck, and we find the accountant pulled off before the bridge. Anyway, she figures you're making a run for it by the river. That's it, man. I just drove my truck where they told me."

That all made sense, and I'd bet once Rogers got out of the woods, he'd trade the jacked-up Silverado for Bunny's car. Not my problem. I had Korpi talking, and I had a pinkie-swear contract to fulfill. "How'd she figure out I had the girl?"

"We searched the woman's trailer for whatever Bunny was looking for—you tell me it's a thumb drive. When she couldn't find it, she decided the kid or old lady had it. On our way out from searching the trailer, we passed you going the other way. Bunny paid someone to learn who you were from your plate number. When we saw you heading to that arts camp in Amasa, she was sure you had the kid and went crazy when we couldn't find them."

How did Bunny learn of the photographs? From Kat? "You know where Kat Serrano is now?"

His eyes flitted everywhere, avoiding looking at me. "I never seen her."

"That wasn't my question. Look at me, Glenn. So far, I've believed everything you said. I'm helping you avoid prison. Don't screw this up. Where is Kat Serrano? Is she alive?"

"I swear, I don't know nothin'."

I leaned into him, putting my nose an inch from his, and stared into his eyes, not blinking for a minute. He broke.

"She's dead. Leastwise, I think so. I heard Aaron and Bunny talking. They drugged her to get answers. And it sorta sounded like, you know, like she died. Honest. That's all I heard. You gotta believe me."

"Where did they take her?"

"I don't know, man. Someplace out where no one could find her. I didn't have nothing to do with that."

I was ninety-five percent sure he was telling the truth, and nothing I could do right now could increase the percentage. While I had him talking, I asked if he knew anything about those two guys who got whacked and dumped at my place. "Were they involved in manufacturing meth?"

His face lost its color. His Adam's apple worked up and down, like he was swallowing bile. "No. No, man. I had nothing to do with killing them. That was Aaron and Bunny. They just got me to drive their stuff to your place and set up that equipment on your propane tank."

"Where did they kill them?"

"I don't know, man. I don't want to know." He started crying, his body shaking with his sobs.

"Stay with me here, Glenn. Are you telling me that besides running a high-class prostitution ring, Bunny was manufacturing meth?"

"No, man. Randy discovered those two yahoos near where they bring guys and her girls for weekend retreats. I've never been there. Hear tell it's a sweet setup. Anyway, Randy stole their operation. Bunny found out and chewed him a new one because she didn't want police coming anywhere near her deal with the girls. Randy supposedly told them to stop. I don't know that he did. Either way, those stupid meth heads kept stealing propane and cooking product. Aaron lured them somewhere, and they whacked them."

He segued into a shaggy dog story about him and his wife arguing over money. He went to blow off steam at the Silver Fox. Ended up hooking up with a dancer, doing some drugs, falling more behind in money. One night, Aaron Rogers suggested he do a little security work on the side to pay them back. Before Korpi knew it, he was in trouble and dependent on them.

Similar to how pimps got girls hooked on drugs to keep them needy and compliant. I interrupted and asked if he had a phone.

"In my truck. You can borrow it."

He had forgotten his Silverado was gone. I couldn't leave him where no one might find him if something happened to me before I called the police. I told him I'd undo the belt, and we'd walk to his truck. If he tried to escape, I'd catch him, strip him, and leave him to starve to death, if bears or wolves didn't eat him first.

He blathered from the moment I released him until he spotted Bunny sprawled on the road. His feet shuffled to a stop. He leaned over and threw up.

I prodded his back. "Don't look at her. You forgot Rogers has your truck and your phone? I brought you here so the police could find you, but I need to secure you to the bridge with your belt until they arrive. Either that, or I shoot you in both legs."

NINETY-NINE

WHEN I JOG, I COVER six miles in forty-eight minutes. Normally, I could walk that distance in ninety. But I was so whipped, it took double the normal time. Three hours of second-guessing everything I had done and worrying if everyone was okay. I reached my property so bushed I could barely put one foot in front of the other.

Cresting the last hill and seeing only my F-150 and the Outback, still up on a jack, was like a slap in the face. I had convinced myself Niki would be waiting for me when I got home, and I'd have my answers. I rarely miss not having my cellphone, but now I desperately wanted to talk with Niki and to verify with Colleen that she had escaped with Valeria and Nana. One of my mother's favorite proverbs popped into my head, "If wishes were horses, beggars would ride."

Niki's SUV not being here meant she was fine. She had responsibilities in St. Paul—business and family responsibilities she had not wanted and had accepted largely because I had encouraged her. She and Colleen and even Mom had done more than I had any right to ask. But I hadn't yet done everything I'd asked of myself.

I retrieved the hidden spare key to the house and found a note from Niki on the dining room table.

Seamus,

I'm dealing with federal bureaucracy. Call me and I'll fill you in.

Niki

I wished she had time-stamped her note so I knew when she had left. It occurred to me the replacement trail cam I had installed on Shank Lake Road would tell me that. I traded my damaged glasses for a spare I kept at the house and retrieved the memory card. I reviewed the pictures while scarfing down a bowl of cereal, a hunk of cheese, and an apple.

The camera caught Agent Carpenter's green jeep heading in, and minutes later, Niki trailing him. Nothing for two hours. Then, a fire department rescue truck drove past. It and Niki returned after an hour. Niki stopped at the house and then headed toward town. The last human was me, dragging up the road.

I told myself Niki was fine. She shot Agent Carpenter and summoned the closest thing we have to an ambulance to transport him to the hospital. Except police weren't involved. Or maybe she didn't shoot him. He injured himself attempting to crash through the second gate to the river. Okay, Seamus, you have no clue what happened. Get yourself into town, call in Bunny's death, and leave before the Sheriff's department shows up.

I removed the tracking device from the truck and stuck it to the Bobcat, just in case it stopped sending signals if it didn't remain attached to metal. Paranoid, I'm sure. But I did not want anybody to follow me where I planned to go.

Glenn Korpi thought Kat was dead. He might have misinterpreted what he heard, and Bunny still held Kat prisoner. While I was free, I would use my time to fulfill my oath to Valeria to try to learn what had happened to her mother.

I loaded the truck with snacks, a fresh can of mosquito dope, and my camera supplies. I realized I should change clothes, did that, and scribbled a quick note below Niki's telling her I was going to Crenshaw's compound—just in case she returned. Not that I expected it.

Not knowing what else I might need, I collected bolt cutters, pry bar, chainsaw, come-a-long, and block and tackle, and threw them into the truck bed.

I raced down to Tall Pines where I used their phone to report Bunny's death and Glenn Korpi's detention. I hung up on their questions. As much as I wanted to call Niki and Colleen, I scratched buying a phone at the Verizon store in Iron River. A replacement phone would take too long to port my information from the cloud to a new one, and a burner phone did me no good because no one would know how to reach me on it. Plus, I relied on my phone's address book and, with a burner, wouldn't know anybody's number to call them.

I was running solo and incommunicado with the police surely looking for me. If anything went wrong, I had no safety net.

ONE HUNDRED

ON THE FOREST ROAD LEADING to the Crenshaw compound, where I now suspected Bunny had taken Kat to question her, I paid attention to the two-track trails I passed. Glenn Korpi had said the meth dealers worked nearby, and, sure enough, a mile before Crenshaw's property line, I noticed one with recent traffic. I stopped and examined the tire tracks. They included wide truck treads and a distinctive set that I figured came from a passenger car. The truck tracks came and went. The most recent passenger car track was heading in. I filed that information away and continued to the locked gate that guarded the Crenshaw property.

I put on work gloves to assure I left no prints. Two snips of the bolt cutters removed the lock, which I chucked into the woods. Littering, yes, but keeping it in my truck as incriminating evidence did not sound like a good idea. I closed the gate behind me and arranged the chain to mimic a locked gate, then drove to the house and was pleased to see no parked vehicles.

The pry bar forced open the rear sliding glass door. Inside, my nose wrinkled at the stench of massive disinfectant use—more than required for a standard cleaning. I called out, asking if anyone was here, and got no answer. With all the people wandering around the first floor over the weekend, the upstairs and basement offered the best hope of finding signs of Kat's captivity.

Upstairs, I counted six bedrooms and a bunk room that could house a dozen. The place was spotless; even the corners were free of dust bunnies. I checked bedroom closets, under beds, in drawers. Loungewear and women's gowns—much fancier than what Kat and the murdered woman had worn at the party given in the Menominee Rapids Resort's private room—filled the closets. Sex toys crammed the bureau drawers. The bathrooms contained only over-the-counter medicines for headache and upset stomach, extra tissues, and toilet paper. Stacked fluffy towels and high-thread-count sheets filled the linen closet shelves. Nothing suggested Kat had been here.

I found an entrance to the attic through a closet ceiling. I dragged a bureau into the closet to stand on and popped the ceiling panel up and out of the way. With no obvious light switches or lights, I retrieved a flashlight from a kitchen drawer and used it to illuminate the area: thick pink insulation cozied between ceiling joists. Nothing stored, and no hidden rooms. I replaced the panel and positioned the bureau feet to fit the original rug indentations. I scuffed the rug with my foot to hide the drag marks.

That left the basement. I opened its door and a wall of disinfectant odor greeted me, even though I had become accustomed to its smell. A light switch at the top of the stairs controlled all the lights. The stairs showed no dust. The devil suggested I was a fool to leave Bunny's P226 and the AR-15 lying next to her for the police to find. I should have them in reach. Until recently, I would never have generated that thought. I told the devil to return to hell and stay there. I swear he snorted.

The main basement area contained a freezer massive enough to hold a body and shelves filled with nonperishable food items. Heart in my mouth, I opened the freezer door and gagged at the sight of hanging slabs of meat. I settled my stomach and inspected each slab, labeled as beef, deer, and elk.

Three padlocked rooms jutted out from one basement wall. I raced to the truck, grabbed the bolt cutter, and removed the first padlock. The door opened to reveal a disinfected bathroom containing a standalone sink, commode, and shower stall. A mold problem in a closed room might require the disinfectant, but I soon discovered that was unlikely the reason for the extreme cleaning. A narrow bedroom lay beyond the second padlocked door. Here, the tang of feces added to the overpowering disinfectant stench. Pushed against the far wall was a single bed, stripped to a plastic mattress cover. An empty chamber pot sat underneath the foot of the bed.

With a bathroom next door, you'd only use a chamber pot if someone had locked you in. The flashlight illuminated several dark brown or rusty spots in one corner that looked more organic than mineral. Disinfectant had burned away my ability to smell even with my nose to the floor. A crime lab could confirm if it was blood.

I unzipped the plastic mattress cover, hoping to find hidden treasure. Nothing. I flipped the mattress up to examine the box spring. One corner had the outline of a stain left by dried liquid.

Breaking into the house, I had been sure I would uncover evidence, but so far, I had discovered nothing that would warrant summoning the police and their forensics. A combination lock secured the third room, which was tucked into the corner and larger than the other two. The bolt cutter made quick work of it, and I entered my last hope.

This space had no internal lighting. The flashlight's beam revealed the walls lined with metal shelves filled with ziplocked storage bags. I slid my feet to make sure I didn't trip on anything, retrieved one bag, and brought it into the light of the main room.

I'd never used cocaine, but I'd seen plenty during my days on Wall Street. This powder had a crystalline structure similar to coke, but yellow shaded its white, unlike the pure white or pinkish tinge I remembered the traders lusted after.

The bag weighed about a kilo. No one locked up bags of detergent. Best guess, this was the meth Bunny had supposedly been furious about. I returned the bag to its place and shut the door on a seven-figure stash of illegal drugs. Now I had something the police would find exciting.

And a problem.

How could I entice the police to raid the place without admitting to B&E?

ONE HUNDRED ONE

I LEFT THE BASEMENT AS I had found it, except for the locks I had removed. I couldn't lock the damaged French door from the outside, so I secured it from the inside and left the house using the front door, which locked behind me. It was dusk, but the sauna and garage still beckoned. I made myself a deal: if I found the doors locked, I'd leave. I returned the bolt cutter and pry bar to my truck to assure I didn't cheat.

The sauna was secure, but the garage was not. God's will. To let in maximum light, I screeched open both garage doors. Kat's rusted Ford Ranger had not been there earlier, but I still registered disappointment to not see it. I weaved around the side-by-sides, past the tractor with a front bucket and a backhoe attachment and examined everything on the workbench that ran across the rear wall. No bloody hatchets, no cellphones, no clutch purses.

Headlights coming down the driveway swept through the garage. Had I triggered a silent alarm and someone from town was checking on the compound? Well, I sure couldn't hide with my F-150 parked in full view. I rushed outside, smacking my shoulder against the backhoe attachment along the way. Randy Crenshaw's blaze orange Caddy Blackwing pulled up next to my truck. I approached as he got out of his car.

He cleared the door and pointed a pistol at me.

I froze. "Randy, it's Seamus. I didn't expect you here." That was true. "Your dad told me to feel free to look around." Total Bullshit. Would Randy call me on it? I resumed walking toward him and offered my hand to shake.

He lowered the gun to his side. A lefty, like his dad, his right remained free to shake mine. He made no move to do that. "Dad didn't say anything about that."

I dropped my hand. "He was exploring options. I don't think he'd decided. I got the impression he didn't come here often. Nice bunch of toys." I waved toward the open garage and brushed my shoulder. My hand came away dirty. *The backhoe.* I wiped my hand clean on my pants.

His eyes jittered, losing focus. Nerves? Drugs?

"You have a key to the house? I peeked through the windows. It looks super in there, but I'd love to see the upstairs."

"Not today." He motioned with the gun toward my truck. "Time to leave. We'll sort this out with dad at a later date."

"Yeah. Sure. Okay." I shut the garage doors. "Could use some WD-40."

He was already walking toward the front stoop. I hopped in my truck and engaged the ignition. While turning the truck around, my lights illuminated his car. I focused my binoculars on his tire tread. I'd bet it matched the automotive tracks I saw entering that two-track a mile before the Crenshaw compound gate. Curiosity got the better of me, and I shifted my focus to the interior. My attention passed over the two-tone leather driver seat, noted a cellphone lay next to the black stick shift, and stopped on seeing dozens of freezer storage bags filled with a yellowish powder on the passenger seat.

ONE HUNDRED TWO

HOW WOULD CRENSHAW REACT WHEN he discovered I had broken into the house and found the drugs? I checked my rearview mirror for him.

Never mind what *he* planned, Seamus. What do *you* do? Because if those drugs escape to the wild, *you're* responsible for the lives lost.

I sped to his gate and parked between the posts to block the driveway, trapping Crenshaw. Now what? The only phone available to call the police was in Crenshaw's car. I sprinted back, hoping I could make it before Crenshaw came back outside.

He opened the front door while I was still fifty yards—six seconds—away.

First three seconds: he raised his head in awareness, retreated two steps, and stopped.

Twenty-five yards to go.

Second four: he leveled his pistol.

Brain calculating: Fifteen yards. Even people trained with pistols have a difficult time hitting a target at any distance. I needed that phone and began an erratic weave.

Second five: he fired three shots.

Second six, I ducked behind his hundred-thousand-dollar beauty.

He sidled left to get an angle. I scooted past his blackened rear window to the front door and looked inside. The phone was a billfold.

"Castle doctrine," he yelled. "I've got every right to kill you."

Bully for him. I'd survived my confrontations with Bunny and Aaron Rogers. Three in one day was pressing my luck. I wanted to keep him here after I escaped so the police could catch him. I extracted my Swiss Army knife and, remembering Niki's advice to take out two tires, not just one, stabbed the awl through the sidewalls of the front and rear tires. Each wound yielded a satisfying hiss. I stayed low, and using his car as a shield, zigzagged to safety behind the garage.

He threw two more slugs in my direction before retreating inside. He could call reinforcements. I could not.

One Hundred Three

I BROUGHT THE F-150 TO a sliding stop scattering gravel, hopped out, and yelled to the folks streaming into the parking lot from the Northwoods Second Coming of Jesus Christ Church, "Anyone got a phone I can borrow?"

The women scattered, either locking themselves in their cars or retreating inside the wooden church. The men gathered in a bunch.

I presented my hands in prayerful supplication. "Please, I need to borrow a phone to call the police. I don't mean to frighten anyone, but it is urgent."

The youngest, smallest guy there walked over and handed me his phone. "You okay, brother? You're bleeding. Press emergency and it dials 9-1-1."

The operator identified herself and asked the nature of my emergency. I was looking down at my arm, which was bleeding, and the first words I spoke were "Holy shit, I've been shot." That got the operator's attention, but not in the way I had intended. My frustration with rules boiled over because she wanted facts about the wound, which was only a crease, and I wanted her to focus on who had done the creasing. Progress went faster when I relented and let her ask her questions.

The operator asked where I was. I handed the phone to the kid to give directions. *Hell, the church is on the highway. Use your head, Seamus.* I leaned against my truck, energy draining through my feet. Now that I had to wait, my body wanted to collapse. Directions complete, the kid said the operator needed my name.

"Seamus McCree."

He repeated my name into the device. His eyes widened. "I understand, but I gotta get home before my curfew." He hung up and jogged to an older guy in the group.

What the hell?

The guy listened to the kid and stepped forward. "You're sure you don't need the hospital?" Behind him, the men were backing toward the church, eyes wide with fear.

"I'm good. Is there a problem I don't know about?"

"We're a Christian community, and if you want help to get medical assistance, I'll take you. But the 9-1-1 operator told young Justin that we should consider you armed and dangerous and to get to a place of safety. I don't know what's going on, and I don't want to know. We believe all people have good inside them. I'm familiar with your work setting up a foundation to help local crime victims. You've shown your positive attributes. I beg you, in the name of Christ our Lord, not to harm any of our flock."

Guilt burned my face and neck for causing innocent people to be fearful. I laced my fingers over my head. "There's a Swiss Army knife in my pocket, which I'm happy to give you. I never intended to make anyone feel threatened. How can I make this right?" I pointed to the picnic table in the side yard, well away from the parking lot. "If I sit there and wait for the police, can everyone go home? I am sorry to have inconvenienced or frightened anyone."

He looked me in the face. "I believe you, brother. Keep your knife. You mind if I wait with you?"

I sat at the picnic table with my back to the parking lot and my legs tucked between the seat and the table. He sat facing me, called someone inside, and told everyone to leave. His name was Christian Fletcher, and he was the church's lay leader. No relation to the HMS Bounty mutineer. He asked if I would pray with him.

I loosely use the term "prayer" to mean sending good thoughts to others or hoping for a good result, like not getting stuck in a mud hole. Christian meant something entirely different, and while I don't believe in an all-powerful God who intercedes on our behalf, it would do no harm. I bowed my head, let his words wash over me, and reflected on my fervent wishes that Colleen and Valeria and Nana and Niki were all safe on their journeys.

And that Randy Crenshaw's poison would never leave the compound.

ONE HUNDRED FOUR

AN IRON COUNTY SHERIFF'S CRUISER, supported by an Iron River patrol car, pulled into the lot, lights flashing. The officers exited their cars, guns drawn, using their doors as shields. "Seamus," Iron County Sergeant Tex said, "keep your hands on your head where we can see them."

I complied and cranked my neck enough to see him. "Tex, everything is cool." I told Christian that the police would feel much better once he was away from me, and he should take a route that didn't put him between the police and me. "Thank you for staying with me. Please give my apologies to anyone I frightened."

Christian told the officers what he planned to do. I yelled at them to hurry. We had a crime to stop.

Tex snapped cuffs on me. "Next time answer your damn phone."

"I can't. It's sitting on the river bottom."

"That's the first time I heard that one." Tex claimed he wasn't arresting me, but that I was a person of interest. *Right, a person of interest with his hands cuffed.*

"You're lucky on that wound. Only a graze, but there's a lot of dirt in it. When did you have your last tetanus shot?"

I lashed out. "Will you stop worrying about me for one minute and focus on the drug bust you need to make?"

Tex contacted Sheriff Bartelle, who reluctantly gave him permission to drive to Crenshaw's compound for a look-see at the supposed drug operation I had spotted. "Block the road if you think you should, but under no circumstances will you approach any suspects until you have backup. And McCree stays caged."

"You heard the man. Into the back." Tex ducked my head under the frame. "I can't wait to hear this story."

Very crafty of my friend. He hadn't asked a question, meaning Miranda didn't apply, and they could, and would, use anything I said against me. I had lots I wanted to tell him, but given I had killed Bunny, let Rogers go, and broken into the Crenshaw compound, I'd be stupid to say anything without representation present. Hell, I'd already been a fool to point Tex to the compound to investigate Randy Crenshaw.

On our way to the Crenshaw compound, I pointed out the trafficked dirt road. "Have your drug guys check down there. I suspect you'll find they've been cooking meth."

"You know this how?"

"Friendly ravens told me."

A red glow painted the clouds as we came closer to the clearing. Tex accelerated down the narrow road and stopped at Crenshaw's gate. Waves of heat poured from the inferno that had been the house. The roar was so loud he had to shout at his phone to call in the fire. The calm night, recent rain, and the distance between house and woods made it unlikely the fire would spread. I might not believe in prayer, but leaving nothing to chance, I prayed the red gouts of sparks shooting into the sky wouldn't start a forest fire.

Randy Crenshaw's car had not moved. The heat had blistered the paint and melted much of the plastic. The garage doors remained open. I pointed out the spot a four-wheeler had occupied, and Tex called dispatch again and issued a BOLO for Randy Crenshaw.

Tex left me in the back seat with my thoughts, which spiraled around everything that was happening. In one sequence, I acknowledged how lucky I was that Randy had only grazed me, tried to picture the circumstances of my most recent tetanus shot, failed and obsessed about the dirt in the wound, remembered the fresh dirt on the backhoe, and pondered the bare area in the garden.

When Tex finally returned to the car, I begged him to let me show him something. Bartelle's orders wouldn't permit it. "That's fine," I said. "You'll need a search warrant, anyway. Check the bare patch in the garden. I could be way wrong, but there's a good chance they buried one or two bodies under there."

ONE HUNDRED FIVE

THE DOCTORS AT THE HOSPITAL cleaned my minor gunshot wound and gave me a tetanus booster. We reached the Iron County Jail at three o'clock Wednesday morning. They took an hour to process me into the facility. The mug shot was not my finest.

They woke me for breakfast and took me from there to the interrogation room, where they read me my rights, but claimed they had not charged me. I made it clear I had nothing to say until I spoke with my lawyer. Years ago, Iron County had arrested me for murder. My attorney then was a force of nature from the Traverse City area. My call found her in Petosky, looking for its famous stones. She'd be here late that afternoon. Irene Frankel had to be in her mid-seventies, but she looked much as she had in her sixties. A cropped helmet of gray hair now replaced the dreadlocks she used to wear.

It took me two hours to share the complete details of everything that had happened. Afterward, should they need it, I engaged Irene's services for Colleen—whose whereabouts were unknown—and Niki, who Irene determined was attending a Pendergast Holdings board meeting in Minnesota. "That's fine," she said. "But if it comes to a conflict of interest, you are my client. I'll make sure they get excellent representation."

That made me feel a little better. "Thanks. Now tell me all the reasons I should not give the police the full truth?" Her reservations caused me to avoid saying anything about breaking into the Crenshaw compound.

My interrogation Thursday morning ran for three hours. Their questions focused on how I "claimed" to have become involved with Bunny and Randy Crenshaw and my version of a timeline of events during the last two weeks.

We broke for a long lunch. Before the afternoon session, Irene had a few minutes alone with me. "Colleen's back. She was successful. A doctor examined Valeria. The meds are working well on her Lyme's disease. By the by, she invited me to stay with her at your place. Generous, don't you think?"

I laughed, the first time in days. "Don't let her fool you. She's an accountant and knows about billing by the hour and travel expenses. She's trying to reduce your charges."

Her eyes twinkled. "Back to business. I have news on your case. Not all the Iron County police think you should be in jail. At least one is feeding info to Niki. She also contacted some FBI friends who confirm the Bureau is looking into the Chicago connections.

"Mike Crenshaw ratted out his son, Randy, who claims the whole thing was Bunny's doing. Randy says he discovered she was manufacturing the drugs and storing them at the compound. He was there to destroy them. They found his prints everywhere in and around the trailer where you guessed they were cooking the meth—not exactly supporting his story. Police recovered several portable generators and the battery bank stolen from your neighbor."

"Did they arrest Mike Crenshaw?"

"Not yet, but the more important question is whether they will arrest you. They can hold you today until they finish talking with you, but they can't keep you overnight without charging you."

The afternoon session concluded at six p.m. I had gone over everything multiple times, showing them on plat maps where the events occurred, including the river segment where I had lost my phone. They had mined everything I planned to tell them, and they knew it. Two hours later, Irene informed me the prosecutor had charged me with involuntary manslaughter, obstructing an official police investigation, and a bunch of other miscellaneous crimes tacked on to use as bargaining chips in a plea agreement.

She had other news. They had uncovered Kat's rusty Ford Ranger in the garden plot. Underneath it, they found the bodies of Kat Serrano and Peggy Dowson, the woman choked to death at the motel.

I hadn't wanted to be right, but at least now we knew, and I had kept my promise to the kids. I told Irene that I hoped Colleen could pass the information to Valeria and Nana.

At the bail hearing, the prosecutor recommended no bail because I was a flight risk. Irene observed to the judge that I had had plenty of opportunity to flee the area if that had been my desire. Instead, I had continued my investigation, without which the police would not have uncovered the burial of two women, a prostitution ring, and a drug operation.

She softened her voice. "And why, you may ask, did he do this? Because he promised his granddaughter and her friend he would try as hard as he could to find out what happened to her friend's missing mother. Not just a promise, a pinkie swear. This, more than anything else I can say, proves my client is a man of his word."

Returning to regular volume, she continued. "If your honor wants to question character witnesses, I have several citizen volunteers in court ready to testify. Frankly, your honor, that's a waste of everyone's time. But I'm willing. I get paid by the hour."

She waited until the chuckles subsided. "We ask for no bail. Mr. McCree will surrender his passport and not leave the state without the court's permission. If your honor decides it's warranted, my client consents to wear a monitor. The defendant wants the court and the prosecutor to understand that he insists on his rights to a speedy jury trial. We will brook no delays."

ONE HUNDRED SIX

Two Months Later

A WEEK AWAY FROM HIGH color in my part of the U.P., the oranges and reds of the maples burned in the bright sunlight at Lake Tranquility. The extended McCree clan had conspired to gather for a long weekend. Colleen's bail—they charged her with obstructing an official investigation—required her to remain in Michigan. I gave her the main house to allow her to work remotely twenty-four/seven and retreated to my unimproved guest cabin.

Megan, her parents, and their dog, Atalanta, drove up that morning from Chicago. They had invited my mother, but she claimed a darts exhibition prevented her from coming. I suspected Mom had had all the wilderness she wanted and preferred her city life.

Colleen and I had shuttled food, extra camp chairs, and hammocks to Lake Tranquility. Once Megan and her parents arrived at the rocks on Lukes Road, we brought them the rest of the way by ATVs, Atalanta loping ahead, her Golden Retriever tongue hanging from her mouth. Megan, with Atalanta at her heels, convinced Colleen to check the trail cameras. Paddy and Cindy, happy to entrust their daughter to Colleen, canoed the lake, leaving me to wait for Niki's arrival.

To keep busy, I built a fire for those less enamored than I of the cool autumn day. My new phone chirped—I should say my primary phone. After losing the one, I vowed never to be without a phone again and had purchased a dozen burner phones for emergencies. Niki's message asked me to bring the two-up to the rocks blocking Lukes Road. Could I also have Paddy come with another ATV? I couldn't imagine why she required both ATVs, but figured I'd soon learn.

Colleen returned with Megan and the dog in time for me to substitute her for Paddy. We arrived at the rocks to find Niki and Valeria (with a signed paper giving Niki *in loco parentis* status for the weekend). "Surprised?"

Colleen helped Valeria onto her ATV for the ride to Lake Tranquility. Niki hopped on behind me and gave me a hug. "Nana is doing well. She wishes she could be here too, but we agreed it was unwise, at least for now."

I plugged my ears to mute the squeals celebrating Megan and Valeria's reunion. They hugged and jumped around one another. As they settled down and I unplugged my ears, I realized I was hearing more than their shrieks. Wheeling above us were George, Martha, and Gonzo. They must have heard the girls. I had continued the eagles' training, adding a special act. I handed the kids fishing poles and told them bait was down in the boat house. They had hungry eagles waiting.

The adult humans gathered around the fire, sipping wine and popping beers. I demanded of Niki, "What's happened with Valeria and Nana?"

"A lawyer who supports the folks harboring Nana persuaded Texas to issue Valeria a birth certificate. That proves she's a US citizen. She's making friends in school and doing splendidly. The organization arranged for her to visit a child psychologist. Her ankle has healed, and the antibiotics did the trick against the Lyme's. All good news."

"Indeed," I said. "And Nana?"

"At least with this administration, Nana isn't the type of person they are targeting. How it plays out long term?" Her shoulders rose and fell, and she let out a sigh. "One gigantic piece of wonderful news, Seamus, is your mother was right about Nana's wood carvings. The organization helped her set up an online store. She's already making enough money to support herself and is accepting special orders."

"Excellent." I caught Paddy and Cindy trading meaningful looks. "Okay, you two, what's up? I haven't seen that much silent communication since you told me you were expecting Megan."

"Well . . ." Cindy prodded Paddy with her elbow.

They were pregnant? "I thought—"

"No medical miracles, Dad," Paddy said. "But we are looking at adopting. We have Nana's permission to adopt Valeria. It's a long process, but the lawyers believe there's an excellent chance it will succeed. Neither girl knows. We don't want anyone getting their hopes up."

"Later," Cindy said, "we'd bring Nana to live with us. Not as an employee, just to stay. Remember, mum's the word around the girls. Have you guys heard what happened to that ICE agent Carpenter who harassed you?"

Colleen and I had not.

Niki's evil chuckle caused Atalanta to raise a questioning head and almost made me sympathetic to the asshole. "On the day he tried to catch you at the river, he made one huge mistake. After seeing how flimsy that first gate was, he thought to save time he'd crash through the second one."

I laughed. "Except, I had embedded those poles in concrete."

"Now he knows," Niki said, "and he'll have a permanent limp to remind him of his stupidity. But that's not where his troubles end. I saved his life that day, which I thought gave me the right to talk to a guy I know who's pretty senior in government."

Yeah, like the assistant director of national intelligence with his strong connections to Homeland Security and ICE.

"I mentioned that Agent Carpenter had a cowboy streak and suggested management should reevaluate his work. Surprise, surprise. To justify the warrants to search your property and put trackers on your vehicles, he fudged facts and exaggerated the situation to the judge. I know this investigative reporter in Chicago." She and Cindy Nelson, my daughter-in-law, high-fived it.

Cindy continued the telling. "And I uncovered evidence that suggests he's part of a rogue group of ICE agents we suspect have links to human trafficking rings. Still not a hundred percent. What is certain is that Vincent Otto is brother-in-law to Bunny Crenshaw. Sources say that before she married Mike Crenshaw, she ran an escort service in Chicago. She never stopped running it. We're pretty sure Vincent Otto is the money behind it. I bet he's feeling heat and lashing out."

She drank a slug of beer. "Drew Dombey, the pimp? Found him in a sewage lagoon with two small-caliber holes in his head. I've tracked down several of the party women you photographed. Some are talking now that Bunny and Dombey are dead. The Feds are also looking at this. We keep crossing each other's trail. We'll be ready for our exposé in another month."

I asked, "Anything on Aaron Rogers?" Everyone looked at everyone else. "In the wind, I guess." I wondered what name he was using and where he was. "So far, they haven't arrested Mike Crenshaw. I hear he has the motel, the resort, the Silver Fox, his house, and all his land for sale. I wish I could've added some of his forest property to Megan's trust, but he won't sell to me given I killed his wife and got his kid arrested for producing and selling meth."

Paddy said, "I thought the house fire destroyed all the evidence you found."

My opportunity to provide information. "Randy left traces of meth on the front seat of his car. His tire tracks went to a travel trailer in the woods a mile away where they cooked the meth, and his prints were all around the trailer. As part of our legal discovery process, we received redacted transcripts of police interviews with Glenn Korpi. He claims Bunny went ballistic when she discovered the two guys stealing propane were also cooking meth for Randy. She ordered him to shut down his operation to protect hers. Randy didn't. Korpi claimed Bunny killed those two local guys to warn Randy and had them dumped at my house to cause me trouble. We know one of the Sig Sauer P226s I took from her was the murder weapon."

Cindy said, "The thing I don't understand is why the prosecutor hasn't dropped charges against you two."

Colleen said, "Irene, our lawyer, speculates that he believed we would cop a plea on a lesser charge. Can you believe they offered me a deal to squeal on Seamus? Failing that, he counted on having the extra time to find evidence to build a case or charge us with something else. Three times wrong. Most defendants try to defer the trial. Irene had told them from the get-go that we'd fight any delays. We want our day in court, and we want it now."

"So," Cindy said, "Irene's confident she'll win—even the obstruction charges?"

My throat tightened, recalling Irene's caution that juries come with no guarantees. "What she said was that she planned to call Sheriff Bartelle, Tex, and the Michigan state officer as hostile defense witnesses. None can testify that any of Colleen's or my actions actually hindered their investigations, even if technically we interfered. And that without the information I provided, they would not have broken up the prostitution ring, solved the propane thefts, cracked the meth operation, etc."

Niki slapped her thigh. "The police will despise the prosecutor if he puts them in *that* situation."

"Which," Colleen said, "is why Irene thinks he will drop all charges. And if it goes to trial, the worst we'll get is a hung jury. But—"

From the lake, the kids yelled, "We got fish!"

Paddy and Cindy wanted to see the girls and their eagles. We tied Atalanta to a tree and made a semicircle of the chairs we carted down to the shore. The eagles were circling overhead, calling with their jittering kri-kri-kri. The kids took turns flinging the fish. Martha snagged hers from the air. George and Gonzo missed and grabbed their fish from the water. Megan had the last fish, which was for Gonzo. Trying to launch it "super-duper high," she threw it behind her. It landed at my feet.

"You do it, Grandpa Seamus." And Valeria chimed in, "Yeah, Grandpa Seamus, you throw it."

I grabbed the fish's tail and held it vertically above my head. "I'll show you something better." Gonzo came swooping in and grabbed it from my hand.

Paddy said, "That is one of the stupidest things I've ever seen you do."

Cindy said, "And we've seen you do a lot of dumb stuff. Do you remember the time . . ."

No way I could defend myself; it was pretty stupid. But it was damned exciting to have an eagle eat from my hand.

Niki came to my rescue. "Valeria, did you have something from Nana you wanted to give to Grandpa Seamus?" Niki pulled a bag from her knapsack and gave it to Valeria, who handed it to me.

Tissue paper covered a heavy object eight inches long. I unwound the wrapping and my eyes stung with tears. From a single block of maple, Nana had carved two bald eagles, wings spread behind their backs, their talons extended and linked by their rear claws.

"Turn it over." Valeria grabbed it from me and flipped it. "Read the bottom."

The base had a brass sliding plate with the etched words "Pinkie Swear."

"Open it, Grampa Seamus." Valeria shoved it into my hands. She was twitching with anticipation.

I slid open the plate. Nestled inside was the granite stone Niki had given Valeria to signify my oath. My heart swelled and pressed against my chest. I couldn't speak. How was I so lucky to have Valeria and Nana enter my life? I motioned Valeria to me and wrapped her in my arms. I regained control of my voice and whispered, "I can't tell you how much this means to me."

Her arms pulled me in tight. "I love you, too, Grampa Seamus."

I hope you enjoyed reading this story. To help me reach other readers, I would appreciate your posting a short review of *Granite Oath* on your favorite retailer or review website.

THIS BOOK WOULD NOT EXIST had it not been for you, my readers. You asked for another story with Seamus and his family, and you wanted it set in Michigan's Upper Peninsula. A special shout out to my Reader's Group who helped pick the name for the "G" novel and choose (and improve) the book cover from several options.

Most of the roads and geography referenced in this story are real. I've spent many enjoyable days exploring the interconnected logging roads, skidder trails, lakes, and rivers of Iron County, Michigan often accompanied by my son, Brad Jackson. Recently, I've been spending more time exploring the adjacent sections of Baraga County accompanied by Lisa, Craig, and Dani Cherry and Courtney Ainsworth. Despite that detailed knowledge, I have taken liberty with the exact locations and numbers of camps, beaver dams, gates, and trails. Lake Tranquility lives only on these pages.

Although I have used many real businesses in this tale of fiction, I have invented several others. The motel in Iron Mountain, the Menominee Rapids Resort, and the Silver Fox are complete figments of my imagination and not based on any existing establishments. You won't find the Northwoods Second Coming of Jesus Christ Church among Iron County's many fine religious establishments. Nor can you reserve a spot for your child or grandchild next summer at the Amasa Summer Creative Arts Academy.

The story refers to several actual police organizations. Over the years I have talked with many professionals from the Iron County Sheriff's Department and the Michigan State Police and watched them work. I've always found them to be great professionals. This is not a police procedural, and I've taken liberties with normal investigation practices.

Gabriel Belanger won a silent auction that benefited The Friends of the Crystal Falls District Community Library. Instead of having me name a character after himself, he chose to give his mother, Kim Belanger, that "pleasure." Neither had a choice in which character I picked, but I did make sure Kim was okay with the idea.

Carl Dickson looked over the Spanish phrases I used. Debra Goldstein told me that it didn't matter how I spelled bupkes/bubkes/bupkis, someone would complain, and I should go with whichever one I preferred. My two eagle-eyed early readers, Carol J. Baldridge and Dottie Caster, prevented me from committing many abuses of the English language. Jan Rubens is always my first, last, and best reader. After all their hard work, I make further "improvements," and so I take full responsibility for any mistakes.

I love to hear from readers. Drop me a note and let me know how you liked the story or that you found a typo so I can correct it for future editions. My email is jmj@jamesmjackson.com.

James M. Jackson
Amasa, Michigan

HIJACKED LEGACY

A Seamus McCree Novel

James M. Jackson

First Edition
Trade Paperback Edition: April 2024

Wolf's Echo Press
PO Box 54
Amasa, MI 49903
www.WolfsEchoPress.com

ISBN-13 Trade Paperback: 978-1-943166-39-8
ISBN-13 e-book: 978-1-943166-40-4
ISBN Audiobook   978-1-943166-41-1
Library of Congress Control Number: 2024930796

Printed in the United States of America
10987654321

HIJACKED LEGACY

A Seamus McCree Novel (#8)

DEDICATION

*For my chosen and given tribes,
united by chaos and love.*

SIX MONTHS PRIOR

TYLER

TYLER GRIPPED THE STEERING WHEEL so hard he thought it might crack. These first five days working back in the office had been the worst. Two wasted hours commuting each day. COVID had proved he could do the work better at home, but it was the boss's way or the highway. Even with unemployment at "record lows," few employers would consider him. He was stuck at his job, stuck on the Mass Pike, stuck in life.

He was curious what had caused Charlene to insist they move their monthly get-together forward to today. It had better be damned important to force him to drive through this rush-hour crap. And parking near her Dorchester apartment was going to be a bitch on a Friday. Zach, who worked from home, would take off early and snag an easy parking space. While Tyler crept toward his exit off the Mass Pike, he patted a slosh of Old Spice onto his cheeks and neck. Charlene liked him to smell nice.

Traffic moved better once he reached the Southeast Expressway. He pulled into the alley that passed for a street near Charlene's place and found a single on-street-parking spot three houses away. Had to be an omen that Charlene's summons was about something good.

At the door of the three-family, he pressed the bell for the second floor. With a metallic buzz, the lock disengaged. He thumped up the staircase. Charlene met him at her door with a Sam Adams in each hand. "Zach's here." She handed him a brew and closed the door behind them.

Tyler swished the sweet combination of malt and honey to warm it up before it froze his throat going down and took a slug from the sweaty bottle. "Hits the spot." He stepped on the heels of his tennies, kicked them onto the mat Charlene had placed by the door, and donned the slippers she insisted they wear. At the time she'd given them the slippers, she said, "I don't want to keep vacuuming your dirt."

He followed Charlene into the kitchen, rinsed the now dead Sam

Adams, and grabbed a second from the fridge. He sniffed the air like a hound on scent, picked up only a hint of lemon from the dish soap dispenser. "I'll bite. What's for dinner?"

Charlene gave him the stare she had perfected during her five years in the Boston City Police Department. He held up his hands in surrender. "Officer Bendick, what's twisted your tail?"

She smiled, swatted his bicep. "That's Officer Bendick, sir, to you, Mr. Kemp. I didn't have time to cook and ordered lasagna from Mama Risa's. Now that you're finally here, I can share all the news."

He couldn't decide from her mixed messages whether it was good news or bad and followed her into the living room. Zach had commandeered the lounger and was leaning over his laptop, eyes squinched like he didn't like what he was seeing.

Tyler tapped the beer lightly against the side of Zach's head. "Wassup, bro?"

Zach pointed to his screen. "I don't believe this shit."

Charlene puffed out her five-three frame. "What, you thought I lied?" To Tyler she said, "The judge dismissed the case because the star witness washed up on the banks of the Charles, all her fingers and toes broken."

Zach looked up from his laptop. "After torturing her, they bashed in her skull." He rotated his computer to show Tyler the information he had pulled from the web where the kid from MIT who had found her posted the cellphone pictures.

Bad news then. Tyler stated the obvious: "She dies. The drug dealer gets away with everything. The guy had a reputation. Why wasn't she protected?"

Charlene began pacing. "The prosecutor offered. Her boyfriend is a rich dude, invented one of those multi-player shoot-'em-up games. He paid for private security."

Zach said, "Phoenix Bluff. It's really the nuts. It launched our sophomore year. I can't tell you how much time I spent playing it. We . . ."

The look Charlene gave him could have frozen lava. "The big news is that rich guy caught me outside the courthouse and offered a quarter million bucks if I quote-unquote made sure the guy could never harm anyone ever again."

Tyler went still. Charlene, no matter how upset she was about the woman getting killed or the drug dealer skating on the charges, wouldn't have gotten them together to cry on their shoulders. They had no secrets between them—well, few secrets—but emotional support wasn't their thing. She called them together because she was considering killing the dealer. Did she realize that or was getting them together some subconscious thing?

She had bent their ears many times since she had become police about how the justice system failed the victims, how something needed to be done to the worst of the worst who seemed untouchable. "Oh sure," she'd once complained, "eventually we get them. But, shit, Whitey Bulger was damn near eighty by the time they caught him." That, she maintained, was not justice. Tyler and Zach totally agreed. But what could you do?

A quarter-million is serious bucks. Like, six times what he brought home in a year before taxes. Somebody offered him that much, he'd do it. That thought gave him a jolt of energy. It would take serious planning to get away with it, but that might be half the fun. He kept excitement from his voice and asked, "You think he meant it, or was he just blowing off steam?"

"Oh, he meant it. Told me he'd pay in bitcoin so no one could trace it. Said if I didn't want to do it myself, he'd give me a ten percent finder's fee and pay whoever I found the two-fifty large." She shook her head, looked like she was replaying the conversation in her mind. "Definitely. And from Zach's reaction to who the guy is, I suspect to him that's chump change."

One thing didn't make sense to Tyler. Why had the guy approached Charlene? He asked her.

A smile twitched across her face. "He might have heard me mutter that the asshole needed to die. Like tomorrow."

Tyler looked at Zach to gauge his reaction. He was still tapping on his laptop. The guy was a friggin' genius in the cyber world—not so much with the real one. If Tyler wanted this, it was up to him to move this conversation forward. "Charlene, are you telling us you want to do it? If you're asking us to help, I'm in."

At Zach's wide-eyed stare, a flash of worry crossed his mind. Tyler hadn't intended to say that, but it was out there now.

Charlene stopped pacing, dropped onto her bean bag, tugged her hair, and stared up at the ceiling.

Zach, seemingly oblivious to Charlene's distress, said, "You guys remember me mentioning Adam Smith?"

Tyler's worry bloomed into frustration. What the hell was Zach talking about? "From history class?" he asked. "The guy who wrote *Wealth of Nations?*"

Zach snorted. "Never heard of it. I mean the high-priced hit man who called himself the Happy Reaper."

Charlene and Tyler shared a look that said, "Here he goes."

"Last I heard," Charlene said, "he was doing life in maximum security."

"True, but—stay with me on this—what if we reincarnated his business model? We," he waved his arm to include all three of them, "become the Happy Reaper. Charlene takes the finder's fee. The new Happy Reaper does the job, and we split two-seventy-five three ways. That's ninety-one thousand, six hundred, sixty-six dollars and sixty-six cents. Two cents left, we can draw straws for them."

Holy shit. This was getting real. The crap about becoming the Happy Reaper was bullshit, but Zach was in. Tyler was in. Was Charlene? Or were they supposed to convince her to forget it? Ever since he had first met Charlene in Mrs. Popovich's third grade class, he'd known she had a dark side. It was ironic that she'd become the cop because she'd been the one who in sixth grade took revenge on that girl spreading lies. While cutting off hanks of the girl's hair, she'd 'accidentally' sliced her cheek. Tyler got suspended for a month for holding the kid down. What was her name?—Molly something. Totally worth it. No one spread rumors targeting Charlene again. Or messed with him.

She'd had the idea in high school to screw with her cheating boyfriend's car. He'd suggested keying the car. Instead, Zach had fried the electronics. That had cost the guy a shit-ton more than buffing out some scratches.

Charlene may not yet know she's planning to take down this miscreant, but she will. He tuned back in to what Zach was saying.

". . . portal, and we can duplicate the cards he left with each victim. They had a Celtic Cross on one side—green and blue colors. On the other is his tagline: Results Guaranteed. We'd set up our own payment system. The bitcoin—"

Charlene leaped to her feet, knocking over her empty beer bottle that rattled on the wooden floor. "Stop."

Now's the time to give her a little shove across the finish line. He walked to her, stooped, and put an arm around her shoulder. "You want to do this. We're with you. I've been practicing at the range. I'm solid to a thousand yards. Happy to help." He thought, don't oversell, and watched her intently.

Charlene hadn't interrupted or objected. Zach wasn't fantasizing. He was definitely in. Charlene's face transformed from thundercloud at what she probably thought was Zach yanking her chain to the faintest curling of her lips. Tyler knew that look. It was the same one she'd had in tenth grade before stripping and accepting the dare to leap naked from the cliff into the water-filled quarry.

Tyler said, "We're made for this. You can even the scales of justice. Zach gets to run the Happy Reaper's websites and set up a payment portal to accept bitcoin. I get to use the sniper skills the Army taught me. And we get paid."

Charlene broke from his hug. "I will not take a penny."

They discussed various scenarios over two more rounds of beer and progressed to specifics during dinner. Tyler still wasn't sure about Charlene's commitment until she suggested they draw straws to determine who would do the hit. He felt destined to win first dibs and suffered a huge letdown when Charlene pulled the winner.

Zach was content to set up all the computer shit. That left Tyler helping Charlene do recon and practicing long-distance kill shots at the range.

It wasn't that $137,500 would make him rich, but it would change his life. And he was confident this was not a one and done.

Monday, October 17, 2022

THE HAPPY REAPER

HIS THIRD FULL DAY ON the lam, and the Happy Reaper figured his luck was holding. He was driving a RAV-4 with a Florida license plate he had lifted from a vehicle of the same make, model, and color, and only a year older. "In God We Trust" the plate said. Maybe, but everyone else was out for themselves, including those he'd hired for $2.5 million to engineer his escape. Which was why by the time anyone official realized he was gone, he'd driven across Massachusetts and traded the "safe" car his liberators had provided him for the RAV-4 he stole from Economy Lot E of the Albany International Airport. That was one dude who should think twice before using a magnetic key holder box again.

He had avoided the interstate system with its toll booths and license plate readers and bypassed cities with their ubiquitous cameras. What with the extra miles, lower speeds, and the frequent stops required to fight his exhaustion, he had doubled normal driving times to reach his storage area north of Chicago. Every stop gave him the willies. One curious cop tapping on the window while he slept in his car could spoil everything.

Phase one—getting here—done. Now came phase two—the hunt.

He punched his password into the keypad. The lock disengaged with an electronic whir. He entered the unit, noted the stale air, and locked the door behind him. Everything was as he had left it, ignoring six years of dust that tickled his nose.

He packed the RAV-4 with more guns and ammunition than an average right-wingnut prepper possessed. All IDs and credit cards had expired during his six-year absence except the Harland Walter Gottkind passport. No credit cards meant he'd continue to use cash. He stuffed his glove box with enough C-notes to last a couple of months. He didn't want to waste time finding the right person to create new IDs before dealing with Seamus McCree. So, he was Gottkind, should anyone ask.

His phone app claimed he would arrive at McCree's place on Shank Lake by two p.m. He drove exactly three miles above the speed limit. With breaks to stretch his legs and grab lunch, he figured three o'clock was more like it.

From then on, he'd improvise based on whether Seamus was home. Either immediately, or once Seamus showed up, they'd have the promised *mano a mano* contest. Wouldn't exactly be sporting because Seamus never carried a gun, but that was on McCree. They both knew what would happen.

Should he say anything or spare Seamus the few seconds of knowing he would die and just do it? He had five hours to decide.

SEAMUS

THE FANFARE OF A TRUMPETER swan family that had taken up residence on Shank Lake woke me that mid-October day. I opened my eyes to the gray of predawn light filtered through the trees. With no reason to rise with the swans, I lay on the bed and stretched: my toes curling down and my arms reaching up. At sixty-one—to be exact, sixty-one years, six months, and two days—my spine lengthened the same way a freight train does, its engine pulling forward, extending tension to the couplings. My spine was quieter than a train starting up, providing only one audible pop. That made me confident that standing, my height would still be its full seventy-four inches.

Three distinct swan voices came from the lake. The calling adult pair resembled loud trumpets with mutes in place that deadened the sound. Their nearly full-grown cygnet's bleats could have come from a toy trumpet like the one I had given my granddaughter, Megan, for her last birthday.

Her parents, especially my stay-at-home son, Paddy, were not thrilled with my gift. I smiled, remembering the back-and forth-negotiations between Megan and her father that resulted in Megan selling the toy to him for three times what it had cost me. Once the money and trumpet changed hands, I told Megan that nothing in the deal with her father prevented her from buying another one and selling him that one, too. Paddy became apoplectic. Hey, every nine-year-old should learn practical economics and to understand the fine print in contracts; who better to teach her than her grandfather?

The cacophony on the lake escalated in a prelude to the swans taking off. Trumpeter swans can't leap into the air like most ducks. They use their wings to propel themselves, running on the water to reach takeoff speed. Their calls cease during their liftoff—I figure they're concentrating on getting airborne. Instead, their wingtips smack the surface, producing rifle-shot percussive slaps. I closed my eyes and counted the wing beats until liftoff. Fifteen. Once airborne, they celebrated with more calls that echoed around the lake as they sped toward nearby feeding grounds.

I let my ears continue birding. A late flock of robins was the loudest, but I also ticked my mental checklist for several other species. An overnight weather front had triggered millions of migrating birds to ride the favorable winds on their journey south. Those I was hearing were some of the later migrants to land around my neck of Michigan's Upper Peninsula. They required rest and food to restore their fat stores for the next leg of their trip—hopefully before the snows flew.

I had already prepared for my nonmigratory winter: plenty of stacked seasoned firewood to warm the house, trails cleared and ready for cross-country skiing and snowshoeing, plow attachment on my Bobcat skidsteer to keep the driveway and roads open.

Best, I had only two projects to complete before I could settle in for a long, contented winter. Plus, a nagging voice in my head reminded, one criminal trial to win. That assumed the damn prosecutor still insisted on bringing the case to trial. Everyone told him he had no chance of convincing a jury to convict me and my sister Colleen Carpetti, even though we were guilty as hell. The trial would waste time and money. Unlike Colleen, I had plenty of both.

Life, I thought, does not get much better than this.

From the foot of the lake a pair of resident barred owls hooted, asking, "Who. Who. Who cooks for y'all?" Since Colleen wouldn't return until Saturday and today was only Monday, if I wanted a hot breakfast, the answer to the owls' question was obvious. With light streaming onto the porch, I had no excuse not to get up. I converted my porch bed into a rustic settee, filled my bird feeders, and scattered seed on the ground.

The day's weather sounded perfect to spend searching for elusive spruce grouse on land held in trust for Megan. My immediate project was to complete a proposal to the USDA to fund habitat improvements on that land. All that remained was to finish mapping every place I spotted spruce grouse. Between today and tomorrow, I figured I could cover all the remaining territories. That left me more than a month to file the application.

With miles of hiking planned for the day, I cooked and ate a thousand calories of buckwheat flapjacks drowned in maple syrup made from my sugar maple trees. Figuring I'd have a late dinner, I filled my day pack with two full water bottles, a twenty-ounce diet Dr Pepper, a brick of cheese, and a baggie filled with gorp.

What else? I included binocs, a GPS device to record the precise location of each sighting, and two spare pairs of socks for the inevitable soakers I'd get trekking through the spruce wetlands the grouse loved. Before heading out, I did a slow spin to make sure I had everything. Sure enough, I couldn't take notes on my cell phone if I left it plugged into the wall socket.

I ATV'd to the farthest site I still needed to map. That area was a bust, but in the second location, I spotted a covey of four spruce grouse feeding high in the trees. While I recorded the details, my phone chirped. I had a message from Colleen. *We need to talk. Now!*

I had hoped my second project would not interfere with today's outing. Arrangements were under control for the party I was throwing in less than three weeks to celebrate my mother turning eighty-five. Colleen lived near Mom in metro Boston and had agreed to handle the invitations. Colleen wanted everything buttoned down, and Mom was . . . flexible.

I checked the phone's signal: enough to text, but not enough for voice.

Me: *What did Mom do?*

Colleen: *Wants a darts competition to raise money for charity*

Me: *OK. It's her party.*

Colleen: *There will be betting. Will Kavanaugh's Tavern allow?*

I hooted, startling the grouse into flight. Their rapid wingbeats pulsed the air. Colleen, who is my half-sister, didn't grow up in Boston and didn't know Kavanaugh's, an Irish cop's bar. After my father's murder in the line of duty, my Uncle Mike had taken me there for my first, decidedly underage, drink. It was where I had held Uncle Mike's wake six years ago. I'd bet they had a bookie *on staff.*

Me: *It's an Irish pub. Bartender will hold the money.*

After a moment's reflection, I added, *What's really bothering you?*

Colleen: *She keeps inviting more people*

I considered repeating "*It's her party*" but decided that was not helpful. We had the entire bar for the afternoon. I had arranged for a couple of off-duty Boston City cops to check invites. My instructions allowed invitees to bring a guest—no party crashers, though. And everyone must be twenty-one or have a bona fide parent in tow.

Me: *Don't worry about $$. It's all good.*

Before she replied, I added: *Will be in the woods all day. I'll respond this evening.*

My phone dinged another message. I placed the phone into "Airplane Mode" and enjoyed the rest of the day.

By the time I returned home, my sports watch recorded I had walked 14.74 miles in eight hours and six minutes. I had used both pairs of spare socks, needed a third, and didn't care. My sightings included twenty-seven spruce grouse, forty-three other bird species, a moose cow with twins, a bobcat, and a bear with triplets—the first time I had ever seen triplet bear cubs.

And, blessedly, not a single human.

That luck did not hold.

CHARLENE

CHARLENE BUZZED ZACH IN. ONCE he'd swapped dirty shoes for slippers, she handed him a Sam Adams. "Tyler beat you here by a few minutes." On their way to the living room, she showed him receipts for the Powerball tickets she had bought the threesome. "Had to, with the expected prize being more than a quarter-billion."

Zach squinted an eye, like he was doing a calculation in his head. "We win, I'm buying a house on Beacon Hill. I'll stand on my balcony and look down my nose at everyone. What about youse guys?"

Charlene clinked bottles with Zach and pointed him to the lounger he preferred. She flopped onto the beanbag on the floor. "You want to live on snooty Beacon Hill? Even with the money, I'd still want to be a cop and take down the bad guys. I'd buy this house from the owner and rent the other two units to pay for the taxes and upkeep."

The thud of something hitting the floor in the apartment above rattled the walls and yanked their attention to the ceiling. "Change that. I would evict that guy and move up to the third floor." She waved at Tyler to let him know it was his turn.

"Me? Dividing the prize three ways we'd each have eighty million before taxes. Plenty to live on, which would be a gigantic relief because this afternoon I told my boss to shove it. I'm officially working full time on our little enterprise."

Zach gave him a high-five.

Interesting. Charlene munched a handful of peanuts, felt a tingle in her right cheek as salt found the spot she had bitten earlier in the day. Didn't stop her from eating more—she loved the taste of salt. She half-listened to the guys talking hypotheticals about winning the lottery while considering how she could move the conversation to the real issue that worried her.

She'd known Tyler since third grade. Even then, he had wanted to achieve results his way. He liked rules, especially if he made them up, and took great offense if someone didn't play by them. He hated in others what he was majorly guilty of doing himself, a flaw he shared with those closeted-gay legislators who were the loudest LGBT-bashers.

The dude did not suffer fools gladly or silently. Bosses included. Insubordination got him in trouble in the Army—that, and landing a right hook on the chin of a major who refused to see Tyler's point. Less than three months after his graduation from the sniper course, the Army expelled him with a less than honorable discharge. The chip on Tyler's shoulder was the size of Nantucket. The jobs he could get without an honorable discharge were crap. And paid crap.

But he didn't learn from that. His intolerance and big mouth had caused him to quit or be fired from several jobs. He was no longer welcome at the LARP events that still occupied many of their friend Zach's weekends. Tyler had loved the live-action role-playing, and some of his costumes were outrageously good. But at any minor infraction, he went ballistic on the guilty party and insisted on informing the guys in charge *exactly* how they should do their job.

Zach may have introduced the idea of taking on the Happy Reaper persona, but Tyler molded the role to fit his style. He fancied himself the personification of Barry Eisler's fictional hired assassin John Rain. He wanted rules like Rain: target principals only, no family members to "send a message." And if someone hired him, they couldn't hire anyone else for the same job. But he fancied himself a modern man. While Rain wouldn't kill women or children, Tyler figured women's rights had earned them the honor of being targets. No kids, though. And no pets. Not that she or Zach had ever suggested targeting kids or pets. Why would they?

Yep, appropriating the role of the Happy Reaper with his principled promise of "Results Guaranteed" fit Tyler like a glove. And now that he had quit his job, he'd push to accept more paying work.

Had Charlene created her own Frankenstein?

Even with all Tyler's faults, she had never had a more loyal friend. He'd had her back, even if she didn't need it. He'd supported her justice platform from the get go—provided they had a plan.

Zach was geekdom at its finest. He still lived in his parents' basement even though he was earning decent six figures doing whatever he did with gaming code. But, like a butterfly in a field of flowers, he flitted from one interest to another. To Zach, this was another LARP event, except the violence was real. Eventually, he'd lose interest in the Happy Reaper and justice killings and throw himself at some new lust.

She shook her head, remembering how he'd approached his first "assignment." He'd devoted all his spare time to hacking into the Happy Reaper's enterprise. That done, he devoured literature on whether killing in real life was as good as killing in online games. Surprise: he liked it even better, and now he just wanted to kill stuff.

With an eighty-million-dollar Powerball win, she wouldn't need Zach's dark-web pages designed to attract people willing to pay big bucks to have someone killed. She could pay the two guys herself—or just Tyler, once Zach lost interest. But who could blame them for dreaming big? She'd been the one who bought the tickets.

Thing was, they had to stop dreaming and deal with reality. This Happy Reaper thing had been the tail on her dog. Now it was the lead, pulling the dog in a new direction.

With a slug of beer, she rinsed her mouth of peanut debris, waited for a conversational lull. "Guys, let's focus. Before we each provide our assignment updates, there's something else we need to discuss. Adam Smith, the original Happy Reaper, escaped three days ago."

That got their attention.

"They transferred him to a hospital. He was suffering shortness of breath and chest pains. The next morning, a nurse went to wake him. Instead of

Smith, she discovered a dead patient their system showed had been transferred to a local funeral home. Someone had rigged the machines to report the corpse had a regular heartbeat, was breathing, the whole nine yards." She looked at Zach. "That something you could do?"

"Sure, if I knew how the machines worked." He accessed his cellphone. "Probably a heart-rate monitor. Let me—"

Squirrel! "Later, Zach. My sources say they have no clue what happened. The security cameras showed nothing. The question is, does the real Happy Reaper being on the loose change anything for us?"

Tyler shook his head, sending his wavy hair flopping from side to side. "An old, dying man? He'll find someplace nice to breathe his last. At least nicer than dying in prison."

Charlene said, "Do we know how sick he is? And he's not that old, roughly our parents' age. Do you think it will bother him that we appropriated his website and Zach left that 'Results Guaranteed' card in Alabama? Should we postpone our planned action against McCree? You know, in case Smith plans to do something himself? And what about Tyler's Silicon Valley angel?"

SEAMUS

IT WAS NEARLY FIVE BY the time I returned home. I planned to hydrate, take a shower, and, after dinner, pop onto the lake in a kayak for a sunset paddle. The jukebox occupying my brain kicked in "April is in my mistress' face," an English madrigal by Thomas Morley I had sung years ago. No longer remembering all the words, I hummed some combination of the bass part and the soprano while bass was tacet. *April is in my mistress' face; July in her eyes hath place; September in her bosom, but December in her heart.*

Before going into the house, I diverted to the garage to dispose of my garbage. The garage door stuck, as it often did ever since the beginning of summer when my Bobcat had tangled with a rope. It had pulled the door off its track and bent the bottom panel. A neighbor and I had repaired the door—well, to be fair, the neighbor did the repairs; I was his go-fer.

I gave the obstreperous door a solid thwack, feeling the reverb in my elbow, jerked the door open, and froze at cold metal pressing my neck.

A voice I recognized from years ago said, "What is it with you and garage doors?"

My mouth dried in an instant. My scrotum clenched. I closed my eyes and expected to see a highlight reel of my life flash by. Instead, the Happy Reaper's words returned me to fifteen years earlier. He had surprised me at a sticky garage door at my then Cincinnati house. He'd spared my life. Nine years later, with tables turned, I had let him live. But I had not let him go, even after his iron voice promised that if I did not, he would feel duty-bound to kill all the McCrees.

Later, I saved his life in prison, and he had magnanimously offered to exact revenge on only me, *mano a mano*. The threat had been hollow. He'd been in a maximum-security prison serving consecutive life sentences. Either he had reincarnated multiple times or he'd escaped.

His sour breath tickled the raised hairs on my neck. If I had my friend Niki's skills, I could disarm him. I visualized a reverse leg sweep, tensed my muscles, and a new thought iced me. Without her skills, I wouldn't succeed. I'd change his aim and instead of killing me, he'd leave me a vegetable.

Don't put that thought out there. Relaxing my muscles, I recognized the hollow feeling in my chest as deep regret for things left undone. Leaving Colleen in the lurch and ruining Mom's party. Not finishing the spruce grouse study for Megan. Oh Megan, I so much wanted to see how you would change the world. For—what was he waiting for?

Was he a cat playing with Seamus, the mouse? I licked my top lip, brushing my mustache with my tongue. "You planning to gloat? Tell me how you've always been better than me?"

He stepped back, pulling away the metal I assumed was a gun. "Amazing how people handle fear. Some pee their pants. Others grovel. I compress mine into a miniature black hole and don't allow it to see the light of day. You do snarky and impatient. Drop the stuff and turn around. I have a proposition."

I considered reminding him that the physics of his fear-eating black hole meant it would consume him from the inside. He may know that and not care. Not the time for a physics lesson. I opened my hands and let gravity take the diet Dr Pepper bottle and plastic wrap that had protected the cheese block.

I faced the Happy Reaper for the first time since I'd saved his life that day a fellow inmate had slit his throat.

No April in *his* face, which was bloated and preternaturally shiny, like someone on prednisone. His gray eyes radiated with the fierceness of July's sun. I did not know what was in his bosom, but December certainly still inhabited his heart. I shivered. "You look like shit. A proposition?"

"Heart failure. A genetic gift from my father, who died at forty-seven. Thanks for asking. If it wouldn't be too much trouble to get a glass of water and sit on your deck? You're smart. You know what happens if you try anything. Thing is, I have a problem. Help me solve it, I'll call us even."

ZACH

ZACH IGNORED THE ANGRY GLARE Tyler directed at him. Sure, he'd left the Happy Reaper "Results Guaranteed" card on the mantel after he'd bashed the guy's head with his own bowling trophy. But it wasn't like they hadn't agreed. Charlene had found an original card in an old Boston case file. Zach had the computer setup to duplicate it and print it off. Tyler had been all in.

Now Tyler didn't like it because the operation hadn't gone exactly as they had planned. He'd even emailed Zach to tell him how disappointed he was with Zach's "judgment." Well, that's life. Right? Time to put that assignment in the rear-view window. "Before we talk new business, let's finish the old-business part of our agenda. There's a reason Robert's Rules puts the old ahead of the new."

Tyler's mouth opened, probably to challenge that statement. Zach pressed on. "The intel we developed regarding my target's routine was spot on." He didn't need to remind them that he alone had developed that information. "I used the electronic lock pick on the kitchen door and ensconced myself in the target's house an hour before he got home. You know how hard it is to wait sixty minutes when you can't do anything that might leave DNA traces? Thank goodness I had installed games on the burner phone."

Tyler spun his hands, telling him to speed it up.

It was his story. He'd tell it as he wanted. "The target returned from his squash match at ten-nineteen, right in the time window we'd predicted. The neighborhood was real quiet. No lawnmowers or leaf blowers. Even with a silencer, I thought neighbors might hear gunshots. So, when I saw the bowling trophies on the mantle, I grabbed one shaped like a bowling pin with a marble base. I could one-hand it, which allowed me to keep the gun in the other hand. Good thinking, huh?"

Tyler rolled his eyes. Charlene said it made sense to her. "But the newspaper said he died in his living room. He came in from the garage, right? Entered the kitchen?"

The details came to Zach clearly, like he had returned to the scene. The garage door squealed up announcing the target's arrival. Zach pressed himself against the wall, gripped the neck of the trophy, and held it low like a cricket bat. The screech of the garage door closing was loud. Had he known, he could have shot the guy right in the kitchen. Something to keep in mind for the future. Funny that a guy that rich had a squeaky door.

He mentally practiced taking one step with his right foot and slamming the trophy up into the guy's chops. All the pro athletes used visualization to perfect their style. The target dawdled in the kitchen. Finally, Zach caught the slap of a sneaker on the oak floor. Two. Three. Four.

At the sight of a hand in the doorway, Zach yelled like an Olympic shot-putter, pushed off the wall, and swung up with an exhilarating power he didn't realize he possessed. The trophy nailed the guy under his nose. His momentum carried him into the living room. Zach laid the pistol down and double-handed the trophy and—"

Tyler said, "We get the picture. The real question is why you didn't get away before the maid showed up."

Leave it to Tyler to spoil his enjoyment of reliving the kill. "I dropped the trophy by the body and realized the perfect spot for the card was to replace the bowling trophy. Get it? A different kind of trophy?"

Neither one seemed to understand the joke. And it was a good one, too.

Charlene drained her beer bottle. "Tell us about the girl."

The cleaning lady was a total surprise. The cops agreed: she was there on the wrong day. The front door opened, and he froze like a Rodin sculpture. She called a hello. He sent her a silent message to leave.

She hadn't.

"What choice did I have?" Zach hated the pleading sound in his voice. "She freaked at the blood and ran. I shot her. Damn fine shooting, too. Only pulled the trigger once and killed her."

Tyler said, "Then why did you put two more slugs in her head?"

"Because, you dumb ass, I didn't know the first shot had killed her.

What did you want me to do, check her pulse? All professionals use a double tap to the skull. Don't you read anything? Nothing I could have done differently."

Zach read disagreement on Tyler's face and pointed at Charlene. "You would have done the same."

Charlene patted his arm. "What's done is done."

"Except—"

Charlene talked over Tyler. "Zach completed the assignment. Dressing like a CSI meant he didn't leave any DNA or prints. It's unfortunate we caused a bystander death. That could have happened to any of us. It doesn't matter what you or I might have done differently, Tyler. We weren't there. Now, can we discuss whether to continue our next assignments or wait to see what Adam Smith does?"

THE HAPPY REAPER

THE HAPPY REAPER FOLLOWED SEAMUS at a distance to avoid any of those soccer-style moves McCree had pulled off in the past. Once in the house, he had Seamus drop his backpack, pour them each something to drink, and arrange the deck chairs to face each other. The Happy Reaper chose the chair closer to the door. He corralled a side table with his foot and dragged it to where he could place his water glass on it.

Seamus sat in the other chair, sipped from the glass of red wine he had poured from a spout on the side of a box, and set the glass on the deck. He said, "Before we get to business, would you indulge my curiosity and tell me how you escaped?"

"What do you know about heart failure?"

Seamus opened his hands and stared at them. "Your heart muscle isn't strong enough to pump all the blood from your heart. Fluids build in your lungs causing you to tire easily. If you're not careful, you'll bloat from fluid buildup. Eventually, other organs, like your kidneys, fail because of chemical imbalances."

"Close. The organ issues apply more to severe congestive heart failure than to me. My heart will stop long before the other stuff happens. Dead is still dead. Thing is, some asshole is pretending to be me."

"That's a common hazard when your name is Adam Smith."

Still snarky. Still afraid. He half-heartedly waved the pistol in Seamus's direction. "My sense of humor is as diminished as my heart capacity. If you still have your Google Alert set up to check for the Happy Reaper, you might have seen a brief article in an Alabama newspaper. Some douche in Birmingham gets whacked—sounded like he deserved it—and the killer leaves behind one of my Results Guaranteed cards with the Celtic Cross on the back."

Behind Seamus's glasses, his steel-blue eyes widened at that information. "Once they convicted you, I deleted the alert, and I don't bother with the so-called news."

The Happy Reaper laid a hand over his heart. "Now that hurts. Not. Your eyes tell me you have questions."

"Any idea if the card was original or a copy?"

"None. Yet."

McCree tilted his head. "Yet?"

"We'll get to that. What else?"

McCree sipped his wine, tugged his beard. "What's his motivation? Copycat? Trying to throw the cops off with a false clue?" A pause. "Homage to your greatness?"

He's engaged, even with the snark. The weight of those questions squeezed the Happy Reaper's lungs. He drank half the glass of water before he could reply. "You jest at homage, but if you saw the complimentary letters I get every week . . ." He paused, caught his breath. "Here's more information for your consideration. Not long after my arrest, someone found and emptied two of the offshore accounts where I hid my money. I waited and watched for more shoes to drop."

Seamus sipped his wine and waved for the Happy Reaper to continue.

"Nothing, which meant I still had plenty to fund my escape. This spring, someone brought live the dormant portal I used to solicit business on the dark web. They solicited hit jobs using my marketing material. Results guaranteed. The card. The whole deal. Don't worry *how* I know. Let's say a satisfied former customer provided proof."

McCree rocked his chair, sipped more wine. "So copycat."

"Thief. And what's worse, they have not maintained my level of ethical practice."

McCree grimaced, probably because the Happy Reaper applied the term ethical to himself. But he *had* applied principles to his work. In fulfilling his contracts, he had never hurt an innocent bystander, let alone killed one. He reminded Seamus of that point of honor. "This guy is sloppy. He lets someone see him making the hit and whacks the witness, a pregnant mother. To claim that botched assignment is the work of the Happy Reaper is intolerable."

His pulse pounded. He set down the glass. Flexed his hands. Performed a quick breathing exercise the prison's anger management instructor had taught him. Inhaling through his nose, he caught a hint of wet leaves and distant wood smoke. The sun was two fingers above the horizon, faint pink streaking the lower clouds. Still McCree didn't respond. He'd wait.

McCree rocked the chair, its creak stopping each time he drank wine. McCree placed the empty wineglass on the deck, matching its base to the condensation ring it had formed. "You're worried he's screwing up your 'legacy' for all eternity. Do you have any idea who he is?"

Good. Let him think vanity is driving me. "That's where you come in."

TYLER

TYLER GREW FRUSTRATED AT CHARLENE because she wouldn't let him shred Zach for not retrieving the Results Guaranteed card after he killed the girl. Would have taken three seconds, tops. And then the Happy Reaper—the new Happy Reaper, he should say—wouldn't have a black mark against him. How will that lapse look to prospective employers? Why did his partners not get that?

But Charlene had shifted the discussion to worrying about the former Happy Reaper. This time, he wasn't letting anyone interrupt him. "Adam Smith has almost three weeks before we plan to take out McCree. If Smith hasn't acted during that window, I say we should proceed as planned. Charlene, you're still assigned to check IDs at Kavanaugh's to make sure everyone's kosher, right?"

At Charlene's nod, he continued. "You let us in, and we find our spot."

Zach spoke up. "I've checked out the place and have some ideas. In the meantime, I'll continue monitoring his dark-web information. Since nothing else has come in, we should reconsider—"

Tyler sprang from his chair, feeling his face heat and his heart race. "*We are not reconsidering that insult of an offer.* We agreed to charge a premium price for a premium service."

Zach waved his hands in surrender. "You're right. But you and Charlene both have projects you're working on."

Tyler collapsed onto the chair and blessed his favorite computer geek with a smile. "I know you want to run another assignment, Zach. If nothing else has come in by the time we're done with the two we have, we can promote our success. Do a little advertising. Research how you can do that on the dark web."

"I can do that. I'll check how competitors market their services, what protocols they use, how we can promote ourselves without giving the authorities anything to pin the crimes on us. That is the tricky—"

Enough already. "We know you can do it, Zach. That's what you're good at." Stroke his ego and send him to his cave. "It was your research on McCree that convinced us to apply Charlene's justice doctrine to him. The cops have turned a blind eye to his multiple crimes. And why? Because he's the son of a cop killed while on duty. Boo fucking hoo. Everybody's parents die sometime. And the *pièce de résistance* is McCree hands the Happy Reaper to the police even though the Reaper saves McCree's life. Not just McCree's, but a bunch of his family's lives, too."

Zach shone like a polished apple.

Charlene said, "I take it you don't think Adam Smith will touch McCree?"

"Unlikely, which is why you need to keep feeding us information about the party at Kavanaugh's. Depending on what you learn, we can decide where and when it makes sense to take out McCree. What we don't want is a situation where we didn't plan well enough, and a maid shows up—"

"Can it!" Zach sliced the air with the side of his hand. "I did what I had to do. Now it's your turn. And I agree we should proceed. If we expect to get more orders, we have to show we can deliver."

Charlene rose, holding up her empty bottle. "You guys are right. Who besides me wants another while we discuss Tyler's assignment?"

Finally. "And we need the money," Tyler said. "I'm not going back to some dead-end job."

SEAMUS

I REACHED FOR THE WINE again, remembered I had drained the glass, and told myself I needed a clear head to consider whatever the Happy Reaper was proposing. No surprise he had fans. The tabloids had covered his trials. That kind of notoriety attracted all kinds of nutjobs. Being a copycat was one thing. Having the chops to find and crack the Reaper's dark-web portal was something Paddy had not accomplished. Not that I planned to mention that Paddy had led the effort to expose the Happy Reaper's assets, drain the accounts, and donate the money to worthy causes. Paddy would be disappointed to learn he had not found it all.

The Happy Reaper clearly wanted to engage in conversation. While we talked, I lived. I would be a regular chatterbox, if that's what it took. "How can I help discover who the imposter is?"

"You agree your life is currently forfeit, right? You saved my life. I agreed to leave your family and friends alone and come after you solo." The Happy Reaper waved the pistol vaguely in my direction. "Bang, you could be dead. And that's still a possibility. However, if you identify this asshole, I'll consider us even."

At which point he would either kill the guy or have someone do it. I unclenched my teeth to avoid both a headache and giving away my thoughts. If I could—

"Seamus, I see that scheming brain of yours working overtime. Looking for a loophole to crawl out from the deal. I won't let that happen. If I don't kill you in the next few minutes, it's because you agree to help me and not interfere with whatever punishment I choose to exact. And you agree you will do nothing to directly *or indirectly* capture, kill, maim, restrain, or otherwise infringe on my ability to live a free man. And you agree to all that with your moral promise to abide by the spirit of the agreement, not squirm out using a technical ambiguity."

His head drooped, and he sucked in a series of raspy breaths. I curled my toes, preparing to rush him. He raised the muzzle of the pistol and pointed it at my chest. I uncurled my toes. "I'm all ears. How do you see this working?"

The corner of his mouth curled into the hint of a smile. "You may have a better idea. Mine is to hire the guy for a job. Give him specifics regarding the where, when, and how. Someplace I can ambush him. You fulfill your end of the bargain, and we go our separate ways. I promise to leave you and yours in peace, and you promise to seal your lips about me."

Now his face broke into a wide grin. "And by lips, I mean any form of communication or lack of communication that could help anyone, anywhere, find me. That moral promise thing we agreed to.”

Which, technically, we hadn't agreed to. If he gave me access to my phone or computer, I could alert—which was thinking like a lawyer looking to weasel on a bargain I would soon have to make if I wanted to stay alive. Thing was, I was sure I had not heard his entire proposal. The Happy Reaper could have some lawyerly trick of his own up his sleeve. “If the idea is to set up a fake hit and trap the guy, why do you need me?”

His smile widened. “Do you agree we should assume this guy is good? Almost, but not quite, as good as me?”

“Hell, if you don't want surprises, assume he's better than you.” Seeing his neck cord in anger, I added, “I'm not saying he is. I'm saying *assume he is*. Prepare for the worst.” His illness had clearly not diminished his self-regard. Could I use that to trip him up? “You're hinting at something I'm not smart enough to figure out. Enlighten me.”

“First, you commit to my offer. Thus far, it's all been theoretical angels dancing on theoretical pins.”

His health issues did not appear to have affected his mental acuity. I told myself I could change my mind once I learned the entire scheme. He'd regain the right to kill me, and that was lawyerly thinking. I should consider what I was unwilling to give up to save my life. And I knew that answer. “I will not put my moral promise on the line until I learn everything that's involved. For now, what if I promise not to do anything to compromise your status? Will that be good enough?”

His gaze settled on the lake, its flat surface reflecting pink striping the pewter sky of a now cloudy evening. His head rotated the tiniest amount from side to side. Weighing alternatives?

As the seconds ticked off, I sent silent messages of love to my family, hoping that positive energy would reach them if the Happy Reaper pulled the trigger.

He cleared his throat. “Time to promise.”

I did.

“Good enough. For now. The secret to my success has been superior skills and meticulous planning. Not just any Joe Blow could hire me. Sure, you had to know the portal existed, but you also had to have a reference I could check. Now before you shake your head at me again, yes, I realize the police could squeeze a reference, and that person could rat me out in a plea deal. It's a risk in my business. I minimized it because references knew that if they crossed me, they were dead. Whether I killed them personally or hired someone, it would happen. Results Guaranteed. The faker accessed the portal and saw my process, including insisting on a reference. Right?"

His breathing had become ragged. I figured he was using the rhetorical question to give himself time to catch his breath. I played along. "Makes sense. You have a way around that?"

He puffed out an exasperated breath. "Does a duck have webbed feet? The reference was only the first step. I researched the buyer and the target. If I didn't like what I saw, I rejected the assignment. That requires us to present him with a legitimate buyer *and* a legitimate target. I'll supply both. You'll front the money. You can get your hands on a hundred thou in a couple of days, right?"

Money was not the problem, although I thought he said he had millions. The Happy Reaper's plan to set up a prospective victim *was* a problem. We had no guarantee that the imposter wouldn't successfully kill the target. Or worse, kill another innocent bystander. Before I could accept, he'd have to convince me that he had a plan that didn't put anyone in jeopardy. Even if it cost my life.

"So far, all I've heard you want from me is cash."

"That's just the ante."

CHARLENE

NOTHING CHARLENE SAID WOULD CHANGE their minds, what with Tyler unemployed and Zach lusting for another chance to kill someone. The best she could hope for was to shape and control the process.

She carted the empties to the kitchen and returned with three more cold beers. "Zach has confirmed William Barret Oceans is not the Silicon Valley angel he claims to be."

At the compliment, Zach sat up straight. It did not take much to stroke his ego. He said, "I dug up the court records. It's true, what the guy who hired us claimed. Oceans legally screwed our client out of a fortune. High eight figures, maybe nine." He handed his phone to Tyler.

"You're looking at a satellite photograph of Oceans' thirty-million-dollar home in Aspen. Fifteen thousand square feet of living space on a two-acre lot. He's hosting a soiree the weekend after next for five of his buddies and their wives, girlfriends, hookers, whatever. The boys are going elk hunting while the girls shop. Total net worth of the six guys is just south of seventy-five billion. I'm thinking if I went with Tyler, we could take them all and do the world a favor while we collect our fee."

Tyler launched off the chair. "That is *not* what we agreed. You two already had your chances. This is mine, and it will be so surgical a neurosurgeon will applaud my technique."

Charlene figured every one of those men had committed multiple crimes to come up with that much money. But—and she emphasized this difference with Zach in the spirited discussion of their rules of engagement that followed—that did not mean they were guilty. Unless Zach came up with proof—and she meant actual proof, not circumstantial evidence, she agreed with Tyler.

Zach grumbled they might never again have this fine an opportunity. Plus, it would confuse the police. They'd have a hard time understanding who the primary target was and waste until forever looking for someone who wanted them all dead.

Charlene agreed that was true. "But I'm not worried about the police. Given the information Zach provided, I have no doubt Tyler will devise a plan that completely covers his tracks." Seeing both guys smiling from her compliments, she asked Zach, "When do you expect the group to arrive at Oceans' modest abode?"

Zach reclaimed his phone and finger-swiped the screen. "Thursday evening, arriving on a private jet. Two limos transport them to the house from the airport. They leave Tuesday morning. Best I can tell, he won't be there before that trip."

Tyler's fingers tapped a merry tune on his thighs, a sure sign he was excited. "Does Oceans have permanent staff at the house?"

Zach looked up from his phone. "No people, only services. Security, grounds, maintenance. That sort of thing. I can give you their names."

Tyler's grin widened. "Thanks, no. My preference is to take him while he and his friends are in the woods hunting elk. Charlene made hers look like a hit-and-run driver. I can make this look like a hunting accident. But if that doesn't pan out, I need to see what I can do at his house. Since I don't have to go to work anymore, I figure I can do a site visit right away. Any objections?"

Charlene liked the idea of the hunting accident. She wished they shared her concerns about the Happy Reaper. At least Zach and his computers were their early warning system if they had pissed off Adam Smith by claiming the Happy Reaper mantle. And, if Zach complained too much about not having his own assignment, she'd ask him to surveil the next criminal she wanted to remove: a pimp with a nasty habit of carving up his girls.

"Tomorrow starts early for me. I'm booting you boys out. Tyler, we look forward to your report on your trip. And Zach, keep your eyes open on the dark web for Adam Smith."

"Not a problem."

Why did his response not comfort her?

NIKI

ASHLEY PRESCOTT RIFLED HER CELLPHONE into the sofa cushions. It bounced back and she caught it one-handed. "Come on, Seamus McCree. Answer me, damnit." Four hours since she'd heard the news. The jerk hadn't responded to her voicemail messages. Or texts. Which didn't exactly surprise her. He often forgot to plug in his phone, and the damn thing would lie dead for days.

He'd been posting daily pictures on Facebook about some bird project he was doing. She'd also left a message on that platform. No response and no post yet today. Maybe he was in the woods? She rarely used email, but he might.

Hey Old Man. Just learned Adam Smith escaped a prison hospital last Thursday/Friday. He's had six years to stew about you stuffing him behind bars. That means he's coming for you. LEAVE NOW!!!

*Do not pass go. Do not collect $200. Meet me in St. Paul. We'll figure this out after I f*ck your brains out.*

Let me know you got this. And turn on your damn phone.
Niki

She'd signed it with her *nom de guerre* because Seamus had been part of its creation, and it was what he called her. Would using "Ashley" get his attention? Shock him into compliance? Not likely. She left *Niki*, deleted what she planned to do to his body, and hit send.

She gave the couch a side-kick. "Ouch." She'd tried everything except her undercover work secure communication system that Seamus had access to. It was against all protocol, which she'd break to save his life, but she had no reason to think he'd see that message any sooner than her earlier ones.

Maybe his son could help. She looked up Patrick McCree's contact info and pressed the call icon.

He answered with, "How's my favorite undercover agent?"

"Desperate. I'm trying to contact your dad. Any suggestions other than the obvious?"

"He's at camp, so good luck with that. Weren't those invitations to my grandma's eighty-fifth birthday party cute? The government allowing you to make it?"

"So far. Look, Patrick, the Marshals Service just issued a BOLO for Adam Smith, a.k.a the Happy Reaper. Why they waited days after his escape is beyond my comprehension. Anyway, your father has to leave the damn woods for somewhere safe until we run the bastard to ground."

"Because you think he will make it a priority to kill Dad for giving him to the police? I'll have Megan text a video chat request to him. She's the one person Dad never ignores. *If he gets it*, he'll call her faster than a starving rat on spam."

Not an attractive picture. And if he doesn't . . .

"Thanks, Patrick. Give Megan a smooch for me and say hello to your lovely wife. And yes, I plan to be at Trudy's eighty-fifth. Should be a blast. Keep me informed?"

She hung up and kicked herself for wasting time. If she had left when she'd first heard the news, she'd already be two-thirds of the way to Seamus's place. However, had she made that choice, odds were she'd discover Seamus was in Chicago or Boston or some such. She ran the mental calculations: forty-five minutes to pack her tactical gear. Six hours' drive including pit stops. An hour to get him packed and lock up his camp. Six hours back to St. Paul, giving her barely enough time to settle Seamus, unpack, shower, and make her eight-a.m. meeting with the Special Agent in Charge of AFT's St. Paul field division. Doable . . .

Ready or not, here I come.

SEAMUS

I PRESSED THE HAPPY REAPER to elaborate on what, in addition to money, he expected from me to expose his imposter. He parried my thrusts like a boxer, dancing away on reminiscences of the times our paths had crossed.

I tried again to focus the conversation. He responded with a woeful head shake. "In due time, Seamus. I'm starved and sleep deprived. First, we hide the car I'm driving. I won't tell you how I acquired it. That way you won't knowingly possess stolen property. Aren't I just the nicest guy?"

That was a rhetorical question I chose not to answer. Once I determined he had no immediate plans to drive the car, I led him to property I owned north of the county line. I set a slow pace with my truck to give him time and space to avoid the worst rocks and holes. Previous traffic had blown the leaves off the road in the first mile and a half. I stopped before we reached the turn onto a less-traveled section and trotted to his car. He lowered the window.

"This looks worse because it's covered with maple leaves. It will be fine if you follow exactly where I go. I'll have to open two gates. No one can drive past the two locked gates, and hunters rarely walk the property to where we're leaving your ride. No guarantees, though."

We made it without problems, and he transferred to my truck a thirty-liter clothes duffel, a plastic grocery bag filled with pill bottles, and a military-style rifle with more ammunition than I had ever seen outside of a store.

On our return, he asked why the trees by my house were mostly bare, but a lot of trees where we'd parked his car still had leaves.

"Different species. My deciduous trees are mostly maple. Down here is mixed aspen and white birch. They hold their leaves longer." I pointed to tamarack we passed. "Tammies are deciduous conifers. Their needles are starting to yellow. They'll soon be gone."

"I can see why you'd like it here. Me, I'd go nuts in a week." His stomach growled. "Now that I think of it, I'm starved."

I, too, was famished by the time we got home. After lugging his stuff onto the screened porch, I reheated soup and created a mixed salad. He picked at the offering, eating less than half what I had served him. Our conversation consisted only of me remarking on how little he ate and him claiming food no longer had much taste. Dinner complete, he surprised me by offering to dry the dishes and put them away. His movements were slow, as though everything was an effort, but he made no complaint.

With the last dish washed, I asked, "You prefer baths or showers?" Seeing his confused expression, I added, "If you want to have a bath, I'll put your towels upstairs. Otherwise, I'll stick them in the downstairs bathroom where the shower is."

"Downstairs is good. Be next to the guest room. I assume you still use the TV room for guests?"

Not so subtly reminding me he had violated the sanctity of my home before. "Until it gets too cold, I sleep on the screened porch. The upstairs bedroom is free, if you want it."

"Guest room is better for avoiding stairs. Fair warning. I snore something fierce without my CPAP machine. Sleep is calling. Remember, you turn me in or shoot me in my sleep, your entire family—every single one of them—will die a slow and painful death. And then they'll come for you."

Despite my desire to appear unfazed by his threat, an icy chill ran up my spine and I shivered. "You already have my promise. Before you rest, help me haul your stuff off the porch. I have a feeling we'll both need to be sharp to pull this off."

With him settled into his room, I dealt with Colleen's concerns about Mom's party. Although trivial compared to my issues with the Happy Reaper, she might think something was wrong if I didn't respond and get my son, Paddy, involved. The last thing I wanted was him driving up from Chicago to check on me.

I answered each of Colleen's four texts. My new-message indicator showed I still had one unread message. My heart performed a joyful leap seeing it was from Megan.

Helloooooooo Grampa Seamus! Papa says to ask 4 your help on my math homework. He says it's a cross between Word Puzzles and Boolean Algebra. I don't know what that means, but it's due tomorrow. FaceTime me! Please! Soonest!

Damn. It was past her bedtime. I'd catch her at breakfast tomorrow morning and see if she still wanted help. I set my watch's alarm and scrolled through a day's worth of notifications: the KP index for northern lights was increasing, my credit score had gone down five points, and I had three phone messages. What was up with that? I didn't normally get three calls in a week.

Niki's first message asked me to call her. Her second, sounding much more concerned, repeated her request. Paddy left one to tell me the Happy Reaper had escaped. He and Niki wanted me to drive to her place in St. Paul. I should check for an email she had sent me with details.

I found two emails from Niki. The first was more of the same. Her second email gave me an instant headache.

I'm leaving now to come get you. If you're still alive and the reason you're ignoring me is the Happy Reaper has you prisoner, leave an outside light on. If you can't do that, leave the mudroom light on or one in the basement. I don't see any lights, I'll assume you're dead.

Despite my earlier promise, I immediately started concocting wiggle room in my bargain with the Happy Reaper. I had not contacted Niki; therefore, whatever happened was not because I broke my commitment. *Sketchy.* I reminded myself to avoid actions that made the Happy Reaper wonder at my motives. He couldn't see a basement light from the guest room. I kicked off my shoes, eased down the stairs, and flicked the switch for the bulb deepest in the back. Its light through the basement windows dimly painted the trees in front of the house.

I put myself in Niki's shoes. What would I do if I saw the light? Go into sniper mode and kill the Happy Reaper. And my nightmares would begin. I had never known the Happy Reaper to not deliver on a threat. His business card had promised "Results Guaranteed."

We'd first met fifteen years ago. I was a financial crimes consultant to the police and exposed his mass-murder plots, solving one and preventing a second. He tracked me down. Threatened to kill me, or maybe Paddy, if I didn't stop pursuing him.

Our paths crossed again six years ago—twice. I had temporarily foiled his plan to kill an informer I was hiding. The Happy Reaper didn't stop. He tracked the man down and killed him before he testified.

A deep ache gripped me, my legs wobbled, my mouth tasted like metal. I sat before I collapsed. I had lost my lover, my business partner, my best friend, Abigail. She had been collateral damage when the Happy Reaper killed the informer.

Later that year, I captured him. He threatened my entire family—first to expose their secrets, then kill them—if I didn't let him go. Despite my mother pleading for me to set him free, I put making him pay for his crimes ahead of my family's safety.

A few weeks later, I saved his life from a prison attack. He canceled his threats against my family and promised to come after only me.

Niki killing him would not bring justice. It might even be a mercy to a guy whose heart problems would cause him to suffer as he lost control of his life. That wasn't worth risking my family's lives. Or voiding a promise.

I turned off the light.

So, how *do* I stop Niki from killing the Happy Reaper or him killing us both?

THE HAPPY REAPER

THE HAPPY REAPER WOKE FEELING perturbed. The semi-dark at his bedtime had become darker than the inside of a gun safe. He stilled his breath and listened. The wind pushing through the trees produced a background whoosh. No footsteps. No breathing. He slid the pistol from under his pillow and pointed it at the doorway. The refrigerator kicked on, and he almost pulled the trigger.

"You stopped snoring." Seamus's voice came from the screened porch. "I assume you're awake. May I come in? We have a problem."

The Happy Reaper shifted on the sofa bed and pointed the pistol in the voice's direction. Still couldn't see a damn thing. "Come in and get the light."

"I'm coming in, but no lights. I need to save my night vision."

A curious statement. His mind fog cleared. McCree was worried. "Come in and you'd better start at the beginning and tell me what stupid thing you did."

The door opened, bringing with it a draft of cool air. A dark form stepped into the room and closed the door behind itself. "I had my phone off and missed people notifying me of your escape. One of them will arrive soon to check on me. I don't want them hurt. I don't want you hurt. And I don't know how to prevent a violent confrontation."

McCree is many things, but stupid isn't one of them. If he could call the person off, he would. "You're leaving out pertinent details."

"Yeah, this friend works for the Marshals Service." Seamus explained the instructions she had given regarding the house lights.

"So now you got your phone on. Use the damn thing and convince her you're fine."

"That might have worked had I seen her messages hours ago. She won't stop now. In fact, she might already be here or close enough to meet us if we try to leave."

Fair enough, but the Happy Reaper figured he was still missing something. "You're saying we don't dare leave? If you leave the lights on, she calls in the hounds. I'll kill you. She'll kill me. My friends will kill your family. Not good for anyone. And if you leave the house dark, she won't know if you didn't get the message or aren't alive. That means she'll wait until she sees you or me. Why not wait for light and let her see you're still breathing? Then you can explain everything." He reached for the light and stopped. "I'm still missing something. Why do you need night vision?"

"Knowing her, the first thing she'll do after arriving here is check the memory cards on my trail cameras. Guaranteed, you're on at least one of them. She'll call in the whole Marshals Service apparatus, which—"

"Is a problem. We take the cards. Problem solved. About the night—"

"You don't think if all the memory cards were missing or blank, or all the trail cameras disappeared, she wouldn't decide it's because you're here? I plan to intercept her and convince her to help us before she finds you on a trail camera or reaches the house. You took precautions and didn't drive straight in. She won't either. I must stop her while she's still in her car."

"Night vision," the Happy Reaper snapped. "Get to the damned night vision."

Seamus nodded. "I have a trail camera by Beaver Creek, which is a mile and a half away. It captured your car coming in. Could have caught you driving it. She spots your picture, she'll park and come in on foot. If that happens, I need to see her before she sees me. Right?"

"That did not make a lick of sense."

"Because you don't know her. If I drive the two and a half miles to the

A Grade to head her off and she's already pulled off the road, she won't stop my truck. She'll continue to the house. We're back to people dying. The only way I can stop her is by walking up the road. But if she sees someone walking up the road at night, she'll assume it's you sneaking away, not me trying to stop her."

The Happy Reaper flicked on the overhead light. The two of them blinked at each other.

"Why did you do that?"

"Because the answer is obvious. Light yourself up like a Christmas tree, so she sees it's you. The bigger issue is what the hell you tell the marshal that doesn't end in my friends killing your family? It better be good, because if this night-vision thing is any indication, you're not exactly firing on all eight cylinders." The Happy Reaper punched a ten-digit number into his phone, listened to the prompt, entered a four-digit code, and hearing a beep said, "Clem, it's me. Everything is copacetic. Use a fresh burner and call me at this number." He hung up and told McCree. "This could take a couple of minutes. While we're waiting, turn on every light in the house, and meet me in the basement cold room. It's the one spot in this place someone can't see in and shoot us."

THE HAPPY REAPER UNFOLDED TWO camp stools in the cold room and propped his automatic weapon against the nearest wall. McCree came down wearing a winter coat and carrying another. "Gonna be cold in here."

The Happy Reaper's phone buzzed before he could don the coat. "Wait a minute. Let me put this on speaker." He tapped the icon. "You still there, Clem?"

"What's so damn important you're calling at one in the morning?" a deep male voice asked.

"I got Seamus McCree here. Tell him what happens if I don't keep calling in."

"You want me to grab the list?"

"Nah," the Happy Reaper said. "Broad brush is fine. He can fill in the details."

"Sure. We don't hear from you, me and the others divvy up the names. McCree's mother, son, daughter-in-law, granddaughter. Sister, too, right?

Maybe two of them? Anyway, the whole family and a few friends. You don't care how we kill them. We can get it done however we want. Last one we do is McCree himself."

If looks could kill, Seamus's scowl would put him six feet under. "Exactly. Throw your burner away. I'll be in touch." He disconnected. "Seamus, I'll wait here while you do whatever you think will work to keep me alive and your family safe." He shrugged on the coat. "Whatcha waiting for, an engraved invitation?"

Seamus left faster than a spooked deer. The Happy Reaper thought that went well. Seamus would do his damnedest to keep the Happy Reaper alive until they smoked out the imposter.

Which didn't guarantee mistakes couldn't happen.

Seamus believed he could convince his marshal friend to get with his program. The problem with federal agents, particularly marshals, is they think they can protect anyone forever. She might blow off Seamus's plan and do her duty and try to bring him in. And if that happened, the feds would surround the cold room. He'd either give himself up or succumb to dehydration. Or go in a blaze of glory like Butch Cassidy and the Sundance Kid in that movie.

He waited five minutes for McCree to clear the area before he and the rifle left the house using the basement door. He plowed through a raft of raspberry bushes and two-foot-tall trees and climbed the hill between the house and the road. Had to stop twice to catch his breath. Geez, in this cold air, he looked and sounded like an old-time steam engine. Cresting the hill, he found a suitable spot beyond the house lights' glare from which he could control the road.

Tuesday, October 18, 2022

Niki

On the long drive from St. Paul, Ashley Prescott shifted her mindset into that of her undercover *persona*, Niki, a special asset of the government, given jobs no agency could legally assign their employees. She mostly dealt with armed militia. No backup. No safety cutouts. Death the penalty for screwing up. Niki stayed alive because she anticipated bad things and prevented them from happening.

With that mindset, she acted as if she knew Adam Smith *was* at Shank Lake. That he *knew* she was coming, *had read her messages* to Seamus, and was waiting for her. Smith had meticulously planned his assassinations. To avoid stumbling into traps he'd set, she wanted to arrive at Seamus's place from a direction Smith would not expect.

Like coming across the water. The moonless sky was dark with cloud cover, but if he—or an associate—spotted her on the water, she had zero protection. If he knew anything about her, he might assume she would try something devious. In that case, coming directly down the road at full speed might be the most unexpected approach. But if he had that covered, she was a dead duck.

Unless something had changed since she was last there, the roads around the lake that might allow her to drive in from the opposite direction had locked gates and blocking boulders. She didn't have time to walk it.

That left walking in using one of the trails that wove through Seamus's property. She knew them all and knew where Seamus had placed trail cameras—unless he had moved them in the last month. The camera farthest away was a mile and a half from his house. Set up by Beaver Creek, it caught pictures of moose, wolf, fox, otters, and traffic on the road.

A few minutes past midnight, she stopped her car a hundred yards before reaching that camera. She affixed her headlamp and, before opening the door, made sure the interior light could not switch on. Listening for any sounds other than the trickling of Beaver Creek through its culvert, she approached the trail cam from behind it.

She opened its cover, turned off the camera, and scrolled through the pictures. A doe and fawn had nibbled vegetation earlier that evening. The next earliest pictures captured a vehicle with Florida plates heading in. Possible snowbird not yet left for winter. That was it for Monday. She continued scrolling, looking for any previous evidence of that Florida plate. More wildlife, Seamus traveling both ways on his yellow ATV. More wildlife. Three trucks of bear hunters hauling their dogs in and out. More wildlife and Seamus's truck.

No evidence of that Florida plate the previous two weeks.

She fought against the pressure of the minutes ticking away and pulled up on her phone a contact who could check the plate. She gave her credentials to the yawning agent on duty, and at his go-ahead, provided the plate number. Five minutes later, she had her answer.

"Plates, not car, reported stolen from a Toyota RAV-4 parked at a Gary, Indiana motel. Owners claim someone swiped it between seven p.m. Sunday night and eight a.m. Monday morning. Twenty-four hours ago, give or take. The replacement plates sitting on those folks' car belong to the same make and model stolen from an airport outside Albany, New York."

Adam Smith could easily have passed those two locations on his way to Seamus. Dread brought an inner chill she couldn't shake off. She muttered a thank you and closed the connection. If that car was Smith, he had arrived before she had even learned of his escape. Dread changed to burning anger at whoever had sat on that information for three days before issuing the BOLO.

Proper procedure required her to call her suspicions in, block the road to prevent Smith's exit, and wait for reinforcements. Screw that.

How close in could she safely drive before Smith might have set his trap? Not much farther on Shank Lake Road, but Seamus had shown her a logging road that looped into the woods and would chop off half the distance to his place.

With the Beaver Creek camera still off, she drove past it, returned and deleted evidence of her opening the camera, and rebooted it. From there, she followed the logging road to a gate, parked, painted her face, and changed into camo tactical gear, including ballistic vest and night-vision headgear. She attached the scope to the sniper rifle and strapped her favorite SigSauer to her ankle.

Niki moved into the woods at least a quarter mile from the road, then paralleled it until she crossed the first of Seamus's ATV trails. A doe threw up her white-tail flag in alarm, and she and her fawn crashed away through the underbrush. Probably the ones she had seen on the Beaver Creek trail camera.

She slowed her pace, scanning ahead before placing her next step to move soundlessly. Good thing it had rained in the last couple of days to eliminate the crunch from the fallen leaves. The path led to the northern edge of Seamus's property. There she planned to cross the road beyond and out-of-sight of his house. Coming closer, she sensed a change in the light from the direction of the house. Had Seamus turned on a light? Moments later, light flooded the house site, highlighting treetops and the underbelly of the low clouds.

What the hell? Had she triggered something that alerted Smith to her presence? Her planned approach no longer made sense. How could she see *into* the house? When she had first met Seamus a dozen years ago, a militia guy had spied on them from the safety of a hill next to the road that overlooked the house. That hill's shadow would protect her from the light until she reached its crest.

She moved sniper low and slow, scanning ahead, placing one careful step after another. Before she crossed the road, she hid behind a mature sugar maple and surveyed both directions. Nothing stirred. She crossed in a low sprint, took shelter next to a tangle caused by a tipped-over cedar a quarter of the way up the hill. Her heart settled, and she picked up the sound of rustling: a mole stuck its nose through the leaf litter, sniffed, and ducked under cover.

She rose into a crouch to plan the safest route up the hill.

"That's far enough," a gravelly voice behind her said. "Hands up, or I'll unload both barrels, and you won't have no head."

If he was planning on killing her, she'd be dead. She froze, waiting to hear what he'd say next.

"I ain't in ta countin. Next and last thing you hear will be the shotgun talkin."

Seamus

I GRABBED A SPARE FLASHLIGHT and left the house at a trot. In daylight, I could cover the two and a half miles to the junction of Shank Lake Road with the A Grade in twenty minutes. But I was wearing boots, I had to be careful of rocks in the road, and I had to use the spare flashlight to illuminate myself so Niki would know it was me. All of which slowed me considerably and made the ticking clock in my head pound louder.

Plus, if Niki had taken the precaution of moving into the woods, she might not see me on the road. In the quiet night, my singing voice would carry a long way. A few minutes down the road, I realized the thudding of my boots provided a steady beat underpinning my brain's jukebox selection that I was singing into the night: The Who's *Tommy,* an entire rock opera about a deaf, dumb, and blind kid.

Not a good omen.

Once the road smoothed, my flashlight highlighted my ATV tracks and a single set of tire treads marking the Happy Reaper's arrival. Good. Niki had not gotten this far. Halfway to the A Grade, Shank Lake meets Lukes Road and makes a left. My ATV tracks followed Lukes Road, leaving only the Happy Reaper's tracks on the road. Excellent, and from that point forward, a grader had smoothed the gravel. No longer concerned with pokey rocks, I stayed centered in the road and quickened my pace.

I was belting the "Acid Queen" track. My voice cracked, and I skidded to a halt. My flashlight revealed two sets of tire tracks. Kneeling, I examined the tread impressions. Both vehicles were heading in. Where they overlapped, the Happy Reaper's RAV-4 track was the older. I had missed the other vehicle turning off.

It could be Niki.

I backtracked and found the second vehicle had taken a road that led to a hunting camp. Niki knew that a half-mile up that road, you could veer off and almost reach Shank Lake Road—and be much closer to my place. Nothing to say it couldn't be the guys from that camp, meaning Niki was still on her way. The acid burning in my stomach supported my conclusion that it was more likely Niki who had made the tracks. She was between me and my house, and all hell might soon break loose.

Either way, following the tracks was a loser. If they weren't Niki's, I'd miss her arrival. And if they were hers, I was unlikely to catch her before she and the Happy Reaper met. Jaw pain alerted me I was gritting my teeth. I opened my mouth wide, tilted my head back and screamed a profanity into the night.

And had an idea.

I hauled branches from the woods and piled them in Shank Lake Road. Not a roadblock, but it would slow Niki down in the event I was wrong about who had made the tracks. Using my boot heel, I scratched NIKI TEXT ME into the road. From a distance, the message wasn't sufficiently pronounced to attract her attention. I used a limb to etch it deeply into the road. If the obstruction stopped her, she'd see the message and not come blundering into an unknown situation.

That safeguard allowed me to operate on my instincts that Niki had taken the alternative route. Finding her would require angels pointing the way. I needed to switch strategies and allow her to find me. I scrambled past my makeshift obstruction and ran toward home, cuing up "Acid Queen" from the beginning. With luck, I'd get there in time.

No, Seamus, if you're lucky, she's still driving in and will text you from the brush pile you left in the road.

I was still a half-mile from home when a gunshot echoed down the lake.

NIKI

NIKI SLOWLY RAISED HER RIGHT hand and placed it on the top of her head. Her mind raced like a greyhound chasing a mechanical rabbit around the track. The rabbit had a crucial trinket of information. Catching the rabbit could save the day. Except the hounds never caught the rabbit, did they?

She raised her left hand to touch fingertips with her right. Something with the voice had her thinking. Sounded Yooper, but that wasn't it. Had Adam Smith picked up local talent? *Get him to talk.*

"Now what?"

"A girl? Well, ain't that somethin. Back your ass down the hill and set it on the road."

Not possible. She hadn't heard that voice in a dozen years. Besides, hadn't Seamus said he was dead? No, disappeared. *Possible.*

She cleared her throat. "Owen?"

"Do I know ya?"

This changed everything. "Remember the woman Seamus rescued? Niki?" No response. Owen was older than Methuselah by now. Did he not remember? Throw a verbal hand grenade to shake free a memory. "Several times, I embarrassed you all to hell. Remember I asked you to buy me tampons, and I stood on Seamus's upstairs deck and flashed that militia guy spying on us from the top of this hill?"

"I'll be ginswoggled. It *is* you. Now, back your purty ass down before I empty both barrels."

THE HAPPY REAPER

VOICES WOKE THE HAPPY REAPER. He made the mistake of looking at the house lights, and now couldn't see a damned thing in the shadow cast by the hill he was on. Did they—whoever they were—know he was up here? Had he been snoring again? His heart hammered his chest like it was pounding a coffin lid wanting to escape. Blast his damned heart.

Owen and Niki. That didn't tell him squat about who the hell they were, or what the hell they were doing here, or why Owen had a shotgun on Niki.

A movement partway up the hill attracted his attention. He stared in the direction, saw nothing, remembered it was better to use peripheral vision, and tried that. Caught another movement. Slowly raised his gun off his lap and pointed it in the general direction.

Niki said, "Don't spit out your choppers. I'm coming. Be a hell of a lot easier if you let me turn around so I can see."

"'Spose so. Nothin fast, hear me?"

"Loud and clear."

By the direction of their voices and brief glimpses of movement, he figured she was edging down the hill. Owen was below her on the road. He owed Owen for stopping this Niki person from finding him sleeping his life away at the top of the hill.

"Whoops." The lady thrashed through brush. "Almost tripped. Be there in a jiffy, Owen. Oh, you bad boy, that's not a shotgun you're toting. Looks like a single-shot rifle."

Which meant the Happy Reaper had them seriously outgunned, and

Niki, whoever she was, was familiar with weapon types. The two knew each other but had come separately. Seamus was off somewhere and neither had mentioned him. The Happy Reaper shifted his haunch to give him a better line to the road and broke a twig. *Shit.* Sounded like a rifle shot to him but elicited no comments from below. Lucky, that.

"Sit yourself down in the middle of the road." They lowered their voices, and he had to cup an ear in their direction to catch their conversation.

"Really, Owen? It's cold and wet. Let's just talk. By the time you actually fire that thing, I'll have ten slugs puncturing your heart from this. What are you doing here? I thought you were gone to Canada or dead? I have to say, I would not have recognized you in that getup. Your accent and droppin Gs at the end of words gave you away."

"Youse still FBI? How come you're sneakin up this hill?"

"U.S. Marshal now, but I'm not here to take you in. Seamus ever talk to you about a guy named Adam Smith? Calls himself the Happy Reaper. No? Not surprising. Seamus keeps that shit close to the vest. Anyway, Seamus put the guy away, but he recently escaped from prison. I figure he wants to kill Seamus, and I came to get the fool to safety. I told Seamus to leave one light on if Smith was already here. The house is ablaze with lights. I'm afraid he's in trouble. Now you talk and make it quick—not one of your yarns that will keep us here until dawn."

Niki is the marshal, and Seamus missed her. Seamus's worry about the two facing off was dead on. Pardon the pun. Except this Owen guy was a wild card.

"I seen the lights and was fixin to check. Seen you sneakin through the woods. I guess maybe we better get up that hill and see what's to see."

Not a good idea. He raised the rifle and fired a single shot over their heads. "This is the Happy Reaper. You two go find Seamus before you do anything else. He's walking down the road looking for a marshal friend, who I assume is you, Niki. I promise you, he's alive and well. Talk to him. If you call in support, it will trigger a killing spree we'll all regret, but especially Seamus and his family."

"Adam Smith," Niki yelled. "Convince me this isn't a tactic to give you time to escape. If everything is copacetic, why didn't Seamus wait for me at home?"

"Because he was afraid one of us would kill the other. Maybe you're asking yourself why he would care if you killed me. Because, if you do, my friends kill his entire family. If all I wanted was to escape, I'd have mowed you down instead of firing a warning shot. Find Seamus and bring him here. You don't have to believe me. He'll tell you what's what."

"Well, Owen, you're the master tracker. Shall we?"

They might split up and try to flank him. He crawled backward down the hill far enough to stand without their seeing him, then he jogged to the path that went to the guest cabin. Mistake. It felt like his heart was clawing through his chest. He doubled over to catch his breath and ease the pain.

SEAMUS

A RIFLE SHOT ECHOING UP and down the lake caused me to dart into the woods and lean against the rough bark of a pine tree for protection. No return fire. Which meant what, besides the obvious conclusion that I had failed to stop Niki?

If she had killed the Happy Reaper, how long before his silence triggered Clem and friends to attack my family? At least six, eight hours. Enough for Niki and me to warn everyone and develop strategies to keep them safe until we could track down Clem. Maybe.

But if the Happy Reaper had killed Niki . . .

From that brain fog came one conclusion: whichever one survived, I didn't want that person to accidentally kill me. I could run the fifteen miles to town in three hours. If Niki answers my call from that safety, I still have time to warn my family.

And if she doesn't answer or the Happy Reaper answers her phone? I had three hours of running to develop a satisfactory response.

Decision made, I pushed away from the tree and stopped at another thought. What if he'd wounded Niki? She could bleed out or die of hypothermia. Or the Happy Reaper might track her down in the light and kill her. If I found her, I could get her to town. I'd still have to deal with the Happy Reaper. Unlikely scenarios, but not zero probability, and I couldn't let her die.

I changed my headlamp into blinking red mode and walked up the center of the road, alternately using my flashlight to light the road and my face. Despair whispered I was a fool to return. I should retreat, save myself, alert my family.

And I'd never be able to live with myself if I could have saved her. I forced one foot in front of the other.

NIKI

NIKI LEANED IN TO WHISPER into Owen's elephantine ear. "Seamus won't be armed. Let's scoot up the road and get away from this guy."

"We can take him."

Niki said, "Maybe later. First, we find Seamus."

Owen left in a brisk walk, hugging the road close to the hill. Niki approved of the strategy to make them smaller targets. They had almost reached the edge of McCree's property before Niki spotted a flash of white light. She formed a megaphone with her hands. "Wait there, Seamus. We'll come to you."

The light moved to point toward them. Niki jogged past Owen, noticed for the first time a blinking red headlamp. She was relieved to hear Seamus speak.

"Who the hell is we? Did you kill the Happy Reaper?"

She saved her answer until she reached him and gave him a hug. "The shot was a warning from him. I met up with someone you know." She motioned Owen into the circle of light. It was the first close look she had gotten of the old coot.

He dressed like an 1840s frontiersman: leather pants, a leather vest over two wool shirts, a beard that Santa would consider extravagant, and a coonskin hat. A stuffed rucksack hung on his back, a dead rabbit dangled from his belt, and he carried a single-shot, bolt-action rifle in both hands.

Seamus's eyes widened. "You're alive!" He raced down the road and pulled Owen into a hug that lifted him off his feet.

Niki coughed to get attention. "You two need to get a room, or can we deal with the issues at hand? I left my car parked in that red pine plantation." She waved toward the east. "Let's talk while we collect it. You can join us, Owen, unless you'd feel more comfortable slipping into the woods. I'm not here to cause you trouble."

Owen wiggled away from Seamus's hug. "He the guy who kilt that nice bodyguard lady, Abigail Hancock?"

Niki was surprised Owen knew that. On second thought, she shouldn't have been. Owen had been a collector and distributor of tales from the entire U.P. Even on the lam, he surely kept his ear to the ground.

Seamus said, "I know you liked her, Owen. For now, anyway, I can't touch him." He lit the way for them toward Niki's car. In a rambling story that convinced her the usually logical Seamus was sick with worry, he filled them in on what had transpired between him and the Happy Reaper. "Here's my plan: I made a promise to help the Happy Reaper find his imposter. I'll return and slow walk that as best I can. While I'm doing that, you warn my family and get them to safety. Get your FBI friends to find Clem and his buddies. Once they do that, you can return the Happy Reaper to prison."

She used her interrogation skills to verify details until she convinced herself Seamus had told her everything of importance. Time to give him a reality check about the feds solving his problem. "First thing, I'm not the only one who will think to look for Adam Smith at your place. At some point, the Marshals service will send a team to check. Given Adam Smith's health, if he hears a bullhorn shouting 'Marshals Service,' he'll probably choose death by cop. That leaves you with a Clem problem. Beyond my—"

"You can't allow that."

"—powers to stop it. You must understand how the Bureau operates. They *might* investigate this Happy Reaper imposter if they think the guy broke federal laws. Which he did if he traveled across state lines to make the kill or solicited a hit using the internet. But it's not like Adam Smith can sit down with them and provide proof. There's no way to even point them in the right direction because we have no clue what the right direction is! As for Clem? I guarantee the Bureau has zero interest in expending resources on looking for someone who *might be a threat* to your family."

Seamus looked like he would interrupt again, and Owen was shaking his head, showing his disgust—with what, she had no time to worry. She rushed on. "You can't hide your family forever, and guys like Clem have long memories. Your—our—only hope is to learn who Clem is. Until then, you must keep Adam Smith alive."

She let Seamus talk himself into the obvious solution, which he had by the time they reached her car. To buy time to neutralize Clem, he and Niki needed to pool resources with Smith and uncover the imposter's identity.

Seamus put an arm around Owen, who had been soaking everything in without comment. "Make yourself scarce. If this goes sideways, cops will soon swarm the area. Niki and I won't tell anyone that we saw you."

Owen gave a shrug. "Maybe so." Without another word, he slipped from the circle of light and vanished into the woods. Niki counted eighteen seconds during which she could hear him moving, and then nothing. "Somehow, I thought he would object to you shooing him off."

Seamus stared into the woods where Owen had gone. "Yeah, surprising. Look, this is my battle, not yours. You should leave while you can."

At his words, her stomach clenched, and a flash of anger ripped through her. *Did he think so little of her?* She tilted her head back and stared into his eyes. "In case you hadn't noticed, I'm not Owen."

THE HAPPY REAPER

ONCE THE HAPPY REAPER ASCERTAINED Niki and Owen had walked up the road past the cabin driveway, he returned to the house, extinguished all the lights, and resumed his position on top of the hill. Nearly three hours passed before a car crawled down the road, headlights on bright, interior light engaged, allowing him to see Seamus driving with a woman in the passenger seat. No third person. The radio blasted BBC news loud enough to cause Canada to disown the Crown.

He grabbed his weapons and shambled to the steps leading up to the kitchen entrance of the house, wishing he'd left one light on to make it easier. The car moseyed down the driveway past the rocks guarding the solar-panels pole and reversed into the parking area in front of the sprawling woodshed.

The motor shut off and took the BBC with it, leaving only a ticking engine to disturb the silence. Seamus got out first, keeping his arms away from his body. The Happy Reaper supposed that was to show he carried a flashlight, no weapons. Big whoop. Seamus hated guns; the woman and the missing Owen were the armed ones.

Seamus called, "Niki promises she won't do anything to jeopardize our agreement. Before she exposes herself to you, I need your promise that you will not harm her. She and I have a plan to share."

"Where's Owen?"

"I sent him off. He, like you, is a fugitive from the law. I swear, it's just you, me, and Niki. I want your commitment. If you say no, she'll leave. But she has skills and contacts that will help us achieve our common goal."

During this conversation, Niki had shifted from the passenger side to the driver's seat. He had no reason not to agree, but delaying might provide more intel.

"What skills?"

"She's a marshal. She knows how to find people. And you can't exactly run a marathon, let alone walk five miles or stay up all night waiting for the imposter. She can, and if that is the only way to stop the imposter from killing someone, she will. Now can we stop dicking around? I'm exhausted, Niki is tired, and you have to be falling asleep on your feet. We all need rest. With three clear brains, we can lock down a plan. Do I have your guarantee or not?"

The Happy Reaper decided he *was* too damn tired to do anything but agree and count on Seamus keeping his word. "You do."

Seamus stepped away from the car. Niki got out, leaving the door open to keep the lights on. She'd slung her rifle over her shoulder. No other weapons visible didn't mean she didn't have them. The car's lights backlit their approach. Gun still at the ready, he walked from the umbra cast by the house into the driveway.

The voice he recognized as Owen's yelled from behind him, "Stay right there. Drop your weapon or I'll drop you like a squirrel from a tree."

Muscle memory kicked in. He dove left, spun in the air to face the threat. Before hitting the ground, he acquired the target and engaged the firing mechanism. Over the gun's roar, he heard Seamus and Niki yelling at Owen.

Owen crumpled. *One secured.* He spun around, his finger applying pressure to the trigger, ready to spray Seamus and Niki.

Niki had found shelter behind the rocks near the solar panels. Seamus lay on the ground, his body arched in pain.

NIKI

NIKI YELLED, "OWEN, NO!" AND dove behind the rocks guarding the solar-panels pole. In sports and moments of crises, everything slowed down for her, allowing her to examine each frame of life's movie. Her mind acknowledged Seamus's shout echoing hers. It observed Smith reacting like a dropped cat, twisting and spinning in the air, a move he must have honed with hours of practice. Before hitting the ground, his rotation brought his aim to Owen. He fired a three-shot burst.

Owen reacted, but not soon enough or fast enough. The rounds struck Owen's torso, punching him off balance. Owen's gun discharged.

Like puppets with strings cut, Seamus and Owen both sank to the ground. Niki ripped her P365 from her ankle holster and aimed it at Smith. "Gun down or you're dead."

Smith lowered the front of his rifle and backed against Seamus's truck. "That one's dead. He might have friends."

Seamus's groan pulled Niki's attention toward him. He was dragging himself toward the house, leaving behind a trail of blood. Keeping her weapon centered on Smith's chest, she yelled at him to put the gun down and scrambled to Seamus, relieved not to see spurting blood. "Swear to God, you don't put that rifle down, you are dead." She added pressure to the trigger and felt a flicker of disappointment when Smith laid his weapon on the ground.

In a calm voice, Smith asked how bad Seamus was.

"I've got a field first-aid kit in my car. Black duffle with a Red-Cross-type patch on it. Bring that and grab the flashlight Seamus dropped. We *did not know* Owen planned to try anything stupid like that."

She heard him mumble under his breath, "I should have killed you both when I had the chance."

He returned with the duffel. While she held the flashlight in one hand and her Sig in the other, he used the scalpel to slice through Seamus's jeans and peel the pants leg away from the wound. He reported, "Through and through. Missed the femoral artery and no bone involvement."

Relief flooded her, threatening to break her focus. She snapped, "Find the hemostatic compound. Once we stop the bleeding, we'll carry him inside." She sneaked a glance at Owen, a silent, dark blob on the ground. *Damn it, Owen. What made you think you were helping?*

Under her instruction, Smith applied the first impregnated dressing to Seamus's neat entrance wound. He did the same for the back of his thigh, where the mess was worse. "Infection and stupidity are his biggest worries now."

Seamus spoke his first word, "Stupidity?"

"Yeah. If you don't take care of the wound." Smith jabbed him with a needle to deliver a local pain killer. "Or you think this changes anything with our agreement." To Niki: "Let's get him inside."

Seamus pressed his hands on the ground. "If you help me up—"

Niki slapped his nearest hand. "You dumb rabbit. Keep that wound above your heart until the bleeding stops." She pressed a hand into his chest and forced him down. To Smith she said, "Get a chair from the dining room. We'll lay that on the ground, get him on it, and carry him up the ramp. Prop open the door to the screened porch and the one from the porch to the main room. That way we don't have to screw around with them while our hands are full."

He looked like he planned to object. She tilted her head. "Just fucking do it. We can compare prick sizes later."

He snorted. "Love your style. Want me to grab a blanket too?"

"No. Main thing is to get him where we can control everything. I'll check Owen while you get the chair."

Smith moved methodically, like he was exhausted and it required effort to move each foot. He wedged a piece of wood under the screened door to keep it open. Good, he was occupied.

She ran to Owen, determined she could do nothing for him. "Godspeed, Owen." She raced back to Seamus and stopped him from moving.

"Really," Seamus said, "If you support me, I can walk."

Niki grabbed his chin, forcing him to look at her. "Seamus, listen up. You are in shock. You're feeling okay because we gave you a shot of synthetic morphine. If you don't behave yourself, I will give you a shot of something that will knock you out."

Smith lay the chair on the ground next to Seamus. "Listen to the lady. I did." The bastard gave her a smile, like they were on the same team.

We are no more on the same team than are Superman and Lex Luthor.

THE HAPPY REAPER

IT WAS CLEAR TO THE Happy Reaper that Niki had much more first aid knowledge than he did. They transferred Seamus to the living room couch, where she created a wedge of pillows to support his legs. To reduce the swelling, she found freezer packs Seamus used after his runs, wrapped his wounded leg with a towel to protect his muscle from freezing, and secured the freezer packs with an ace-bandage.

She pressed her fingers onto the pulsing of Seamus's neck. "Fifty-six, a bit elevated from his normal resting forty-four. He might have neurological damage. I agree nothing caused the bullet to fragment, but embedded fabric may be in the wound. If it gets infected, his being in outstanding physical shape won't be much help."

With McCree stable, it was time for the two of them to confab, and not where McCree could butt in. The Happy Reaper motioned toward the porch door. "Let's talk. We can leave the door open and hear if he stirs."

She leaned down and brushed Seamus's forehead with her lips. "You know my rules, Seamus. I'll have to kill you if you die on me."

The Happy Reaper waited for her to choose where she wanted to sit. No way would he sit first and gift her a strategic edge. She showed him she was thinking along similar lines by placing her chair to rest her back against the lakeside door.

He thumped another one across the floor and parked himself facing her. The seat was hard, but it felt good to get off his feet.

She didn't wait for him to start. "Let's be clear. Seamus and you may have looked deeply into each other's hearts and decided you could trust each other. You and I share no such history. If you or your cohorts so much as look cross-eyed at any member of the McCree clan, I will not rest until you all lie in unmarked graves."

Her putting her cards on the table made him more comfortable. He needed a separation agreement with Niki should Seamus die. "Thanks for your candor. Way I see it, you and I have three common concerns. First, make sure McCree doesn't die. Obviously, I can't allow police involvement. I get the feeling you have your own reasons for not reporting this, and that limits our options."

She acknowledged the point with a head bob.

"Good. Two, Owen made a fatal mistake. We have a body to disappear. Again, without involving the police."

"I agree. We can't notify anyone about what happened to Owen. What's third?"

"Fulfilling Seamus's promise to help me remove the Happy Reaper imposter. He said he had ideas, and that you had a plan. What?"

"The general plan was for me to help hide you until we determine who your impostor is. Seamus had an idea how to accomplish that, but he didn't have time to tell me what."

What had they been doing during those three hours if not making plans? First things first. His idea of how to physically take care of Seamus had to wait until the world woke up. Same with finding the imposter. That left dealing with Owen. "McCree has a Bobcat. I saw he has a backhoe attachment. Once he's with it, he can tell us the best place to dispose of the body around here. My guess is we dig a deep hole and cover it with good sized rocks so critters can't dig up a meal. That's what I would want if it were me. For now, we should cover him with a tarp."

"Why? It's not like he cares. You can barely hold your head up. Rest is our priority."

He felt like he had run a marathon. He knew she was a hard-ass, but that was callous. Some things decency said you had to do no matter how tired you were. "Scavengers? Somebody shows up in the morning? Until we can bury it, we should keep his body hidden and cool in the basement storage room."

He got up. She didn't move. Well, screw her. "I can do this myself, but it would be a lot easier if you helped." An idea popped into this head. "You ever see a dead body?"

She closed her eyes and shuddered. Interesting. She had, and the experience had left its mark. "We'll cover him with a tarp. Seamus must have some. That will make it easier to move him. Come on."

She wiped her face and pushed herself from the chair. "I can see you're on a mission. Save yourself some time and effort. Turn on the outside lights."

He walked through the house, past a sleeping Seamus, to the mudroom. She trailed behind. He flicked on the floods and stared through the window. No body. The shooting had happened quickly. Had he misremembered where it lay? He shifted his focus to the truck, where his rifle still lay on the ground. Using his finger, he tracked a line to his position where Owen had stood. What the hell had she done? "You knew and you let him go?"

He reared his fist to punch out her lights.

She did not flinch. "If you want to live, don't try."

Gravity brought his arm down to his side.

"Owen stole one of my bulletproof vests. You hit him full on. Probably broke a rib or two. He played possum and now he's long gone."

SEAMUS

I WOKE, LYING ON THE living room couch with my legs elevated. It was full light, making it past seven-thirty, and I had a lot of bladder pressure. After considerable effort, I pushed aside the wool blanket covering me and attempted to swing my legs off the couch to stand. Pain radiated from both ankles. I looked down to discover rope tied my ankles, and a cargo strap secured me to the couch.

I yelled, "What the hell?" Then I remembered the hell: Owen surprising everyone; the Happy Reaper killing Owen; Owen's bullet smashing my leg; the two of them carting me into the house on a chair. After that . . .nothing. "Niki?"

From the upstairs bedroom I heard her, "Coming. " She padded down the stairs barefoot, wiping sleepies from the corners of her eyes. "Can't a girl get her beauty rest anymore? How's the pain?"

I looked at my bandaged leg, aware that it should be killing me, but it wasn't. "Aches a little, but I need to go to the bathroom."

"I gave you a second morphine shot a couple of hours ago, which is why you feel okay. Just to be clear, you are not okay. One or two?"

"I think I only got hit once."

She hooted. "I mean, do you have to poop?" Hearing my answer, she told me to hold on a sec and stepped away. Kitchen cabinet doors opened and closed. She handed me my favorite water bottle.

"Just help me stand."

"Not happening. I'll undo the strap that kept you safe from falling off the couch and roll you onto your left side. Can you handle the rest?"

I could not. She had to hold the bottle. The awkward situation prevented my urine from flowing, but once it started, I worried whether the container was large enough.

"You're a human, not a horse—even if you are a stud." She laughed at her joke. "Speaking of horses and elephants, being a math guy, I'm sure you'll be interested to know scientists determined it takes an elephant, a horse, a man, and a cat the same time to pee. Twenty-one seconds, give or take."

I had read that, but chose not to spoil her fun, given my exposed situation.

That immediate issue taken care of, my mind shifted to my next concern. "Is the Happy Reaper still alive?"

"Can't you hear him sawing wood? He and I have a truce. We agreed to discuss moving forward once everyone's awake. First thing I gotta do is cancel a meeting I was supposed to attend this morning."

Lying back on the couch, I listened to her end of the conversation. She reported she had gotten the dreaded two pink lines on a Covid test. She was isolating and would reschedule once she was safe to be around. She disconnected, and I laid into her. "Why the hell aren't you wearing a mask? Just because you feel fine doesn't mean—"

"You bonehead. It was an excuse. I'm perfectly fine. Switching gears, what do you think happens regarding the mysterious Clem if Smith dies before we figure out who the imposter is?"

I heard her words clearly, but they made no sense. Clem was the guy the Happy Reaper had contacted, but I didn't remember any Smith or why he might die. Plus, wasn't there some question I wanted to ask? I closed my eyes and concentrated. Nothing. Concussion? I didn't remember smacking my head and gave it a shake to determine if I saw stars. No stars. Morphine fuzziness? Unbidden, the thought came. "Owen's dead?"

She leaned in and whispered. "Rabbited. He stole one of my tactical vests. It saved his life. I told Smith—"

"Who the hell is Smith?"

She put a finger to her lips. "Quiet. You remember Adam Smith showed up?"

"Oh, the Happy Reaper. Why don't you—"

"I refuse to give him the pleasure of calling him that. I said Owen had known and liked Abigail, and I suspected he wanted frontier justice. My guess is Owen planned to make Smith an offer he couldn't refuse."

"But—"

"Yep. You know, and I know, that wouldn't work. What does Clem do if Smith dies tomorrow of his heart condition?"

"Clem wouldn't know or believe natural causes. He'd take revenge."

She gave me a peck on the cheek. "I thought you'd say that, which is why Smith is still alive. Stay here," she patted the couch. "I'll get a long stick and poke him awake."

NIKI

NIKI POUNDED ON THE GUEST room door. "Rise and shine. We got places to go, people to see."

The snorts changed timbre, then stopped. The sofa-bed springs squeaked. "That's it? No breakfast in bed. No fresh flowers to brighten the room?"

Be thankful I didn't slit your throat while you were sleeping. "Seamus is awake. I have an idea for getting him treatment."

"So do I. Be there shortly."

While Smith rattled around in the kitchen, Niki reminded Seamus of the time the FBI had spirited her to a private doctor in St. Paul who had removed eight shotgun pellets from her. No one had reported anything to the authorities. "We kill two birds with one stone. We get Deputy Director Ambrose to authorize their doctor to treat you and they bury the required gunshot paperwork. And we can tap into Bureau resources to help stop the imposter from completing his next assignment once Smith provides enough info to convince them he's a federal criminal."

"No way." Smith brought a glass of orange juice and a plate piled with cheese and fruit. "My idea is similar, but without cops. I know a doc in Jersey who specializes in gunshot and knife wounds. Does fabulous work and is discrete. He's not inexpensive, but in my experience, he's worth every penny. We bring Seamus—"

Niki wanted to close that down hard. "Drive him to Jersey? That's eighteen hours, minimum, with Seamus suffering the whole time. He'll have to lie down on the rear seat. That doesn't leave enough room in my car for us and my gear, which I cannot leave behind. We can't take Seamus's truck, because he doesn't have a topper, and I can't leave my gear in the truck bed. That means taking two vehicles. You aren't healthy enough to drive straight through, which means stopping at a hotel. More time and more risk. I plan to have the FBI send the doctor here. What do you say, Seamus?"

Another idea popped into her head, and she didn't give Seamus a chance to respond. She pointed a finger at Smith. "Besides, can you guarantee your doctor is still practicing and uncompromised? A lot happens in six years. Covid killed more than a million people. If he's Jersey, he's tied into the mob. They've had some turmoil recently." She didn't know if that was true.

It sounded reasonable and would force Smith to disclose the guy's name if he wanted his idea to win. "Seamus?"

"Both plans suck. The ride to Jersey won't do me any good. And, as Niki observed, we don't know if the Jersey doctor is still alive and practicing. I'm sure Deputy Director Ambrose *could* arrange a house call— or at worst, for us to drive to St. Paul. Problem is, Niki, even if he agrees— and I'm not sure why he would—you have too many enemies inside the Bureau. Someone will sabotage it. Then we have a thousand agents swarming in to capture our guest, leaving me with Clem and his cohorts gunning for my family. Plus, realistically, the FBI's bureaucracy would take at least a month to pull together a task force to do the massive forensic computer work necessary to uncover the imposter. I don't think we have that kind of time."

Smith said, "We don't."

She was about to object, but Seamus saw it coming and held up a hand.

"Hear me out. I agree you can't drop me off at the emergency room. The county prosecutor, who wants my ass, will have the Sheriff's Office swarming this place regardless of what tale I told. Your FBI idea gave me a better one. Substitute Averell Harrington Park for Ambrose. Surely the assistant director of national intelligence can arrange an off-the-books doctor to pay a house call. And we enlist Paddy and his buddies to hack into the imposter's dark-net websites."

Seamus was right. Niki's initial relationship with Park had been fraught, but they had grown to trust each other—within limits. She knew how to frame it so Park would help. Convincing Smith they had clout with the assistant director took some doing since she couldn't exactly reveal the true nature of her undercover work and that she, Ambrose, Park, Seamus, and one other ally, Rick Kaska, used a secure messaging system to communicate privately. She stopped selling when he asked if he could still listen in on all the conversations. She said, "Sure. We're agreed?"

Smith toasted her with a raised orange juice glass. "My tax dollars at work." He lowered the glass and focused hard eyes on Seamus. "You positive? It's your family's lives on the line if this goes sideways."

"Thanks for the reminder. Niki, something to do before you call. I left a brush pile and a message for you on Shank Lake Road, just before Beaver Creek. Remove it before someone sees them and wonders what's going on."

TYLER

TYLER LOOKED OUT THE FIRST-CLASS window and marveled at the Rocky Mountains, which he had never seen. Mid-October and already sun glinted off snow-capped peaks. Good thing he brought cold-weather gear.

He stretched his legs, curled his toes, felt his calves stretch all the way to his knees. He couldn't imagine how cramped his six-four frame would be in coach. What would Charlene and Zach say to his upgraded ticket? Whatever. They could take it from his share of the fee if they objected. Wait until they saw the other costs. Mary, Mother of God, an Aspen hotel for two nights cost more than he earned in a week. He corrected himself— used to earn in a week. Well, when in Rome . . .

His phone app claimed the flight was on time. The full-sized rental was waiting for his four-hour drive to Aspen. He'd check in, grab a bite—no drinks—he'd read alcohol made adjusting to altitude worse, whereas staying hydrated helped. Aspen's altitude of 7,908 feet was roughly 7,900 feet above what his body was used to. One goal of this research trip was learning how that would affect his stamina.

Mostly, it was to determine how much of Zach's intel he could have gotten himself. Not that he planned to ditch his pals, but Charlene made him nervous. He'd been afraid Zach's killing the maid would cause her to withdraw. She'd taught him everything he cared to know about police procedures. And Zach was batshit crazy. His hair-brained idea to mow down the entire hunting party proved he and Zach did not have the same vision for the Happy Reaper.

No detail was too minute for the perfect "Results Guaranteed" kill. His fingers tapped a comforting rhythm on his legs. Good thing he had escaped from the Army. He was born for this.

THE HAPPY REAPER

THE HAPPY REAPER WAS AT a loss to figure out what the two of them were up to. He didn't think they were good enough actors to have planned a charade this complicated while he was sleeping. Especially since they both believed Clem would come for the McCrees if something happened to him. Or, he reminded himself, they acted as though they believed.

His priorities to remain free and stop the imposter had not changed. Last night's activities and Owen getting a drop on him had only strengthened his resolve to avoid recapture. He still had his guns. If he sensed betrayal, he could kill them both. And himself if it came to it.

While Niki cleared the brush pile, McCree put his cell phone on speaker and called his son, got his granddaughter, and had to chitchat first. He'd bet Niki had contacted Paddy because Seamus's son did not seem at all surprised by anything his father said. Paddy insisted it would work best to understand the web design if he was physically with the Happy Reaper. A friend of his named Lisa was visiting. Would it be okay to bring her up?

Seamus muted his phone. "She and Paddy founded a company together. I was on their board, and we've kept in touch. She's good people, an excellent hacker. We need her, and she knows how to keep secrets."

Hackers weren't exactly establishment people. "It's your funeral if she screws things up."

Seamus unmuted the phone, said Lisa could come. Seamus again had his ear bent by his granddaughter. At Niki's return, he wrapped up the call and shared that Lisa and his son would pack and leave.

Niki motioned at the Happy Reaper. "We ready?"

Nothing had changed his mind. "Do it."

Niki borrowed a burner phone from Seamus and placed a call to Assistant Director of National Intelligence Averell Harrington Park. After three holds and two transfers, ADNI Park answered and asked for her code name.

"This is Niki. I am on an unsecured line with an unauthorized party listening in and am unwilling to provide my code name. I require assistance."

Park said, "Understood. I'll call you in five minutes. This number?"

"Perfect." Niki pressed disconnect.

The Happy Reaper thought that conversation odd. "Why's he calling you back?"

"If I had been under duress, I would not have agreed to the five-minute delay. This way, he'll make sure no one is recording the conversation. He'll want to know who you are. What shall I tell him?"

Seamus piped up from the couch. "Say he's an old acquaintance, come to make amends before he dies."

That struck the Happy Reaper as too much information. "Let's leave it at old acquaintance. He'll be suspicious if you don't give him my name. Tell him Harry Gottkind."

The phone in Niki's hand rang. She answered with, "You're on speaker."

"May I know the name or names of the unauthorized parties?"

"Harry Gottkind. He's an old acquaintance of Seamus's and a suspicious bugger. Seamus is also here. Here's the situation. Seamus was accidentally shot—not by himself, me, or Mr. Gottkind. He's stable with a through-and-through wound in his upper leg. For various reasons, we cannot report the gunshot wound, which means we cannot take him anyplace for medical care.

"Mr. Gottkind has information concerning an active murder-for-hire scheme. Previously, I might have contacted Deputy Director Ambrose and convinced him to use Bureau services to treat Seamus and stop the killers. Given my history with the Bureau, we think that solution won't work. Furthermore, the computer expertise necessary to stop the murder-for-hire requires a faster approach than the FBI can muster.

"I am committed to seeing this through, which makes me unavailable for other projects. I hoped you could arrange a house call from a safe doctor to make sure Seamus's wound is clean and healing. And maybe you could provide computer expertise to supplement what Seamus has available."

Park cleared his throat. "Excellent analysis regarding the FBI. With the election less than a month away, they are buttoning everything down. They know once the Republicans retake the House, everyone and their sister in the Bureau will be up on the Hill testifying. Where are you?"

"At Seamus's place in Michigan's Upper Peninsula."

"That works. A qualified medical professional will arrive by the end of the day. The computer expertise issue is more fraught. This is a domestic situation, and we have our own issues to consider. What does Seamus have in mind, or should I talk with him?"

Seamus spoke from the couch. "My son hopes he won't get in trouble for tracking down the participants in the murder-for-hire by utilizing some of the software he developed, or tested, or used for you in the past."

"Let me consider that for a moment before I respond."

From the speaker came the sound of a creaking chair. The Happy Reaper pictured some fat guy leaning back and scratching his stomach.

The chair creaked again, and Park said, "If I correctly read Seamus's suggestion, we can provide Patrick a contract to test certain aspects of various software packages for vulnerabilities. If caught using that software in a manner that does not follow U.S. laws, Patrick and anyone he involves will be on their own. We'll want the contract signed in triplicate. Federal rules."

The Happy Reaper wanted to see that contract to make sure it contained nothing that it shouldn't have. He said, "Send the contract here. Seamus's son is on his way to join us."

Park said, "I will arrange for the paperwork to arrive with the doctor. Please have Patrick sign the top two copies and give those to the doc. He should keep the bottom copy in a safe place. Is there anything else? If not, I have a meeting with the President regarding Ukraine."

Niki thanked him and disconnected.

What the hell pull did these two have? And why? He looked at the clock on the wall. Already ten o'clock. Time to feed their fears of Clem. While neither one was paying attention to him, he reduced the volume on his phone to its minimum, dialed a number. The ring changed to a message informing him the number was no longer in service. "Hey Clem, get your beauty sleep? Yeah, well, sorry about the late-night call." He paused, pretending to listen to Clem's half of the conversation. "Fine, hold it over my head. Yeah, you know I'm kidding. All's well here." He paused again. "Yep, by noon. If not, check the web. If nothing there . . . Yeah, I know you'll handle it."

SEAMUS

I WAITED UNTIL PARK'S RETURN call engaged the Happy Reaper's attention before I entered a nine-digit number that opened the secure messaging app used for Niki's secret undercover work. I selected Park to receive the communication. Every line or two, I pressed send, which transmitted it to Park and eliminated it from my phone, a precaution should the Happy Reaper notice my actions.

"Guest" is Adam Smith, escaped convict a.k.a the Happy Reaper. If something happens to him, he has a dead-man switch in place, which will trigger his allies to kill my family and friends.

Someone is copying his Happy Reaper persona. Uses same business card, same dark web portal, etc. At least one murder committed in Alabama.

He wants me to smoke out the imposter to kill him. With threat to family, I have no choice but to help. Except I want to capture imposter, not kill.

FBI has people who want to harm Niki, so cannot involve them or any other normal law enforcement group that would bring in the Bureau.

I'm engaging my son and a hacker friend to 1. Break into imposter's dark web and determine who he is and what his plans are. 2. Find the Happy Reaper's dead-man switch and neutralize. Can you provide Paddy access to proprietary software without involving your people?

A message showed in my inbox from Park: *Will send medical help with other skills to assess entire situation.* I deleted his message and continued typing.

Message received. TY. Adam Smith claims heart failure, but not conjunctive heart failure. Confirm?

Damn autocorrect. Congestive heart failure. Signing off before you hang up with Niki.

I exited the app, causing all evidence of it to vanish from my phone, and opened a word game in case the Happy Reaper checked what I was doing.

Niki ended her conversation, and the Happy Reaper made a call to Clem that sent chills up my spine and anger pains stabbing behind my eyes. Getting Clem and his buddies off the street had to be Paddy's number one priority—all the while making the Happy Reaper believe identifying the imposter was job number one.

"Now that's taken care of," the Happy Reaper said. "I'll police the grounds."

I said, "Meaning what?"

"Meaning I have casings to pick up. And now that it's light, I can see what's what with your Owen. We can't have him lying dead somewhere in the woods with a blood trail leading to us."

Niki said, "You don't believe he's alive?"

"An old man like that could have died of cardiac arrest a hundred yards from here. I didn't get to be the best by being sloppy."

I agreed that cleaning up from last night was critical, but the idea of him tracking Owen was unwise. "If you follow Owen's trail, and he's alive, he'll see you way before you see him. He'll assume you're hunting him and kill you. Then everyone is screwed."

Niki patted my good leg. "You're both right. I'll go with Smith. If Owen is dead, we can take care of his remains. If he's alive and injured, we can help because we know he won't go to a hospital or the cops."

I threw up my hands in frustration. "And if he's alive and waiting for a shot?"

Niki gave me another pat. "I plan to talk loudly to Smith. Remind him Seamus needs everyone's help, including Smith's. Owen may or may not show himself, but he'll get the message and won't kill Smith."

I did not share Niki's confidence that she understood Owen and his motives. She hadn't predicted his ambush last night that nearly got me killed. But it was two to one, and the morphine was wearing off. "Do me a favor and clean up the evidence outside the house first and leave Owen for later."

NIKI AND THE HAPPY REAPER had been gone an hour when nature demanded I visit the bathroom. The wounds had stopped leaking through the bandages, but the throbbing increased in intensity. Standing was a bad idea. With difficulty, I eased myself to the floor, rested the injured leg on the good one, and inch-wormed into the bathroom.

My business complete, my next trick was to return to the couch. I wrapped a towel from the towel bar around the wounded leg to control the fresh blood now darkening the bandages. The rumble of an approaching vehicle alerted me to company. A mental calculation that took way longer than it should told me not enough time had passed for Paddy and Lisa to get here. I sent a silent message for whoever it was to drive by. The alternating brake squeaks and engine acceleration allowed me to follow its progress down the road.

The crunch of tires turning onto my gravel driveway dashed my hopes. I felt vindicated that I had insisted the Happy Reaper and Niki eliminate evidence of last night's confrontation with Owen before searching for him.

Then realized they hadn't agreed.

Nothing I could do but cross fingers on both hands and hope they found everything. My job was to avoid letting the visitor see me bleeding from an obvious gunshot wound. I crammed myself against the toilet, gritted my teeth, and used my good leg to help raise the injured one to rest on the sink. I was safe, unless they entered the house.

A car door creaked open and shut with a thump. Footsteps on gravel approached the kitchen stoop, clumped up the three steps. The screen door whined in protest. A fist pounded on the door.

"Iron County Sheriff's Department. You in there, Seamus?"

Chief Bartelle. My brain spun in confusion. Had Owen contacted the police or gone to a hospital? Had someone found him and that triggered the police to investigate? And why the chief?

Where were Niki and the Happy Reaper?

Bartelle couldn't see me, but if he went through the screened porch to the front deck, he would see the couch with the blanket and pillows. And blood-stained dressings that forced his hand, and he *would* come in.

Acid poured into my stomach, its burning an unwelcome relief from the leg pain.

Bartelle pounded on the door again. "Got a request for a safety check." In a lower voice, like he was talking to himself, he said, "Those Minnesota plates mean someone else is here. I'd better look around."

NIKI

NIKI CONSIDERED HERSELF AN OKAY tracker. Smith was better. He followed Owen's trail with few pauses, pointing to disturbed leaves, a freshly bent stalk, a drop of blood. Owen had taken the path toward the cabin, walked down the cabin driveway, and crossed the road into the area where Seamus had once intended to plant an orchard. Seamus still called it that even though a neighbor had talked him out of the project after he had cleared an acre of trees.

Owen continued through the orchard, down the hill, and picked up a cleared trail Niki had taken the previous night. A mile and a half later, and a hundred feet from a passable dirt road, the tracks vanished.

Crap. Had Owen circled around? Was he stalking them now? She prattled on about Seamus needing everyone's help. Smith was crucial to his plans. She had no clue if she was making any sense, but she kept at it even after she and Smith separated and the only one listening was a curious blue jay. The jay heard enough, gave a dissatisfied squawk and flew off. No one wanted to hear her. She shut up.

Smith called it quits after a quarter hour of walking ever-wider circles and still not reacquiring Owen's track. "It's like a helicopter picked him up."

"Up" triggered her to spin around, checking the tops of nearby trees. She pressed her hands over her pounding heart to prevent it from escaping her chest. No Owen.

He had vanished. It was Smith's outing, so she asked, "Now what?"

Smith threw up his hands. "I wouldn't believe it if I hadn't seen it with my own eyes. Nothing to do except retrace our steps and obliterate his trail with ours. Once we get to that so-called orchard, I want to find every leaf with even a speck of blood. We'll burn them to destroy that evidence."

She heard a vehicle approaching on the road and pressed Smith into a crouch. They watched in silence as the Iron County Sheriff's car drove past.

She whispered her optimistic thought. "With luck, they're here to warn Seamus about you. I know some of the deputies. I'll try to prevent them from seeing Seamus."

Wearing her tactical vest would make any cop suspicious. She stripped it off and dropped it next to Smith. "Don't lose it. Stay hidden. I'll return for you when it's safe."

"Probably find me snoozing. I'm whipped."

She raced to the house in time to hear Chief Bartelle say he should look around. "Yo, Chief. How they hanging?"

He spun toward her voice. She stepped from behind the garage and gave him a wave. "What's up?"

"Where's Seamus? We got an anonymous call suggesting we do a safety check. Something suspicious going on."

She shrugged a who-knows gesture. "Really? What did they say?" Was Owen behind it? "We were walking in the woods. Seamus spotted some rare bird." She continued up the driveway and stopped next to the patrol car, guaranteeing Bartelle's gaze didn't wander in the opposite direction toward Owen's blood trail. "A half hour of tromping through stickers and underbrush looking for some little brown jobber was enough for me. You're free to wait, but I honestly don't know how long that will be."

Bartelle didn't take her implied hint to come off the stoop and chat with her by his car. "I'll check eBird and see what he posts. Your wheels?" He pointed at her ride.

She made a mental note to ask Seamus to explain eBird. "Got here last night. Plan to stay maybe a week. Love it with the leaves down and the woods open to view. Want me to have him call you?"

"Please do, so I can close this inquiry." He tromped down the steps. "You going to be up for rifle season?"

Rifle season? Oh, he meant deer hunting with a rifle. She laughed. "With what Michigan charges for out-of-state licenses? No way. Seamus likes to photograph them. I enjoy watching both him and the deer. But this bird-watching stuff with nothing to see? That's for the birds. Pun intended."

He humored her with a smile. "Have Seamus leave a message with the front desk if I'm not available."

She gave him an emphatic thumbs up—as much for his leaving without triggering a crisis as confirming she'd have Seamus call. Watching him drive away, she had a bad feeling that this would not be their last scrape with the law.

SEAMUS

NIKI FOUND ME IN THE bathroom, blood soaking through the towel I had wrapped around my leg.

"Ah crap, Seamus. You opened it up." She raced from the bathroom and returned with the pillows and a blanket from the couch. "You're not moving until that doc gets here."

She tucked one pillow under my neck and arranged the others to support my leg. "Keep warm." She draped the blanket over me. "I have to collect Smith."

SHE DID, AND THEY TOLD me about Owen's vanishing trail. Whether

Owen or someone else had called the police was moot. The damage was the same. I waited forty-five minutes before I called Bartelle and told him I was hunky-dory.

"Good to hear. What rare bird were you looking for?"

I restrained myself from saying, "Huh?" and shot a look at Niki in hopes she could give me a clue.

She whispered, "Little brown one."

"I couldn't decide between winter wren or house wren. It had the cocked tail of a winter wren, but the supercilium wasn't sufficiently pronounced. And the bird seemed a little large, which made me think it might be a house wren. Would the danged thing sing and resolve the question?"

I whistled the warble of the house wren. "I can't do that long continuous song of the winter wren. Didn't matter, because it stayed silent and only offered glimpses as it flitted from one bush to another. Just when I thought I'd have a good view, the sucker flew off. I wasted another half hour trying to find it. It's late for either of them to still be here, but we've had such unseasonably warm weather, who knows what they're thinking. This hot, the deer—"

"Gotta go, Seamus. You take care." He ended the call.

The Happy Reaper asked, "What was all that wren nonsense?"

Niki said, "I told the chief that I got bored with Seamus looking at some rare little brown bird."

The Happy Reaper pointed at me. "And I can see why. We have a plan before you bleed out on us?"

I gave him my brightest smile. "We do."

"That," Niki said, "must wait for Smith and me to finish eliminating Owen's trail. Seamus, you stay right here until the bleeding stops. Keep that leg elevated"

"While you do that," I said, "I'll create a bird list on eBird from today's quote-unquote outing because Bartelle knows I always do."

The Happy Reaper patted my head. "Good to see your brain rebooted and is functioning again."

Niki rolled her eyes. "Let's not celebrate until we hear his plan."

I DON'T KNOW HOW MUCH time passed with me on the bathroom floor. Niki and the Happy Reaper left, returned, and ate lunch, denying me food on the theory the expected doctor might use anesthesia. Another set of tires crunching to a stop in the driveway brought me bolt upright from my nap.

The Happy Reaper appeared at the bathroom door holding his assault rifle. "You know a seriously fit black dude, six-six? Drives a white Mercedes van. Niki's talking to him."

"The doctor? If not, you better make yourself and that weapon scarce. Upstairs is good."

He padded slowly up the staircase. The next thing I heard was the bed creak—his lying down. I hoped he was smart enough not to close his eyes. His snoring would surely give him away.

Footsteps came up the ramp to the porch, and Niki appeared in the hallway with two strangers. She introduced the buff, black guy as Gerry with a G, the mid-twenties Latina with serious muscle definition as Carla. Gerry unwrapped the towel, peeled off the bandages, and gave Carla a shrug. "Boring."

Carla said, "That's his response to any through and through wound. Gerry and I will operate on Seamus in the van. We have everything we need in there, including Seamus's blood type, should he require a transfusion. What we do not want are any additional unhygienic people around while we work."

While lying in the bathroom, I'd had nothing to do but sleep and worry. That had conjured a fresh concern: would anesthesia affect my ability to keep secrets? I did not want to say something unintended about the Happy Reaper or reveal Niki's undercover work. "I hate that brain-dead feeling I get with general anesthesia. Can you use a local?"

Gerry asked about my experiences. Yes, I had had several surgeries—he'd see the scars. No, I'd never had an adverse reaction, other than being brain-fogged. No, I did not want to watch through a mirror.

"It will take us up to three hours, depending on the damage. We'll use a combination of local anesthesia and IV sedation. Our plan is to do a debridement and irrigation. You may hear us and possibly feel a little tug, but you should be comfortable and avoid most post-anesthesia issues."

I asked what that meant in English.

Carla said, "Debridement is a fancy term for removing everything that shouldn't be in you. Next, we flush out—i.e. clean—the canal the bullet left. We'll start you on IV antibiotics during the surgery. We want to prevent an infection from all the germs blasted into you by the bullet going through clothing."

They loaded me on a stretcher, carted me to the van, and laid me on a black examination table. The air smelled antiseptic. The ceiling sprouted green, red, and white ports. Silent machines covered counter tops, above and below which were various labeled cupboards.

Carla engaged an exhaust fan, which I soon realized was to mask sound as much as circulate air.

Gerry leaned close to me. "We're alone. Let's talk. Anything we shouldn't say to Niki? No? Good, that makes it easier. You're lucky. The bullet did not hit bone, sever a major artery, or disrupt a major nerve. You have suffered significant trauma to your biceps femoris and semitendinosus muscles—two of the three muscles of your hamstring. You may have a permanent limp. You will require extensive rehabilitation to regain maximum flexibility. Questions?"

"None that matter."

"Good. I'm a trauma surgeon and honed my skills during a few of our recent overseas wars. Carla is a fine vascular surgeon. Neither of us are plastic surgeons. Despite our best efforts, you will have two ugly scars at the end of this process that may require skin grafts later."

Carla draped me with surgical cloths, keeping only the wound area open. "Gerry didn't mention that we are both Special Services veterans. Before we operate, what should we know about this Adam Smith individual?"

Park had passed along all the information I had provided him, plus a lot of additional information regarding the Happy Reaper—and, apparently, me. "He says, and I believe, his heart is failing. I can't have him corking off on me before we find his cohorts and eliminate the threat against my family. I don't know if there's anything you can do to help keep him alive, but that's my biggest concern. Well, that and I guess I have to reconcile myself to knowing my legs will no longer support my supermodel career."

They both laughed. Gerry said, "Good attitude. We'll examine him and make sure he has the right meds. Alright, Carla, let's find a vein, start an IV, and try not to disappoint Adam Smith by killing Seamus."

NIKI

NIKI PACED OUTSIDE THE MOBILE operating room, waiting for news. She checked her watch: two hours since Gerry and Carla had locked themselves inside the van with Seamus. For the last hour, Smith had been snoring away in the camp chair he had found in the garage and set up in the sun. She couldn't ask for a nicer autumn day: bright sunshine had brought the temperature to the mid-sixties, and a previous killing frost had done in the mosquitoes. Could you still call it Indian Summer, or was that now a racial slur like Indian Giver? It was great, whatever you called it in "polite company." An oxymoron. By being polite, they were impolite, and who wanted that kind of company, anyway? And now when she heard the word oxymoron, all she could think of were the morons who had foisted the OxyContin epidemic on the US.

She hit her forehead with the heel of her hand to knock away the dull roar of miscellaneous thoughts flitting through her mind. Dull roar, another oxymoron. If she couldn't focus, she'd silently scream about the civil war between the clearly misunderstood hemispheres of her brain. It was becoming old news in a bittersweet manner that she must dismiss with deliberate speed and leave behind an eloquent silence.

Good grief, that crap was something Seamus would come up with. She circled the van, plunked into the seat next to Smith, checked her watch. Two hours and five minutes. Stood and paced. Kicked a piece of gravel up and down the driveway. Gave that up and—

The distant clunk of a vehicle jarring a pothole in the road grabbed her attention. There it was again, shocks reacting badly to the rough road. Distant but heading their way. She shook Smith awake. "Someone's driving down the road. Could be Seamus's son, Patrick. But if not, we don't want them to see you."

He cupped his hands behind his ears and tilted his head. "Good ears." He stretched and walked toward the house. "I'll cover you from inside."

Not after I pulled your firing pins. She raced the camp chairs into the garage—no reason to explain their presence in the driveway—sprinted to the van, and pounded on the door. "We may have company. Do not leave until I tell you it's safe."

Gerry responded, "Roger that."

If the vehicle got more than a hundred feet down the driveway, it would see the van. She had to cut them off at the road. Wouldn't look right to be breathing hard. She slowed to a fast walk, reached the road, heard the sounds more clearly. Two vehicles. Not Patrick. Bird hunters? Chief Bartelle bringing reinforcements? *Screwed if it's police, so assume it's not.*

She adopted the mannerisms of someone on their daily stroll. Told herself to put on a cheerful face.

The Happy Reaper

Seeing a green Prius and dark blue SUV drive down the driveway, the Happy Reaper's stomach knotted and pain flared behind his eyes. Niki hopped from the Prius passenger seat, and a guy who looked like a younger, more muscular Seamus exited from the driver's side. Aha! Patrick McCree had arrived. Niki made a beeline for the van. Patrick led the driver of the SUV, a short woman with a baby bump, toward the house.

The Happy Reaper ditched his weapon in the guest bedroom and met them on the screened porch. Patrick introduced him to General Lisa Latoya, who up close had intelligent eyes and the body fat of an Olympic athlete. He shook her hand and asked what she was a general of.

Patrick said, "Regular army. CyberOps."

"No shit. I've never met a general in person before. Seen a shit-ton on television and met a retired one in prison." Why was he running off at the mouth like a gobsmacked cretin?

She graced him with a smile that could melt cheese. "I'm sorry to disappoint. You still haven't met an active general. My promotion doesn't officially take effect until I return from leave. I've asked Patrick to do the honors of pinning on my star."

He glanced at her stomach. Not that pregnant. "When are you due?"

"Oh, that's not for a while. I'm on a two-week leave before I report for my next assignment. I'll have to disembark here in four days. Five tops."

"CyberOps sounds interesting. What's your assignment?"

"Are you aware that the air force has pilots trained to act like our enemies? You might have heard them called the aggressor or adversary squadron. The Army makes no secret that they want to build the best group of hackers the U.S. has ever encountered. Better than the Russians. Better than the Chinese or North Koreans. Our job is to try to break into anything and everything."

Confidence radiated off her. He was sure she would succeed.

She continued. "I'd love to be one of the troops." Her expression matched her wistful tone. "But my job will be five percent thinking and ninety-five percent paperwork. When Patrick asked if I would help find your imposter, I jumped with both feet." She leaned in. "Between you, me, and the lamppost, Patrick is good at this stuff, but I am way better."

Her mannerisms were disarming, and he told himself to be wary and not fall under her charm. "Where did you and Patrick meet?"

"College. Four of us founded a cybersecurity firm after graduation. Only lasted a couple of years before we cashed in. Seamus has been advising me on how to invest my money. I'm happy to repay the favor."

Patrick chuckled. "You make it sound like we sold our souls for the money. Lisa and I had an idea we wanted to pass by you, Mr. Smith. From what Dad told me, the imposter hacked into your dark websites and hijacked them."

Lisa placed a hand on the Happy Reaper's arm. "We hoped you'd detail for us the structure you set up. The initial client contact, how you verified the client and subject, payment protocols, etcetera. Our working assumption is the imposter made only minor modifications to your structure. Or do you have another idea?"

The Happy Reaper considered exposing the back doors he had left in all his software. That would save time, but he had used similar techniques for other programs not related to the imposter that he did not want them to gain access to. No go. "Happy to help, but a lot can change in six years."

Lisa gave him the biggest smile, like he was something special. He'd bet her troops thought she walked on water.

Patrick, whose vibe made it clear he still wished his father had killed the Happy Reaper six years ago, kept on the business track. "We'll make the guest cabin our command center. I understand you get winded walking. You okay using one of the ATVs?"

Like he was some kind of invalid. "No problem."

Patrick offered a head bob. "Once I help Lisa set up a generator, create a separate satellite link, and unpack all our hardware, I'll fix dinner. Lisa will link the servers and activate a bot network to assist us."

To hide who you are. Nice.

"Can we debrief you this evening? Or must we wait until morning?"

No moss would grow on these two. "Evening's fine. I'll let you get to your work." *And I'll do my own cyber-intelligence gathering on Lisa Latoya.*

Niki

GERRY INFORMED NIKI THE OPERATION was complete and a success. Her nervousness surprised her. Would Seamus fully recover, and how long would his rehab take? Would that constrain how they could deal with Smith? And what the hell was Seamus's grand plan? Time was a-wastin'.

At Gerry's invite, she climbed into the van and stopped at the foot of the table on which an unconscious Seamus lay. He looked serene, and she wondered how long that would last once he came to.

She made notes covering details of changing bandages, how long to expect the drain to remain in his leg until it fell out on its own, the technique to inject antibiotics into the peripheral IV catheter, and timing for Seamus to take pain meds. Then before her eyes, magic happened: in one breath, Seamus transitioned from unconscious to awake. "Welcome back." She kissed his forehead. "The docs officially made me your nurse and insist you do exactly what I tell you."

He batted his eyes. "Don't I always?"

She snorted. "Who are you and what did you do with Seamus McCree? Kidding aside, if you don't follow orders, you'll screw up your recovery."

Gerry went through the bandage and med routine with Seamus. Carla said, "We want you on bed rest today and tonight. Tomorrow, we'll make sure everything looks good and get you using crutches."

Seamus nodded his understanding. "Hey, Niki. Don't I have crutches in the attic storage from the last time I destroyed my ankle?"

Destroying his ankle had occurred in the Boston area. Was he remembering his ex-wife's place where he had recuperated? Or could he mean the basement here? "Where are they?"

"By the front windows or leaning on the wall behind the attic door."

Giving the doctors an eye roll, she said, "He doesn't have an attic. Do I need to go into town and buy some?"

Carla: "We brought adjustable ones. Is there space for us to stay? Or should we try to get rooms in town? I saw Tall Pines has a hotel, and we passed one in Iron River if Tall Pines is full."

Seamus: "You can stay in the guest cabin. Or I can stay there, and you can have the house."

Oh boy. "Seamus, do you remember that Patrick and Lisa are here and are staying at the cabin? There's room—"

"You bumb dunny. Paddy's wife's name is Cindy, not Lisa. Are the kids sleeping in the cabin, too?"

Seamus had warned them about brain fog, but this was something else. Niki told the doctors there was room. She'd give them a tour of the house once they were ready to move Seamus.

Gerry: "Seamus, your vitals are looking good, but we need to let the anesthesia effects wear off before we move you."

Seamus gave him a two-handed wave of dismissal. "It's all gone. Leg's still numb. Otherwise, I could walk."

Carla to Niki: "I see what you mean about him being a handful." To Seamus: "I'm sure you're right. But the AMA has protocols we must follow. They insist at least an hour in post-op before we release you and twelve hours before you use the leg. You still have, oh, at least forty-five minutes left."

Thank goodness these two were quick thinkers.

"What time is it?" Seamus asked. "I'm not keeping you from wine time, am I? Five o'clock on the deck."

Gerry: "Sounds like a plan. Now, why don't you close your eyes and rest up for us, Seamus?"

Seamus: "Niki, there's an open box of Cabernet, and I'm sure I have some white wine chilling in the cold room. You'll take care of them?"

His befuddlement was endearing. "Tell you what, Seamus. Since they came all this way to make a house call, I'll serve the good wine you've been hiding for an undefined special occasion. Now shut your trap and close your eyes." She put on a stern face. "Or I'll tape them shut."

"That's the Niki I know and love."

Her heart did a jitterbug. His voice had become tender. Did he actually mean that? And if he did, what did that mean for their relationship?

Gerry snagged her attention and motioned her to follow him from the van. Shutting the door behind them, he said ADNI Park had ordered them to ignore Seamus, who Park called a civilian in a bind, and follow Niki's orders regarding how to handle Smith. "He authorized us to remove Smith if that's what you want."

Tempting, but she had to live with Seamus. Well, not had to, but—and not live with, but . . . Nothing she wanted to explain. "Not necessary. I've pulled the firing pins from his AR and his pistol. He has a knife, which is why I'll sleep on the porch with Seamus." At Gerry's questioning look, she added. "His preference and best we accede. He can listen to the birds and stuff. It'll make him less antsy, meaning less likely to do something stupid."

Gerry: "And you don't want to take away Smith's knife because it alerts him to check his firearms. Besides, he could find another knife from the kitchen. Good thinking. Seamus wanted us to examine Smith and make sure he has whatever meds he needs."

"Good. How long before Seamus starts making sense? He says he has a plan, but . . ."

"Wait until morning. Anything we, meaning ADNI Park, can do for you?"

She gave that some thought, decided until she heard Seamus's plan, she didn't know what would help. "Got anything to give me the patience of Job?"

"No. But if you end up with boils from the top of your head to the soles of your feet, we can cure that."

THE HAPPY REAPER

A KNOCK ON THE DOOR woke the Happy Reaper from his nap. He sat upright and arranged the pillows to support himself and hide his handgun and knife. "Come in," he said. "You caught me catching up on my Zs."

"I'm Gerry. This is Carla."

They both had a military vibe. His estimate on Gerry's size had been accurate. He looked like he might have played wide-receiver in college. His entire face smiled, letting you know he delighted in life. She was average height but projected a larger presence. He waved them in. "How did you get the short stick?"

Carla sat on the lone chair. Gerry leaned against the doorframe and squinted. "Short stick? I don't get your meaning."

"Well," the Happy Reaper drew out the word. "Seamus is shot. Niki calls an assistant director of national intelligence, and you two materialize like genies from a lamp. Who do you work for, anyway?"

"Private practice," Gerry said.

Carla said, "I figured since we were here, I'd give you a quick check-up. I understand doctors have diagnosed you with heart failure. Did they have you on oxygen before your unexpected release from supervision?"

What the hell did Seamus tell these two? He must have tongue-wagged while under the influence of whatever they gave him to knock him out. "I don't quite get your meaning."

Carla rose from the chair. "I am tired and want to take a shower to wash off the day, so I'll be blunt. We know you're Adam Smith and that you escaped from prison while hospitalized. We downloaded your patient records. Your doctors sometimes had you on oxygen. Looking at the pulse in your neck and the way you're leaning to suck in air, I'd guess your oxygen level is low. I don't see a CPAP machine. Slip on this pulse oximeter and let's get a reading."

It required a moment for him to take in her words. He preached to all who would listen that no one should assume they had any privacy. And yet he had foolishly assumed his medical records were actually safe. She sat next to him, the couch cushion releasing an exhausted sigh. He allowed her to place a device on his index finger. She shook her head and tisked under her breath. She checked his wrist for his pulse. "Ninety."

Gerry said. "High. They told you that you could live three months. But that's if you do everything right. Keep your oxygen up, sleep well, avoid stress, take your medicine. Low oxygen makes your heart work double shifts. It should be on disability pension. You're sleeping poorly without your CPAP. This situation is highly stressful. At least you grabbed your meds."

Carla handed him several prescription scripts. "CPAP, oxygen concentrator, and refills of all your meds to get you through three months. Without health insurance, they're expensive. If you don't get the machines, don't worry about the refills. You won't need them."

So much for bedside manner. He checked the scripts. They used his real name, which was like taking out a Super Bowl ad telling the Feds where he was. They surely had someone checking prescriptions for Adam Smith for his medicines or these devices. "Money's not the issue. Can't you write the scripts for one of the others to fill for me?"

Carla rubbed her eyes. "That's fraud. Those machines are Class II Medical Devices. We could lose our licenses for that. Adam Smith is the one who might not make it another week without those machines. Adam Smith is the one who gets the prescription. You didn't think to grab your DNR, did you? I'm not telling you what to do, but if it were me, I'd get one in place ASAP. Without it, first responders will resuscitate you. The medical establishment will put you on a ventilator and artificially pump your heart and lungs to keep you alive. I see by your reaction you don't want that. Create a DNR. Soon."

Without another word, the two left and closed the door. What the hell was that? They'd treated Seamus. They weren't reporting his gunshot wound. That was against the law, but they weren't willing to put the prescription in a different name, even though they knew he'd use it appropriately. That did not compute, but he was too tired to deal with it now. Maybe after he napped, a solution would come clear.

Closing his eyes brought the specter of imminent death. He sat bolt upright. What was important here? It didn't matter if Patrick and Lisa used knowledge of how he constructed software back doors to crack where he stored his money. After he died and the money remained unclaimed for enough years, some government or another would eventually glom onto it through their escheatment laws.

The *only* two things that mattered right now were to avoid the lingering death Carla described and make sure the imposter who hijacked his legacy became a footnote, not a successor.

Yet right now, his clenched teeth, tight neck, and headache were proof he was still reluctant to tell Patrick and Lisa about his secret access. Why? Without interference, his autobiography would be the definitive statement of his life and times. If he gave those two the keys to the kingdom, and they opened his code up to others, he'd lose control of that narrative.

He held his arms like lady justice, weighing the desire to erase the imposter versus losing control. Erasing the imposter won. He'd give Patrick and Lisa time to hack their way through the front. If that took too long, he'd say open sesame and let them in the easy way through the back door.

If it still existed. The imposter might have found and sealed it. That thought convinced him he had no reason to offer the back door yet. He was wired and alert. Time to research Lisa Latoya.

NIKI

WITH SEAMUS SETTLED ONTO THE daybed on his screened porch, and the Special Services doctors talking with Smith, Niki decided she had time for a quick confab with Patrick and Lisa.

She followed the purr of a generator and found them both in the guest cabin. Closing the door behind her, she said, "You obviously have a plan. What can I do to assist?"

Lisa asked, "You any good at climbing trees?"

"Been years. What do you have in mind?"

Lisa handed her a spool of cable. "Ever heard of cell-site simulators?"

Guessing their plan, Niki felt a warm glow. "Used them with the Bureau. You're creating an antenna to monitor Smith's cell phone."

Patrick pointed to a massive pine tree. "Where he can't see it and guess what it is. Lisa thinks an antenna near the top of that pine will provide a tower strong enough to capture any signals within a mile radius. We'll run the line down the trunk, under needles and leaf duff, and into the crawl space under the cabin. From there, we can bring it up through the grate Dad installed in the floor to allow air flow in the cabin." Seeing Niki's confusion, he added, "He's got another grate up high in the wall. Those allow air to flow and prevent mold forming on the rafters, even in the winter when the cabin's closed. Sorry, too much information."

Niki saw they had already brought the generator cable from outside through the crawl space and floor grate. That made it easy to hide another wire through the same space, especially once they set up the banks of computers and monitors now resting on the bed. The fake tower would allow them to capture conversations and numbers called. Niki spotted a flaw in their solution. "This guy Clem uses throwaway phones. Even if you determine the number Smith calls, you won't know who's holding the phone."

Patrick booted up a computer. "Sure. But we get to hear their conversations. Maybe they have a code word to tell Clem the Happy Reaper—I'm sorry, I know you don't want to call him that. If Smith and Clem are indiscreet, they might drop clues. It may gain nothing, but it might."

Lisa handed Niki a handful of zip-ties, and a handsaw. "Set it up a few feet below the top making it invisible from a distance. Avoid clearing more branches than you must. Zip-tie the end of the cable to the tree for a few feet and leave the rest loose. The cable can flex with the tree. Patrick tells me it can be very windy here. The antenna is only one prong of our attack."

Patrick picked up the thread. "We want to tap Dad's internet and capture all its traffic. His router has the capability for a guest network. If we can segregate Smith's traffic onto that, it would minimize what we have to analyze."

"Too late," Niki said. "Your father already gave Smith the regular password."

Lisa: "We get the same effect if we switch all the other devices to the guest network. Seamus has a cellphone and computers. I'll bet you're also linked to it."

Patrick: "And me. But to Lisa's point, the more traffic we can shunt to the guest network, the easier it will be to isolate and evaluate Smith's stuff. Do you know how to set up the guest network and assign a different password?"

"I could Google or YouTube it."

Lisa tugged Niki's arm. "We can figure that out later. I need that wire up. If you can't do it, I'll have to. Patrick is too heavy. Truth is, I'll piss my pants because of the height."

Niki could tell she and Lisa would get along famously. "Can Seamus make the router changes remotely using his laptop?"

Patrick chuckled. "He was so zonked the last I talked to him, he's liable to take down his entire setup and fry the Starlink receiver. If you can't do it this evening, we'll get to it tomorrow. I'll give you a boost to the first limb."

She tucked the zip ties into a jeans pocket, tied the handsaw onto her belt, and cinched the cable around her waist using a bowline hitch. The tree was a big sucker. Patrick lifted her onto his shoulders, plenty high enough for her to grab the lowest limb. Ignoring the pain from the rough bark, she pulled herself onto it. The next few limbs were difficult because they were far apart. Thereafter, she scampered up the tree, making sure not to tangle the cable behind her. Eventually, her weight caused the top of the tree to tip. She wished she had brought a rope to secure herself while she worked.

The view up and down the lake was spectacular. *You're not here to sightsee.* She wriggled through the next few branches until the tree's top canted thirty degrees. An eagle's kri-kri-kri sounded from up the lake. She cranked her head and watched a fully mature bald eagle cruising toward her, its deep wing beats audibly compressing the air. Further away, two eagles glided in circles above the deep end of the lake. What the hell had the kids named those eagles? George, Martha, and Gonzo. Gonzo was the juvenile.

"Hey, George or Martha, if that's who you are. Stay the hell away from me. I have nothing for you." She waved a hand, relying on the bird's superior vision to see she had no fish.

Still it came, on a strafing run. Yellow legs extended. Claws the size of a grizzly bear's. She pinned the tree between her forearm and biceps, grabbed the handsaw with her free hand, and waved the weapon at the bird. George—it had to be George; no female would treat another woman like that—gave an ear-piercing call. The tree top swayed with her flailing.

Fewer than fifteen feet away, the damned thing banked and cruised over the water.

Patrick called from below, "What's happening?"

Next time Lisa can piss her *pants.* Niki breathed deeply to pretend the calm she did not feel. "Trimming branches. I'll be done in a jiffy."

THE HAPPY REAPER

THE HAPPY REAPER LOVED DRIVING the yellow ATV from McCree's house to his guest cabin. Wind pulled his hair, and the cool air brought him fully awake. Maybe instead of taking naps, he'd be better off taking the four-wheeler for quick pick-me-ups.

He couldn't drive around Colonel Lisa's SUV, which she'd backed into the driveway, its trunk and doors wide open. He dismounted and peered into the car as he walked past. One red duffel sat on the passenger seat, otherwise the car and trunk were empty. A portable gasoline generator roared, a sound barrier pushing the noise toward him and away from the cabin. On the other side of the barrier, the roar changed to a purr. What a difference.

Patrick held open the door to the screened porch. A cooler, on which rested a battery-powered lamp, separated two sleeping bags lying on air mattresses. Like father, like son, he supposed. He preferred sleeping inside four walls. Looking through the door into the cabin, he realized they were sleeping on the porch from necessity. They had pushed the bed, dresser, and futon to the far end of the single-room cabin. Folding tables covered with monitors and laptops lined the exterior walls. Cables snaked down from them to what he guessed were servers. Fans pushed warm, metallic air through opened windows.

In the central area devoid of electronics, they had crammed three chairs. "Impressive layout."

Lisa gave him another big smile. "It's only half as impressive as it looks. We've built in one hundred percent redundancy. It's not like we can drop into a Best Buy for a spare part if something goes haywire." She gestured toward the chairs. "We'll try to make this quick for you. Could you start by giving us an overview of the structure you employed, including URLs, if you remember them? Patrick tells me you had a portal where people inquired about your services. If you were interested in the proposed contract, you allowed them to contact you through a second portal. Was that one unique for each contract?"

The Happy Reaper didn't remember giving Seamus or his son that information. Had he forgotten or had they learned on their own? He explained how he'd organized his online presence. The first website was like a traditional retailer's contact page, except on the dark web. After he learned of the imposter, he had checked that URL and discovered the asshole now used it. Boy, had that ticked him off.

An interested party had to leave contact information, details about who had referenced them, the services desired, and the proposed fee. Once they completed the form, a pop-up informed them that if the Happy Reaper approved them, they would receive login details to a second site. That's where the client provided specifics for the assignment: who, what, where, when, and sometimes how. If the Happy Reaper accepted the assignment, he opened a module to receive the fifty percent down payment.

Lisa and Patrick scribbled notes. Patrick asked the first question. "If we crack that contact portal, can we access buyer information?"

"Not the way I did it. I copied the information to an encrypted cloud server and wiped all data from the server. I also had an automatic wipe of any info older than ten days."

Lisa leaned forward at that last piece of information. "Meaning a cloud server contains contact information for all your contracts?"

The Happy Reaper laughed. "Wouldn't the cops love that? Once I received final payment, I wiped that information everywhere. And, before you ask, the server routinely wiped backups more than a week old. No way was I leaving digital fingerprints lying around for prying eyes. I know the imposter kept the first site's URL. I did not verify whether he left the coding. If he did, the only way you could see who had contacted him is to hack that site during the short window opening when a buyer made contact and closing when the imposter checked the website and the information disappeared."

Patrick: "Or hack the website's server and leave code to forward new information as it arrives."

Good thought, but he'd been smarter than that. "Nope, I'd know. My code includes a self-check. If anyone adds or subtracts anything, the self-check triggers a wipe of the entire code. Never happened."

The two of them exchanged a knowing look that gave him pause. He spent a moment trying to understand what he had said that elicited that response from them. Gave up and continued his lecture. "The second website contained a similar self-check mechanism. The login ID and password for the first website changed daily based on an old-fashioned book code. Plus, you could only use it once per day. If you tried a second time, the code erased itself. I randomly generated a year's worth of numbers for the page, line, and word for both the ID and password. I tacked the results onto a ten-digit base comprising capital letters, small letters, and symbols. Even if you found the database with the numbers, you'd have to know which book they referred to. It's the *Complete Works of Sherlock Holmes*. That means—"

Patrick interrupted. "Am I correct that the program reference froze on the last line in the database?"

That sounded like Patrick *knew* that would happen. The Happy Reaper considered how he had structured the code. Patrick *was* right, which made it likely he—with Lisa's help?—had cracked open that server. Meaning Patrick was the one who'd stolen his money. "What did you do with the money you stole?"

Lisa reached into a backpack and withdrew a handgun.

The Happy Reaper laughed. "You won't need that. At the time, it pissed me off. More than pissed me off. Now I'm just impressed and curious." A new thought hit him. Six years ago, Seamus shooting him had been more luck than skill. Enmity boiled off Patrick. The kid was super smart and wanted revenge. Had Patrick created the imposter to tarnish his reputation?

He could picture Seamus wanting revenge for the accidental death of his partner, lover, whatever, Abigail Hancock. To hijack the Happy Reaper's legacy, he thinks of this idea of an imposter who screws things up. To Seamus, it's a mental game. But he tells his son—and maybe Niki, she definitely had killer in her genes—and they decide to take some rotten people off the earth, blame it on the Happy Reaper. Double win. Except they hire someone for the work, and now that person jumped the shark and is doing stuff on his own, leaving these yahoos trying to put the cat back in the bag.

He ignored Lisa's gun and stared at Patrick. "Did you create the imposter too?"

Patrick looked at him like he had two heads. "You're as loopy as my father. Yes, we combined my IT skills and Dad's forensic accounting knowledge to find your money and distribute it to various charities. That led me to the server that held your contact website. Since I could enter through the server, I didn't need the user ID and password to have access. Your coding self-check was a good idea to catch someone who made changes before understanding the entire program. Didn't work on me. I spotted it and simply changed the check digit to match my revisions, and I removed the notification."

The Happy Reaper's brain hurt. Well, his head and neck and shoulders hurt; his brain acted like a computer processor with throttled speed. He could not take it all in. "If you know all that, why are you asking me?"

Patrick held up a single finger. "The imposter kept the URL but changed the server. We haven't cracked *that server.*" Patrick raised a second finger. "I added a separate username and password to your coding to avoid having to go in through the server. Those do not work on the imposter's website, which makes sense because he would surely change those." Patrick's third finger rose. "But if the imposter didn't delete or replace your old-fashioned book-code-login routine, maybe we can use that to peek behind the curtain."

And that, the Happy Reaper realized, was a half-brilliant idea. "With no additional entries, it *would* stop overwriting. I had no reason to renew the cloud server contract. It's long expired, leaving you no way to access that old database and learn the last ID and password."

Patrick raised a fourth finger. "Except I have the copy I downloaded six years ago. What we need is the *Sherlock* book."

"Still not enough," the Happy Reaper said. "I don't have any idea what I used for the ten-digit base to which I appended the code words."

Patrick raised his fifth finger and gave Lisa a high five. "Told you it would work. That was in your program, which I downloaded."

The Happy Reaper could not remember a time he had felt so outclassed. He had used an online PDF edition of *Sherlock.* Lisa downloaded it and cross-referenced the information from the last line of the database that Patrick provided. The resulting ID/password combination was Jephro/said. Patrick added those to the ten-digit base (&Qe34^l!Wn) and entered the resulting ID and password. The screen turned black. They double-checked *Sherlock* to make sure they had counted pages and lines correctly. Patrick tried again with Lisa verifying the letters and numbers. Same result.

The Happy Reaper stated the obvious. "I suppose it was asking a lot for the imposter to ignore that code. You have a Plan B?"

Lisa gave him another of her smiles. "It was worth the try. B stands for brute force."

ZACH

ZACH IGNORED THE FIRST ALERT that someone had entered an incorrect username/password combination on the Happy Reaper website contact page. Bots occasionally stumbled upon the page and tried something uninspired, like "admin" for both username and password.

Given the measures he had taken, he was not worried someone would stumble onto the right combination. The first thing he had done once he had access was to extract and examine the entire code before making changes. Good thing. He avoided the bomb the Happy Reaper left to destroy the code, and that allowed him to learn how the Happy Reaper conducted his business.

The guy had been good, but old school. Zach made minor improvements, like modifying the website's display to look elegant regardless of whether the user used a cellphone, tablet, or computer. His coding now captured the routing information for anyone who opened the contact form, even if they didn't complete it. And if they completed the form, a database stored the offered username and password. Seven failures caused the site to lock down. He had to reset it before anyone could try again. This had stopped bots in their tracks.

The fourth alert in less than five minutes triggered him to learn what login credentials the bots were trying. He entered the ID and sixteen-character password for administrative access and dumped the contents of that database.

His fingers and the tip of his nose tingled with cold. Knowing it was a hard-wired response to a perceived threat didn't make the blood draining from his exterior to his core any less frightening. The database showed the first attempt used the credential structure the Happy Reaper had employed before Zach changed it. The next three attempts tried variations on the theme.

Had to be the Happy Reaper. What would he do if he concluded someone was using his website?

Zach lowered his head between his legs and sucked in several deep breaths. *Panic is not your friend.* He checked the routing information. Purportedly Belarus, which meant whoever this was knew how to hide.

An escaped prisoner would hide his location. Maybe the Happy Reaper was curious whether anyone had contacted his website. The knot in Zach's stomach didn't buy that. What if the Happy Reaper already realized he had absconded with the website and wanted to discover who had stolen his work? The guy *was* a killer. What if he targeted them?

Well, the hacker—whoever it was—couldn't do that unless he learned who ran that website, which required getting in. The hacker was a long way from doing that. Even if he did, he wouldn't find anything else because Zach had isolated the portal on a separate server.

No reason to panic the others. He had this under control. He'd monitor the situation. All was fine, although he'd lay off spicy foods today and let his stomach settle.

Wednesday, October 19, 2022

SEAMUS

PAIN BROUGHT ME FROM TROUBLED dreams. My right leg felt like a goalie had booted it to the center line. Compared to that, the catheter was a minor inconvenience. I pushed physical thoughts away and focused on the world around me. The moon lit the woods beyond the screened porch. Ducks, most likely mergansers this time of year, were restless on the lake, paddling around, managing their business with percussive quacks. My breath puffed before me in white clouds that floated away on a light breeze.

A snort followed by a long snore from the guest bedroom focused my thoughts on the recent past: the Happy Reaper, me, Niki, Owen, the shots. I sorted through a collage of images from the day before. Texting ADNI Park, the medical van, two doctors, and secrets. What secrets I could not recall. And Paddy had arrived, hadn't he? With secrets of his own. I closed my eyes and cleared my memories. The replacement image became Abigail telling me, "It was just an accident. You should be more careful."

"Seamus." A hand jostled my shoulder. "You okay?"

I opened my eyes to find dawn painting the world with a rose brush and Niki hovering, a look of concern on her face. How to answer her question seemed beyond my abilities. I did not feel okay. My leg ached and my mouth tasted furry. But I was alive, and that felt like an accomplishment. "Still on the right side of the grass, but you look like the roof is about to fall in."

"You were yelling something that sounded like a warning."

I closed my eyes and regained the vision of Abigail, now six years dead, telling me something was an accident. Did she mean my being shot, or was she referring to her own death at the hands of the Happy Reaper? I had not thought of her for a while. Why now? She'd been an extraordinary bodyguard. Was she still protecting me from beyond the grave? I didn't believe in an afterlife, but I didn't *not* believe, either. "A dream, I guess. I have a feeling I don't remember everything that went on yesterday."

Her face cleared. "A few things . . ."

Talk about understatements. I remembered some of what she told me. Other information, like Lisa Latoya arriving with Paddy, was a complete surprise.

At Niki's request, I created a shockingly long list of all the electronic devises that attached to the internet. Without being obvious, she'd gather them to allow me to switch them onto the guest network to isolate the Happy Reaper on the main network.

The door from the main room to the porch cracked open. Niki dropped my hand and stepped away from me. "Good morning, Gerry. Did you sleep well?"

"Like a rock, except for the snoring." He waved toward the guest room where the Happy Reaper was noisily sawing wood. "Time for you to give Seamus his next dose of antibiotics."

Niki performed the task, and Gerry pronounced her fully qualified to do it on her own. He snapped on Nitrile gloves.

Niki said, "Since you're watching him, I'll go for a run. I have a feeling it will be my only chance for a while."

Gerry waved her off. He asked me twenty questions, changed the dressings, checked the drain, and said everything was healing well. He removed the Foley catheter, a process I did not enjoy.

He said, "Niki tells me you're a tough guy dealing with pain. Recent studies show that how we process pain has more to do with our brains than our so-called pain receptors. A positive attitude goes a long way. But you will heal faster if you stay ahead of your leg pain. I'll leave enough codeine-laced ibuprofen for two days. After that, take your favorite extra strength analgesic. As needed, but no more than the bottle recommends."

"Niki's right. I hate taking painkillers."

"We'll see what you say after Carla puts you through your PT. I'll get her."

Without further explanation, he carried the stinky catheter and urine bag inside.

ZACH

ZACH HAD WOKEN UP AT least once an hour wondering what was going on with the website. His parents were light sleepers, and he didn't want them pestering him to keep regular hours. He had forced himself to stay in bed until seven o'clock. At 7:01, he logged on.

Three more unsuccessful login attempts had triggered the solicitation portal to close. The hits came from the same Belarus IP address, all variations on the old login paradigms. That approach would never work, but it might be interesting to see how long they kept trying. He reset the counter and watched in real time. Nothing, meaning it was human-driven, not an automated attack.

He followed his daily routine: showered, ate breakfast, and did up the dishes, all before his parents rose. While on morning autopilot, he put himself in the Happy Reaper's shoes and considered how he would try to hack into the website once he had instigated the incorrect password shutdown. Obviously, give up on passwords. Focus on cracking the server side. With that in mind, he sketched the outline of a honey trap to lure hackers in. He'd bait the trap with a known vulnerability. They'd find the vulnerability, search for the honey, and he'd capture their information before leading them into a brick-solid dead end.

He spent his morning doing his actual job, mostly fidgeting in useless online meetings. During his lunch break, he coded the honey trap and tested it in a sandbox. Worked perfectly, and he brought it live. The first hit arrived in under thirty seconds. In rapid succession, additional probes struck from India, Russia, North Korea, China, the US, and fourteen other countries. A botnet attack, and he was watching it in real time!

The honey trap did its job, shunting the attackers into the sterile dead end. With a sophisticated botnet attack, he wouldn't discover who was behind it. He had installed the best security protocols for his server, but that didn't mean it didn't have any vulnerabilities. Rather than risk a breech, he knew he should shut the portal down.

Problem was, with their recent disagreements, Charlene and Tyler—especially Tyler—might construe any unilateral decision as evidence he wasn't a team player. With Tyler in Colorado and Charlene working the day shift, the three couldn't physically meet. The burner phones he had bought for each of them to use for the Silicon Valley angel job would work. Using his, he left text messages on theirs: *Call me. Urgent.*

The Happy Reaper

THUMPING FROM THE SCREENED PORCH made the Happy Reaper curious. He cracked the door and stuck out his head. Seamus, using crutches, clumped to the far end of the porch. Gerry and Carla walked on either side, prepared to steady Seamus should he wobble.

Carla spotted the Happy Reaper and said, "Let's see how you're doing this morning." She hustled him into the room and pointed to the bed. "Sit." She checked his pulse, blood pressure, blood oxygen. "Pulse and blood pressure are high, and oxygen is low. You should be on oxygen and in a hospital."

"A hospital is not possible." He paused and caught his breath. "You swore the Hippocratic oath." Paused again. "Get me the damn oxygen."

"Mister Smith," she said in a tone a teacher might use on her most recalcitrant student. "My oaths do not give me carte blanche to break laws."

Seamus stopped at the doorway. "I take it he needs an oxygen machine and oxygen?"

"And a CPAP," Carla said. "And I gave him scripts for everything.

The Happy Reaper burned with indignation. "As Adam Smith. Like we can use that."

Seamus cleared his throat, which got everyone looking at him. "I'll go on Telephone Time and say I'm getting them for a friend who flew in for a visit and wasn't smart enough to bring his along."

Seamus had to explain that Telephone Time was a program on WIKB produced in Iron River that allowed people to buy, sell, and swap items.

"Totally illegal," Carla said. "Both machines and the supplemental oxygen require prescriptions."

Seamus leaned against the door frame. "And what? You think half the items listed as 'never been used, still in the original packaging' aren't stolen?"

This was getting nowhere. The Happy Reaper hoped a middle-ground solution would work. "Can you rent? Maybe raise fewer eyebrows?"

Carla rolled her eyes, released an exasperated sigh. Seamus's eyes lit with understanding. "Sure, especially if I say I need the CPAP so I can get some sleep and keep the roof on my house. Get everyone laughing. Say I'm desperate. I'll bet I get multiple calls. If the cops ring me up, I'll tell them nothing happened because a doctor told me it wasn't legal."

The Happy Reaper saw a flaw in that. "You can't have people come here."

"Yeah, yeah. Paddy has to go in town to stock up on vegetarian food, anyway. He'll collect it."

Gerry snagged Seamus's arm. "Carla, it's not our affair. Seamus, that's enough exercise to see how your leg is holding up. Bed rest for you."

The Happy Reaper followed Carla from the room and watched them unwrap Seamus's bandage and remove the covering. The exit wound leaked a few drops of fresh blood. He didn't catch any sniff of putrefaction. Seamus would have two ugly puckers on that leg.

Gerry said, "Remember, infection is your enemy. Complete the course of antibiotics. Don't stop because you feel fine. Keep the wound covered and use the Neosporin. That should also help keep the stitches from itching. If any redness shows at the wound's edges or red streaks start running up your leg, you must give me a shout. *Do not wait.* Anything else, Carla?"

"Keep your leg above your heart whenever possible. These wounds will take time to drain. Use your crutches until we say not. And in moderation. To and from the bathroom, to eat, to change rooms. I'll email detailed care instructions. We're off. We'll each send you a text message, so you have our numbers. You are an incredibly lucky man, Seamus McCree. Don't press it."

The two doctors gave a last wave from their van and were gone.

The Happy Reaper watched Seamus struggle to make up his bed. "Didn't you listen to what they said? Sit your ass down and let me do it." He rolled the sleeping bag and stored it under the futon, situated the pillows to keep Seamus's right leg elevated, and helped get him settled. The effort was enough to make the Happy Reaper want a nap. "I hope like hell your idea to score oxygen supplies works."

Seamus pointed to the cellphone resting on the table. "Could you hand me the phone? I'll call now."

Seamus unlocked the cellphone with his fingerprint. "Before I call, please make your daily check-in with Clem. Let him know I haven't done you in." Seamus offered him the phone.

How stupid did Seamus think he was? No way would he dial Clem's number on Seamus's phone and allow Seamus to learn the number. Even if Clem used a burner paid for with cash, it wasn't safe. Given Niki's contacts and Patrick's hacking skills, they could discover the origin of any phone. If the store had security cameras, they might learn what the buyer looked like.

But, if he had Seamus's phone for a few minutes, he could download a piece of software onto it and use the local Wi-Fi to monitor everything Seamus did. He accepted the phone and, to Seamus's obvious dismay, went into his bedroom. He left the door open a crack to allow Seamus to hear. While the software downloaded onto Seamus's phone, he used his own phone to leave Clem a message. "Everything's copacetic. Talk to you tomorrow."

SEAMUS

FORTUNATELY, THE HOST OF TELEPHONE Time was not familiar with the prescription requirements to obtain (or as I had defined it, borrow) a CPAP and an oxygen machine with spare oxygen tanks. We chatted amicably about what a pain it was flying, what with security, baggage restrictions, crowded planes, and rude passengers.

In under an hour, I lined up everything the Happy Reaper required. The CPAP was from a guy in Crystal Falls whose mother had recently died. He'd rather sell me the contraption than have it around reminding him. Fine with me.

I negotiated with someone from Florence, Wisconsin to secure the oxygen. He'd rent me the machine but also wanted the oxygen tanks replenished. He had a script but didn't want to have to drive to fill it. We were happy to take care of that for him. His name, unlike Adam Smith's, wouldn't trigger any red flags.

I had no sooner hung up than Niki completed her ten-mile run. "Sorry, Seamus. I didn't realize the docs were leaving so soon. They passed me on the road."

Unspoken subtext was she didn't want me alone with the Happy Reaper. I filled her in on both his and my medical check-ups and on my recent negotiations.

She asked Smith if I had described what had happened. He confirmed my memory was functioning. "Good," she said. "We've been waiting to hear your plan."

I suggested we move the conversation to the cabin so Paddy and Lisa could take part.

Niki adopted her Wonder Woman pose. "What part of not overdoing it do you not understand?"

Instead of admitting I was wrong, I got huffy and told her time was wasting. Paddy would soon have to leave to pick up the oxygen and equipment. She could do a little more running and bring them here.

Niki returned with Paddy in tow. Lisa had taken the final overnight shift to monitor the progress of the attempted hacking, and the two of them agreed to let her sleep.

Paddy summed up their results. "The guy's got chops or good staff. In two hours, he put together an impressive honey trap. Lisa found it and did a spectacular job leaving false tracks. The imposter knows someone is attempting to get in, but he can't be certain if it's a random attack or targeted. Bad news is that since we haven't gotten in, we don't know if we should look for a second website on a different server."

Which gave me the opportunity to segue into my plan. "If we provide him a new client, we'll know exactly what he asks for, and we'll have a specific website to attack."

Three sets of eyes stared at me.

"I know it sounds crazy. If he follows the old script, the client has to come with bona fides. Who has better credentials than the Happy Reaper contracting to hire a hit on me? He can explain that he's not well enough to do it himself, and he wants it done before he's gone. While he's not thrilled with them using his Happy Reaper moniker, it would fit in this case."

Still they stared, and a burn made my face warm. "What? Why are you all looking at me like I'm nuts? I'm totally recovered from the anesthesia."

The Happy Reaper was the first to find his voice. "I wondered how long it would take for you to arrive at that solution."

Paddy: "You presume he can't pull it off."

Me: "Given a little time, I have confidence you and Lisa can crack the websites. You and I can follow the money. If he moves faster than that, this is as safe a place as any to trap someone gunning for me. We can establish a perimeter defense with trail cams and detection devices like Niki and Abigail did that time at Owen's place. Niki is a sharpshooter. I assume the army trained Lisa, and Paddy knows how to shoot."

Oops, if the Happy Reaper caught the implication, I'd just admitted that Paddy had found and repatriated millions of the killer's monies. I slid a glance his way. No reaction. Did he not catch it, or did he already know?

Niki clapped her hands. "Bravo, Seamus. Well thought, with only a few minor problems. What prevents the guy from hiring a helicopter, loading up a Hellfire missile, and obliterating your house with us in it?"

THE HAPPY REAPER

THE HAPPY REAPER WAS DELIGHTED McCree had come up with the staked-goat idea on his own. Over the years he had known McCree, he had periodically wondered how much they were alike and where they were different. Their chosen professions were an obvious dissimilarity. He had made a killing, pun intended, from his "Results Guaranteed" slogan. He had only reneged on an assignment once, and that was when he chose not to kill McCree, even though McCree had thwarted his plans. Full disclosure required him to recognize that his client, having both lied and being dead and unable to pay the rest of the agreed fee, might have factored into that decision.

He had concluded that McCree's most fundamental core value was to keep his promises. Not like a skeezy lawyer who combs the fine print to find escape hatches. No, McCree adhered to the spirit of the commitment. Wasn't that another way of saying "Results Guaranteed?"

It would surprise McCree to hear him say it, but the two of them also shared a strong desire to see justice served. Provided, of course, the same justice wasn't applied to themselves. Oh sure, there were different degrees. McCree tried not to kill anyone. The Happy Reaper had no qualms, although he had principles: he never killed kids and prided himself on killing only his targets. Paradoxically, McCree's interference had resulted in his only collateral killing.

But the Happy Reaper wanted to see justice brought to the drug cartels, and the corporations that polluted the environment, foisted opioids on an unsuspecting public, bought and sold Congress and presidents to line their pockets. Thank God he had no children. The world we were leaving them—well, that was off-topic.

He rooted for the Seamus McCrees of the world to take on white-collar crime and money laundering, and he cast no blame on McCree and his son for figuring out where he stored most of his wealth. He was curious how they had done it, but fair was fair.

That was the key to both men: fairness. And yet, McCree went a step farther, didn't he? Sure, perhaps McCree was arranging for the oxygen only because he was worried the docs were correct that the Happy Reaper was not long to carry this mortal coil. And McCree believed that if Clem didn't receive his daily call, dark forces would smite the McCrees one by one.

Feeling Niki's stare, he asked her to repeat her question. She wanted confirmation that a helicopter attack on Seamus was possible.

"A helicopter and rockets call for a level of resources most don't have. Even in my day, a Hellfire setup would cost a quarter mill on the black market. Seamus is not likely to command that kind of price tag." He quirked his eyebrows. "Unless there's something I don't know?"

Niki had retaken her Wonder Woman pose: commanding space, her legs wide, hands on hips, arms akimbo. Her voice rose in annoyance. "Kamikaze drones, then. Get a squadron from Amazon. My point is, time and ingenuity are on the killer's side, not ours."

That is correct. He alone had the knowledge to tilt those odds. To Patrick, he asked, "How do those odds change if we—you—hacked into the portal?"

Patrick extended his hands in a "Lord, why me?" pose. "Because you have a back door."

Holy moly, he was quick. "At one time, I had them for each of the websites. The imposter might have found and eliminated them. Patrick, can you take me to the cabin on your way to collect my breathing equipment? Lisa and I can see what's what?"

Niki

WITH SMITH AT THE CABIN working with Lisa, Patrick collecting medical supplies, and Seamus behaving himself—for the moment—on the screened porch, Niki relaxed post-shower on the deck off the second-floor bedroom. Squeaking brakes and abused springs announced a vehicle was coming down the road.

For being deep in the woods, this place sure got a lot of traffic. The deck's height allowed her to spot the Iron County Sheriff's car driving past the cabin's driveway. She pounded down the stairs, yelling for Seamus to get off the screened porch.

Seamus must have heard the car because he and his crutches met her at the door from the porch into the main room. "He shouldn't see me. You need to take care of this. Since Paddy has my truck, insinuate that I'm in town. Do not let them inside. I'll hide in the bathroom." A rueful smile played on his face. "Again."

"On it." Not only could she not let in the police, she couldn't let them near the porch where they would spot Seamus's medical supplies. And Smith's stuff decorated the guest bedroom, including an AR lying on the bed. Everyone knew Seamus didn't have weapons. If it came to that, she'd have to claim it.

She pushed past the screen door, down the ramp, and met Chief Bartelle rounding the front of his SUV. *The big guns are here.* "Hey Chief, long time no see."

"Concerned citizen called regarding someone on Telephone Time trying to get medical equipment without a prescription. She copied down the phone number, which I recognized belongs to Seamus. We had a domestic situation down on Deer Lake I had to get involved with, so it made sense for me to come the extra few miles and give Seamus a heads up. He can't legally do what he wants to do. You, being former law enforcement, should know that."

"Chief, you're sweet and all, but you didn't drive all this way when a simple phone call would do. Why are you really here?"

"Mind if I come in and set myself down?"

"I don't, but with Iron County, Michigan versus Seamus McCree and Colleen Carpetti still on the court docket, his attorney forbids it without a court order."

He crooked his arm over his head, scratched his ear, shifted his weight.

This was a hard one for him. She wanted him gone before Smith showed up, but she couldn't push. She caught herself tapping her toes and forced her feet to be still.

He pinched the bridge of his nose. "Thing is, I don't agree with the prosecutor's decision to charge them. Oh, they're guilty. But no way will twelve of Iron County's finest citizens vote to convict them once they hear the full story. I've told the prosecutor it will make him and us look like schmucks. He can't ask for a change in venue because that looks like he doesn't trust his own county to be impartial."

Bartelle was talking more than usual. She sure hoped he'd soon come to the reason he was here. It required all her willpower to not look toward the cabin, where Smith was with Lisa. She made several noncommittal noises to show she sympathized with his position.

"This CPAP and oxygen tank? Prosecutor gets wind of those, he'll have us arrest Seamus. Who are they for?"

"Now that we know it's illegal, they're for naught. I appreciate you passing on that information. Was there anything else? If not, I'll wish you a blessed day, and see if I can catch Seamus on his cellphone."

"One more thing, although seeing you here, I'm guessing it's old news. The guy Seamus shot in Massachusetts, Adam Smith? Got sent to jail for life?"

She raised an eyebrow to encourage him to continue.

"We received a BOLO 'cause he escaped from a hospital. Given the earlier report of gunfire, I thought I'd make sure Seamus was still alive."

"Very much so. You can wait and see for yourself. Or call him."

Chief Bartelle scrolled through his cellphone directory and punched ten numbers. Her heart sunk hearing Seamus's phone ring from the screened porch. Didn't it figure: the one time it would have been useful for Seamus to let the battery run down, he hadn't.

Niki shook her head in disgust. "My mother's line about people like Seamus was, 'It's a good thing his head's attached.' Shall I have him call you?"

"Think I'll wait."

THE HAPPY REAPER

THE HAPPY REAPER STAYED OUTSIDE the cabin while Patrick woke Lisa. Patrick rejoined him while Lisa performed whatever her wake-up ritual was. He figured it was a good time to pump Seamus's son for information on Colonel Lisa. His online searching had provided her age, education, information about the business she, Patrick, and two others had formed and sold. Not a word explained why she had joined the army or how someone her age would soon become a brigadier general. To get to the answer, he asked a question he knew the answer to. "Is Lisa a West Pointer? My understanding is they have a leg up on being awarded stars."

Patrick squinched his eyes shut and hooted. "That is hysterical. Weeks before the statute of limitations expired, the Feds nailed her for youthful hacking exploits. They dropped all charges, gave her immunity for any other prior hacking offenses, and all it cost her was a six-year army commitment. Officer rank."

"Why did they want her that badly?"

"That's classified. Whatever the job was, it required at least a captain, which was her initial rank after she completed basic training. Her commands keep getting shit done in record time, and the Army keeps promoting her to take more responsibility. Fortunately, the army has two ranks: official and brevet. Brevet has all the authority, pay, and perks of official rank, but is temporary. During the Civil War, George Custer was a brevet Major General. After the war, the highest official rank he achieved was lieutenant colonel."

Nothing to be gained by admitting he knew about Custer. Lisa joined them outside, giving him the opportunity to ask her why the army was currently using brevetted ranks.

"Competition with the private sector. I've got guys working for me who could earn mid six-figures easy in IT. No way for us to compete on bucks. We have an excellent retirement plan though, and we keep the country safe. Listen to me, the little recruiter. Anyway, it helps get the right people into the right position. And I'm benefiting from that, becoming the first O-7—brigadier general—brevetted in modern times. But that's not relevant to what we need to do today. Let's get cracking. Patrick, will you fill the generator before you take off?"

The Happy Reaper didn't think you were supposed to pour gasoline into a running generator. He supposed that's what you did if you didn't want a power interruption and didn't have an alternate source. Seeing no reason to blow up with Patrick, he walked to the screen door and held it open for Lisa, using the courtesy as an excuse to catch his breath. Damn, he couldn't do anything without huffing and puffing. If he didn't know better, he'd think he was wearing a hundred-pound straight jacket.

She politely thanked him, slid open the door to the cabin proper, and motioned him in. Code scrolled down the banks of monitors, lights blinked, and it was warm and stuffy inside despite there being no fire in the wood stove. She motioned him toward the seats and asked what he required to try his back door.

"Access to the internet." He talked her through the process and, hallelujah, in less than a minute they were in. They downloaded the database with the collected information, crossing fingers they had avoided booby-traps that alerted the imposter of their presence.

Lisa ran the database through a program the Happy Reaper was unfamiliar with. "Looks for unpleasant surprises," she said. "Databases are great places to tuck malware." A green check appeared, and she displayed the contents of the database: four lines of unlabeled information. "Either he's extremely busy, or he doesn't clean this file like you used to."

He waved at the screen. "He's sloppy. The earliest contact is from five months ago."

She asked him to interpret the data.

He pointed as he explained. "This gives the inquirer's information. Name, phone number—should be a burner, but it's surprising how many people are stupid or lazy and provide their regular cellphone or land line. This next text provides information on their reference. Once, a guy put down that an angel told him to use me. I'll admit, that tempted me to contact him just to get the details."

She tapped the next column. "This the planned victim?"

"And their basic info. Name and address, a reason, and their proposed fee. The website automatically collects the rest of this stuff, like time stamp and IP address. I used how long they remained logged into the website to gain a sense of their frame of mind. The information takes at most two minutes to enter. I figure if they take a long time, it's because they're conflicted or disorganized. Either way, I don't want to work for them. If conflicted, they might change their mind—or worse, feel guilty and try to set me up."

Lisa prompted, "And disorganized?"

"The risk of capture increases if I can't trust them not to screw up something vital. Let's see if anything happened to the proposed targets."

Lisa opened a browser and typed in the first name. A news article said two days after the date in the database, he had stopped on the way home from a bar to fix a flat tire. A hit-and-run driver had killed him. The police found the vehicle involved—a stolen van—abandoned several miles away. No witnesses and no suspects.

Two days was way too fast to have pulled off a hit. He had to know where the target would be, set up a tire leak slow enough that the guy didn't notice before he started driving, but fast enough to disable the car before the target reached his destination. And have a freshly stolen car at the ready as the instrument of death. Something with this deal was fishy. Then again, a quarter million was real bucks. Maybe the imposter had more chops than the Happy Reaper had given him credit for.

Or maybe the imposter already knew the victim. That likely meant the two lived in the same general area. Boston—.

She interrupted his thoughts. "What do you see that I don't?"

"Just thinking," he said. "I assume the second target is still alive."

She tapped her keyboard. "Yep. What made you think that?"

"Look at the pittance offered for the contract. It's ten percent of what he got for the first one, which was a pretty big number. I figured he wouldn't take the deal. The third one is more reasonable. That's where he left the Results Guaranteed card. A total screw-up. No way a pregnant cleaning lady should have died."

He let Lisa confirm the details he already knew. Screw-up it was. Two victims. The killer had bashed in the target's head with a bowling trophy the homeowner kept on his mantel. In its place, the police found the Results Guaranteed business card. Police theorized that the second victim, a substitute cleaning lady, had surprised the killer. She had made it off the stoop and a few feet up the sidewalk before the killer shot her in the back and finished her with head shots at point-blank range. And that botch-up did not compute with the first hit—maybe the first was luck? "And the last one?"

Lisa reported the guy listed in the fourth line was still alive and asked if he would take that job.

"Me, no. But the imposter doesn't command the same fees I did. In his shoes, I'd go to the next step." He leaned in and read the information on her screen. William Barrett Oceans was a mega-wealthy venture capitalist. "Guy like him probably has lots of enemies, which is good. Makes it harder for the police to zero in on my employer. If they do, the employer inevitably decides it's your fault. I'd want to know the backstory. Did someone not get funding and lose their company? Did he screw someone else's wife or boyfriend? Is it an inheritance thing?"

Lisa tilted her head toward the door. "Hold those thoughts. You hear an engine?"

TYLER

FIRST THING IN THE MORNING, Tyler chugged a twelve-ounce glass of water to help him stay hydrated. He sifted through the coffee offerings, shook his head at the pumpkin spice crap he could smell through the wrapper, chose a hazelnut coffee, and set the in-room Keurig to brewing. The view through the window was stunning: snow dusted the tops of the peaks, a scattering of aspens down in a warm valley microclimate flaunted their yellow leaves.

While the coffee steamed and hissed, he planned his day. Talk with the guide service. Assuming he learned where the elk hunt would take place, tour the area. For a backup plan, he'd visit the target's house and, depending on what he saw, maybe chat up a sales guy from the security firm that monitored the house.

He placed his phone call a minute after the guide's office opened. The magic words "Administrative Assistant" unlocked the details of the elk hunt, including the guide's name, meeting place and time, even GPS coordinates of the hunt area so his boss could remotely study the topography. He thanked the employee and promised a five-star review on Yelp, which would not happen.

The hunt area looked promising on Google Earth, but unlike Zach, he wouldn't rely on computer images. The rental car's navigation system brought him to a secluded valley high in the mountains. Awesome scenery and elk were around. Two walked from a field into an aspen patch and vanished. How something that massive could disappear before his eyes amazed him. Probably why elk genetics had chosen that hide color.

No phone coverage. That bonus would provide time for him to leave the area before anyone could call in the "hunting accident."

The more closely he inspected the area, the less practical his plan became. The hunters would park in a small gravel lot close to the hunting site. He obviously couldn't leave his vehicle there, and, for miles in either direction, the road was too narrow to park along its edge. He found a weedy lane that ended at a locked gate located two miles before the lot, but even pulled all the way in, it was visible from the road. No good.

The road continued ten miles beyond the lot and dead ended. In that section, he found several places he could hide the car. After the kill, he guessed the hunting party would split into two groups. One would track him. They wouldn't catch him before he reached his car. The other group would rush to their vehicles to summon the authorities. Those guys, armed and pissed, would try to stop him when he drove past. Minimally, they'd report his make/model/plate number to the cops.

And that assumed the guide didn't have a satellite phone, in which case he might meet the cops coming in.

Way too risky.

Zach would plant an IED and blow up the entire party. Or wait in ambush and gun them all down. Good thing they chose him, not Zach, to do this one. He had really wanted the hunt area to be the kill spot, but a "hunting accident" entailed too much risk.

That left the house and the airport as two spots he could target Oceans. The airport seemed unlikely with all the security post 9-11, but you never knew until you checked.

NIKI

WITH CHIEF BARTELLE SETTLED IN his squad car to await Seamus, Niki called Patrick and warned him to stay away until the coast was clear. She brought blankets, quilts, and pillows from the linen closet to make Seamus a semi-comfortable lair in the bathroom.

"Thanks," he said. "You gotta see this." He started a video on his cellphone and handed it to her.

First came a nausea-inducing journey from the porch to the guest bedroom, ending in a steady view of the ceiling. Its audio caught a clicking sound, followed by Smith's half of a conversation with Clem. Hearing fifteen seconds of nothing, she halted the recording. "Yeah, and?"

Seamus stopped arranging a quilt around himself. "Keep watching."

Soon, the Happy Reaper's face stared at the phone. Following more keys clacking, Smith said, "Good. That should do it." The remainder of the recording captured the herky-jerky path of the phone's return to Seamus.

"I asked myself why he took my phone if he didn't use it to make any calls. He's put spyware on my stuff before. I think he did it again."

Niki rubbed her eyes. "Well, isn't that special? With luck, Patrick and Lisa recorded both sides of his call to Clem and have Clem's phone number. What are the odds it's a landline?"

"Slightly less than you winning the Powerball."

"For which I don't buy tickets."

Seamus gave her a thumbs up. "Precisely that little. Chief Bartelle could sit there forever. What if you tell him you contacted me. Since I can't legally have the medical supplies for my mother, I decided instead to fly home to Boston?"

She rubbed her eyes. "Yeah, no. The judge gave you and Colleen permission to leave the area for your mom's birthday bash, but that's not until—"

"Yeah, I was talking, not thinking. He won't wait forever. We're screwed."

Footsteps sounded on the mudroom porch steps and landing. *Maybe even sooner.* She shut the bathroom door behind her and found Lisa entering the dining area.

"What?" they said at the same time.

Niki said, "Me first. Where's Smith?"

"At the cabin until I retrieve him."

"Good. The Iron County sheriff is waiting for Seamus. I told him Seamus is in town, and I told Patrick not to return until we sort it out."

Outside, a car door slammed.

Niki continued. "My guess is the sheriff spotted you and is right now coming to the house. We've got to prevent Smith from showing up."

Lisa said, "Know his name? I'll occupy him while you secure Smith."

"Lon Bartelle." Niki followed Lisa onto the porch.

"Just the person I wanted to see!" Lisa's voice boomed with unanticipated pleasure. "You're Sheriff Lon Bartelle, right?" She opened the screened door and shoved her hand up at a forty-five-degree angle for Bartelle to shake. "This saves me a trip into town." She pumped his hand twice with a firm grip, slid her other hand down his arm, and had him turned around and walking down the ramp. "Thank you. Thank you. Let's chat."

Niki had seen politicians project excitement at meeting their constituents, but she had never seen anyone handle someone significantly larger with the ease and finesse Lisa had shown with Bartelle. He hadn't gotten a word in edgewise, and she had him strolling up the driveway, her hand gently resting on his arm as though they were entering a grand ball.

Niki rarely found herself jealous, but she wouldn't mind having Lisa's presence in certain situations. Lisa would surely lead Bartelle down the road, away from the house and the cabin. She *could* rely on Lisa keeping Bartelle occupied for a few minutes. She *could not* rely on Smith staying away.

Once Lisa and Bartelle were no longer visible, Niki sprinted up the path to the guest cabin. The generator purred in the makeshift shack Patrick had constructed to deaden its sound. She checked the outhouse on her way past: door latched from the outside. Not there.

She scanned the screened porch. Not there. He had better be inside. She pushed the door open and didn't see him. Like a phosphorus flare, her rage at him burned.

Then, she looked down.

A puddle of the man lay on the floor.

SEAMUS

I HAD FINISHED WORDLE, QUORDLE, Octordle, and a dozen other mindless games, perused all the news articles Google suggested for me, the same with Microsoft, and was reading a Mick Herron novel on my phone when Niki yelled my name with an urgency that meant a crisis. I struggled to my feet—well, foot—and opened the bathroom door.

Niki stopped at the other end of the hallway. "Where are your car keys? Lisa's car has mine blocked. I can't find her keys or Patrick's. Smith's passed out at the cabin. I need to get him to the hospital."

Her words struck me like a kidney punch. The Happy Reaper could not die on me. Not yet. My mind recycled to the problem at hand. "Won't work. I pulled the battery to replace it the next time I go to town. That's why Paddy drove my truck. Can we push Lisa's car?"

"The damn thing's locked."

It was the midweek. No neighbors were up. The ATVs wouldn't help if the Happy Reaper was unconscious. "Paddy's got oxygen. How close is he? Never mind." I leaned against a wall to retrieve my cell phone from my pocket. "I'll call him and find out where the keys are."

She fried me with a how-stupid-do-you-think-I-am look. "I tried. He didn't answer."

My phone's speaker buzzed to let me know it was calling Paddy. He answered with, "I was returning Niki's call. Is the coast clear?"

"No. Where are your car keys?"

"In my pocket. I'm having a bite to eat in Covington. I figured that way I wouldn't accidentally—"

"Niki has to take the Happy Reaper to a hospital. Do you know where Lisa keeps her keys? She's blocking Niki in."

"Sorry, no. If it's a matter of saving his life, have Sheriff Bartelle drive—"

"Stay where you are until we call." I disconnected. "Take Bartelle's cruiser."

"This is a level past FUBAR." She rubbed her hands over her eyes, down past her nose, mouth and chin, muttering profanities. "Fine. I'll call 9-1-1 to get the EMTs to meet us. You'll have to level with Bartelle. And let Park know a shitstorm is coming. I'm not taking a fall for *this*."

Shitstorm was an understatement of what would happen once Lisa and Bartelle reappeared. I had to prioritize. Bartelle could show at any time. That required me to concoct a story. It would take time for news to reach Park. He could wait—a little, not forever. First thing was to provide Niki the Happy Reaper's fake ID information.

I crutched into the spare bedroom, searched through the Happy Reaper's bags and found a business card holder. My nervous hands shook it open. My eyes had involuntarily pinched shut, not wanting to see his "Results Guaranteed" business card with the Celtic Cross on the other side. I forced myself to look and felt like the Cowardly Lion. The Happy Reaper wasn't that stupid. The expired Illinois driver's license claimed he was Harland W. Gottkind. I kept digging and found zipped in the bag's internal compartment two defunct credit cards, an old AAA card, and an unexpired passport, all with the same name.

Niki answered with, "Speak." In the background was the whine of a stressed engine and the rattle of a car nailing potholes.

"He's going by Harland W. Gottkind. You want his birth date?"

"Text me pictures of whatever you got. I can't take my eyes off the road. EMS is coming to meet us. Smith came to, but he's totally foggy. You call Park yet?"

"Next. I'll let you go." I hung up, not waiting for her response. I snapped pics, texted them to Niki, and dialed Paddy.

"Come home. I'll tell Bartelle I got back and sent you with the truck to deliver ah, deliver lumber to—you remember that camp up on Bone Lake? The guy who pulled my Bobcat from the ditch with his tractor that one winter? He's off horse-back riding in Montana or some place. Before you quote return unquote from dropping off the lumber, leave the oxygen equipment somewhere Bartelle won't see it."

"Dad, don't lie to him. I don't mean tell him everything, just don't lie. If they catch you lying, they'll throw you in jail again."

"Gotta go. He and Lisa are here."

TYLER

ON THE DRIVE TO ASPEN from the elk-hunting area, Tyler's burner phone chirped with an incoming message. He waited until he could safely pull off and listened to Zach spouting bullshit. What the hell was he thinking? You didn't project a high-quality service with a website 404 error—page not found.

He called Zach's burner and made his position known.

"I hear you loud and clear," Zach said. "It's not permanent. The chances of a new job coming in while I figure out what's going on with this botnet attack are low, and the risk is—"

Tyler's head felt like it would explode. Why did Zach not get it? "Low is not zero. If we miss even one assignment, I'm screwed. You get that? Keep the damn portal up and let me do my job and find the perfect way to fulfill our contract on Mr. William Barrett Oceans. Agreed?"

"Sure, sure. Sorry I bothered you."

Tyler disconnected, hoping he had nipped that in the bud. Zach was a react first, think later kind of guy. That was fine for computer games, but it was causing problems with molding the new Happy Reaper the way Tyler wanted him to be. Zach's knee-jerk reaction to kill the maid had tarnished the new Happy Reaper's image. Zach had worn a mask. He could have let her go and escaped. His over-reaction about the security of his precious websites was just—

Let it go. He inhaled through his nose until his chest filled, held to a count of ten, and emptied his lungs with a long, steady hiss.

The time to address the issue was after he completed this assignment and showed Zach how planning and foresight worked. Unless Zach lost his nerve again. Then, he'd have to take care of the problem. Permanently.

SEAMUS

HURRYING TO MEET BARTELLE, I worried we might have another victim on our hands—either Bartelle from a stroke or me from the blow it looked like he wanted to land. He stormed down the driveway, yelling at Lisa, his fists clenched, face purple.

I waited to speak until I judged him to be four strides away. In a calm voice I said, "We had an emergency, and yours was the only vehicle available for Niki."

My words, or Bartelle's good sense, stopped him a foot from my nose. I tilted my head to talk past him to Lisa. "She couldn't find your keys, otherwise she would have borrowed yours instead of the sheriff's."

"Sorry," Lisa said, "They're on a branch of that coat tree you have on the cabin porch. What emergency?"

"All I know is Niki called 9-1-1 and EMTs are meeting her and our guest on her way in. I assume they're headed to the hospital in Iron River."

Bartelle walked away, phone to his ear.

I motioned Lisa close and said in a quiet voice that Niki had found Smith unconscious at the cabin and thought the only way to keep him alive was to get him to a hospital.

Bartelle ended his call. His face had lightened from plum to raspberry. I figured both he and I were likely to live a little while longer.

"Where's your truck?" Bartelle asked.

"Paddy's got it."

He echoed, "Paddy's got it."

I felt no obligation to provide more details. I eased myself onto the largest of the rocks guarding the solar-panels pole. A few awkward seconds passed before Bartelle asked what I had done to myself.

So far, I hadn't lied, and I wanted to keep it that way. "Injured myself through stupidity. Doc wanted me on crutches. Hopefully, it's only a few days."

He looped his arm around his head, scratching the back of his opposite shoulder. He pointed to the drain in my leg. "You drove with that?"

I'd forgotten the drain. He had to know it was a gunshot wound. Crap. "'Course not. Paddy drove." Absolutely true. If he got the impression that Paddy drove me, well, that was on him.

"Where are your son and your truck?"

"He was grabbing a bite in Covington. He should be heading back. Did dispatch tell you where your car is? Lisa can take you to it."

Lisa seconded the offer. "Give you a chance to complete your sales pitch."

Bartelle finished scratching and switched to fidgeting his thumb at the corner of his pant's pocket. "She tell you laws prohibit you getting that medical equipment?"

"Yeah, I heard." Though not exactly because you told her and she told me.

"Who was the equipment for?"

"Guy Niki had to take in."

Bartelle shook a finger at me. "I thought you said on TT it was for your mother."

I shrugged. "Figured I'd generate sympathy and get a better deal. Everybody has a mother."

Bartelle's eyes narrowed. "This guy have a name?"

Lisa said, "I have to get my keys if I'm giving you a ride. You want it?"

Bartelle shifted his stare to her. She blessed him with a 10,000-watt smile. He said, "Yeah, sure."

Lisa took off toward the cabin at a trot.

Bartelle to me: "I know I'm just a dumb Wop cop, not a certified genius like you. That does not mean I will swallow the load of horse shit you're trying to shovel down my throat. I try to help you, and this is the thanks I get? Screw you, Seamus. Once I deal with my stolen cruiser, I will be back. You will tell me how you got shot. If I don't believe you, I will haul your ass into jail, where the prosecutor thinks it should be anyway. Are we clear?"

I felt like a heel. Even though we'd had our run-ins, I liked Bartelle a lot. He was doing a good job despite a tight budget and several open positions. But I kept breaking laws—for all the best reasons—and until I mended my ways, that was a problem.

He expected me to say something. I stayed with the truth. "It's far weirder than you think." Lisa's car beeped open. Hoping to distract him, I pointed toward her. "Here comes Lisa."

"One last time, Seamus. What's the guy's name?"

"Harland. Harland Gottkind." Among others.

NIKI

NIKI MET THE EMTS NEAR the two-mile marker on The Grade. She suggested the patient suffered from low oxygen. They transferred him into the truck and strapped him to a pallet to prevent his bouncing on the rough road.

Niki locked the cruiser and tucked the key on top of the passenger side rear tire. Not exactly secure, but a deputy should intercept them soon, and she'd tell him what she'd done. She flashed her Marshals badge and insisted on staying with Harland Gottkind, as she was forcing herself to think of him.

The EMT slipped a pulse oximeter on Gottkind's finger and let out a low whistle. "Holy crap, I've never seen a reading that low." He secured a nasal cannula around Gottkind's head and started oxygen. "That should help. Let's see how your vitals are doing, bud." He jotted readings of Gottkind's breathing, pulse, and blood pressure on a pad. "Not bad considering."

Moments later, they were bouncing toward Amasa. At the sawmill, they regained pavement. The ride smoothed and the siren came on. She caught splashes of red and blue flashing on the trees they passed.

With nothing to occupy her physically, Niki's worry mechanism kicked into high gear. Would Smith—Gottkind—suffer permanent brain issues from the oxygen deficit? Assuming he lived. They had the better part of a day until his next check-in with Clem. A lot could happen in twenty-four hours.

At the hospital, Niki discovered an Iron County deputy had joined them. While the EMTs transferred the patient to the ER staff, Niki approached the deputy. "Did the EMT driver let you know where we left the sheriff's car?"

The deputy, who looked like he still belonged in junior high school, stuck out his hand. "Ma'am, I need to see some ID." His other hand hovered near his revolver.

So much for a "thank you so much for taking the initiative and saving the guy's life." She produced her badge, transformed her body posture from supplicant to federal officer with an attitude. "Deputy Marshal Ashley Prescott."

The Iron County deputy's posture relaxed, and his hand moved away from his holster. She took advantage of his surprise and said, "Since I have to be there when he regains consciousness, there's no reason for you to stick around. About the sheriff's car?" She lifted her eyebrows with the question.

"Yeah, he's en route to collect it."

She told him where she had left the key. "Let me see how the patient is doing."

"I'll come with you. I need to confirm a few details with the crew."

Made sense that Bartelle would want to determine what the EMTs knew while the information was fresh. In the ER, indistinct conversation came from behind a set of drawn curtains. The other bays were empty. The two EMTs chatted in low voices on the periphery—probably waiting for someone to sign paperwork. She half-listened to the deputy confirm details with the EMTs. Nothing she didn't already know.

One side of the screening slid away. A doctor stepped out, leaving the room open behind him. "He has you guys to thank if he recovers," he told the EMTs. "His oxygen is rising quickly."

With Smith's next call to Clem on her mind, she asked, "Will he have permanent damage?"

"Too soon to tell, but I hope not. You're a relative?"

"Not exactly," she said. "I'm—"

"No shit," the deputy said, using his outside voice.

Niki spun toward the disruption and discovered the deputy was staring through the screen's opening.

"That's Adam Smith. You caught the guy the sheriff told us about."

Well damn, Niki thought, this changes everything.

TYLER

TYLER SCOUTED THE AIRPORT. NO way that would work. After grabbing lunch downtown, he drove into the hills to Oceans' house. It never ceased to amaze him how accepting people were of strangers if you carried a clipboard and occasionally wrote things down. If anyone had asked, he would tell them he was preparing a quote to manage the place, the whole nine yards: maintenance, grounds, snowplowing, and rentals, including preparation and clean-up. No one asked.

A tasteful sign suggested a national security firm guarded the premises. A quarter of the people who had the signs had *only* the signs, having snagged one from a friend or brought it from another house they owned. Because this confirmed Zach's research, he figured this was for real. He recorded the name for show.

He paced the length of the driveway, calculated distances from the patio fireplace to various trees, measured the house dimensions, windows and doors. On many of the downstairs windows, he spotted devices that triggered an alarm if the window opened while the system was armed. He created several sketches on which he recorded the details. Despite not spotting any exterior security cameras, he assumed the doorbells had embedded video cameras and positioned himself to avoid their capturing his face.

A neighbor strolling by walking a Great Dane paid some attention to him. She subjected him to more scrutiny on her return. He gave her a friendly wave with the clipboard, making sure she could not observe much of his face.

The lady's interest was a sign for him to skedaddle. A good, professional, first visit: he found several places to hide and take his shot. Pro that he was, he wouldn't stop here. No, he would not. He'd observe what changed at night, learn the areas streetlights lit and where they didn't, determine if the security system worked, and get a sense of police response times.

Oh yes, he'd show Zach how a professional planned a hit.

SEAMUS

WITH BARTELLE TEMPORALLY GONE, I summoned Paddy. He parked my truck in its usual spot in the driveway. Lisa reported no issues with dropping Bartelle at his car. They left me resting on the screened porch with a propane heater for warmth and retreated to the guest cabin to review recent data. An hour later, they had news.

Paddy confirmed the cell tower simulator had captured several calls, including the Happy Reaper's to Clem. From that, they learned Clem's number and determined that six days earlier someone bought it from a store in Natick, Massachusetts.

Damn my brain. The Happy Reaper had used my phone to call Clem. Why hadn't I remembered and retrieved that number for Paddy. I checked—different number, but the same area code and prefix.

"I'll check it," Paddy said. "Likely bought from the same place. If the store keeps surveillance video, we need Niki to arrange a court order to gain access."

I shook my head. "Probably won't happen. I've had no luck getting any response from Assistant Director of National Intelligence Park and we agree right now we can't risk contacting the FBI, not even Deputy Director Ambrose." I included all the titles for Lisa's benefit. "We're S-O-L until Park responds. Besides the specs on Clem's phone, did you learn anything else?"

They had. The Happy Reaper's conversation with Clem had been one-sided. Clem had not uttered even a hello or goodbye. Bartelle's phone call had been two-sided, proving the equipment was working. Bartelle had ordered a deputy to "stick with that woman like spots on a dalmatian" but leave her for Bartelle to question.

Lisa continued the commentary to bring me current on the imposter front. "The back door worked, and we found a database with detailed information on four prior contacts."

"Including who ordered the hits? Who the victims are?"

Lisa's expression flattened into a grimace. "And more. Two of the four are dead. One of those relates to the murder in Alabama where he left the Results Guaranteed business card. The Happy Reaper thinks the imposter would only be interested in one of the other two. But—"

I didn't need to hear more. "We should contact the intended victims and tell them someone is targeting them. And give all four client names to the police."

Patrick coughed to hide his laugh. "I told Lisa you'd say that. How do you propose we do it? It's not like we can fess up to what we've been doing."

The jangle of my cellphone saved me from admitting I had not considered the ramifications of my suggestion. I picked up Niki's call and learned that news of escaped murderer Adam Smith's presence in the Iron River hospital would soon become widespread.

I popped my phone to speaker. "Can't you swear them to secrecy? Tell them it's for their own safety."

Niki said, "Come on, Seamus. How long have you lived here? This is small-town America. Everybody swears they won't tell a soul and calls their best friend because they know their buddy can keep a secret. Soon it's common knowledge, and someone posts a picture of Smith in the hospital bed on their favorite social media."

She was right. It might already be on Telephone Time if the show wasn't finished for the day. "So, we assume the world will soon know. Do *you* have a plan?"

"Did you contact Park?"

"Wait. Wait. Wait. Remember the spyware I think's on my phone? I'll call you right back." I disconnected, explained to Paddy and Lisa what I suspected the Happy Reaper had done to my phone, and borrowed Lisa's phone while she took mine to "disinfect it."

I ended up in Niki's voicemail and left Lisa's number for her to call.

But the phone didn't ring.

FIVE MINUTES OF NOT HEARING from Niki caused me to wonder if I had given her the wrong number. I called and left a second message. Another five minutes passed. My stomach churned with anxiety. The only reason she wouldn't call was because she couldn't, and the only reason she couldn't was because she was in trouble.

I retrieved the phone with the secure message app I used as the backup to Niki's primary contact while working undercover, FBI Special Agent Rick Kaska. I did not know him well, but Niki trusted him. I'm old school and believe meeting in person is better than talking on the phone, which is better than texting. I used the secure app to ask Kaska to call me ASAP, with the condition that he had to be somewhere no one official could overhear. Not willing to tie up Lisa's phone while I waited for Niki's call, I gave Kaska Paddy's cell number.

A few minutes later, Paddy's cell rang. He looked at the display. "DC area code."

"It's private." I shooed them away. Kaska had no insight regarding Park's location or when he might respond. In broad strokes, I painted the situation with the Happy Reaper, the imposter, and the database.

His long sigh came down the line. "The FBI will do nothing with an untraceable, anonymous phone call offering murder-for-hire details. Even if I say the info came from a CI—confidential informant—the bureaucratic nightmare is impossible. The manual on CIs is thicker than the DC phone book. Niki, with her special—what do I call it?—status might pull it off without using your name. Nothing I can do. Why don't you warn the targets? But buy a burner, maybe use software that disguises your voice. You don't want this coming back at you."

After being without a phone had nearly cost me my life, I had made it a practice to have multiple burner phones available. "Good idea." I thanked him for his help and signed off. I hated the idea that the people who solicited hits might get away with it but reminded myself that was not an immediate concern. Protecting the two potential victims was the priority. Then, my focus had to be on uncovering the imposter's identity.

I yelled to Paddy and Lisa that I was done with the call. Lisa had returned to the cabin. Paddy's internet searches found phone numbers for both potential targets. Instead of using a burner phone, he set up voice scrambling software on his computer. He used the TOR browser and made the phone call through the internet, the combination concealing information about his computer and our location. "Dad, going through all those connections means the quality won't be great, but no one will know it's us."

I first tried the venture capitalist and had to leave a message on his business phone. "This message is for William Barrett Oceans. I recently learned through illegally hacking the dark web that someone wants to hire a hit man to kill you. This was a few weeks ago, so please, please take precautions."

The second guy I called—a Kevin Porwall, the assignment the Happy Reaper thought the imposter would not accept—answered. It shocked me to learn he was aware of the threat. Police had arrested the alleged perpetrator, who a judge had locked away for psychological evaluation.

Paddy gave my shoulder a slap. "That should do it."

"Get me the number for the guy who ordered the venture capitalist hit. I'll tell him to call it off or pay the consequences."

I had to leave another message. Just as well. I was twitching with outrage and wasn't sure how I'd handle talking to the guy. Paddy and I agree we had done what we could, which did not make me feel one iota better. Time to switch our efforts to uncovering the imposter. "What do you and Lisa have planned?"

"We've mined everything we can from the website he uses to collect the initial contact information. We figured he might become suspicious if we stopped the bot attack. To avoid scaring him off, we significantly reduced the effort. We've ramped up searching for the website he uses to further the discussions if he's interested. Given we've determined he uses a different server to house it, we're searching for that needle in a haystack. More like the universe."

I used the crutches to stand and do laps on the screened porch. Stopping in front of Paddy, I said. "To summarize, we've made excellent progress and are no closer to learning who the imposter is."

"Correct. So, let's refocus on finding Clem. We do that, we remove that loaded gun pointed at our families. Face it, Dad. We're running low on options. Niki insists we can't use the FBI. Kaska agrees. Since Park isn't contacting you, you can't sweet-talk him into issuing a warrant to tap into Clem's phone records. Niki's gone silent, and locals have uncovered the Happy Reaper's identity. There's a category five hurricane heading our way. I know you don't like hacking the phone companies, and given her position, Lisa can't risk it. I have to try."

He was right: I did not like illegal hacking in the abstract. What caused me heartburn was the thought of Paddy doing it. I'd acquiesced in other situations in which that seemed to be our only choice. But it had to be *the last resort.* Yes, Clem was an issue, but bigger in my mind was uncovering the imposter and having the police arrest him. Despite everyone else thinking it was a terrible idea, I still had one more thing to try before I conceded we had reached the last resort stage.

"Let's hold off until we hear from Niki. Humor me, would you? Bring up that first website so I can see what it looks like."

Paddy again used the TOR browser to hide our location and entered the imposter's portal. The website looked innocuous if you didn't know why it existed. Leaving that browser open, I dramatically slapped my forehead. "What a dummy! The Happy Reaper left his phone in his room. If you can open that . . ." I left the statement hanging for him to fill in the blank.

Paddy swallowed the bait, found the Happy Reaper's phone, and started playing. With him fully occupied, I set up a new Gmail account, thehappyreaper followed by an eight-digit number. Using the TOR browser, I typed in a request from the Happy Reaper to "off" one Seamus Anselm McCree. Under reason, I typed "I'm dying. Can't do it myself. I want to outlive the bastard."

Paddy was humming some song I didn't recognize, a sure sign he was not paying attention to me. I rechecked my entries and clicked the submit button at the bottom of the form. The form cleared and the single word,

DELIVERED, showed on my screen for ten seconds before the screen went blank. I had the sinking feeling I should have had Paddy capture what happened after I hit submit. Too late now.

THE HAPPY REAPER

THE HAPPY REAPER WOKE TO a bright room and jerked his hand to cover his eyes. Metal dinged metal and pain shot up his arm from his wrist to his elbow when a force field stopped his motion. He rolled his head and discovered his hand cuffed to a bed rail.

He curled his fingers around the rail and jerked, triggering angry beeps and alarms from multiple monitors.

A woman, hard face, hawk eyes, pinned him to the bed with one hand. He arched his body and realized she had secured his other arm to his chest.

"Don't say a damn thing until we're alone. Got it? Nod your head."

Footsteps entered the room. "What are you doing to him?" a strident voice asked.

"Thank God you're here! He woke up and started struggling. I was calming him until you arrived."

The hard woman removed her hand, stepped away, and a taller blonde replaced her. "Welcome back, Mr. Gottkind." She silenced the beeping machines. "You've had us worried. Do you remember falling? Your low oxygen level caused you to pass out."

He closed his eyes. Hospital made sense. He felt certain he'd seen the hawk-faced woman before. The blonde? He thought not. Gottkind was not his name, but he didn't feel any urge to object. Until he understood what was happening, he would take the hawk's advice—command—to stay silent. Well, not silent, but not answering questions.

He pointed to his throat and said, "Thirsty." It came out a rasp. How long had he been unconscious?

"I'll bet you are," the blonde said. "Those IVs work wonders at keeping you hydrated, but they don't help for dry throat. Your vitals look good. I'll let the doctor know you're responsive. She'll decide whether you can have liquids. Be right back."

The hawk leaned over. Didn't touch him this time. "Your fake ID says your name is Harland Gottkind. You're handcuffed to the bed because I had to use my U.S. Marshal credentials to claim custody and prevent the locals from taking charge. None of this may make any sense to you right now. Regardless, for your own good, do not answer questions. Trust me, we are in this together."

At the sound of approaching footsteps, the hawk moved to a corner of the room, and white coats surrounded him. Asking questions. Some were stupid, like who was the president, which he did not answer. He complied with their instructions to follow their fingers with his eyes. Part way through the exam, he remembered the hawk's name was Niki, and she was a friend of Seamus McCree.

He listened with amusement to the white coats argue about the extent of damage caused by the lack of oxygen. They agreed his speech functions were intact. He'd asked for and received water and thanked the nurse. He had not answered questions about today's date, who the president was, what his name was, etc. They would rerun the tests in a few hours and see if he improved.

The nurse bustled around the room, checking this and that before leaving the two of them alone. Niki arranged her chair to be next to him. "Please keep your voice down. Do you remember who I am?"

"Seamus McCree's friend Niki. But—?"

"Listen first, then I'll answer all your questions. I promise. I found you unconscious on the floor in Seamus's guest cabin. To get you to the hospital, I borrowed a sheriff's car, had to call 9-1-1. EMTs met us part way and put you on oxygen. A local cop recognized you from a BOLO— an alert his department received to be on the lookout. He knew your real name is Adam Smith and tagged you the Happy Reaper. You with me so far?"

The pieces fit like a jigsaw puzzle coming together, borders complete, middle still missing. "I'm all ears."

"Because the cop recognized you, I showed my credentials and said I have you in custody and insisted the hospital records show you as Gottkind. That's why I locked you to the bed. The nurse restricted your other arm because you were thrashing around and threatening your IV. Do you remember why you were at Seamus's place?"

Jigsaw complete. "Yeah, and I remember we had a deal." He rattled the handcuffs. "And this isn't part of it."

"Save your tantrum for later. If the two of us don't agree on a rock-solid story, nothing I say or do can prevent you from going back to jail. They'll put you in solitary and forget to give you your meds and oxygen. The next time you become unconscious, no one will find you until you're dead. The imposter will have his way, and you lose all around."

That put a different spin on things. "What's the story?"

"You escaped—I'm sure you're smart enough not to say how or who helped you. I guessed you would want to kill Seamus, got there ahead of you, and stopped you. Hold on and hear me out before you get all angry. Because once I had you, you cut a deal with the feds. You help them find the guy who wants to become the next Happy Reaper. We keep you under guard at Seamus's place. That makes you look like a decent guy and explains all the electronic equipment Patrick and Lisa—you remember them?"

"Hackers. Seamus's son and she's soon to be a general."

"Good. Because believe me, a ton of people will soon be asking questions. If either of us says the wrong thing, you're in prison, and I'm screwed."

"Why did I agree?"

"Stick with the truth that you didn't want the imposter to hijack your legacy."

Could work. "Why don't I remain silent? Let you do all the talking."

"Doctors are already confused by your behavior. Can you pretend you were doing a silent, pissed-off-prisoner act, but now you're cooperating?"

It wasn't like he had a better alternative. He'd say little and follow her lead. "Got it. You don't want me telling him Jimmy Carter is the president. More water?"

She held the straw to his lips. He sucked in half a glass. Its cool soothed his raw throat. She said, "I'm starving. We both missed lunch and dinner. You want me to see if the nurses can rustle up something?"

"Sure. In the prison, they chained my feet to the bed."

"The handcuffs were all the sheriff's deputy had. Added complication if we have to sneak you out of here: he has the key, not me. I can at least release your other arm."

"Get me a piece of stiff wire or a paper clip. I'll have them off in no time."

That got her smiling. "You probably should not have told me that." She released his arm. "I'll see what food I can arrange for you."

She reported success at ordering him food and marched to his bed. Lowered her head to his level and whispered, "I'm calling your bluff."

His heart raced. How the hell did she figure it out? He couldn't have said anything while he was unconscious. Not responding was admitting to the bluff. "What are you talking about? You're calling what bluff?"

She showed him a paper clip. "Tick tock. Timer's on."

He bent the paper clip to perform its new task, a lock pick. In fifteen seconds, he freed his wrist of the cuff. He knew by her surprised face that he had far exceeded her expectations.

She snapped the handcuff back on his wrist. "Show me how you did that?"

"Show you how he did what?" asked a male voice from the doorway.

SEAMUS

PADDY WOULD NOT REACT WELL to my telling him what I had done, so I waited until he was cooking dinner and Lisa's presence might provide a buffer. They both had glasses of wine. I was stuck with water until I was off the pain meds and antibiotics, which Paddy had administered in Niki's absence.

Paddy blew a much bigger gasket than I had anticipated. Lisa slipped past the verbal volcano that was my son, gave me a tight hug, and whispered in my ear, "Has he told you he's the father of my kid?" She stepped away, gave me a conspiratorial smile, and patted her belly.

What the hell? I was unaware of any issues in Paddy's and Cindy's marriage. Last I knew, they planned to adopt Valeria, who had come into our lives that summer and was the same age as my granddaughter. Seeing Lisa's smile brought me back to a time she had been just a name to me, one of the three partners Paddy was starting a business with. She had bet Paddy that she could fool me into thinking she and Paddy were getting married. She'd won. Which was uproariously funny to them because Lisa is gay.

Clearly, she was acting the trickster to get my mind off Paddy's outrage, which had gone on long enough.

"Paddy," I said, "give it a break. I heard all the arguments you and Niki and Lisa made. I used a VPN. All the imposter has is an email address I set up just for his response. Tell me I'm not right that if he contacts me and gives me a link to the next dark-web page, you aren't a billion times more likely to crack it and identify him? This gambit makes perfect sense. We can still choose not to respond."

Lisa said, "True, that. Patrick, your father does not believe that my kid has half your DNA."

Paddy threw his hands up and waved them down, a pantomime of total disgust.

I said, "Lisa, I don't think your diversionary tactic is working."

Lisa laughed. "Busted. With my luck, my guy will get the same pig-headed gene you two share. Having decided to have a child, I asked Patrick to be the sperm donor, but only if Cindy approved. The first fertilized egg implanted and here we are. I have plenty frozen if I decide baby needs a sib. Patrick and Cindy have agreed to be his godparents. I hope I can convince you and your ex, Elizabeth, to be great-godparents. What do you say to having another munchkin calling you Grampa Seamus?"

Humor sparkling Lisa's eyes, anger still in Paddy's. It all fit. Lisa's parents had disowned her after she came out. And yet, these two could play me the fool. "I might become more angry than Paddy if you're pulling my leg, Lisa."

"Cross my heart."

She made the sign, and *my* heart filled with warmth. I had surprised myself at how quickly and how deep my feelings for Valeria had grown in the brief time since she had come into our lives. Lisa's munchkin would surely be another rich blessing for me.

I wrapped her in a hug. "I'm honored, and I'm sure Lizzie will also agree." Holding Lisa at arm's length, I said. "Now I should wipe the tears from my eyes and check my new email account to see if we have a response."

ZACH

ZACH TOOK A LATE-AFTERNOON BREAK from his day job to check whether the portal was still under hacking attack. His server diagnostics showed someone was still poking around, and—wait, what's this? The database included a new contact.

His mind spaced out reviewing the information, and he had to reread it from the beginning. Someone claiming to be the Happy Reaper wanted to hire them to off—his word—Seamus McCree. This, after someone with the Happy Reaper's knowledge had tried to enter the administrative area of the website, and hackers had attempted to pry it open with a digital crowbar.

He knew what Tyler would say: They planned to do McCree anyway, so why not get paid for it? *Because, you money-obsessed cretin, it might be a setup.* He left another text for Charlene to call after her shift ended.

Forty minutes later, she did. Zach forced himself to go through the meaningless pleasantries before explaining everything that had happened that day. At the conclusion, Charlene told him to shutter the portal. "Tyler can complain if he wants, but between the rich guy in Colorado and McCree, we already have all the work we can handle."

And she didn't even know about his planned adventure this weekend. Keep this focused on the Tyler aspect. "Right. Tyler has twelve days left to earn the bonus on the VC guy. That's what should be his worry."

"We're on the same page. Let him do that while you and I handle McCree's visit here next month and whatever's going on with this recent contact. Can you put up a notice that says we're temporarily closed to new assignments?"

Excellent. Zach left the connection open, listening to Charlene banging pots around in her kitchen while he made the change. "Got it done. Can you make sure it looks okay to you? I don't want Tyler crawling up my butt on this."

The pot banging stopped. "You reversed the N and G in assignments. Otherwise looks good. I'll handle Tyler."

Her words lifted a weight off his neck. "How should I respond to this purported Happy Reaper request to kill McCree?"

"Who did he use as a reference?"

Zach checked the database. "Instead of a name, his message stated that only he knew the old passwords to the portal's administrative module. I could verify that he had used them."

The sound of an exhaust fan came over the line. "Five minutes to cook. That's totally unconvincing. All it proves is this is the guy who tried the passwords. I'm confident I can gain access to police files related to a hit he performed in Boston. A case they didn't bother bringing to trial because he admitted to it. I'll go in tonight and search for something odd that we can use to verify it's him. The guy will have to wait."

Perfect. She has no clue, but Tyler might smell a rat. "Sounds great, but Tyler will be pissed if we don't tell him first."

"Negative. If he calls, don't answer. Let me know, and I'll take care of him."

Zach saw the hole in that. "But you can't call him while you're on patrol."

"Then he'll have to cool his jets. It's not like he can do anything while he's in Aspen. My dinner's ready. I'll let you know if I find something. Relax, Zach. You done good. I promise I *will* handle Tyler if he gets out of line."

She disconnected, leaving Zach elated. That could not have gone better. Charlene did not know his supposed LARP outing this weekend was cover for him to deliver on the contract Tyler had forced them to decline. The guy had it coming, and Zach was happy to be the instrument of his demise. He wouldn't leave the Happy Reaper's business card—no reason to thumb his nose at Tyler—and he didn't care about being paid. Personal satisfaction was the only reward he wanted.

Zach could now blame shutting down the website on Charlene. He planned to support Tyler in the inevitable discussion in which Tyler insisted it was a lot of money and they had nothing to lose. That would keep Tyler from sniffing out Zach's extracurricular activities this weekend.

Two days and he'd be on the road to Cincinnati. He and Mr. Kevin Porwall had an appointment, except Porwall didn't have any idea he was coming.

Niki

"SHERIFF BARTELLE," NIKI SAID TO the voice behind her. "I trust you found your cruiser okay?"

"Let's you and me walk and talk."

Niki faced Bartelle. "I do not wish to leave my prisoner. I've already told him I borrowed your ride to save his life. Whatever you have to say, I'm happy with him hearing." *Which will help Smith keep his story consistent with mine.*

"Fine." Bartelle left and returned dragging a chair screeching across the tile floor. "Let's start with why your prisoner was at McCree's instead of sitting safely in my jail?"

She reminded herself Bartelle was a skilled investigator and interrogator. Do not offer extraneous information. "Mister Gottkind, the name we are using to protect him, is assisting an investigation of someone who is impersonating—" At Smith stirring in the bed, she amended it to, "*Attempting to impersonate him* as a master assassin. For his support, the government agreed to keep him in a remote spot. McCree's place fits. Agreed?"

"You're telling me the government staged his escape?" Bartelle's voice rose with incredulity.

Niki thought briefly of spinning that line, decided the truth was better, and informed Bartelle that Smith's escape was real. She repeated her line about how she had anticipated his revenge and captured him at Seamus's place. And since he was there, keeping him there made the most sense.

Bartelle asked Smith, "Were you armed?"

Before Niki could caution Smith not to answer that question, he did.

His eyes flashed with anger. "Of course, numbnuts. Do I look like someone who could wrestle McCree to death?" He closed his eyes. Gathering strength?

Hoping to end that line of questioning, she asked if Smith wanted her to hold the cup so he could sip through the straw. He did and took his time.

Bartelle waited for him to finish. Smith pushed the empty cup aside and Bartelle pounced. "We received a report of gunshots around Shank Lake. Did you shoot McCree?"

"He wouldn't be alive if I had shot him."

"Who did?"

Smith opened his eyes wide with feigned surprise. "He's shot?"

Bartelle turned to her. "Tell me what happened to McCree?"

She met his stare. "I can't tell you what I don't know." A true, albeit misleading, statement.

Bartelle released an exasperated breath, switched his glare to Smith. "What are you armed with, and where are the weapons now?"

"A semi-automatic rifle and a Glock. And a knife. I don't know where they are now."

Bartelle rolled his eyes. "Where were they when you last saw them?"

"In the room where I was staying at McCree's."

Bartelle crooked his arm over his head. "Loaded?"

"The knife wasn't."

"I'll take that as a yes. What agreement do you think you have with this lady?"

"Here's the thing, Sheriff—Bartelle, is it? I signed a non-disclosure agreement, which I can't break. I have no desire to spend my last few months, weeks, or days behind prison walls. If you want to ask the lady questions, ask away, but I believe I've said all I'm going to say."

Praise the Lord. Why hadn't they thought of the nondisclosure agreement idea earlier?

To Niki Bartelle said, "A nondisclosure agreement. Learn that from Trump, did you?"

Niki did not want Smith to get into it with Bartelle. "You've heard that 'loose lips sink ships' expression? He's not allowed to tell anyone what he's doing. It's that simple. He posed no risk to you. He was never within fifty yards of you and, if he had examined his firearms, he'd know I removed their firing pins. I'm sorry I inconvenienced you by borrowing your ride. I shouldn't have allowed anyone to block in my car. We need him alive to catch the new killer. I'm sure you'll agree I had the right to commandeer your cruiser to save his life." Left unsaid was that if they had no longer needed his assistance to catch the imposter, she would have let nature decide whether he lived or died.

Bartelle shifted in his chair. "I'm more pissed that you trust Seamus, his son, and an army colonel with information, but not me. Word that Adam Smith is in our hospital will soon be everywhere. I need to understand your plans and what they mean for my department."

From her unconscious came a fresh worry. On any real Marshal's assignment, she'd be working with a partner. Her lack of backup was a major issue, but not one she wanted to address with Bartelle. "I could use your help keeping unwanted media at bay."

The sheriff scratched his head. "You're not worried the same people who extracted him from the first hospital won't try again?"

Niki put on the same expression she used for news conferences. "He knows that is not in his best interest."

Bartelle's tone dripped with skepticism. "Even if he succeeds?" His mike squawked. "Be back in a sec." His leaving was brief. "That was the prosecutor. I'm off, but we're not done. Not by a long shot."

Bartelle left the extra chair and closed the door after himself. Smith pointed at the door. "I know a threat when I hear one."

"Keep that paper clip handy."

TYLER

DARK CAME ON QUICKLY IN the Colorado mountains. Following a late dinner at a ridiculously overpriced restaurant, Tyler drove to the target's neighborhood. He liked that there were no streetlamps, although half the houses had their outdoor lights on. Not even Halloween yet, for Pete's sake, and one even had its damn Christmas lights up.

He parked in the driveway of a house under construction a half-mile from the target's residence. Carrying only the car fob, he walked a circuitous route to avoid all patches of light and arrived at the line of trees marking the target's property line.

Excellent. That meant he could slip in at night, take his shot, slip out, and no one would ever see him. Now to learn how good the security is. He found a fist-sized rock and threw it through one of the upstairs windows. He retreated to his car. If police had responded, they had taken a different route than he anticipated and had not used lights or sirens. His best guess was that the upstairs windows had no protection. Good to know should he decide to get into the house.

On the return drive to the hotel, he called Zach to let him know he had a plan and would leave the next morning.

Zach answered the phone with, "There's been a development." With hardly a breath, he poured out the story of the contact from the real Happy Reaper or someone posing as him. Because "Charlene freaked." Zach had followed her advice. "Assuming we can confirm it's him," Zach concluded, "Do you agree we should take the job?"

The fee was substantial, exactly what Tyler would expect from the Happy Reaper. If only one person in the world understood the value of a good hit, he was the guy. "Why the hell not? Nothing wrong with someone paying us for doing what we planned to do anyway. And if it's not him, or someone acting for him, let's learn enough to take that person off the stage."

Zach's next words sounded much calmer. "I'm glad we're agreed on that. I don't think Charlene will see it that way."

Which may mean it's time for the two of them to go on their own.

"Seeing how easy it will be to shoot Oceans while he's in the boonies, I think a similar approach would also work better for McCree than trying something at the party for his mother."

Zach cleared his throat. "Charlene already has a plan."

"Yeah, well, nothing wrong with us coming up with a better one with less risk. I'll change flights and do a little scout of McCree's place in the U.P. on the way home."

Another throat clear came down the line. "Maybe we should talk with Charlene first?"

Screw that. "Don't tell her anything. If nothing comes of this, she won't have to know."

Thursday, October 20, 2022

SEAMUS

I AWOKE IN THE NIGHT to a thumping heart and sweat-drenched sheets. The Happy Reaper's phone was sitting in the guest room. He was in the hospital. Tomorrow morning, he either called Clem or—assuming the Happy Reaper had told the truth—the clock started ticking and Clem would soon begin targeting my family. The Happy Reaper might be leery of using any phone other than his. No problem. Paddy or Lisa could deliver it to the hospital.

Resolving that concern should have let me sleep. *Should* being the operative word. One result of the terrible, no good, rotten night's sleep was I was awake to hear engines approaching on the road. I left the bed and spotted two Iron County Sheriff's cars pulling down my driveway, their cars tinged pink from the sunrise.

Because the night temperatures had dropped into the twenties, I already had on sweatpants, wool socks, a turtleneck, and a beanie. No time to grab a coat. I crutched down the screened-porch ramp to meet Bartelle and Tex. Bartelle held a piece of paper. My stomach flips told me it was a search warrant.

The leg wound must have been enough to convince a judge. Unless the Happy Reaper or Niki had triggered this response from the county? Niki would have let me know, unless—I pulled my cellphone from my sweats pocket and checked. Battery at 64%, airplane mode off, Wi-Fi active, plenty of bars. Niki had not called or left a message. Whatever this was, she had not anticipated it.

A car door slamming from the guest cabin driveway drew my attention that way. A third cruiser had parked, and an officer was making his way to the cabin.

Bartelle pointed Tex toward the kitchen stoop before hitching up his belt and walking in my direction. I reminded myself to let him speak first.

They could hold anything I said against me. My breath steamed the morning air and the cold air cut through my turtleneck. I willed myself not to shiver.

Bartelle skirted a puddle skimmed with ice. A dead expression painted his face. This was bad. Terrible.

He stopped at arm's distance. "I wanted to give you one more chance to tell me what's going on. The prosecutor didn't agree. Here's a search warrant that covers everywhere on your property. Under the terms of your bail, you may not have any firearms on your premises. Nor drugs. The warrant allows us to determine if you are meeting the conditions of your bail."

Now I got it. The prosecutor, who had a hard-on for me and was running for re-election on being tough on crime and criminals, had gotten wind of the Happy Reaper's guns. Or Niki's.

I skimmed the warrant, relying on experience to understand the gist.

"Let your deputy up by the guest cabin know two people are inside. One is Lisa, the Army member you've already met. I don't know if she's armed. I don't want any accidents. The guns you're looking for are in the TV room—the room off the screened porch. I'm sure Niki has weapons locked in her vehicle."

"Yep, that's where Smith said they'd be. I knew I'd have to take you into custody for violating your bail conditions, so we got here early enough to bring you to Crystal in time for you to attend a bail hearing today. Otherwise, the prosecutor would keep your ass in jail overnight."

"Thanks, I think."

"You're welcome, I think. I'll accompany you while you collect your stuff before I take you in. Remember your cell phone. First, let me get Tex and my other deputy started."

He yelled for Tex to collect the guns from the TV room and search the rest of the house. He used the mike clipped to his chest protector to pass my information to the deputy at the cabin and direct him not to enter until Tex was there to assist.

My head felt like a vise was crushing it. How could I make sure the Happy Reaper got his phone with Bartelle dragging me into town? Bartelle assisted me to the house, watched me down my first dose of antibiotic pills. Good thing Lisa had pulled the port last night after giving me the final IV treatment. He helped me don a parka, and carried the sling pack with my wallet, address book, and cellphone while I crutched to the cruiser. He ducked me into the car and said, "I'm leaving you for a few minutes. I'm not telling you what to do, but I'll confiscate your phone before we leave. Fifteen minutes good?"

Message received: call my lawyer. "Thanks." I'd buy him several thank-you cases of beer. Had to wait, though. Otherwise, the prosecutor would charge me with bribery.

I first called Niki and briefed her on the situation. She assured me she'd coordinate with Paddy to retrieve the Happy Reaper's phone. My stress level dropped several notches. My call to Irene Frankel, my Michigan criminal defense lawyer, went to her answering service, which promised to pass on my message.

Twelve of my promised fifteen minutes had ticked away before Irene responded. She could not travel from her place in the Mitten in time for any bail hearing. "I know anyone representing himself has a fool for a client, but that's better for you today than trying to get a local attorney up to speed. Let me pass an idea by you."

NIKI

NIKI HAD BARELY ENDED HER phone call with Seamus before Smith asked, "What was that? It didn't sound good."

"That was Seamus being thankful his half-sister was not staying with him. If she wasn't away for a court-approved business reason, she'd also be heading to jail."

Smith scratched his chest. "You lost me."

"You told Sheriff Bartelle you brought firearms into Seamus's house. That broke Seamus's bond restrictions. The prosecutor has it in for him and sent the sheriff to bring him in. Bartelle confiscated your weapons and is taking Seamus to jail. That's now spilt milk. Unless you want to join him behind bars, you have a task you must complete today."

"You're talking riddles. Are you always like this when you don't get enough sleep?"

"Call your pal Clem and let him know you're okay. If you don't and he sets the hounds loose on Seamus's family, there's no reason for me not to send your ass away."

Push came to shove, she'd have Patrick or Lisa bring his phone to him.

She hoped by not offering that option, he would propose a different solution, which might lead them closer to determining Clem's identity.

Understanding dawned on Smith's face. Then he looked worried. "I need my phone. I don't have the number memorized."

Good try. "The number's in your phone's memory. Patrick or Lisa can unlock your phone and get it for you."

"The finger that unlocks the phone is here." He waved his fingers at her. "Get them to bring me the phone."

"Gosh, I never thought of that," Niki said in her most sarcastic tone. "Except until the cops finish searching the property, they can't take anything. There's a password. There's always a password. Look, I don't care a rat's ass who your contact is. I just want to see Seamus's family safe and the imposter behind bars. What's the deadline for making your call? Does one missed day trigger Clem?"

Smith's expression suggested that he was engaged in some heavy thinking. If she stayed patient, she might learn something from this exercise. Before he decided, her phone rang. Unknown number with a 703 area code. Who was calling from Northern Virginia? She answered with a tentative, "Hello?"

"Is this Ashley Pendergast Prescott?"

Very authority sounding. She straightened her spine, as though that would make a difference to her caller. "You have me at a disadvantage."

"This is Deputy Director Drake. Who the hell *are* you, and what the hell is going on?"

She'd never spoken to the man that agents referred to as 3D behind his back, a play on words of DD Drake combined with his habit of wanting the "big picture." She wanted time to think. "Sir, as a precaution, I will call you right back. Please make sure your assistant accepts my phone call." Niki disconnected.

Smith's eyebrows rose into inverted half moons. "Who's that?"

Niki grabbed her bag and headed for the door. "More problems. When I return, I expect an answer from you on how you will handle Clem." She shut the door behind her, found an empty room, and left that door cracked open to make sure Smith didn't take a walkabout. An online search provided the main number in Arlington for the Marshals Service. She asked the switchboard operator to connect her to DD Drake.

Soon, she heard the same man's voice in her ear. "Satisfied? Before this morning, I'd never heard of you. Now I discover you're some political hack who got special treatment to become a marshal. Somehow, you captured an escaped murderer in East Jesus, Michigan, and the Director chewed my ass for not keeping him informed."

Despite warning herself to be the adult in the room, Niki's voice came out hot. "Did you have a question, sir?"

"Do you know who you're talking to, young lady?"

"Yes sir. I have established to my satisfaction that you are Deputy Director Drake." She mentally kicked herself for being a jerk, but he was acting like an ass. "What I meant was, did you have a specific question, or did you want the big picture?" She smacked herself on the forehead when she realized what she'd said.

"What I want is—never mind. Here are your orders. You will relinquish the prisoner . . ." The connection picked up papers rustling. "Adam Smith, really? Relinquish Adam Smith to the two marshals who are heading your way. You will be in my office tomorrow morning at eight o'clock and not a second later. You will not talk to the press. Have I made myself clear?"

"Crystal." After a pause, she thought to add, "sir."

"Very well. Now give me the big picture. What the hell is going on?"

And here we go. Time to offer rope to tie him in knots—or hang herself. "I'm sorry, sir. I don't know whether you have proper clearance. My understanding is this is on a need-to-know basis. Before we can discuss this, I must determine if your security authorization allows you to receive this intel."

"What the—"

Niki disconnected before he could swear. She opened her secure app and typed a message to ADNI Park, copies to Rick Kaska and Seamus, not that she had any hope Seamus could retrieve it given his current situation.

I am standing directly in front of the fan the shit is about to hit. Please intervene with Deputy Director Drake before his agents arrive and grab Adam Smith.

She strode toward Smith's room. A nurse veered from her path, a look of concern creasing her face. *I must look a terror.* Niki formed her mouth into a smile, but suspected it looked more like a mentally unstable grin. Entering Smith's room, the first thing she saw was the empty bed.

SEAMUS

BARTELLE LEFT ME IN A holding cell in the county jail. I paced the room on crutches and prepared my plea to the judge to convince him he didn't have to revoke my bond because of the weapons violation. A few minutes before ten a.m., a deputy brought me to the courtroom and sat with me. Sunlight streamed through the massive courthouse windows and lifted my spirits until I remembered why I was here. The judge and deputy prosecutor briskly resolved several cases. The court clerk announced Seamus Anselm McCree in the matter of a bail violation. My deputy escorted me to the defense table, and remained standing nearby, ready, I supposed, to grab me should I try to escape.

The prosecutor joined the deputy prosecutor at the other table. Wasn't that special? He didn't look my way, keeping his attention on the papers he shuffled before him. Sensing movement in a room they often kept witnesses in, I spotted Tex and another deputy standing at the ready. With the Happy Reaper's weapons, I'd bet.

The judge looked up from the material the clerk had handed him. "I'm disappointed to see you today, Mr. McCree. Where is your counsel?"

I rose. "Could we approach the bench, your Honor?"

He motioned us forward to stand in front of his elevated perch. The prosecutor waited until I positioned myself and then crowded my space. Had he read a Books for Dummies on intimidation? I'd dealt for years with banking titans. This was amateur hour.

"Make it quick," the judge said.

"Your Honor, I am representing myself today. Ms. Frankel, who has been representing me in this matter, told me to request an *ex parte* meeting in your chambers to allow me to provide you with information I cannot share with the prosecutor."

The prosecutor objected loudly. The judge hushed him and said to me, "Why did your counsel think I would accept such an . . . unusual proposition?"

"She believes that if I present you with the facts regarding why this violation occurred and the ramifications of placing me in jail until the prosecutor stops dragging his feet and lets me defend myself in court against the charges he's brought, that you will agree the greater societal good is to allow me to remain free on bail. However, I can not and will not provide those confidential details with the prosecutor present. I must choose silence and jail."

The judge signaled for the prosecutor to respond. His argument was I had already admitted to the bail violation, which was no minor technicality, given the weapons included an assault weapon, semi-automatic pistol, and a six-inch blade.

The judge asked if I was prepared to have the court clerk sit in on the *ex parte* conversation. "Provided she gives your Honor her assurance that she won't repeat anything she hears."

The judge removed his hand from the microphone, announced a ten-minute recess, and told me and the court clerk to join him in chambers. The prosecutor stomped to his table, reminding me of the cartoon character Yosemite Sam with steam pouring from his ears. When the sheriff's deputy made to accompany us, the judge waved him off.

The three of us sat in his chambers. The judge asked what happened to my leg. I said it was a stupid accident, and summarized my past interactions with Adam Smith, the bargain he and I had recently made, that U.S. Marshal Ashley Prescott had the escapee in custody, and how we were working with law enforcement to entrap the imposter. "If I'm in jail, your Honor, the staked-goat trap we've set will fail and lives may be lost."

The judge asked the clerk, "You believe him?"

"Yes."

"Please return to the court, Mr. McCree. I will deliver my decision shortly."

Two good things: the clerk believed me and the judge didn't follow up on asking about my leg. I ignored the poisoned-dart glare the prosecutor threw my way and sat at the defense table. When the judge and clerk reentered the courtroom, we both rose. The judge sat and pulled the microphone to him.

"I have decided the following. First, the Iron County Sheriff's office shall maintain possession of the weapons confiscated this morning from the defendant's premises. Second, I shall amend the bail provisions to strike the requirement that the defendant may not have any weapons in his residence. Others may have such weapons; the defendant may not. Nor may he borrow or otherwise use any weapons belonging to others. I remind the defendant he must remain in the State of Michigan, except for immediate transit through Wisconsin to get from one place in Michigan directly to another. Questions?"

The prosecutor barely waited for the judge to add the 's' in questions before exclaiming, "Your Honor. Mr. McCree is a known—"

The judge straightened in his chair. "Stop right there. I asked if you had questions, not to hear your opinion. Is that clear?"

The prosecutor mumbled a yes. I asked if the previously approved trip to attend my mother's eighty-fifth birthday celebration was still acceptable. The judge said it was. "Remind me," he asked the clerk, "what the trial date is for this case?"

I said, "The first Monday in December, your Honor, provided the prosecutor doesn't invent another excuse to delay it."

The prosecutor looked like he wanted to throttle me but held his tongue. There being nothing else, the judge asked the clerk to call the next case. "And see you transport Mr. McCree directly home."

I SOON LEARNED THAT "DIRECTLY home" did not mean I would leave immediately. Sheriff Bartelle was the only one available, and a budget meeting would tie him up for an hour or two. The department clerk gave me my phone, told me I couldn't stay in their office, and agreed Bartelle or whoever first became available would text me when they were ready.

A pinched stomach reminded me I had not eaten breakfast. I ambled the couple of blocks to the Curious Pig and ordered a smoked turkey sandwich. The place had just opened, and I had it to myself. While my cellphone was not in my possession, I had received one phone call and a bunch of text messages from Paddy and Colleen.

Paddy had kept a running text commentary of what the police were up to at camp. Tex had insisted they open all the vehicles. They inventoried the weapons found in Niki's and Lisa's but did not confiscate them. I wondered if weapons locked in vehicles didn't count against me. Or were Tex and Bartelle bending backwards to minimize the damage, despite Bartelle's aggravation at my refusal to cooperate? The police finished their work, and Paddy's last message said he and Lisa were both driving to Iron River to bring Niki her car and the Happy Reaper his phone.

My shoulders relaxed when I read the news about the Happy Reaper's phone. I caught myself whistling an upbeat tune of unknown origin. I called Paddy. He and Lisa were nearly at the hospital. Once they made their deliveries to Niki, they would pick me up and take me home.

That problem solved, I read the first message from Colleen: was I still available to pick her up at the airport in two days? My stomach did a back flip with a half-gainer. Her bail required her to remain in Michigan except for court-approved absences. With everything going on, I had forgotten her court-authorized work in Boston concluded this week.

Without the changes I had negotiated, she still had the original no firearms provision in her bail agreement. I left a message with Irene Frankel to let her know her tactic had worked and warn her Colleen required the same exemption to her bail terms.

The sandwich arrived. Using one hand to eat and one to hunt and peck, I responded to Colleen that either Paddy or I would meet her. Her other messages related to Mom's birthday bash. I deferred dealing with those.

What else was I forgetting? The heat of embarrassment bloomed on my face. I hadn't checked the secure communication system to see if we had heard anything from ADNI Park.

Nothing from him. The sandwich lost its taste when I read Niki's message that the shit would soon hit the fan. A search brought me the information that Deputy Director Drake was the number two guy at the U.S. Marshals Service. Oh crap. This time, I had dropped Niki in boiling water.

Rick had left messages containing news about Park. The ADNI had undergone a routine colonoscopy yesterday. Something, Rick did not know what, had kept Park in the hospital. Rick speculated that because Park underwent anesthesia, he did not have any secure communication devices with him and did not know Niki was trying to contact him. Rick would try to physically track Park down, bringing his own secure device along, but he could not break away from his job until late afternoon. Did Niki want him to contact AD Ambrose? She did not.

I could do nothing to help bring Park into the loop. Knowing that did not prevent my stomach from knotting. No longer hungry, I had the waitress put the second half of the sandwich in a to-go bag and moseyed toward the bench in front of the courthouse where Paddy was to pick me up.

The judge was walking down the courthouse steps. I changed my path to intercept him. "Excuse me, your Honor. May I have a minute?"

He stopped at the bottom of the steps. "Another *ex parte* conversation?"

"I was so concerned about my problems, I did not remember my co-defendant, Colleen Carpetti, was returning in two days from the business trip you kindly allowed her to take. Is it possible to extend the bail changes to her?"

He pinched his nose. "Any changes in bail require a hearing. Her counsel should request one. Until I can approve the change, Ms. Carpetti must stay elsewhere. Why are you still in town? I thought I made it clear—"

Time to protect Bartelle. "I preferred for my son to pick me up. He should be here any minute. Thanks for the information, sir. My apologies for interrupting you."

I sat on the bench and watched the judge walk down the hill into the main business district. No new messages, no new voicemails. I decided to handle my email. Everything was routine until I came to one in the spam folder. The subject was "Your recent inquiry." I nearly skipped it, but my eye caught the email of the sender: HR@resultsguaranteed.com.

Addressed to the new account I had recently opened, the email comprised a single link.

I opened the link in a sandboxed browser to prevent malware or a virus from infecting my phone. A ghost background image of a Celtic Cross grew increasingly visible. The words scrolled from the top, like an ancient Star Wars movie.

This is a one-time-entry system.
Before you start the process, make sure you have funds available
for an immediate transfer of 50% of the fee before starting the process.

ONCE YOU CLICK THAT YOU ARE READY TO PROCEED
DO NOT CLOSE YOUR BROWSER!

After the words scrolled to the bottom of the screen, a checkbox appeared.

Both me and my money are ready. LET ME IN!

NIKI

NIKI DASHED INTO THE HALLWAY, yelled at the nurse, "Where did he go?"

"He's using the facilities. The doctor said—"

"He was cuffed—never mind."

She re-entered the room, raced to the closed bathroom door, and heard the whistling notes of some aria she remembered from freshman year music appreciation. The doctor on rounds entered the room, preventing her from reaming out Smith for showing off his paper clip skills.

The doctor examined Smith and gave him a positive assessment. Putting a chipper note in her voice, she said, "Now that he's recovered, how soon can you release him?"

"He's stable while on oxygen. We still must determine how long his heart can maintain a decent oxygen level when he's not connected to it. That takes time to assess."

Not what she wanted to hear. How could she get Smith discharged before the two U.S. marshals arrived and screwed up everything? "I don't understand. He's antsy to leave, and frankly, so am I. He's doing great on the oxygen. Why not keep him on it?"

"Good question. The only way his insurance company will go for that is if we determine a continuous supply is necessary to keep him alive. That requires us to perform the test under controlled circumstances where we can immediately administer oxygen. I don't think we're anywhere near there. Mister—" his eyes scanned the chart. "—Gottkind should have another month, several weeks anyway, before that will be necessary."

The doctor was recognizing the realities of insurance companies determining medical practice more than AMA recommendations. Niki made sympathetic noises. "But *scientifically*, it wouldn't hurt him to be on oxygen all day long."

"His nose might get chapped, and he'll suffer a dry throat if he doesn't drink enough."

She pressed for something definitive. "But he'll breathe fine all the time?"

"My father was a doctor before insurance companies ruled the world. He'd have Mr. Gottkind carting a portable oxygen unit and tell him to use it whenever he felt tired or struggled even a little to breathe. The good old days."

Niki said, "I hear ya. Anything else we should know about how his condition progresses?"

"He'll grow more tired. Require more sleep."

Smith cleared his throat. "What will my end be like?"

The doctor pushed his glasses up on his forehead. "We don't know for sure. Given your ticker, I'd expect something like what brought you here, except you won't wake up."

"I'm good with that."

Niki considered that outcome too good for him by half. She escorted the doctor to the door and closed it behind him. Keeping her voice low, she said, "We gotta escape."

"You heard what the doc said."

Niki gave a quick reprise of her conversation with Deputy Director Drake. "To prevent the cops from finding it and charging Seamus with fraud or whatever, Patrick stored the CPAP and oxygen equipment in the woods. The issue is how to avoid detection. You have more experience at this than I do. What do you suggest?"

"A dead body worked well last time."

He must be feeling better. "I didn't see any lying around in the halls."

Happy Reaper

THE HAPPY REAPER CHANGED INTO the sweats Patrick had brought, then put his ear to the bathroom door to hear the conversation between Patrick and Niki. He couldn't hear the words, only Niki's agitation and Patrick's calm. Which meant they couldn't hear him when he made his "daily call to Clem" using his phone, which Patrick had brought.

What a sad state: he had access to a phone, no restrictions on how he could use it, and he had exactly zero people he wanted to talk to—at least until he discovered the imposter's identity. Clearly Niki and Seamus were scheming to capture the imposter rather than let him kill the guy. Once they identified him, he might choose to make some calls. For now, there was not one damned thing more Clem or anyone else could do for him.

He dialed a random 617 area code number, connected to an AI-voiced recording telling him to listen until the end because menu options had recently changed. When the beep signaled for him to make his menu choice, he hung up and deleted the call from his phone's memory. If they got a court order to tap into his account, the gig was up anyway, and he didn't accidentally want to tip the cops to those who had helped him escape.

In his absence, a nurse had brought a portable oxygen tank. "I understand you want to stretch your legs. A little exercise is good. Are you both accompanying him?"

Niki pointed to Patrick. "Just him."

Interesting that Niki did not use Patrick's name.

The nurse handed him the contraption. "If you stop feeling the oxygen flow, you might have pinched the tube. It happens more often than you'd think. When both lights are green, the tank is full. The low warning changes one green to red. Shouldn't happen, but if it's depleted, both lights show red. Questions?"

He had one. "Is it better for me to drag it or for him to handle it?"

The nurse said, if he was game, it worked better for him to push it. "After you're discharged, you might talk to your primary care physician about a backpack or shoulder bag model."

He thanked her for the information and maneuvered the apparatus and himself into the hallway.

Patrick pointed him left. The Happy Reaper trudged off, taking it easy, making sure the air felt secure. They trooped past the nurses' station and a waiting room decorated with orange plastic chairs before Patrick spoke. "It's pleasant out. We'll get some fresh air."

Sticking his nose outside sounded nice. They waited for an empty elevator, rode it to the first floor, and followed signs for the entrance. He expected someone to challenge them, but the automatic doors parted at their approach.

Patrick helped lift the oxygen device over the raised threshold. "We'll wander down the sidewalk."

The Happy Reaper's legs were feeling leaden. "The sun's warm here. Let's—"

Through clenched teeth, Patrick said, "Keep moving, don't look back, and keep quiet." He gripped the Happy Reaper's arm and steered him around the front of the building.

No shit, he thought. We're just walking away. Was there a world record for escapes from hospitals?

SEAMUS

I SPOTTED PATRICK'S CAR TWO blocks away. Driver, no passenger. I thought I had understood him to say Lisa would be with him. Now what had gone wrong?

I crutched to the curb, looked into the backseat to make sure I could stretch out, and did a double take. The Happy Reaper and Lisa sat in the foot-wells, resting their heads against the front seats.

"What the hell?"

Lisa opened her door. "Toss your crutches in and sit in the front. We didn't think he should be visible when we drove by the sheriff's office. I had to show him even a future general can hide when it makes sense. I'm glad you avoided jail."

With some difficulty, I disposed of the crutches, shut Lisa's door, shuffled to the front, and buckled myself into the passenger seat. "I thought he had to stay in the hospital. Where's Niki?"

Paddy eased from the curb and took the first right. "Pretending to guard her prisoner. I'll pick up Smith's oxygen supplies that I hid in the woods. If I take Deer Lake Road to Four Corners, it reduces chances of anyone spotting us. From there, Lisa and I will walk the seven miles to camp. She'll stay to monitor the electronics. I'll use your truck, gather the equipment, and meet you somewhere. He's willing to drive my car, since you can't. Right?"

The Happy Reaper confirmed he was happy to drive.

"Good plan, but better for you to stay on the highway past Amasa all the way to Lukes Road. Take Lukes in until you get to the dilapidated bridge. That route is much faster, you're less likely to run into people or cops on the way to my place, and it's a couple miles closer than Four Corners. Once you hoof it to Shank Lake Road, keep to the woods. That way, you'll see anyone before they see you."

Paddy slowed for a turning truck. "Will do. And that way Lisa and I avoid Beaver Creek. Water was starting to run over the road."

I said, "I noticed that when the police took me out this morning. I've been fighting with the beaver blocking the culvert. He works on it overnight. I clear it the next morning. What with the distractions, I totally forgot. I should have warned you."

Paddy said, "It's not too deep. I'll get to it when I can. Let's meet at that park in Michigamme by the river. I'll call if something holds me up. You two can sit up now."

"You know, Paddy, in case we can't go home tonight, you should also bring my antibiotics, stuff to change my leg dressings, and all his meds. I suspect my drain will soon fall out." With that settled, I switched gears and explained my contacting the imposter had elicited an email with instructions and a link. I asked the Happy Reaper if that was how he had handled it.

"Similar. The one-time-only entry is a new wrinkle. I'll know better when I see the website the link takes you to. It feels like he's not convinced it's me. He might ask something stupid, like what my grandmother's maiden name was."

Lisa said, "Forward the link to me. I'll see what I can learn."

"You can't delay responding too long," the Happy Reaper said. "He might pull the plug if he feels like you're—I'm—stalling."

"But before I can click the link, I need to have money ready to transfer. Don't you think that would buy time?"

The Happy Reaper leaned forward, sticking his head between Paddy's and mine. "No. He knows I'd have the money ready before I made the initial contact. My gut tells me it better be this afternoon, and I should prepare a damn good reason to explain why I haven't already contacted him."

"Better start thinking. It will take Paddy hours to get to my place and retrieve the financial records I need to make the transfer, pick up your oxygen equipment, and drive to Michigamme. We'll be lucky if he gets to us by four. Which is five in the Eastern time zone."

The Happy Reaper huffed out a breath. "That's pushing it. Just drive straight to your place."

I spun around. Gave him a disgusted look. "Get your head out of your ass. Paddy and Lisa are voluntarily helping you. That does not mean they should—nor will I allow them to—take unnecessary risks that could ruin their lives, their careers. We will take whatever precautions we deem necessary. If that screws up this attempt to learn more about the imposter, so be it. One more fucking complaint from you, and we'll strip you naked and leave you."

For several seconds, no one broke the heavy silence. Then Lisa said, "You're a real hard ass, Seamus. I'd let him keep his skivvies."

NIKI

NIKI DIDN'T WANT TO MAKE the nursing staff suspicious by leaving right on the heels of Patrick and Smith. Fifteen minutes seemed like it should work. She checked her secure message service in the hopes Park had replied. He had not. Nor had Rick left any recent messages. This was flipping worse than working undercover. At least then, the opposing side was unaware she was undercover. Here, the Marshals Service knew she was not behaving in an approved manner.

With minutes still to kill, she opted to use the facilities before slipping away. She shut the door to the bathroom, did her business, and found two bulky males standing outside the door. They wore blue windbreakers she'd bet had U.S. Marshal stenciled on the back. Crap on a stick. How to play this?

"Prescott," the older one said, "where's the prisoner?"

She stifled her flippant reaction to say he's strolling the grounds. *Slow walk this. Gain time for Patrick and Smith to get away, pick up Seamus, and become scarce.* She planted her feet shoulder width, pressed her feet hard into the floor, put her hands on her hips, and said, "Attending to human nature." With luck, they'd assume he was taking a dump, rather than the natural human reaction to want to escape.

Guy two moved away from the older one, blocking her from leaving—had she considered trying, which she had not. The older guy held his phone to his ear and soon said, "Yes, she is." He thrust the phone toward her. "Deputy Director Drake wants to talk to you."

To avoid stepping between them, she made him walk the phone to her. She kept her eyes on the guys and brought the phone to her ear. "Yes?"

She recognized Drake's voice from earlier. He demanded that she release the prisoner to the custody of the *authorized* marshals. When she reminded him she still knew nothing to inform her he had proper classification, he exploded with a string of curse words worthy of the toughest drill sergeant, ending with, "This is a direct order. You are hereby relieved of your duty. Relinquish your badge and government-issued arms to the U.S. marshals with you, who *are* trained to handle prisoners. They will take this from here. Give me Deputy Marshal Stinger."

"He wants to talk to you." Niki surreptitiously disconnected the call and tossed Stinger the phone.

She pressed her heels onto the floor, forced herself to take centering breaths while Stinger redialed. She wasted no effort trying to guess the other end of a conversation, instead, concentrating on the two guys' body language and micro-movements. Stinger's end went, "Yes, sir. . . . She won't, sir . . . On the next flight. . . Yes, sir. . . Of course, sir."

Stinger hung up and motioned to his partner, who pushed his sleeves up. "Give me your badge and your guns. We're ordered to take custody of your prisoner and secure him in a local facility. You, we stick on the next flight to D.C. Someone will meet you at the airport and take you directly to DD Drake."

Not if she could help it. Keeping her eyes on them, she yelled, "Stay in there and no matter what happens, do not come out." Striking a more conversational tone, she said, "Gentlemen, you have no warrant for my arrest, and you have no evidence of a crime. The local sheriff and I go way back. He'll charge you with kidnapping if you take me from this room. And consider this before you make your move: if you try to get past me to *my* prisoner, one, two, or all three of us will learn how well the emergency room takes care of trauma cases."

The young guy blew out a puff of disdain. "You think you can take us?"

Niki gave him a withering stare and told an outright falsehood. "In this space, you can't make it two on one. Whichever of you is stupid enough to touch me will end up with broken bones and injured organs. You'll have to shoot me. If you do, neither one of you will be a marshal tomorrow. Guaranteed."

She had them thinking. Good, but not good enough. Soon, they'd coordinate a two-pronged attack, with one coming in low and the other high. Time to play dirty. "If you don't leave in five seconds, I will scream rape. One. Two. Three."

At four, the older guy in charge motioned his partner to leave. Niki continued her centering breathing. She had bought time, but they'd be waiting for her. She scrolled through her phone's address book and came up with the personal cell number for Sheriff Bartelle. It had been years since he had given it to her. She'd soon learn if he still had the same number and carried the phone with him during the day. She hit connect and heard it ring.

"Hello?"

"Sheriff, it's Niki. I hope you can do me a humongous favor."

"You've got a brass set. I should hang up, but since you're taking me away from a budget meeting, I'm willing to hear what humongous favor you have in mind."

She explained that two armed individuals claiming to be U.S. Marshals had tried to force her to leave with them, supposedly to put her on a plane to D.C. She believed they were waiting for her to leave. Could one of his deputies come to the hospital and verify their identities?

"Where's your prisoner?"

"He's been released." The passive-voice answer wasn't a lie, if you looked at it the right way.

"Reading between the lines, it sounds to me like these two guys are there to pick up your prisoner, who you spirited away. And now they want to take you to D.C. to explain yourself to the big bosses. How close am I?"

"Oh, I'd say the outer bullseye. If you don't intervene, people *will* get hurt."

"When this is over, I'm starting a Go Fund Me campaign to buy out McCree and send him to another state. Maybe another country. Of everything you've said, the one thing I totally believe is about the injuries. The hospital is inside Iron River city limits. That makes it the Iron River police department's responsibility. I'll contact them. They can reach you at this number? Oh, one more question. Are you currently armed?"

"I am not." True now, but not once she got in her car.

TYLER

TYLER WAS PLEASED HOW WELL the day had gone. Nary a hitch driving to Denver. His flights to Iron Mountain, Michigan were on time, and he appreciated how easy it was to breathe at 1,200 feet above sea level compared to his struggles in the rarefied air of the Colorado mountains. His only complaint, and it wasn't much of one, was that he couldn't get a full-sized rental. With temperatures in the low fifties—unseasonably warm according to his weather app—he rested his elbow through the open window and enjoyed the warm air on his skin.

He followed his cellphone map through several totally forgettable towns and blink-and-you-miss villages, and onto passable gravel roads with monster logging trucks that forced him to move to the side and stop until the dust settled enough to see. He could picture himself living in the mountains with their extravagant vistas. Here, he'd caught an occasional okay view from atop a rolling hill, but mostly the place was trees and bogs and more trees. Once he hit the gravel, all he saw were trucks, SUVs, and one of those side-by-side contraptions. His rental felt conspicuous. Not a problem for this scouting trip, but he wouldn't make that mistake again if he returned to shoot McCree.

After ten miles of gravel, the map's voice said to make a left onto Shank Lake Road, which became so narrow two cars couldn't pass. With a mile and a half to go, he stopped in front of water running across the road. Two car-lengths wide. It didn't look deep, but he didn't like the sound the rushing water made. McCree had to get through this thing, right? His memory brought up images of drowned vehicles washed away by innocuous-looking water. The rental's clearance was like four inches. Best to find a stick and test the depth and water flow.

Movement at the side of the road stopped him from exiting the car. An otter popped up at the edge of the marsh, stood on its hind legs sniffing the air, scampered through the water, and dropped over the far-side edge. Tyler laughed at himself. "Thank you, Mr. Otter."

He eased the car into the water, which splashed in the wheel wells. The bumper pushed a two-inch wave ahead of the car. The tires maintained a firm grip on the gravel bottom. Once through, he flexed his fingers to shake out the tension of holding the steering wheel too tight. Another quarter mile and the road made a sharp right. Soon he saw the lake on his left. He had the car up to twenty-five when he spotted a trenched area with water flowing through it toward the lake. He slammed on the brakes and nearly lost control when the front tires dropped into the depression and smacked the far side. His seatbelt grabbed him, and he bit his lip.

A damn tank trap. He probed his cheek with his tongue. Tasted blood. That sumbitch was going to hurt. Better than cracking his nose, though.

He drove at crawl speed. Good thing, too. Just over a hill, he entered an intersection with a rougher road heading away from the lake. Immediately after, Shank Lake Road became a minefield of protruding rocks. He pussyfooted the car around them, only scraping the rocker panel once. Well, twice. Next time, he'd order something with higher clearance.

Like magic, no more rocks. McCree's work? Why the hell hadn't he done the rest of the road? Well, fool me once, shame on you . . .

He maintained a ten-miles-an-hour pace past an old unoccupied cabin—or at least with no vehicles around—after which the road smoothed and widened. *Must be McCree.* He drove past a two-track driveway to a log cabin, and then a graveled driveway to an attractive house where Google Maps had marked McCree's place. He slowed and craned his head out the window to see down the driveway. Garage door closed, a truck and car parked in the driveway. He sped up in case someone was looking, faced forward, and slammed on the brakes. The low-slung vehicle scraped a rock in the middle of the road.

He held his breath and crept forward, hoping the damn thing didn't punch a hole in the exhaust system or catch the differential. The drawn-out scraping ended, and he wiped his brow. Rocks littered the road ahead. He put the car into reverse. The damn backup camera showed a brown smear, a present from the mud puddles he'd driven through. No choice but to proceed and look for a safe place to turn around.

Three minutes of creeping through rocks brought him to more water over the road. This stream was faster and no friendly otters showed up to help. He got out to check how deep it was, couldn't tell, and tossed a couple of rocks into the middle. They hit the water with a glug-glug and drowned. He found the largest stone he figured he could toss, gave it a heave, and watched it vanish with a stomach-wrenching plop.

At the edges, the crowned road went from terra firma to mid-calf mud in less than a step. He damn near didn't get his shoe out. The shoe and sock smelled like fresh shit. Rinsing his shoe off in the water, he had an idea. He dipped the corner of his shirt in the water, hopped to the car's rear, and cleaned the backup camera lens. Success!

Driving with one shoe off and one shoe on and memories of his mother singing the nursery rhyme "Diddle, Diddle, Dumpling" running through his head, he executed an eighty-seven-point turn. He avoided any additional bottom-scraping incidents and returned to McCree's property, where the road looked divine.

He stopped at McCree's driveway, put on his soaked shoe, and got out. He checked to make sure no vehicle fluids were leaking—dripping water but no leaks. Kneeling next to the car, he observed the area around the house. Lots of maples, but also a nice collection of evergreens under which he could hide. The open space between the house and the parked cars provided a window where he could pick off McCree walking from one to the other.

Talk about deserted. That otter was the only living creature he'd seen, ignoring himself in the mirror, since he had turned onto Shank Lake Road. With the right transportation, his risk of capture here had to be way less than pulling off the hit in Boston. Damn, if only he had thought to bring a long gun, he could take care of this tonight. Wouldn't that put frosting on the cake?

Except that would put the old cart before the old horse, wouldn't it? Get the down payment, perform the hit, receive the rest. This scouting had accomplished what he had hoped. With everything fresh in mind and a solid cell signal, now was an excellent time to convince Zach to agree to take the assignment.

He described the setup to Zach, who sounded excited, but the damn wet blanket wouldn't commit. A little face-to-face would convince him. And if it didn't? Tyler was doing this job, anyway.

Only the wind heard his whisper. "I'll be back."

NIKI

MINUTES STRETCHED INTO A HALF hour with no sign of the Iron River police. Her delay had given Patrick plenty of time to effect his getaway. Soon, the nursing staff would check on their patient and discover his absence. At that point, if the local police had not intervened, she'd have to either surrender or resist in what would likely be a violent confrontation.

No way, if she could avoid it, would she meet with Drake until she had spoken with ADNI Park. Time to slip the noose. Or try.

She opened the door and found the younger marshal sitting in a chair tipped against the wall. Niki glared. "You touch me or my prisoner, and bad things will happen. Guaranteed."

He rose and held his hands in a surrender posture. "Look, lady, my orders say you're not allowed to leave with the prisoner. You try, and you're right, bad things *will* happen."

"Where's the boss man?"

A sly grin crept on his face. "Arranging your funeral."

She bit back a nasty retort about who would bury whom and retreated into the room, shutting the door behind her. She checked her secure app one last time, hoping for something from ADNI Park or Rick.

Only a series of messages from Seamus detailing what he and "his guest" were doing. At least they had made good the escape.

Replaying the young marshal's words, she decided his primary task was to make sure "the prisoner" didn't leave the room. If she was right, the marshal would stay by the room, even if she left.

Provided the senior agent—Stinger?—wasn't sitting on her car, she had a pretty good chance of evading him. Much better chances than dealing with both of them.

She yanked open the door and strode past the marshal. He scrambled to get up from his chair. Over her shoulder she said, "He's taking another crap. I have to talk to the nurse. You go in there, I'll break your kneecap."

She quick-walked down the hall, past the nurse's station, and followed signs to the exit. No footsteps echoed behind her. No sign of Stinger in the lobby. The door to the outside sensed her presence and opened. She had one foot out before she spotted Stinger standing near her car, chatting with a cop in blue. *Crap.* She spun around, intending to shield herself with the building, and heard, "That's her."

"Hey you, miss," the cop yelled. "Hold it right there."

Instinct said run. Experience told her that was useless. At least the Iron River police had responded to Bartelle. Stinger wouldn't be able to cart her off and throw her in a trunk.

Probably.

She adopted her Wonder Woman pose.

SEAMUS

THE HAPPY REAPER AND I watched Paddy and Lisa help each other through the obstacle course of the washed-out bridge and disappear around the first curve on Lukes Road. With the Happy Reaper driving, we regained the highway. That reduced my stress level by—oh, three percent.

A lot could still go wrong. Paddy and Lisa could run into the police. Niki hadn't responded to my texts keeping her updated on what was happening on my end. The Happy Reaper kept harping about missing our window to respond to the imposter. I thought he was wrong, but worried whether he could pass the imposter's tests. Even if he did, would that help Paddy and Lisa identify the imposter? The itching around my leg drain was becoming more intense. Good thing or bad? Plus, every moment the Happy Reaper was exposed to the public was a chance for someone else to recognize him as the Iron County deputy had.

The Happy Reaper stopped at a gas station mini-mart. I left him in the car and, hobbling on crutches, bought a variety of sandwiches to supplement my unfinished lunch, a soda for me, and beer for him. Not able to carry it all in one trip, I ferried half the stuff to the car and found the driver's seat reclined and him fast asleep.

Low oxygen issues? At least he had thought to turn his head away from the window.

LUCK, OR MORE LIKELY A nippy weekday in the third week of October, provided a deserted Michigamme picnic area. The Happy Reaper parked in a sunny spot to keep the car warm while he snoozed.

With the Happy Reaper sleeping, I tried to make myself comfortable, sitting with my leg stretched out on a picnic table. The spot was in full sun, shielded from the wind, and provided a pleasant view of the foot of the Michigamme reservoir. I checked for messages—not even spam—and tried meditation to control my angst. That was a waste of breath.

Paddy had texted me when he left my house. Four o'clock came and went. He should have been here by now, and still no word from Niki. The Happy Reaper, looking battleship gray, rested in the car. I had a sore butt to go along with an aching leg whose bandages needed changing.

A half hour later, Paddy pulled up to my picnic table and buzzed down the window. "Sorry I'm late. Got trapped by a pair of logging trucks that took forever to load. I've got Smith's oxygen stuff set up in the rear."

Paddy parked the truck next to his car. He helped the now wheezing Happy Reaper into the truck, strapped him into the seat, and handed him the cannula. Once it was in place, Paddy switched on the machine. The Happy Reaper's color improved. One crisis averted.

While the Happy Reaper recovered, I settled into the front passenger seat. Paddy handed me a laptop and clunked a magnetic antenna on the truck's roof. "It picks up a satellite signature and uses a VPN that goes through a server we installed in your cabin."

"You're pointing them directly—"

"Not to worry. Lisa set that server to claim it's in New Orleans. The key is, she'll capture all the traffic to and from this laptop."

I asked the Happy Reaper, "You ready?"

"As I'll ever be. I'd like to look at the screen and see what's changed. Can you put the laptop on the console? Don't know if that will tell us anything, but—"

Paddy thought that was a great idea. He plugged in a keyboard and handed it to me. "So you don't have to reach. This good?" He held the laptop so all three of us could see it.

My arms would get tired if I were him—but I was the soccer guy, and he still rowed, which showed in his sculpted upper body. I retrieved the email with the link and copied the URL into the browser Paddy had prepared. The scrolling message reappeared. I ignored the lousy grammar and ticked the box next to *Both me and my money are ready. LET ME IN!*

The screen darkened, a faint Celtic Cross glowing in the background. Several seconds later, writing materialized, like a ghost becoming visible.

Good afternoon, Adam Smith. Please confirm it is 17:46 where you are.

Next to the statement were check boxes for YES and NO. I looked at the truck's clock. It read 5:46, 17:46 on a twenty-four-hour clock. I moved the cursor to the Yes box. Hesitated. Michigamme and, therefore, my truck, were in the Eastern time zone. "New Orleans is Central Time zone, right? You sure your VPN is working?" I flicked the cursor away from the boxes.

Paddy said, "I'm sure it *was* working."

The Happy Reaper blared, "You gotta answer now."

Uncertainty painted Paddy's face. I moved the cursor to the "no" box and clicked. "Check, Paddy. I have a few seconds to fess up to forgetting how to add twelve.

The screen changed.

What time is it? (hh:mm)

I typed 16:47, looked at Paddy, who was frantically thumbing his phone. I hit enter. The screen went blank. I could not breathe.

The screen produced a line of scrambled letters and numbers. With a flash of color, the screen scrambled the letters into a new question with a drop-down menu.

What is your astrological sign?

"Show off," the Happy Reaper said. "It's Aries."

I clicked that response, and the screen changed again.

On your 1996 assignment in Brookline, what specifically did you not kill in that house?

A blinking cursor waited to record my answer. Had to be a trick question. I looked up from the computer. "Not multiple choice. What do I say?"

The Happy Reaper pounded the back of my seat with both fists, jolting me. "I have no clue. Give me context. What geo-political events happened then?"

I said, "Clinton was re-elected that November."

He clapped his hands. "Got it. An old Irish Setter and an unknown number of houseplants."

I entered his answer. "Would you type houseplants as one word or two?"

"One. What idiot would make it two?"

I completed the response, hit enter.

Assignment Accepted upon payment of 50% of fee to this bitcoin wallet.

Beneath was a QR Code.

I must receive payment within three hours. Upon confirmed receipt, I will let you know how we can safely discuss specifics.

The Happy Reaper said, "This is not how I did it. I verified identity through the messaging app, and only after we discussed the specifics would I agree to the contract and accept payment. I gave them much more time once I used cryptocurrency. Most people have to set up accounts, buy the bitcoins, or whatever."

Paddy said, "But if he cracked your dark web sites, he knew you used bitcoin, right?"

"The structure was there to support it. I also did wire transfers to banks in places no regulator could go. That was part of my discussion with the client. We'd talk timing. Often, they knew the person's schedule or had an idea where they might be alone. That kind of thing. Not that I'd necessarily accept their plan, but it was good intel. This is amateur hour."

His pride poking up its ugly head.

"You're still going to do it, Dad?"

"I see no reason not to. Do you?"

Paddy settled the computer on his lap and rapidly clicked keys. "Last chance to say stop before I send your money. Hearing nothing, here goes." He dramatically lifted his pointer finger high above his head and plunged it onto the key. "And done. Now we wait for the confirmation, which should be one, one and a half hours, give or take."

"And we've still heard nothing from Niki. Let me check to see if I have any messages."

Nothing from Niki, but one from Rick, relaying information from ADNI Park. He apologized for being incommunicado. His colonoscopy proved a life saver. The surgeon found cancerous polyps and removed a portion of Park's colon. Between the anesthesia and the pain meds, he'd been in la-la land. He had to remain in the hospital for several more days and summoned U.S. Marshals' Deputy Director Drake to shift his priorities.

Rick would not be there when the two met—that would raise unanswerable questions. He would return at nine p.m. Eastern to pass on the results of the meeting. Park had total confidence that Niki would know how to handle herself.

I said, "Hopefully we'll hear from Niki before then. Paddy, you should go home and help Lisa analyze whatever data she captured from our imposter contact. It's better for the Happy Reaper and me to stay away from my place until we know it's safe. Hopefully, Rick will tell us in three hours."

"Before I leave, Dad, let me show you something. Good thing you warned Lisa and me to stay in the woods once we reached Shank Lake Road. We were close to the cabin driveway area when a car heading toward town drove past. Don't worry, he didn't see us. Once I confirmed no cops were waiting for us at your house, I retrieved the memory cards from the two trail cameras by your driveway. Look at this."

He spun the computer, and I played several video clips of the rental car—the sticker was clear. It drove past and a few minutes later returned and parked by the driveway. The guy checked his undercarriage—made sense, given how rough the road past my place is for a low-slung car. The next half-dozen fifteen-second clips showed him looking intently down my driveway from various positions before he drove off.

What was he doing? "Usually, lost people come down the driveway to ask where they are or if there's a road to US 141. You have any ideas?"

The Happy Reaper said, "He's scouting your place, looking at shooting lanes. I'm sure of it."

NIKI

IT DIDN'T SURPRISE NIKI THAT the Iron River police officer decided a dispute between three U.S. marshals was above his pay grade and better handled at police headquarters. On the drive from the hospital to the police station, the officer followed Niki, a border collie waiting to nip at her heels at any deviation.

The officer stuck her in a room while he and the two marshals met with the police chief. Fine with her: every minute they wasted on her was a minute they weren't looking for Adam Smith, who they had by now surely determined was not still in the hospital. When the two marshals and the chief came in, the chief's attitude and questions made it clear the marshals had convinced them she was a menace. Wouldn't surprise her if DD Drake had talked to the chief directly.

Niki didn't plan to tell him anything more than name, rank, and serial number. She didn't play the I-want-a-lawyer card, but said she would if they violated her rights one iota. The chief gave her an earful regarding how appalled he was at her behavior and attitude, allowing a dangerous convicted murderer loose in his community. He had issued a BOLO using information provided by the marshals and contacted the county and state police. He was waiting to hear from the Iron County prosecutor to determine if they could charge her with gross negligence.

The more he ranted, the wider Niki's smile became until he noticed and said, "What? You think this is funny?"

"Here's the problem, Chief. My prisoner is still secure and has caused no harm to anyone. The prosecutor will tell you I've done nothing to justify a gross negligence charge. Second, if you force me to go with these two, you will probably find yourself on trial for aiding and abetting the kidnapping of a private citizen from *your* police building. Third, I've said everything I plan to say until you either charge or release me."

She crossed her arms to show her defiance.

Left alone with nothing to do but think, her stomach increased the intensity of the SOS-feed-me signals, reminding her she hadn't eaten since last night's dinner. She guessed Drake would order at least one marshal to stay near her. Forcing the marshals to split their efforts between her and Adam Smith could help give time for Smith and whoever was with him to become invisible.

Two bozos she could handle. But that wasn't typical Marshal Service strategy. Drake would order reinforcements from Minnesota or downstate Wisconsin or even Illinois. He might have already done that, which gave her three hours grace before they arrived. Defeating a gaggle of testosterone with guns, all wanting to please a deputy director, was asking a lot—even for her.

She let two hours pass before making her move. Listening at the door, she heard nothing. She walked into a deserted hallway. No one said, "boo," let alone stopped her from leaving by the front door. She half-expected to see a boot on her car. Nope. Those doofuses—she stopped with her hand on the doorhandle. Doofuses or doofi? Jerks, she could spell and knew the plural. Those jerks thought she would lead them to Adam Smith. *We'll play that game after I get something to eat.*

She exited the parking lot and headed for US 2. A nondescript gray car followed. *Really? They didn't care that she knew?* She pulled into the shopping center with the food store and yep, the tailing car parked where its occupants could observe her.

She doubted they were relying solely on direct sight to follow her. Had they placed trackers on her vehicle? Had DD Drake pressured a friendly judge to allow them to tap her phone? Were other cars part of a surveillance team? She hummed "Every Breath You Take." Caught herself and mused at the irony of a generation of newlyweds adopting Police's classic stalker tune for "their" song.

The Bureau had trained recruits in surveillance techniques by having them try to follow her. They never gave her a heads up, but her standard daily evasion protocols always lost them. Often she'd flip the script and follow them for fun. This was her first time on the other side of a Marshal's surveillance. The only question in her mind was how long she wanted to play with them before she slipped the leash. Food first.

She purchased a variety of items she could eat while driving, bottled water and a couple of "healthy" snacks, and made a preemptory restroom stop before exiting the store. She placed the groceries on the front seat of her car, dug into one of the duffels stowed in the back, and retrieved a second phone. The Marshal's Service knew nothing of its existence. Nor were they privy to its secure messaging software. From another bag, she found a cloaking case for her regular phone.

"Gentlemen, start your engines."

She drove from the parking lot without a glance toward the surveillance car and hung a right toward Iron River proper. In her mirror, she watched her pursuers allow a pickup and a semi to get between them. She stayed on US 2 through town.

Hung a left on MI-73, Wisconsin bound.

Her tail kept at least one vehicle between them until they crossed the bridge into Wisconsin. At a bar near Nelma, the rusted green pickup that had been the last shielding vehicle pulled into the parking lot. "Whatcha gonna do now, boys?" she called to her rearview mirror. She maintained her speed at a couple of miles above the posted limit, making it easy for them to follow her without showing their hand. She had driven this route multiple times and knew where she'd make her move, assuming they didn't do something stupid first.

At the village of Alvin, the speed limit dropped to thirty-five. She maintained her fifty-seven and, once through town, accelerated to sixty-five for the mile to the stop sign at WI-70. Slowing only to check for traffic, she swung a tire-squealing left turn onto WI-70. Gripping the wheel hard, she accelerated through a half-mile curve and on the straightaway pushed her speed to eighty.

The adrenaline junkie in her wanted to push them, but her purpose was to see how they reacted, not get busted by a local cop for speeding. A mile later, she eased her speed to sixty-two, tapping her fingers to burn off energy.

At the top of a hill in a ruler-straight section of the highway, she spotted them a half mile in the distance. At the next hill, they were still there, no closer, but not falling behind.

Their actions supported Niki's suspicions that they didn't need to physically see her because they had placed a tracker on either her car or phone. Or both. Time to confirm that supposition.

Partway through a series of curves, she spotted a well-used dirt driveway, stood on her brakes, and, in a stench of burned rubber, stopped fifty feet beyond it. She speed-reversed into the driveway, pulling far enough down it to avoid them seeing her if they drove by. She shoved the transmission into park, left the car running, and ran back far enough to watch traffic on the highway.

If they didn't know she had stopped, she should see them in under thirty seconds. When her count hit ninety, she was positive they had pulled off to see what she would do next. No reason to keep them waiting.

Using her regular phone, she dialed a random number in the 906 area code. Delighted to get a message machine, at the beep, she said, "I'm pretty sure I lost them. Deliver the package to me at that bar in Eagle River where we had a few Leinies. I'll call again when I get there."

If they had tapped her phone, that should get them thinking.

Eagle River was the opposite direction on WI-70, which gave her an opportunity to spot where they had pulled off. She drove at the speed limit but didn't see them. Halfway to Eagle River, she realized she had no phone reception. *That's right, this is a dead zone.* She steered with her knees and secured her regular phone in the cloaking case, eliminating her followers' ability to track her phone once she re-entered cellphone coverage. That still left the possibility they had attached a GPS tracking device to her car.

Not wanting to risk the possibility anyone could visually pick up her presence near Eagle River, she stayed on secondary roads. Approaching Three Lakes, she parked at the edge of a dirt road. Knowing the best spots to hide a tracking device, she made a thorough search and came up empty. No guarantees, but it made it more likely they had used her phone to track her.

She linked up with US 45, at Gagen cut west to Rhinelander, where she pulled her cellphone from the cloaking case and exposed her position to anyone who was interested.

She would love to be a fly on DD Drake's wall when his boys told them they had regained contact with the phone twenty-five miles south of where they expected to find her in Eagle River. They'd wonder whether it was her, or if she had ditched it on a long-haul trucker, or what.

She pumped a fist in the air in celebration of her temporary victory. Her moves had likely forced them to spread their resources thin. Someone to check all the bars in Eagle River that served Leinenkugel, which in October, she guessed, included them all. Someone to intersect her phone's path and determine if it's her or not. Everything involving her was miles away from wherever Seamus and Smith were.

Round one was all hers. Problem was, championship fights these days usually ran for ten or twelve rounds. And the judges were not in her corner.

SEAMUS

WITH PADDY HEADING TO MY place to work with Lisa, the Happy Reaper convinced me to let him drive to see Lake Superior. Even though he had been to the U.P. several times on "business," he had never seen the greatest of our Great Lakes from any closer than thirty-thousand feet. We were driving the Presque Isle loop in Marquette when Paddy's call arrived on my phone, which had a bluetooth connection with the truck. I pointed for the Happy Reaper to grab a parking spot we were approaching and asked Paddy if I needed privacy.

Paddy said, "Speaker's fine. This affects him, too."

I told Paddy where we were and asked what was up.

"You should stay away for the night. We had two extremely pissed U.S. marshals visit us. Niki gave them the slip, and they accused me of taking Smith. We learned they didn't have a search warrant and used our phones to video-record me telling them to leave. Our cell site simulator caught them making a phone call from their car to Deputy Director Drake. Drake said they had two agents checking the bars in Eagle River for Niki, me, you, and/or Smith. Niki's cellphone keeps popping up. They've concluded it's heading toward Minneapolis-St. Paul. He's assigned three sets of agents to find that phone and determine if Niki is with it or if she dumped it.

"Drake told these guys to drive to Crystal Falls and pick up a search warrant. They are to tear your place apart and not worry about what they break. Lisa is scrubbing our servers and transferring everything to secure cloud storage. It'll take them ninety minutes to get to town and back. By then, all they'll find are detritus from a massive multi-player role game scenario."

The Happy Reaper had closed his eyes, but his eyelids fluttered at the mention of the cell tower simulator. He now knew we had eavesdropped on his calls. Why hadn't Paddy talked with me privately?

"I'm sorry." I said it reflexively, even though I could have done nothing to prevent it. "Sounds like either Park hasn't talked to Drake, or the conversation did not match Park's expectations. We're not scheduled to hear from Rick Kaska for another half hour. I'll let him know. Maybe Park can still stop it."

"We'll be fine, although I'm not sure how much damage they'll do. But that wasn't the only reason I called. I had been hyper-focused on getting Smith's breathing stuff to him, and I screwed up. I grabbed those trail cam videos from the cameras by your driveway, but I never thought to check the cell tower simulator for phone calls from around that time. Smith was right. They plan to kill you."

True to form, I went into analytical mode regarding my planned assassination. The emotional impact would hit later. Not the Happy Reaper. His eyes popped open, his fists clenched, and his neck muscles corded. He leaned into the truck's touchscreen, as though that was where the microphone was located. "There's two of you, you bastards," he yelled. "That's cheating."

I made Paddy repeat what the Happy Reaper had talked over. Instead, he read a transcript he had made of the call. At its conclusion, I asked the riled-up Happy Reaper for his take.

"I told you the guy was scoping out a place to shoot from. Using two people to replace me is total bullshit. I want them both."

I gave him a thumbs-up to acknowledge his statement. "You've got both phone numbers, Paddy?"

"Yeah, and Lisa and—"

"We don't want to do anything to screw up a conviction. I'll tell Niki when we hear from her, and we can figure out how to legally use that info. Be sure you dismantle the cell tower simulator before those marshals can find it. Love you, Paddy. Stay safe."

"Love you, too, Dad."

The Happy Reaper had a big grin on his face. "Nothing like a good hunt to make me forget how shitty I feel." He wagged a finger at me. "You tried to get Clem's phone number, didn't you? Tricky, Mr. McCree. Very tricky. I'm proud of you. Not that it did you any good. Now, I do have one itsy, bitsy problem with what I heard. Your concern to not screw up a conviction is irrelevant. There won't be any conviction, because our deal is that you smoke out these bastards, and I punch their tickets. Remember? That's what keeps Clem on a leash."

The grin was still on his face, but it no longer reached his eyes, now taking on the blue and icy look of a February sky when temperatures dropped to thirty below.

Oh boy, I screwed that up. I held my hands like a priest opening himself to the Spirit. "You and I have that deal. The others aren't party to that. I need their assistance to learn who these two are. They might not help if they knew the full scope of our agreement. In fact, if they knew what you planned, I'm pretty sure Niki would haul your ass to prison and set a trap to capture Clem and his crew when they came after my family."

That sounded so plausible, I nearly convinced myself it was true. "You threatened my family. Of course I'll try to discover who Clem is. And, since we're being honest with each other, Paddy found and removed the spyware you put on my phone."

That got a startle reaction from him.

"Remember, I used myself for bait. Without that and the systems Paddy and Lisa set up, you still wouldn't know there are two of them. Keep your priorities in order. Learn who they are. Then take your revenge." To which I mentally added, *if you can.*

The Happy Reaper stared silently at the gray expanse that was Lake Superior. The distant sky looked ready to boil. Waves, each more massive than its predecessor, crashed on the rocks with a throaty roar. A storm raging over Lake Superior was heading our way, and I did not want it to catch us in the open. The Happy Reaper gave no evidence that he planned to respond to my soliloquy. Time to move. "You had enough sightseeing? Shall I get us rooms?"

"Not yet," he said. "I miss the ocean. This may be as close to that feeling as I ever get, and I'd like to enjoy it a while longer." He cranked the car's heat to seventy-eight.

Thank goodness for dual controls. I dialed my side down ten degrees, and that's when it struck me that the timing of the imposter's visit was suspect. Within twenty-four hours of my approach to the imposter—well, imposters—one of them was scoping out my place in the U.P., not an easy place to get to.

I explained my confusion to the Happy Reaper. "You wouldn't do that, would you? It's hard to believe Paddy and Lisa screwed up in their hacking to allow the imposters to pinpoint our location."

"No Seamus, it's you they want. If he'd been looking for hackers, he'd be scanning for electronic signals. We saw and heard no evidence of that."

Okay, made sense. "You're saying the offer was sufficiently attractive, one of the two dropped whatever he was doing and came to check the layout. Why?"

"Maybe he was already coming out."

He remained staring at the glowering lake, not making eye contact. Purposefully? "What do you know you haven't told me?"

That got him to shift his attention to me. Hard eyes. Nothing to read.

"I don't *know* anything. In my memoir, I made it clear it was your fault I was rotting in prison. What if these imposters think the way to become the Happy Reaper is to do what I claimed I was going to do if I escaped?"

"Kill me."

He pointed his finger at me and mimed pulling a trigger. "Or maybe they have oodles of money and time and figured they'd do some exploratory field work after the Happy Reaper contacted them. Or maybe Paddy and Lisa did screw up, and these guys put two and two together and decided you were behind the so-called hit on yourself."

My head swam with the many possibilities. I was riding a tiger, blindfolded, my hands tied behind me, and trying to stay on by squeezing my knees. "Let's go. I want a drink."

He gave me a side glance. "You're on antibiotics."

"I didn't say I'd have one, just that I wanted one. Drive."

NIKI

A HIGHWAY SIGN ALERTED NIKI that the Minnesota welcome center was coming up in two miles. It wouldn't surprise her to have U.S. Marshal Service greeters when she arrived in St. Paul. Time to check for messages. She parked in the first spot, the easiest location to check arriving cars.

Rick Kaska had left a quick note on the secure app reminding her he was meeting with Park at nine pm. Eight central, which was in ten minutes. She responded, telling him she was available if they wanted to call her.

Seamus had left several messages. The marshals showing up at his place didn't surprise her.

The news that two people collaborated to become the imposter was a shock but didn't change much. She'd have Patrick provide her the phone numbers for the two imposters and send her a picture from the trail cam video of the guy who had scouted Seamus's place. She'd worry later how to use the info legally. Her immediate problem was that she didn't want to call Patrick if the marshals had confiscated his phone during their search. What a hot mess.

Time crawled. Eight o'clock came and went. Each tick of her watch was like a ratchet, cranking up the tension in her shoulders and neck. Would Rick and ADNI Park call? How long should she wait? Did Drake have other marshals following her and staying here made her a sitting duck? Well, all they'd learn was she didn't have Smith with her.

At seven minutes past the hour, her regular phone announced a call from Rick Kaska. She refused the call to prevent others from listening in—although just by his calling, they could link her to Rick and might wonder why an FBI agent was contacting her. She called him on the secure phone. After a quick explanation detailing why she was using a different device, Rick handed the conversation to Park.

He said, "I have only one question. Can you assure me that your prisoner is one hundred percent secure? Before you answer, be aware that if you say yes and you should have said no, after the dust settles, you will be unemployed and awaiting trial on numerous charges. Some will stick. Are we clear?"

For sure. My ass, not yours, is on the line. Nothing new with that. "Can you tell me what happens if I do not say yes?"

"No charges, but you won't be a U.S. marshal. We'll have to assess the rest."

So, it will be like any other day. "I can assure you with one hundred percent certainty that my prisoner is secure."

Over the line she heard Park tell Rick to take a ten-minute walk. In the background, she heard a door click shut. "Mute your phone and stay on the line," Park said. "I want you to hear this next conversation. Understand?"

"Yes, sir."

THE HAPPY REAPER

THE HAPPY REAPER ACQUIESCED THE third time Seamus said they should check into the hotel. He waited in the truck with the engine on to keep himself warm while Seamus checked them in. Given their heart-to-heart that afternoon, he wasn't sure what would happen if Seamus lost his fear of Clem coming for his family. Seamus might keep his promise—it was one of his core tenets. But since he'd made the promise under duress, and the others hadn't bought in, if they learned the Clem threat wasn't real, one of them would likely take him prisoner. Or die trying.

For now, to protect himself he must continue the pretense of Clem's revenge. Once—if—they returned to Seamus's property, he could rearm using weapons he had cached outside when he first arrived. *Always have a backup plan.*

Seamus crutched to the truck, holding keycards in one hand. "You able to get a luggage cart and wheel all your stuff in? I didn't want to ask the clerk for help."

What a pair they were: him tethered to an oxygen machine, and Seamus hobbling around on crutches, a drain still operating under his sweatpants. He choked back a bitter reply, disconnected the cannula, arranged his COVID mask, and retrieved the cart.

Their connecting rooms were on the top floor with views of solar lights rimming the lakeshore and the black of the water beyond. He wondered where east was and whether they might see a spectacular sunrise if the clouds lifted a little. He set up his oxygen equipment in the room. Seamus had pulled a toothbrush, travel tube of toothpaste, and dental floss from the truck's center console. No extra toothbrush, though. Through the open connecting doorway, the Happy Reaper asked, "This place has cheap toothbrushes for guests, right?"

"Probably. There's a drugstore not far away. We can drive there."

"A crappy toothbrush will do fine. It's not like I have to keep these teeth going for a long time." He shook his head and laughed at the gallows humor that seemed to pop from his mouth all on its own. "I'll stretch my legs and walk down to the front desk. Don't look at me like that. It's not like the clerk didn't already get a good look at me. I'll wear my COVID mask, and I've been sucking oxygen for hours. I'm perfectly capable for a brief time."

To his surprise, Seamus didn't insist on doing it himself or accompanying him. All he got was a reminder to make himself scarce if he saw a cop. He had opened the door when Seamus called, "Don't forget a room key."

Seamus pointed to the top of the dresser, where both room keys sat next to the truck fob. An electric current ran up the Happy Reaper's spine. He had to try. He stashed a room key in his pocket and palmed the fob with his other hand.

"If I'm not back in fifteen, come find me."

Niki

FOR TWO MINUTES NIKI HEARD only the beep of a monitor and the creak of the hospital bed when ADNI Park adjusted his position. A double tap on a door announced an arrival. Park told the person to come in. "Doug, thanks for coming by to discuss this situation. I spoke with Deputy Marshal Prescott. She assures me that the prisoner is one-hundred-percent secure. Given that, an excellent move on your part is to tell your boys to stand down."

"On what basis?" Deputy Director Drake's tone made it clear he was not at all happy.

"Blame it on an administrative screw-up, paperwork misfiled, whatever you want. Don't name names. Some faceless bureaucrat. Tell your two agents that you're willing to overlook their judgmental errors. In fact—"

"Their errors?" Drake's voice screeched his incredulity. "Prescott lied to them, threatened them, lied to me, she's—"

"Tell me how it will look, Doug, when the Washington Post publishes an exposé of the snafu under your supervision that nearly derailed a critical national security operation. Give your guys a plumb assignment to make them feel better."

"Averell, we've known each other for a lot of years, but that does not give you the right to interfere like this. First, you insert an untrained individual into our organization. One, I may add, that I learned you must be paying off the books because we have no payroll records for her. Now you have her obstructing my organization from performing its core function."

"If you are offering to resign, Doug, the president authorized me to accept. You look shocked. You shouldn't. Who do you think approved assigning an *extremely well-trained* undercover agent to the Marshals Service and paying her off the books?"

The president? Niki rolled her shoulders to stretch them from hunching over the phone. She had never asked how they pulled it off, but the president? Or was Park lying? A lot of that going on recently.

The beeping machines assured Niki the connection was still open. When Deputy Director Drake spoke, his voice had lost its bombast. "Are you ordering me to do this or you'll fire me?"

"You know better than that. I don't fire people. Your Director has that responsibility. He wisely refused my offer to read him in on this situation, plausible deniability being all the rage these days. But how will he react when he discovers that instead of the U.S. Marshals Service receiving praise for apprehending a notorious hit man in record time and using him to expose others in his former profession, you get zero credit, national newspapers expose the Services' dirty underwear, and social media explodes in indignation?"

"You—"

"Or that you rushed to a pet judge to get permission to tap the phone of one of your own agents, and search warrants on three individuals, one of whom is a decorated member of the army who I understand is on the brigadier general promotion list. Oh, your agents didn't tell you that? What else do you think they forgot to tell you while they stepped all over their dicks covering up that Prescott ran circles around them?"

"That's not—"

"That's not what, Doug? What happened or what everyone will think happened? I will sleep much more comfortably tonight after you call your agents off the hunt. If you had nothing to do with it and it goes south, it can't reflect badly on you. And if it works well, Prescott will not be the one basking in the praise. That will be the Marshals Service and its hard-working agents. Put your anger aside and make the call. Or not, the choice is all yours."

Niki had a newfound respect for Park. In her undercover roles, she had walked the razor's sharp edge, one screw-up away from losing her job—or her life. Yes, she loved her country and wanted to protect it from those who would do it harm. But few comprehended how much she enjoyed the rush of traveling that thin line separating success from disaster. Seamus did. She was now fairly certain Park did, too.

If Deputy Director Drake had ever known that feeling, he had lost it in his bureaucratic climb. He called the agents she had met, learned they had served the warrant and were waiting for others to cart off "a shit ton of computer stuff." They were royally ticked when he ordered them to return everything and leave. He'd talk to them later.

Drake completed the call. "Satisfied?"

"I won't be able to sleep well until I hear you tell the judge to pull that search warrant. And the one you have on Prescott's phone. And the others you have to search her house and car. I'm sure I don't have to remind you to rescind the order to arrest Deputy Marshal Prescott once she reaches Minnesota. Did you read the transcripts of her interviews by your agents? There's a big difference between not answering questions and lying to federal officers. Shocked again? Your people were being thorough. So were mine. We understand each other, yes?"

Niki pressed the phone tight to her ear, but Drake's response was nonverbal or too quiet for the phone to pick up. The next thing Niki heard was Park saying he hoped Doug would also sleep better tonight, and he could leave the door open.

She pulled the phone away when Park's voice boomed down the line. "That didn't go as well as I had hoped. He left like a beaten dog, and those often become vicious. He'll pull everything official, but you should assume they are still monitoring you. In the past, you made it clear that my actions had left you with trust issues. I want to eliminate your concerns in that regard. What else can I do to help make this endeavor a success?"

She unmuted her phone and told Park that a cell tower simulator constructed by Patrick and Lisa had captured a conversation between two suspects who planned to kill Seamus. She had both cellphone numbers from that call and one of Seamus's trail cameras had captured one suspect's image. Based on that information, she hoped to use publicly available sources to identify the two individuals. She neglected to mention the computer work Lisa and Patrick had done or would do.

Park said, "Rick has returned and heard what you said. Correct me if I'm wrong, but I assume you won't be worth jack shit for anything else until we fix this situation. I shall encourage AD Ambrose to assign Rick to a special task force looking at the interstate commission of murder for hire. Will that be sufficient, Rick, to give you access to Bureau resources?"

Rick said yes, provided Ambrose approved the task force. Having listened to Park in action, Niki had no doubt that Ambrose would approve.

"Good. I'll let you and Ambrose hammer out the details. Assume Drake will double his efforts to find Adam Smith. If he does, the second you're not with him, his guys will take Smith into custody, and there won't be a damned thing we can do about it."

SEAMUS

I USED THE TIME WHILE Adam was finding his freebie toothbrush to check the secure message app and determine if Niki had responded. She provided a call-back number I did not recognize and insisted I use one of the burner phones I had purchased in bulk. Good thing I had two stored in the truck.

Except the fob wasn't sitting on the dresser where I thought I had laid it. I patted my pockets, lowered myself to the ground to check the floor, pulled myself to standing again, turned my pockets inside out. What started as a gnawing in my stomach grew to full-fledged heartburn. I stuck the room key in my front pants pocket, grabbed my crutches, and left to verify my suspicions.

A lime green SUV occupied the spot where my truck had been.

My immediate reaction was pure spite: call the local police, report my truck stolen. They'd fingerprint him, discover he was an escaped murderer, and they'd remove him forever from my hair.

Clem, however, would still be a problem. As, I suspected, would the imposters who were targeting me.

I burned off anger and frustration, weaving a convoluted path between the two connected rooms. On the five hundred and eighty-ninth circuit—at least my burning leg felt like that—I glanced at the phone on the nightstand. Using it would cost a pretty penny, but it was a phone with a number no one knew. I followed the instructions for dialing long distance and soon connected with Niki.

In normal Niki fashion, she listened to my vitriol and angst until I grew quiet. "He still needs you, so he'll show up. Remember, he's been in prison for six years. He's probably getting laid."

That was a picture I did not want stuck in my head. "You're saying I do nothing more than twiddle my thumbs?"

"Not at all." She filled me in on her conversation with ADNI Park.

"Park is right that we can't let the Marshals Service get their hands on Smith. I have an idea to make your camp into a sanctuary from them. Have your lawyer sue the U.S. Marshals Service, DD Drake, and the two agents—I have both their names—for wrongful search and seizure. She files the suit, the Marshals Service lawyers won't let them anywhere near you until they understand what's going on."

Sneaky, something I should have thought of myself. "That takes care of the marshals, but not the imposters. And probably not the Iron County constabulary, if the prosecutor can conjure a reason to have them bother us."

"The judge slapped him down the last time, so I don't think the prosecutor will risk anything—at least until after the election. And hell, Seamus, you *want* the imposters to come, remember? Your trap won't do any good if you're not there. Set up your trail cameras for early warning. Lisa and Paddy and Smith are all good shots. Heck, this weekend when Colleen gets there, you have another good shooter. She's a cop's daughter. In defending home ground, she won't blink at doing whatever's necessary, even if that means killing them."

That reminded me to ask Irene Frankel to file for a bail amendment for Colleen, who was arriving the day after tomorrow. "You know I don't want to kill them. Just send them away for a long time."

"Which we will do *if* we have enough time before they come for you. Remember, everything has to hold up in court. That takes time. But, if they come after you before we get them, you may not have a choice. It's you or them. Remember, before you aim a gun, you'd better be willing to pull the trigger. Get some sleep. Smith will show up and the sun will rise tomorrow."

Niki nailed one thing: I could accomplish nothing tonight. If someone identified Adam Smith while he was wandering, we were all in the shitter. He would return safely or he wouldn't. Paddy and Lisa would make electronic headway or they wouldn't. The FBI would set up Rick with a task force to identify and capture the imposters, or they wouldn't. Same applied to finding Clem and his associates. The county prosecutor would behave himself or he wouldn't.

I stared up at the ceiling. "Did I ever mention how much I hate not being able to do anything?"

My hollow words echoed in the room. From the distant past came the wisdom of a physical therapist who had told me my job was not to focus on what I could not do, or what I might do tomorrow. My responsibility was to accomplish everything I could do today.

I could take care of myself. I emptied my leg drain and checked the wound for signs of infection. Looked good. I changed the bandage and swallowed my daily antibiotic. "Okay, tomorrow. Bring it on!"

NIKI

DESPITE HER ASSURANCES TO SEAMUS, Niki had no way to know what the hell Adam Smith was up to. She wished she could head back to the U.P. now, but the whole reason for leaving had been to lessen the chances of the U.S. Marshals getting the drop on Smith.

She drove into St. Paul and parked in the driveway of a house devoid of any residents. She punched in the security code and rearmed the system once she was inside. Her sister had converted their father's home into a shelter for abused mothers with children. Whenever clients were in residence, at least one staff member remained in the house. Sometimes the kids' noises filled the place. Sometimes there were only a couple of people. Rarely was it empty, but its silence, broken only by the ticking of the grandfather clock, suited Niki's mood. She had work to do and the fewer interruptions, the better.

Niki secured all her guns, using the personal gun safe in her private room for her SigSauer 345 and storing the other weapons in the basement gun safe. She left a note on the kitchen table alerting the manager that she was in residence, separated her clothes into lights and darks, and put a load in the washer.

She brewed a pot of herbal tea to help settle all the junk food she had consumed on the ride. While the tea steeped, she called Patrick, confirmed the marshals had left, and had him send her the imposter's picture captured by one of the trail cameras covering Seamus's driveway, the imposter's phone number, and the number he had called to discuss the hit on Seamus.

She used Park's desire to have this "side issue" cleared up as permission for her to employ Rembrandt, NSA's super-powerful face-recognition program. She set it working on the image. Even running on high-speed computers, the program took bloody forever.

Typical facial recognition software converts the geometry of a target's face into a digital file that it compares to measurements from other known (and unknown) subjects. It is difficult to fool the software regarding some measurements, like the distance between eyes. But others, like the shape of a person's nose, ears, or chin, are easy for a makeup artist to alter. A skilled person can even fake underlying bone structure, provided x-rays aren't involved.

Niki had proved that. With the right clothes and make-up, she could look like a seventy-year-old bag lady. She'd even passed as male on more than one occasion. She knew how to make standard facial recognition fail to identify her.

Rembrandt did that same job, just much better. It also worked at a deeper level, ignoring anything other than immutable measurements, and had a sophisticated system to correct for camera angle differences.

Plus, it had an unparalleled subject database covertly created based on high-resolution photographic images. Only a few individuals knew how precise. She wasn't one, didn't want to know where those pictures came from—although she guessed spy satellites were involved. If only it was faster.

While Rembrandt did its thing in the background, Niki searched for data on the cellphones used by the two imposters. She confirmed they were both Verizon numbers assigned to R G Services. That sounded more like a company name than an individual person.

Searching for R G Services came up with a shit-ton of contractors from across the country. The area code pointed to Massachusetts, so she concentrated her efforts there. None of the R G Services listings from any New England state included either of the phone numbers.

Tea drunk. Laundry done. Rembrandt still chugging away, its counter spinning past ten million already. What it was counting, she didn't know. Watched pot and all that.

She showered and shaved her legs and pits. Refreshed, she checked the monitor. A smile crept onto her face. She had a name to go with the imposter's face.

Tyler Kemp, Rembrandt proclaimed with a 95.37% probability, was her suspect. Last known address in the Brighton area of Boston.

Friday, October 21, 2022

Charlene

Charlene opened the door for Tyler. "You smell nice. Always loved Old Spice. Zach's here, and I have to leave in fifteen. Coffee's in the living room."

Tyler entered, swapped shoes for slippers, and dropped his backpack next to one end of the couch. He poured a cup, inhaled the aroma, and tested it with a sip. She'd made it hot and bitter, just the way he liked it. "So why the summons?"

Charlene sat on the other half of the couch and waved for Zach to answer since he had been the one to call the meeting. He stopped the rocking chair. "Since I'm driving to my LARP event today, this was the only time we could get together. The money was there when I woke up. Thing is, I'm still not sure we should take it."

Tyler slammed his fist on the couch's arm. "Why the hell not? He passed all the tests, right? And he sent the money within the window, right? And we already planned to do McCree, right? What's the damn problem?"

Zach crossed his arms. "It's a feeling. I can't put a finger on it, but my gut tells me to walk away from this. We have a plan to deal with McCree at that party they're throwing at Kavanaugh's. And we have excellent alternatives and contingencies."

Tyler asked Charlene, "You hear anything more about the Happy Reaper's escape?"

She tapped her lips with her fingers. She'd previously been the cautious one. What was *really* going on with Zach? "I talked to a guy who had a shift at the hospital the day before the escape. He said they planned to transfer the Happy Reaper to a prison that had hospice care. If he's that sick, it makes sense he wouldn't be able to do the job himself. Zach, tell me more about your feeling."

"Nothing I can put a finger on. It's just we're hit by a hacker trying to get in. Then the Happy Reaper—or someone who knows enough to answer your deep background question about the dog being left alive in that Brookline house—contacts us. And soon after that, the hacking attack nearly disappears. Timing seems . . .”

Tyler filled in the words. “Too much of a coincidence. But what difference does that make? Yesterday afternoon, I checked on McCree’s place. It is truly in the middle of nowhere. I found a perfect spot under an evergreen at the edge of McCree’s driveway where I’ll have a clear hundred-yard shot. I can fly tomorrow and get into place at night. The moment he leaves the house on Sunday, bang—the job’s done. Still gives me plenty of time to fly to Colorado and take care of the hedge fund guy the following Thursday or Friday.”

“Venture capital, not hedge fund,” Zach said. “I don’t like it. Lots can go wrong. Let’s finish the Colorado assignment. We can decide once that’s complete whether to tackle McCree at his Michigan place or, like we planned, at the birthday party.”

Ah, Charlene thought. Now I get it. Zach wants in on killing McCree. Not the right reason to put the brakes on Tyler, but she’d take Zach as a temporary ally. “Plus, that gives me more time to gather intel on the Happy Reaper’s escape, the hunt for him, and the party. The guest list keeps growing. I wonder how many Kavanaugh’s can hold.”

Tyler leaned forward, eyes lit, mouth in a got-you grin. “Which is a reason to deal with McCree at his place.”

Zach said, “Fire code says two hundred forty-seven. Not that anyone will be standing at the door counting.”

Actually, Charlene thought, I’ll be there, and I will be counting, but she’d gone off track. “It’s from noon until five. They won’t all be there at the same time. The key point is that we do not want to do anything that screws up the Colorado situation for next week. When Tyler finishes that, we can decide how—” seeing both of them about to interrupt, she lifted her hand like she was stopping traffic at Copley Square “—and where to target McCree. And one more thing. We should stop meeting so often in person. Keep it to no more than once a month, our level of socializing before we started this . . . enterprise.”

Zach’s face scrunched in confusion.

“Because, numbnuts,” Tyler said. “If they catch one of us, there’s no reason for them to catch us all. That’s why we’re using burner phones.”

Before he and Zach got into another argument, she said, "Last thing, and I know this is pricey." She checked to make sure she had their attention. "I suggest Tyler flies to Colorado tomorrow." Facing him with an encouraging smile, she said, "Your first scouting tour was a great success. You wisely eliminated our initial idea to make it look like a hunting accident. It's dangerous to have only one plan. If something changes, we're back to square one. You visited during the week, but you might have your best opportunity on a weekend. This gives you a chance to see how Aspen differs between work week and weekend. And we want to get it done while he's there because that earns us the bonus for completing the job before Halloween. Right?"

Tyler's head bobbed at that. Point scored. "And," she said, "it's a little thing, but going early allows you more time to adjust to the altitude."

Zach stood and settled the rocker. "I like it. And it gives Tyler a little bonus vacation time on us. He's doing more of the work right now. Seems fair. All agreed?"

They did. Too easily to be comforting, but with three minutes before she had to leave to be punctual for her shift, she didn't have time to probe. She dashed to the bedroom and finished dressing. Returning to the living room, still fiddling with her duty belt, she spotted Zach slipping something into Tyler's backpack before he scooted out the door. *Interesting.*

Hearing the toilet flush, she checked her watch. "Tyler. Lock the door behind you. I gotta boogie."

THE HAPPY REAPER

RAPPING ON THE DRIVER'S WINDOW. The Happy Reaper blinked awake to a gray world dusted with snow. Another tap-tap-tap drew his attention. He buzzed down the window. "Yeah?"

The guy standing there wore no hat. Frozen breath frosted his beard. "Wanted to make sure you were okay. It's been an hour since I jogged past you, and you were in the same place with the engine on, and . . ."

"Must have fallen asleep," the Happy Reaper said. "Thanks for checking up on me. You should finish your run before you freeze." Looked like the guy might say more, so the Happy Reaper zipped the window up and swished the wipers to clear the windshield of the melted snow.

The guy jogged off with a story to tell his friends about the dude he'd found sleeping at a parking area overlooking Lake Superior. The clock said 7:15, but it looked much darker than it had yesterday at the same time. He laughed at himself. They'd changed time zones. Marquette was Eastern Time Zone; McCree's place was in Central, where it was 6:15. You had to be a Yooper to remember which counties in Michigan's Upper Peninsula were in the Eastern and which were Central.

He'd been damn lucky the jogger had roused him, not the cops. He clunked the transmission into reverse, backed into the road, and drove to the hotel. An early bird had left an empty slot close to the door. He pulled in, saw the sign stating they reserved it for the chain's elite members, parked anyway. Donned his mask.

He waved to the clerk, busy at the desk with a guest, took the elevator to the top floor. The door lock whirred open at the touch of the keycard. He turned the doorknob, heard nothing from inside, and pushed the door open.

From the floor where Seamus was stretching came a laconic, "Did you at least fill the tank?"

The Happy Reaper snorted. "I forgot. You're not going to ask what I was doing?"

"We've got all day together. Why spoil the suspense? For now, I'd prefer you remain in the room and not provide more chances for people to recognize you. Later today, I'll let you drive me around the U.P. to your heart's content. If you want something from the breakfast buffet, I'll get it, provided it fits in a bag I can carry." Seamus used a crutch on one side and the bed on the other to pull himself to a stand. "Did you call your buddy Clem yet?"

Good, Seamus is still worried that if something happens to me, his family will be in extreme danger. "Finish stretching, then maybe a muffin and a big thing of OJ? Clem should be up soon. You're not curious where I went?"

"Niki thought you were getting laid. I figured you found a spot you could park with the engine on to stay warm and watch the breakers roll in."

Nailed it. "How'd you figure that?"

"Once I got over being furious at you risking everything, I gave it some consideration. You don't have a lot of time. Given that, I might do the same." Seamus extended his hand. "I'd like the fob to retrieve my phone charger from the truck."

The Happy Reaper handed it to him. "I don't get why you're not still angry or at least curious or I don't know . . ."

Seamus closed his eyes like he was drawing strength from somewhere and inhaled while his fingers extended one-by-one. Counting to ten? He exhaled and repeated the process. Part of his stretching routine? Meditation? The guy's actions definitely had the Happy Reaper intrigued.

Seamus faced him directly. "I know you think we're a lot alike. In some ways, you're right. We're both driven by a will to keep our promises. I'm uncertain whether that's a great strength or hides a great weakness. Maybe we started out worrying what people would think of us if they knew who we really were. You've said that if circumstances were different, the two of us could have switched places." His mouth momentarily curled into a moue of distaste. "I don't think that's true. We have motivational differences I don't think you understand."

The Happy Reaper prompted him to continue, curious what he thought the motivational differences were.

"In your remaining days, you say you're focused solely on reclaiming and polishing your legacy. It's true that you desperately want people to remember *you* when you're gone, not remember that two guys attempted to create what ends up being a lousy sequel. You want everyone to praise your skills, express awe at how much people paid you to murder. Yada yada yada. It seems to me you're more interested in being the center of attention than you are in finding the imposters."

He sucked in air to object and fought off a coughing jag.

McCree kept talking. "It took me way too many years to realize this, but I did. My key understanding is that I must choose my promises carefully. I will not make one I do not intend to keep. Doesn't matter if it's to you or to myself. If it's important enough for me to make, it deserves my full attention. I find something stands in the way of keeping my promise, I'll change it. Give it my best shot, anyway. If I can't change it, worrying about it or using energy to knock my head against a wall is a waste of time. That's where your shenanigans last night fall."

The Happy Reaper pulled his shoulders back. "Meaning what? I'm a distraction?"

"Before you showed up, I was working on a project I might choose for a legacy if I cared what people thought after I'm gone. I'm creating habitat to help endangered species, so when my granddaughter is old enough to manage the land, they'll still be there. So, yes. In that sense, your appearance stands in the way of my promise to the land and the birds. But you miss my point. Your adventure last night was a distraction from our mutual objective: finding the imposter—imposters. Basically, I don't give a crap what you were doing."

McCree rubbed his eyes, gave a shrug. "Your breathing is getting ragged. You'd better get on the oxygen. What kind of muffin?"

Seamus left him alone to deal with the oxygen and call Clem. Why had McCree's words felt like a rapier stabbing his gut? What did he care what one person thought made him tick? Especially a guy who damn well knew he was alive only because the Happy Reaper let him live. Seamus might keep his promises because he was worried what other people thought. In his Happy Reaper role, he kept his because he was a pro. It was good business. Excellent business. And he was all business.

He installed the cannula, opened the oxygen flow, and made himself comfortable in the easy chair.

Oh sure, that was all true, but McCree's rapier had found its way past that defense and pricked the truth. Well, it was too late to change that stripe, wasn't it? What McCree had not said, which had also been true, was they both adjusted to circumstances to achieve their goal. He had nothing to prove. He admitted that tying to his belt the scalps of the guys impersonating him had been overkill. Pure revenge for their hubris. Exposing them for the frauds they were was sufficient to the task. And judging by the looks of the man with the gray, lined face peering at him from the mirror, killing them might now be beyond his current powers.

Let's see how quickly we learn *who* they are before deciding *how to deal* with them. That approach felt good.

What didn't feel accurate was Seamus McCree's self-claimed motivation. No way McCree understood his own workings. Sure, the man painted a noble picture, but in the end, didn't everyone want to be remembered?

Niki

DESPITE WORKING HALF THE NIGHT, Niki was up at dawn. With

nothing remaining for her to do regarding Tyler Kemp until FBI AD Ambrose appointed Rick to a one-person "Interstate murder-for-hire task force," she pushed her body with a fast ten-miler. Wearing only a tank top and shorty-shorts, she damn-near froze to death for the first two miles. She felt comfortable for the next three miles. Sweat poured off her by the time she finished.

Just what she needed. Actually, what she needed was a good roll in the hay, but Seamus had disappointed on that account—temporarily, she told herself.

Exercised, showered, breakfasted, she faced a day of domestic chores, balancing her checkbook, and working on her cover job of translating documents from Mandarin. With relief, she remembered her postponed meeting with the local ATF leader and snagged a mid-morning appointment. They compared notes on an overlapping assignment targeting a local militia and agreed they had nothing actionable. It was a waste of Niki's time but allowed the ATF guy to tick a box and keep Washington happy. That meant he was in her debt, always a good thing.

She performed a standard surveillance check, found no evidence of a physical tail, and arrived home to discover a message from Rick on the secure app. Because he wasn't sure what her situation was, he'd leave it to her to contact him to talk. For all her original issues with Rick, he'd become an excellent partner.

She found a patch of sun on the front porch and used her secure phone to call Rick's cellphone. Rick updated her on Park's health issues and switched focus. "My one-man task force is official. Ambrose made sure I understood he and Park want this distraction wrapped up *tout de suite*. If I need something, all I have to do is ask. We'll see."

Excellent news for her, but what about for Rick? She asked if she had screwed things up for him. "You'd let me know, right?"

"We're good. What info do you have for me?"

"I'm forwarding the trail-cam picture of the guy who plans to kill Seamus along with the URL for an Instagram post you'll quote-unquote discover. Once you confirm his name is Tyler Kemp, get warrants to check with the airlines and rental car agencies to determine how he transited to McCree's place and where else he's been. You'll—"

"Niki, I know how to do this, remember?"

Yep. She had slipped into Miss Bossypants mode. "Sorry. It's my worry talking. Not just about Seamus. We can't let anything happen on our watch to the other guy they're targeting."

"Let me nail down Kemp's ID, get the warrants, and have Ambrose assign a bunch of agents to learn everything about him down to his hat size."

Niki gave him the Verizon phone numbers and the name R G Services. "For now, that's additional information you don't officially have. Maybe Park can have someone accidentally monitor them."

Rick laughed. "Anyone tell you that you have a way with words? I'm just a lowly FBI special agent on a task force. You want to suggest that to Park, be my guest."

SATURDAY, OCTOBER 22, 2022

SEAMUS

THE HAPPY REAPER WAS CHAMPING at the bit to leave the hotel and go meet my sister's flight. I settled our hotel bill, and the Happy Reaper drove us to Ford Airport in Kingsford, a name people associated with charcoal, not the city located cheek-by-jowl with Iron Mountain. He bristled at my command that he remain in the truck while I met Colleen.

"You can't come in. Would you prefer to drive around and take the grand tour?"

He snorted. "Is there anything that tops the ski jump we passed?"

"Not above ground. The airline app says the flight's on time. Shouldn't be long."

While I waited for Colleen, I looked up the history of Kingsford charcoal on Wikipedia. I had recalled Henry Ford had come up with the charcoal idea to deal with the voluminous scrap generated by the sawmill he owned that produced wood products for Ford cars and trucks. Kingsford was the real estate guy (his wife was a Ford cousin) who bought the land and managed the manufacturing process. Got the city named after him. Now I knew.

Colleen exited security and greeted me with, "What the hell happened to you?"

I gave her a hug. "It's a long story. Let's save it for the ride."

"Fine. I have news. We can go to your place. Irene filed suit yesterday afternoon against the U.S. Marshals Service and put them on notice that she will not tolerate any harassment. Even better, the Iron County prosecutor did not object to extending the changed bail provisions to me. I guess the judge told the poor guy that he could waste everyone's time in a hearing, but the judge would approve the changes no matter what."

"Never thought I'd hear you sympathetic to the prosecutor."

"Slip of the tongue. I do appreciate not having to stay in a motel room for the duration. Crutches suck. Did you drive left footed?"

How to respond? I led her to the baggage claim area where the metal grate was still closed. "Someone drove me. That's part of the long story." *And after I tell it, you may decide a motel room is better than getting involved in my latest mess.*

The grate scraped up to display the cargo arranged for the grabbing. Colleen plucked two roller bags. "I'd like to stop for a quick bite. Is this mysterious driver someone I know? Will I be pleasantly surprised?"

"Surprised for sure."

Colleen let out a long breath. "Oh Seamus, what have you gotten us into this time?"

THE HAPPY REAPER

THE HAPPY REAPER RAISED THE temperature in the truck and flipped on the windshield wipers to remove the light snow beginning to accumulate. Who would want to live in a place with snow on October 22? What he wouldn't give to be teleported to his pied-à-terre on the Mediterranean. Through the screen of snow, he watched Seamus and Colleen exit the airport. Their legs were the same length, but Seamus had become comfortable with his crutches and had no trouble keeping up with her confident strides.

He weighed whether he should help her store her bags in the truck bed, there not being enough room in the cab given all his medical supplies. If he got out of the driver's seat, she might want to drive, and he was enjoying the relative freedom of being behind the wheel. Besides, Colleen did not look like a woman who needed a man's help. What she looked like was a McCree: closely resembling Seamus, his son, and the picture he carried in his head of Seamus's mother, Trudy.

Colleen peered in the rear door window, wheeled her bags to the tailgate, and hefted them directly into the bed without dropping the tailgate. Good thing he hadn't offered to help. She pointed Seamus to the front passenger seat and sat in the back. She reached her hand toward him. "Knowing Seamus, he might not have told you my name. I'm Colleen Carpetti."

The Happy Reaper reached around the seat and shook her hand, warm and firm. "Adam Smith."

Her hand became a vise. "Jesus, Mary, and Joseph. You're shitting me." She released his hand, which he thought she'd bruised, and sighed. "This I have got to hear."

"Well," Seamus said, "that went better than I expected. Culver's drive-through okay? We're trying to avoid showing his face in public. I'll tell you my story, and you can decide whether you're coming to camp with us."

The Happy Reaper was delighted to hear he and Seamus were returning to the house. He had stopped complaining about wearing a mask after hearing the news that COVID cases were again on the rise. Between the mask and the cannula, his nose constantly itched. Ditching the mask and having freedom to move about sounded like heaven. It also allowed him to monitor Patrick's and Lisa's progress uncovering the imposters' identities.

Seamus waited until they had left Culvers to relate his version of why Adam Smith was driving his truck. The Happy Reaper added a detail here and there to Seamus's story, felt guilty when Seamus explained about Clem gunning for the McCree's if anything bad happened to Adam.

"Good thing you made that deal with Seamus." Colleen said in a voice that could cut hardened steel. "If I'd been him, I would have lied through my teeth, taken the first opportunity to kill you, and called it self-defense. I'd beat those charges like Seamus and I are going to beat the current ones. Another thing, if these imposters show up at Seamus's place, they deserve to die."

Whoa, he thought. She's a tough one. "Didn't Seamus tell me you were a cop's daughter?"

"I am. And my daddy told me that if someone points a gun at me, I should never let them pull the trigger."

ZACH

ZACH DROVE FOURTEEN HOURS FRIDAY, collapsed in the Cincinnati hotel, and slept well. He rose early, breakfasted, and drove across the river into Kentucky and parked at Doe Run Lake in Erlanger.

The birds were active in the sun's warmth, high in the trees, singing their little hearts out. Zach shivered in the cold air that had drained off the surrounding hills into the valley with the lake. That would soon change, and he did not want to make the mistake of overdressing. He looped ten-power binoculars around his neck and crammed the central pocket of a two-water-bottle fanny pack full of protein bars. With that strapped around his waist, he was prepared to stay the whole day. He followed the hiking trail he had used before to gain access to the rear of the condo community that Kevin Porwall called home.

The trail was in the same lousy shape it had been a month ago, but he appreciated it once he veered off and bushwhacked up the hill. He was soon huffing and puffing and warmed by the time he gained the summit. Keeping to the woods, he rediscovered the excellent position from which he could watch Kevin Porwall's activities.

Porwall still left his sliding glass door onto his deck cracked three inches. Good, no armed security system to deal with on the inside. Zach found no external cameras on either Porwall's condo or the ones on either side of his.

Watching, waiting, Zach could not control his excitement. His feet tapped the ground, and if he stopped them, his free hand patted his leg. He was going to get to do this. Yes he was.

Porwall began his walk eight minutes later than he had the last time. It lasted forty-three minutes and twenty-eight seconds from when he shut his front door to him reopening it—a minute and a half longer. Well within normal variations in a routine. No one walked with him.

Afterward, Porwall spent an hour on his open deck reading the paper and sipping from a steaming cup of coffee or tea. That routine had not changed with the cooler weather. If Zach had chosen to use a long gun, he could have easily ended the guy's life then and there. He had rifles in the car, but that wasn't his plan.

He wanted to see Kevin Porwall's eyes open in surprise, know he was soon to die. Witnessing that moment of understanding and watching the eye-sparkle fade to black was the best. The Best! He'd been skeptical when he'd read other killers say that. But once he experienced it himself, he was a convert.

If all continued according to plan, he'd taste that wave of pleasure between two and three Sunday morning. That gave him plenty of time for a nap, although his twitching fingers and toes suggested he was too cranked to sleep. He'd blame the caffeine in all those protein bars. Next time, he'd get a brand without added caffeine. Live and learn.

He connected his computer to someone's Wi-Fi "secured" with admin/admin, navigated to the dark web, and what the hell? His heart raced, his vision narrowed, the hairs on his neck prickled. Something he had thought could never happen sure looked like it had.

He punched Charlene's number into his burner phone.

THE HAPPY REAPER

LATE THAT AFTERNOON, THE HAPPY Reaper found himself unattended in the McCree TV room he now considered his bedroom. Despite the weather forecast calling for temperatures that should melt the six inches of snow in the next two days, McCree had asked his son to plow the road with the Bobcat. Colleen had tagged along to learn how to run the skidsteer, since Seamus shouldn't until his leg healed. Colonel Lisa had holed up in the guest cabin doing God only knew what. Because Patrick and Lisa were both leaving tomorrow, he was disappointed to learn they had not reestablished their servers in the cabin. And Seamus, who had claimed he had slept well, had apparently lied. He was fast asleep on the living room sofa.

Which meant no one was monitoring his computer or cell phone use. Well, Patrick and Lisa might still have their cell tower apparatus in operation, despite claiming they dismantled it before the U.S. marshals returned with their search warrant. Good for him to keep in mind. His planned deep search on Colleen Carpetti wouldn't cause any problems for him or her.

He found she had never married. Was adopted, which explained the Italian last name attached to someone who looked Irish. Father was a Massachusetts state cop, died of cancer some years ago. Mother remarried. No siblings growing up. Smart as a whip—what the hell did that expression mean, anyway? Googled the expression, discovered it came from the mid-nineteenth century when whips made a sharp crack.

Her career began as an accountant for a boutique firm in Boston. Won a sizeable suit against a partner for undisclosed reasons—he guessed sexual harassment. Became a forensic accountant and joined Criminal Investigations Group. Wasn't that who Seamus worked for when they first crossed paths? He confirmed that memory and discovered Seamus had created the entire financial crimes division of CIG. For two peas in the accounting-world pod, they sure had different attitudes toward guns and violence.

She and Seamus had been arrested on several charges here in Iron County. Hard to know the facts, but a death had been involved.

Seemed like he should have a one-on-one conversation with Ms. Colleen Carpetti to prevent any misunderstandings that ended up in someone dying.

SEAMUS

I AWOKE TO LISA JIGGLING my arm. She placed a finger on her lips. "Time's short. Let's talk while Colleen's gone with Patrick."

This could not be good.

She helped me to the dining room table and brought us each a diet Dr Pepper. She handed me a page from a steno notebook. "Patrick and I moved the cell tower simulator across the lake. We figured the marshals wouldn't find it there, and we have more to learn about Clem. Smith has not made any calls, but he's been busy. These are the websites Smith accessed this afternoon. He's searching for Colleen's past and the recent troubles up here that resulted in your arrest."

It made sense for the Happy Reaper to be curious—but why not ask? The Dr Pepper turned acidic in my mouth. Colleen hadn't actually threatened him, but she sure let him know her feelings. The line goes that when you're a hammer, you treat any problem like it's a nail. The Happy Reaper's hammer was to kill.

An iron lung squeezed the air from me. I pulled at the collar of my shirt, but I was wearing a t-shirt, not a too-tight tie around my neck. My eyesight blurred until I forced myself to focus on the snow-tipped balsam at the edge of the vernal pond.

I had to make sure he didn't see Colleen as a nail. If I couldn't, I'd have to go against my word and turn him in to the police.

I crumpled the notepaper and asked Lisa to toss it onto the glowing orange coals of the wood stove fire. "Have you and Paddy made any progress on Clem or the imposters?"

"Nothing on Clem. The imposters have taken offline all the servers we discovered for both the original portal and the follow-up communication with you. I'm sorry."

And I hadn't thought the day could get worse.

"Patrick and I have agreed on an approach to scour the dark web in case they revive the portal. But . . ."

"You're not hopeful."

"Who knows? Unfortunately, we taught them where their security flaws were. It will be harder to crack next time. We'll keep working, but honestly, your best bet to find them is with Niki and the FBI's investigation. Same with Clem, unless Smith gives something away with his phone or computer use."

Not comforting. "I hear the Bobcat. Before you go, can you or Paddy show me how to monitor the Happy Reaper's internet use?"

"We'll install an app on your phone to monitor the cell tower simulator. Patrick can show you how to monitor the internet, but it might be easier for him to do that remotely for you. I'll make sure he takes you for a drive before he leaves tomorrow, and you can talk in private. Sorry I don't have better news."

"I can't thank you enough for everything you've done." We shared a hug. "Time for me to check with Niki and see if she and Rick are having any luck."

TYLER

TYLER HAD ENJOYED HIS DAY in Aspen. He'd people-watched at breakfast and lunch to make sure his clothes and actions fit in with the locals. They did. He'd spent the morning hiking around the elk-hunting area with the dual purpose of getting acclimated to the altitude and confirming he could not safely use the area for the hit. That afternoon, he'd driven around Oceans' neighborhood without the aid of maps. Lots more activity, which made sense for a Saturday. He was delighted to see his rental car looked exactly like several he passed. Oceans' house still looked empty. Unfortunately, he couldn't tell whether anyone had fixed the window he'd broken. That meant another visit after dark.

He was occupying himself before dinner by checking the in-room movie selections when the burner phone rang.

To his hello, Zach replied, "We've got a situation."

Tyler dropped onto the bed, rolled his eyes at the ceiling. "What now?"

"Someone hacked into the server that held information on the job you're on."

He bit back his angry question about how and when that had happened and instead asked what that meant.

"Worst case. They know the name of the target. The info we gathered on the contractor. The proposed fee. Nothing that says we agreed to kill the target. But—"

Tyler pictured Zach, agitated about stuff that hardly mattered, pacing, tugging his earlobes. He asked, "Can they track the money?"

"No. Different servers. That same server held McCree's info. What if the Happy Reaper was behind the website attack, and he contacted us only to find out who we are?"

Zach's panic was making him stupid. "Why the hell would he bother paying us the money?"

"To bait a trap. Look, I talked with Charlene. She agrees on us backing off from everything. I shut down the servers. They can't get anything else. Our contract requires us to complete the Oceans assignment by year's end. That gives us more than two months. If everything is quiet for a month, we'll find another opportunity. Oceans usually skis in Aspen in December, so your scouting work can still pay off."

This bullshit was why he should go solo. But now was time to play nice while he executed his plan. They'd expect him to bitch about losing the Halloween bonus, so he did, stomping around the room. His feet slamming the floor helped bring anger to his voice.

When Tyler simmered down, Zach said, "Charlene and I discussed that. Since it wasn't your fault, I agreed that once you complete the job, I'll use part of my payment to reimburse you for your half of the lost bonus."

Huh, Zach was no longer in panic mode. Like he was following a script. Time to switch gears and sound grateful. "Thank you. That's thoughtful and generous. Just thinking out loud. We've already paid for the room here and it will cost more to change the plane ticket. Are you guys okay with me staying here? I can watch to see if Oceans still shows and whether he beefed up security. That would tell us something, right?"

The relief in Zach's voice was obvious. "That's an awesome idea. I'm sure Charlene agrees. After you return, we can decide what to do with Seamus McCree. Yeah?"

"Absolutely." Tyler added a mental *not*. "I'll let you go."

How stupid did Zach think he was? Whatever Zach had screwed up on the computer side would lead only to Zach. Unless he squealed.

No way would Tyler expose himself to some security guy capturing his picture while he "checked if Oceans showed or had extra security." He'd still do Oceans when the time was right. The others might not believe in the Results Guaranteed part of their business, but he knew it was critical. If the Happy Reaper was involved with the hacking, it was part of a test to make sure they—no, he—is a worthy successor to that trademark. Huh—could he trademark that expression? Nah, too risky. Well, maybe. Anyway, what could prove his worth more than quickly and efficiently fulfilling the McCree contract?

His eyes crinkled in a smile. Absolutely nothing. He'd do McCree and present his so-called partners with a *fait accompli*.

Niki

Niki had to give the FBI credit: when they threw resources at a problem, they could quickly uncover a ton of information. Rick had used the FBI's face-recognition software which was, unless they knew about NSA's Rembrandt, considered state-of-the-art. Combined with the inside information she had provided, he'd "been lucky" and discovered a Facebook group that included a picture of the unsub. The software identified Tyler Kemp in minutes. The name, a search warrant, and access to Bureau resources allowed Rick to track Kemp's trip the day before from Boston to an uber-expensive hotel in Aspen, Colorado.

Niki booked a flight from MSP to Denver, rented the same SUV model Kemp had from the same kiosk at the Denver airport, and made a reservation at the same Aspen hotel. Before checking in, she toured its parking garage but did not spot Kemp's vehicle.

She chatted up the older man who checked her in. He was the manager, filling in at the front desk. The normal receptionist was quarantining because her boyfriend had tested positive for Covid. They had an extremely strict policy and paid their employees, blah, blah, blah. She wanted this guy to like her, since she might have to deal with him if she later obtained a warrant to bug Kemp's room. She smiled, nodded, and uh-huh'd in all the right places instead of tapping her fingers because he was taking forever to get her a room key. She got him to confirm that Kemp still had two nights on his reservation. Her flirting scored a room on Kemp's floor. The rooms next door, ideal for listening through the walls, were not available, and she settled for one several doors away.

Niki allowed the bellhop to cart her four pieces of luggage to her room, learned his other job was as a ski instructor qualified for the local rescue team. Hard to know what kind of snow year it would be. Autumn had been ten degrees above normal, but one good blizzard could give them a sufficient snow base. Blah, blah, blah. Did she want to make sure the bed would suit her back?

Niki arched a brow at the double entendre. Chose to play it straight and said she preferred putting her own stuff away, and no, she didn't need him to tell her how to run the jacuzzi. Worried the chatterbox would ask why she had four bags, she escorted him to the door and gave him a generous tip. Seamus always reminded her to treat staff well because you never knew when you might need them. Like possibly to slip her into Kemp's room.

She unpacked and stored the bag that held all a girl might want for a stay of up to ten days. The luggage rack proved perfect to hold the bag that contained everything necessary to create a myriad of disguises: wigs, cosmetics to change her skin color, putty to modify the shape of her nose, dye to color her eyebrows, lenses to create various eye colors. She didn't expect to have to use the contents, but if she did, Niki could look old, young, or of indeterminate age. A biker babe with tats in all the right places. A washerwoman, hunched by years of hard work.

Electronics filled bag three. Rick had given her a lesson in state laws on attaching a tracker to someone's car. Wisconsin was crazy: anybody can put trackers on anybody else. In Colorado, it was against the law. Besides, she was law enforcement, not a private citizen, and that required a warrant to be legal.

From the last case, she removed her Sig 365 and holster and the modest ankle rig she used for backup. She strapped both on, tucked several zip ties into her all-purpose sling bag, and verified that all the parts to her long rifle with scope were in their padded slots.

She checked the garage again. Still no car there or on the surrounding neighborhood streets. Time to learn if Rick had gained permission to tap Kemp's phone. To her surprise, Rick answered her phone call.

"Yes, I am monitoring Kemp's cellphone. Won't do you any good, though. It's fully charged, sitting stationary in his apartment. The judge blocked our request to monitor the two numbers owned by R G Services. I was unable to satisfy him that the phones are currently under the suspects' control. The judge ruled incomplete our Hail Mary to allow us to monitor Clem's phone number, and he threatened to flag us on a fifteen-yard penalty for unsportsmanlike conduct."

"Enough with the sports analogies, please. What else did you learn about Tyler Kemp?"

"Never married. Lives alone in a dive in Boston. Recently quit his tech job. Apparently doesn't get along well with authority figures. We mined public records and social media but are avoiding contacting known associates. Don't want to tip off Kemp's partner, who is most likely among them. Nor do we want his friends mentioning our contacting them. Kemp enjoys multi-player online shoot-'em-up games. Got a decent rep there, but again bounces around 'cause he keeps getting into arguments about strategy. Spends beaucoup bucks at the range. He was good enough to graduate from the Army's sniper school before they booted him out with a less-than-honorable discharge. It's not much. Sorry."

A shooter with a bad attitude, then. "Good start for a Saturday. I'll drive around and get a feel for the area. Develop a mental map of where the nouveau rich live. Have you—"

"I can't ask anything about the Bureau's response to the anonymous tip identifying the VC guy as a target. How would I know you made it? You want intel on that, you'll have to get it through Ambrose—and he'll wonder how you knew to ask. Leave it alone, Niki. Go scout your territory and find Kemp."

Becoming predictable, even enough that her work partner could anticipate her questions, was the last thing she wanted to become. Too dangerous in her line of work.

Sᴜɴᴅᴀʏ, Oᴄᴛᴏʙᴇʀ 23, 2022

Zᴀᴄʜ

Aᴛ 1:50 Sᴜɴᴅᴀʏ ᴍᴏʀɴɪɴɢ, Zᴀᴄʜ parked in a deserted lot off Richardson Road in Erlanger, Kentucky that was used by golf course maintenance people. From there, he walked the mile and a quarter to the rear of Porwall's condo, snapped on the nitrile gloves, and shimmied up the 6x6 post to access the deck. The sliding door into the condo was open three inches.

He let his heart calm to a steady beat, listened to the hum of the refrigerator inside partially drown the soft snoring coming from the bedroom window, also cracked to let in fresh air. The screened door remained locked, but he'd YouTubed that issue and discovered a way to lift the locking mechanism from the outside. He waited until the refrigerator motor kicked in again and had the screen unlocked in seconds.

Easing the screen and sliding doors open without making noise required three minutes. A little silicone spray would have done wonders, but a steady hand and patience sufficed. The snoring never stopped or even varied much. He stepped into the living room and caught a whiff of something sweet.

He extracted the blade from its leather sheaf with a whisper. The snoring continued. His eyes had sufficiently adjusted that he didn't bother to use his headlamp. Five steps brought him to the bedroom door. One more brought him inside.

Porwall lay face up—a perfect position for Zach's intended knife-thrust into his target's black heart. Porwall had tucked his right hand under his pillow. His curled left rested on the covers. The miasma of the guy's bad breath smothered the scent of oil coming from a night light glowing in the ensuite bathroom. *Didn't your mama teach you to brush before you go to bed?*

Zach planned to approach the head of the bed from the far side to strike over Porwall's left shoulder and reduce the possibility of a jerked reaction blocking his downward blow. He didn't have to worry about tripping over slippers; they were on the near side of the bed. The only thing not perfect was Porwall lay in the center of a king-sized bed. Zach would have to lean a long way to see the guy's eyes.

Using the technique he'd read top athletes used to prepare themselves, he mentally rehearsed his approach and the killing stroke. He moved to the foot of the bed, one slow, sure step following another. With a snort, Porwall rolled onto his side, facing away from the side of the bed Zach had planned to use. Phooey. Zach remained in place, mentally rehearsing his revised approach. He walked to the near bedside and swept the slippers under the bed with the toe of one foot.

Extracting that foot, he dinged his boot's topmost hooked eyelet against the bed frame.

His target's head raised; his eyes opened. In the dim light, Zach witnessed the fear he had hoped to see. In a flash, he filled with a warm glow, like he was basking under a heat lamp.

One heartbeat later, Zach executed the downward arc of his knife, noticed Porwall's hand moving from under the pillow. With a handgun.

Zach adjusted his swing and slashed deep across the exposed forearm. Porwall's scream cut off when Zach plunged the knife into Porwall's neck. In the melee, Porwall landed two glancing blows to Zach's face. Zach stabbed and stabbed and stabbed until the target no longer moved. Blood covered everything: the corpse, the bed, the walls, and Zach.

His breathing was ragged. His hands shook from adrenaline now leaking from his system. Had Porwall only screamed the once? A quick glance outside assured him both neighboring units remained dark. Stop and think, Zachary. You do not want this guy's blood in your car.

He found a garbage bag under the kitchen sink and clothes in the closet to wear on the walk to his car. He'd have to wear his own boots; Porwall's feet were several sizes smaller. Taking everything to the bathroom, he stripped in the shower, leaving on his nitrile gloves, and stuffed all his clothes into the garbage bag. He showered until the last drop of blood circled down the drain. Remaining in the shower, he dried off. He dressed while standing on the used towels, then stuffed the towels into the garbage bag and added the knife, which he had left on the bed.

He wasn't foolish enough to think he hadn't left any DNA, but local

CSI would have to be damned lucky to find it. He left the bedroom window open, closed both the screen and sliding door to the deck. With no reason to expose himself by clambering down the deck post to the ground, Zach exited from the lower level and checked his watch. Three-twenty.

He used the return walk to his car to ask himself what lessons he had learned.

Even with the extra time for food and rest stops, he'd be home near to when his parents expected him from his so-called LARP weekend. That was well-planned.

A bowling trophy worked better than a knife.

He had enjoyed seeing the guy's eyes, but the safety of using a gun at a distance might be a better alternative.

He wasn't one of those sickos who had to follow a pattern. Nope, he was good at adjusting on the fly. Learning from his experience.

And he knew he wanted to do it again. Soon.

SEAMUS

THE DITTY I FIRST HEARD from my father goes: red sky at night, sailors' delight; red sky at morning, sailors take warning. What did it mean when the pre-dawn eastern sky glowed fuchsia? I shook off my dread that it was an omen, reminding myself I wasn't important enough for the gods to paint my skies.

The thermometer recorded the pre-dawn temperature at twenty. The roads would be frozen for Lisa's drive out, which was good. Waiting meant rising temps melting the remaining snow, creating slick roads.

The white noise from the CPAP machine and silence from upstairs suggested the Happy Reaper and Colleen were both sleeping. I left my sleeping bag on the screened porch, minced into the house in socked feet, and changed clothes in the bathroom. By the time I had my outer gear on, the fuchsia sky had leached its color to become gray.

I wanted to say goodbye to Lisa but, with a dusting of snow covering the icy road, was loath to crutch to the cabin. I called Paddy and asked him to pick me up in his car.

By the time he carted me to the cabin, Lisa's car was warming up. She left the outhouse and came to meet us. She beamed at me. "One thing I won't miss is that cold toilet seat."

I reminded her that she could have used either bathroom in the house.

"Oh, I'm just complaining to hear myself talk."

"I'm sure you could have enjoyed a thousand better places during your leave than coming here to help me. Please tell me how I can thank you for all you've done."

"Like I told you last night when you thanked me, it was a wonderful break from my routine and helped clear my head for taking on my new responsibilities. And who knows, you might see a lot more of me. I plan to recommend locating my new command nearby. Alright, hugs all around. Good luck with your trial if I don't talk with you before."

Lisa had always been a good hugger, and even through our winter coats, I felt the power of her squeeze.

I held her away from me to look at her face. "Gosh, you hugged me like it was the last time."

"You never know. Old man like you could keel over any second."

I laughed. "I take back everything nice I've ever said about you. Off you go." We traded a second hug and separated.

Paddy and I watched Lisa ease her car down the cabin driveway and travel Shank Lake Road until a hill hid her. I suggested he should also leave before the roads thawed. "But first, Lisa said you'd install an app on my phone so I can monitor the cell tower simulator."

Paddy downloaded an app for the simulator and another to monitor traffic on the regular Wi-Fi network, which would only be the Happy Reaper, given Niki and I had moved everything else onto the guest Wi-Fi. I practiced using both apps. While I retrieved prior call data, a notification on my cellphone said the cell tower simulator had detected a new phone call.

Paddy said, "Good timing. I can show you how to do it in real time. Hopefully, this is Adam calling Clem."

The phone numbers popped up, and we heard the start of a conversation between Colleen and her girlfriend before we exited the app to give them privacy.

"Call me if you forget something," Paddy said. "The simulator battery will only last two or three days. Fingers crossed you won't need it any longer. I'll return next week and remove it."

Niki

NIKI LAY IN A STRANGE bed at four a.m.—five o'clock body time. Her mind churned with possibilities. No way she'd get more shut-eye. She dressed in layers and went for a run through a sleeping Aspen, checking all the nearby streets and alleys for Kemp's rental. No sign of it. The altitude had her huffing and puffing more than usual. She cut her planned ten miles down to a hard six. After showering, she paced an oval in her room's carpet until seven o'clock when the Sunday buffet breakfast opened.

On her way to the stairs, she stopped at Tyler Kemp's room. No light under the door. She tapped on the door—loud enough for anyone inside to hear, not loud enough to bring protests from other guests. No answer.

Downstairs, she grabbed a complimentary copy of the Denver Post and dropped it on a two-top to claim the table. She filled her plate with fruit and yogurt. Hearing a group of four middle-aged women with frozen botoxed faces praising the buns on offer, sounding like Meg Ryan's fake orgasm in "When Harry Met Sally," she snagged one. It was good, but not *that* good.

Breakfast done, her phone said 7:23. She formed her face into a worried look and approached the front desk. "I'm getting really concerned. I tried calling Tyler. He was supposed to meet me at seven for breakfast. I've tried his cellphone several times. Maybe he's got it on airplane mode or something? Can you call his room for me? It's Tyler Kemp." She spelled his name.

She could dial herself using the interior phone, but the whole point was to get the clerk invested in what had happened to dear Tyler, and she counted on a place that catered to rich people to bend over backwards to accommodate both their guests' stupidity and their sense of entitlement.

The clerk placed the call. No answer.

Niki dabbed away tears from the corner of her eyes. "That's not like him. Not like him at all. Is it possible for you to do a wellness check? You wouldn't think it with someone his age, but with the altitude and his heart . . ." She trailed off, blinking another tear into existence and allowing it to track down her cheek. What else could she do to get this guy to offer to open the room?

His face showed a mixture of well-trained concern and new-situation confusion. Confusion was winning. One more push would do it. She said,

"If you can't help me, I guess I should call the police, right? I could ask them not to use their sirens, right? I don't want to do anything to upset the guests, but . . ." She fumbled with her knapsack, mumbled, "Where did I put my phone?"

The guy was wavering. One more push.

She dropped the bag and burst into tears. That acting drew attention, which must have been enough to tip the balance.

The clerk said, "I can't leave the desk until my morning receptionist comes on at seven-thirty. She should be here any moment. Would that be okay?"

Niki nodded her appreciation, snuffled her tears, and offered to try Tyler's cellphone one more time. She made a production of swiping open her cellphone and making a call, letting her shoulders slump in dismay when no one at her bank in St. Paul answered the phone.

The clerk didn't even let his replacement take off her coat before explaining the situation. Motioning Niki to join him, they elevatored to the top floor and walked to Tyler's room. He rapped on the door with his wedding band. "Mr. Kemp, are you okay in there?"

No answer. He repeated the wedding-band knock, each attempt louder than the one before. To spur him to open the door, Niki said, "Oh God. He's dead, isn't he?"

Worked. The clerk tapped the card reader with his master card. The lock whirred and a green light flashed. He opened the door three inches and called inside. No response. A trickle of sweat rolled down behind his ear. He pushed the door open.

Light from the unscreened window painted the room with the blue of mountain dawn. On the right, the door to the darkened bathroom was open. The clerk stepped past it and stopped at the opening to the main room.

Niki followed him in, flicked on the bathroom light. No dirty towels. No toiletries on the counter. Faint whiff of cologne: citrus and a hint of musk. Passing the partially opened closet door, she noted the luggage rack held no bag. Another step allowed her to scan most of the room. Chocolate bites still on the pillows. Desk and bedside table empty.

The clerk spun around in a circle, pushed past Niki, and examined the closet. "Nothing." Niki opened the dresser drawers, which contained only an extra blanket.

She held her cheeks with both hands, the personification of shocked concern. "Oh gosh. I hope nothing happened to his wife and kids. He didn't check out, right?"

"He's still in the system. We'll have to charge him for the night."

Niki thanked him and wrung her hands, modeling great consternation. "I'll call his assistant and see if she knows anything. I'm sure she'll be in touch to cancel the rest of his reservation. Again, thank you. Looks like I have to do this on my own."

What she had to do was warn Seamus to be on the lookout.

THE HAPPY REAPER

THE SMELL OF BACON CONVINCED the Happy Reaper to get up. He'd slept well, felt rested, and the finger pulse oximeter confirmed his oxygen level was good at 96%. He showered and put on his last clean clothes—oh boy, laundry day, something to look forward to.

He found Seamus and Colleen sitting at the dining room table, Patrick in the kitchen cooking.

"About time," Seamus said, "I'm starving, but Paddy said he wouldn't start the pancakes until everyone was ready."

Patrick said, "The bacon is done, and the omelet is warming. Start on those while I prep the pancakes. Save room for the last of the wild blueberries Dad collected. Plus, he made the maple syrup this past winter. The bacon's for you and Dad. I'm vegetarian and Colleen doesn't like it. Sit. Eat."

He did. Patrick had not oversold how wonderful everything tasted. Amazing what a good night's sleep did. The mealtime chatter was catchup on McCree family happenings: Seamus asking questions and offering little. Colleen still loving her forensic accounting job and worried about Trudy McCree's upcoming birthday party. Patrick regaled them with anecdotes of life with his daughter, Megan, and Valeria, the girl he and his wife planned to adopt.

The Happy Reaper asked for Valeria's backstory, and the three recounted the events earlier this year that had brought Valeria into their lives and resulted in the criminal charges against Colleen and Seamus.

He found the breakfast experience discombobulating. He knew the only reason Patrick and Colleen (and Niki and Lisa for that matter) hadn't either killed him or returned him to prison was because Seamus forbade it. And yet, during their hour together at the table, neither one showed any animosity—like the McCree clan was adopting him, too. Which was crazy thinking.

Patrick made the first move to end the breakfast conversation. "The dishes won't do themselves, and I need to pack and get on my way."

"Off you go," Seamus said. "You know the deal. You cook and I clean. I have the same arrangement with Colleen."

The Happy Reaper saw his opportunity. "Speaking of cleaning, I should do laundry today. Anything special I need to know?"

Colleen asked if he had ever used a front loader.

Fact was, the prison had been doing his laundry for him. Before that, he had mostly used dry cleaners. He admitted it was his first time.

"In that case, while Seamus takes care of the dishes, I'll do your laundry. That's easier than recovering if you put in too much detergent. Seamus, are all your dirty clothes in the laundry basket?"

Seamus raised his voice to be heard over water filling the sink. "All there. While I'm doing dishes and Colleen starts your laundry, you can give Clem your daily call."

The Happy Reaper closed the door to his room and flicked on the TV to further mask his voice. He eased onto the couch, adjusted the pillow behind his shoulders. With the night's rest, he felt better than he had in a couple of weeks. Which, he had to admit, was not exactly great. In his current condition, even if Seamus fully cooperated, the only way he'd be able to kill both imposters was if he caught them together. And was lucky. That sucked.

He read the news ticker scrolling under a talking head spouting many words with little substance. Same old, same old. Ukraine war. Midterm campaign nonsense. Trump investigations. Another mass shooting.

And they called him a monster?

He should tell Seamus that he'd changed his mind about killing the imposters. Better: tell Seamus that his arguments had caused his change of mind. That should improve Seamus's attitude.

And why not? It made him, the Happy Reaper, look magnanimous. With luck, he could spin the story and get credit for their capture. None of them wanted the publicity, so why not polish his own halo? That was using the old noggin.

He retrieved the last number he had called, hit redial, and listened to the same greeting. At the beep, he hung up. Time to give Seamus the good news.

SEAMUS

WHILE I WASHED DISHES, COLLEEN sorted the clothes into lights and darks, put the darks in the washer, and plunked down at the table, her hands wrapped around a steaming cup of tea. Something was bothering her. I could try guessing, but wisely chose silence, which she eventually broke.

"I didn't sleep well last night."

I responded with an open-ended, "Oh?" I figured now we'd get to it.

"Do you think this will be resolved before we're supposed to leave for the big birthday bash?"

Paddy burst through the mudroom door. "Dad, can you show me how you want to arrange your furniture in the cabin?"

Whatever this was, it did not concern rearranging furniture.

I threw on a winter coat and grabbed gloves and a hat. Even with Paddy's implied urgency, I used care crutching my way to his car.

Once Paddy had the car moving, he said, "Smith called a furniture store, listened to the recorded message giving store hours, waited for the beep, but didn't leave a message."

I considered the possibilities. "Is the act of calling the message?"

"It's a legitimate business. Been at that location for two generations. He's jerking your chain."

When the Happy Reaper had handed me the phone, I had talked with someone. Who that person was, and what agreement he had made with the Happy Reaper were unclear. They could be playing me. "Even if you're right, Paddy, I won't do anything different. At least, not until we thwart the imposters."

"But if you made yourself a target for no good reason, we should throw his ass back in jail where he can rot until he dies. It's the least we can do for Abigail. And you and Colleen should get the hell out. Let Niki and Rick and the police find the imposters."

Was my son accusing me of not caring that the Happy Reaper had killed

Abigail, my best friend and so much more? I closed my eyes to regroup. This was not an argument that would do either of us any good, but given our history, one we couldn't avoid.

"I hear your words, Paddy. I agree, it seems increasingly likely he lied to me. We don't know the shape of the lie. Did he and Clem lie about what would happen if harm came to Smith? Or only on how the two of them would keep in touch? Is whatever satisfaction you or I might feel if he spent his last days in custody rather than breathing fresh air worth risking sending killers after everyone in our family? If you're wrong, we could be looking over our shoulders for years. I think not."

Paddy slapped the steering wheel with his open hand. "And I don't have any say in this? We're talking about my family."

Exactly why this argument would do us no good. "And your grandmother's, and your two aunts', and your wife's. Shall we do a family Zoom call and take a vote? No. Until we know more, you have two choices, Patrick McCree. Either do it my way or go against my wishes and contact whatever authorities you want and tell them I'm harboring a fugitive."

He blew out disgusted air. "Yeah, right. Like that's an option."

"One last thing to keep in mind. Do you think the Happy Reaper could make a phone call from prison and order an actual hit? I do. I'm not saying we do nothing forever. Let's give Niki, Rick, and the FBI a little time to develop their case against Tyler Kemp and find the second imposter."

"It won't do you a damn bit of good if Kemp comes here and shoots you in the head."

"He's in Aspen. Niki's on his ass. I'm not worried about Kemp. You shouldn't be either."

He slammed on the car's brakes, and we nearly skidded into a tree. "Fine. Just promise you won't do anything stupid."

I snorted. "You know I don't make promises I can't keep."

TYLER

TYLER WOKE RESTED AND PREPARED to score a big payday sometime in the next thirty hours. The weather looked good both Sunday and Monday: partly sunny, warming into the low forties. Chance of snow overnight, but that would quickly melt off. With the clothes he had brought for Colorado, he'd be plenty toasty, no matter how long he had to wait outside for his shot at McCree.

He was stuck at the motel until the local side-by-side rental place opened up at ten. The more he thought about Zach and his servers, the more he wished the damn computers would disappear. He called Charlene, provided her his fictional plans for the day in Aspen, and shared his worries.

"I was thinking the same thing," Charlene said. "I'll visit him today after he gets back. Make him prove to me that nothing related to us or this Happy Reaper stuff is on his computers."

A perfect solution. "Thanks, Charlene. And thanks again for being so understanding."

He could only hope her understanding nature would hold once she learned he had completed the McCree assignment without letting either of them know. Screw 'em if they didn't like it. It wasn't like they'd be able to do anything.

SEAMUS

PADDY DROPPED ME AT THE house and drove away, promising to let me know when he arrived home. I remained outside in the freezing air until the thrum of his engine disappeared, which was a long time, given how silent the woods were. No wind disquieted the branches. No distant logging machines operated. Road noises from the highway seven miles away were blessedly absent. Even the birds chose silence. The only way I knew they were present was the gentle patter of seed husks dropping from a flock of nine purple finches amicably munching sunflower seeds at the feeders.

It's like the world is holding its breath. A raven croaked in the distance, breaking the spell and causing me to realize I, not the world, had been holding my breath.

I entered the house and found Colleen at the table creating a shopping list and the Happy Reaper, wrapped in a wool blanket, sitting in the chair closest to the wood stove. Having come inside from the cold, I was roasting. I hung up my outer clothes and checked the indoor temperature. Seventy, and it had to be several degrees warmer close to the fire. I asked Smith if he was feeling okay.

"Other than cold, which, I guess, is a forever thing. Can we talk now?"

"Let me first check and see if I have any messages from Niki." I settled into the chair opposite him, brought up the secure message app, and discovered several messages between Niki and Rick.

As I read through them, I replayed my argument with Paddy. I had assumed Niki had Kemp under observation in Aspen. Her failure to find him blew a massive hole in one of my arguments. The last message was from Niki to me, confirming what I had surmised from her exchanges with Rick.

I shared what I had learned. "Kemp and his rental are MIA. He didn't sleep in his room, but he hasn't checked out. Niki asked Rick to check with the rental agency to see if he had turned in his car. Rick says he's on it, but even with the warrant, it usually takes several hours to get information from any big corporation like a car rental company. This is where the NSA has an enormous advantage over the FBI. They'd just hack the rental car company's reservation system."

Colleen flopped onto the couch, creating a conversational triangle. "That's jaded. Do you think your warning messages worked? Maybe the contractor let Kemp know that someone was onto him?"

Maybe. "Then why not check out of his hotel?"

Colleen said, "My bet? For whatever reason, he decided it wasn't the right time to kill that venture capitalist. Maybe his partner convinced him. Maybe the venture capital guy listened to Seamus and canceled the trip. Or the guy who wanted the hit waved him off. If Kemp leaves early, he points a spotlight on himself, right? That's something the FBI would look for. Instead, he packs up and leaves. He might head home. But he might come for you, Seamus."

She leaned forward. "The question is, what are you going to do?"

THE HAPPY REAPER

THE HAPPY REAPER LISTENED TO Seamus describe Niki's failure to find Kemp in Aspen. He put himself in the imposter's shoes and considered why he would make such a move. He never wasted money, and he had way more than Kemp. The only logical reason was Kemp wanted someone to think he was in that hotel when he wasn't.

The only person—other than Niki and the FBI—who knew where he was staying was his partner. He doubted Niki had scared him off, or that Kemp was strategic enough to keep his room because he was worried police would check lodging reservations to look for cancelations. That was Colleen's logic, not Kemp's. To him, Kemp's actions hinted at a disagreement with his partner. And given Kemp had already scouted McCree's place, he figured Colleen's suggestion that Kemp was coming here to kill Seamus had a decent probability.

Which suited him perfectly if he could sidetrack the discussion before Seamus suggested they leave. He cleared his throat and got their attention. "On some assignments, I set up my position for the kill a day or even two ahead. Camoed myself and became part of the scenery. If I were doing that in Aspen, I'd keep the room to hide in after I fulfilled the contract. Stay there until I thought it was safe to move from the area. If Kemp or his partner studied me enough to know an Irish Setter was at that house in Brookline, he would know how I operated. He's taking a page from my playbook."

Colleen said, "I still think the buyer got cold feet, canceled the venture capital guy's hit and—"

Dominate the room, now. He rose from his chair and looked down at them. "Not the way it works. If a contractor cancelled, he'd have to pay me the rest of the fee. And if he reneged, I'd remind him I knew who he was, but he didn't know who I was. And if he had to pay me anyway, I might as well whack the guy as not."

Colleen said, "Except he's not you. Kemp could have driven anywhere by now. How do we know he isn't here already?"

That one he could honestly answer. "Because Seamus is still alive. If Kemp had arrived and set up last night, Seamus would be lying in his driveway with a bullet through his heart." To Seamus, he added, "Tell Niki to look for him wherever she thinks he might take his kill shot. I'd like to get some air. Can I have the car keys, Dad? Please?"

Seamus tilted his head, like he was contemplating what the Happy Reaper really wanted. The Happy Reaper folded the blanket and placed it on the chairback, as though Seamus had already agreed to his request for the keys.

"Roads are slick," Seamus said. "You're safer with an ATV. Bundle up against the cold and wear the helmet with the smoky visor. It will keep you warm and hide your identity should you meet someone."

The Happy Reaper made sure not to show how pleased he was with Seamus focused on his request for the keys and not his weak argument to explain why Kemp was still in Aspen.

From the laundry room came the beep of the washer finishing a load. Colleen's eyes did a quick check in that direction. He attempted to add to her distraction. "Colleen, want to join me on a loop around the lake? I can wait until you start the second load of laundry."

A flash of distaste crossed her face, one she probably didn't realize she had made. She politely refused, rushed to the laundry room, and attended to the washer.

Fair enough. She didn't have to like him, she just had to be open to his plan. He ran some risk that in leaving them alone, Seamus would convince her to leave. He thought that with her combination of a hard edge and stubborn streak, she'd go along with him if he presented a credible plan to dispatch Kemp.

He had spent his working life creating plans that worked. He donned the gear and went outside to explore their options and develop one more.

ZACH

ZACH WAS FURIOUS WITH HIMSELF for not checking earlier. He'd wasted several hours driving toward Boston when he could have driven straight to the U.P.

Tyler had given him no reason to suspect he planned to abandon Aspen and fly east to execute McCree. But the AirTag he had slipped into Tyler's backpack the last time they were all together now showed Tyler in a motel in Iron Mountain, Michigan. He should have realized when Tyler had been so agreeable that he was blowing smoke up Zach's ass.

Killing McCree now was not what they agreed. No damn way Tyler got to decide that on his own. Tyler was not the world's best planner. Sure, he'd visited McCree's property, but things could go wrong, and any error could cause them all to rot in jail.

Zach did not plan to rot in jail.

His mapping software said it was under 700 miles and ten and a half hours to McCree's place on Shank Lake Road. He gained an hour moving from Eastern to Central time. Busting hump, he could get there at sunset.

He paid for gas, bought a bunch of food and drink, and set his phone to follow Tyler's AirTag. Assuming Tyler hadn't totally lost it, he wasn't rash enough to try something during daylight. That gave Zach the entire trip to develop multiple scenarios to cover whatever Tyler had planned.

His parents expected him back around dinner time. He'd wait until mid-afternoon and call with a last-minute change. The boss wanted him in—hmmm, where? He'd mentioned the LARP was in the Catskills. It had to be a location he would drive directly to from there rather than travel home and fly or take the train. *Philly.* Boss said he could buy chinos and a polo shirt. He already had his laptop. That took care of Monday's story. He had plenty of time to create Tuesday's.

No reason to tell Charlene about Tyler's actions or his own plan. She'd object, and who wanted to hear that? Let sleeping dogs lie.

Lucky thing that in planning for contingencies while killing Porwall, he had packed his military-style rifle with its auto sear to convert the semi-automatic rifle into one that could empty an entire magazine with a single pull of the trigger. He had ten magazines. More than enough for whatever happened.

His so-called LARP provisions included camo gear, night-vision goggles, binoculars, another AirTag, and a bunch of other stuff that might come in handy.

"Tyler, my man. Ready or not, here I come."

Niki

NIKI HADN'T THOUGHT OF IT before, but ski resorts, even ones with booming populations, didn't take up a lot of physical space. Homes were confined to the valleys and lower slopes. She depleted her gas tank checking for Kemp's rental and came up empty. When she saw Rick's ID pop on her phone, she was prepared for him to tell her Kemp had left the area.

Rick did that and dropped a bombshell. "Kemp returned his rental to the Denver airport and flew to Iron Mountain, Michigan. Arrived last night and rented a pickup with a hitch. I'm working on getting warrants for his credit cards and phones. What do you think he's up to that he wants a hitch?"

Her stomach lurched. She had already alerted Seamus that Kemp was missing. Him being in the U.P. jacked the danger from DEFCON 3 to DEFCON 1. She was a day behind him. A day in which anything could happen. "Where are we on getting information on Kemp's partner?"

Rick released a long stream of frustrated air. "Far as I know, nowhere. There's a reason you get things done while the bureaucracy pushes paper."

She pulled into a gas station to fill the tank. "Okay, Rick. Let me know if you hear anything else."

"For sure. What are you going to do?"

"If I don't tell you, you won't have to lie." *And pray I'm not too late.*

THE HAPPY REAPER

THE HAPPY REAPER HAD NOT felt this well in days. The oxygen he'd been sucking down had something to do with it. And the crisp autumn day, sunlight bouncing off the snow like it was a mirror. He figured the biggest reason for his increased endorphins came from his renewed sense of purpose.

Seamus and Colleen were good thinkers and smart, but they had a flaw. They thought like rational and decent humans. He thought like a trained killer. That's why his gut said Kemp was making a move to eliminate Seamus, probably because the other imposter didn't approve.

Using the ATV to save steps and energy, he scouted McCree's property from an assassin's perspective. Looking for the best places to set up his shot. Shooting lanes to the target were important. So were ease of entry to the selected spot and the ability to escape if things went sideways.

To his surprise, he agreed with Kemp's choice: waiting under the evergreen near the head of the driveway was the best location if your plan was to ambush Seamus leaving his house. And unless you had inside information about Seamus's movements, that strategy made perfect sense.

He wasn't sure if Kemp was skilled to have chosen that spot or just lucky. Either way, the guy had proved he was impatient and changed plans midstream. A good plan took just as long as it took. Rushing it led to errors. Given Kemp's impatience, how would he react if Seamus stayed inside his house?

Kemp might try to shoot Seamus in the house. Two places had obvious appeal for a shot through windows. He had proved already that the top of the hill had easy access and suitable cover. But it provided clear views only at the upstairs bathroom window and the downstairs room the Happy Reaper was using. Seamus was not in danger from that spot. Kemp would grow frustrated and seek a better location. Conclusion: no reason for the Happy Reaper to waste time counteracting that scenario.

From the edge of the vernal pond, Kemp could find excellent views deep into the house through the dining-room windows. Melting snow would make the pond wet, a minor inconvenience. Getting there required Kemp to move past the guest cabin. The driveway into the cabin had lots of tracks, and Kemp could not be certain no one was staying there. That might be sufficient risk to put him off.

It might not, though. To prevent Kemp from considering the vernal pond, the Happy Reaper had to make the approach appear not just risky, but treacherous. Something to consider.

But that was a minor issue. The larger concern was to develop a workable strategy to surveil the place that Kemp had chosen, with its shooting lane down the driveway. Examining it again, he decided the upper branches of a nearby sugar maple provided a fine and relatively safe shooting platform. Nothing else with a direct bead on the evergreen was safe. Before this heart crap, he could have free-climbed the tree and sat up there all day. The good old days.

Seamus could no more climb the tree than he could. That meant if the Happy Reaper didn't kill Kemp before he reached the evergreen, Colleen had to do it from the tree. He could set obstacles to steer Kemp toward an ambush site of the Happy Reaper's choosing. That didn't mean Kemp would cooperate. Colleen had to agree to his plan or he was screwed, and McCree's house would be a trap they must flee.

He sucked in a long breath. Felt like a basset hound was lying on his chest. Time to tap that oxygen. But before he did, he had one more thing to do.

SEAMUS

COLLEEN AND I WERE SITTING near the fire, discussing our options, given Kemp had left Aspen yesterday and flown to Iron Mountain. Our points of disagreement focused on whether to turn in the Happy Reaper, let him loose to fend for himself, or take him with us to a not-yet-defined safe location.

That discussion stopped mid-word when the Happy Reaper entered the house carrying three automatic rifles, his grin splitting his face. "From your conversation, I take it the imposter is on his way."

How long had he been listening and where had he gotten those guns? I asked the second question.

He laid the rifles on the table. "One for each of us. You didn't think I'd keep all my toys where you could find them, did you? Congratulations, Seamus, you got Kemp where we want him. I've spent the last hour analyzing how to spring the trap. Just a few last details to resolve."

I glanced at Colleen to gauge how close she was to exploding. To my surprise, her head tilted in interest, a quizzical expression on her face. "Do tell," she said.

Getting him talking was smart—even though hell could freeze before Colleen and I would agree to his plan. The Happy Reaper presented his conclusions and his proposal of how to limit Kemp's choices and force him to do what he wanted.

As he described his plan to kill Kemp, my stomach clenched and threatened to spew breakfast. But my curiosity about how a killer thought had me sitting on the edge of my seat. Colleen smiled at each of his points, which seemed to encourage him, his enthusiasm for his plans evidenced by his rapid speech and wild gesticulation.

"And the last few details?" Colleen prompted.

"If he makes it to his spot under the evergreen, the best place to shoot him is from a maple tree that overlooks the top of the driveway. You're the only one of us who can climb it." He gestured, indicating he was open to her response.

How could the guy think Colleen would agree? More to the point, what would he do when she rejected him? He had the guns. Were these our last few minutes of life? I felt strangely peaceful.

The Happy Reaper added what he must have thought was a clinching argument. "We kill Kemp, I'll release you of any obligations to me and drive away from here. The FBI will get the second imposter, or I'll have others do it. Either way, we're square. You have enough worries without me adding to your burdens."

Colleen gnawed at her lip. "You believe him?"

"Yeah, but you're not—"

"I will. And I'll tell you why. I know you don't believe in the death penalty, but I do. Anyone who plans in cold blood to murder someone should die for it. Doesn't matter if they succeed. In my book, Kemp deserves to die."

To the Happy Reaper she added, "You don't have to worry about giving me a gun and me killing you, too. Seamus should have done it when he had the chance. If he had, we wouldn't be here. But I respect Seamus too much to break the pact you two have."

Fixing me with her steel-blue eyes, she said, "And since I believe Kemp should die, I have no right to say I won't be his executioner. That's like politicians sending other people's kids to war and making sure their own progeny never get near harm's way—or worse, profit from it. They're spineless." She shook her head in disgust.

"Smith's plan can work with tweaks. I can and will pull the trigger. We'll rid ourselves of Kemp. Then we'll retrieve Smith's car from wherever you hid it and off he goes. I have complete confidence that Niki will soon uncover the second imposter. You and I beat the charges in court. I go to Boston to the job and the woman I love. You get back to giving your granddaughter the legacy you hope for her." Her steel-blue eyes burned with the passion of conviction. "If we're voting, it's two to one against you, Seamus."

On her deathbed, my friend Lt. Tanya Hastings, Cincinnati's first woman to head homicide, had challenged me to tell myself every morning that "I am responsible only for my own actions, not anyone else's reactions." Some mornings I remembered to contemplate those words, other mornings I forgot. Now was an excellent time to keep focused on my response, not on how Colleen and the Happy Reaper reacted.

I had killed people when I thought I had no choice. And each time, my soul darkened. This was worse. I had a logical alternative. I could drive off and try to protect my family from whatever retribution the Happy Reaper sought. That course had been open to me for some time. By not taking it, I had made this situation worse.

Regardless of what I did, the two of them would stay and kill or be killed. Despite the wisdom of Tanya Hasting's mantra, no matter my choice, that blood was on me.

Unless I stayed and provided Kemp every opportunity to leave or give himself up.

Decision made, I agreed to help only if we made it clear to Kemp that we were prepared for his arrival by putting every possible impediment in his way. If he took the hints and departed, Rick and the FBI would soon have him.

If he stayed the course, it was him or us. I would do my damnedest to make sure it was him, even if I had to pull the trigger.

TYLER

TYLER REQUIRED SEVERAL TRIES USING the backup camera to line up the rental truck's hitch with the trailer that carried the side-by-side. The manager of the place showed him how to lock down the hitch, connect the electronics to link the trailer's lights to the truck's. Lesson complete, the two walked around to the rear of the trailer. The manager demonstrated how to convert the rear gate into a trailer ramp. Easy enough, just a couple of pins.

"Store the clip with the pin," the owner said. "I put them in the glove compartment. That way, I know where they are." He showed how to secure the side-by-side onto the trailer bed with tie-downs. "You want to try, or are you all set?"

"Think I got it. And if I decide to keep it an extra day, you'll put it on my card."

"Yep, but the next reservation for this UTV starts Wednesday at five. Make sure it's back before then. Key's in the ignition and the tank's full."

"I'm a little confused," Tyler said. "You called it a UTV, but your website uses the term side-by-side."

"Same difference. UTV stands for Utility Task Vehicle. Ours have space for more than one rider to sit side-by-side and people call them that. I use UTV because it's quicker. Most people think of them as side-by-sides, so that's how we advertise them. Remember, with that trailer attached, you make wide turns."

"Thanks. Since no one's sitting at my side, I'll follow your approach and call it an UTV."

They shook and the guy gave the truck a friendly pat. "Drive safe."

Tyler cautiously exited the lot, the warning concerning wide turns ringing in his ear. An S-curve in Florence, Wisconsin gave him a chance to practice before his full left at an intersection in Crystal Falls. He made it through Amasa and onto The Grade, having run over only one curb and that with only one tire. Not bad, but it convinced him not to try backing with the trailer attached.

He recalled passing a wide triangle intersection where the Grade split with the A Grade and parked on the triangle's base at the edge of the road. Ten minutes later, he had the UTV zipping up the A Grade toward McCree's place. Figured he'd do a reconnaissance drive-by, then after full dark he'd bring his weapon and slip into the spot he'd found with the excellent sight lines.

That plan died when he discovered a Bobcat skidsteer blocking the road less than a mile from McCree's place. No one was around and the engine was barely warm to the touch. Walking to find the owner could expose him to more observation than he wanted. No biggie. He and his buggy would go around the lake and approach McCree's place from the other direction.

Which worked fine until he hit locked gates blocking the road. What he wouldn't give for a pair of bolt cutters. He could buy them in Crystal Falls at the grocery/hardware store he had passed. That meant storing the UTV on the trailer and schlepping twenty miles each way. And could he avoid backing up? Screw that.

The UTV came with a winch. He examined the two gates held shut with a locked chain. The pins holding the right gate to the post wobbled a little when he shook it. He spooled out the cable, wound it around the gate, and worked on destroying the weak link.

An hour later, the gate slightly bent but unbroken, and his neck sore from the whiplash he'd caused, he gave up and considered his options. GPS said it was three and a half miles on the road from here to McCree's. Seven miles total. Fourteen if he scouted and retraced the route to get into place to kill McCree. It was comfy now, but temps were supposed to drop tonight, and that was a hell of a lot of walking. He'd wait for nightfall, park somewhere near that Bobcat, regardless of whether it was still there, and walk to his sniper's nest.

Tyler thought of being snug under that evergreen, crosshairs centered on McCree's chest, slowly putting pressure on the trigger. Despite his desire to act the pro, he could not wipe the smile off his face.

CHARLENE

CHARLENE USED HER COP FACE to hide her surprise when Zach's mother said her son's boss had asked him to attend a meeting in Philadelphia. He was driving there straight from his LARP and planned to be home sometime late Monday night.

She had dropped in on Zach to confirm he had nothing on his computers and to get his take on a Google Alert she'd received to the effect that Erlanger, Kentucky police had responded to a call and found a Mr. Porwall dead in "suspicious circumstances." Zach had never mentioned any Philly-area clients that she recalled. This sudden change in plans did not sit well. Had Zach only taken his normal LARP gear with him? Or was the whole LARP trip a ruse?

While Mrs. Canon rambled, she hmmed and uh-huhed and spent her brain power deciding her approach to get Mrs. Canon to let her into Zach's room. When Mrs. Canon talked herself silent, she said, "Gosh, Mrs. Canon, Zach had invited me to play with his VR headset while he was off LARPing. I haven't had a chance until now. Will that be okay?" She put a look on her face that suggested that it was the most natural thing in the world.

Mrs. Canon patted her cheek. "Of course, dear. Herb and I are off to visit our grandkids. You know where snacks are. Grab whatever you want to drink from the refrigerator. You'll lock up after yourself?"

She promised.

Down the stairs, but before entering Zach's basement room, she pulled nitrile gloves from her purse and snapped them on. At first, she only looked, making mental notes of what was missing or moved since she'd last been in the room. Zach's new laptop and burner phone weren't there. No surprise. His missing gun case *was* a surprise. She unlocked his gun safe using the combination he had once used in her presence: the European style day-month-year of his birthday.

Most of his guns and a third of his ammo were missing.

Damnation. Zach had gone rogue and killed Porwall. This was going off the rails. She could apologize if he got away with it. If he didn't, she had a short window to eliminate everything she could find that linked her to Zach.

Starting with the burner she had brought with her. She wiped it down and dumped it in a drawer where Zach had kept his own burner phone, which she noted was missing.

She searched the entire basement for anything that could lead cops to her. The only thing she found was a picture of the three of them he had stuck in a drawer.

That left his computers—four big ones and his previous laptop.

She used her phone to learn how to scrub Linux system hard drives, followed the instructions on all four machines. He surely had everything stored in the cloud, but she didn't know enough to eliminate that. If Zach confronted her, she'd claim she was overly cautious because he was gone for longer than expected.

God only knew what was on his laptop. She booted up the old one and was delighted when it used the same password she had seen Zach use for his new one. She opened the Find My app and discovered Zach had modified the standard Apple app to provide current *and past* locations for the old laptop, his new Mac, his phone, and three AirTags. The old laptop was here, and everything else other than one AirTag was moving near Marquette, Michigan. What?

The current location was less than two hours' drive from Seamus McCree's home and past pings showed Zach was heading in that direction. First Porwall and now heading toward McCree. *The crazy bastard is on a killing spree.*

She went to close the app, and the oddball AirTag that showed "out of range" sprang to mind. She zoomed in to discover it had last pinged at Tall Pines Grocery in Amasa, Michigan. It had been in Iron Mountain, Michigan earlier that day, and before that, in Denver and Aspen, Colorado.

A jolt of pain blazed behind her eyes. She let loose a string of curses that would make her sergeant blush. She'd bet a million bucks, if she had them, that AirTag was with Tyler. That was what she had seen Zach slip into Tyler's backpack when they were last at her place.

The out-of-range made sense. Zach used an iPhone, which updated his location whenever his phone connected to a network. Tyler's phone was Android. The AirTag he was unknowingly carrying around required an Apple product in its vicinity to ping its location. The last place Zach had crossed paths with an Apple device must have been several hours earlier at Tall Pines.

Those two were scheming behind her back to do McCree.

But wait. If they were in it together, why had Zach hidden that AirTag in Tyler's backpack? Maybe they *weren't* working together. Either way, neither of them had wanted her to know he was homing in on McCree.

Which, if one or both succeeded, didn't much matter. She'd sever her ties and wish them luck. But if they didn't succeed. Oh, God, what did Zach have in the cloud? And on his new laptop?

If she grabbed the computers, could the police still find his cloud-based stuff? She had no clue, but what would she do with the computers?

She could burn down the house. That would destroy the computers.

And destroy Mr. and Mrs. Canon. Having *that* idea was worrisome in the extreme. She was not the kind of person who would harm an innocent, even if it was to keep her own butt safe.

The Canons weren't due back for hours. She had time to perform a thorough search. She tapped walls and floors for hidden storage, pushed up ceiling tiles, checked behind furniture and pictures. The only thing she found was Zach's stash of porn.

She checked the Find My app to see what had changed. Zach was now in the woods south of Michigamme, a half hour from McCree's place. No change for the other AirTag. She would "borrow" Zach's old computer to keep track of those AirTags.

Wait. Tracking works both ways. If she could follow them, Zach—or any police organization—could follow the laptop. That she did not want. She wiped the laptop's hard drive and put the hunk of useless metal where she had originally found it.

She was officially flying blind.

ZACH

ZACH TOUCHED THE METAL OVER the Bobcat's engine. Colder than air temperature. The skidsteer had been blocking the road for some time. His intuition told him it was intentional, and McCree knew Tyler was coming. Tyler had clearly screwed up. How was not his current concern. He checked his phone to see if Tyler's AirTag had pinged anything since Tall Pines. Nada.

Marks in the dirt and gravel showed one vehicle had arrived at this spot before him and turned around. Zach kicked himself for not paying more attention to vehicle tracks on his way in. He reversed direction. This time he observed, in addition to his own tracks, the two sets left by the one vehicle coming in and leaving. At the head of the lake where Shank Lake Road intersected Lukes Road, the number of tracks doubled.

He used his phone to take pictures of the tracks, compared them, and concluded the same vehicle had left them all. Using the pattern of overlapping tracks, he decided the vehicle had driven from the A Grade down Shank Lake Road to the skidsteer, reversed course and followed Lukes Road. Sometime later, it returned on Lukes Road and kept going toward the A Grade.

Whether Tyler or someone else, the individual was no longer around. Zach followed the tracks up Lukes Road, discovered an abused gate with the road in front of it torn all to hell. Fresh scars on the gate made him think the Bobcat had frustrated whoever he was following, and when this gate stopped him, he'd tried to pull it down.

That sure sounded like Tyler. If Tyler was smart, he'd ditch the idea of killing McCree. The AirTag would ping and show he was long gone when it eventually met a connected Apple product. A dumb Tyler, however, meant he could still be in this great wilderness, biding his time until dark to move into position at McCree's place. Under that scenario, it didn't matter whether he'd been following Tyler's tracks or someone else pissed off at the obstruction. Zach's original plan to clean up any Tyler screw-ups still held.

Nothing said Zach couldn't wait to see who came to move the Bobcat. Wouldn't that frost Tyler's cake if Zach nailed McCree? The thought made his heart go pitter-patter, as his mother would say.

He found a driveway off Luke's Road near the head of the lake and backed his rental in until it was invisible from the road. He dressed in warm layers, slipped foot warmers into his boots, and hand warmers in his pockets. Still nothing from the AirTag. He adjusted the helmet with the infrared scope to allow him to swing the scope in place to help after dark. He beeped the vehicle locked and hiked to a spot where he sat and watched the Bobcat.

Sunset triggered him to eat six energy bars for dinner. Dark settled in. Zach gave up on McCree coming to move the Bobcat, and a new thought brought him a moment of anxiety. Tyler may have gone to town to purchase a bolt cutter or hack saw or something to force open the abused gate and allow him to drive around the lake and get to McCree's place. He hadn't heard any vehicles, but would he? Zach retreated to the head of the lake. No new tracks on Luke's Road. Relief flushed his system of tension.

He settled into a spot where he could observe anything moving on either Shank Lake Road or Lukes Road. He'd give Tyler until midnight or the first sign of the missing AirTag. No way Tyler had the patience to wait longer than that.

SEAMUS

I LOOKED IN THE MIRROR at my camouflaged face and neck. The swirls of white, gray, green, and brown made my cheeks nearly unrecognizable. The Happy Reaper had painted my face using Niki's supplies that I'd found in the basement. My neck blended with the mossy oak bug shirt I wore on top of two wool layers I hoped would keep me warm through the long night. He'd painted my tan pants white and gray to blend in with the remaining snow on the ground.

What did I want to happen tonight? Best case, Kemp would see our preparations and leave. All that would cost us was an uncomfortable night in the woods. Second best, he came in from a direction that allowed me to shout one last warning before he reached a spot where either the Happy Reaper or Colleen could shoot him. I forced myself to admit that if he'd ignored all the other signs, the likelihood that he'd listen to my warning and leave was damned miniscule. Still, I had to try.

Worst case—I didn't want to think about worst cases. I reviewed the preparations one more time, looking for holes.

The Happy Reaper had prepared a detailed plan. Scary how that guy thinks. I suggested minor modifications based on my local knowledge, successful use of trail cameras to provide early warning of trespassers, and a previous failed attempt to prevent bad people from driving down the road to my house. We batted around ideas and agreed on a plan.

Colleen, following my instructions, blocked Shank Lake Road with my Bobcat. The spot I chose was a half mile from my house and featured a steep ravine on one side of the road. The other side dropped into a gooey marsh that would swallow any vehicle, including a Sherman tank. Locked gates, strategically placed boulders, and downed trees that had already been in place and would take hours of chainsaw work to clear, blocked all other vehicle approaches to my property. If he came, it would have to be on foot.

The Happy Reaper had structured impediments to persuade a walking Kemp—assuming he did not see them and retreat—to make choices we preferred and funnel him into areas we could cover.

The Bobcat barricade met its first test that afternoon. The trail camera I had installed sent pictures of a stopped UTV. Not a UTV I recognized, but on a Sunday, it could have been a bird hunter or someone scouting for deer sign three weeks before the opening of rifle season. Its male driver got out, surveyed the area, and left.

The closer we got to sunset, the more I worried. I stared hard at the image in the mirror. Had we thought of everything? I'm sure we had not. *Had I done everything I could to prevent Kemp's death?* The mirror refused to comment.

My leg ached from the day's exertion. The spot the Happy Reaper chose for me was in the woods on the opposite side of the road from the lake. I'd bundle in warm clothes, tuck my legs into a sleeping bag, and have at my side my phone, a battery-powered million-candlepower light, and crutches. And a rifle loaded with a full magazine. When the time came to move, would I be able to maneuver the crutches to walk the dark woods without falling?

Colleen would wait strapped high in the maple Smith had chosen. She continued to maintain that she could and would take the shot. Saying and doing are two different things when a human is the target. Although her father had trained her to be a fine shot, hours in a tree would stiffen her muscles and give her icy hands. She'd be a sitting target if she missed.

The Happy Reaper assigned himself the perfect ambush site if he had correctly predicted how Kemp would react to the impediments we'd placed in his path. It all sounded good while we discussed it, but humans are, by nature, unpredictable when stressed. If nothing else, the impediments should stress Kemp.

At some point, the Happy Reaper would disconnect himself from his supplemental oxygen to eliminate the machine's sound. With temps dropping into the teens, would he remain alert through the snowy night to make an accurate shot?

I could think of nothing else we could do to prepare. Time to face the night, and my thoughts, my fears, and maybe Tyler Kemp.

* * *

I WAS COLD AND BORED for the first three hours of our vigil in the woods until my cellphone vibrated in my front pocket. The trail camera at the Bobcat roadblock showed a triptych of a side-by-side similar to the one that had been around that afternoon. One driver, no passengers. I triggered the camera to take more pictures, and followed the individual, partially obscured by the UTV, walking past the Bobcat.

Could not tell if that person carried weapons.

I mentally repeated the signals I had devised to let the Happy Reaper and Colleen know we had an intruder arriving: From Bobcat and the south, Barred Owl. From the north, Bobwhite. I sucked on my tongue to create saliva to moisten my parched mouth, formed a megaphone with my hands, and hooted a reasonable version of a barred owl's call.

What would Kemp do when he saw the lights? If he ignored them and walked the road at a brisk walking pace, it would still take him seven minutes to arrive. Hopefully, the lights would convince him to give up. At a minimum, they would slow him down. I coached myself to relax.

My body was having none of it, going on full alert to hear a twig crack or sense any movement in the woods.

Four minutes later, my cellphone vibrated again. It worked! He'd seen the lights and retreated. Hold your horses, Seamus. That seems a little too quick.

I scrambled open the app. The three pictures showed a person *heading in*. This person walked between the camera and the UTV. He wore what I guessed was IR headgear and carried an AR-profile weapon. I pulled up the earlier pictures. Definitely different people—the first guy took up much more space than the second. I repeated my barred owl call, sounding it twice to signify two individuals coming from the south.

Our discussions had covered how to deal with Kemp. We'd briefly considered the complication of dealing with two people who stayed together. We had not anticipated a scenario that involved two people arriving separately. Maybe we'd be lucky and the second would catch up with the first. They could both still turn around, and if they didn't, they might walk together into the trap we had set. That scenario would allow me to shout my demand for them to surrender.

What are the chances of that? By starting separately, they were being more tactical. The Happy Reaper had thought the imposter would loop around the lake and arrive from the north. If not that, he'd avoid the light and take to the woods to circle around. If Kemp went down to the lake in front of the house, he'd funnel into the Happy Reaper's area. I was waiting if Kemp approached using the woods on the other side of the road.

Did tactical include also sending someone around the lake? I had received no warning pictures from the northern trail camera. My luck, it would stop working. It responded to my signal to take a picture with a perfect image of empty woods.

The Happy Reaper had insisted that once we were in position, we must remain in place. Anything else risked the strong possibility of friendly-fire casualties. Yet I thought it was important to consult with him on how to handle these two. Every second I delayed was another second the invaders drew closer.

I checked the time: seven minutes had elapsed since the first person had triggered the camera. He could be close enough to hear anything I said. Shit. Shit. Shit. I put my hands behind my ears and rotated my head to pick up any sound.

My phone vibrated again.

Same camera. The first frame showed a person approaching directly. The second frame caught the individual several steps closer, a gun barrel protruding past his body. That silhouette reminded me of someone. I held my breath waiting for the third picture to resolve on my phone screen.

Gone.

I did my barred owl routine again, now signaling three people. But that didn't do justice to how screwed up this was with three separate intruders. I transitioned from hoots to a loon rain call. Since we had not talked about loon calls, I hoped it would alert them to something strange going on.

I tried the hands-behind-the-ears trick again. All I heard was the pounding of my heart.

ZACH

AN ENGINE'S RUMBLE ALERTED ZACH to an approaching vehicle. To avoid its headlights blinding him, he flipped up the night-vision goggles through which he had been watching a porcupine in shades of green. A utility vehicle puttered by, driven by a big guy—large enough to be Tyler. Zach jogged after the vehicle jouncing up the road, its suspension creaking in protest at the bumps. He lost sight of the red taillights and was relieved when the engine noises went silent.

Zach moved to the edge of the road and slowed to a walk, not wanting anyone to see or hear him in the now quiet woods. He flipped the goggles in place and soon reached the parked UTV. Once he was past it and the Bobcat, he spotted a Sasquatch carrying a long gun at the top of a rise in the road. Beyond Tyler—surely it was Tyler—was a hint of lights in the forest. Zach attributed them to the cabin 3/8ths of a mile before McCree's place.

Pulling up his mental map of the area, he realized that couldn't be. Tyler's current position had to be close to the cabin that occupied a clearing tight by the road and only 220 yards away. These lights were more distant and encompassed a broader area. Had to be from McCree's property.

First the Bobcat blockade, now the lights. They absolutely, positively knew Tyler was coming.

He put his hands to his mouth to yell to Tyler to abort his mission.

Don't be stupid, an inner voice coaxed. Tyler was more likely to shoot him than thank him.

With each step, Zach felt his resolution strengthen. If Tyler pulled this off, fine. He'd offer his congratulations, take his share of the money, and call the business complete. The one thing that he wanted to prevent—must prevent—was for McCree or anyone else to capture Tyler.

The crack of a snapped twig behind him sent Zach's heart into full throttle. He spun around, cursing himself. Just like Tyler, he had neglected to watch his back. His headlamp caught eyes shining a half-foot above the ground. He relaxed. Humans didn't have eye shine. The snowshoe hare hopped off.

He returned his attention to Tyler.

Gone.

Zach froze mid-step.

Silently lowered his foot to the ground. Took slow, silent breaths and willed his heart to stop pounding. No movement ahead. Underneath the dub-dub of his heart, he sensed a low thrum. An engine?

Standing still wouldn't accomplish anything. He was here because Tyler was here. Forward.

Zach followed Tyler's path past the dark cabin close to the road. There, Tyler's tracks, visible in the remaining snow, veered into the woods, eventually leading to the top of a hill. From there Zach glimpsed the real-life version of McCree's rustic cabin he had seen while studying satellite photos of the area. The low thrum had resolved into multiple sources. A nearby portable generator lit the cabin interior. A truck with doors open, lights on, and engine running sat closer to the road. Its lights, combined with cabin light spilling onto the surrounding snow, created a massive kill zone.

He knew from the satellite photos that McCree's house was beyond the intervening low hill. That area was lit like a sports stadium.

Tyler's trail veered off toward the darkness of the lake. In Zach's online war games, defenders used light to make it easy to see invaders, hard for invaders to see in, and had the effect of encouraging attackers to use the "safer" areas of darkness.

His chest constricted with foreboding. Tyler was walking into a trap. Zach could not succumb to the same trap if he was to ensure Tyler didn't talk if they caught him.

Reluctantly, he let Tyler go and retreated into darkness. When it felt safe, he crossed Shank Lake Road and looped deep into the woods to approach the north end of McCree's property from that safe route. He used his night-vision headgear and scanned ahead for any hidden people or booby traps.

A careful forty-five minutes, during which Sunday ended and Monday began, brought Zach to the top of a hill that commanded the area where McCree's driveway exited onto the road. He used the rifle's night scope and found an evergreen that matched Tyler's description of the place he planned to hide and wait for his kill shot. Not there yet.

Monday, October 24, 2022

The Happy Reaper

THE HAPPY REAPER WAS IN his happy place. Colleen had followed his instructions and had aligned the two vehicles to shine their lights on Shank Lake Road, both north and south of the spot he was sure Kemp planned to use to gun down McCree. If he were Kemp and saw those lights, he would bug out immediately. But if he were Kemp, he wouldn't be here. Rule one: if you don't control the situation, you leave. Which was why he would never bring two other people onto the scene. Plus, whatever that loon call meant.

Although, come to think of it, he was working with Seamus and Colleen. Showed he was flexible. Just like he agreed to Colleen's suggestion to keep him on oxygen. She had helped him drag the portable oxygen to where he waited in ambush, and he plugged in. At the sound of the first owl call, he had shut down the machine and stowed it next to a tree.

The intruders were taking their time—it had been more than an hour since Seamus's third set of hoots. Or they had left, and he was freezing his butt for no reason, slowly becoming covered by the snow flurries. His instinct said they were still coming. Time was when he could lie still for hours without feeling any discomfort. Now everything hurt. Some more than —

The brush of cloth on a branch brought him to focus. In his peripheral vision, he caught movement through the screen of the flurries: shadow in shadow. Could be human. Could be a deer. He relaxed his muscles and silently drew in a breath through his nose.

Aftershave.

The dark form moved cautiously on the exact trajectory he had anticipated Kemp would take. He raised the rifle. Aimed center chest. Squeezed the trigger. Felt the jolt of the recoil. Heard the rifle's bang and the target's scream. Watched the body drop, followed by caterwauling and thrashing on the ground.

How the hell had he not killed the guy? He looked at the betraying gun. He should have test-fired it. How to proceed? If their places were switched, he'd lay there silent, plotting how to kill whoever had shot him. He shook his head. The guy's crying was one more reason Kemp, or whoever this was, had no reason to think he could replace the Happy Reaper.

He'd admit Seamus was right: killing this asshole was too good for him. Let him rot in prison. See how he liked it.

In a clear, low voice, he said, "I'm coming to administer first aid. Try anything and you die."

The Happy Reaper kept his finger on the trigger, ready to pull it if the guy made any move toward his fallen weapon. He slid his feet along the ground to avoid tripping and followed his pointed rifle. His right toe detected a fallen branch. To create a solid stance, he drew his left foot under him and—

Someone punched his gut.

The Happy Reaper sat, though he had no recollection of the process of transitioning from standing to sitting. *Shot. Fully automatic burst. Not close.*

The guy he'd wounded was dead silent. Nothing nearby moved, and he heard nothing beyond a dull ringing in his ears. He removed his glove and probed through the hole in the front of his coat. His finger found warm liquid spilling from his stomach, the entry wound smaller than his finger tip.

Bad, but not too bad.

He gritted his teeth against the pain and lay on his side, resting the rifle on the ground. He twisted his bare hand under his coat. Wetter than the front. He pushed his thumb higher and found blood pooling from a hole more than an inch wide.

Nothing spurting. Who was he kidding? If he were a betting man, he'd give good odds that he would not see the sun rise.

ZACH

ZACH FOUND A HIGH STUMP that made a perfect stool and waited for Tyler to show up at the spot he had chosen for his lair to take his shot at McCree. The lights around McCree's house gave the surrounding area a glow, but under the evergreen it remained dark. It was still a suitable spot. Without the night-vision gear, he couldn't have seen if Tyler was hiding or not.

He'd had no problem quietly waiting before he snuffed out Kevin Porwall's lousy excuse of a life. So why was he having trouble staying awake? Sure, he'd been up for hours, but he should be excited, maybe even antsy, not jerking his head to keep it from hitting his chest.

One big difference was that at Porwall's, he'd been following a narrative he had created. Here he had none. If he treated this like a LARP with Tyler and Seamus McCree and himself live-playing their roles, they'd each have freedom of action, but within the context of the narrative.

Good. So, Zach, let's create some narratives. Say, Tyler gets smart and leaves. Zach, not knowing Tyler is gone, stoically sits on a stump all night. When the sun rises, Zach must decide whether to leave or stay and do the job for Tyler. The boring night left him possibilities to exercise judgment and strategy come daylight.

In another, Tyler kills McCree and escapes. Also boring; leaving Zach nothing to do but successfully escape himself. In a third, Tyler screws up, either before or after killing McCree, and is captured. Not boring. Zach must play terminator, killing off whoever captured Tyler, or eliminating Tyler from the game to protect himself and Charlene. His blood warmed thinking through those possibilities. He controls a weapon that can discharge an entire magazine in a few seconds. And he has plenty of ammo. No reason to be fussy. Kill them all. Or kill Tyler. Or both.

He could picture it: Tyler being held by one or two people, and Zach, kneeling to provide a steady aim, loosing a magazine worth of projectiles taking them all down. Oh yeah, and he'd quickly discard the used magazine, ram in a replacement that he had ready at his feet and be prepared for anyone who dared challenge him.

Now that was a narrative! He did a body scan. He was no longer tired. Okay, Zach. Let's see where that story takes you.

He inched a magazine from his pocket and laid it on the ground between his boots.

SEAMUS

I PRAYED MY CELLPHONE WOULD buzz with a picture showing all three invaders leaving. Minutes passed, nothing. They were still coming. I was waiting in an increasing screen of snow flurries that made it more difficult to hear and see what was in front of me.

Even tucked into a sleeping bag rated to -20F, the cold slowly seeped in, finding my weak points: my leg wound and the finger on my left hand I had once frostbitten. My leg pain reached four on the pain scale of zero to ten that doctors are fond of using. I walled that pain off into a mental compartment I could mostly ignore.

The finger was more exposed. When its pain reached seven, I pulled off my glove and buried that hand in my crotch to warm it up.

A rifle crack and a man's scream of pain jerked me back to the present. The sounds came from the area in which the Happy Reaper lay in wait. One imposter down? Or was the Happy Reaper down? I squinted through the flurries, finding nothing in front of me, and for no reason other than to do something, counted seconds, like I was waiting for thunder after lightning.

At nine, a burst of automatic gunfire tore into the night from a spot not a hundred yards away from me. I cradled the rifle with my left arm, grabbed the million-candlepower light with my right, and pointed it toward the muzzle flash. I rested the light on my knees and thumbed on the switch. Brilliant light exploded like a sun. Through squinted eyes, I spotted a kneeling individual wearing night goggles, sideways to me, hands jamming a magazine into a rifle.

I used both hands to aim the rifle and ripped off two quick shots. The gun recoiled into my shoulder and dumped the light upside down in the snow. I clenched the rifle to my side, and legs still entombed in the sleeping bag, rolled down the hill to avoid return fire. A stump jarred my funny bone and stopped my tumble. I extracted my legs from the sleeping bag and pulled myself behind the snag—not that it would provide cover against bullets.

I was in a pickle. I couldn't hear him coming down the hill because the shots had deafened me. I couldn't see anything more than a couple feet away because I'd obliterated my night vision. My frostbit finger ached, but that was nothing compared to my elbow, which suffered with the ferocity of a gazillion bee stings. That pain gradually disappeared, replaced by my leg awakening to the abuse I had subjected it to. It throbbed with each heartbeat. I gently patted the injured area. Not wet with blood, but I had ripped away the drain. Probably tore the stitches.

Nothing to do for it now other than acknowledge the injury and remain vigilant.

Minutes crawled past. My ungloved hand turned numb.

My cellphone vibrated. *They're leaving?* I tucked it deep inside my jacket to block its light when I thumbed it on. Not a trail cam picture. Colleen had texted *you alive?* Good question since we couldn't see each other from our current positions. I texted her a *yes* and to the Happy Reaper the same *You alive?* before I remembered he had argued against taking cell phones, calling them a distraction he would do without.

I thumbed a second response to Colleen: *We wait for light.* Colleen responded with a check.

Forty minutes later, a single shot sounded from the Happy Reaper's area. I texted Colleen. She was fine.

Little by little, my hearing and night vision returned. My leg pain decreased to the four it had been before I rolled down the hill. The only way I could stand the ache of my frostbitten finger was to keep it warming against my body.

At one point, I realized the snow had stopped falling. Later—much later, the eastern sky hinted at the sun's arrival. Still no pictures of anyone moving near the Bobcat or taking the parked UTV. The northern trail camera had caught no movement but still worked when I told it to take pictures.

Alive or dead, the gang was all here.

Another hour to wait until the sun poked its rays through the woods. And then what?

* * *

THE WOODS LIGHTENED IN THE pre-dawn, enough for me to discover blood had soaked through my leg bandage and created a fist-sized stain on my pant leg. Not good, but not fatal.

I leaned left and right to learn whether I could see where the shooter had been when I fired at him. Not without exposing myself to him—if he was still there. Why would he be? *For the same reason you froze yourself to the ground.* My minor movement woke muscles that responded with messages of distress. Suck it up, Seamus. You're still alive and this is nothing a hot shower and stretching won't fix. I texted Colleen, *Can you see anybody?*

She couldn't but noted that a fox had recently trotted by on the road. *Didn't look the least concerned.*

This might be one of those situations where the one to stand was the one shot. Something or someone had to break the stalemate. Another fifteen minutes passed with me on high alert and hearing nothing more than the call of two chickadees, I texted Colleen again: *Don't shoot me, I'm getting up to find out what happened.*

She responded, *I'm ready to provide cover.*

I left the sleeping bag next to the stump and elbow-crawled to a decent-sized maple. Using that for cover, I pulled myself into a kneel, stretching my injured leg behind me. Couldn't see jack. I pulled myself to standing and peeked around the side of the tree. A snow-dusted body lay face down, arms outstretched. A stubby rifle lay across its back.

I killed him.

Wait.

He didn't pose himself that way. Did one of the other guys find him and bait a trap?

Silence no longer worked to my advantage. I hollered, "Adam Smith, you alive?"

The body didn't twitch at my voice. Nor did the Happy Reaper reply. Was he dead? More cautious than I?

I didn't want to expose Colleen's presence and texted her. *Still nothing moving?*

Nada

What did I know? I had killed one of the three invaders. The gunfire coming from the area the Happy Reaper had chosen for his surveillance had comprised two shots together, followed much later by a single shot. I wanted to believe those shots had all come from the Happy Reaper, but just because the dead guy in front of me had let loose an entire magazine at a go, didn't mean one of the other two invaders wasn't more circumspect. And the Happy Reaper hadn't answered my query.

Curiosity killed the—

Not the expression I was looking for. Regardless, an irrepressible urge drove me to take charge. To let Colleen know what I was doing without exposing her, I pretended to yell to the Happy Reaper. "Adam, I'm checking what looks like a dead body."

Colleen texted me a checkmark. Good, she was on the same page.

I looked for my crutches and remembered I'd left them with the spotlight that had fallen off my lap and had run its battery down during the night. My initial place to wait was uphill and in the wrong direction. I converted a branch into a staff and inched my way to the body. This person was not sufficiently tall to be the guy who arrived in the UTV. Could be either of the other two. A ragged hole in his back, partially covered by the assault rifle, looked like an exit wound. I was wondering why someone placed the rifle on him when I noticed a neat small-caliber wound at the back of his head. Entry wound.

Someone had walked up to the wounded man and killed him. My stomach erupted. I barely missed the corpse with my vomit. Its smell elicited another stomach contraction that doubled me over. I dry-heaved twice more, scooped a handful of clean snow and soaked leaves, and rinsed my mouth of the acrid taste.

My phone vibrated with a new text from Colleen: *Smoke coming out the house chimney!!!*

SEAMUS

I WANTED IT TO BE the Happy Reaper who had laid a fire in the wood stove. That would explain why he didn't respond to my hollering. Problem was, my trail camera had recorded three people coming in, and zero departing. One was dead. But two were unaccounted for, and the UTV parked by the Bobcat remained at the side of the road. This could be a crafty way to lure me to the house.

I texted Colleen to stay in place until I reached her tree. The staff was working well enough that I temporarily abandoned the crutches, sleeping bag, and million-candlepower light and picked my way through the woods burdened only by the rifle.

Colleen met me at the base of the tree. The Happy Reaper had confirmed the two best spots to see inside my house from a distance were from the vernal pond and atop the hill between the road and the house. Colleen's perch had given her a view of the hill. She had seen no movement on it, meaning it was devoid of intruders, unless they had climbed it from the house side. We discussed the risk and decided it was safer than the longer approach to the vernal pond. I covered Colleen while she scrambled to the top of the hill.

She reported by text that the hill was clear. Somebody had walked up the house ramp to the screened porch, leaving a single set of footprints. Another set of footprints started at the mudroom door, circled the garage, proceeded to the generator shed, and returned to the house. That text got me to realize my big generator was silent. The generator used to power the cabin lights still ran. Under that purr, I caught my truck's engine still running in the cabin driveway.

Colleen reported she did not see any internal or external house lights on. The chimney smoke was white, meaning a hot fire. From what she could see, the vernal pond was clear, and no footprints had approached it from the house side.

That all made sense if the Happy Reaper was inside because he had been with me when I turned the generator on. But it didn't eliminate an intruder being the one who might have turned off the generator to hear better what was going on outside the house. Colleen agreed to cover me from the top of the hill while I looped around to the cabin and scrambled down the hill to the vernal pond.

I followed the fox's prints up the road to the cabin driveway. The snow on the driveway was devoid of any prints. So far, so good, although if I were hunting me, I'd stay off roads and driveways, too. I switched off my truck, whose headlights had played their part by lighting a patch of Shank Lake Road. At the cabin, I killed the generator, which extinguished the lamp we had placed inside to radiate light from all the cabin's windows.

The steps up to the cabin screened porch showed no new footprints, nor did I see any in my walk around the cabin. From there, I used a screen of balsam to shield me from the house and sneaked into the vernal pond. I positioned myself behind a substantial rock where I had excellent views to the house's south windows, kitchen porch, and a corner of its front deck.

I texted Colleen to let her know I was in place and received *yep I saw U.* In short order, I sensed movement inside. The inner mudroom door opened. An arm pushed open the storm door. My mink-fur winter hat appeared, pulled low on the guy's head. He was too short for the Happy Reaper and wore clothes I recognized were mine.

Not armed—at least not with a rifle. What to do?

I texted, *Unknown male exiting house.*

Colleen: *Yell if you want me to shoot*

The man backed through the door and pulled the inner door closed. I stowed my phone and sighted the rifle on him. I mentally urged him to move away from the house where Colleen could cover him while I yelled for him to surrender.

The individual closed the storm door, presented a profile of his hirsute face. I knew that third person had seemed familiar.

"Owen," I yelled. "Stay right there. Don't move or Colleen might shoot you."

Colleen scrambled down the hill, weapon at the ready. Owen greeted us with, "Lots ta tell ya. First, I gotta see a man about a horse."

Colleen spun this way and that, her rifle at the ready. "What's that mean? Is it safe? Are they all gone?"

Owen threw a "You betcha" over his shoulder.

I explained he had to take a leak and didn't believe in wasting water by using a toilet. To Owen's back, I asked, "Do you know where the Happy Reaper is?"

He waved in the direction where the Happy Reaper had stationed himself. "With his maker. Got breakfast ready for ya. Keeping it warm in the oven. Serve it up. I'll be right back." He must have caught my look of disbelief. "You need energy, Seamus. Go eat."

He ambled to the far side of the garage where he would take care of business. I had so hoped the Happy Reaper had been in the house that it took a moment for Owen's words to sink in. A sadness filled my chest, a feeling I had not had when I looked at the body of the attacker I'd shot. Wondering about those feelings had to wait until I had time to contemplate my navel. The current situation required a clear mind. The big guy who came in the UTV was still at large, and I had decisions—which if I screwed up would land me in prison for a long time.

* * *

COLLEEN AND I LEANED OUR guns against the wall in the corner where Owen had left his along with an old Army rucksack. Owen had the house heated to the high sixties. Stepping in from the cold, it felt like a sauna. Colleen handed me her coat to hang along with mine in the closet. "I want to change clothes. Be right down."

Colleen had either missed or decided not to comment on my blood-stained pants. Not wanting to mark the floors with my staff, I used the walls for support and made it to the bathroom, where I shucked my top layers and unwound the bandage. The exit wound looked fine. Bleeding at the entry wound had stopped, but the area looked inflamed, and several stitches had popped.

I slathered on antibiotic ointment, re-bandaged my leg, and swallowed two ibuprofen. Owen and Colleen were conversing in the dining area when I arrived. Owen had set the table for three. He had poured orange juice, and the coffeemaker burbled and hissed, finishing its process.

I hadn't realized how hungry I was until Owen opened the oven door and the aroma of bacon, sausage, and scrapple hit me. He must have brought the pork with him, because I didn't have any in the house.

He placed everything on hot pads. "Hope you don't mind my cookin for youse. Figured we got a shit ton of work to do and need full bellies. I hope, Colleen, that you ain't one of those vegetabletarians like Seamus's son."

Owen hadn't lost his knack for inventing words.

Once everyone had enjoyed their first forkful, I asked Owen to tell us what happened.

"Near as I can read the sign, the first of the guys wantin to kill you avoided all the lights you had on by goin down to the shoreline and cuttin past the house with the ideer of coming up from the far side." He waved toward the area the Happy Reaper had positioned himself. "I thought that Reaper fellow was supposed to be an excellent shot? Couldn't have been twenty-five yards away and all he did was shatter the guy's right shoulder."

Colleen said, "And the guy shot Adam?"

"Ah nope. That ain't it at all. The guy Seamus kilt had been sitting on a stump. Responding to the first shots, he knelt and sprayed a full magazine toward that general area. Obviously didn't care who was down there. Kilt the guy the Reaper shot. Relieved him from his misery in a hurry. The Reaper—now that's just tough luck. You know, I remember—"

I had no patience for one of Owen's shaggy dog stories and asked him to get to the point.

"Fine," Owen said, clearly disappointed. "Reaper got hisself gut shot. Didn't get no major artery, but he was gonna bleed out, sure as I'm standin here. I put him down."

I blurted, "You killed him?"

Owen put his fork down and gave me a hard stare. "No, Seamus. He was already dead. I did the decent thing and ended his earthly suffering. Even though he kilt Abigail, and I powerfully wanted to see him pay for it. He'll do that in hell for all eternity. I didn't do nothin I wouldn't do for any animal. What kind of person do you take me for?"

What kind indeed? I slid a glance at Colleen to gauge her reaction. She sliced a bite off a turkey sausage, dipped it in brown mustard, and sucked it off her fork. Maybe she was in shock? Maybe I was?

"You did the same thing to the guy I shot?"

"Hell no. You lit him up with that torch. The way I figure it, you musta shot just afore me. He was dropping by the time I pulled the trigger, which explains why I hit him in the head, not the heart. Seamus, that was some fine shootin. You're a man of many talents. Time to address the elephant we ain't talkin about. What we gonna do with them bodies?" He shoveled a forkful of scrapple into his mouth and smacked his lips. "Glad I thought of makin it when I seen your cornmeal."

The picture of the dead guy wouldn't go away. I set my fork across my plate. Owen's explanation made sense. I hadn't heard another shot to explain the hole in the guy's head. What to do with the bodies? I had not considered for a second calling the Iron County Sheriff's Office and reporting a dead body—not even after I learned the Happy Reaper and the second guy were also dead. But I had no plan. "Explain yourself."

"Welp, I was looking for pancake mix and then I seen—"

"No, Owen. The bodies?"

"Fastest thing is drag 'em deep into the tammy swamp. Critters will clean up the mess in no time. No one goes in there."

Not true. Both bears and I picked blueberries in tamarack swamps. And we weren't the only ones.

Colleen said, "Seamus, your mind is working, but I can't read the little bubble floating above your head."

Owen scratched his beard. "Say what?"

"He's thinking and not talking."

"Right." Owen shoveled in another forkful of scrapple. "He does that a lot."

"Okay, you two," I said. "Enough with the tag team comedy act. I agree we must dispose of the bodies. Colleen, all you did was sit in a tree all night. If you leave—say, safely to a Marquette motel—you're free of this mess. Owen's already on the lam. He returns to hiding. We wipe the weapons down and dump them in a river. Who's to say exactly what happened or where?"

Colleen threw up her hands in pantomimed exasperation. "First, you and I texted, remember? I'm linked. And second, given enough time, the cops will put it together. Remember, we sicced the FBI onto Kemp? We have to disappear the bodies, clean up the brass, get rid of their transportation, etcetera. Owen does his Owen thing, and you and I act like nothing happened."

"She's right," Owen said. "Snows already melting. It and the tracks will be gone soon. The thing . . ."

I stopped listening to Owen. Watergate didn't end badly for Nixon because of the initial break-in, but because he and his cronies tried to cover it up. Same with Clinton and his sex scandals. If he'd simply said, "my bad," they never would have impeached him. If anything eventually brought Trump down, it would be his cover-ups.

I'd lost my opportunity to disclose the entire story to the police. I had already covered up my involvement with the Happy Reaper. The only way I could explain what happened last night was to reveal everything that led up to it. Doing that exposed not just me, but Niki, Colleen, Paddy, his wife, and soon-to-be brevetted Brigadier General Lisa Latoya. Paddy and his hacker friends could eliminate last night's incriminating messages between Colleen and me from the phone company's servers, but that involved more cover-up with even more people involved.

Keep it contained. Keep it simple. Only the three of us knew what had happened. Owen had buried bodies before and was on the lam because one had surfaced after thirty years. I might not live thirty years, but Colleen would. We had to do a better job.

SEAMUS

WHEN COMMITTING ILLEGAL ACTIVITIES, THE risk caused by writing things down is huge. The risk of not getting everything right was higher. Normally, when presented with multiple tasks, priorities, time constraints, and limited resources, I would create a spreadsheet. Deleted electronic data has a nasty habit of resurfacing, a chance I would not take. I made a chart on a piece of notepaper. The five columns included task, priority, and our three names.

Owen may have buried a body before, but my experience of reading a few true crime books and thousands of crime novels proved more valuable. Colleen looked at my writing and insisted she complete the chart so we could read it. I kept the master sheet in my pocket. When someone completed a task, I crossed it off. If someone thought of something else, I added it, and when Colleen became available, she rewrote it to her satisfaction.

According to Owen, none of the bodies was visible from the road. That meant their disposal was a lower priority. Colleen suggested we cover the bodies with tarps until we were ready to bury them. "Ain't a good ideer," Owen said. "They're all wearing camo. Hard to see even if you're lookin. A tarp in the woods is a flashin neon invite to snoop to see what's underneath."

True, that.

First, we had to move vehicles we didn't want anyone to see. That included my Bobcat, the UTV Kemp arrived in, the car Owen said the second guy had left on Lukes Road, and the Happy Reaper's stolen car, which we had used to block Shank Lake Road to the north of my house.

I distributed gloves to prevent us leaving fingerprints on anything we touched.

While Colleen used one of my ATVs to transport Owen to retrieve the Bobcat, I stripped the bodies of identification, keys, and anything else they had that might prove useful.

I started with the guy I had killed and extracted a wallet from his left rear pocket. His Massachusetts driver's license identified him as Zachery Canon. I pulled dead hand-warmers, an iPhone and car fob from his coat pocket and laid them on the ground. No watch. I looked at the Garmin on my wrist. It had a GPS that tracked me. Where did that information go? *Shit.*

I added another line to the paper chart: make sure no electronics can track where we bury the bodies.

To get to Canon's front pockets, I had to roll him, which I did without looking at his face. I retrieved two Apple AirTags. *Double shit.* I checked Canon's iPhone: on and locked onto the Verizon network. Those AirTags were transmitting their location. Anyone with access to Canon's iCloud would know he had been here. I powered down the phone.

I scribbled on the list, "Destroy AirTags(2) and iPhone at appropriate location." I'd decide what *appropriate location* meant later. Until then, neither the phone nor AirTags were going anywhere. I stored the fob in my knapsack.

Good thing I unzipped and unbuttoned his clothes. He wore a slender USB flash drive on a chain around his neck. Paddy sometimes used a similar device to lock his laptop when he traveled. I added it to the knapsack.

One body down, two to go.

The Happy Reaper and Tyler Kemp were within twenty feet of each other. The Happy Reaper lay face down, covering his rifle. The bullet that had entered his stomach had ripped a large hole in his back. Nothing could have saved him. Stippling surrounded the small hole in his head. Owen had been close when he pulled the trigger and had done him a favor to end his suffering. Best I think of it that way.

My stomach flipped when I got close enough to Tyler Kemp to see the damage done to him. He was a big man, which confirmed Owen's statement that he had been the first person past the trail camera by the Bobcat. He lay face up, his night-vision headset pointed uselessly to the sky. One round had ripped his throat apart; a second penetrated his chest. A third had shattered his shoulder. Blood pooled underneath him.

I made another note on my chart: Rent metal detector and comb the area for bullets and shards.

My search of the Happy Reaper's pockets came up with an uneaten granola bar and an empty wrapper. Kemp's pockets yielded a fob for a rental truck and a key to what I guessed was the UTV. No phone. No AirTags.

I added locate and remove rental truck to the chart.

List tucked safely in my pocket, I steeled myself and unzipped his coat, unbuttoned his shirt. Nothing around his neck. No watch. I put everything into my knapsack, confirmed these bodies were not visible from the road. By the time I got home, the snow had already melted from the road except in deep shade. Soon those tracks would disappear. One thing in the plus column.

Owen had parked my Bobcat and already switched its bucket for the backhoe attachment. Colleen had located both the UTV and Canon's car sporting Massachusetts plates.

When I asked if she'd seen a truck, she had nothing.

I said, "We know Kemp flew into Iron Mountain. There's a place on the main drag that rents UTVs and trailers for transport. I'll bet he trailered it into the woods and left the rig parked. Before we search for that, let's take care of Canon's car, the UTV, and the Happy Reaper's ride. My leg's sore, but once my pain meds kick in, I can manage the UTV."

What I couldn't do was ride triple on an ATV. Colleen drove my truck, dropped me off at the UTV, brought Owen to Canon's rental. We soon had the rental and UTV hidden in my garage. While I collected my crutches, sleeping bag, and million-watt light from where I had abandoned them in the woods, Colleen shuttled Owen to retrieve the Happy Reaper's stolen vehicle. Once we tucked it into the garage, the garage was full.

We emptied the vehicles of their contents. I searched the backpack from Kemp's UTV, finding a bunch of miscellaneous junk and—*shit, shit, shit*—another AirTag, which may at one point have been close enough to Canon's iPhone for them to connect. I pulled the battery from the AirTag.

Canon's rental car produced a suitcase with clothes, a gun-carrying case, what we guessed was a cheap burner phone, and a MacBook Pro. I'd bet the flash drive around his neck unlocked the computer. That experiment could wait for later. The burner phone was off. Curiosity begged me to take a peek and learn if its number was the one our fake cell tower had captured Kemp calling. No way I could risk turning it on and triggering an electronic trail. The glove box held registration, insurance, a tire gauge, and a half dozen cards that looked like the ones the Happy Reaper had used: a Celtic cross on one side and "Results Guaranteed" on the other.

I caught myself feeling bad that the Happy Reaper had not known he'd gotten his wish for both imposters to die. What was it with these feelings I had about the Happy Reaper?

I slapped my head. Colleen gave me a strange look and snagged the list from my pocket. "What's next?"

* * *

DRIVING THE UTV CONVINCED ME my leg had not sufficiently recovered to operate the Bobcat. Owen could, and he knew the woods around us better than I. Using a plat book, I showed him the location I had in mind for burying the bodies.

It was two miles behind a locked gate on land held in trust for my granddaughter. The public could legally walk the land, but two miles from the gate made it a long trek, especially since it (1) wasn't near water that might attract anglers, (2) was too mature for deer habitat, (3) wasn't good for hunting birds, and (4) moose didn't frequent that area, so neither did moose-shed seekers. Bonus points, it was near an old gravel pit that had a pile of discarded boulders available for covering the grave.

Owen said, "Scarpi brothers used that gravel pit when they logged that area 'bout sixty years ago."

Who knew? It would take Owen a couple of hours to drive the Bobcat there. I gave him a key to the gate and sent him off with the promise that Colleen or I would pick him up. Colleen and I ditched our electronic devices in the house and used my truck to search for Kemp's rental.

We found it parked seven miles away, where the Grade splits from the A Grade. Its glove compartment contained pins for the folding gate at the back of the trailer and two rental agreements. One was for the truck, which came from the Iron Mountain airport. The other covered the UTV and trailer. Nothing was due until tomorrow, which gave us flexibility.

Since I had towed trailers before, I drove the truck and trailer to my place and stored it on a woods road invisible from the main road. Colleen accompanied me while I moved the rented UTV from the garage. She helped me strap it onto the trailer. On the way to the house, we strategized how to get the rented vehicles to Iron Mountain.

Owen was a fugitive and without a driver's license. We couldn't risk him driving the hour and a half to Iron Mountain. That meant two trips and six hours of driving time for Colleen and me. My frustration boiled. "We're running on no sleep, and we still have to clean up everything—every single thing—that ties into any of the dead folks. Let's pick up Owen, grab lunch and a little shut-eye. Refreshed, we can do the cleanup, eat dinner, and move the bodies tonight. What am I missing?"

Colleen pointed down the driveway. "That."

Tex leaned against an Iron County Sheriff's car, sipping from a coffee to-go cup. He hadn't been there long, but probably long enough that if he wanted to, he could have snooped in the garage and seen Canon's car and the one the Happy Reaper had stolen. Unless he had a search warrant, anything he discovered became fruit of the poisonous tree, inadmissible in court.

Even an innocent move like peering through the mudroom door—totally legal--would have let him see the rifles we had left in the mudroom. I had no explanation for them without Niki being here.

CHARLENE

CHARLENE ENTERED THE PRECINCT EXHAUSTED from worry and lack of sleep. She hoped no one would notice her head seemed to lag six inches behind the rest of her body. At the end of roll call, the sergeant told her to see the lieutenant.

At her knock, the lieutenant motioned her in, handed her a slip of paper. "FBI wants local support for a raid. Don't get excited. All they need is someone to keep away lookie-loos. It's your old neighborhood, and I thought of you. Here are two addresses. The first is the meet and the second the target."

The first was a bodega she'd visited a ton growing up. She scanned the second and wobbly knees forced her to grab the desk.

"Something wrong?"

Everything's wrong. What the fuck happened? *No way to hide that I know Zach.* She forced iron into her legs, looked him straight in the eye. "I know that house. A high school buddy of mine lives there with his parents. They're the sweetest people. I was there yesterday afternoon, playing with his VR headset while Zach was away for the weekend. What's going on?"

"So you know the house's layout?"

"First floor and basement."

"Let the Feds know. I'm sure they'll want to pick your brain before they turn you into a doorstop. Dismissed."

Her legs carried her from the lieutenant's office, through the warren of cubicles, and into the ladies, where she threw up breakfast. She flushed the toilet and watched her vomit and life swirl down the drain.

Maybe it had nothing to do with Porwall's murder. *Maybe.* At least they couldn't link any money to her because she had refused to take any. And it wasn't like she could run away and become someone else. You gotta act natural. Shocked by whatever they suspected Zach had done. Sure, she could do that. Keep her trap shut. She could do that too.

She rinsed her mouth until the taste went away. Patted her cheeks to bring back some color. She stiffened her spine and left—just a cop wasting her time babysitting the Feds.

* * *

THE OFFICER AT THE BODEGA door directed her to an agent from DC who wore cowboy boots with his nice suit. The short guy introduced himself as Rick Kaska. "We're serving a search warrant. Boston wants one of theirs guarding the door against lookie-loos."

The Feds blame the lieutenant; the lieutenant blames the Feds, and she was still destined to be a doorstop. Use it to your advantage. "Lieutenant assigned me because I know the family who lives there. Been in their house."

Kaska waved over a couple of agents, locals judging by their accents. They spread a blueprint of the house on a table and machine-gunned questions. She confirmed the ground floor remained unchanged; she'd never been on the second floor. The son—they called him Zachery—lived in the basement. She sketched on the blueprint the location of rooms recently added. Put an X in the one with his computers; a W for the weapons safe. Both parents worked during the day. Zach normally worked at home. Sensing they had finished questioning her, she asked, "What do you want him for?"

Kaska said, "Murder for hire. Late last night we raided the apartment of a Tyler Kemp. Didn't find him, but we did find a printout of an email Kemp sent this Zachary Canon. It berated him concerning specific details of a murder the email says Canon committed. The local police confirmed the email included details not released to the public. We think the two are in cahoots and Canon's computers will provide the proof. Although I'd take a notarized confession."

Her stomach clenched like it wanted to spew her guts again. They already knew about Tyler, had linked him to Zach. Was this a trap for her? She eased into the chair, feeling stronger with the wood supporting her.

"Unbelievable. I know those guys. No way they're killers." She rubbed her eyes. "Isn't that what neighbors say when they've been living next to a psycho for years and didn't know it?" She threw her hands in the air, like "who knows anything?" and waited for the boom to fall.

Kaska gave her a wan smile. "I agree. You never know, do you? Let's saddle up."

Somehow, she reached her patrol car without falling down or throwing up. She followed the FBI caravan to the house, decided against telling them the Canons kept a key hidden in a fake rock in the side garden, and watched them break the door lock and pour into the house. Now the only one outside, she hoped if Zach drove up, he'd see her and keep driving to the end of the earth.

With nothing to do but worry, she wondered what else they had found at Tyler's place. They'd find phone calls between them, but she had already admitted she knew the guy and had been at his place. No one could know what the calls were about. She had insisted he didn't email her. Police loved emails.

She replayed everything she had done yesterday at Zach's. Worn gloves—no prints. Wiped the servers—they'd get nothing physical. But if there were external hard drives or cloud backup . . . *You did what you could.* Good thing she hadn't taken the old laptop. Right now some FBI techie might be monitoring it through a warrant on Zach's cellphone. Phones—she had left the burner and wiped it clean. They'd check the call logs and find it had called two other burners, which they would eventually discover someone (they'd determine it was Zach) had bought at the same time. They might trace one to Tyler, but nothing would come back on her.

Unless Zach or Tyler cut a deal to deliver a wayward cop. *No regrets. Think positive.*

When she got off duty, she'd rid her apartment of any evidence that Tyler and Zach had ever been there. Lots of cleaning to do, including tossing their slippers into a Goodwill bin.

The fact that she still had her weapon meant they had no clue she was the third leg of the tripod. She'd let time pass before deciding if she wanted to go solo to deliver her own brand of justice to those who deserved it.

First, she had to get through the day.

SEAMUS

I KICKED MYSELF FOR MY first words. "You remember Colleen?" Of course Tex did.

Tex tipped his cup, draining the contents, his throat audibly bobbing. He crushed the cup and set it on top of the cruiser. "Same property owner on Long Lake called to complain of a machine gun firing. Since the chief wasn't in the area, he sent me to check."

"Sorry. I slept the sleep of the dead." What a terrible choice of words, and to emphasize the lie, my body decided it was a perfect time to yawn.

Colleen said, "It woke me up. Sounded like it came from one of those camps off the A Grade." She pointed in the general direction. "Heard one more single shot later on. You think someone's taking early deer?"

Tex scratched his chin. "Those gates on the A Grade were locked when I went by, but I suppose illegal hunters might do that. I take it your guests are gone. Anyone else up on the lake?"

I said I had heard no generators nor seen any lights. True enough, provided it was someone else's generators and lights I was referring to.

"Nothing suspicious on that satellite trail camera I see you have on the road a half mile from here?"

Damn. I'd forgotten to have Owen take it down when he retrieved the Bobcat, or the other one I'd placed near the Happy Reaper's car. They had documented all our comings and goings. *Double damn.* The pictures were also sitting on my phone, accessible with a warrant. "I'd spotted a big buck in that area. Soon as I installed that camera, he ghosted. Most excitement that camera has had was to catch you and us today."

My heart sunk. I had opened the door for him to ask to see the pictures.

Tex chuckled. "Ain't that always the case? I'll make sure everything's locked up tight at the other camps. Have you heard anything more about your case? I keep hoping the prosecutor will get smart and drop it."

Colleen gave him two thumbs up. "Maybe after he gets re-elected and has nothing to prove."

Tex grabbed the crumpled cup off his car. "Hope, they say, springs eternal."

We silently watched Tex drive away. I considered whether Colleen's confirmation of the shots was a good thing, a bad thing, or a neutral thing. My conclusion was my brain was too tired to compute. "Owen will have to wait for us to retrieve him until Tex clears the area. I'll clean the house of any evidence the Happy Reaper was here. You search for his cache of weapons."

Colleen tilted her head. "You hear that?"

A car coming up the road. Ah shit. What did Tex see that tipped him off?

Niki

NIKI SPOTTED A COP CAR crawling down Shank Lake Road from the opposite direction, and she broke into a sweat. Was she too late to save Seamus? She pulled to the road's edge to let the vehicle pass, saw Tex, Iron County's crime scene guy, was driving, and her anxiety spun into the atmosphere. Tex driving away meant whatever had happened had occurred hours before. Was Seamus incapacitated, and that's why he didn't answer her phone calls? Dead?

She thought of her joking comment that she'd have to kill him if he died on her. She had not had time to tell him why.

A new thought hit her. Had something happened to Adam Smith? Had he succumbed to his bad heart? Park would not be happy if the Marshals Service discovered Smith wasn't under her control. Better her getting buried from a ton of crap than something happening to Seamus.

Wait, wasn't Colleen supposed to be there, too? Niki pried her hands from the steering wheel, flexed her fingers, and told herself to drive. Answers were in two miles.

No Iron County deputies waited to stop her at Seamus's property line, which did not settle her stomach in the least. No flashing lights painted the house. Garage door closed. Truck and Subaru parked in their usual spots. No extra vehicles. The place looked dead.

She pulled around the garage to face her car up the driveway. Stopping, she tapped her ankles together, confirming she wore her ankle holster. She checked the load of her Sig and got out. Keeping the pistol at her side, she called using her cop voice, "Anyone home?"

Colleen appeared through the mudroom door; Seamus hobbled out behind her. They looked like they had seen ghosts. She tucked the Sig in the waistband of her pants, saved berating Seamus for not having his phone on until they were alone, and opened the conversation with, "Where's Adam Smith?"

They traded looks that told her he wasn't there. Seamus said, "If you drive away now, I can communicate with the secure app, and you can deny everything."

SEAMUS

WHILE COLLEEN GAVE NIKI A detailed description of recent events, I picked up Owen, who had dug a grave exactly where I had suggested.

While the four of us ate lunch, Niki reviewed my paper chart of tasks. Asked a few clarifying questions about lines I had scribbled that Colleen had not had time to make legible. "For amateurs, it's not bad. Owen, those AirTags mean the police could show up at any minute. You can't be here if that happens. Change back into your clothes, take your gun, and make yourself scarce. Take whatever food or other supplies you want. Seamus, give Owen all the cash in your wallet." She retrieved her wallet and tossed a wad of bills on the table in front of Owen, who had not moved an inch. She gave his shoulder a squeeze. "I know you want to keep helping. This is how you can help the most. Honest."

The stormy expression on Owen's face made it clear he did not cotton to her ideas. I'm sure Niki also saw it because she said, "If you don't want the money, that's fine. He told me you need new boots. But if you don't leave, I'll forget myself and thank you the way I know best: I'll give you a big kiss, probably stick my tongue in your mouth, maybe grab your ass."

Owen's glower broke. He held up his hands in surrender and a grin crept across his face. "You are a pistol."

He disappeared to swap my garments for his, which gave me time to gather five hundred dollars. "Consider it payment for breakfast with a tip. Thank you, Owen." I gave him a hug, threatened to grab his ass. He left with the money, all the bricks of cheese I had, and a smile.

I asked Niki why she wanted him gone. "I talked to Rick on my drive here. The FBI already raided Kemp's apartment. Rick didn't tell me what all they found, but they discovered a printout of an email Kemp had sent Zach Canon that makes them suspect Canon is the other imposter. They're preparing to raid Canon's residence. If they can track Canon's AirTags, they'll be here soon. Even if they don't, Kemp's and Canon's trails might still lead them here. That puts Owen at risk. Plus, I know he can keep a secret, but he's old and stuff happens. He might say something he shouldn't."

Colleen said, "He dug the hole. It's not like he'll forget."

"Which is why," Niki said, "I plan to fill it in and dig a new one somewhere else. Seamus, find me another spot and drop me off at your

Bobcat. You two grab some Zs, then Seamus can pick me up before dinner. We're going to be up all night burying bodies, returning Kemp's rentals, and repositioning those two cars you have hidden in your garage and creating a fresh trail for my FBI friends to follow that does not lead here."

Knowing I was running on fumes, my leg was throbbing, and I was missing something big, I focused on a minor detail. "When did you learn to operate a Bobcat?"

"I figure twenty minutes from now. I'm a quick study."

* * *

UNLIKE THE BOBCAT, WHICH NIKI mastered with a few minutes of instruction, she had no interest in driving a strange truck with a trailer. That fell to me. The sun set over the lake during dinner. With darkness upon us, Niki and I left Colleen to catch another three hours of sleep.

We had debated during dinner how to handle the AirTags. I didn't know exactly how they worked. According to Colleen, they reported last known position, but didn't leave a history.

If the one Kemp had been carrying in his backpack had recorded itself on my property, I wanted to replace that electronic pin at my first opportunity. But if it hadn't recorded being on my property, I didn't want the first ping to be close to my home, especially if the FBI had learned that AirTag existed and was monitoring it. The ones Canon carried posed a different issue that we'd take care of later.

If anyone was monitoring the AirTag from Kemp's knapsack, they saw it wink into existence in the Florence, Wisconsin grocery store. I replaced the battery in the AirTag, donned an N-95 mask to hide my face, and wandered the place, figuring at least one shopper carried an iPhone. Back in the truck, I removed the AirTag's battery.

At the UTV rental place, I again donned a mask to guard against security cameras catching my face. Niki waited in her car a few stores farther down the road while I unhooked the trailer. I left the key to the UTV in its ignition. A twinge of concern tightened my neck. I laughed off the worry. Having someone steal it was the least of my problems.

At the Iron Mountain airport, I reversed the truck into a slot reserved for rentals. I again replaced the AirTag's battery and stored it in the truck's console. Cinching my hood tight to my face and with the mask in place, I walked the fob to the drop off box, slotted it, and walked from the airport parking lot to where Niki waited.

That disposed of everything Kemp had rented. We returned to my place to collect and ditch Canon's car and the Happy Reaper's stolen RAV-4. Niki searched the vehicles, found nothing new in Canon's but discovered a roll of 100-dollar bills in the glove box of the RAV-4. She returned the stash. "That's going to tempt someone. It'll be interesting to see if that money gets logged into confiscated inventory."

We pulled onto the road on the dot of nine. Niki led our caravan in the RAV-4. Her theory being that if she got stopped, she'd use her U.S. Marshals credentials to talk herself out of trouble. I followed in Canon's car and dry-swallowed two extra strength Excedrin. Colleen brought up the rear in Niki's vehicle.

Because we had no personal electronic devices with us, we maintained visual contact. Niki kept driving and driving and driving until three and a half hours later, she stopped at a weedy driveway off a gravel road in the general vicinity of Ladysmith, Wisconsin.

We piled from the vehicles. I asked, "How did you know this was here?"

"I didn't, although I knew we'd find something like it. It's not in town, but close enough to have cell service. Seamus and Colleen, you two switch cars. My plan involves some walking and Colleen can do that and Seamus, you shouldn't. Seamus, you'll drive my car to that intersection a mile back and wait. Colleen and I will drive the other vehicles back and forth to obliterate Seamus's tracks. Then we'll park both vehicles behind the barn. I'll replace the batteries in those two AirTags, start Canon's iPhone, and we'll walk to Seamus. Even if the Bureau sees any of it come online, they'll take hours to scramble people here to check."

Colleen asked, "If they aren't tracking the phone or AirTag, how long do you think before *anyone* finds them?"

"Tomorrow."

"Tomorrow?" Colleen sounded skeptical.

I said, "It's after midnight, so today is tomorrow. Or did you mean Wednesday?"

"Wednesday. When an anonymous source—" She tapped her chest. "—will contact local law enforcement."

AFTERMATH

CHARLENE

CHARLENE HARDLY REMEMBERED WHAT SHE did the rest of her shift on Monday after FBI Special Agent Kaska dismissed her from door duty at Zach's. Tuesday had dragged, and she couldn't keep her mind off wondering what Tyler and Zach were doing. It didn't help any when Zach's mother called, told her about the FBI raid, and asked if Charlene had heard from Zach. He hadn't come home Monday, wasn't answering his phone, and his boss knew nothing of a Philadelphia meeting. It was damned hard for Charlene to offer assurances to Zach's mother that she was almost certain were misplaced.

She could find no updates on Porwall's murder. She didn't know if that was good or bad. That night, she cleaned her apartment again and thanked her lucky stars she had left her burner phone at Zach's.

Wednesday found her fretting and scattered. She rose early and drove past their places. Didn't spot either of their cars. Her online search found no news relating to murders or hunting accidents in McCree's vicinity. Problem was, he was so isolated, when would anyone know?

Later that morning, an officer-needs-assistance call resulted in her joining a foot chase that captured an attempted car-jacking suspect. That temporarily allowed her to forget everything except being part of a team that took down the suspect. She and some others were standing around in the aftermath when she received a call to return to the station.

Icicles instantly filled her insides. She acknowledged, got funny looks from her mates. She managed a nonchalant, "No clue," and walked away like a normal person, not the zombie she felt like.

FBI Special Agent Kaska was waiting for her. Before he could ask or say whatever he planned, she jumped in with, "Get what you were looking for with the warrant?"

"Some, not all. Zachery Canon's parents gave us a list of names of people their son knew, which included you. We've added a few people to their list. I'd like your take on everyone. Have you had lunch?"

They ordered in and sat side-by-side at an empty desk. She scanned the list, mostly kids she knew from high school, a couple she knew were gaming buddies of Zach's, and a few names she'd never run across. It wasn't a long list.

"In high school, Zach and this guy—" she tapped Tyler Kemp's name, "were inseparable, and I was like their girl buddy."

She caught a brief brightening of Kaska's eyes. Had he known that already from talking to others, or had she just given him new intel? *Keep talking, Charlene. Paint him a picture.*

Calm replaced her nerves. She tapped Tyler's name again. "As kids, I knew Zach pretty well. He went to college. By the time he graduated, I had joined the force and was mostly hanging with other cops. I'd see him and Tyler occasionally for a beer or dinner or to play some computer games. Zach was kind of like that guy in the Springsteen song, talking about how great high school was." She knew its name, but it was time to get him talking. Pump him for a little information. "You know it?"

"Glory Days," Kaska said.

She gave him her best smile. "That's the one. I still can't believe he had anything to do with murder for hire. I take it you haven't found him or Tyler?"

"Not yet."

"And no activity on their credit cards?"

"I'm not at liberty to say."

Typical Fed. Suck information from everyone and disclose nothing. She interpreted the way he responded to mean neither one had used his credit cards recently. Having learned all she would, she decided that unless he asked specifically about Tyler, she didn't plan on saying anything more about him. She filled Kaska in on the others. When she finished the list, Kaska asked, "Any of these people have a connection to Northern Wisconsin?"

Maybe one of them *had* used his credit card. "Not that I'm aware. Why?"

"This morning, police followed a tip and found two abandoned vehicles stashed behind an old barn outside Ladysmith, Wisconsin. One was a car stolen last week from New York State. The other was Zachery Canon's car."

"That makes no sense to me." And that was no lie.

"Agents from our Eau Claire office are on site. Someone wiped both vehicles clean. Canon's car contained his iPhone, a bunch of weapons, some clothes, and a newish laptop. We're working on cracking passwords on his phone and laptop. Fingers crossed, they'll tell us something. The stolen car's glove compartment contained thirty-five one-hundred-dollar bills."

She whistled at the money. Zach's phone and laptop would surely have one of those programs to wipe the memory after a few incorrect password attempts, right? She thought of a little misdirection. "Zach participated in live-action role-playing games. LARPs? Maybe some of those people can help?"

He thanked her and wrote a note. They batted ideas around for another quarter hour in which she learned nothing. He claimed he had another interview, and he'd better let her return to work.

She had already deduced that Zach had driven to the Cincinnati area and killed Porwall. Before she deleted the tracking program by wiping Zach's old computer, the last report from Zach's AirTag had shown him a half hour from McCree's place, presumably to meet with Tyler. Ladysmith was halfway between Nothing and Nowhere and far from any logical route Zach would take from McCree's. Unless he and Tyler had left McCree's and planned to drive together to Aspen to kill William Barret Owens, the VC guy. But why abandon his car? She could make no sense why police found it in the same location as a stolen car from New York that contained $3,500 of cash.

Her cop instincts said Zach and Tyler were no longer alive. Was McCree? She called Kavanaugh's Tavern and confirmed Mrs. McCree's birthday bash in eleven days was still on.

She would be there to see who showed up.

SEAMUS

EACH DAY THE POLICE DID not arrive, my anxiety dropped another notch. Nightmares continued to interrupt my sleep, but days became more normal.

Niki left on Thursday, letting Sheriff Bartelle know that Adam Smith was no longer in his county. True statement: the spot I picked for his burial was across the Baraga County line.

I made one additional invitation to Mom's upcoming birthday party. With Paddy's blessing, I invited soon-to-be General Lisa Latoya to give Mom the opportunity to meet the mother of her next great-grandchild. We forwarded the final list to the two off-duty Boston police officers I'd hired to man the front door and to check IDs. Colleen and I dotted I's and crossed T's for the party until even she believed we had nothing else we could do to prepare.

Paddy made a quick visit to dismantle and remove the fake cell tower. He and Niki had worked together remotely, without success, to uncover who Clem was. They'd rung up the furniture store the Happy Reaper had called and were told no Clem worked there or ever had. Also disappointing, no law enforcement agency had developed any information on the individuals who had sprung the Happy Reaper from the hospital. Without my knowledge, Paddy had conferred with the rest of the McCree clan, and they had concluded that the Happy Reaper never intended for Clem to kill them. They'd all be mindful but take no greater precautions than they ever did.

I hoped they were right.

That week, Colleen and I finished another old piece of shady business when I made the last filing to close a charity my Uncle Mike had set up to distribute money of questionable origin to families of fallen first responders.

Despite the abuse I had subjected my wounds to, antibiotics and less strenuous activity allowed them to resume healing. One day, Gerry and Carla used a zoom call to look at my wounds. They pronounced me officially on the mend.

I moved to the cabin to allow Colleen full use of the house to do her work whenever she wanted, day or night. That worked to my advantage when she worked at night to make up for daylight hours she spent helping me complete the spruce grouse project for Megan's land that the Happy Reaper's arrival had interrupted. I had a modicum of work that had to wait until next spring, but I knew—well, God willing and the creek don't rise— that I could finish that and get that portion of Megan's land certified for her.

Alone at the cabin with the lights extinguished, my brain kept circling around to the question of what I could have, should have, done differently to have avoided the three deaths. Eventually, I remembered to recite the mantra, "I am responsible only for my own actions, not anyone else's reactions."

I don't think it helped.

Our impending trial still hung over our heads. The Iron County prosecutor made no move to drop the charges. The day following the party, Mom planned to fly to Savannah and spend the winter at the place I bought on Tybee Island as a summer rental and winter retreat for her. Colleen and I would return to Michigan. Our lawyer, Irene Frankel, planned to join us to prepare for the trial.

The preparation and trial would force Colleen to remain here and be away from her home and honey for several months. I still hoped the prosecutor would drop the charges after voters re-elected him in two weeks. But if not, all the trial would cost me was money and time. I had complete confidence at least one juror would vote not guilty. Probably want to shake our hands and thank us.

The fallout from the Happy Reaper imposters continued. Niki informed me that someone had stabbed Porwall more than thirty times in a murder of great passion. Police had no viable suspects. Paddy funneled to Rick Kaska and his "independent" FBI task force information he recovered from the files on Canon's laptop that I had copied before wiping its hard drive. The FBI issued arrest warrants for Tyler Kemp and Zachary Canon and seized their offshore bank accounts. The FBI also arrested everyone who had solicited or attempted to solicit the imposters.

Local news in the various locations modestly covered those events. The Happy Reaper's belief that eliminating the imposters would restore his legacy proved optimistic. Some articles mentioned his name, Adam Smith. Half of those indicated he had escaped from a hospital. One identified it as a psychiatric hospital for the criminally insane. None mentioned his promise and nearly total delivery of "Results Guaranteed." Two Twitter accounts with a bazillion followers confused him with a serial rapist.

I found myself disappointed on his behalf and more disappointed in myself for having those feelings. At least, I thought, if my legacy was to restore the flora and fauna on Megan's land, that was nearly in the bag and required nothing more than a bit more time and effort on my part next year.

The night before Niki drove here to allow us three to travel together to Boston for Mom's birthday weekend, I had the rare pleasure of being by myself at the cabin with everything crossed off my to do list. I bundled up against the cold and gently swung in the cloth hammock hanging from the rafters on the screened porch—the same hammock where I had first laid eyes on Niki. So much had happened since then.

The world outside held its breath. The wind a dead calm. The lake frozen, sending the last of the ducks to seek open water. Without wind or extreme cold, the lake had no reason to creak or groan. The squeak of hammock rope rubbing against the rafter provided cover to any small animals that might be about. Even the barred owls chose to keep their hoots to themselves.

My thoughts flitted through the years, covering the good and the great and the disappointments and disasters, and spiraled around to the most recent trauma.

I stilled the hammock and closed my eyes. My chest rose and fell with deliberate breaths. The slow pulse of my blood vibrated deep in my ear. In that pure, calm moment, I experienced an epiphany: if right now my biggest disappointment in myself was that I had become fond of the Happy Reaper, life was good. Superior, even.

Mom's Birthday Bash

SEAMUS

AS MOM'S PARTY WAS WINDING down, Colleen found me talking with an old copper who had been on the force with my father. To him she said, "Could you excuse us for a minute?"

The former police officer thanked us for a great party.

"Everything okay?" I asked.

"I wanted to apologize. You were right. Everything about the party was perfect. I was a worrywart over nothing. Sorry I put you through that."

"The reason it all went so well is because you made sure everything was nailed down. I'd better find Mom and start to extract her from her adoring public."

* * *

I FOUND MOM HOLDING COURT in one of Kavanaugh's private rooms. "They've made last call, Mom."

"Oh gosh, how did it get that late? This was so much fun. You and Colleen made this the best day ever—the best weekend ever, with the family together. I should have turned eighty-five earlier."

Mom was right: it had been a nearly perfect weekend. We had banned any discussions of the election on the coming Tuesday, Colleen's and my trial in a month, and anything related to the Happy Reaper or the two imposters who moldered with him in their now snow-covered grave.

I had mentioned to Niki on our flight that I wished my older sister, who still called herself Ailish, could have made room in her heart to attend. Paddy and I had made sure she knew she was welcome. Niki remarked that in years past, I would have fretted over what I could do differently. "Congratulations, Seamus," she'd said. "You've learned that not everything is your responsibility."

The family card and board games were vicious, no-holds-barred affairs, filled with trash talk and laughter. Colleen's new girlfriend, a winsome redhead post-doc chemical engineer working at MIT, was appalled when my ex-wife, Lizzie, called my mother "an old bat" and me a "wastrel gimp." By the second day, she was fully engaged in the McCree banter. Even Niki, who on previous occasions had kept herself aloof, had participated in the antics, teaming up with Megan and Valeria to make an unbeatable Jenga team.

I told Mom to make sure she told Colleen, who had done the lion's share of the work, how pleased she was.

"Stop worrying, Seamus. I have and will again. Now, anyone for a last game of darts?"

At Mom's offer, everyone, except for one guy I didn't know, begged off. Off on a side table sat a huge fishbowl stuffed with twenties, fifties, hundreds, and many checks. Mom's charities had done well today. I didn't recognize the guy who was up for taking on Mom in one last game of 501. "What, a newbie you haven't yet fleeced, Mom?"

"Ha," she said. "He's the current Minuteman League champion. He's giving me a handicap, though. We agreed to play left-handed."

I shook the guy's hand. "Do you know she's ambidextrous?"

He laughed. "Trudy, you are a sneaky one."

"Seamus." My mother's head shook in mock disappointment. "Don't you have to settle the bill or something? I promise I'll leave after this match."

"Fifteen minutes, Mom. I'll wait near the door."

* * *

THE BARTENDER SLID A STACK of paper across the polished wood. "Colleen double checked, and here's your credit card."

Of course, the accountant double checked. The tab was what I expected, given four hundred people had attended. I verified it included the twenty percent tip I had requested. "Thanks for everything you all did to make this special for my mother. I'll try to catch each of the staff, but if I miss anyone, please let them know Mom was thrilled."

Niki, Colleen, and now General Lisa were chatting with a group of women at the far corner of the bar. I told them we'd leave in ten with Mom, that the rest of the family had already left to allow the kids to wind down at the hotel from their Shirley Temple sugar highs before we concluded the weekend with the dinner.

I expressed my great appreciation to the staff I caught tidying up and also to the two police officers, one male, one female, posted at the door to make sure only invited guests entered Kavanaugh's for the duration of the party. "You're free to go," I said. "If you want something from the bar, tell her to put it on my card. I know it was a thankless task, but this could have been a disaster without you. Any idea where the nearest restroom is?"

Both cops pointed across the main room toward a hallway on the right.

"Tell you what, Ken," the female officer said. "Can you order me a stout? I believe I'll follow Mr. McCree and take care of business."

The jingle of her belt followed me into the hallway. I had passed the ladies and was three steps from the gents when the cop called, "Mister McCree, got a sec?"

I turned to a silenced pistol leveled at my chest. "Justice for the Happy Reaper and my two partners." The pistol coughed three times.

My legs folded under me. Three blooms of red sprouted on my chest. There were three of them! I promised the Happy Reaper to stop his imposters, and these three red roses on my chest is the price of failure. I rested my head on the floor and looked at the ceiling. Sorry, Mom. I spoiled your celebration. My heart pumped more blood into my hands. My eyelids fluttered shut. No. I did everything I could. This isn't on me.

A blaring noise accompanied white flashes that penetrated to my optic nerve. *Not what I thought they meant by God's trumpet call.*

NIKI

NIKI HAD JOINED A CONVERSATION with several of Colleen's friends when Seamus gave them the ten-minute warning, breaking up the chatter. Colleen whispered something in her honey's ear and gave the redhead a quick pat on the butt before pointing her toward the front door.

Niki asked Colleen, "Want to share the secret?"

"It's a hoot. She's buying Seamus a box of that cabernet he likes. He chose one of Boston's fanciest restaurants to complete today's celebration. I bribed the sommelier to present the box to him with all the pomp and ceremony they'd use for a three-hundred-dollar bottle of wine. I can't wait to see the look on his face. Or hear what Trudy has to say."

Niki laughed so hard her ribs hurt. This weekend had proved that, despite all the collective McCree traumas, they had pulled together as a family. "I envy you this." At Colleen's confused expression, Niki clarified. "Being part of the McCrees."

Colleen put her hands on her hips, rose on her toes to exaggerate her height advantage, and looked down at Niki. "Don't you realize you *are* part of the family? Come on. Let's hit the loo before they ask everyone to leave and there's a line."

Niki read Colleen's tone and expression to mean she was not joking. *Was Niki part of what Seamus called the clan?* She'd ponder that when she was alone. "I didn't have to go until you put the idea in my head." Hooking one of Colleen's elbows, Niki pulled her toward the hallway with the bathrooms. "Shall we?"

They were halfway across the main room when Niki heard three coughs—silenced shots from the direction of the restrooms. Dropping Colleen's arm, she drew her Sig from her shoulder harness and sprinted toward the sound. She entered the hallway accompanied by the blare of an emergency alarm. Still sprinting, she scanned the scene. White strobe lights pained her eyes. Her nostrils twitched against the acrid smell of gunpowder and propellant. Near the men's room, Seamus lay sprawled on the carpet. His chest gushed blood. A female uniformed cop pointed a service weapon out the fire-exit door.

"He went that way," the cop yelled. "Call 9-1-1. I'm going after him."

Bullshit. Niki glanced at Seamus in passing—a glug of blood bubbled through his fingers. "Get a medic!" She reached the door before it closed, slammed through, and drove the cop to the ground. The suspect's gun skittered into the alley. Feeling her pushing up with her hips, Niki smacked the woman's skull with the butt of the Sig. "Move and I'll fucking blow your head off. Marshals Service. You're under arrest."

Niki used her FBI training to control the woman's thrashing. She knelt on her prisoner's lower back and pinned her head to the ground with a forearm. The woman shouted that she was a Boston cop, and the killer was getting away. Ignoring her, Niki's one-handed pat-down found a silenced pistol, warm to the touch, in an easy-to-access, magnet-sealed sling pack. She ripped it off and tossed it aside.

In one continuous motion, she power-lifted her prisoner to a stand and body-slammed her against the door, not bothering to protect the woman's face. She muscled her to the side and tried the handle—locked, as it should be. Using the flat of her hand, she pounded on the door, then pulled out her Marshal's badge, and held it out.

The door cracked open, and a Boston cop's gun pointed at her head.

"U.S. Marshal." Niki waved the badge. "This is the shooter. How is he?" Peering past legs, she spotted a red first-aid kit, two guys working on Seamus, and Colleen kneeling at Seamus's head. Through the cacophony came Colleen's clear voice. "Stay with me, Seamus. You can't leave us now. We just bought you a box of your favorite wine."

THANKS FOR READING THIS STORY. To help me reach other readers, I would appreciate your posting a short review of *Hijacked Legacy* on your favorite retailer or review website.

Author's Note

I KNOW I AM ONE lucky guy. So many people have helped bring this story to you and make it better than what I could have done on my own.

My Reader's Group helped pick the name for the "H" novel and provided excellent insights about the cover options I offered them. Paco Aguilar offered advice on treating Seamus's injuries and on the Happy Reaper's health status. Terri Bishoff's developmental review of an early draft provided valuable insights on plot and character elements.

Throughout the year and a half it took to complete this novel, my blogging partners at Writers Who Kill and author friends at Behind the Crime Tape provided terrific support. I especially want to shout out Maggie Toussaint and Kim Striker, whose comment on a late draft allowed me to make a small tweak with a big impact. Carol Baldridge's eagle eyes caught typos I missed. Jan Rubens is always my first, last, and best reader. I credit her as being my editor. Despite everyone's hard work, mistakes surely remain, for which I take full responsibility.

Most of the roads and geography referenced in this story are real, as are many of the businesses. Some descriptions are intentionally vague or misleading—I don't want people searching for dead bodies on private property. Despite appearing in previous Seamus McCree stories, Kavanaugh's Tavern in Boston still does not exist. Any real "RG Services" has nothing to do with the fictional organization invented for this story. While Tall Pines in Amasa does have a hotel, the motels and hotels my characters used in the story are figments of my imagination and not based on any existing establishments.

The story refers to individuals from the Iron County sheriff's department, prosecutor's office, and court system. Over the years, I have met the real individuals who occupy these positions. I've always found them to be great professionals. My characters say and do things these professionals would consider inappropriate. That's on me, not them. This is not a police procedural nor a legal thriller, and I've taken liberties with normal investigation and court practices.

Charlene Bendick won a silent auction that benefited The Friends of the Crystal Falls District Community Library. Her "prize" was to have me give her name to a character. She didn't get to choose which one; that choice was mine.

I love to hear from readers. Drop me a note and let me know what you thought of the story or that you found a typo so I can correct it for future editions. My email is jmj@jamesmjackson.com.

James M. Jackson
Amasa, Michigan

James M. Jackson authors the Seamus McCree and Niki Undercover Thriller series.

Jim has also published an acclaimed book on contract bridge, *One Trick at a Time: How to start winning at bridge.*

He calls the deep woods of Michigan's Upper Peninsula home. You can find out more about Jim or sign up for his Readers Group newsletter at his website, https://jamesmjackson.com.

www.ingramcontent.com/pod-product-compliance
Lightning Source LLC
Chambersburg PA
CBHW050955180726
48291CB00006B/1842